DEMON'S RISE

About the Author

R.E. Sanders was born in England and moved to Wales to study archaeology. *Demon's Tear*, Book One of the Jantakai Saga was released in 2024 and he has also published the novella *Tann's Last Stand* and the novel *A Path of Blades,* both set in the same world as the Jantakai Saga. He lives in Cardiff.

Visit https://resanderswrites.wixsite.com/r-e--sanderswrites for more information about R.E. Sanders.

THE JANTAKAI SAGA

BOOK TWO

DEMON'S RISE

R.E. SANDERS

This novel is entirely a work of fiction.
The names, characters and incidents portrayed
in it are the work of the author's imagination.
Any resemblance to actual persons, living or
dead, events or localities is entirely coincidental.

No generative AI was used in the production of
any of the text or images that are included in
this book.

Copyright © 2025 by R.E. Sanders
Cover by getcovers
Maps by Inkarnate
All other artwork by P.A.Bennett

All rights reserved. No part of this publication
may be reproduced, stored in a retrieval system,
or transmitted, in any form or by any means,
electronic, mechanical, photocopying, recording
or otherwise, without the prior permission of
the copyright owner.

First edition August 2025
ISBN: 9798288959202

https://resanderswrites.wixsite.com/r-e--sanderswrites

Sing, muses of life and death, of war and peace. Of betrayal and hope, of two brothers and of the forging of the Swords.

- Prathin Pra Mithrin

THE STORY SO FAR...

Young soldier Eain Connow is caught up in a situation beyond anything he could have expected when Banahgar is invaded by their neighbouring country, the greedy Kotev. Trying to lead the troops under his command to safety, he instead walks into an ambush and is the only survivor.

Fleeing for his life, his path leads him over the mountains of the Banahgarian border and into exile in the Lands of the Great River. He finds sanctuary at an isolated farm owned by Carilton Tann, but no peace from the guilty memories that haunt him. He travels on eastward into further danger.

Meanwhile, petty thief Ellyah Jerim plans and executes a daring robbery; stealing a mysterious gem from right under the noses of a dangerous criminal gang – the Mackems. With the help of her old friend Nastja Mjette and former assassin Luara Orsini they evade the clutches of the gang and escape northwards through the country of Anish.

Unbeknownst to the three women, the jewel was part of a dark plot by a secret organisation led by a priestess, Evane Claes. She will stop at nothing to reclaim the jewel and uses magical means to track the women as they cross the mountains that form the northern border of Anish, descending into the Lands of the Great River.

The women and Eain are now both travelling westwards across the same lands, heading for Ben Gedrin; a trading town in the frontier zone of Kiraband.

Luara leads them to a village she knows called Feorhryc, where they steal horses and travel onwards more quickly. Eain arrives in the same village a day later, where he encounters the criminals who are pursuing the girls - the Mackems. He confronts them and drives them off, but then decides to follow the Mackems in case the women will be put in danger.

In Ben Gedrin, Luara helps them make contact with one of the two of the criminal gangs who control the city; the Cyfres, so that Ellyah can sell the jewel. An overheard conversation leads Eain to pledge himself to the same gangs, hoping he can protect the women from the planned double-cross at the jewel trade.

The first jewel trade fails when the gang contact is killed by the deadly power of the jewel. Meanwhile, Eain is captured by the other gang, the Sticasts, and forced to switch his allegiance to save his own life. Ellyah and Nastja manage to arrange a meeting with the Sticasts to trade the jewel, and Eain is sent as a guard for the meeting.

On Demonsnight, a fire festival, the trade is supposed to take place but the Sticasts secretly plan to kill Ellyah and Nastja and take the jewel. Eain intervenes, letting the two women escape but keeping the jewel himself. A running battle ensues in the crowded, dirty streets of Ben Gedrin; Sticasts and Cyfres and both ambushed by the city militia, who are in an alliance with the Mackems. In the chaos, the city is set alight and Eain escapes, with Ellyah and Nastja close behind.

CONTENTS

The Story So Far	*vii – x*
Map	*xii-xiii*
PROLOGUE	1
PART ONE	5
PART TWO	83
PART THREE	155
PART FOUR	243
PART FIVE	337
PART SIX	429
EPILOGUE	512
GLOSSARY	519
AUTHOR'S STATEMENT	523
THANK YOU	524
SECRET SCRIBES	525

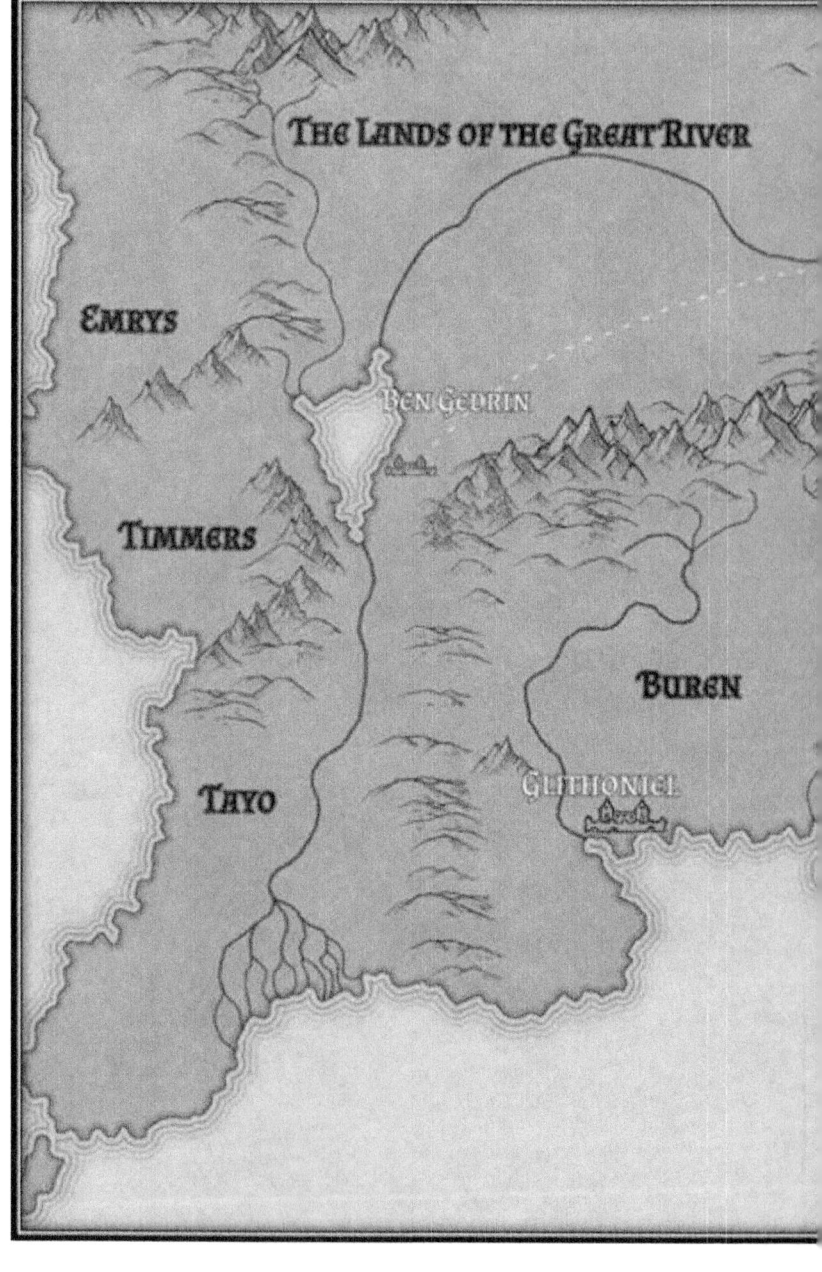

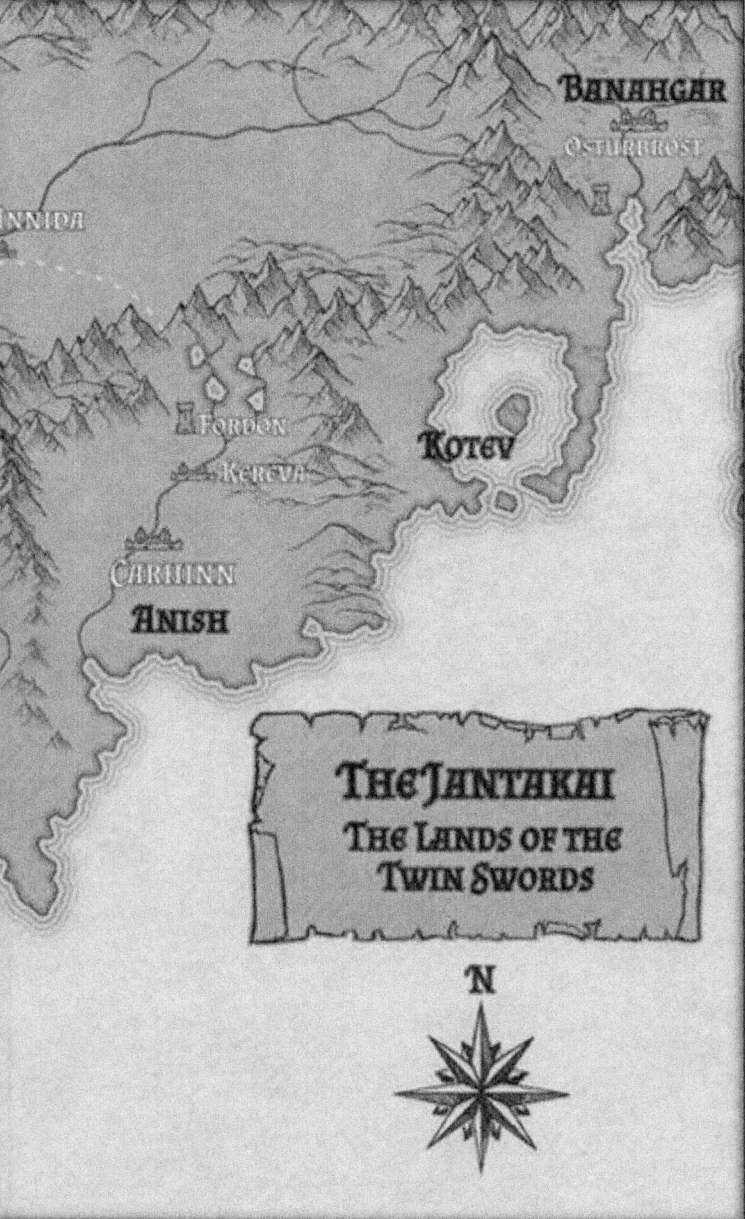

PROLOGUE

Tureank the Hunter knelt before his queen.

His eyes rose to her face; pale and haughty, twisted with cold arrogance. He hated her. He loved her. He craved her embrace and was prepared to destroy her.

If only he had the strength.

The sword in his fist felt light and cool. It was surely too insubstantial to use as a weapon, flimsy as a fleeting rain shower. Yet, he knew that the power it held could be as devastating as a tidal wave.

Its twin was clutched in Queen Conferan's slender fingers, and was more than its match. Swift as a viper's bite and deadly as venom, the Serpentsword writhed with malice and foreboded death.

'Give me the Riversword,' she said, and her voice hissed like sliding scales. 'Give it to me now, and die swiftly.'

He shuddered. She had fallen so far. They were both children of the gods who bore immortal power, and yet the malevolence of the Serpentsword had been too strong for even her to resist.

He felt unutterable sadness, mingled with pity. And loss. Keen loss of the woman he had known; the woman he loved.

Shaking his head, he summoned what remained of his strength and climbed to his feet.

He had come too far and suffered too much to surrender now. His mother had set his feet on the path that put the Riversword in his hands, and led him to this place. He could not betray her trust, and her hope.

He made the only response he could: 'No.'

She smiled, and the expression was as cold as a frozen lake.

'Then,' she replied in a low hiss. 'Die.'

She screamed, a piercing, high-pitched death scream and as she raised her pale, slender arms, dusk fell.

And from the sudden shadows, her army swarmed. A scuttling horde of beasts flooded forth with skin like tree bark and claws like iron nails.

His own followers stood against them, ranks of brave warriors girt in polished bronze and bearing long spears. The lines clashed with a sound like breaking branches.

Death was everywhere and Tureank fought through the chaos. Crows and kites gathered above the field. Tureank reached deep inside himself to find the courage he knew he would need.

He had to challenge Conferan herself.

Clutching the Riversword before him like a protective totem, he strode towards the bright queen. She pulsed with power, a clear white jewel against the dark cloak of the untimely night.

Tureank knew only fear. He raised his blade.

They fought.

Conferan attacked with demonic fury. Her strikes were like thunderbolts, flashing again and again in the darkness. Tureank defended, but could do no more than desperately withstand her storm.

He would soon be swept away.

Blood fell across the battlefield like rain as Conferan's savage beasts tore the flesh of Tureank's painted warriors. Tureank wanted only peace, not victory. He prayed. With the powers that were his birthright he reached out through the clouds and veils that shrouded the land, and beseeched his mother Mordea for aid.

The only response was an echoing silence.

The Serpentsword whistled past his head, and he barely ducked aside. His defence had faltered in his moment of disappointment and Conferan attacked with renewed ferocity.

Blade met blade; a smith pounding on an anvil. The only light was the sparks that flashed with each impact. It felt like the end of times.

Tureank staggered back, riven with pain. The Serpentsword had pierced his side, and the pain of it filled his body as though he burned from the inside. Conferan's grin of triumph was feral.

'Mother, you have forsaken me,' he whispered as he fell to his knees. 'I could not do this alone.'

A reply filled his ears, the rush of a beck in spate.

'You are not alone,' came the voice of Mordea.

Even as Conferan raised her blade for the killing stroke, there came a mighty wind. The beasts quailed as Conferan's unearthly darkness was blown away. The queen herself gasped and flinched, warding her eyes with a long-fingered hand. The light came from the gods themselves. It came from beyond the mortal lands, from the distant Veil.

Tureank forced away his pain and stood once more. His mother had given him this chance, this one opportunity to make things right. And he knew he must take it.

Fighting his instinct, he swung the Riversword at his lover, his queen. She had no time to defend herself. Tureank's stroke took her wrist, and the keen edge of the ancient blade cleaved through her flawless, immortal flesh, skin and bone.

The hand which still clutched the Serpentsword fell, cut from her body. Tureank hated himself for inflicting such a hurt on one so fair.

But he had no time to grieve.

When that magical blade touched the earth there was a mighty flash, a blinding burst of white light. When it died away, Tureank the Hunter and Conferan the Queen had gone, and the beasts had fled for the distant hills.

What had happened to the two warring lovers?

None could know for certain.

Some say that as soon as the Serpentsword was cut from her body, Conferan remembered her great love for Tureank and used what remained of her godly power to save him from death. She lifted them both from the mortal realm to dwell forever in the stars. Together.

Others say that Tureank perished from Conferan's strike and that she removed his body to the Shining Veil before ending her own life in a torrent of grief.

The only certainty was that the Twin Swords, the Riversword and the Serpentsword, were gone from the land once more.

They would reappear in the lands of mortals again after many years, and their presence would once more leave a trail of enmity, destruction and death.

PART ONE

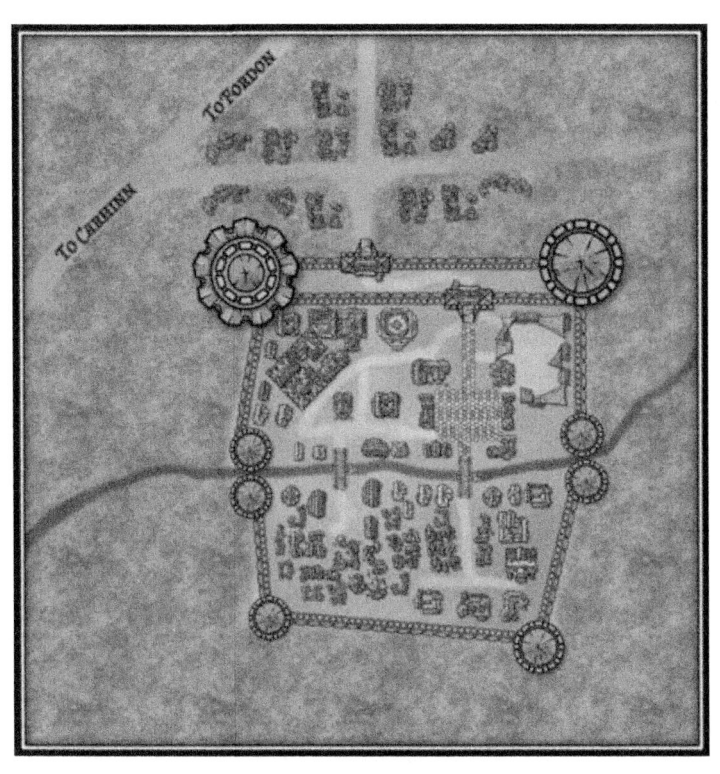

KEREVA

ONE

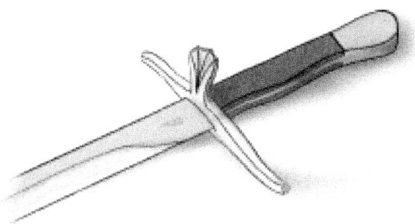

As heavy clouds gathered, the snow began to fall.

At first it was the finest dust, tiny crystalline specks driven into a swirling dance by the nagging wind. Soon the fall was heavier, and the mountainside was painted white.

The blizzard raged on, and the mountains were blanketed, peaks so high that none would ever set foot on their sharp summits. But, the clouds spread out to cover the lower slopes, brown-shaded darkness reaching further and further.

Soon, the storm would cover everything.

The Baron of Kereva stared down at his sword.

The patterns folded into the steel seemed to ripple and flow as they caught the afternoon light. He studied it as though it might hold answers to his questions. So far, he had learned little.

It was a traditional sabre, well-made but unremarkable in his country of Anish. The single-edged blade was forged with a subtle curve and was about the length of his outstretched arm. It was light enough to swing one-handed although the straight wooden handle was long enough for two.

The trappings were simple and understated: a forged iron hand guard and undecorated pommel. The nobles of Kotev, the neighbouring country, were known for their flamboyant versions of this simple design, with silk-wrapped hilts, gold ornamentation and enough gems encrusted in the scabbard to feed a family for a year.

They were not like this sword. They were swords designed to be seen, to boast of their owner's wealth and status. The sword in his hands was meant to be used.

He tightened his grip as his lip curled in frustration. He was like one of those Kotevari swords. He was little more than an ornament. A status symbol. A ceremonial blade, brought out for symbolic occasions and otherwise left to go blunt.

The point of his sword wavered, seeming to echo the roiling uncertainty that coursed through him. He attempted to still it, to summon the calm and focus that his fencing teacher demanded.

He had learned to concentrate until he found peace, and through that; insight. His teacher, Morehai, had encouraged this state of mind: blank and unquestioning, yet open to intuition.

He sought it now, needing answers and craving surety, but it was elusive. His emotions bubbled like a hot pan. The events of the last few days had unsettled him, shaken his very foundations.

What was he going to do?

Earlier that day, he had stormed up to his lavish quarters in the mighty keep that loomed over the city of Kereva. He had thrust the door open with such fierce rage that it had bounced back off the russet stone of the adjacent wall.

He had been heedless of the noise.

The room was large, but the walls seemed to close around him as he strode inside. At that moment it felt like a cage.

Then, he stopped.

He was not alone. He eyed the smooth-skinned body of the girl spread across his bed with weary disdain. She was naked, and already curled into a seductive pose. Her wide eyes showed surprise at his abrupt entrance, but a slow smile began to spread across her painted lips as he stared down at her.

Another gift from Coril. Clearly, she thought this was enough to buy his compliance. Anger and shame warred for primacy.

'Be gone by the time I return,' he snarled, and the smile died on her lips. He turned on his heel and stalked from the room.

This was not the reaction she had expected. Surprise, perhaps, followed by shy arousal. She had probably seen it all before. If she was not a simple prostitute then she was the daughter of a minor noble, hoping to gain favour with the Council by offering services to the new baron. It amounted to the same thing.

He had descended the staircase again, body falling heavily onto each step as he struggled with the weight of his frustration and disappointment.

Was this to be his life now? A tame hound performing simple tricks in exchange for titbits from his masters' table?

He had reached the bottom of the stairs, and his body steered itself towards the courtyard in the outer keep. He would do what he always did when faced with a problem he could not yet solve. He would train, practice, and immerse himself in study.

Yet, as he thought about the events of the last days, calm eluded him. He stared at the sword.

Coril. It was all Coril. Pulling the strings. Showering him with gifts. Doing what she could to keep the young baron placid, content and above all silent.

His name was Styoyan Jukeev, and the day of his investiture as Baron of Kereva had seemed the culmination of everything he had worked for. His whole childhood had led to it. The honour was all he had ever wanted.

Lessons in statecraft, politics, languages and history, in addition to training in martial arts and singing. He was the model of everything that a noble of Anish should be. The youngest of his brothers, he had always been determined not to be the least. He would stand in their company as an equal, and his father would finally be proud.

He had sung the ancient words that bound him to his duty, standing proudly in the great hall of the keep of Kereva. The rich, resounding notes of harp and bell had rung out to accompany his words, and his hands had shaken slightly as he grasped the golden rod of the barony.

The hall was filled by the voices of the congregation, all raised in song at the climax of the ceremony, and he felt as though he must actually be glowing, such was the feeling pride and vitality within his body at that moment.

'The Five shall guide the steps of the baron,' Coril had intoned. 'Courage, fortune, luck, unity and long life shall they grant.'

It had been Coril that had introduced him to the girl. Dressed in fine silks, she had smooth skin the colour of young oak and bright, wide eyes.

Styoyan had not been able to restrain his enthusiasm in tearing her from her dress, once she had led him to his quarters, her soft hand in his. It had been his first time, and the frantic, heart-racing pleasure and joy he had felt as she wrapped her long legs around him seemed a fitting climax to the day.

His chest heaving, her delicate hands had stroked his body gently as he talked afterwards. Gabbled. Told her all his hopes and heroic dreams, like a grand fool.

Her presence was intoxicating, and for Styoyan the warmth in his body and the ache in his balls was the same as many other young men had mistaken for love.

She had cut him off abruptly when she stood to dress.

'Will payment be through Coril, as usual?' she asked. 'I can return any time to suit your lordship, daily or weekly. Coril knows how to reach me.'

Only then did it dawn on him that she was nothing but a common whore. He supposed, as the door banged shut, that she was not that common. More like a high-class working girl to service the needs of the wealthy and powerful. He had been too excited at first to notice the slight upsweep of her ears that showed her half-elven blood.

Just a little gift from Coril. A taste of what Styoyan could enjoy as baron, if he played along. If he kept his head down.

Coril ran Kereva.

That truth had hit home over the days that followed. Coril and the High Council of Kereva held all the power, not Baron Styoyan Jukeev. He had been summoned to the great hall the following day and had that hard truth spelled out.

The hall had felt much bigger then than during his investiture. The benches were empty, and the harps and bells were still. The voices of the council members, grey, aging men and women sounded hollow as they spoke down to him.

Coril had said the most. She had been quite persuasive.

'There is simply no need for you to worry yourself with the petty details,' she explained. 'Myself and the other councillors have many years of experience. I'm sure you don't want to be bored by it all.'

She had deflected his attempts to argue.

Styoyan was not so naïve that he could not understand the implications.

The council had carved up the business of the city between them and had become very wealthy as a result. They did not want, or need, an idealistic young noble interfering.

'Of course,' Coril had continued. 'Your new title endows various estates in the country outside the city. The orchards are beautiful this time of year, and the eternity trees in the borderlands will soon be in blossom. They are a stirring sight, if you've never seen them.'

Styoyan had declined to take the hint.

But, now he was clear on the true nature of his title. It was a gilded cap. To be worn, and seen, but serving no practical purpose.

He should accept the lavish comfort it provided and keep his mouth shut. It was bribery of the worst sort. And it seemed he had little choice but to be party to it.

Styoyan stared down at his sword. The silver-grey ripples in the blade were like the shifting autumnal clouds that swirled above his head. The words of Morehai, his fencing master, returned:

'In life, you have but two choices. You can endure your troubles, or you can instigate change. Complaints and regret achieve nothing but wasted air. It is leaves blowing in the wind. Endure, or change. That is all there is.'

Change something.

Styoyan picked up his scabbard and slid the blade home. He paused. In his haste to leave his chambers he had forgotten his sword belt. He held the scabbard beside his hip, his left hand near the collar.

There was something. Some flicker of insight. A premonition of change.

He focused on his breathing, calming his emotions and putting his anger aside. Empty.

His right hand hovered near the hilt.

Exhaling, his mind floated as his weight sank down on the balls of his feet. Was this it?

Without his sword belt, he could not draw the sword from the scabbard, but he now saw there was another way.

With a rush of certainty, he set his hand to the hilt and in the same motion thrust the scabbard backward, off the blade.

The sabre scythed out and there was a dull thud as the bundle of reeds he used for cutting practice fell to the ground cut cleanly in two. Instead of drawing the sword from the sheath, he had pushed the scabbard off the blade. He knew that he had to grasp control from a different direction.

He needed to visit his father.

TWO

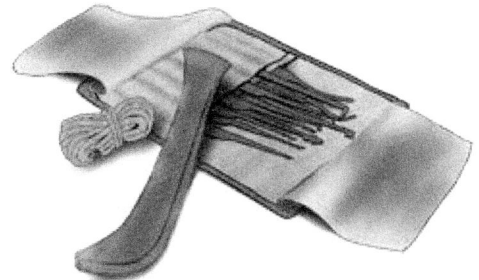

'Shit! Shit and shitting demon's blood!'

Ellyah could not contain her rage.

'That thief! That cheating, traitorous thief,' she continued as she paced around the small room. 'I knew we shouldn't have trusted him. Didn't I say? I can't believe that we helped him escape!'

She glared at Nastja who looked up silently from where she was sitting, legs crossed neatly beneath her. A heap of silver money rings and several finger-sized gold marks were arranged before her.

They had fled the burning chaos of Ben Gedrin without a backward glance. The Demonsnight fire festival had descended into a running battle through the crowded streets.

Criminal gangs had faced off against each other while the city militia sprung a trap to capture them all. As blood flowed and screams rent the air, the ceremonial fire-bulls escaped their pens and charged through the melee. At the same time, one of the palanquin-borne model houses was knocked over, falling in flames into the front of a tavern.

Fire quickly engulfed the building, the timber old and dry, and soon the city was lit by coruscating orange light.

That is how Ellyah recalled the events of that night, but she acknowledged that she was already thinking in the way that she would tell the tale.

The truth was that she had been the one that had released the bulls, and she was the one who had started the fire. It had been the only way that she and Nastja could escape together, and she did not regret it. Ben Gedrin was a city that would be improved by the cleansing touch of flame.

It had not seemed significant at the time but the chaos she created had also allowed a man to escape from the gangs, and from the militia's cordon. A man who was a complete stranger. A man who, it seemed, had orchestrated a sophisticated double-cross that night.

'Are you sure?' she asked, turning to Nastja once more.

The gold and silver spread at her feet had been their payment for their part in the deal. The gangs of Ben Gedrin had both been eager to get their hands on something that Ellyah and Nastja had possessed. Something rare, and unearthly. Something valuable.

The Demon's Tear ruby.

It was a fist-sized jewel that Ellyah had stolen from the Mackems, a criminal gang based in her home country of Anish. When rumours reached her ears of this object, she had been unable to resist its call.

A long chase ensued, the Mackems following the trail of the jewel and Ellyah, Nastja and their friend Luara staying a scant few steps ahead.

The deal had been done. The sale had been made. Ellyah had handed over the ruby and taken this sack of silver and gold as payment. Enough money for her to escape forever.

But, moments after taking the gold, the gang leader's own bodyguard had lashed out with his blade and killed both him and his son. It had been a trap, claimed the assassin. The gang had planned to ambush Ellyah and Nastja and take back the gold. They would have had their throats cut.

They had certainly seen enough gang fighters on the streets that night for the story to ring true, but now Ellyah was not sure what to believe.

'The silver is fine,' said Nastja, indicating a heap of money rings, grey and yet gleaming. 'And this mark,' she reached out and picked up a finger-sized ingot of gleaming gold, 'is real. Look, you can see the maker's mark here, and these runes at the end tell the striking date. Only a few months ago. Vainkeev. That's when we were in Carhinn with the jewel.'

Ellyah waited. Nastja would answer the question, eventually.

'The clearest sign is that if you scratch it deeply,' she pressed a fingernail into the ingot to demonstrate. 'It's the same colour all the way through the scratch. Look.'

She held it up.

'Yes,' said Ellyah, trying to keep the impatience out of her voice.

'But these,' Nastja went on, 'are fakes. Good fakes.' She picked one up. It was the same shape, the same size, and shone with the same rich, lustrous gleam. She weighed it in her hand.

'Right weight. Right colour. They have even copied the maker's mark, but they are all for the same date. It's a hint but most wouldn't spot it. The forger managed a really good colour match. It's probably a mixture of lead and tin, to make it shine, and then the surface is varnished.'

She pressed her thumbnail deeply into the ingot.

'It's slightly harder and – look, it's less golden below the surface.'

So,' replied Ellyah in a level tone. Nastja was oblivious to her growing annoyance. She dragged the words out. 'You're certain that most of our payment for the jewel was in fake marks?'

'Looks that way, yes.'

Ellyah swore again. She stooped and picked up the fake ingots, drawing back her arm as if to throw them from the balcony and into the narrow, rocky gorge below.

'Wait!' Nastja's voice was suddenly urgent. Ellyah paused, turning. 'The fakes are still worth something,' she said. 'We might need them.'

Ellyah sighed and dropped the lumps of metal to the floor. They bounced off the floorboards with a hollow sound. Nastja quickly gathered them and put them neatly beside her.

'So how much have we got? Of real money.'

'One gold mark and…five pounds in silver rings. I counted them. Enough to last most of a year, if we are careful.'

Ellyah was silent for a moment, then stamped her foot. She knew that it was pure petulance, but her blood was boiling and she could not hold it in.

'That man!' she growled. 'This is all his fault. If he was working with the gangs of Ben Gedrin, or the Mackems, or on his own, I don't know. But he's left us with a pittance while he walks away with the jewel. He's just a thief!'

'And a good one,' put in Nastja. 'He walked out of Ben Gedrin with the Demon's Tear, even though he had the gangs of the city, the militia and the Mackems after him.'

With my help, thought Ellyah, grinding her teeth.

She looked up at the dyed linen curtain that separated their small partition from the rest of the house. Her thoughts ran through the curtain, through the house and out of the front door to the great south road. He was out there somewhere.

Nastja guessed her thoughts.

'We can't chase him now,' she said. 'It's not safe to be on the road at night. Besides, it'd be easy to miss him in the darkness. We could walk straight past him.'

Ellyah clenched her jaw. 'But, he'll be getting away with it. With the ruby. *My* ruby.'

'Do you remember what he looked like?' asked Nastja, her voice flat and overly calm.

'Of course!' replied Ellyah. 'Huge bloke! Fair hair and shoulders like chiselled stone. He had a bloody huge sword on his back.'

He had been a striking-looking man: tall and solidly built with pale eyes and skin that had a glowing, golden tone. Ellyah kept seeing his face when she closed her eyes. It made her angry.

'He was really distinctive,' agreed Nastja. 'So, don't you think he'll be easy to find? He's heading south, obviously, and the only place he's likely to be heading is Glithoniel.'

Ellyah turned to Nastja, surprised but not wanting to show it. Glithoniel was the capital city of Buren and the confederacy of Re'Emsser. It was the biggest city in the world, hard on the south coast and with docks that thrived with the world's trade. Nastja was almost certainly right.

Nastja continued. 'He'll have to call in somewhere along the road between here and there, and people will remember him when he does. We just have to follow. Follow the trail he leaves behind. There's no sense in running out into the road in the middle of the night. We'll find him in the end.'

'Right,' said Ellyah. 'Right. You're right. We'll track him down, and get the jewel back.'

He owed them. He had stolen from them. There was no way she could let him escape. She still needed that jewel. It was her future.

'So come and lie down,' said Nastja gently. 'We were tricked. But we're also lucky to be alive. It's gone dusk and time to sleep, if we are to chase him hard tomorrow.'

'Right,' repeated Ellyah. 'We need to be on the road at dawn tomorrow. We can ask everyone we meet if they've seen him. Follow his trail, find a way to take the ruby back.'

'We can do it.'

Ellyah sniffed. 'Just wish I had a change of clothes. This shirt has seen better days, and now it stinks of smoke too.'

'Wait.' Nastja dug her hand into her bulging pack, and pulled out a clean shirt in pale linen.

'This my size?' asked Ellyah, puzzled.

'Yes,' said Nastja. 'I brought spares for both of us.'

Of course you did, thought Ellyah, as she doffed the dirty shirt and pulled the clean one over her head.

'Tomorrow,' she said, as she lay down on the floor and tried to find a comfortable position on the rough bed of rush matting. Tomorrow, they went from hunted to hunters.

Two full days' walking had been enough for the two women to feel like they were in a different world. As dusk fell on the second evening they looked uneasily around at hard-edged stone buildings. Pale lights glimmered. Shadows shifted.

They had set out at dawn on the first day, when clouds filled the river valley below the road with deep, woolly mist. Fat, heavy droplets had glistened on the underside of the guesthouse's low, curling eaves as they hastened down the steps.

Ellyah peered down the road. The light was dull and grey, and the steep mountainside to her left was only visible as a looming dark mass through the foggy gloom.

There was no movement on the road, but Ellyah knew that their quarry was out there somewhere.

'Fare you well,' called the master of the house from the doorway. He placed his splayed fingers over his heart and inclined his head gravely. Ellyah nodded back before turning her eyes towards their onward road.

The first of their silver was spent. How long would the rest last? Not long enough.

'The roadside houses are mostly owned by Tayans,' said Nastja, as they followed the hard packed trail steadily downhill. 'Did you know that?'

Ellyah did not care. 'Oh?' she said, putting a question in her voice to encourage Nastja to continue. It would pass the time.

'After the last Tayan uprising,' she went on. 'When Buren took the Swarthland in the southeast of Tayo and forced the ruler to forswear the title *brehnan* for *taosach*, they made the Tayan rulers sign up to the terms of Re'Emsser. Plenty of the northern Tayans realised that they would be a lot worse off under the new treaty and left as quickly as possible. Some went all the way north to Ben Gedrin and out into the Riverlands, or took boats across the lake to the Alrean Empire. But, some realised that this valley, where the road runs, wasn't actually formally part of either Buren or Tayo. It existed outside the terms of Re'Emsser.'

Ellyah suppressed a sigh as she continued walking. She was much more interested in finding the man who had robbed them of the jewel. But when Nastja wanted to share her knowledge, there was really no way of stopping her.

'It's why all the houses are built in the Tayan style, with those curving eaves and balconies. It made sense to open up their spare rooms to travellers, and now the road is lined with them.'

She gestured upward and to their left.

The steep hillside was dotted at intervals with those ornate houses. Thick curved beams stained a deep red showed below steeply pitched roofs covered with bamboo tiles. They looked nothing like the houses of their native Anish, and Ellyah realised in that moment just how far they were from home.

There is nothing for me there, she thought. *There is only the onward road, and the jewel, and the fortune I need to escape.*

'Makes sense,' she said aloud. 'Think we'll find that thief in one of them?'

Nastja shrugged. 'We'll be in Buren if we keep walking until tomorrow night.'

So, it had proved.

The mist lifted throughout the morning, although the sky above remained filled with thick grey clouds. The Great River thundered away to their right, narrower here than above the shimmering expanse of Lake Gedrin, pounding down its rocky valley with relentless vigour.

As they descended from the mountains, moving further south, the colours of autumn were everywhere. The season had turned as they had been travelling across the dull, colourless plains of the north and the only sign had been the greyness of the sky and knifing chill of the wind.

Here, sparse forests huddled in the base of the valley and the leaves that shook in the gentle breeze were every shade from deep, dark brown to vivid yellow. The lower slopes were clad in a verdant gown and rows of birch on the higher fringes edged them a royal purple. The occasional evergreen fir stood out like an embroidered emerald.

The ground beneath their feet, and between the trees, remained a pale dun shade but in the distance green hills rolled away southward. Ellyah knew that they were seeing the northern extent of the great country of Buren.

They would cross the border by the next nightfall.

'Careful here,' said Ellyah under her breath around noon on the first day.

The road had flattened out and the rocks and boulders to either side were sharp edged and reddish. The river gorge was much deeper here, a sheer-sided ravine that fell away abruptly to their right. The voice of the churning water was a baritone, echoing roar.

A bridge spanned the gorge in a single arching leap. An impossible bridge. The top surface of the two-hundred-foot span was flat and straight as the smoothest road, but no pier or buttress supported the underside. It was as though a single tongue of rock had stretched out across the yawning gap.

Ellyah took a step closer. It did not look like something that had been built, but as though it had been formed by nature itself. The edges were bound by neither parapet nor wall, but a flimsy and insubstantial fence of woven willow had been raised on either side. Fathoms below, the river foamed and crashed.

Nastja silently reached out and grasped Ellyah's arm, steering her away from the bridge of solid, unjointed stone and from the rift that yawned below.

Where the road passed the mouth of the bridge, a barricade of slim, stripped logs barred passage. Men and women dressed for war, in baked leather and bearing long spears, stood belligerently around the barrier.

'Bureno guards,' whispered Ellyah as they hurried past. A tall warrior in shimmering scale-mail stepped forwards, hand on the hilt of a scabbarded longsword.

'Yea,' agreed Nastja. 'They guard this as the border between them and Tayo in the north.' She gestured to the far side of the span where a group of brightly dressed figures stood. Tayans, on their side of the border.

Relations between the two nations were frosty.

The two women turned to put the bridge and its guards behind them, and hurried away.

'Could he have crossed the bridge?' asked Nastja in an undertone. Until this point, the road had been channelled down the river-cut valley with no turnings or alternative routes. At the bridge, though, the way split; straight on southward to Buren, or westward across the gorge to Tayo.

'Why would he?' Ellyah answered quickly. She thought for a moment, then dismissed the idea. 'He's got the jewel and he clearly knows what it's worth. He wouldn't waste his time in Tayo. There's no money there, just war. He'd keep heading south to the Star City.'

'Glithoniel.'

'Right. So, that's where we go. We'll find him there if we don't catch him on the way. He'll have left a trail, right?'

Nastja nodded.

Ellyah was glad that Nastja agreed. The pair walked on.

The night was spent at another simple guest house, and the next day they followed the river as it surged down towards the lowlands. The sky remained roofed with grey and only a vague glow indicated the sun's passage as the afternoon wore on. The mountains to their left dwindled in height and soon gave way to brown slopes of bracken and heather.

The Great River's gorge wound away westward, and a low range of green hills spread across the path of the road. These formed the historic border between Buren and Tayo, but banks and walls to their right showed where Tayan land had been taken and fortified.

Ellyah and Nastja turned away as the road wound up a shallow slope and towards a cluster of houses in a cleft between two rounded peaks. Fields stretched across the hillsides like a patchwork quilt of green and brown, colours fading in the evening light.

They walked past single storey cottages on the outskirts of the village, but taller buildings rose to either side of the road as they neared the centre. A sturdy wall ran across the hillside, split by a gateway where the road passed through. The gates were thrown open and unguarded, and the two women hurried into the village.

Most of the buildings had at least a foundation or lower wall of pale stone, and were square and solidly-built. Orange lights glimmered through shuttered windows as hearth fires were kindled into life. Shadows lengthened as Ellyah and Nastja strolled into the heart of the village.

'What's that?' asked Ellyah, pointing ahead.

The street ahead was darkened by a looming archway. Almost like another fortified gateway, it stretched across the street, connecting the buildings on either side and forming a gloomy tunnel beneath.

On one side, the dancing light of a blazing fire shone through an open doorway, while on the other a wider opening led to a dark area that smelled of hay and horses.

'It's the inn,' said Nastja, as though stating the obvious. She pointed left. 'Stables,' then up. 'Rooms. Let's have a drink,' she said, moving towards the beckoning door.

The fire crackled and conversation hummed as Ellyah followed Nastja inside. Her eyes darted around the room. She half-expected to see that tall, fair-haired stranger at the bar or huddled in one of the corners.

Would he think they would track him, or would he be surprised to see them again? He had played the parties grappling for the jewel in Ben Gedrin so adeptly that he would probably be very cautious on the road.

'Don't stare at everyone.' Nastja's voice intruded on her thoughts. 'They'll think you're looking for a fight. Here, drink this. I've paid for a room here for the night.'

She passed a wooden cup filled with dark red wine and led the way to a small round table near the hearth. The warmth was welcome and Ellyah suddenly felt her fatigue like a heavy hand on her brow.

She took a deep drink. The wine was heavy and bittersweet.

Where was that man?

His face, golden-skinned and youthful, flashed before her each time she closed her eyes. She could clearly remember his expression when she had seen him trapped by the Ben Gedrin militia's defensive line.

Pure fear.

And it was her actions that had saved him. As she was dragging Nastja away from the fire and the fighting, she had seen him striding off in a different direction. The charge of the fire-bulls had broken the militia's line and allowed him to escape their trap, and the city.

She remembered feeling a surge of relief at the time, although she could not have said why.

She wondered about it anew. And now she realised why.

She had believed his story at the time, believed that his actions had saved their lives. That the Sticasts had planned to ambush them and kill them both to recover their silver and phoney gold was probably true. People like the Sticasts killed without a second thought.

Ellyah *had* believed him, and so had felt a stab of guilt when she had seen him in such danger. She had felt that she would be left with an unpayable debt. She hated owing anyone.

She assured herself now that she had done the right thing, even if it turned out that the man she had saved was a thief and a double-crosser.

The chaos had helped them escape Ben Gedrin, too. Without it, Nastja could have been captured by the militia or worse. Their other friend Luara had fled into the night; they had not seen her again but knew she had left the city on horseback. If Ellyah had not acted, then the jewel would have been captured with the thief and would now be the prized possession of the governor of Ben Gedrin.

I had no choice, she thought.

They just needed to find that man and reclaim the jewel. Ellyah still felt that the ruby was hers by right, until she had sold it for a fair price. Until she had pocketed the gold and silver she needed to escape for good.

The crimson glow of the jewel was an indelible memory. Magical, unique and extremely dangerous. She *had* to get it back.

'I'm going to ask the barman some questions,' she murmured to Nastja. If the man had passed through, then the barman would be sure to remember him.

'Be careful,' said Nastja, unhelpfully.

'Be you well,' she said to the barman as she leaned towards him. He was middle aged, with white wings in the dark hair above his ears, and with skin that was the rich brown common in Buren. He nodded.

'I'm looking for a friend,' she said, voice low. 'He's a tall man, nigh on ceiling height. Might have been carrying a sword with a long hilt on his back.' The barman was already shaking his head. 'Sure?'

'Na, he sounds distinctive. He'd have been noticed if he'd passed through. Not seen his like. Sounds like the sort as could find his way to Tayo.'

She thanked him and returned to her seat.

'If he's travelling fast, and knows he's hunted,' she mused. 'Then maybe he isn't stopping at inns.'

'He'll leave a trace somewhere, though,' said Nastja. 'We know what to look for and we'll notice things that others might miss. Maybe we'll have more luck in one of the bigger towns.'

'Maybe.'

Ellyah took another sip of her drink. She could develop a taste for Bureno wine when she had recovered the jewel and sold it for what it was truly worth.

Nastja stiffened as the door banged shut behind someone leaving the inn. Nastja was staring straight at it.

'What? What is it?'

'We need to get out of here, now.' Her eyes were wide.

'Don't be daft!' said Ellyah. 'We've just paid for the room.'

Nastja leaned closer. 'Someone just got up and left. A woman. She had been sat in the far corner. As she walked out of the door she looked right at us.'

Ellyah scoffed.

'I'm not joking, Ellyah. She looked at us, at both of our faces, exactly as though she was expecting to see us. She was waiting here for us.'

Her face was grave. 'We're in danger. Again.'

THREE

Skane wiped his hands down the coarse fabric of his smock as he stepped out of the house. There was something about these guest houses that set his teeth on edge.

Too neat. Too clean. All precisely placed decorations and polished wood.

'I hope we can find a proper tavern today,' he said, looking in Jhari's direction.

Jhari's first response was a chesty grunt. Jhari was a giant, a monster nearly seven feet tall and with hands like shovels. The subtle upsweep of his ears and the mahogany darkness of his skin betrayed his elven blood, but most half-elves were a foot or more shorter, and probably half his weight.

'Good wine in Buren,' he said, eventually. He was a useful right-hand man. People often admitted to things as soon as they saw him, and a locked door was not an obstacle.

'I'd prefer a mug or two of ale,' said Skane as they headed south, following the broad wagon road. They left the house behind them empty. The owner of the guesthouse had not been eager to tell them anything, at first.

'My guests' business is their own,' he had whimpered after Skane had barged through the door. 'I cannot be known as a house-keeper who breaks trust!'

Jhari had broken one of his fingers. That had encouraged him to tell them what they wanted to know, while his wife and daughters wailed and pleaded from the doorway.

Two women had stayed there two nights previously. One was tall and dark haired, the other shorter and with dark skin but fair hair. They seemed to have some money although their garb was simple and plain.

Yes, they had headed south. No, they had not mentioned whether they were for Buren or Tayo.

'That's all I know, that's all I know,' said the house-keeper, again and again. 'Please spare my family. Please.'

Skane had ordered Jhari to let the man go, and he had dashed out of the door with his wife and daughters. They hurried up the road and the evening gloom had swallowed them.

'Got to be heading for Buren,' said Jhari, as they walked on, the following day. 'Nothing to do in Tayo but fight.'

'Yea,' agreed Skane. Good fighting though, by accounts, for good coin. The saying went that there were two types of mercenary in Tayo; rich or dead. It was tempting for Skane. Fighting for a living sounded simple. He liked things simple.

His work with the Mackems used to be simple. Break down that door, bash that head, squeeze that mark until the gold fell from their nerveless fingers.

Lately, though…things had changed. Chasing people across three different countries in pursuit of a dangerous, magical jewel and seeing the dead walk ?

No, none of this was simple.

He did not dare voice those concerns. He was in too deep, and his masters held too much mysterious power. They could be watching him right now. He could not appear weak or indecisive in front of the band of thugs and thieves he led on this quest. He had to keep going until the job was done.

He had his orders.

The governor of Ben Gedrin had summoned them the day after Demonsnight. A pall of smoke still hung over the city and several of the buildings around the central square had been reduced to blackened husks. Charred spars and beams jutted out like the ribs of a decaying corpse.

The atmosphere in the governor's broad timber hall was jubilant. It stood uphill and to the north of the city's centre, far enough from the previous night's chaos to have been spared the flames.

The polished trunks of at least twenty mighty redwoods held up a wide roof, the lattice of rafters carved with intricate designs. Morning light beamed in through open shutters, illuminating the equally beaming face of the governor.

'Come!' he boomed. 'Come closer, that you might all hear me easily.'

Governor Ceolbaght was a tall but rotund man in his middle years. His hair was cropped short, with the colour and texture of dry straw. He wore a long robe of the southern style and a drooping yellow moustache that was intended to make him look like a warrior.

He could not have looked less like one, in Skane's opinion.

'Bar the doors,' added Ceolbaght, smile fading. The bars thudded into place, and he continued: 'We have won a great victory! With the help of our new southern friends,' he gestured to the corner where Skane, Jhari and the other Mackems stood, 'we trapped and defeated the fighting core of the Sticasts and the Cyfres. Many were killed and we shall not weep for them. Many more were taken and will soon be put to work to pay off the great debt they owe to this city.

'Rest assured, my friends, any who are known to have killed any of your fellow militia will have their throats slit and their bodies thrown into the old mounds where the ghosts abide. They shall not find their way to the Veil.'

He paused, and the gathered militia cheered their approval.

'The sovereignty of the government will be restored, and the city will prosper!' More cheers.

He spoke more quietly now. 'However, the work is not done. Not all the criminals were caught. Three women came to our city in recent days. They brought an item of great worth with them, and used it to initiate the disturbances from which we wrested our victory. We had hoped to capture those criminals and take the item from them on Demonsnight.'

The jewel, thought Skane. *He was talking about the three girls from Anish and the ruby they had stolen.*

'But, they escaped. We do not know how, but they are no longer in the city. The item they carried has also slipped away, and we suspect they still have it. The item must be recovered and brought to me, and those girls must meet justice for their part in what happened.'

The governor paused, looking directly at Skane and the Mackems.

'I have spoken with your *master*,' he said, emphasising the last word. 'And your orders remain to pursue the women and recover what they carry. They are likely to be taking the southern road towards Buren. You will go that way, and quickly.

'I will send my own guards out across the Riverlands. We will find them. Now, go!'

Skane, Jhari and the other Mackems had collected their things and readied their wagon, before rolling out of Ben Gedrin that afternoon.

The governor's speech had given Skane a lot to think about, in his slow, quiet way. Ceolbaght claimed to have spoken with the Mackems' master. Skane had to assume they meant the masked figure who spoke to them through portals conjured in the air, and not Cannis Flett, their leader back in Carhinn.

Did that mean that the masked sorcerer was in Ben Gedrin? Or that they had magically communicated with the governor? Skane did not know, but both alternatives posed further questions.

Also, they seemed to believe that the girls still had the jewel. Why would that be the case? They had travelled to Ben Gedrin to trade it, so how could anyone know that they had not done just that? One of the gang leaders, Cyfres or Sticast, could have it by now.

'This stinks,' he had said to Jhari, sat in the other seat at the front of the wagon. The big half-elf grunted an agreement.

As the wagon rocked and swayed through the city's south gate, Skane caught the vague rumble of Jhari speaking.

'What?' Skane asked impatiently. 'Speak up!'

Jhari sighed, turning so that Skane could watch his lips. Jhari coped well with Skane's deafness, speaking loudly and clearly and making sure to face him as he spoke. He just needed the occasional reminder.

'I said, what happened to the big guy? The young one.'

'What big guy?' Jhari was nearly seven feet tall, and did not describe many others as "big".

'The one from the village,' said Jhari, slowly, brow furrowed in concentration. 'The one with the big sword.'

'Oh, him.'

Skane remembered. They had been trying to follow the girls' trail across the Riverlands, and at a roadside inn a tall stranger had chased them away brandishing a heavy sword he had pulled off the wall.

It had been in the look in the man's eyes that had persuaded Skane to back away from the fight, rather than the weapon itself. Those pale eyes had been...dead.

'What about him?'

'He was in Ben Gedrin,' replied Jhari, in a matter-of-fact tone.

'What? Where? Where'd you see him?'

That sort of coincidence seemed unlikely.

'The first night. You went into the fighting club." Jhari paused between each sentence, thinking hard. 'He went in after you. He didn't have the sword and he was wearing a hood, but I recognised his eyes. And his shoulders.'

Skane nodded. In their line of work, quickly assessing someone's capacity for violence became second nature. It was easy to forget how observant Jhari could be.

'You didn't tell me,' said Skane.

'Didn't ask,' said Jhari, shrugging. 'Didn't seem important. But I saw him again, after that.'

'Right.' This was interesting, and for some reason, worrying.

'Demonsnight. When the fight started and someone ran away from the warehouse, and we all chased them? That was him.'

Skane was silent, thinking back. They had been closing in on the jewel, guided to the location by the magically animated corpse of the thief, Clayton Moore. That had been months previously, but their mysterious master had used a dark spell to bid his dead sinews to work, and to lead the Mackems towards their prize.

Skane shuddered. He had been glad to see the end of Clayton Moore. His head had rolled grimly across the cobbles, lopped from his body by the blades of a dark-clad assassin. But, by that time they had been close to their destination, weapons in hands and ready to fight.

They had not been the only ones though, and they found themselves confronted by one of the gangs of Ben Gedrin: the Cyfres. *Someone else to fight*, Skane had thought at the time. Looking back, he realised that they were probably also searching for the jewel.

That was the moment when a lone figure had distracted them all. He had burst from the door of the darkened warehouse and sprinted away. They had given chase, without a word. The Cyfres seemed to recognise him, and the Mackems knew they were all heading into an ambush.

Soon, knives were flashing and the gangs were painting the cobbles with each other's blood. All the Mackems had to do was watch, shoulder to shoulder across each end of a narrow lane, blocking any escape.

'He was fighting with the Sticasts,' said Skane, suddenly remembering.

'Yea,' replied Jhari. 'But he didn't go down. And I didn't see him get caught, either. I think he must have escaped.'

Their trap had been sprung, the militia advancing with their spears level towards the grappling gang members. The noose was tight. But then, the night was lit by the flare and glow of flames. The city was on fire.

And through the flames came the thunder of hooves. The sacrificial fire-bulls which were due to be hunted down and slaughtered at the climax of the Demonsnight festival had been released into the melee.

They galloped across the square and down the narrow lanes of the city's centre, causing chaos and destruction. Many who were in the way were trampled down or gored by their sharp, curving horns; criminals, militia fighters and common citizens alike. It had been a fiery vision of the underworld itself.

Jhari was right. That boy had been fighting in Ben Gedrin, and he seemed to have escaped capture.

'What if...?' he began, but tailed off, reluctant to finish the thought.

'The jewel trade was done.' Jhari said it instead.

'And he had it. And escaped with it. That's why he ran.'

'Yea.'

'Shit.' Skane swore, with feeling. 'Well, we got our orders. We'll do what we're told. But the jewel could be anywhere by now.'

Skane hated difficult decisions. He liked his life to be simple.

He was faced with a dilemma now, though, and he did not like it at all. The rest of the Mackems, a couple of handfuls in number, milled around uncertainly. They had overheard his conversations with Jhari and knew that something was troubling their leader.

That Jhari had to bellow every word to make sure he was heard made that impossible to avoid.

Now, they were waiting for him to tell them what to do.

They stood where the Great River had cut a deep gorge through the arid landscape. Sheer cliffs of reddish rock stood to either side, making the ravine impassable apart from a single narrow bridge.

It was guarded at either end, and the Bureno knight and his armsmen glared balefully at the Mackems as they approached, hands on weapons. Skane eyed them as he considered their options.

He had never been so far from Anish before, but knew that the river was used as the border between Buren and Tayo. The two nations held an uneasy peace, since Tayo had been defeated in the last border wars and made to sign up to the terms of the Re'Emsser confederacy.

The guards at both sides of the bridge looked ready to act at the slightest provocation. Which way should Skane lead the Mackems?

The girls had probably come this way. Buren was relatively safe and Glithoniel was big enough to hide away, busy enough to buy and sell all sorts of goods. They could even jump on a ship. It seemed very unlikely that they would have turned towards Tayo. There was nothing there but war.

That young man, though…

'That boy,' he said, turning to Jhari. 'Good fighter? Handy with that sword?'

'Yea,' replied Jhari. 'Lethal.'

Skane sucked his teeth. It was well known that there was solid work for warriors in Tayo, just across the bridge. What if he had gone that way and taken the jewel with him?

Their orders had been to follow the girls, though. It was much easier just to follow orders.

'South,' he said, loudly enough for everyone to hear. 'We continue south.' He hoped he would not regret this decision. The wagon rumbled on, and the other Mackems trudged along beside it.

That evening, they arrived at the first village in Buren, a small but prosperous hilltop settlement.

None of them expected the scene of confusion and distress that they found there.

FOUR

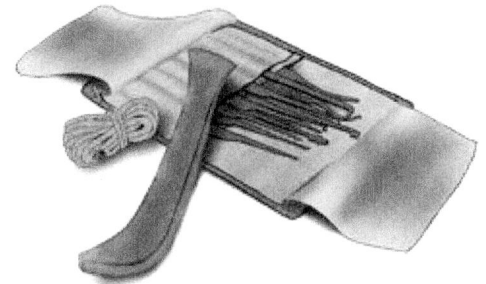

Ellyah woke up in a bad mood.

A few short paces away was a bed. A bed with a well-stuffed mattress beneath a sturdy roof and with a glowing hearth nearby. A bed that she had paid for.

Yet, here she was, in the inn's barn, huddling in the straw to keep warm and scratching the bugs off her skin. It would be a strange thing if she was not in a bad mood.

She turned, glowering, to where Nastja was sleeping in her own pile of matted straw, and saw the other woman's pale eyes staring back.

'We need to go,' she said, as soon as she noticed that Ellyah was awake. 'Now.'

They had gone up to their chambers from the inn's common room the previous night and argued bitterly. Nastja had been adamant that the woman who had stared at them the previous night had been looking for them specifically, and that they should act accordingly.

'We've been chased all the way from Carhinn,' she had said, voice flat. 'Why would they have stopped now?'

'They were chasing the jewel?' replied Ellyah quickly. 'We don't have it anymore.'

'They don't know that!' retorted Nastja, raising her voice.

'How could they have even got here so quickly?' said Ellyah. 'You said yourself they were waiting for us. No fast horses passed us on the road from Ben Gedrin, did they?'

'No, but—' Ellyah rolled her eyes and Nastja spoke more insistently. 'But! They've always trailed us before. How do we know they didn't have people here in Buren already? We know nothing about them or what they are capable of.'

'It seems really unlikely, Nas…'

'Maybe,' agreed Nastja. 'But if we've already been stabbed in our beds it'll be too late for you to admit I was right to be cautious.'

Ellyah pressed her teeth together. The sense of it was infuriating. 'What do you suggest?'

'Normal business. If they think they know where you are, make sure you're not there.'

They had waited until the inn's evening bustle had died down, the sounds of movement and conversation in the common room below fading away into the still of the night. Then, cracking the shutters open they slipped out of the window, clinging to the outside of the inn wall like brooding spiders.

'I'll go first,' hissed Ellyah. She was the better climber, and could find good foot and handholds for Nastja to follow. She edged away from the window, moving with all the stealth that she could muster.

Until now, she had not even considered that they might still be being followed, but Nastja's fears were infectious.

Their room was in the overhanging extension that spanned the road, so below her feet was nothing but dark, inky space. She could not tell exactly how high she was, but the sensation of height was inescapable. She had no intention of falling.

Placing her feet on the rough wooden lip of the thick beam that supported the rooms, she sidled along, inch by inch. The gnarled timber of the walls and window frames provided plenty of room for her fingers to grip.

She glanced back to make sure that Nastja was following, before swarming rapidly into the corner where the jutting extension joined the inn's main wall. Nastja was a great observer, and would have watched Ellyah's technique carefully. Ellyah knew she would fall to her doom before admitting there was anything she could not do. With the other bedrooms so near, Ellyah did not dare to utter even a word of encouragement.

The blocky walls of quarried stone were well furnished with ledges and cracks, and Ellyah scrambled down to ground level with ease. As her feet touched the earth, there was a scraping noise above her and a sharp intake of breath.

Looking up, she saw the soles of Nastja's boots waving through the dusky gloom, several feet above her head. She hung from a small edge by her fingertips. Ellyah bit her lip and spread her arms wide, as if to catch the other woman if she fell.

But Nastja held on. She had grabbed a window ledge as her feet slipped, and after a moment's airy dangling, she pulled up and continued the climb. Nastja dropped the last few feet to land beside Ellyah heartbeats later. Her expression was hidden in the low light, but her breathing was even. Calm.

Behind the stables was a darkened barn. They darted inside, their movement quiet and careful. There was not a chink of light inside so they felt their way around the edge until the rough, spiky stalks of a haystack prickled their fingertips.

'This will do,' whispered Nastja. Ellyah grunted in reply.

Once they had bedded down, she had decided to stay awake all night. It was much too uncomfortable in the barn to sleep. And cold. She kept thinking about the soft mattress in their abandoned room, and the thick woollen blanket they had left behind.

She lay awake, staring into the darkness, silently fuming.

When she woke, she had firstly been surprised that she had slept at all, but as soon as she remembered where she was, her bad mood returned swiftly. She had a stiff back and cold hands, and it was Nastja's fault for overreacting.

'Are you ready?' asked Nastja, as the two of them stared at one another, faces lit only by the grey shards of dawn's light creeping through cracks in the timber walls.

'Ready for what?' asked Ellyah, grimacing as she heard the sulky tone of her own voice.

'We need to get out of here. Quickly. It's just before dawn.'

Ellyah paused, then nodded. They had agreed it was wise to be cautious, so they might as well get moving. People began to rise at dawn to begin their day's tasks. If they wanted to leave unnoticed then now was the time.

Brushing off the straw, they crossed to the door and Nastja opened it a crack. Ellyah leaned across to peer out. No one could be seen.

Nastja pushed it wider and they edged through. Sparing a glance left, Ellyah noticed that the front door of the inn was wide open, despite the early hour. It swung loosely in the gentle morning breeze. Nastja was staring in that direction.

'This way,' hissed Ellyah. 'Let's get away from the street until we're out of the village.'

She was still not fully prepared to admit that Nastja's worries were justified. Not yet. But, something was prickling her survival instincts. She felt the urge to run. To escape.

Something was wrong at the inn.

The houses set back from the main road were less grand than those facing the street. Fewer were stone built, and most were timber-framed but sprung up off a stone foundation. Some were little more than huts with straight branches as uprights and infilled with flimsy walls of woven hazel, others were daubed with dark clay.

Soft sounds of waking and movement came from within, groans and snatches of indistinct conversation, but as Ellyah and Nastja passed between the houses they saw no one else. More importantly, there was no one here to see them

They caught each other's eyes more than once, indicating with nods, head motions and hand gestures when to go left or right, when to go forwards, when to stop. They had known each other long enough that words were not necessary. The road was a bowshot away to their right as they headed south and towards the outskirts of the village.

The day had begun overcast, and the light was dull and flat. Everything looked grey, including the thick clouds that roiled overhead in the freshening breeze. A cold touch against Ellyah's cheek, it whipped a few stray strands of her long dark hair across her face, nagging at the corner of her mouth.

As they moved away from the last of the simple houses on the outskirts, something caused them to look up. A watchtower stood at the southern extent of the village, built next to the road. Ellyah looked again and blinked. It was not a watchtower, she realised. It was a temple.

Five square columns of age-darkened wood rose from the ground, to twice Ellyah's height. Nastja ran one of her hands down one as they walked around the base. It was heavy with deep carvings, with one motif repeated on each side of the column. It was a female face, stern and noble. Her eyes were hard, but they held a depth of wisdom and power.

This was the face of Conferan the Queen, one of the five gods. The other four columns would depict the faces of Ome, Tureank the Hunter, Kaled the Glorious and Mordea the Mother. Faith in their existence faded but they were still remembered, still revered.

At the top of the columns was a five-sided platform. Built as high as possible, to be nearer the gods, it could hold a handful of people, a family perhaps, who wanted to offer prayers.

Ellyah wondered what they prayed for. Did they ask for help doing things they could not achieve by themselves? Things that they were not prepared to work for, or risk for, and yet they wanted so desperately that instead they shouted their wishes to the unhearing heavens. She shook her head.

Nastja stopped, raising a warning hand.

'Wait,' she said. Her voice was clipped. Tense.

Before them, beyond the edge of the village was a wide area of flat, cleared ground. The perimeter was marked by five tall wooden shapes. They resembled trees, but were each formed from three stripped logs of pale wood.

Each one had a single upright, a waist-thick trunk about ten feet in height. Two spars of the same girth crossed the upright about three-quarters of the way up to form a five-pointed star: a *pentang*.

But, these *pentangs* were many times larger than any Ellyah had seen as grave markers back home in Anish or as they had crossed the Riverlands.

A house stood at the centre of the circle formed by the five looming *pentangs*. Or, more accurately, a house-shaped structure.

Nastja stepped cautiously into the circle, and Ellyah followed.

The house was a model, built from smooth, polished white stone. It was the same style as the bigger, more substantial houses of the village but was barely more than six feet high to the very peak of the pale, pitched roof.

'What is it?' hissed Ellyah.

Nastja waved her hand dismissively. 'A house for the dead. A communal memorial.' Her answer was unusually perfunctory, and her eyes were fixed on a spot just beyond the house. 'Look,' she said, in a hoarse whisper.

Ellyah took a single step closer, then froze.

A pathway led from the road into the centre of the circle, stopping just before the white memorial house. Pale, chalky chippings had been laid as the surface, mirroring the bare wood of the pentangs. White stone, white wood.

A figure was lying spreadeagled at the end of the path, near the house. Even from a few paces away Ellyah could tell that they were dead. Their body was limp and deflated, and a dark, congealing pool around them showed where they had bled out, staining the stones of the path.

'Look who it is,' said Nastja, voice hushed, before correcting herself. 'Was.'

Ellyah forced herself to look at the face as she sidled closer. The skin was also pale, leached of colour just as the body had been drained of life. Her breath caught. It was the innkeeper.

Dark stripes marred the cuffs of his earth-coloured smock where his wrists had been slit. Another ugly gash gaped across his throat, cut by a sharp blade. Patches of blood had also pooled beneath the backs of his spread legs.

'Hamstrung,' said Ellyah. 'They cut his hamstrings too.'

'Who did it?'

Ellyah just shrugged. 'Someone who badly wanted answers.'

It looked like he had been tortured.

'Or, someone who wanted to send a message,' said Nastja, taking a step back to look at the scene.

Ellyah followed Nastja's eyes, trying to see what the shorter woman was seeing. She did not want to have to ask.

The unfortunate man had both arms and legs spread, positioned deliberately to point towards four of the five *pentangs*. Ellyah supposed his head was pointing at the fifth, beyond the memorial house.

And then there were his wounds…

'Cuts to his neck, wrists and legs,' she said, speaking as she thought it through. 'Five wounds for the five-pointed star.'

'Six.'

Nastja was pointing to the ground between the dead innkeeper's legs. A pale scrap of flesh lay there amid a small smear of drying blood. There was another dark patch spreading across the man's hose, between his legs.

'They cut off his…' Ellyah did not complete the sentence.

'Yea.'

'Why?'

'To make six,' replied Nastja, unhelpfully.

Ellyah did not understand, and was about to ask Nastja why she thought this had been done, why six injuries had been inflicted in such a calculated way, when she heard raised voices from the village.

Her head snapped round, as did Nastja's.

The tone of the voices was telling, even if they could not yet hear the words. Worrying. Questioning. Calling. Searching for someone, someone who was missing.

Ellyah looked back to the dead man.

'We can't be found here!' she said, feeling panic rising in her breast. 'They'll think we did it.'

She glanced around, thinking quickly. Thinking to run.

The pale strip of the road was a few paces away, but once on it they would be visible for miles as it wound through the low hills nearby. To her left, east and south, fields rolled away into the green-grey distance.

It was an open land with little cover. Their options for escape were limited.

Where were they going to go?

FIVE

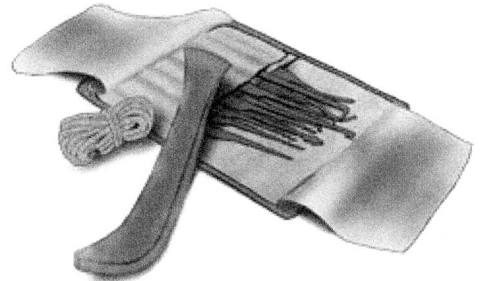

The shouts were getting louder. New voices joined as more people were roused to continue the search. Someone was not where they were expected to be.

'We can't be found here,' said Nastja. Her eyes darted. 'We need to run.'

Ellyah looked from her anxious face to the mutilated body of the innkeeper, spreadeagled across the path. Nastja was right. If they were found anywhere near, then they would be blamed. But, they would be fools to just run.

'We won't outrun horses on the road,' she said, turning back towards the village. 'Follow me.'

The wind was cool on her face as she darted back past the tall temple. The important thing was not being caught out in the open, or while obviously trying to escape.

Do not be the runner.

Dashing across the last stretch of open ground, she pressed herself against the rough clay wall of the nearest house. Nastja huddled down next to her. Behind this south-facing wall they were screened from the rest of the village, giving them a moment to think.

Nastja had looked puzzled at first, as Ellyah had headed back towards the village, but she had not protested. Ellyah assumed she understood. Flight was futile.

The shouts continued in the distance. As Ellyah tilted her head to hear better, the door of the house was flung open. She and Nastja cowered, thinking that they were about to be found.

A voice rang out from inside the house. 'What's going on?' They were speaking the Common Speech, accented but clear.

'Not sure,' came the reply from the doorway. Another woman's voice. 'Something's happening up by the inn. Something's wrong. We should go up to help.'

'Aye,' replied the first woman. 'Lerin, get your boots on.' Quiet mumbling followed, words Ellyah could not make out. She listened intently as people shuffled around inside the house, and then footsteps receded as they headed north towards the inn.

She turned back to Nastja, who was holding up three fingers. Three people had just walked away. Ellyah reckoned it was the woman in the doorway with a couple from inside. The house must now be empty. Ellyah caught Nastja's eye, and the shorter woman nodded. The understanding was immediate, with no need for words.

Together, they stood. Ellyah edged around the corner of the squarish house, eyes darting as she checked for anyone moving nearby. There was no one.

With fluid speed that was nonetheless short of clumsy haste, she moved around the corner and opened the door of the house. As she held it slightly ajar Nastja darted inside, and Ellyah followed.

Then stopped suddenly, and stared.

A table of rough wood stood in the centre of the single-roomed house. Behind the table, a partly drawn curtain showed the bed, and a low fire smouldered in the hearth set against one of the walls.

Sitting at the table was a young child, a small girl several years younger than ten. At her feet in a woven basket, a baby wriggled and gurgled. The girl was staring directly at them, a serious expression on her face.

Ellyah's breathing deepened. The girl could be moments from screaming an alarm.

Her hand dropped to her right hip, to the smooth handle of her belt knife. Could she do it? Nastja's head turned at the movement and she shook her head, brows furrowed. Ellyah put her hands on her hips.

'We could offer her silver to be quiet?' she whispered, feeling for the silver money rings on her wrist. Nastja rolled her eyes, stepping forwards.

'Hello,' she said, brightly, and the small girl's eyes were drawn to her. 'We need to get ready for the day, and we're wearing the wrong clothes.' She gestured ruefully to her travel-stained leggings and coat. The girl giggled slightly.

'Can you help us find some better clothes?' The girl nodded vigorously, smiling now. 'Your mother won't mind.'

Ellyah stared. This approach had not crossed her mind. She was ready to run, but even in her astonishment she noticed that none of what Nastja had said was untrue.

They were indeed wearing the wrong clothes if they wanted to blend in. Nastja was still dressed in the peasant garb of Ben Gedrin, and Ellyah was in her well-worn breeches and a coat. Ellyah reckoned that in the scheme of things, any mother would not mind losing a couple of sets of clothes if it meant their children escaped unharmed.

Nastja took a few steps towards the table, then crouched down before the girl.

'Do you like dates?' she asked, swinging her sack off her back and plunging in a hand. She set two plump dried fruits on the table. 'One each,' she said. 'But he's too small to eat them, so you can have both.'

The girl smiled broadly, beaming at being part of the conspiracy, before stuffing both dates into her mouth. Nastja left her chewing and stood, moving towards the curtain at the back of the room which partially obscured the bed.

Apparently, a deal had been struck and now they were trusted friends.

'Clothes,' said Nastja, beginning to rummage through some wooden storage boxes at the foot of the bed.

Soon, they were both clad in Bureno-style work smocks, dyed a brownish-red, and dark hose. Ellyah felt awkward and uncomfortable in the strange clothes, and stashed her own away with some reluctance.

'Burenos wear hats,' stated Nastja. It was Ellyah's turn to dip her hand into her own sack, and she triumphantly produced two plain cloth caps. Nastja showed no surprise.

'Turn around,' she said. 'I need to tie your hair up to fit underneath.' Ellyah turned. She saw the sense. They both had memorable hair. Hers was long and dark, and Nastja's was shorter but unusually fair. Plaited, it could be mostly hidden beneath their caps.

Once their caps were pulled down tightly over their heads, they turned and stepped towards the door.

'Wait!' came the shrill voice of the little girl. She jumped off her chair and hurried over to them before tilting her head upward. 'Me too!'

Ellyah rolled her eyes as Nastja moved over to plait the girl's hair.

A few moments later they slipped back out of the door, heading towards the south side of the house.

'She'll tell her parents she saw us,' said Nastja.

Ellyah spoke briskly. 'It won't matter. By the time she does, we'll be far away.'

'That's going to be hard. We'll be noticed and followed if we leave the village.' The sound of anxious voices came from near and far. The search continued.

'That's why we're not going to leave. We're going to walk in.'

Ellyah led the way as they moved through the outskirts, wary of being spotted by anyone in the houses. They darted between the thick columns of the raised temple, and Ellyah paused by the last, holding up a hand.

The southward road was a few paces away, clear as far as Ellyah could see, but most of the houses were north of where they stood. Many eyes could be watching them from darkened windows. By luck, the road turned a curve just beyond the temple, screening much of the village from their view. And they from it.

'Now,' said Ellyah, and darted into the middle of the road, boots skidding on the hard dirt. Nastja followed and they strolled up the road towards the inn. Ellyah forced herself to walk with a casual gait, putting thoughts of the murder and the ensuing hunt from her mind. She had done nothing. She was no one.

She was confident that they would not be recognised from the previous night, but Nastja looked anxious. Her hands gripped the hem of her smock, the knuckles whitening.

'Relax,' Ellyah whispered. 'They will have forgotten our faces.'

Normal people only recalled the most basic details, and even then, only if they had good reason. The only person she had spoken to in the village was the innkeeper, and he was in no state to remember anything. With their change of clothes and with their hair hidden, they would appear completely different to the women who had passed through the village the previous night.

They rounded the slight bend and found the street ahead busy. The doors of the houses were flung open, and people were peering out anxiously. Others dashed here and there, asking questions with worried faces.

None of them spared Ellyah and Nastja a second glance.

'Let me do the talking,' said Nastja in an urgent undertone, before approaching a local and speaking in a completely different voice.

'What is happening?' she asked, and suddenly her speech was heavy with the accent of Buren. She sounded just like the frantic voices that called out from all around them.

'Innkeeper's gone missing,' replied the woman before them. Her dark hair was tucked beneath a cap alike to theirs, and her short over-smock was a dark, woody green. 'Looks like he was taken in the night by a couple of outlander women. His place is all smashed up.'

'No! That's terrible!' exclaimed Nastja, in a convincing show of surprise.

'Aye. We're going to have to start barring the gates. Too many strange folk passing through.'

'Well, we're not stopping,' said Nastja. 'But maybe we should keep moving quickly, in case the rogues are still around. Anyone around here with horses to sell?'

The woman's attention was captured by sharp shouts from the south. Ellyah's head jerked in that direction. The woman waved them away.

'There's sometimes a few mounts for sale up at the inn. Ask for Frenos.' She hurried off, barely looking at them as she spoke.

Ellyah beamed inwardly. The woman had not seen them as anything other than a couple of fellow locals. The morning's drama was a distraction that would let them slip away. She caught Nastja's eye and raised a slight eyebrow. This was working.

A small crowd had gathered before the inn. An older man with a drooping moustache was standing up in front of the crowd. Ellyah and Nastja quietly joined the rear of the group. No one looked around.

'They must be found!' the man was saying. His jowly cheeks shook with worry and indignation as he spoke. 'These criminals, these savages, emptied his strong box and then took him in the night. Perhaps they are thinking of asking a ransom.'

A narrow-faced woman at his side wrung her hands. Her face was drawn and anxious, eyes rimmed with grey.

'How do we know he didn't go willingly?' came a voice from the crowd. The woman, who Ellyah assumed was the innkeepers wife, stared.

'There were signs of a struggle,' replied the moustached elder. 'I saw—' he hesitated. 'A splash of blood.' There were gasps from the crowd and the widow covered her face.

Ellyah tapped Nastja's arm and beckoned her away. She moved calmly but her heart was racing. They had not been caught, yet, but that did not mean they were safe.

They passed beneath the broad arch of the inn and turned into the dark warmth of the stables. Timber beams and columns, gnarled with age, framed the space, and wickerwork walls enclosed and divided the pens.

The sweet smell of hay filled the air and tickled the back of Ellyah's throat. The scraping sound of brushing came from the gloom to the rear, but ceased as a broad young man stepped forwards into the light.

'Yes?' he asked, in a hesitant, stammering tone. 'Can I help?'

He came forwards with small steps, a broom of birch twigs held loosely in one hand. His sleeveless smock was a dark, muddy brown, and his hose were work stained.

'We're looking for horses,' said Nastja, still putting on that Bureno accent. 'Seems there's trouble around so we want to move more quickly. Your mother sent us.'

Ellyah scowled in surprise, but then looked more closely at the lad and realised that Nastja had made a wise gamble. The lad had the same eyes and nose as the murdered innkeeper. It seemed possible that he could be the man's son.

'Looking for horses,' he repeated. His face twitched. He was distracted.

'To buy,' clarified Nastja. 'We have silver.'

She lifted an arm and the silver money rings on her wrist gleamed in the low light.

'Yes, yes. We have a pair of mares to trade. Ten rings each, in silver.'

'We'll give you fifteen for the pair,' said Ellyah. 'And we need tack too.' If he noticed her odd accent, he gave no sign. Ellyah could feel Nastja's irritated glare without having to look around.

Ellyah did not care. It had seemed like an opportune moment to get a good deal. Their supply of gold and silver was limited, after all.

At that moment, a new chorus of shouts and yells rose outside. The stable boy's eyes widened.

They have found him, thought Ellyah. *They have found the innkeeper's body. This boy's father.*

He dropped his broom and dashed towards the door. 'Wait here,' he called over his shoulder. 'I'll come back.'

'Well,' said Ellyah once his footsteps had died away. 'We can't just wait. Let's saddle up and get out of here.'

'Without paying?' Nastja's expression was incredulous.

Ellyah sighed. 'We'll leave the silver behind for him. Can hang it on that nail over there. Some of the silver, anyway…'

Nastja's brow furrowed. 'Oh. I see. I hadn't thought of that. I'll saddle the horses.'

She moved further into the stables, towards the pens that the lad had indicated. Ellyah set down her sack and carefully counted out twelve silver money rings. Hanging them on the protruding nail, she went across to the doorway and peered out.

The crowd had gone. From what she had been able to hear from within the barn, everyone had rushed off south, in the direction of the shouting. Cries in the distance were surely over the discovery of the mutilated body.

She could not dwell on it. They just had to escape.

Someone in the crowd would make a connection. They would remember the two women they had seen the previous night, and the two travellers passing through the village this day. They would point a finger. How long did they have?

'Nas! Hurry!'

'Yes,' came the muffled response.

What was truly going on here? Nothing that had happened over the last few days felt like coincidence. The way they had been tricked at the jewel trade and then been forced into a pursuit, to find someone at a distant inn who seemed to be waiting for them.

And now this? A brutal, ritualistic murder for which it looked like they would be blamed. What had they stumbled into, and why did they seem like targets?

The muffled thud of hooves behind her broke into her thoughts. Nastja was leading two horses: one chestnut, one grey. They looked in good condition, but Ellyah was no expert on horses. She could just about stay on one while it was trotting, but she trusted Nastja's judgement.

They mounted quickly, Ellyah on the grey, and set off southwards along the road.

'From the temple, we need to ride,' she said, leaning towards Nastja. 'Ride hard and don't stop.' Nastja nodded seriously.

As Ellyah had guessed, a large crowd was gathered just beyond the tall temple. It looked like most of the village had followed the sounds of alarm and were stood beneath the shadows cast by the five tall *pentangs*.

They were looking down at something on the ground. As they drew closer, Ellyah could make out horrified, grief-stricken faces and the sounds of moaning and weeping grew louder. She felt a stab in her own heart as she contemplated their pain, their confusion. But this was not their problem. They did not do it and could not help. They should not be blamed.

'Ride!' she urged, as soon as she noticed the first set of eyes turn to regard their approach. 'Ride now!'

She tapped her heels to the grey mare's flanks, and the beast broke into a trot, and then a jolting run. Hooves drummed on the hard earth as they flashed passed the milling villagers.

'Those strangers!' came shouts from the crowd. 'It were them! Stop them!'

But Nastja and Ellyah were moving too quickly, rocking in their saddles as their new mounts ran along the road. In moments, the chaos and the noise were at their backs and the village receded into the distance.

They were back on the road, and now had even more reason to keep moving.

SIX

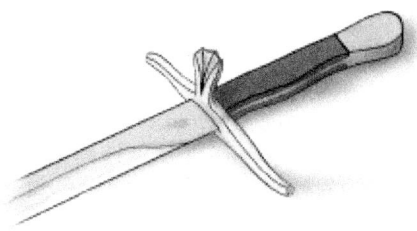

The rings on Styoyan's hands glittered in the morning sun which filtered through his high, arched windows. He would have preferred to wear riding gloves against the autumnal chill, but did not want his hands to be hidden. Not today.

He glanced down. Five slim silver rings shone on each of his index fingers. He had received them from his father on his tenth birthday as part of the ceremony formally marking the end of his childhood.

The singing in the great hall of Fordon Keep had been loud that day. He remembered the sensation of his ears burning as the gathered crowd all turned to look at him. He recalled the stern face of his father and the blank looks of his four brothers as they stared down.

He had been determined not to forget any of the words of the ancient songs. He wanted to be worthy of his noble name, of the title he would one day hold.

Five more rings of the same type encircled the base of the middle finger of his left hand, but on his right hand there were only four. Just four silver rings, because the fifth ring was of gold. He looked at it and could not help smiling.

He had received this one at his twentieth birth day, the same day as he had been invested as Baron of Kereva. Only the highest-ranking nobles in Anish - dukes, earls, barons and counts - could wear gold.

None but the royal family could wear the richest, most valuable metal: the rare blue-black of *pluitone*.

Recalling his investiture reminded him of the machinations of the High Council of Kereva, and the hollow hopelessness of his impotent status as baron. Reminded him of the reason for his journey today.

Leaving his quarters quietly, Styoyan stole down to the stables and saddled his own horse, a chestnut stallion called Mahdesht. There were few people stirring as he approached the gatehouse of Kereva in the grey cold of dawn, which was good. The council could not stop him going. They could not hold him in the city. In theory. However, Styoyan had thought it wise to deny them the opportunity to try.

He was dressed simply in a long, plain robe, divided for riding, and was unarmoured. He wore a short coat of soft leather over the top, dark and plain. His sabre hung at his side, the hilt a reassuring presence at his hip. He had wrapped a short cape edged with black fox fur around his shoulders to keep out the worst of the chill, and his breath misted as he passed through the gateway and out onto the road.

Movement in the corner of his eye caught his attention and he fumbled for the hilt of his sword, but relaxed when the sound of familiar, deep laughter reached his ears. He knew that laugh.

He reined in and turned.

'Morehai,' he said, and then in response to the raised eyebrow of the approaching figure added: 'Master Morehai,' before slightly inclining his head.

'Early for a ride, Baron Jukeev,' said Morehai, bringing his own mount to a halt beside Styoyan's.

Morehai's face showed mild amusement, a knowing wisdom in his dark eyes. Those eyes were level with Styoyan's now, but when standing he towered over Styoyan by a hand's length or more. This tall, slender build and coal-dark skin revealed that he was an elf, even if his pointed ears were missed.

Unusually for an elf, he wore his age. Fine wrinkles creased the skin around his sharp eyes and his curling hair, cropped short, was tinted with silver. He was dressed in a simple robe and as far as Styoyan could tell, he was unarmed. Not that Morehai would need a weapon, were he attacked.

'I must visit my father,' replied Styoyan. He summoned his defiance. 'The council can't stop me. I am the Baron of Kereva. I can go where I will.'

'Interesting that your first thought is that you might be prevented from leaving, if you are so certain that it is your right to go.'

Styoyan struggled to keep a grimace off his face. Of course, Morehai had the right of it. He always did.

'Return and tell the council you did not see me,' said Styoyan. Morehai gazed at him, unmoved. 'I could order it. I am the Baron.'

Morehai bowed low in his saddle. 'Of course, my lord,' he said, voice level but with a trace of amusement 'Unfortunately, I already have other orders.' He reached into a pocket inside his thick over-robe and pulled out a rolled strip of linen. 'Messages from the council to your father. Accounts. I am tasked as messenger this day. It seems as though we will be travelling in the same direction, and would seem unnecessary to be strangers to one another.'

Styoyan sighed. Morehai always talked like this, tying knots with his words. And yet, he was rarely wrong.

'Fine,' he replied. 'Let us make haste.' Then, he smiled. 'It will be a pleasure to have your company, my master.'

They heeled their horses into motion once more, riding side by side along the northward road. Their progress was quick. Both were light riders and the road was well-maintained, flat and free of sharp stones. Beyond the verges, serf labourers were already in the fields. This time of year, they toiled from dawn until dusk, turning the swaying golden fields into bare, brown expanses. Thus was the Vale of Fordon fed through the winter.

'What accounts do the council require you to deliver?' Styoyan asked, breaking the silence. Morehai had almost certainly volunteered to be the messenger, guessing Styoyan's intention to make this journey, but Styoyan felt he had to at least play the game.

'Incomings, outgoings,' said Morehai, enigmatically. 'The city prospers and your father may want to strengthen the garrisons if the news from Kotev is true.'

'Why were they not brought to me?'

'These are for the accounts of Fordon, not of Kereva,' replied Morehai quickly. 'And the council felt they might…uhh…bore you, my Baron.'

Styoyan's hands tightened on the reins in rage, the action involuntary.

'And your business with your father?' asked Morehai.

Styoyan turned to him, but did not speak immediately, searching for the right words. Morehai found them first.

'Your experience of lordship as a baron is...not what you hoped?'

Styoyan sagged. 'My father must know,' he said, relief coursing through him as he let the truth out to his fencing master. 'He must know how Coril abuses her position. How the council has marginalised me.'

Morehai nodded. 'It is time you confronted the issue in this way. It will help you. And yet—' The tall elf looked him in the eye. 'You fear what may happen next.'

Styoyan swallowed. Morehai was right. He had no idea how his father would react to the news.

'My father can be—' Styoyan paused, thinking of the right word. 'Stern. He has many worries.'

'Yes, you should not expect sympathy. But you must do something, change something, or live with things as they are.'

'You always say that,' said Styoyan reproachfully.

'And am I wrong?' responded Morehai, with a smile. Styoyan rolled his eyes and Morehai laughed. Styoyan turned, pressing a fist to his open left palm and ducking his head in exaggerated deference.

'The student bows before his master,' he said, gravely.

Morehai chuckled and they rode on.

The tall, softly spoken elf had been part of Styoyan's life for as long as he could remember. As fencing master, he held a prestigious rank in Earl Gevrin's household, but Styoyan had learned a lot more from him than just swordsmanship.

From a young age he had taught Styoyan to fight, armed and unarmed, taught him to think philosophically, and made him consider the wider consequences of his actions.

'We are all drops of rain falling into a still pool,' he would say. *'We are small, but our ripples stretch out to touch others in ways we cannot anticipate.'*

In truth, Morehai had been a greater influence on Styoyan's younger years than his own father. He had certainly spent more time with the elf than with the earl. His thoughts came around once more to the conversation before him, and he fell into silence.

The road wound through green countryside. Ahead, the bare and rounded summits of the Singing Mountains rose above Styoyan's eyeline. Beyond them, the rocky slopes of the central Derufin climbed higher still, rising to black and white spires and pinnacles; the very peak of the world.

One hill drew his attention more than the others, though. Barely a hummock compared to the great ranges beyond, it was far more important. The hill of Fordon was where he had grown up and was the place he felt at home. Where he had first met Morehai. It was the centre of his world.

It had always been important to Anish, too. Back in the days when the country had been a patchwork of warring fiefdoms, the hill and fort of Anish had been an intimidating stronghold. It was easily defended and commanded a view over much of the surrounding countryside, as far as Kereva and including the trade route to and from Kalojne Pass. Whoever held Fordon also held wealth, and power.

So much so that when the Many Kings of legend had gathered at the table and made their peace, it was the ruler of the fiefdom of Fordon that had been elected as the first High King of all Anish. The country was united behind the influence of Fordon.

And now his father sat in that seat, lord over all the surrounding lands. How would he react to the news that the High Council of Kereva had effectively usurped his son's authority as baron? His rage would be primal.

Styoyan would rather not be the one to tell him, would rather be far away when Gevrin found out. He knew though, that no one else would raise the issue. It had to be him.

He gathered his courage as the causeway rose ahead. A serpentine path had been cut into the southern slope of the hill, meaning that any attacker would be exposed for a long time as they attempted to approach the gate.

In peacetime the ramp merely served to ease the sharp gradient of the hill, and Mahdesht turned this way and that as he carried Styoyan upwards and through the gate. Morehai followed close behind on his own mount, a dappled grey he called Nihda.

If the guards noticed his rings or recognised his face, they gave no sign. He and Morehai rode past them and into the town. It was past noon and the streets were bustling, despite the chill in the air. From the gate, a narrow lane led north but soon opened out into a broad, busy marketplace.

Styoyan barely saw any of it. From the moment he had entered the market square, his attention had been fixed on one thing.

The keep.

It rose behind another staunch gatehouse in the inner wall, three or four times the height of any other building in Fordon, including the Crossways Inn. Grey, solid and eternal. It was where he had spent his early years, where he had grown up and he still considered it his family home.

And today, it was where he would meet with his father.

Morehai reined in.

'I have a thirst,' he said. Styoyan noticed that he had stopped beside the Crossways Inn, and smiled. 'If the Five smile I will see you soon.'

'I will see you soon, Morehai,' said Styoyan, reaching out to grasp his teacher's hand. 'Be you well.'

'The threads of fate cannot be foreseen,' replied Morehai, gripping Styoyan's hand tightly. 'Go with courage, young Styoyan.'

As he swung himself effortlessly down from his horse, Styoyan was already riding away.

'Your mother meant nothing to me. And neither do you.'

Earl Gevrin Jukeev's words fell into Styoyan's ears as though they were a headsman's sabre cleaving into his neck. If he had not already been kneeling before his father's great chair, he might have fallen to the ground.

The great hall seemed to swim around him. The cold flagstones beneath his knees buckled and swayed. How could this be real? How could this be happening?

'What is it?'

His father's tone had been impatient as he had entered the hall, leaving Styoyan to fall into step behind him. The blocky shape of his father's broad shoulders filled Styoyan's vision as he trailed across the room. Impatience bloomed. He wanted to speak to his father's face, not his back.

Gevrin reached the end of the hall and turned, his intricately carved chair just behind him.

'My youngest son has demanded to see me,' he snapped, in his usual brusque tone. 'And so, I have come. I'm sure this is more pressing than any other business I may have had. Speak.'

The earl had been a renowned warrior-general in his youth and had retained that imposing physique even now. There was a thickness to his arms and shoulders that suggested great strength, and his scarred hands were thick-fingered and robust.

Those hands were clenched into fists now, as he stared down at his youngest son.

'I need to tell you about the impropriety of the High Council of Kereva,' began Styoyan, uncertain about how to word his complaint. 'Led by councillor Coril.'

His father was silent. Styoyan went on.

'The High Council denies me the authority of the barony. I should have a seat at the council and a casting vote. They will not even let me enter the chamber.' The words tumbled out in a rush. After a pause, he spoke more quietly. 'They act unlawfully.'

His father was silent for a long time. His heavy brows were lowered, his forehead creased like old linen parchment. His dark eyes regarded Styoyan, the rest of his body as motionless as a statue hewn from granite.

His dark hair, which was streaked with more silver than Styoyan remembered was gathered up atop his head and pinned, in the traditional style. Styoyan found his eyes drawn to the golden pins, another sign of his father's many years of noble rank, mirroring the many golden rings on his fingers.

'Do you have any idea why I decided to give you this barony?' he asked, eventually. 'Have you thought about what you might have done to deserve such an honour?'

Styoyan was silent. He knew that his father did not want answers to these questions.

'Perhaps you have led a brilliant military campaign like your brother Siylen, repulsing an attack from Kotev and shoring up the border defences. Or, maybe you attended the court of the

High King and negotiated for lenient tax levies on goods from Fordon and Kereva, like your brother Nadezd?

'Did you travel to Buren, or the Severed City as an emissary of Anish and return with gifts and favour?' His father's voice had become harsher and more impatient as he spoke, and it took Styoyan back to his childhood. He had not forgotten the feeling that used to fill him as he stared at the floor, his father's bitter words piercing him like knives.

The knowledge that he could not match his brothers, that he was not good enough; it had faded but as his father spoke it returned heavily.

'Have you done these things?' asked his father, his eyes boring down on Styoyan. Styoyan looked away.

'No, father.'

'No,' repeated Earl Gevrin. 'You have not. And it seems unlikely that you ever will. Why then, do you think I wanted to grant you the title and estate of Baron of Kereva, a city run most adequately, and profitably, by Coril and the High Council on my behalf?'

On my behalf. The words repeated inside Styoyan's head. They could not mean what he thought they did. His father could not have known about how Coril and the High Council would treat him. Could he?

'I do not know, father,' replied Styoyan honestly, while a score of flippant answers fought to break free of his mouth. He restrained them, tempered by his growing unease.

He had thought his father believed him mature enough to become a landed noble like his brothers. They, dukes and counts and he now a baron. It had made sense. It had completed Styoyan's journey from child to man.

'No, of course you do not know,' said his father. 'You have not the wit. You never did. Yet another strength you lack.'

Styoyan's guts lurched. His father had never spoken to him so, at least never so openly. Never so hostile. True, in the past his father had barely deigned to speak to Styoyan at all, but these words were worse than the silence.

'I appointed you baron,' he continued, 'because I wanted you out of my sight. I wanted you elsewhere, in a place you could do no harm. Where you would not offend me with your weakness and with your lack of spine.'

Styoyan could only gape. He kept his eyes lowered to hide the hot, bitter tears that were threatening to spring forth. His last meal battled to reappear through his mouth and gush out onto the flagstones. He swallowed.

'I hoped you would take the hint, along with the fat purse that I offered so generously, and take your scrawny backside away from my home, the noble home of my mighty ancestors. But you remain dull, and blind to reality.

'So, here you are before me once more. Whining like a gelded pup.'

Earl Gevrin's jaw was set in a grimace of anger. His voice had got louder and harsher the longer he spoke. It echoed from the distant corners of the great hall, laden with the weight of words long unsaid, striking forth suddenly and violently like a thrown spear.

Styoyan thought of his mother then, and words sprang from his lips before he could restrain them.

'I thought this is what mother wanted. To see me stand alongside my brothers.' Childish words.

That was when his father had thrown his most jagged stone.

'Your mother meant nothing to me. And neither do you.' Styoyan flinched from each word like they were physical blows. His father went on. 'All I wanted was you out of this house and far away from me. It worked to get that half-breed woman away from me, but it seems as though you are a tougher stain to shift.'

Half-breed!

The insult burned in Styoyan's ears. His mother was half-elven, the child of a southern Anise knight and his elven wife. But, she was still of noble blood and should not be dismissed with such a slur.

'Father—' he began angrily, but was interrupted.

'It would have been better had I never married the mongrel,' his father continued, each word another blow of a cruel hammer. 'But in life, compromises must be made. Alliances are required, considerations must be given and taken. Concessions made. The court must see an earl with a stable home, not a lonely man weakened by grief.'

Styoyan glanced up, and met his father's eyes which were suddenly wary and sharp. It was as though Gevrin had been speaking to himself.

'Grief over your first wife?' asked Styoyan in a small, careful voice.

'Krasohta was my sun and moons,' came the growled reply. 'All that the presence of your mother did was remind me of what I had lost with her passing. But I had no choice but to remarry. No choice. I wouldn't expect you to understand. I wanted no other wife, and no other child. But duty…'

His glare towards Styoyan became more hostile. He knew this was his one chance to convince his father of his worth.

'All I wanted was to prove myself to you,' he said, eyes fixed on the floor once more. 'I wanted to prove that I was as worthy of my noble name as my brothers.'

'And in that you have failed.'

Styoyan felt as though he were ten years old again, dwarfed by the stature and deeds of his older brothers. He was nothing more than a useless, clumsy child who could not be trusted with anything. From where he knelt, the walls of the hall rose up vertiginously, making him feel like a speck in the centre of the broad floor.

'What am I supposed to do?' he replied. He felt frustration and some anger, but his voice was little more than a whimper.

'Go,' said his father. 'Climb back into your feather bed in Kereva with your whores and do your duty. Or retreat to the countryside and let the council get on with governing with the competence you lack. I care not which. I just want you out of my sight.'

Styoyan's whole body trembled at the words, but he found the empty emotionless place within himself and mastered his emotions. He knew further words would be futile. He could rail against his treatment, protest the unfairness and wail about how he was misjudged and undervalued, but it would only harden his father's heart further.

'One way or another, though,' added his father. 'I expect you to do your duty. Attend the functions that require you. Wear the right clothes. Wave and at least try to look grateful for the comfort I have generously provided you. Failure in this will be considered treason and I will not hesitate in enforcing the law against you. Do you understand this?'

Styoyan stood. Words could not change his father's mind now.

'Earl Gevrin,' he said, as a reply. 'I thank you. May the Five protect you in life and guide you in death.'

He turned and strode briskly from the hall. His father said nothing.

'Silla! My precious Silla is here!'

Styoyan's mother rushed forwards to embrace her son. She still insisted on using his child-name, "Silla", no matter how often he asked her not to. He had left that name behind when he reached ten years old and received his first finger-rings.

'I am Styoyan now, mother,' he replied, but wrapped his arms around his mother's slight figure. After a moment she stepped away and gazed at him.

'Baron Styoyan!' she exclaimed. 'My little boy is a baron now!' She grasped his right hand. 'Let me see that golden ring.'

Styoyan let her examine the narrow band of gleaming gold that sat behind the knuckle of his index finger. Her maids and grooms stood on the veranda, a respectful distance away but near enough that Styoyan could see them whispering to one another.

His mother's country house rose behind them; two stories of neatly dressed stone daubed with thick white paint that made the walls seem smooth and almost jointless. The roof overhung on all four sides, rising to a point above the centre of the house, leaving the attic room beneath. Thick, carved timber columns held up the edges, forming a colonnaded veranda around the perimeter of the house.

Flowering vines ran up the columns to spread up the roof, and bright shrubs were planted all around. It was a riot of colour in the greenery of northern Anish.

Such a house was a grand dwelling for a single woman, and Styoyan felt a stab of sadness at how his father had dealt with his mother; provided her luxury that he hoped she would not spurn. It was the same way he had tried to placate him in Kereva.

'That is why I came here, Mother,' he said, quietly, after she had cooed over his ring. He gathered the courage to say the next words aloud. They would be hard for his mother to hear.

He took a deep breath. 'I have just come from bringing a complaint to Father. The High Council of Kereva would not acknowledge the authority of my title. They excluded me from council business.'

His mother was staring at him, her eyes wide. They were dark but flecked with a scatter of lilac, matching the purple tints across her temples.

'The council treated my rank as a mere formality, Mother. I had no power there. No honour. No chance to prove my worth. So, I went to father.'

'Sounds like there's been a misunderstanding,' replied his mother, eyes still wide. 'I'm sure Gevrin will resolve the problem. He's so strong, so sure.'

Styoyan took a step closer. 'That's the thing, Mother. That's the problem. Father knew. He knew that the High Council would ignore me. He knew that they would exclude me, denigrate my authority. It was his idea.'

Styoyan felt an uncomfortable tightness in his chest as he said the words. Hearing them aloud made his father's dismissal seem real in a way it had not before.

His mother was still staring at him, eyes wide and a half smile on her lips.

'Oh, no,' she said, shaking her head in dismissal. 'That can't be right, my Silla. I think it's all a misunderstanding. I'm sure your father will fix it. He's probably on his way to Kereva now.'

'I don't think you understand,' said Styoyan, reaching out to grasp his mother's slender shoulders. 'Father told me that it was what he wanted. He said he wanted me away from Fordon, away from him and didn't care about Kereva. He said these words earlier this day, Mother.'

She was shaking her head.

'You are mistaken, my son,' she said. 'Your father wants only the best for you, for us. He cares for us deeply even when he finds it hard to show it. The pressure of governing wisely and fairly weighs heavily on him.' She looked back at Styoyan, conviction in her eyes. 'You'll see when you go back to Kereva. The High Council will welcome you with honour, and give you the highest seat. You are a Jukeev after all.'

Styoyan opened his mouth to speak again. Why was his mother not listening? Why could she not understand?

The words "mongrel" and "half-breed" came into his mind, his father's voice returning to him as he had described this woman. If she knew his father felt that way about her, surely she would believe what Styoyan had told her?

He looked at her. Her mouth was smiling, and her eyes were wide. The smile did not reach those eyes. They were open, but a flicker of terror haunted their speckled depths. Her chest heaved with deep breaths, although she had not moved.

He realised, then, and the knowledge washed over him like a cold rain. She knew. She knew all this already but could not bring herself to acknowledge the truth of it. She clung to her denial fiercely. The fear that Styoyan saw in her eyes was directed towards him. She was terrified of what he might say next.

He could break her. He could shatter her world with a few simple words. All he had to do was to tell the truth.

He sagged. 'Maybe you're right.'

'Of course,' she said, smile broadening. 'There is a stew on the hearth. Come in, you must be hungry.'

She grasped his arm and led him into the house.

The next day, as dawn broke, he was already far away.

SEVEN

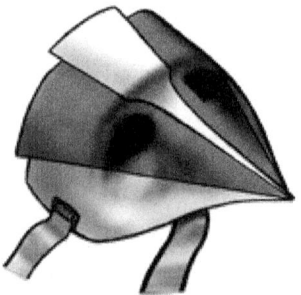

Her feet slapped against the worn, ancient flagstones of the keep of Kereva, the muted echoes repeating from the dark, angular corners of the corridor. The feeling of age and tradition was carved heavily into the very stones of this looming building. The square-cut, reddish stones felt eternal.

But, things were about to change.

A curving staircase of the same, solid stone led away from a tall portal in the wall of the corridor, up to a higher level. She followed it, lifting her feet high to ascend the steep steps. Fatigue built quickly in her legs and she resented it. Nevertheless, this was important and would pay her efforts back handsomely.

Coril Faduile, head of the High Council of Kereva, reached the top of the staircase and stepped out into a narrower corridor on the floor above. Her robe brushed the ground as she turned to the right and continued.

Her mind worked furiously although her steps were slow and sedate as she passed the offices of the rest of the High Council, which opened off each side of the corridor. The other councillors would be in many of them now, meeting important merchants and landholders, increasing their holdings and status.

Petty schemes, for small gains. She would rise above them all, and soon.

The door to her office was at the end of the corridor, and she swiftly opened it and passed inside.

She had already secured the grandest office, a wide room that filled one entire corner of this floor of the keep. Broad windows let the evening light into the room and huge tapestries filled the spaces in between, the blocky stones concealed behind. She locked the door, double-checking the bolt before moving away.

Kicking off her wood-soled shoes of the softest leather, her toes curled into the warmth of the furs which were spread from wall to wall. A broad desk sat beneath one of the windows and several scrolls awaited her mark. To her right, a long table suitable for closed-door council meetings or private dinners, stretched towards the opposite wall.

A flask of wine, still cool from the cellar, was waiting on the table. Glistening beads of moisture ran down the intricate glazing. She poured a generous splash into a clay cup and drank it swiftly. Before the council, she was confident of her power and authority, but for what she needed to do next, courage was needed.

She knew that she was destined to rise to the heights but accepted that allies were important. Not the squabbling fools of the council, but allies with true power. Allies who could offer Coril much but who required service, obedience and dedication.

Coril had found one such, or perhaps had been sought out, and now she must secure this alliance, offer the service, and secure her position.

A locked box lay inside a locked chest, and she found the keys and methodically opened the locks in turn to access what lay within. She forced herself to be calm as she reached into the box and withdrew the items.

A gold chain went around her neck with an unusual symbol hanging as the pendant: a six-pointed star, brightly gilded. It hung against her chest, and she could see the gleam from the corner of her eye, reflecting starkly against the subdued tones of her fine silk robe.

Next, she lifted the mask and raised it to her face. It was charcoal-dark but striped with silver and grey. It hid her face and revealed her allegiance.

A bell chimed in the city below. The appointed time had arrived. She was ready.

The furs softened the firm sensation of the stone beneath her knees as she lowered herself to the floor. She would give service, but she would not be subservient. Not for long. The lesser of equals, that was what she was, for now. But not forever.

She waited.

Her mind worked as the moments passed. She had news to give and was anxious to show off what she had done. But she did not want to give too much. Did not want to seem eager for praise. The right approach was important to guide the path of this relationship.

She could not afford to put a foot wrong.

The importance of what was about to happen weighed on her as she continued to wait. A bead of sweat trickled down her brow, behind the mask, and she resisted the temptation to lift it.

Then, it happened.

It began as an almost imperceptible swirl of light in the space before her eyes. Several motes of dust, perhaps, caught in a draft and whipped into a dazzling dance in a shaft of sunshine. But from there it grew, swirling and radiating a purplish glow which gained intensity until it shone like a lantern.

The purple shape coalesced and solidified in the air, becoming a five-sided portal to…she knew not. But to somewhere else. As she watched it opened and shifted and another face appeared, framed by the mystical portal.

'It is done?' the masked figure asked. No preamble, no greeting. Coril relished this. Straight into the meat of the conversation.

'He has done it himself,' she replied, her voice muffled and metallic in her own ears. 'The young baron has spurned the comfort and decadence I offered. His pride could not let him settle for an empty, but easy life.'

'As you predicted,' came the voice from the other mask. It was the voice of another woman, but that was the limit of Coril's knowledge of her mysterious ally.

'I gave him little choice,' said Coril, humility in her voice. 'He would accept my offer and become my docile vassal, or he would reject it. I thought the latter more likely.'

'As did I. Where did he go?'

'He was followed, on your orders. I suspected he would go running to his father, and so it proved.'

'The boy will have received a cold welcome.'

Coril could not restrain a wry chuckle. 'Indeed. I have worked tirelessly to gain Earl Gevrin's trust, and forbearance. I knew he would prefer I retained authority over Kereva. He knows I will look after his interests. We are fortunate that his youngest son is not one of them.'

'No, this is true. And yet- he is of value. Do we know where he is now?'

'No, he has not been seen, and this also works in our favour. Should he abandon his duty here he will become an enemy of the state. His father has indicated to me previously that he would consider it treason. He has long suspected that this boy lacked the backbone to bear his responsibilities.'

'So, he will not be missed?'

'No, he will not,' said Coril, unable to keep the satisfaction from her voice. 'There would be…value, in capturing him and returning him to the Duke to face justice. But you have indicated that you have other plans?'

There was a pause, as the mind behind the other mask seemed to consider how much to tell Coril. The more she was let into the other's plans, the more trust was implied. Trust that Coril would make sure she capitalised upon.

'Yes. He can be…used. That he is out of the picture and you are free to secure your power base here in Kereva is a victory in itself, but one of that heritage, that bloodline…he must be found, and restrained. Once he is, I will come to him in person, when the time is right. He can strengthen our cause mightily, even as he…uh…passes.'

So, the boy was to die. Coril cared not, just so long as Earl Gevrin did not discover she had a hand in preventing him facing the Duke's justice. She knew many ways that necessary acts could be hidden, however.

'Find him. Capture him. Keep him restrained.' The voice from the masked figure in the portal was now brisk and authoritative. 'I do not care what becomes of him, so long as he lives long enough for me to come to him in person.'

Coril bobbed her head. 'It shall be done. What will you do to the boy, when you come?'

A slight pause. 'This is for the privileged few to know.'

With that, the masked face receded, and the portal began to close.

'I can help make preparations!' urged Coril as the masked face vanished from view. Coril cursed as she was left alone in the empty office. The note of pleading in her voice had been desperate and childish.

She hung her head as she remained kneeling on the floor, but only for a moment. She would not give up.

Climbing to her feet, she removed the mask and symbol and locked them back where none would find them, before moving to her desk. She had work to do.

Shre Evane Claes, priestess of the Veil, removed her striped mask slowly from her face. Her narrow chest rose and fell deeply as she gasped in air, and her arms and legs felt heavy, empty.

She had recovered her health and her energy in the weeks since the climax of her frantic pursuit of the jewel, but working these spells still took a toll. When she closed her eyes she could still see those scenes; through the eyes of the magically animated corpse of the thief Clayton Moore she had seen the fires of Demonsnight and Mackems closing in on the jewel, before swift blades had destroyed that body and left her swimming in the void.

With the strength to communicate with those far away once more, she had found out that they had failed. The jewel had escaped, in the hands of another thief. She had expected punishment and maybe death for her failure, but instead had been given another task.

The pleading voice of her vassal in Kereva had been cut off mid-word as the portal closed. Claes permitted herself a wry smile. That one was awed by power and would do anything to grasp more.

Claes had let Coril believe that she was special, that she was important, and that her service to the cause would place her alongside Claes herself. Let her think that. It kept her working diligently, and gave Claes a robust hold on Kereva and northern Anish, on behalf of her mighty master.

She sat down on the bed, weary and suddenly cold at the thought of the one she served. Chained but powerful, hidden but ever-present, capable of so much and yet depending so utterly on Claes and a few other devotees. The demon, Desya.

He had punished her with torture as her Mackems minions fruitlessly pursued the jewel from Anish, across the Lands of the

Great River and to Ben Gedrin. He had dragged her down to his underground lair and hurt her, humiliated her, methodically and regularly. He had drained all her strength with the pain he inflicted, only returning enough for her to continue to supervise the chase.

When she had been summoned after it all was over, to tell him that the jewel had escaped her grasp, she had expected the worst.

And yet, pain had not come. Death had not come. She lived, and was given a new task. He had shown her an image, a vision of a shining sword. This was her new goal: to find the fabled Serpentsword along with one with the strength to wield it, as the leader of Desya's army when he emerged back into the world.

She had buried herself in scrolls and tablets of ancient writings, for the very existence of the weapon was little more than a rumour. A myth. She had found little so far, and before she could learn more the demon had summoned her again.

Braced for pain, she was surprised when he beckoned her further into the cavern in which he was chained, moving aside to show her something.

Look, he said, the voice like granite boulders shifting against one another.

This is why the jewel must be found.

She had looked.

At the rear of the cave, which was usually shrouded in near-complete darkness, was a crimson glow. She saw it with her eyes but still was not sure if what she experienced in this place was real. She knew she could feel pain, only too well, but the torture that had been inflicted left no visible mark once she returned to the surface, and to her real body.

Was she here? Was it just her mind, or consciousness, or soul that was drawn down to this deep, dark place? She did not know and could not ask.

The red light surrounded two silhouettes, patches of blood-red darkness amid the glow, and shaped like people. Claes looked closer and with a flash of realisation *knew* that one of them was, in some way, Clayton Moore. The thief was dead, his body rotting even as she had animated it with the power of the jewel, but this was somehow the essence of his being.

It was just a lifeless shape surrounded by a crimson halo, but she knew that it was him. She did not get that sense of recognition from the other shape...not at first...but then she realised who it must be. After Clayton Moore's remains had been hacked down, she had managed to inhabit another body. Another person who must have been killed by the jewel, their lifeforce stripped away.

The demon's voice rang in her mind once more, grating and painfully loud.

Touch.

Reaching out tentatively with one hand, or with something that her own mind suggested was a hand, she edged towards the light. As her fingertips got to within a handspan of the glimmering shape, she felt a jolt go through her body, a shock of power.

It was like the flow she had drawn into herself to do the demon's will, to animate the corpse of Clayton Moore and to follow the jewel. It filled her body, flooding in through her fingertips. It was so strong...she felt as though she could do anything.

She realised the implications with a sudden shock, and almost staggered.

This was the true purpose of the jewel. This was its function; not to kill and create biddable husks with the remains, but to strip away the essence of a person and to store it. This patch of glowing red light was a store of power, a stockpile.

You understand.

And she did. The force that flowed into her was the essence of just two people. She could not help but imagine how it would feel with more. Many more. She glanced around to where the bulky shape of the demon lay on the floor of the cavern. The dark iron of thick chains glinted in the low light but mercifully, most of the demon's form was still in shadow.

The jewel will be found. We will use the finder to increase my power. With the sword in their hand they will be unstoppable, and I shall have my freedom.

She had been dismissed but her mind was reeling. Previously, she had followed the demon's orders with the goal of releasing him from his subterranean prison, but had not truly believed that it was possible. Now, she knew that it was. A collection of souls from the jewel would provide the power that was needed to break the chains and to let Desya climb back to the surface.

And when he was there, the world would tremble.

He had been quite specific in his instructions. He did not order her to find the jewel, not this time. It was his belief that fate would carry it to the hand of one who was destined to use it, and not be consumed by it. This one would be able to carry it, to wield it, and would lead Desya's conquest of the world.

They did not need to be found; they would make themselves known when the time was right.

Her next task was different.

The demon had explained that some souls were more valuable than others, and that those with a strong fate or a renowned bloodline could be sources of greater power. Those that had defied him previously were to be hunted, and captured.

The thieves who had stolen the jewel and led Claes and the Mackems a merry dance all the way to Ben Gedrin, would have to be found. The Demon's Tear jewel would consume their souls, and Claes would be thrilled to watch them die.

Whoever found the jewel would be next, if they were tempted into picking it up. Desya had stated that the finder would wield it, but Claes knew it could not be touched without killing the holder. When that happened, though, she would be able to find them. Perhaps, *she* could be the wielder. *She* could be the one to lead Desya's armies across the world.

First, though, was the boy. He was out there, somewhere, and Desya would be well pleased when she found him. She hoped Coril would do her work well, and find a way to capture Baron Styoyan Jukeev.

EIGHT

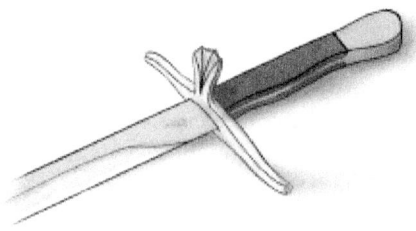

Styoyan regarded the border town, and a stab of anxiety pricked him like the point of a slender blade.

Was he really going to do this?

High stone walls rose ahead, but buildings spread within and without as though the boundary was an irrelevance. Kufiria stood amid the hills that bordered Anish and Buren, and the relationship between the two countries was cordial. A peace had existed for many years. Trade flowed.

As Styoyan approached, heeling his tired mount forwards at a slow walk, he joined a great throng of people. The town gates were thrown open and a steady stream of traffic passed through.

He would have to join them.

A Bureno merchant in a long, fine robe passed the other way, atop a heavily loaded wagon. She inclined her head graciously. Styoyan frowned to himself as he glanced around. Only then did he realise that the other travellers were giving him exaggerated space on the road. A simply dressed man, face smeared with dirt, noticed his gaze.

'My lord,' he said, bowing his head.

Styoyan's stomach lurched. Of course, he was still dressed as the Baron of Kereva. Even though his bright rings were covered by his soft leather riding gloves, his fine clothes, steed and the silver pins in his hair marked his status.

None here would know that his position was little more than a convenience for his father. A child's crown of gilded wood.

Travelling like this could be problematic- he was much too conspicuous. He thought quickly as he rode through the gates.

Within the walls, the town swarmed. Styoyan was glad to be raised above street level, high on Mahdesht's back. The passage of hooves, wheels and many feet had churned the dirt road ahead into thick, dark mud. It caked Mahdesht's lower legs and the folk that passed Styoyan were splattered with brown up to their waists.

The houses of the town were built in the traditional Anise style, with the lower walls of stone and the upper storeys of overhanging timber. In the alleyways in between, stretched canvas formed a warren of covered markets. Hawkers cried their wares, meat sizzled on charcoal grills and people in clothes of all styles and cuts mingled, talked and traded.

Styoyan let his gaze travel across the stalls and barrows. He had not seen what he wanted. He did not want to buy any food or trinkets; what he needed was an ostler.

The street opened into the town's central square, and he finally beheld what he sought.

Ahead and to his right was a grand house. Two storeys of well-dressed stone were capped with a tall and wide upper level. Many shuttered windows looked out over the square and a pair of armed guards stood to either side of a broad doorway.

This was clearly the townhouse of a local lord, a baron or a duke. Styoyan had probably been told their name at some point, but he had always struggled to find that sort of thing interesting. The fortunes of the Jukeev family had been his only concern. The owner of the house did not matter, anyway. Styoyan was finished with the nobility.

He turned away and headed towards another looming building in the opposite corner of the square; a tall and solidly built inn.

The foundations of the building were a series of parallel stone arches, wide as a man and perhaps twenty paces each in length. Long timber beams were laid across the arches, spanning the gaps and the bulk of the inn was built on top.

The narrow, gloomy spaces between the arches were partitioned into pens; stabling for the customers' horses. Styoyan rode across the square and dismounted beside the nearest pen.

'Do you have space for my horse?' he asked the ostler, as she shambled forwards. Her smock reached down past her hips and her rings were bright. It seemed as though the inn was prosperous, with a good business for ostlers minding the steeds of its wealthy patrons.

She looked him up and down.

'To you, lordship,' she said. 'A silver section will cover it.'

'I only want the pen for one night. I don't want to buy it off you.'

'That's the price. Demand is high.'

Her face was impassive as Styoyan tugged a silver money ring from his wrist, where it had been cool against his skin beneath the sleeve of his over-robe, and handed it over. She snipped a section from the end with a small pair of shears and passed the rest back.

'Take care of him,' he said, but she had already turned away, leading Mahdesht beneath the arches without a word. 'Being busy doesn't mean you don't need manners,' he muttered towards her retreating back.

She stopped.

'What was that, lordling?' she shot back, glaring over her shoulder.

'Nothing,' said Styoyan, and turned away.

He suppressed his annoyance as he strode towards the entrance to the inn. He could have responded with a withering put down, but he did not want to risk Mahdesht being mistreated. A creaking flight of wooden stairs led up to the open doorway. The doors were flung open wide and fires roared in several hearths as the sound of merry singing filled the air.

A few moments were all that it took for Styoyan to exchange another silver section for a small room with a narrow bed. It was humble and overpriced, but it would have to do. A lockbox at the foot of the bed fit his sabre and most of his silver money rings and sections, along with his soft leather purse which contained several small gold ingots.

It would be unwise to walk out into a strange town while carrying a sword, and equally foolish to bear all the wealth he still owned while unarmed. Lastly, he withdrew the silver pins securing his hair and dropped them into the trunk beside his scabbarded blade. His long, dark hair hung loose in unruly curls, so he gathered it back and tied it with a cord.

Pulling his cape about his shoulders, he strode from the room and out of the inn looking somewhat less like a noble at court. That was to the good.

On the opposite side of the square, he spotted a large shop with a bolt of cloth mounted above the door. More were spread on tables beneath the wide awning. He hurried over.

Brightly coloured reams of fabric hung from the shop's ceiling. Styoyan swayed between them, feeling as though he was inside a rainbow. Tayan silk in pink, yellow and opalescent green hung next to fine Bureno linen in more muted colours.

He was not interested in any of them.

He edged further into the shop, glancing around, left and right. Near the back of the shop, he found what he was looking for.

An old woman, silver hair tucked beneath a plain cap, sat behind a broad counter. As Styoyan watched she cut a section of bright silk from a roll before her with a sharp knife, then reached for a needle and thread.

'Yes?' she asked while staring intently at the eye of her needle. She passed the thread through and only then did her eyes flick up. 'Sir,' she added.

Styoyan pointed behind her.

'I would like to buy that,' he said. She followed his pointing finger with her eyes, then looked back at him, shaking her head. He was looking at a simple robe in a plain, dun fabric that hung on the wall.

'No, sir,' she replied. 'Those are just samples. They are just to show our customers the styles. We make those robes up with one of these fabrics.' She gestured to the swaying streamers of cloth that hung all around them.

'And fine robes they would be,' replied Styoyan with patience. 'But that is not what I want. A plain robe is what I need, and I would like to take it now. Please.'

It took a lot more negotiation before the seamstress could be persuaded to part with the plain grey robe. Styoyan had ended up paying two silver sections for it, which was three or four times what it was worth.

'Thank you,' said Styoyan, eventually, as he turned to leave with the folded robe beneath his arm.

'I'll have to make a new sample robe now,' she grumbled.

'I appreciate what you've done for me,' said Styoyan before leaving the shop. As he crossed the threshold, he chewed his lip. He hoped he had not left her thinking ill of him.

He turned and headed towards a different shop that he had spotted from across the square. This one had a narrow, heavy door and the windows were screened by a mesh of decorative but heavy iron rods. A strongarm stood beside the door, a thick leather arming jacket over his work smock and his hand resting on the butt of an iron-shod cudgel. He looked Styoyan up and down briefly as he pushed the door open, then looked away again, disinterested.

The interior of the shop glittered. Everywhere Styoyan looked, the light of candle lanterns reflected from a multitude of polished, shining objects. It was as though the nighttime sky of stars was in the room with him.

'How may I serve, sir?' came a voice. A small, neat man stood behind a small, neat counter at the rear of the shop. His robe was of fine cloth but with little adornment. This was someone who had wealth, had earned it and had no need to show it off.

'Fare you well,' said Styoyan, greeting the merchant as he moved closer to the counter. 'Do you sell finger-rings?'

'Of course, sir,' replied the merchant, a metalsmith. He indicated a nearby shelf which was set with long dowels. Rings of almost every colour and metal were threaded onto them, although Styoyan saw only a few gold and none of the rare, royal *pluitone*. 'Does sir approach a birth day? Or perhaps it is for someone else?'

'No, and no,' replied Styoyan. Now for the awkward part. 'I require a new full set of twenty, and they are for myself.' He tugged off his gloves and tucked them into his belt.

'Sir, I cannot—' began the ring dealer as Styoyan began to pull off his rings, beginning with the golden barony ring.

'I just need to exchange them,' said Styoyan, cutting him off mid-sentence. 'For something more plain. Something that will not stand out. Mostly copper, maybe a couple of steel? I am a trained soldier.'

As Styoyan talked, the man's lips moved soundlessly as though he could not summon the words he was trying to say. Eventually, he found his voice and his cheeks reddened as he spoke. 'Sir, you cannot ask this. You cannot be serious!'

'Why would I ask it if I were not serious?'

'These are your rings,' he said, gesturing at the small pile that Styoyan had created on the counter. 'This is your life! You cannot just swap them! It's not seemly, and I will not be party to it.'

Styoyan was taken aback by the man's obvious unease. Of course, to wear false finger rings was vulgar and against the unwritten Anise code of etiquette, but surely, he must see that these circumstances were unique? The man should even profit from it.

Of course, Styoyan had never had to buy his own rings before. Or, in fact, ever had to buy anything much for himself. Nevertheless, he could not see the problem.

'Look,' he said, affecting a conciliatory tone. 'I don't need money. You can have my rings as a pure exchange for a less valuable set. It's a good deal for you.'

The merchant drew in a deep, calming breath. 'Sir, I'm sure it is not your intention to offend, and yet your suggestions, and your insistence are an affront to my honour as an honest trader. If word were to spread that I was party to this subterfuge, this…' He searched for a suitable word. 'This travesty, then my reputation would be ruined. I must ask you to leave. Take your rings and go. Sir.'

His face was stony and Styoyan knew he would not be able to talk him around. The word 'but' rose to his lips but he suppressed it. His frustration rose.

'You have missed an opportunity today,' he snapped. 'Fare you well!' He marched from the shop, jamming his slim rings back on his fingers as he went.

What would he do now?

The ring dealer's voice came quietly from behind him. 'I would suggest you find your way to the Burkotil and ask the same questions. You are likely to get a different response.'

When Styoyan turned, the metalsmith was facing away. On the threshold, he stopped to address the bulky guard.

'Where is the Burkotil?' he asked. The guard looked down and his heavy brows creased, clearly surprised to be addressed.

'South,' he said after a moment, in a voice like trodden gravel. He pointed away to his left. 'Hard on the river, where the streets get narrow.'

'Thank you,' said Styoyan, turning away.

'Uhh...' The guard's voice came again, an uncertain rumble. Styoyan paused, tilting his head. 'It's a bad place,' said the guard. 'Be careful.'

Styoyan walked away, his hands curling unconsciously into loose fists. He would be a surprise for any thug who chose to attack him.

Beyond the southern extent of the square the buildings dwindled in size and the streets were narrower. Styoyan walked along twisting lanes where the lower storeys were mere pillars of rubble walling and the upper floors of timber shacks perched on top. The sounds and the smells of everyday life surrounded him as the light began to fade from the autumn sky.

Familiar scents of woodsmoke and cooking food mingled with the pervasive aroma of damp earth. The sharp, unpleasant tang of what might be a tannery was borne on the gentle westerly breeze.

Styoyan walked on, and soon a gap in the buildings indicated the line of the river. It was a narrow but deep-cut waterway, fed by streams which ran off the hills lining the border between Anish and Buren. It flowed southeast through this town and out towards the coast, where it emptied into the Southern Ocean at Savin Tides.

As he looked down at the cinnamon waters, slender barges floated away or were drawn into the docks on the opposite banks, small teams of thickset ponies towing them with rough ropes.

Styoyan stepped back from the river and glanced around. The ring dealer had said that there were other merchants in this area, and where he stood matched the guard's description of the Burkotil. Lanes and alleyways so enclosed by overhanging buildings that they were like tunnels stretched away in each direction, turning sharp corners and twisting haphazardly until out of sight. It resembled a maze. Which way should he go?

'Any help, my lord?'

The speaker was a tall, skinny woman. Her hair was dark and so was the skin of her dirty cheeks. She wore a short smock and Styoyan noticed with surprise that she was barefoot. Nevertheless, she held herself with a confidence that he recognised from his dealings with noble men and women. This was someone totally at ease in their surroundings.

'I'm not a lord,' he replied, automatically. 'But I'm looking for a ring dealer. Do you know of one?'

'It's your lucky day, sire,' she replied, smiling broadly and showing too many teeth. 'My brother is a trader of rings, jewels and trinkets. He'll be sure to give you a good price, if you have my recommendation. Follow this way, my lord.'

She led him down a twisting alleyway, no different to the others, as the light dimmed. Sunset was near and the houses closed in over Styoyan's head. Commoners with simple caps stared at him with curiosity as he passed. Cur-dogs barked as they chased black foxes into dark spaces between the ramshackle buildings. Babies wailed from within the cramped, tumbledown houses.

'Not much further,' she called back over her shoulder. 'This way, my lord.' Styoyan grimaced and followed. He was not sure he would be able to find his way out of this rat's nest of lanes without help.

At last, they stopped before a plain door in a simple timber house. A low foundation of stone rose above the muddy street, but the rest of the house was built of darkened planks that were cracked and warped. No sign or symbol was hung above the door.

Styoyan's unease was growing, but he could not back out now. Besides, if this was the only way he could exchange his bright rings for something less obtrusive, it was what he must do.

He felt a brief pang of sadness at the thought of turning his back on the past, but then his mother's resolute insistence on not accepting the state of things and his father's stern, uncaring face repeated in his memory and his resolve hardened once more.

'Here we are,' said his guide. 'This is where my brother does business.' She knocked twice, quick and sharp, then opened the door and stepped inside.

It was clearly not a shop. A small group of people were sitting around a table in the centre of the room, and a pile of copper and silver money rings lay between them. As one, they looked around to regard the arrivals. Their eyes were flinty.

'What is this, Amien?' asked one. He had dark eyes and an unruly mop of brown hair. Styoyan noted that the rings of his early years were dull colours; iron and lead, but the most recent were the brighter tones of pewter and brass. This was someone who was on his way up in the world.

'A customer, Amek,' replied Styoyan's guide, Amek's sister. 'He was looking for somewhere to buy finger-rings, and I told him how my brother was a reputable dealer who would give him a fair price.'

'Finger-rings?' asked Amek, before continuing. 'Quite so. I have a good stock right now, and you've come at just the right time to get some real bargains.'

Amien coughed, a slight sound. 'I'll leave him with you, my brother. I need to…round up my dogs.' She turned and left.

'Quite so,' repeated Amek, nodding. As the door clicked shut his unreadable eyes turned to regard Styoyan. 'What exactly are you looking for, sir?'

'Finger-rings, like your sister said,' said Styoyan. 'A full set of twenty.'

If the trader was surprised, he gave no sign. Neither did any of the rest of the group around the table. They were a mix of men and women, and their robes that hung to mid-thigh suggested that they were all merchants and traders.

Watching Amek's face carefully, he tugged at each finger of the glove on his left hand, before tucking it into his belt. The silver of the ten rings on that hand gleamed in the low light of the room. His right glove followed and Styoyan held out both hands. The single gold barony ring almost seemed to glow. Amek barely blinked.

'An exchange,' said Styoyan. 'I need some plainer rings and I'm happy to exchange these.' Amek raised an eyebrow, just a tiny twitch. 'Consider the difference a fee for your discretion.'

'Sir is generous,' said Amek. 'And fair. I would be very happy to help.'

At last, thought Styoyan. He could not have taken any more histrionics like the metalsmith in the square.

Amek stood, the room silent, and moved to an iron-bound chest beside one of the walls. Opening it, he returned with a small case. He brushed the pile of silver and copper away with a clatter, making a space on the table. The case was brimming with rings of every size, shape and colour.

'The choice is yours,' said Amek, with a subtle bow.

A few moments later Styoyan's own silver rings had joined the collection in the case. He held his single golden ring between his thumb and forefinger. Amek's eyes were fixed upon it, though his expression had not altered.

Could he really trade this away? Receiving it had been the greatest honour of his young life. He had been so proud to slip it onto his finger, so full of hope. It had finally made him into a true noble, a hero of the bloodline of Steyfan Jukeev. Wearing it, he had been able to imagine himself as a benevolent ruler, a resolute protector of his people and a warrior of virtue.

And yet, it was naught but artifice. A child's paper crown. It meant nothing. It meant less than nothing; it was an insult, a stain on his honour. A sign of the contempt with which his father had treated him.

Styoyan could not forget the unsympathetic expression on his father's face as he had spelled out what Styoyan and his mother truly meant to him; nothing. It hardened his resolve. Gevrin would not be pleased unless Styoyan proved his worth, and that needed action, not golden trinkets.

He cast the narrow band of gold into the case.

To replace them, he picked out another twenty rings. He chose mostly copper; the metal of a moderately wealthy minor noble. The last two he took from the case were steel. He liked the idea of appearing as a military man, and, after all, he had military training. He could have led fighting forces.

The disapproving face of his tutor, the old elf Morehai, appeared in his mind for a moment but Styoyan waved it away. This was not deception, it was reinvention.

Moments later he stood, the new rings resized by Amek's thick but deft fingers, and securely in place upon his fingers.

'Thanks to you once more, sir,' said Amek as he also stood. 'May the Five protect you on your onward journey.'

That seemed like a strange thing for a trader to say, and Styoyan thought he noticed one of other men around the table smirking, but the expression was gone before he could be sure.

'Brunek,' said Amek, looking to the man who had given that fleeting smirk. 'Show our friend out.'

Styoyan nodded in thanks, before heading for the door. Brunek got there first, striding past Styoyan then reaching for the handle. The man's hand was blocky and thick-fingered, and Styoyan could not help noticing that the knuckles were puffy and scarred. The hand of a brawler.

An uneasy feeling began to grow in his stomach. He suppressed it.

'Fare you well, sir,' came Amek's voice from deeper in the room behind, then Brunek had pulled open the door and Styoyan stepped out onto the street.

He looked up into many pairs of unfriendly eyes. The thump of the door shutting behind him was ominous, like a single beat of a war drum. He had time to notice Amek's sister Amien at the head of the small crowd before a solid force hit him in the back and he stumbled forwards.

He whirled to be confronted by the heavy shape of Brunek, who had followed him out before shutting the door. The thickset man had his fists clenched, his face blank.

'You can make this easy, my lord,' said Amien. Styoyan turned again. She stood slightly forwards from the rest of the crowd. A thick wooden cudgel was held loosely in one hand.

'Turn out your purse, and bare your wrists,' she continued. 'And you can walk away. You don't want to try the hard way.'

Cold rage rose in Styoyan's breast. Rage, and indignation. They had tricked him, and now they would try to rob him. He had been stupid. He had no intention, however, of handing over a single copper section. His fingers twitched.

The words of his tutor, Morehai, came to his mind in that moment.

If you are outnumbered, attack the enemy where they are strongest. Disable their strongest hand and the rest of the body may quickly follow.

The thought shocked him into action.

He spun on the ball of his left foot, both hands moving. With his left, he batted away Brunek's arm, thrown across his body in instinctive defence. His right lashed out towards Brunek's throat, Styoyan's knuckles catching his windpipe with a solid blow.

Brunek staggered, but at that moment crushing pain bloomed in Styoyan's ribs. The breath exploded from his lungs as Amien's cudgel struck him from behind. His back arched against the impact and another blow struck, this time to the back of his head.

Cold dirt slapped wetly against his face as he dropped to the ground. He urged his body to rise, but dark spots swam before his eyes and water seemed to have filled his limbs.

Strong hands gripped him and flipped him over. Fingers groped over his body, quickly stripping him of his purse and the silver money ring he wore on each wrist. They did not touch his hands, or his new finger-rings. There were boundaries, even for thugs and criminals.

When they were done, mere heartbeats later, they left him without another word. He heard their treads recede as they strolled away down the narrow street. He gathered his resolve and began to push himself to his feet. As he looked up, a face appeared above him. It was Brunek. His eyes were narrow.

'You're lucky to walk away,' he hissed, his voice rasping and wheezing. 'If I see you in the Burkotil again, I'll kill you.' Styoyan felt dampness on his face as Brunek's words showered him in spittle.

His face lifted but his leg swung, and Styoyan was left gasping once more as the thief's boot struck him hard in the ribs. The world swam in a haze of pain. Shame and anger warred within him. This was not fair, but he had been a fool.

He lay in the mud, the urge to run and hide washing over him like cold rain. Where could he go now?

PART TWO

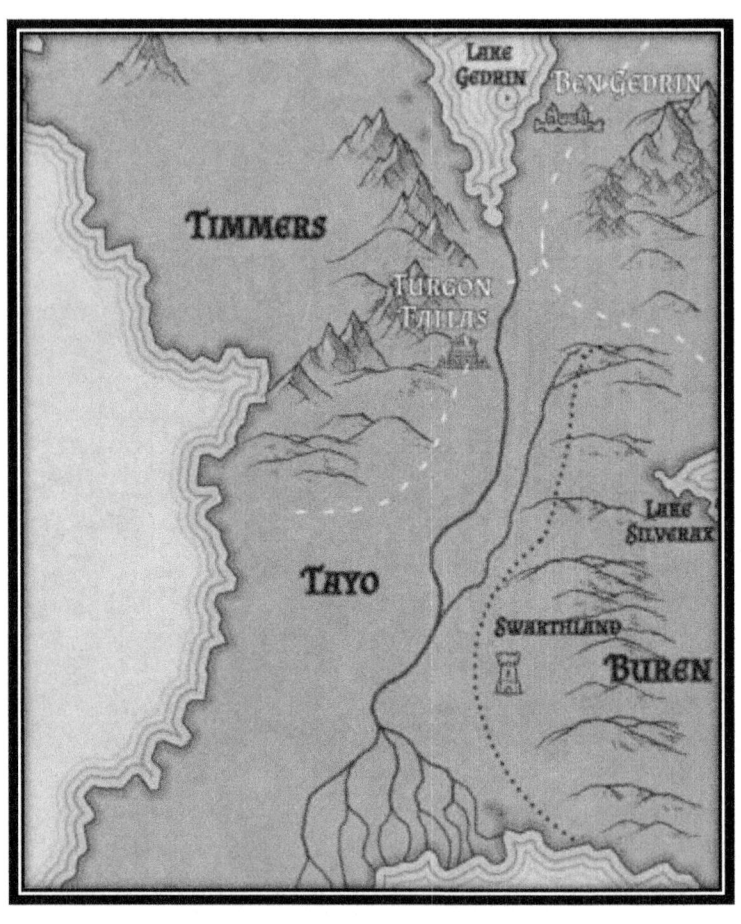

TAYO

NINE

He had known this day would come.

His father, Duke Teleri, had given him a great deal of advice as he had aged.

'I am Duke,' he had said, 'for now. But soon I will abdicate the duchy in your favour. I grow old, Daeron, and you are coming into the full strength of your manhood.

'I tire of this endless relentless strife. You must master it. I grow weak, and I see you grow stronger every day. I don't mean in strength of arm. Relying on physical might is for savages and simpletons. You are growing in strength of will, and that is what you will need to face the challenges ahead.'

They were playing *sadawch*. Daeron had a heap of tiles in his hand, the palm-sized slates etched with twisting paths that seemed unlikely to meet, until they did.

'Yes, father,' Daeron Teleri had replied, laying a tile onto the grid marked on the square of cloth before them, and moving the small wooden peg that was his piece along the pale, scratched path until it reached an end.

'We are Tayan,' his father had said. 'True Tayan, not this new breed of lapdogs who beg for scraps at the feet of the Boian. You know of who I speak.'

'The Taosach.'

'Quite so, and all the lackeys in her court. My opposition to Re'Emsser becomes a bigger problem for her but Teleri is still too strong a house for her to rebuke. We remain too powerful to challenge. Too many Tayan lords on both sides owe us.

'Added to that, Turgon Fallas, this great home of ours,' he threw up his hands, indicating the huge red stone blocks of their ancient fortress, 'is unassailable by force.'

Daeron looked around, seeing the great hall anew. It had been built by an elder Teleri in times gone past. A Teleri who bore the title *distan* as a trusted advisor to the Tayan *brehnan*, or war-leader. Before the Boian had abolished that royal title after their conquest.

Before Re'Emsser had been forced on the country, and Tayo had been proudly independent.

'For now,' continued Duke Owaen Teleri, placing another tile without seeming to look down at the board. 'But not forever. The Taosach knows the risk we pose to her authority, whether it is our will to do so or not. There are many who would go to way to see a Teleri take the title of *taosach* and yet more who fear what would happen next.'

He moved his small wooden piece, a peg with a rounded head and curved belly, along the scratched path. It ran perilously close to the edge of the board, and would hand Daeron the victory if it went out of bounds, but somehow curved back towards the centre and safety, tracing a devious path that Daeron had not noticed.

'Rejection of Re'Emsser. Defiance of the Boian. A claim to the title of *brehnan*, with a Teleri in Turgon Fallas holding that office. A great many Tayan nobles would see their status and fortunes vanish. They rely on the flow of Bureno silver and gold to them, and them alone, through the stranglehold of Re'Emsser. They would risk war to avoid that.'

'And is that what would happen, father?' asked Daeron. He did not know if he would want to become *taosach*, and even less *brehnan*. It was a title that meant little less than king, and in some contexts meant "warlord". The High King in Buren had outlawed it as a Tayan title following their victory in the border wars a decade ago. Membership of Re'Emsser beneath the yoke-like rule of the Bureno High King had been another condition of Tayo's defeat.

Duke Teleri spread his wrinkled hands.

'When you have power, you are faced with a choice. You may do your best to retain that power, trying to keep things as they are. Or, you can initiate change. To try to do what is right. You cannot do more. You cannot control all outcomes.'

Daeron laid a tile. His piece, which had been close to his father's, immediately veered away along a serpentine trail which led into a corner of the board. His position suddenly looked parlous.

His father had barely glanced at the board, but continued speaking. 'Do you think that striving for a free Tayo is the right thing to do? Do you think the people of our country would be better off unchained from the shackles of Re'Emsser?'

Daeron paused while he thought. This was another lesson from his father. Think before you speak, and be honest in what you say when you do.

He had seen first-hand the conditions that the common folk of the land were forced to endure. He knew how they laboured from dawn until dusk in their marshes and paddy fields, and yet barely grew enough to live on. And, he had also seen the opulence of the Taosach's palace in the west, the comfort enjoyed by her inner circle of dukes and barons as they mimicked the airs and graces of the Bureno court.

'Yes,' he replied after several moments. 'Tayo must be free. It is the right thing to do.'

'You are truly my son,' said Owaen Teleri. His ruddy-skinned face cracked into a broad smile for a moment, then became serious once more. 'Yet, they all know that we think this way. They know how we would act given the chance, and they fear that the people would rise up in support. They will not let it happen.'

'They will come for you?'

'No, they dare not. Too many of them owe me honour-debts still. They cannot move against me. Not openly, and not unless I grow weak.'

Duke Teleri fixed his eyes, shockingly pale against the dark skin of his face, on his son once more.

'They will wait until I am infirm, or in the ground. Then, they will come for you. But, you will be ready. Remember this as you remember what we have lost. The Tayo that should have been. The Tayo stolen by...*them*.'

Daeron lifted his eyes, recalling that conversation as he stared out across the sloping, ochre rocks of the high plateau. His enemies would be searching for him now, and he heard the bark of a hunting hound, muted by the distance.

His father had been right. He had to keep moving.

The nobles subservient to the Taosach had muttered about the Teleri family, and when his father had abdicated from the title and passed it down to Daeron, the volume of those mutters had increased. But, Turgon Fallas was too strong for any force to conquer it by direct attack.

The fortress-town was built into the walls of rocky ravine, where terraces in the smooth red stone provided the foundations for the high, blocky walls. Within were dwellings, armouries and granaries, as well as the grand house that was the ancestral home of the Teleris.

This huge, circular keep was built against the cliff wall and was impossible to approach or assail from the rear; sheer cliffs guarded it well. A sequence of walls, easily defended by few against many, lay between the keep and the main gate, which itself could only be reached by a steep, narrow rampway.

Another sturdy tower stared across the gorge from a terrace on the opposite side, and between them lay the reason for the Teleri's enduring prosperity; the great north road of Tayo.

It was a busy road.

Trading to Buren along the routes in the south of Tayo incurred heavy taxes, another stipulation of Re'Emsser, but trading through the north avoided that. Kiraband and northern Buren had healthy appetites for Tayan rice, spice and cloth, and there was only one route. This road.

Turgon Fallas sat astride this route, and took a small fee on everything that passed. This included a passage levy on the steady stream of mercenary companies that flowed into Tayo to strengthen the garrisons of the northern nobles. That alone had always made it very difficult for the Taosach and her allies to muster an army strong enough to challenge Teleri and Turgon Fallas.

The toll bar across the dusty road was kept busy, and was heavy with guards.

So, when the offensive that Daeron had been waiting for finally came, it was not a military assault, it was a political one.

The day was fine, with inconsequential white clouds sweeping across a pale blue sky towards the east. Autumn was here but the air had not yet chilled, and Daeron stood on the highest wall of Turgon Fallas in just a light shirt.

A gentle breeze tugged at his baggy sleeves as he stared back south, eyes fixed on the great north road where it appeared around a bend in the canyon. Movement had caught his attention. The words of his father rang in his mind: *they will come.*

And today, it seemed they had.

Slumping down to rest his elbows on the cool, honey-coloured stone, he waited.

The sun had not travelled much further across the afternoon sky before the figures in the valley below had approached closer, striding forwards to stand beneath the gates. A soldier appeared at his elbow.

'Sir,' they said. 'It is the Taosach.'

Everyone in Tayo knew of the strength of Turgon Fallas. As a fortress, it was unbreakable. Most people would assume that it was equally difficult to escape from. The Taosach certainly thought so. With the ruler of Tayo knocking on the door and her army, unseen as yet but surely nearby, waiting further down the road, Daeron was trapped.

'I will speak with her,' said Daeron. Even he could hear the weary resignation in his own voice. Yet, he had to play the game.

He strode down the steps behind the wall, binding a strip of purple silk into a formal headscarf with the ease of repetition as he went. As he passed through the second gate, his chamberlain Trwys was waiting, and passed him a blue woollen coat.

'We must open the gates!' urged Trwys. 'We cannot leave the Taosach waiting outside.' Even though his hands were now empty his fingers still clenched, white at the knuckles. Daeron held up a hand for peace, before shrugging into the coat.

'The Taosach has travelled far to be here,' he said, keeping his voice calm. 'She can wait another few moments.'

With the chamberlain trailing in his wake, he climbed the next flight of stairs to stand above the main gate. The court bard, Teulu, was already there, the braids in her dark hair swinging as she turned to face him. Her long-hilted sword was unsheathed and held in one hand, and she leaned her hip against the hilt.

'Why is she here?' she asked. The bards always made it very clear that they regarded themselves as the equals of all, rich or poor, common or noble.

'Let's find out,' said Daeron, with a flash of a smile. He leaned over the thick battlement towards the small delegation below. 'Welcome, my noble friends,' he called down. 'Be welcomed to Turgon Fallas.'

At the head of the group, from which the Taosach herself was conspicuously absent, was the Taosach's seneschal Ffiore ap Bywyn. He was flanked by the dukes Siaben and Pentyr. Daeron knew them, understood their ambition and liked them not at all. They were leeches who embodied all that was wrong with the Taosach's regime.

The seneschal spoke. 'A welcome would feel warmer if the gates were opened. I am filled with worry about how my lord will react if I tell her I was shut out.'

'Our enemies are everywhere,' replied Daeron in a loud voice that echoed off the walls of the canyon. 'They could be stood beside you.' He looked openly in the direction of Siaben and Pentyr. 'It saddens me to keep the gates shut for now, but are you requesting admittance? Or does the Taosach request it?'

'Neither,' Seneschal Ffiore called back. 'Taosach Wenas wishes to pass along the road with a small force to check her borders are secure.'

'A noble mission. Let her know she can call on assistance from the forces of House Teleri whenever she requires it.'

'This is assumed but your confirmation is received with gratitude. That is not why we approach your gates, however.'

'What other service can we provide?' asked Daeron, although he already knew where this conversation was headed.

They will come. And you will be ready.

The words of his father, ringing in his head as he looked down towards the group of nobles that seemed likely to bring doom and disaster to his house. They had come indeed, and Daeron was ready. But he had to be sure.

'Turgon Fallas is your domain,' said the seneschal. 'We acknowledge your authority here, and would pay the levy due for moving troops past your toll bar.'

Daeron tried not to sigh. 'You can tell the Taosach that any and all levies are waived, now and ever more. Pass through as pleases you, with my blessing.'

The seneschal did not miss a beat. 'The Taosach would not dream of dishonouring a faithful friend so. A debt is owed and must be paid. She would feel great sadness to ignore the precedents.'

'I will calculate the fee, and collect next time I am at court,' called Daeron.

'That would not be proper,' replied the seneschal, quickly. Far too quickly. 'The Taosach insists on paying what she owes before she proceeds, and paying in person. Face to face. To refuse her this wish would be insulting and would leave us in distress.'

So, there it was. The trap set.

His choice; to open the gates of Turgon Fallas to the forces of the Taosach of his own free will, or to refuse and to defy and disobey his lord. Whichever decision he made, the Taosach won.

Occupying Turgon Fallas would be a great victory, even if it was done peacefully and with Daeron's permission. He could imagine the concessions he would have to make, and the oaths he would have to swear to the Taosach in order that her army would ever leave again. Likely, they would be enough to prevent him from ever challenging for power.

His life's task left for him by his father would be over when it had barely been started.

Or, Daeron left the bars on the gates and was besieged. His influence would likewise be hobbled, and he would be squeezed for money and resources until he begged for the siege to be lifted. In this case too, he would be reduced to an impotent vassal of the Taosach and her court.

He turned to the chamberlain.

'Prepare the great hall to formally receive the Taosach. Make sure everyone is in attendance.'

'My Duke?' The expression on Trwys' face was one of curious worry. He was no fool and knew as well as Daeron that the whole fortress lay beneath the headsman's blade.

'Do it,' he confirmed. 'And trust me. All will be well.' The chamberlain nodded and scurried away.

'Your answer, Teleri,' came the seneschal's voice from below the walls. The pretence of friendliness was gone. Daeron fixed the bard, Teulu, with a stare.

'The gates will be opened,' he called out, holding her eyes. Teulu opened her mouth, but Daeron held up a warning hand. 'But we must prepare to receive the Taosach in the glory she deserves. It will take an hour.'

'Very well,' called the seneschal, voice resounding from the uncaring ochre rocks all around. He turned and rode away, closely followed by Siaben and Pentyr. Neither had spoken, and Daeron doubted that either had the wit. He leaned in closer to Teulu.

'You shall open the gates,' he told her, lowering his voice.

'But—' she tried to interrupt.

'You will do this,' he spoke over her protest. 'For me. You know I trust you more than I trust most others. Open the gates when the sun has passed another hour, and welcome the Taosach and her soldiers with all courtesy.'

'Soldiers?'

'Yes, they will come. I expect a full company of Kingsguard to arrive as her bodyguard.'

'So many Gluttons?' Her eyebrows rose. The huge, heavily-armoured soldiers of the old Kingsguard were commonly referred to as the Gluttons thanks to their insatiable appetite for both food and battle.

'They are no simple escort. Guide them all to the great hall. Do as you are bidden.'

She nodded, braids swinging. 'Yes, my duke.'

'And, Teulu.' She paused as she turned to climb down the steps. 'Put your sword away.'

He followed behind as they both stepped back down to ground level, before heading away to his own quarters. He had to move quickly.

The trap was obvious, which meant that it was not the real trap. It was a long knife that glittered in one hand to distract from a shorter, sharper blade in the other, thrust towards the guts. He wished he had the strength to wrestle both knives away and deliver a strike of his own, but it was not yet the right time.

The Taosach would be prepared for a siege but hoping to stroll in through opened gates. Once in, she could force Daeron to bend the knee. But, that would not be enough. His name was too powerful. Teleri.

The click of his chamber door shutting behind him was loud, and final. He knew what the Taosach truly planned. The signs were clear even if he wished in his heart that it were not so. Wished in his heart that there was another way out.

The Taosach was planning to kill him and end his challenge. Today.

'Bravery is one of the great lies.' His father's voice once more. 'Men do not fight in battle because they are brave. They fight because they would live. And the only reason they march to war in the first place is because the fear of what may happen there is less strong than the fear of defying their own masters. Us. Do not compare bravery with foolishness.'

He had placed one more *sadawch* tile and moved his piece. It described a looping path that returned it to the centre of the board. Daeron looked down and realised that he had been fooled. He could not play another piece without the path leading him off the edge and to defeat. Death.

He knew to pay attention to his father's advice. He held the words close to his heart and lived by them.

Daeron was no fool, but he could not help feeling like a coward as he pulled his bed, the heavy, carved wooden frame scraping on the stone, away from the wall. Behind it, and known only to the head of House Teleri, was a small slot carved through the ancient stone of the wall.

He breathed in and squeezed through the narrow gap, face pressed against the cold masonry and the swell of his belly tight beneath him. He dragged a small leather sack behind him before pulling the bed flush against the wall once more.

The Taosach had given him an impossible choice; to be caged and powerless, or to die. Daeron would follow the advice of his father and choose neither. He would choose life.

Behind the small carved slot in the wall was a void. It led to a hidden system of natural caves and cracks that spread behind Turgon Fallas. One of Daeron's ancestors had traced a path through the squeezing darkness, back and up, to find a narrow cave at the summit of a rocky hill. And, they had kept it secret, lest a Duke Teleri ever needed to escape the fortress unseen.

Daeron had emerged from that cave like a cavy startled from a burrow, and set off south across the plateau. The oche rock echoed the hazy orange of the autumn sunset.

He would be far away before dark.

The plateau sloped away south in rocky shelves and ledges, until it dropped into the dappled shade of a forest. The pursuit would be furious once it was discovered that he was no longer in Turgon Fallas, but hopefully his absence would spare his household.

He bit his lip against his worries. He could do nothing more. Dying with them would help them not. Alive, he could hope to return.

And he was determined to return, in vengeance, and to reclaim what was rightfully his.

First, he needed to evade the hunt and survive the night. Then, he needed shelter, allies and silver. He knew where he could find all three.

The light faded from the sky but the fury in Daeron Teleri's heart burned more brightly as he jogged away from his home. He swore that he would return to Turgon Fallas, and when he did, it would be with the destructive rage of a forest fire.

He would remember.

TEN

Klay Garrant had just seen a ghost.

He was sitting on a low wall that bounded the grounds of a roadside teahouse, minding his own business and watching the other mercenaries file into the muster when he saw it. A ghostly relic. A symbol from his past. A past he had almost forgotten.

It was common knowledge across Re'Emsser that the best place for mercenary work was Tayo, and the teahouses in the north of the country acted as muster stations. They were staging posts before the companies of sellswords marched into the interior to draw blood and earn their money rings.

This teahouse sat beside the Great North Road that ran from the south of Tayo, through the rocky hills of the north and on towards the Leaping Bridge. From there, a traveller could join the road that linked Buren or Kiraband, south or north. Mercenaries were arriving from both directions, gathering on the verges of the road and in the grounds of the teahouse.

In a bright knot to one side, nobles in colourful headscarves had gathered, come to inspect the goods. Butchers eyeing the meat market.

No, Klay did not like it but like everyone else in the world, he needed to eat and hiring himself out as a soldier enabled him to do that. It just so happened that he was very good at it. While others were sickened by the waste of life or unmanned by the danger, Klay revelled in the bloody work. He had been doing it long enough to have learned how to survive.

'Could be peace, this time,' said Klay's neighbour on the wall. He was a burly Bureno who went by the name of Elras and had tired of the formality of his own country. His skills had taken him into the turmoil of Tayo where he earned well, and had become one of the regular captains of this company.

'Goatshit,' replied Klay.

'Na, true,' chuckled Elras. 'Taosach has chased Teleri out of that huge fortress of his. Some are saying he's dead. He was the main figurehead of the Separatists, his family has always been against Re'Emsser. With him gone, the Taosach can oust or cow the rest, and there'll be a united Tayo for once.'

'Won't 'appen,' grunted Klay.

There was always war in Tayo. Even if Teleri truly was dead, which Klay would doubt until he saw the body with his own eyes, some other crusader would spring up and there would be more fighting.

In any case, Klay was only half listening as Elras went on, insisting that their next commission would be easy money. His gaze was fixed on what he had just seen, wanting to be certain he was not mistaken.

It was a sword, strapped across the back of a tall, fair-haired mercenary. Not just any sword, though. It was a very distinctive weapon; two-handed with a broad, heavy blade and a long, thick grip. A sword forged for someone with ferocious strength in their hands, wrists and shoulders. A killer's sword.

He knew that weapon although it must have been twenty years since he had last seen it. He remembered the details of it particularly sharply because he had faced it in single combat. He had faced that long, deadly blade and won, leaving the owner, a dwarf named Sturi, dead in the dust.

So, how in the name of the wolf-god had it come to this man?

Klay eyed him up as he edged through the crowd. His movements were studied and wary, careful to keep his distance from the other mercenaries. He had broad shoulders, clad in a coat of stitched skins, and he stepped forwards with the unmistakable balance of a trained fighter. His eyes looked older than his face. They were hooded and sharp, but his face was youthful with smooth cheeks but a bristly moustache.

And, he was about to get into a fight.

Careful as he was, his gaze was in the other direction when a Tayan mercenary turned suddenly. There was a small collision. A touch of shoulders.

'Who are you, lanky?' snarled the Tayan, before the young warrior could move away, The Tayan was wearing a baked leather breastplate over a verdigris-coloured shirt. His long dark hair was pulled across and tied to one side in the country's traditional style. Klay recalled the man's name was Morlen, and he was trouble.

Morlen fancied himself as a hard-nut and made sure that everyone knew it.

'Looking at me?' he raged, confronting the new man.

'I look at nothing,' replied the new man. 'I'm here to join as a mercenary. This is the right place?'

His accent was unusual, the consonants soft but the syllables hard and blocky. His voice was calm but there was uncertainty in his expression.

'You're in my face,' spat Morlen. 'So, you're in the wrong place. It makes me angry when people don't show respect. That's how I feel right now – angry. With you.'

The new man shrugged, and made as though to walk past. Morlen took a step to the side to block his way.

'Are you ignoring me now? No one ignores me. It offends my feelings. Makes me think I don't matter to you.'

The fair-haired stranger stopped, directing a blank, grey-eyed stare in Morlen's direction.

'I heard you,' he said, the words spoken softly, but clear and dangerous. 'But I have nothing to say. Let me pass.'

'I have things to say, though.' Morlen squared his shoulders and took a step closer. Several others crowded behind him, friends of his who fancied a fight where the odds were stacked in their favour. 'You're new, so you don't know this works. Around here, you show your betters respect, right? Or you'll end up in the ground before your first battle. You hear me?'

'Betters,' said the new man under his breath, a chuckle in his voice.

Morlen was instantly furious. 'Are you laughing at me?' Klay got to his feet and took a few steps closer. Elras. They both knew when trouble was brewing.

'Now, you're making me angry. Really angry.' Morlen squared up to the new man, chin jutting forwards. The young mercenary stared back, impassive.

With no warning, Morlen gestured with his head, left and right. His cronies lunged forwards, grabbing the new man's arms at his bicep and elbow. At the same time, Morlen drew back a fist.

Before Morlen could strike, the tall stranger moved. Instead of trying to escape from the grip of the two men, he surged forwards. Neither were expecting this and were unable to restrain him. His weight crashed into Morlen as their chests collided, and the smaller, lighter Tayan was flung backward.

Dropping his weight and twisting to one side, the new man freed his right arm and struck the Tayan who had been grabbing it a stinging blow to the chin before turning to the third. He grabbed the man's wrist, and then twisted violently. The Tayan was pulled off his feet and tumbled to the ground.

Morlen had recovered his balance and surged forwards, fists clenched.

'Enough. Enough!'

A strident voice rang out. Klay was still ambling closer as Elras dashed out of the crowd to stand in Morlen's path.

'We fight when we are paid to,' said the burly Bureno. 'And with the enemy, not with each other!'

'He addressed me with disrespect,' complained Morlen, gesturing towards the new man. 'He needs to learn where he stands.'

'He stands equal to any other,' said Elras. 'Including you. You created this quarrel, now put it aside. It will achieve nothing.'

Morlen glared sullenly, eyes twitching between Elras and the new man. 'Fine,' he said, eventually.

'And you?' continued Elras, turning to the younger man. 'Do you agree to this truce?'

'Yes. Of course,' he replied. 'I just want to join the company.'

'Very well then,' said Elras, clapping his hands together. He turned away, the new man moving to follow.

Something kept Klay's eyes trained on Morlen's back. Something about the way his fists clenched, and his shoulders remained tense. His hand twitched and Klay sped up.

'Turn!' he shouted, unable to think of another way to warn the man of the danger quickly enough.

Morlen's right hand came up, and a jagged knife glittered in the morning light. Klay pumped his legs, curiosity driving his desire to intervene. If Morlen stuck his knife in the new man, then he might never find out how he came to be carrying Sturi's sword.

The tall stranger had half-turned, seen Morlen's blade and quickly dropped back into a fighting crouch. He was no fool. Klay had already decided to put an end to this though, without waiting to see if anyone got hurt. Seriously hurt, anyway.

Morlen's fist was near his right hip, the blade a menacing gleam. He would use it. He liked shedding blood too much. Klay's approach had been quick and quiet, though, and Morlen did not know he was there.

Klay's lack of height was his ally. He reached between Morlen's legs from behind, took a firm handful, and squeezed. With his other hand, he reached up and grasped the hand of the wrist holding the knife.

Morlen shrieked in surprise and pain, and started to struggle, but Klay held him firmly.

'Get your hands off me!' he howled. 'I'll kill you, whoever you are. I'll kill you!' He turned to his companions. 'Get him! Get him off me!'

The Tayan thugs to either side turned to help, but after one look downwards their faces fell.

'It's Klay,' said one, voice subdued.

'Klay?' Morlen suddenly sounded worried; his aggressive tone gone.

'Aye, it's meself,' replied Klay. 'Put knife down else ah'll have a go at crackin' these pebbles.' The hand between Morlen's legs gripped slightly harder. There was a squeak of discomfort, and the knife clattered to the ground. Klay kicked it away.

'Ah've had enough of thy cack, Morlen,' Klay went on. 'If I catch yer at it again we'll have us another little chat, but this time it'll be the Capper doing the talking.'

He let Morlen go and the Tayan staggered away, dropping a hand to his crotch as if to check he was still intact.

'Yes, Klay,' mumbled Morlen. There was still a glimmer of anger in his face, but he had put his hands behind his back submissively. Even he knew better than to challenge Klay.

Klay knew he would have to watch his back, though. The man would not forgive.

'What is wrong with you?' came a voice from over Klay's right shoulder. The tall, fair-haired newcomer was starting forwards. 'We agreed a truce, and then you come at me with a knife? Have you no honour?'

Morlen simply gazed back, his lips twitching into a half smile. He shrugged.

Klay saw the movement in the corner of his eye as the tall man stepped closer. Almost as a reflex, he reached up and laid his hand on the outside of the man's elbow. A bare touch, it was just a grip and a twist away from an armlock that could bear even a strong man to the ground, or be used to propel them in a direction of Klay's choosing.

He had done it a hundred times, and did not consider it a violent gesture. It just made him ready. Usually, as his hand touched their arm there was a slight flinch as they went to pull away. He was used to following this, not even needing to grip. Not if they cooperated.

His fingers wrapped around the new man's upper arm, and there was no flinch. No tightening of the shoulders or twisting of the body, no intention to escape. The tall man sank his weight down, bending his knees slightly. His left arm pressed back against Klay's hand, just slightly, and the man's right hand came across, moving towards Klay's own.

Shit, thought Klay.

This never happened. People tried to get away. Mind working quickly, he realised that he was now in a dangerous position. The taller man could clamp his own hand over Klay's and by sinking down it would give him the leverage to twist. It would lock Klay's right arm up and throw him to the ground. He might escape a broken arm, if he was lucky.

He turned towards the man, lifting his right elbow. Raising his fingers towards the sky, he held his left hand out, palm facing away. That changed the situation. Now, before the taller man could lock Klay's right arm, Klay could spin and drop. His low centre of gravity and weight meant that it would be impossible to resist. The man would be flung outwards, all his own weight on his shoulder and elbow.

It would be difficult to fight back after all the joints in that arm had been disconnected.

There was a moment. Other figures moved in Klay's peripheral vision but he ignored them. His concentration was focused on the point where his right hand touched the other man's arm. Tension or relaxation, weak or soft; Klay would feel it instantly and react. Whoever reacted slowest might never fight again.

Klay breathed out, a slow, calming breath to centre his energy, as he had been taught all those years ago. He did not want to do this, and was cross with himself for getting into this situation. He had underestimated the man, that was certain. Would he pay for his foolishness?

The man's fingertips flicked upwards. He stared down, hands now out, palms flat in a gesture of peace. Klay removed his hand from the other man's arm and copied the motion as he stepped back. The exchange had taken mere heartbeats, but had happened with glacial slowness for Klay. He was not sure anyone else observing would have even noticed.

'Drink?' he said, craning up to look the taller man in the eye.

'Yes,' came the reply.

The inside of the teahouse was gloomy and made hazy by gouts of steam from the boiling kettles and smoke from the hearths. Klay weaved through the shifting vapours, across a large circular common room that was packed with other mercenaries waiting for the order to march.

He looked around, eyes narrowed, until he found what he was looking for. A small round table stood beneath a narrow window, occupied by a single veteran mercenary nursing a small and almost empty cup. His face was lined with age and his dark moustache was streaked with grey.

Klay had fought alongside him many times.

'Finishin' up, Caryl?' said Klay as he approached. Caryl looked up, then started when he noticed who it was.

'Oh...uhh...Klay,' he muttered, before reaching for his cup and hastily draining the last of his tea. 'Yes Klay, all done. Table's all yours.'

'Much obliged, friend,' said Klay, before lifting himself onto Caryl's seat. It was tucked in near the wall and gave a good view of the main room of the teahouse, including of the door. The new man glanced around, brow furrowed in consternation before sitting.

Klay felt instantly more at ease once they were both seated. He could now look the man in the eye. He was never relaxed, and knew that trouble could start at any time. But at least now he was comfortable.

Klay Garrant was a dwarf. He felt that this made him the perfect height, and he was as strong as any human man, and heavier. The fact that the top of his head only reached chest-high on most men sometimes made it difficult to have a straight conversation, without having to crane his neck awkwardly.

He fixed his stare on the young man sat across from him.

'I'm Klay,' he said. Then waited.

'I am Eain,' said the man, after a pause. 'No moons?'

Klay waved that away. 'Ah've no time for that stuff. Think we know each other now, any road.'

He eyed the new man, Eain, as he spoke. Did they need to talk about the confrontation that had almost happened outside the teahouse? Probably not. They had both walked away knowing where they stood, and what could have happened, without needing words.

'I don't understand...' began Eain, then stopped, considering what to say. 'We agreed a truce. And then he came at me with his knife? He would have stabbed me in the back. What about honour?'

Klay grunted to himself. This one was young. Too young to be here, doing this.

'First time in Tayo?' he said, and he could hear the weariness in his own voice. Eain nodded. 'Forget about honour. Forget about loyalty. Forget trust. They don't exist here.'

Eain's face was a mask of confusion. 'But—' he began.

'Look,' interrupted Klay. 'That Morlen, he's nothin' unusual for a Tayan. They tell the truth about what they think, but lie about what they're going t'do. If yer goin' to survive you've got t'expect it. And if yer can't hack it, yer need t'tek yerself elsewhere.'

Eain's brows furrowed, and Klay waved to one of the servers. Moments later they set a steaming pot of tea in the centre of the table, and placed cups of turned wood in front of Klay and Eain.

'What is it?' asked Eain, gesturing towards the teapot.

'It's tea,' replied Klay, lifting the lid and letting a gout of steam escape. It had a rich savoury scent, rain on pine mixed with jasmine and rosemary. He replaced the lid and poured a small measure into each cup. 'Leaves and herbs and the like. And a healthy slug of that rice wine they brew all over. Not had tea before?'

Eain shook his head.

'Where're you from?' asked Klay. He was burning with questions, but did not want to seem too curious. This man was still a stranger.

'North,' replied Eain, with a vague wave behind him.

North made sense, thought Klay. He could be from Ben Gedrin or the Riverlands. That would explain how he came to be in Feorhryc, the village where Klay's battle with Sturi had taken place, although how he had left with that sword in his hands was another question.

A thought occurred to Klay.

'Did you come past Ben Gedrin?' he asked, and Eain started. There was suddenly a look of slight guilt in his eyes. There had been rumours of strife in the city, only a couple of days march up the Great North Road. Travellers fleeing south spoke of fighting, fire and death. Maybe this man had been there, been involved. Yet another question, that Klay could not bring himself to ask outright.

'Well', he said, before sipping his tea. 'Things're different here. You won't be facing skirmishes in the street. We'll be in a battle afore the month is out, you mark me.'

'They said we would be defending a fortress. The risk is how we earn our money rings, no?'

'Aye, that's true,' replied Klay. He nodded toward the sword that Eain had propped beside his chair. The long hilt loomed menacingly over the table. 'That's a battle-weapon and a half. Not many warriors around with the skill to use something like that.'

Eain did not respond. Klay kept his face blank but inside he seethed. How could he find out what he wanted to know? He had to ask.

'Where'd you buy it?' He knew that the man had not bought it, but hopefully the question would provoke a useful answer.

'I did not buy it,' he replied. 'It was a gift.'

'A gift?' Klay could not hide his surprise. 'A gift from who?'

'A man I met on the way here. He thought I might need it.'

Klay scowled. This was not the whole story. He knew that sword had been kept in Feorhryc as a trophy of their victory over Wolt Wose and his bandits. The idea of it being given away as a gift seemed deeply unlikely.

'Did he have a name, this man?'

'Why is it important to you?'

Klay ground his teeth. He had to admit that it might seem a strange question, but a suspicion was growing about this young man.

He had clearly passed through Feorhryc and come away with an heirloom sword. Next, he had passed through Ben Gedrin and left as it burned. Then, as soon as he had arrived at the muster a bad feeling had fallen over Klay, and fights had begun to start over nothing.

Was this man a bandit, and a murderer? Or, was he something even worse? Klay was not superstitious, but he paid attention to his instincts, and they were all screaming at him to be very wary of the smooth-cheeked young man sat before him.

'I just like to know something of the fellows I'll be fighting with,' said Klay. 'I like to be able to trust the man on my left and right.'

'You just said that trust does not exist here.'

'Your mouth is going to get you in't trouble, youth.'

'I am used to trouble,' replied Eain, blandly.

'Aye, and that thinking almost got you knifed just now.' Klay felt his irritation rising but kept his voice even.

'He would not have stabbed me,' replied Eain, his voice still annoyingly devoid of expression. 'I could have dealt with him. And I did not need your help. You should have stayed out of it.'

Klay clenched his fist. He wanted to roar at the young man. The worst part of it was- he was right. Klay had no reason or right to intervene. So why had he? That wolf-damned sword, that was why. And he had still got no answers. His frustration rose.

'I'll leave you to be stuck full o' holes next time, youth!' he growled, his voice rising.

Before Eain could respond, a horn blew outside, long and loud. Klay lifted his cup and downed his tea, hiding his fury behind the drink. All around, the other mercenaries were doing the same. Eain looked around, confused.

'C'mon, youth,' said Klay, standing. 'News. Probably goin't be on our way.'

Eain stood without speaking and followed Klay as he elbowed his way through the crowd filing out of the warm, dingy confines of the teahouse and into the weak afternoon light. Every fighter at the muster, and Klay could see armed warriors from Buren, Anish and the Riverlands, as well as native Tayans with their dark hair contrasting with their bright shirts, was gathering in the open space beside the teahouse.

Klay was immediately confronted by a forest of backs, blocking his view of the captains who were about to address the muster.

'Bloody lanky arses,' he muttered, and stuck his elbows out to each side. Jabbing them left and right, he forced his way forwards. He noted that the new man, Eain, was following. He might be close-mouthed, and Klay still had not ruled out him being a bandit or worse, but at least he had some sense.

'Oi!' came a voice as an angry face turned to look down towards the source of the intrusion. Then: 'Sorry, Klay', as they saw who it was.

Once at the front, Klay had a good view of proceedings. Agerys, the mercenary captain-broker, was already speaking.

He was a tallish man, compared to others nearby. He was a native Tayan with coppery skin and hair so dark it was almost black. He was not young but creases around his eyes and mouth were the only real signs of age, although his hair was cut in an old-fashioned style; trimmed short at the front and grown long only at the back. A slight paunch was hidden beneath a tooled leather breastplate.

He was a handy fighter, and the hilt of his curved sword was well used, but Klay was used to him commanding from the rear these days. Klay supposed he had earned the right.

'The deal is done,' he said, projecting his voice to be heard by all of those assembled. 'Sir Crenant, emissary of the honourable Duke Siaben, has accepted our offer and I have passed him the rod. He now commands the Legion of the Steel Hounds.'

There were cheers. Klay did not join in. Agerys said one thing but meant another. The offer, of course, was made by Duke Siaben via his messenger Crenant. "Fight for me, and I'll pay you." But, tradition ran that the mercenary captain-broker offered their services. Once negotiated and accepted, the captain passed their company's rod across and delegated command until the contract was fulfilled.

The title "the Steel Hounds" sounded grand, but in reality it was just Agerys and whatever force he could gather to satisfy the demands of the contract. Agerys had a solid network of captains though, and did well from mustering good numbers quickly. Klay glanced around at the gathered warriors. This time, it looked like about five hundreds.

'The contract is simple,' Agerys went on. 'Dukes Siaben and Pentyr have occupied Turgon Fallas. They need extra numbers to man the walls while the Taosach's forces scour the northern country for rebels.'

That was revealing. If Teleri were dead, why the need to defend his old fortress, or to worry about putting down further rebellion? Teleri was one of the last nobles to openly align himself with the Separatist cause. Who else was there? Someone was worried.

For Klay, this was an ideal scenario. People with worries paid well to have those concerns eased. And an armed force to do as bid was often comforting for those with the means to employ them.

'Turgon Fallas is a four-day march from here, so get your shit together. We'll be moving out in the next hour.'

The crowd broke up, dispersing across the rough land that surrounded the teahouse, and the indistinct murmur of conversation filled the air.

'*Man the walls*', Agerys had said, as if that was all there was to it. Klay would keep the Capper, his brutal warhammer, close to hand. Something smelled off about this job, as if part of the story had been kept back.

Klay did not need to pack. All his possessions were in a tough leather sack across his back, and he was ready to move out. He glanced across to the road and saw the new man, Eain, also stood ready. He had a similar bag slung across his back, alongside the long shape of that sword.

Someone else who isn't telling the whole story, thought Klay, and felt his annoyance grow again. He strolled south, finding a low boulder to sit on, waiting for the others to finish faffing around.

They had some miles ahead, and plenty of time. Maybe he would manage to pry this man's tale from him on the way, and find out how he had come by that sword and what manner of man he was. Or, maybe he would be able to put these pointless questions from his mind and concentrate on the job in hand.

ELEVEN

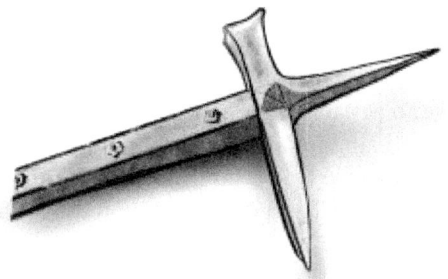

The mercenary camp was disorganised.

Klay cast a critical eye over the haphazard clusters of tents and poorly banked fires and sucked his teeth.

'I 'ope we're not called t'fight any time soon,' he grumbled. 'Easy pickins' for any general worth 'is salt.'

'There's time yet, Klay,' replied Elras, the broad, silver-haired Bureno. 'I'm sure we'll be able to knock them into shape. Besides, they're not going to need too much discipline to just stand on a wall at Turgon Fallas.'

Klay grunted. 'Won't be that simple.'

He had already said the same thing, many times during the first couple of days of their march south. No one wanted to hear it. No one wanted to see sense.

'Easy money,' Agerys had announced, loudly and frequently. Of course he bloody did. He wanted a happy, relaxed and motivated army. Easier to keep moving, far fewer brawls.

'Someone's goin't end up lookin' a fool,' said Klay, 'If we 'ave to draw swords after all this.'

Swords. As he said the word, he glanced across towards the new face. The new member of the company, with that young face and the hilt of that familiar sword still rising above his shoulder.

'D'yer hear any more about what 'appened up Ben Gedrin?' Klay asked Elras. The army had camped out the back of a teahouse the previous night, and a bard had arrived soon after to tell tales and spread news. Klay had not felt like being in a crowd, and had cooked himself his usual bowl of frumenty, a coarse barley porridge, before rolling himself into his blankets early, eager for his first sleep.

'Aye,' Elras replied. 'The bard told all about it. I'm sure they exaggerated. Some things they said sounded a bit far-fetched.'

He paused. He fixed Klay with a beady glare.

'And?' asked the dwarf, after a few slow heartbeats had passed. Elras gave a wry grin before answering. Wölfin chew his bones.

'Gang war,' said Elras, with dramatic emphasis. 'The gangs of Ben Gedrin are always trying to backstab each other, and the city militia do sod all about it. But this was different. The way the bard told it, the streets were filled with gang fighters, hacking and stabbing each other in front of the people celebrating their autumn harvest festival. The streets were red.'

'Aye, aye,' replied Klay. This news did not surprise him. He had spent plenty of time in Ben Gedrin and knew it was a dangerous, edgy place. The dark corners were all filled with swift dagger points.

The last few weeks, though, it had been worse. He had been there as a growing tension had descended on the city. Something had been building. Some ember was smouldering in the darkness, waiting to set everything ablaze.

So, he had left. He had hoped to find guarding work on the wagon trains, but rumours of Wild Elf attacks were causing more wagon leaders to stay put in the west, or to roll down to Buren instead of risking a journey across the Lands of the Great River. It made sense.

There was nothing else for him there, so he had slung the Capper over his shoulder and headed south to fight for his supper in Tayo, like he had so many times before.

That had been a week ago.

'What else?' asked Klay. As he spoke, though, he glanced once more across towards the young man with the two-handed sword. Now that Klay thought about, the same sense of tension and danger that he had felt in Ben Gedrin had been present when they had first spoken.

Could there be a connection? Probably not. More likely was that Klay was frustrated because of how evasive the boy had been.

Elras was still talking.

'The bard said that by the end of the night, all of Ben Gedrin was burning.' Klay barked a humourless laugh.

'Aye, whole city is dry wood. That's no shock, that.'

'No, but she claimed that it was the firebulls as started it. Like they were possessed by the demons themselves. They broke their fences down and stampeded through the city.'

Klay laughed again, a harsh coughing sound. 'Weren't no demons,' he scoffed. 'Some bugger's let 'em out as a burst.'

'A what?'

'A burst! A prank. Thought it was reet funny.'

'Many were killed!' insisted Elras.

'More fool them fer standin' in't way.'

Elras shrugged. 'That's just what the stories say. The gangs were all but wiped out, and the militia arrested those that weren't gored or trampled or burned.'

Klay nodded. It did sound noteworthy. Big victory for governor Ceolbaght. Why did he still have a sneaking feeling that the new man had been involved somehow?

If he was ruthless enough to take on the gangs and had the strength and skill to fight his way free of that burning city, then Klay needed to keep a close eye on him. He could be dangerous. To the enemy, or to his own side; Klay did not know yet.

A gout of grey smoke wafted across from the nearest fire, blown on a gust. Klay clamped his eyes shut but they were already stinging. Irritation surged. He turned to the campfire where one of the younger, newer mercenaries, a Tayan local, had just dumped an armful of branches onto the flames.

The dark, mottled wood was fresh from the nearby forest floor, damp and rotting. It spat as the flames engulfed the twigs and branches, the wet wood belching dirty steam.

Klay was on his feet in a moment, blinking the smoke from his smarting eyes. He kicked the soggy sticks off the fire, his heavy boots scattering chips and sparks across the damp ground.

He rounded on the young soldier.

'Bloody hell d'yer think yer at?' The young man took a step back in the face of Klay's fury. 'That wood's wetter'n Southern Ocean!'

'You told me to fetch wood, Klay,' came the nervous, stammered response.

'Wood to put on't fire, tha' steamin' idiot. Not a bunch of soggy twigs an' leaves!'

'It's just what I could find—'

'Then you've got nowt between yer ears.'

Klay reached up and caught the young man a clout around the ear with the back of his hand. His head was knocked aside, and he cried out, before scurrying away. Klay watched his retreating shape, sucking his teeth. The sound of a chuckle behind him caught his ear, and his head snapped around.

Elras was laughing behind his hand.

'What?' Klay grunted, feeling his fists clench.

'You're tense,' said the solidly built Bureno. 'It's not like you.'

Klay pressed his teeth together for a moment. Was everyone here trying to annoy him? Irritation bubbled within him, a kettle simmering on the low embers of a dying hearth. It passed as he let out his held breath in a quiet but expulsive hiss. Sitting back down on the flat rock that was his chosen seat, he scowled back at Elras.

'Aye, you're right,' he admitted. 'Ah don't like it when ah'm not tole the whole truth. And there's more t'this,' he gestured to the mercenary camp that surrounded them, 'that's been made plain.'

'You're probably right. But that's never made you so tetchy before.'

'Tetchy?' Klay rounded on Elras. The Bureno soldier just laughed. The worst part was, that he was right.

Klay cast his eye over the rest of the camp.

Agerys had called a halt to the day's march after the ragged column had wound through a steep-sided valley between rocky hills. A broad, bare plateau opened out before them, and the camp was ordered beside the road, on a flat patch of dirt and weeds just to the west.

To the east, slopes fell away steeply into dense, tangled forests. Even with autumn's arrival, the canopy was lush and green. Klay knew from bitter experience that the forest floor would be choked with thorn-ferns and barbed vines, and would remain damp, dark and humid all through the year.

In the other direction, ochre-coloured hills rose; bulging rock that was rough and flaky like tree bark. Loose, arid and inhospitable.

That was Tayo: rough and rocky or damp and uninviting, with little in between.

'Food!' came a call from the centre of the camp. A large pot had been set on a blazing fire, stewing up some Tayan filth of rice, beans and spice, to dish out to the waiting mercenaries.

'Coming, my ray of sunshine?' asked Elras, standing up.

Klay grunted once more. 'Eaten.' Elras shrugged, unconcerned, and walked away. Klay dug into his pack for his blanket, dwarf-made of a mix of different wools to provide warmth, softness and durability. It was much better than the roughly woven blankets the other mercenaries insisted on using, and lighter too.

He was just laying down on some moss he had gathered to soften the stony ground, when a tall figure joined the throng waiting for food from the pot.

The new mercenary, Eain.

Once again, Klay sucked his teeth in frustration. There was the reason he was tense and…tetchy. Another day where he was no nearer unravelling that mystery. Another day where the long hilt looking over the young man's shoulder seemed to taunt him.

He flung himself onto his blanket and rolled it around him. If the answer was not going to be forthcoming, he would just have to forget about it. Let it go. He had more important things to worry about, like what they were going to be doing at Turgon Fallas, and what had really happened to Duke Teleri.

But, as he drifted off to sleep it was that young, beardless face that swam before his mind's eye.

Klay awoke. It was the still dark of the deep hours of the night. It felt familiar, and the quiet was welcome after the noisy bustle of the daytime camp.

He unrolled himself from his blanket and rose. The stars were shrouded by a low mass of cloud, that Klay could feel more than see. A fleeting breeze chilled his face, causing the leafy boughs of the forest below to stir and sway. The shifting leaves hissed and whispered like the mocking voices of lurking forest spirits.

None of this concerned Klay. Not the hushed chatter of the woodland, not the darkness, not the sensation of being alone.

He was a dwarf. His race had grown and flourished in tunnels, caves and mines and the simple darkness of the night was no veil to his sight.

He raised himself like this every night. Nearly all dwarves did. Klay found it hard to understand how folk could put their heads down at dusk and not stir until dawn. This quiet time was useful. Back in the Severed City, the night waking was used to sing as a family, and to have a small, simple meal and to pray to Wölfin. Out here, Klay used the time to train.

Reaching down, he grasped the Capper and turned towards the road. But, something gave him pause. A sound drifted across the still camp, distinct and jarring against the muted sounds of men and women sleeping and the hushed voices of a few other dwarfs who were sitting quietly talking.

It was the sound of someone sobbing.

The sound was plaintive, an irregular mewling that was loud in the still of the night. Klay was suddenly curious.

Klay was heavy and his boots were sturdy, with thick soles and metal plates stitched around the ankles, but he could still move quietly when needed. Stepping over and around the humped, indistinct shapes of sleepers, he made his way steadily closer to the source of the gasped cries.

Standing over the blanket-wrapped shape that was making the noise, he was unsurprised by what he saw.

The young mercenary Eain twitched and writhed in troubled sleep. His hands, outside his rough blanket, grasped and clenched, the fingers curling like claws. As Klay looked closer, Eain's eyes flickered and his mouth worked, soft moans and gasps punctuating his tortured, jerky movements.

He dreamed, and it must be a nightmare.

Klay had seen this before. He recognised the signs of one who had seen too much, one who had been deep in blood and death. An experienced warrior, then, but where had he fought? What had happened?

More questions, with no answers.

Klay shook his head and moved stealthily away. The new man had a tangled history, that was clear. He had seen many troubled young men come and go, many unable to live the life of the sword, many buried in shallow graves. Why was this man bothering him so much?

As he hefted the Capper and began his practice of the forms that would fill his time before his second sleep, his mind was filled with that young mercenary's face. Just what was behind those night terrors? What was his story?

The morning sky was bruised and unsettled. Iron-grey clouds jostled overhead, driven by a surging wind that shivered the leafy branches and whipped up the blankets of the mercenary army as they bustled to pack up and move out.

Klay had been ready for some time.

He had stirred the ashy grey embers of the nearest campfire to life and made another panful of frumenty, while the rest of the camp slowly wakened. To Klay it seemed agonisingly slow, and painfully late. Why could they not just get on with it?

'Are rest of 'em doin' their knitting or summat?' he grumbled to Elras as the burly Bureno approached. Elras just chuckled again. 'Beats me how it teks 'em so long.'

'We lack your efficiency,' replied Elras. 'Well, not all of us.'

He pointed across the road to where the tall mercenary, Eain, was also ready and waiting, sitting easily on a flat-topped orange rock. The long hilt of that sword loomed over his right shoulder like a guard standing sentinel.

Klay grunted. 'Mebbes 'e 'ad a decent teacher, the youth.'

'Like you.'

Klay snorted, and turned his back on Elras before striding away across the road. The youngster looked up as he approached.

His eyes were ringed with grey; evidence of his disturbed night, but his gaze was sharp. They were the same colour as today's sky, a shifting pale grey. Dwarf eyes were often the same colour.

'Ready to march?' Klay asked.

The man made a noise that sounded like 'ice', before saying simply: 'Yes.'

'What was that noise you made?'

'I am sorry,' replied the young man. 'Your accent makes me think of my own country.'

'And where's that?'

Eain waved his hand. 'North.'

'Aye,' said Klay. 'So you told me afore. And there's plenty thou 'asn't told.'

'Why do you care?' The words were defiant, but spoken with a tone of genuine curiosity.

'Cos I like t'know when them that marches wi' me is a murdering bandit!'

He spoke from frustration, the words jumping forth to his lips. He thought, more strongly than ever, that this man must have a trail of death and destruction behind him, across the Riverlands and perhaps beyond. Including Feorhryc. Klay had fought to protect that village, and the thought of a common robber causing the people harm suddenly caused his anger to rise.

The sword was surely evidence of that. How could this man have it otherwise?

Klay realised that he was staring at it, his eyes on the ox-horn quillons and the thick, leather wrapped hilt as if he might find answers there. Then, he glanced towards the man's face. That youthful face was cast with dismayed confusion. His expression was one of total incomprehension.

Before he had time to wonder what that might mean, Agerys' voice rang out across the camp, followed by a single blast from the company's war horn.

'The sun is rising, the day is wasting,' he bellowed. 'All of the company to be ready to march before half of the next hour passes. If you're left behind you won't get paid!

'We march south, and with the favour of the Five we shall be at the gates of Turgon Fallas by dusk. It is a fine and rich abode, and I'm sure we can expect a grand welcome!'

There were cheers at that.

'Now! Get your packs slung and make ready to march. The Steel Hounds hunt!'

Klay turned away from Agerys and the chorus of dull cheers that followed his words, looking for the northerner once more. The tall man had stood and slipped away into the crowd while Agerys was speaking.

'Stand back, old boulder!' came a cry as Klay stepped forwards to follow, along with a restraining hand on his shoulder. The next moment, the pounding of hoofbeats on hard earth sounded nearby and several tall horses trotted past, followed by Agerys on his scruffy nag.

The colourful headscarves of the Tayan knight Sir Crenant and his retainers snapped and fluttered in the breeze as they rode past and up to the head of the column. The hand was quickly removed when Klay glared at its owner, Elras.

'Fookin' high and mighties,' he muttered to himself as he hurried along the gap formed in the crowd. Elras would have to hang back and make sure the soldiers in his division were ready and marching, but Klay had no such responsibility.

He would much rather be at the front of the column than sucking in the dust from others' feet at the rear.

Behind the few mounted figures, the mercenary company began to move. Klay could feel the tremble of the ground itself beneath many feet, and somewhere towards the back a drummer began to pound out a steady rhythm. Voices rose in a marching song.

✕

They marched beneath a leaden sky. The rocky hills rising to their right were dun and colourless, scabby and rough. The beaten trail hugged their flanks, twisting and turning before descending through dry, craggy valleys.

Klay stretched his short legs, striving to remain near the head of the column. The Tayan nobles all rode slightly ahead; separate, lofty and aloof. Nobles were all the same.

He eyed the steep sides of the ravine. This road was the only route through this part of Tayo, from the rocky north into the greener south. It carved through a highland plateau of broken, jagged rock which ran away in every other direction. All traffic was channelled this way, which led inevitably south towards the mountain fastness of Turgon Fallas.

Their destination.

It was near noon and Klay guessed they had covered about five overground leagues, with the same distance still ahead of them. Agerys turned his mount and held up a hand.

'A halt!' he cried, imperiously. 'Rest for a short while. Be ready to march on when the horn blows.'

It was a timely and diplomatic time to call a halt. Klay knew that many of the Tayan warriors in the Steel Hounds remained worshippers of the old gods, the pagan gods; animal deities of air, earth and sky.

It was no longer the official religion of Tayo, the defeat by the armies of Buren and the enforcement of Re'Emsser forcing the nobility who would remain on good terms with their conquerors to adopt the veneration of the Five and the devotion to the Shining Veil.

Klay quickly found a rock and sat down. He was not tired, not after so short a march, but he had learned long ago to never spurn the opportunity for a rest. As the rest of the camp halted, several Tayans drifted quietly off into the trees. The old practices were not banned, but it could be foolish to be too open.

'Making good progress,' said Elras, coming to stand beside where Klay was sitting. 'Should arrive before nightfall, if we can maintain this speed.'

'If we were t'go faster, we could march straight past the Teleri place an' go somewhere safe.'

Elras laughed. 'Come, surely you'll be happy with a sturdy wall to rest behind?'

'Can't 'elp thinkin' we'll be wishin' for that, afore this is done and dusted.'

'You're such a pessimist!' scoffed Elras.

'I just live in't real world,' replied Klay.

A broad shadow loomed over Klay and Elras at that moment. A shadow with the hilt of a long sword over one shoulder.

'Holt,' said the man who cast the shadow.

'Eh?' grunted Klay, squinting upwards.

'The man who gave me this sword,' said the new man, Eain, stepping closer. 'He was named Holt.' There was a pause. 'You wanted to know.'

'Aye,' said Klay slowly, thinking.

Holt. Yes, Klay remembered the boy called Holt from the village of Feorhryc. He and a woman called Fion had been sent out to seek help when bandits had besieged their village.

The two of them had found Carilton Tann, and Tann and his old friend Ingvar had found Klay. He was still unsure how they had managed to persuade him to get involved. Ingvar was always a smarter operator than his bluff face would have you believe. There had been some negotiations around debts and pardons.

It had been bad business, for Ingvar particularly.

'Human chap?' he asked, watching Eain carefully. 'Round face. Fair hair like ripe corn?'

'Yes, that is Holt. He is a leader in their village. He was a soldier, but a long time ago.'

Klay raised an eyebrow.

'Did he tell you that?'

'No. I saw it.' Eain pointed to his own eyes. 'I saw it there.'

Klay knew exactly what the young man meant. Years had passed but he recalled the same look in Holt's eyes. They were not the eyes of those who were members of this company, fighters and killers with no remorse, but the eyes of one who had seen the horrors of war and wanted no further part in them. Poor boy.

The main question remained unanswered, though.

'And the sword?'

Eain glanced back over his shoulder as if he had forgotten that the huge weapon was there.

'Yes,' he said. 'Holt gave it to me. He thought I might need it.'

'Did you leave him alive?'

The question tumbled from Klay's lips before he could stop it. Eain's eyes widened and Elras shifted uneasily.

'What? Of course. I helped him. We parted as friends.'

'Of course. Right.' Klay sucked his teeth. The young man's reaction seemed genuine. 'And did yer need it?'

'Yes.'

Eain's face had hardened. Klay had more questions but did not think it was the moment to push. He looked away, glancing up towards the ridge.

Why?

Had he seen a flicker of movement there? Should he bring the Capper to hand, or had he just noticed the feathery flicker of a bird's flight?

There was nothing to be seen there now. So, why did he feel on edge? Klay trusted his instincts, and something felt off. His eyes narrowed and scanned the ridge once more.

Up ahead, Sir Crenant and his retinue had mounted once more, ready to move out. Agerys threw his leg across his own horse and turned to face the waiting column, raising his arm to signal to his herald.

The air was split by a harsh whistle. Then another. And another. They were followed by hollow thumps.

As Klay's head swivelled towards the sound, a groan of pain echoed down the ravine.

Sir Crenant was sitting very upright in his saddle, back arched with pain. His hands clutched uselessly at several dark-fletched shafts that protruded from his chest. Arrows.

Another volley hissed from the ridge and side walls of the canyon, and an arrow took Crenant in the throat. He gasped and fell.

His retinue and their mounts had also been peppered with barbed points. Men and women groaned, slumping over the pommels of their saddles, or falling to lie in the dust. Horses screamed and reared, and several tumbled to the ground.

Panic rose among the mercenaries. Klay looked up in time to see a red-clad figure, hooded and bearing a curved bow, ducking out of sight below the ridge.

'Protect the Broker-Captain!' roared Elras, surging forwards. Brave, stupid Elras. The burst of movement turned him into an obvious target.

Two whistles. Two thumps, hollow and fleshy. Elras froze, body arched, before stumbling to the ground with two shafts buried deeply in his back. Agerys stared, before turning to scan the chaos, panicked fury on his face.

'Traitors! Bandits! Cowards!' be bellowed. 'Show yourselves and face the wrath of the Steel Hounds!'

Beside Klay, Eain took a step forward and reached back over his shoulder as if to draw that great sword. Klay held out a warning hand, palm outward.

'Stay, youth,' he said. 'Look!' He gestured upward towards what he had noticed.

The top of the rocky ridge was now lined with figures dressed in red, hooded robes. All held bent bows, ready to shoot. It was an ambush.

'Steel Hounds!' thundered Agerys. 'Form ranks! Draw your weapons!'

'I would not do that,' rang out a new voice. It was a soft, female voice and the words were spoken quietly. The surrounding rocks amplified the words though, and Agerys turned toward the sound.

The sheer walls ahead of the column of mercenaries had concealed a narrow gully, little more than a crack in the rock. Figures began to issue from this hiding place and moved forwards to stand just beyond where the Tayan nobles had bolted and were now lying; dead or dying.

Klay recognised what he saw from descriptions he had heard, but had never believed they were anything more than just a myth.

Five slender figures moved to stand just beyond the downed nobles. All were dressed in red robes that hung down to just below their knees, with deep hoods over their heads. Their arms were left free and all five held bows, and four had arrows nocked.

The fifth carried a great curved bow, taller than herself, and a cloak of eagle feathers hung down her back. She stepped forwards, pushing back her hood.

'How dare you?' blustered Agerys.

She held up a single hand, without looking at him, and he fell silent. Her eyes were bound with dark gauze, which looked fine enough to see through but gave her a mysterious and menacing appearance.

'I am the High *Offerad* Brynder, and I come with a message,' she said. Her voice was flat and calm, and rich with age, which also showed in the slate grey of her short, cropped hair. 'Your surrender is accepted, and your company has a new sponsor. You will follow us to receive your new orders.'

Agerys was furious 'New orders? New sponsor? What is this nonsense? You have no authority over me.'

'No?' she said, as she began to turn away. 'I may not, but my master does.'

'And who is that?'

'His name is Duke Daeron Teleri. You will meet him soon.'

TWELVE

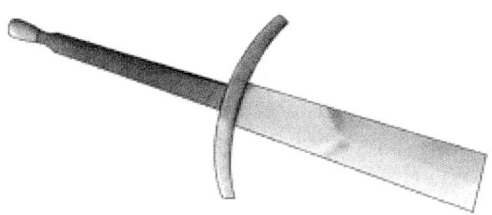

Eain drew in a deep, raking breath. Fear and panic rose through his body, and he ground his teeth to suppress them.

He looked around, his hands starting to shake. Clenching his fists like he had clenched his jaw, he tried to control himself.

It was no use. He felt trapped. Threatened. He had the urge to run, to hide, to do anything to escape this place.

The stony walls of the boxy ravine rose to his left and right. The rock was very different to that of his native Banahgar; honey-coloured and flaky, where Banahgar's frowned solidly in grey and black. Nonetheless, he was transported back to that fateful day, with the sheer walls of the box quarry looming up around him.

He shivered at the memory. As the leader of a group of young soldiers, Sverlaeggare and Hniffare, he had led the way into what had become a trap. Finding their escape blocked by those steep walls, the enemy army from Kotev had closed in and his own force, his friends, had been cut to ribbons. They had all died, and he alone had escaped.

His night terrors were still fuelled by images from that day: dark red blood on bright green grass. And now, here he was again. Trapped by rocky walls, and with enemies closing in from all around, he had nowhere to run.

'Daeron Teleri,' scoffed the mercenary leader, Agerys. 'You'll not fool me with that sort of talk. Teleri is dispossessed and probably dead. We're on our way to his manor now, to reinforce it against his return or the attack of any who would try to avenge him. I assume that is why you stand in our path, but you scare me not.'

The woman before him smiled slightly. Her eyes were hidden behind a strip of black cloth, but her lips were thin, and her short hair was streaked with silver. She was not young.

Yet, Eain could tell from the breadth of her shoulders and the sinewy cords in her forearms that she had strength in her slight build. The strength to pull a bow, in any case. She said nothing, but raised her fingers to her lips and whistled, three shrill blasts. The sound was piercing, and echoed from the canyon walls while the mercenaries around Eain shuffled uneasily.

'We will not be restrained by such as you,' snarled Agerys, drawing his broad, curved sword. 'Steel Hounds! Form ranks! We shall fight our way free.'

The warriors around Eain began moving reluctantly into organised lines, and he found himself close to the dwarf, Klay. His shoulder dug firmly into Eain's ribs. There was something granitic about his presence, something solid and imperturbable.

'Mebbes we'll find out if you can use that blade, after all,' muttered the dwarf, his accent rough and earthy.

Before Agerys could signal the advance, the sound of footsteps came from the hidden gully. Steadily coming closer, there was an ominous rhythm to the treads. A hush fell.

Then, in the pregnant silence, someone stepped out into the light.

Eain would recall later that his first impressions of this man had been underwhelming. He slouched out into the open, a shabby figure despite his fine, colourful robes. He was tall, but his stooped posture made him seem less so. His shoulders sloped and there was a roundness to his middle that spoke of an easy life. Despite the mace hanging at one hip and the long dagger on the other, this man was no warrior.

His hair was long and dark, and his skin the colour of roasted spice. Then he turned, and his eyes flashed across the mercenary ranks.

Those eyes. They were strikingly blue like a crystal lake, and with the unblinking stare of a hunting eagle. The gathered ranks slowed their advance.

Then he spoke. And they stopped.

'Tayans and outcomers,' he began. Quiet words, but resonating with authority. 'As you can see, you have been misled. I live.'

There was a fleeting ripple of hushed laughter which quietened as he continued talking.

'I am Daeron Teleri, rightful lord of Turgon Fallas, and I have found you just in time. Re'Emsser has made paupers of the Tayan people while a few line their pockets and grind the rest of us beneath their bootheels.

'You know of whom I speak.'

There were murmurs around Eain and he glanced to his left and right. The Tayans in their bright colours whispered in each other's ears, and even Agerys was silent, for the moment.

'The Taosach!' cried Teleri in a louder voice. 'And her cronies. She would have us tied ever tighter to the Boian until we are little more than a province of Buren, kneeling at the feet of their High King and begging for scraps.'

The gathered company was nodding now. Teleri's words seemed to echo in Eain's mind, and even though he did not understand their politics he felt the desire to rally to this man's cause.

Teleri raised a clenched fist. 'Have we forgotten? Does our memory fail? Do we not remember how the Boian assaulted our borders? How they razed villages full of innocent people as they invaded our land? Have we forgotten the blood spilled, women and children cut down, the screams rising in the evening sky?'

Eain could feel the agitation in the crowd around him now. Teleri's words were cutting them deeply.

'Have we forgotten how Buren stole the Swarthland? Annexed to satisfy their own ambition, their own greed. The heads of brave Tayan knights still sit on spikes along that wall!

'And then they forced us into Re'Emsser, forced us to pay for our own shackles, iron chains that will destroy our country, our culture and our very lives, if we do not throw them off!'

Angry shouts came from the crowd. 'Down with the Boian!' and 'Robbers and oppressors!'

'House Teleri remembers,' said Teleri. His voice was quieter now, smooth and dangerous like a silk sheath around a polished blade. 'I remember. I remember what was, and would fight for it. Die for it. A united, independent Tayo once more. The Tayo that should have been. It is time to rise up, to make our voices heard.

'I come to you now with an opportunity. A proposal. Halt your march to Turgon Fallas. Join me instead, and when we return to that place it will be as a conquering army with a united Tayo behind us.'

He raised his arms. 'What say you?'

Vague noises of agreement rose from the crowd around Eain, but he could feel Klay shifting uneasily.

'Stay sharp,' muttered the dwarf quietly, so that only Eain could hear. 'This could all kick off.' The dwarf squinted upward, eyeing the archers on the ridge unhappily.

A bark of cynical laughter sounded, a raven's croak, and heads turned towards the sound. Agerys had dismounted and was stepping forwards, a bared sword still in his hand.

'This is desperate stuff, Teleri,' he said, face twisting to a sneer. 'You have already lost. Your castle is taken and you will never be allowed to return. This crusade of yours is over. You cannot beat the Taosach, and I am filled with joy at the thought of you in chains and Tayo returned to peace.'

There was a pause before Teleri spoke again. 'Your words sadden me, because they betray our country, and are rooted in falsehood. The Taosach does not want peace, she just wants profit and power. She will do anything to achieve this, including appeasing the Boian, those who encroach on our borders.

'I think only of Tayo. I fight for Tayo. I cannot stand by while the long arm of the Boian picks the pocket of our people. I give you and those who follow you a chance, a chance to fight a noble war. A war that I intend to win. For Tayo.'

Agerys laughed again. Dismissive. 'You will win nothing! You are nothing but a grubby outlaw and my contract is with your enemies. Stand aside, or blood will be shed this day.'

The movement happened with such casual ease that the speed was deceptive. Agerys did not even have time to raise his sword. Teleri's right hand swept up and the short blade in his fist took Agerys' throat.

Blood bubbled from the ugly slash, and Agerys clutched at the wound as desperate noises issued from his mouth. Teleri took a step back as the mercenary broker-captain collapsed. His knees buckled like they had been deboned, and he fell with a dull thump and a puff of dust.

'Our proud country is on its knees because of men like this,' said Teleri, addressing his words towards the mercenaries who were standing in mute, stunned silence. 'Those who would raise weapons against their own, in exchange for Boian silver. This will end, I swear it. I will not forget what they have done.'

He paused, and took a few steps back to where the bodies of Sir Crenant and his retinue lay. Stooping, he scooped up Agerys' rod of command. It was a leg-length shaft of pale, carved wood, as thick as a thumb.

'I claim the rod,' he said, holding it aloft. 'And with it I assume the contracts of this company.'

Swiftly, he laid the rod across his knee and snapped it in two with a splintering crack. There were a few gasps. He threw the pieces away.

'The contract is broken. This company is disbanded. You are mercenaries no longer. I would enlist you into my own army instead.' The gasps were replaced by curious mutters. 'Rates of pay to remain the same, of course. March with me! Avenge those we have lost! Reclaim that which was stolen from us!'

There was an uncomfortable pause, the hissing of conversations held in undertones like the sighing of the wind. Warriors looked to their neighbours, unsure of what to do. A flash of movement caught Eain's eye, and a figure surged out of the front line and turned to face the company. With surprise, Eain saw that it was Morlen.

He raised a fist. 'I stand with Teleri. I remember. I had family in the borderlands, murdered by the Boian. I know we cannot trust him, as we trust none who would put themselves forward as leaders, but I know he has the strength of will and cunning that is needed. I fight for Tayo!'

Another Tayan joined him, leaping from the ranks. 'And I! I will not weep for Agerys. He was foolish and greedy. I will bloody my weapon for Teleri!'

A different voice called out from the crowd. 'And what if we don't want to join you? What if we just walk away?'

Teleri smiled, a hungry wolf. 'I'm afraid it's too late for that. I have enlisted you. And I do not tolerate deserters.'

His eyes flicked upward. The archers, the red-robed priestesses, lined either ridge, arrows nocked. Eain swallowed. Teleri had made their choice very simple; follow him or die.

Eain swam in a lake of confusion and grief. Everything around him was indistinct and the vague shapes shimmered and shifted whenever he tried to bring them into focus.

The only clear thing was the pervading feeling of horror.

Horror at what he had done. Horror at what he had become. His hands were stained with blood.

A figure rose from the depths of the swirling darkness. Its features were blurry but Eain's gaze was drawn immediately to its eyes. They were blood-red and glowing with an unearthly inner light.

It surged forwards, clawed hands reaching for his throat.

He woke.

With the dream still alive in his senses he jolted himself up onto his elbows, ready to dodge back, or to run.

The earthy darkness of the camp was around him, and the horror of the dream ebbed away as reality enfolded him like a blanket. His heartbeat was a rapid drumming in his ears, his breathing deep and ragged.

'Bad dream?' asked a voice nearby, and Eain turned. Klay, the dwarf, was sat on his own blankets. 'Dreams can't hurt yer. Here, 'ave a drink of this.'

He handed Eain a small clay flask, stoppered with a cork. Eain took a careful sip and winced as the fiery spirit burned a trail through his middle. Eain had been allowed a sniff of *vochvior*, a potent Banahgarian spirit, at feast days, and a sip when he had been older. This was stronger.

'Why are you awake?' he asked, when he could speak again. 'Is there danger? Is something happening?'

He thought immediately of his sword, wanting its solid, heavy presence in his hand. Then he cursed himself for the urge to hold and use the weapon.

'Ah'm awake because ah'm awake,' replied Klay, gruffly and obliquely. 'There's nowt wrong. Well, nowt worse. Be best if you got some more sleep though. Got a feeling we'll 'ave another hard march tomorrow.'

Eain eased himself back down towards his blankets, but did not relax. His heart was still beating like an angry fist pounding against a locked door.

The dwarf was right, he did need to rest. But, of late, sleep was a window with shutters flung open on the terrible memories within. He could suppress them while he was awake, but in his dreams they tormented him. Memories of violence and death.

He remembered the faces of the first men he had killed, as though he had swung the blade that very day.

Striking the enemies of Banahgar down had seemed so simple in training, but his years as a member of the Claihed had not prepared him for the moment where his blade had cleaved flesh, shed blood and taken life. His disgust at his own actions had haunted him as he had fled headlong from Banahgar.

He had thought that would be the end of his fighting life. Yet, how many more had he killed since then?

As a wagon guard he had fought his way from a wild elf raid, striking several down with his bare fists. It had been that or to die to their spears, axes and arrows. He had no choice but to fight, and yet he had still failed to save any of his companions.

That had led him to the chaos of Ben Gedrin.

He had told himself that he was doing something right, something worthy, when he got involved in the criminal politics of that city. Something where he could feel a sense of redemption.

He had trailed a gang of bandits who were hunting three women, with plans to kill them and rob them of a treasure they carried. Eain had been forced to fight and kill again, but he had at least prevented the women being ambushed before fighting his way clear of the burning city.

His blade had been red by the end of that night.

Red.

The colour made him think of the treasure they had all been fighting for: a fist sized ruby.

Eain carried it now, hidden in a wooden box at the bottom of his pack. He had not wanted to open it. When he had dared handle it, something about it had made him uneasy, and he had considered throwing it away several times. Yet, he had not been able to follow through on that, either.

'Wish your feet had tekken you elsewhere now, youth?' asked Klay quietly as Eain laid his head back down.

'I had nowhere else to go,' replied Eain. It was true. He had fled Ben Gedrin, unwilling to retrace his steps east, and yet having no knowledge of the lands west and south either. 'This is my trade now. This is how I must live.'

He had seen the mercenaries crossing the bridge that leapt across the steep, rocky river valley, and had followed.

'I took one down!' one was exclaiming. 'I slayed one of the firebulls, and tasted the *torro*!'

'You're full of shit,' said another, a Tayan with their dark hair drawn to one side. 'I saw you running when the bulls broke out. There was piss down your breeches.'

'Shut it,' said the first. 'You weren't there when we caught the bull. You were scared to follow. The blood was like dark wine.'

The boasting and banter continued as they walked on, and Eain had paused by the bridge. He had a decision to make; should he follow the mercenaries, walking the same path, or should he turn south.

'You have doubt,' said a deep, rich voice, close to his ear. He turned to be faced by a tall, dark-skinned figure who had appeared as though out of the air. He wore an orange skirt of trailing strands, and a makeshift vest of fabric wound around his shoulders. Eain noticed he was an elf.

'I don't know where to go,' said Eain, simply.

'You are far from home,' said the elf. 'Loyanivah sees and hears. Loyanivah knows. You come from war, but is war also in your future? That is your choice to make.'

'What will I find over that bridge?' asked Eain. He had heard the stories of the turmoil that constantly beset Tayo, and he remembered the furious aggression of Sarm, from Tann's farm. He feared he already knew the answer.

'War,' replied Loyanivah.

'And south?'

'Maybe something different. Maybe peace. Maybe you will take what is within you wherever you go.'

That made Eain stop and think. Maybe, if he headed south he could put down his sword. He could find work labouring and he knew how to till and harvest. But he had tried that at Tann's farm and had known no peace. In the quiet times his demons had screamed ever louder.

And then he recalled the chaos and fear of Ben Gedrin. He had fought in the very heart of the maelstrom and had felt…nothing. He had been calm. The inner voices had been silent.

He made a decision.

'Thank you,' he said to the elf, and turned toward the bridge. As he followed the mercenaries, he did not look back.

'Ah'm worried about where this Teleri'll lead us,' muttered Klay. 'He's got a head full of grand dreams alright, and men like that tend to come and go quickly in Tayo.'

Eain nodded, but he did not agree.

Daeron Teleri had impressed him from the moment he started talking. Eain had no idea of the bloody history between the two neighbouring nations, Buren and Tayo, but Teleri's words had filled Eain with sorrow at the injustice Tayo had suffered.

When he had announced that the Steel Hounds were no longer mercenaries but were enlisted into his army, Eain had felt the thrill of a new purpose. He would follow this man.

They had been given no choice, in any case.

'Desertion will be punished by death,' Teleri had announced. 'And I would feel sorrow to lose any of you fine warriors in such a way. But do not think of that. Think instead of what you can achieve in life.

'I fight only for the nation of Tayo, the true nation. The water of our country runs in the blood of my veins. I will not rest while I lead you in this.'

'What about pay?'

Teleri waved the question away. 'Standard rates, and I'll give every warrior who is with me when I take back Turgon Fallas four weeks' pay as a bonus.' There were mutters of interest in the crowd at that.

'I need a captain to step forwards. I need leaders you know, and trust.'

Silence followed. Gazes went from the limp figure of Agerys to the slumped, bloodied shape of Elras. The reluctance of any other to put themselves forwards was palpable. A noise that was somewhere between a groan and cough broke the peace, and Klay stepped forwards from where had been standing to Eain's right.

'Humans,' he grumbled, before glaring up at the tall duke. 'Looks like it's going to 'ave to be me, Sir Teleri.'

'Name?' asked Teleri briskly, glaring down his aquiline nose at the dwarf.

'Ah'm Klay Garrant, sir,' said Klay. His words were respectful, but he met the duke's eyes unflinchingly.

'Klay,' repeated Teleri. 'Will they listen to you, Klay? Will they obey? Will they fight and die on your command?' He leaned in, pale eyes scanning the massed ranks of mercenaries.

'They had bloody better,' grunted Klay in response.

'Yes,' agreed Teleri with a slight smile. 'They bloody had. Keep them in line and in order on the march, or it is you who will be answerable.'

Klay shuffled back into line, brows lowered and face set in a deep frown as Teleri straightened to address the crowd.

'We must make a camp far from this place, and remain hidden, for now. We march. Do not fall behind!'

> *This day is the dawn*
> *Of righting our wrongs*
> *As we ride, we remember*

The lines of the poem faded into echo and Teleri turned and stalked away without another word. The red-clad archers followed behind, although when Eain glanced up at the ridge, it still bristled with bows. Arrows remained nocked.

Flight would be foolish.

Klay stepped up onto a rough-sided cube of rock.

'You heard the man. Nowt has changed about the day but the destination. Any as lags behind that dodges the arrows'll 'ave meself t'answer to. Get on't!'

'Well done,' said Eain as he moved forwards to walk beside the heavily built dwarf. 'Well done for volunteering.'

Klay grunted. 'Someone 'ad to. If I 'adn't spoke up, he might 'ave picked someone as didn't know what they were about.'

Eain knew what he meant. Sometimes you just had to do something yourself rather than risk the consequence of another failing. It was a sign of someone who cared, although he was sure Klay would not admit to that. The dwarf was a complex puzzle of outward aggression and belligerence, but Eain could tell that beneath the gruff exterior was a keen mind.

Eain had studied him as they had marched that day, picking their way through a complex maze of narrow ravines and gullies, always heading south and downhill.

As dusk had fallen they dropped around a low crag and beneath the swaying canopy of a forest. Trees that Eain could not name loomed over the vague path in the gloom. He saw no oaks or birches or pines, but passed beneath dark-trunked trees with leaves like his splayed hand, and fronded ferns many times the height of a man.

As he had looked up, he could not distinguish between the shifting screen of the upper canopy and the dull blanket of the low clouds. The stars were veiled.

'Do you know these lands?' asked Eain, returning to the present and sinking back to lie on his blankets, head pillowed in his hands.

'Aye, some,' replied Klay. 'But Teleri has led us well away from't beaten track. Reckon he has to.'

'What do you mean?' asked Eain. Sleep was stealing over him once more and his head felt heavy, his thoughts fuzzy.

'Use yer brain, youth,' snapped Klay. 'Yer not daft, that's plain. Think. Why's Teleri captured us?'

'Captured?'

'Aye, aye. He said we were enlisted but you know as well as I do we 'ad no choice. We're prisoners. Why?'

'To strengthen his army.'

Klay chuckled. 'Yer've still not got in't the Tayan way of thinkin'. We're not joining his army. We *are* his army. Us and those priestesses. That's it.'

Eain was surprised for a moment, eyes opening and widening, but then he realised the truth of Klay's words. Teleri was dispossessed of his castle and lands. He had nothing. Just this band of mercenaries and the red priestesses.

'Who are they?' asked Eain. Their hooded robes were emblazoned with eagle motifs, and a vivid red. It reminded him uncomfortably of Banahgar.

'Sisters of t'Eagle,' said Klay. He wrinkled his nose and gave a deep sniff, as if what he was about to say had a bad odour. 'Ah must admit that ah've not seem 'em before. Heard of 'em, o'course. Been told they don't leave their temples often.'

There was nothing like this in Banahgar, though. The Sjonacaidh were the wardens of Banahgar's history and the sagas. They presided over weddings, coming of age ceremonies and funerals, but they did not invoke the gods. The animal pantheon was respected and remembered with small rituals and offerings, but they were not worshipped.

'They are priestesses of the five gods?' asked Eain. He had learned enough of the gods of these lands by now and seen the *pentangs* that people raised to revere them. Yet, people spoke of the five with sadness and regret, as though they were absent. Gone.

Klay shook his head. The dim light of the camp's dying fires illuminated his craggy face, and his reddish hair and beard gleamed with golden strands.

'Of the old gods,' he said. 'The animal gods. Yer must have heard the tell? Before the Five, twas nobbut beasts that roamed the land. Their chiefs became the first gods. That's why they wear an eagle. 'E became their king. They call 'im the Skyfather.

Maneg, thought Eain, but then he remembered that Anndra had used the name Skyfather when she gave him the small carved eagle he still carried in his pocket.

'Kid's tales,' said Klay dismissively, and Eain stayed his tongue. Voicing his wonder about the similarity between the Banahgarian gods and the old gods of these lands might make him sound a fool. He did not want to dwell on the existence of another red-clad military organisation, either. He was sleepy again. The dream had faded until he could not even bring the fear of it to mind.

'Wait,' he said. Something Klay had said a moment ago returned to him, just as he was about to drift off, and he suddenly needed an answer. 'You said Teleri had to lead us into hiding. Why?'

'Thought you'd started thinking,' replied Klay, gruffly but without heat. 'We're the private army of a dispossessed Tayan duke, who's planning to oppose the Taosach herself. We're fighting against the Tayan state. So, what does that make us?'

Liberators, thought Eain, but he stayed his tongue.

Klay answered his own question. 'Outlaws, youth. It makes us outlaws.'

Eain could think of no reply, so he let his head loll back onto his blankets once more. As he felt sleep stealing over him, that word came again and again, echoing inside his head.

Outlaws.

Across the camp, shrouded by the shadowy veil of night, hidden eyes observed the tall outlander warrior as he conversed with the dwarf.

It was unexpected, and as man and dwarf settled down to sleep once more the owner of the eyes slunk away into the darkness, wondering what this alliance might mean, wondering if it was for good or for ill.

None saw any trace of their passing.

THIRTEEN

Trailing vines and sprays of damp leaves, heavy with morning dew, groped out across the narrow trail. As the long line of mercenaries filed along, the overhanging foliage touched their hands and faces like the touch of clammy fingers.

Outlaws.

The word echoed around Eain's skull like the ring of an anvil struck by a hammer. Despite his bloody dreams and violent memories, he had believed he was doing something simple when he followed the Tayan fighters into the mercenary muster. Something that was neither good or bad; just a way to live.

Draw his sword, and get paid for it.

Perhaps somewhere in his heart he had hoped that any fights would be for a worthy cause, and so Teleri's impassioned speech had stirred him deeply. It contained a fresh breeze of hope. Teleri's campaign had seemed a noble one, the liberation of a people under the yoke of oppression.

It had not occurred to him, until the midnight conversation with Klay, that doing so would place him and this army outside the laws of this country.

'If Teleri is defeated, or forced to surrender?' he had asked Klay as they struck camp that morning. 'What happens to us?'

Klay shrugged, unconcerned. 'Likely as not we'd fall in battle.' He rolled his blanket up deftly and strapped it to the outside of his pack before hoisting it up onto his broad shoulders. 'If not, we'd be executed.' He mimed the swing of a sword.

He looked up and must have noticed the expression of alarm on Eain's face.

'Not such a surprise, is it? Taosach Wenas can't let uprisings against her go unpunished. No leader can.'

Eain nodded, thinking immediately of Banahgar. With the Claihed to enforce the law of the *witans*, few would be fool enough to rise in protest against the ruling nobility.

'It is a crime in my country too,' Eain admitted. He had never seen it, but rumours persisted of particularly outspoken dissidents being taken away in the dead of night. It was said that their throats were cut and their bodies dropped into remote mountain lakes, just like murderers.

The *draugr* would take their souls, and they would never find rebirth into the land.

'Your country, eh?' said Klay, a sly note in his voice. 'Yer've still not tole where that is, or what it's named.'

'North,' replied Eain. Klay chuckled.

At that moment, the steady murmur of conversation quietened as Daeron Teleri stood up, his height emphasised as he climbed onto the trunk of a fallen tree. A bright blue headscarf, mirroring the tone of his sharp eyes, bound his long dark hair, tied to one side.

'We march soon,' he said. Voices stilled and his words carried to all, despite being quietly spoken. 'Be ready. This night we will make a better camp, and our path to victory will begin!'

Cheers followed him as he climbed down.

Eain hoisted his pack onto his shoulders and began forwards, but a hand slapped down onto his shoulder, and he whirled away defensively. He found himself looking straight into the grinning face of Morlen.

'It's the new man,' he said. 'I'm happy to see that you're still here and still drawing breath, new man.' He was bouncing on the balls of his feet, and the same bunch of friends were clustered behind him.

Was he looking for another fight? Eain clenched his fists.

'Back off, Morlen,' growled Klay, moving forwards to stand beside Eain.

'I am just greeting my brothers-in-arms this morning,' said Morlen. 'All is well. You are one of us now, new man. Except you are not, because you have not drawn blood with us. You have not joined us in battle. Only then, will you truly be one of us.'

'Shut yer trap,' said Klay. 'Don't hearken to him, youth.'

'No, it is fine,' said Eain, fixing Morlen with a steady stare. 'I will fight alongside you. I will be one of you. I will prove myself, you will see.'

Morlen took a step closer. 'You talk big, but do you have it in you? We shall see. Our glorious new leader Duke Teleri has a surprise coming his way. Be ready.'

Then he and his gang moved away into the crowd, leaving Eain to puzzle at what he had meant.

The morning's march had given him plenty of opportunity to think. To worry.

Teleri and the Sister of the Eagle had led them through thick, moist woodland, the only sounds the rustle of foliage being crushed under any feet and the sporadic alarm calls of startled birds.

Eain saw flashes of bright feathers as they fluttered away through the greenery, but did not recognise the colours or the shapes.

From their previous camp, Teleri led them deeper into the forests that hugged the flanks of jumbled, low hills. Eain reckoned they headed consistently southward, with the road somewhere on the higher ground to their right.

The paths were narrow and overgrown, weaving between looming trees and trailing up and down steep banks. The sky was barely visible beyond the dense, swaying canopy above, and the ends of the marching column were both out of sight as the path twisted and turned.

It did not help Eain worry less about his new status as an outlaw. A hunted man, and an enemy of the Tayan state. Fighting for Teleri was now his only choice.

Then, the path turned a corner, and the anxious thoughts were driven from his mind.

The trail bent, curving right to follow the contours of the steep hillside. It passed between two tall trees, their smooth, russet-toned bark framing the wide vista beyond. Eain's eyes were drawn forwards as he followed Klay, seeing the interior of Tayo for the first time.

The hills fell away, the steep wooded slopes merging with rolling green plains in the distance. Here and there, the verdant flats were punctuated by ochre domes of smooth rock. Chains of lakes like jewels and expanses of shining marshland gleamed in the day's grey light, but nevertheless the broad, green land reminded Eain inevitably of Banahgar.

A pang of homesickness hit him then, an icy stab in his belly that was followed quickly by the cold claw of guilt. He pushed those feelings down, hardening himself against them in a way that had become practice.

'Keep moving!' came a grumpy voice from behind him, and he started forwards again hurriedly. He had not even realised that he had stopped to stare.

As he followed the path downhill, he glanced over his left shoulder. There it was. It seemed to have been present, near or within consciousness, for much of his journey since he had left Tann's farm behind.

The Great River. It flowed across the dry plains of the north, winding its way ever westward until it emptied into Lake Gedrin. Eain had seen it, when he was in Ben Gedrin. Amid the chaos, the violence, and the swirling fear he had gazed out at that metallic expanse of flat water; wider than he could have imagined, the opposite bank barely visible. That, at least, had been peaceful.

Here, it coiled across the lowlands like a huge, ancient serpent. Dull green waters shimmered like innumerable scales, snaking through the lands and broadening still further in the hazy distance.

The path turned another tight bend into a narrow cleft in the hillside and the river, together with the rest of the Tayan lowlands, was lost behind a tree-clad slope.

The way forwards was by a narrow, rocky trail that hugged the slope. Out of the trees, it was bounded by ferny greenery as it led them deeper into a cleft-like valley between two overgrown hills. The bubbling melody of flowing water filled the air.

Eain could feel cool dampness on the gentle breeze, whispering lightly against his face. Klay's beard was jewelled with tiny drops.

Around another corner, the path curved sharply to the left and the ground before them lurched down into a deep, mossy gully. White water foamed along the base as it hurried towards the lowlands.

A simple bridge of a couple of cut logs formed a walking route over the gully, and the mercenaries filed over it in turn. The unplaned wood was slick and damp, and Eain minded his steps. A fall would be unpleasant.

And then, the endless chatter of the stream was receding at his back as the path led away, deeper into the trees once more. However, this time the trees screened a broad plateau. The mercenary force, led by Teleri and the Sisters of the Eagle, filed into a cleared area of flat, grassy land.

Tall, mature trees grew around the perimeter, hiding the area within from eyes outside. It was big enough for a large camp, and would be able to hold twice the numbers they had.

The centre of the clearing was open to the sky, and as Eain looked up the heavy clouds were shifting, a dull grey sheet becoming a moving mosaic of blue and white, tinted with dusky pink where the sun touched the edges.

To the west, another band of trees grew, these with slender, russet-tinted trunks, and the setting sun gleamed between them. The western sky was suddenly washed with molten gold with the imminent sunset.

'Steel Hounds!'

Teleri's voice boomed out across the clearing, and heads turned. He was stood on a boulder to the north of the camp.

'This is our base. This is our camp. This is where it begins. The bards will sing of this place in years to come as the place Daeron Teleri planned his revenge, planned how to take back what was stolen from him, and began assembling the force that would return our country to its people!'

The uphill edge of the plateau butted up against a rocky scarp, twice the height of a man. As Eain watched, several of the priestesses worked together to roll a round stone away from the rockface. Behind was a dark opening.

As the mercenaries pressed in closer, Eain could see that there was a void behind, packed high with sacks and crates.

'Now, you know the secret of this place,' continued Teleri. 'This is our store. Many days' worth of food lies here and—' he jumped down and stooped to the low opening, turning with a barrel in his hands. 'Wine!'

There were loud cheers.

'Tonight, we drink! Tomorrow, we plan.' He stepped forwards, ignoring the roars from the crowd, and approached. 'Klay Garrant,' he said, remembering the dwarf's name.

'Klay,' he said. 'You are my camp warden. Keep them in order. My tent will be pitched here, before the rock face. Make sure none are sleeping within ten paces. This is important.'

Klay nodded.

'Keep the peace, or you'll be answerable.'

'Aye. Sir,' said Klay, and they watched as Teleri strode away. Eain turned to Klay, to say something about the day, and the place that they found themselves, but Klay spoke first.

'You 'eard 'im!' he snapped. 'Yer've got work t'do. Step to it!'

He bustled off without glancing toward Eain, shoulders hunched and his whole body bristling with annoyance. Eain could hear him snapping orders as he moved across the camp, his gruff voice harsh in the quiet of the evening.

Eain was left alone in the middle of the clearing, as the controlled bustle of the emerging camp went on around him. In front of the rock face, Teleri's tent had already sprung up. The man himself was deep in conversation with the grey-haired head priestess, head bowed low.

Other red-garbed figures moved purposefully across the grass, clustering around Teleri's tent and erecting their own screen-sided shelters at the far end of the plateau, well away from the mercenaries. As Eain considered what he should do next, the head priestess stepped away from the duke.

'Sisters,' she proclaimed, voice pitched to carry. 'We are safe here. We are at peace.'

She put her hands to the back of her head and untied the knot holding the strip of dark gauzy cloth in place. The other priestesses followed, revealing their eyes at last. To Eain, they changed before his eyes from fearsome warriors to nothing more than normal women. The difference was stark and surprising.

The nearest priestess turned and looked directly at him, and a new shock stopped his breath.

'Anndra!' he said aloud, recognising he woman he had met at Tann's farm, all those months ago. The carved wooden eagle he carried in his pocket had been her parting gift.

She turned at the sound of his voice, one eyebrow raised and a puzzled expression across her face.

It was not Anndra. Of course it was not. Anndra had reddish hair and pale eyes, and this woman was Tayan with dark hair that curled, tied tightly. Where Anndra was slender as a willow, this woman was broad shouldered with a full chest.

For an instant, though, he had been certain it was her.

She turned away, brow furrowed, and returned to her labour as Eain moved off quickly in the opposite direction, hoping that the dusk would hide the flush in his cheeks. How could he have made such an error? What was wrong with him?

Eain woke from his dream as though trying not to drown, thrashing desperately towards the surface. Coldness surrounded him and his whole body felt heavy. Weighted with grief and regret, reaching the life-giving sanctuary of the surface seemed impossible.

Words. He could hear spoken words, mumbled and indistinct but still near enough to pull him from the grasping water of his nightmares and into the air of wakefulness.

'New man,' hissed the voice. Eain blinked, his vision filled with darkness whether his eyes were open or shut. 'New man, listen,' it said again, low and urgent. Eain peered upward.

Morlen's face was inches from his own, barely lit by the paltry light of the moons; Jura a half and Kalua a bare crescent. It was deep in the night.

'Leave him be, Morlen,' came another voice, gruff and deep. Klay. What was going on?

'You've had your chance, dwarf,' shot back Morlen in a sharp whisper. 'You know what you're missing.'

'Don't get him mixed up in this,' said Klay. 'He needs nowt to do with your foolishness.'

Eain lifted himself onto his elbows and looked towards Klay. The dwarf was sat on his bedroll, knees drawn up to his chest and with his back to Morlen and a few other dark shapes that Eain guessed were Morlen's usual cronies.

'It's for him to decide,' said Morlen, before leaning closer to whisper in Eain's ear once more. 'We need to take Teleri down.

He's going to lead us to nothing but death. His crusade doesn't need to involve us.'

'But,' said Eain. 'You spoke for him. You swore your loyalty.'

Morlen stared for a moment, confused, then shrugged. 'He's not telling the truth either. All he wants is his fancy castle back and that's no concern of mine. He'll never get it, and I'm not dying to help him try. I want out.' He gestured to the others. 'We all do.'

Eain stared into the long shadows of the dark camp. He was shocked. Teleri had impressed him as a speaker and a leader, and the war he hoped to wage seemed righteous, and just. It would be for the good. But these traitors wanted to turn against him so soon? After pledging themselves?

'He won't defeat the Taosach,' continued Morlen, as if guessing Eain's thoughts. 'Ever. He can't win. My heart is filled with sadness because I know he believes in his cause, but all he will win is death. For himself and any that follow him.'

Eain still hesitated, unsure of what to do, or what to say.

'Draw your sword. Follow us. Our attack will be swift, while he sleeps. Then, we will be free.'

Eain sat up and glanced towards Klay. The dwarf's craggy profile with its heavy brows, prominent hooked nose and bush of beard was like an onyx statue in the moonlight. The dwarf did not move, but his nose swung, just slightly. A shake of his head.

'No,' said Eain. 'I gave Teleri my word.'

A sigh hissed from Morlen's lips, and he straightened.

'Your loss,' he whispered. 'Let's go.'

Softly as stalking foxes, the mercenaries spread out, moving away across the silent camp to be swallowed by the gloom. Eain could see the outline of Teleri's tent, their target, and could not make himself look away as the dark shapes—five or six of them—materialised around it and closed in.

His mouth was open, an uncomfortable lump in his throat.

'Bloody fools,' muttered Klay.

A wisp of cloud passed over the moon Jura, darkening the camp for a fleeting moment. When the silvery light returned, crouching shadows were close around the tent, and blades shone in their fists.

A slash. The hiss of heavy canvas parting beneath sharp steel. More followed and the shadowy figures surged through the gaps, one by one. Then, there was silence.

Eain's heart hammered and he imagined the blood being spilled within. There were no screams, but it had all been so fast. So easy.

Moments passed.

Movement caused Eain to look up. There were suddenly figures in the treeline at the top of the crag. One of them stepped forwards, to stand on a rock ledge that almost overhung the shredded tent.

It was a tall figure, but little more than an inky shade in the moonlight.

'Come out of the tent,' said the voice of Daeron Teleri.

As he spoke, figures sprang up from where they had been lying, wrapped in blankets and feigning sleep. Even as they leapt to their feet, they were stringing arrows to the bows they held.

'Come out now,' said Teleri, firmly. 'Those who would betray me. Those who would do murder. Come out and face justice.'

The tent rippled and Morlen and his friends filed back out through the slashes in the canvas. Seeing the archers, they dropped their blades and raised their hands. At the same time, priestesses close to Teleri lifted the cowls off several small candle lanterns they bore.

The scene was bathed in flickering light, leaving Morlen blinking with an expression of incredulous shock on his face. Equally surprised, his cronies huddled close.

Teleri climbed easily down from his perch and moved to stand before them. A dark cloak covered his bright robes, but he still looked regal and full of authority, casting a long shadow as he towered over the Tayan conspirators.

'I should thank you,' he said. 'Because now I know which of you are my enemies. Which of you would kill me in my sleep, given the chance. Although it does offend me that you think I would be so foolish.'

'We had to test you—' began Morlen.

'Silence, assassin!' snapped Teleri, his kindly manner vanishing in an instant. He looked out across the camp. 'Where is the dwarf?' he called into the darkness. 'Where is my camp warden?'

Klay stood. 'Ah'm right here. Sir.'

'These traitors are your responsibility until the morning. If they escape, you will take their place and face their fate.' He raised a hand, pointing a finger at Eain. 'You, swordsman,' he said. 'Be ready at dawn tomorrow. Sharpen that blade.'

Teleri turned to address the whole camp, where most were now awake and standing to watch. Eain's heart was hammering as he guessed at what was to come.

'Justice must be done, and done properly. The gods must be satisfied, and bear witness. The punishment for treachery is death. They will die at dawn, in a place that is within sight of the gods. This is my will.'

He turned to look at Eain, his pale eyes flashing like a flame close to ice.

'You will be the executioner. Be ready.'

Eain could think of no response to make, but his mind raced.

Tomorrow, he would have to kill again.

FOURTEEN

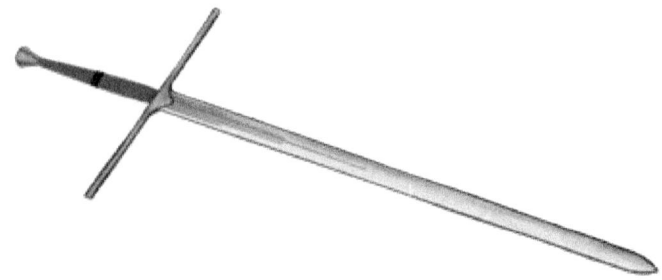

Eain. Eain. Eain.

Where is my grandson?

The words echoed around Cerle Connow's head, over and over. He bellowed the question, but it was sucked away by the void. There were no answers.

He woke.

It had just been a dream, but he could not escape the questions, even as he slept. Unanswerable questions. Dilemmas with no way of reaching a decision.

He sighed, swinging his legs from the narrow bunk and raising himself to a sitting position. He just wanted to take action. There had been too much waiting.

The room was cold and Cerle's skin puckered to goosebumps as he pushed the blanket of coarse wool aside. He slept in just a small strip of cloth, wrapped around his hips. His sleep was better when he was not too warm.

The other men in the bunkroom were still as he rose and began to stretch. It was a habit, long formed, and eased away some of the stiffness of age, as well as the fatigue of travel.

His body was gnarled and twisted with old muscle. A lifetime of practice with weapons left its mark, but his body did not have the smooth curves and bulges of the young; his arms, legs and trunk had the sinewy ridges and lumps of a life lived hard.

He thought of himself as an old oak tree, branches still strong but stiff, bark rough and creased under the assault of the seasons. Just waiting for the next storm strong enough to tear up its roots and send it crashing to the ground.

It was coming. He knew it was. He could feel it in his bones. A storm was building, and he knew it would be his last.

Shaking the morbid thoughts away, he bent to dress. No point in worrying about tomorrow when there were decisions to be made today. Tugging on his worn leather trousers and shirt of pale linen, he ducked through the doorway of the bunkroom and out into the main hall of the house.

The house of Carilton Tann.

His eyes went immediately to the small figure sat at the hall's long table, a steaming mug between her delicate hands and an embroidered shawl around her shoulders. His wife. His Indaella.

'Well met, brave soldier,' she said, her face breaking into a smile of mild amusement. It was a ray of sunshine to warm Cerle's heart, but he could not help noticing how tired the eyes behind the smile were.

Her hair, once brown as beech bark, was more grey than brown now and her eyes were shadowed, creased at the corners with crow's feet. If only he could lend her some of his strength.

'And a good morning to you, fair lady,' said Cerle in exaggerated formality, bowing at the waist as he spoke. A chuckle from the corner of the room revealed that they were not alone. Cerle turned and bowed in that direction too. 'And another fair lady. Good morning, Ma.'

Ma Tann laughed uproariously, rocking back in her chair.

'Sit, sit, and have some breakfast,' she chuckled. 'You big foolish ox.' Cerle laughed as he sat on the bench.

When he and Ma Tann had first met, they had argued about what he should call her.

'I can't call you "ma",' he had blustered. 'I'm an old man!'

'Reckon I'm older'n you,' she had said. 'And I ain't telling you my right name so you've got no choice. Everyone else calls me Ma.'

They had argued back and forth, and it had been Indaella who had thought to ask their ages. Once Cerle had been assured that Ma Tann was indeed a few years older, he had relented. She could be his Ma too, for the few days he planned to stay here.

He reached across the table and took Indaella's hands in his own. They were so delicate, so small. They disappeared beneath his thick, scarred fingers.

'Did you sleep?' he asked, voice low.

'Some,' she answered quickly, the tiredness in her eyes giving away the lie.

'Dreams?' he asked. It was a blunt question, and he saw her flinch, but the decision they needed to make was so important. They had to know all they could.

She shook her head. 'Nothing I can remember. Not last night. Just...feelings. Impressions.'

'What did you feel?'

'Eain,' she said, as if the name alone was enough of an answer. And in a way, it was. Just the presence of their grandson's name on her lips was remarkable. A question, and an answer in itself.

Cerle's wife Indaella dreamed. Her dreams were unlike others.

They had started just after the birth of their son, Reid, and at first they had been terrifying for her. When she slept, Indaella was assailed by images of battle and death. To Cerle it had seemed as though she was going mad.

Until, she had touched him as she slept, and suddenly Cerle could see what she saw, and feel what she felt. At that moment he shared her fear, but even more so than her because he recognised the scenes in the visions, and knew what he was seeing.

He had seen the King of Banahgar. He had seen mighty Leowrac himself, the last King, battling against the beasts of legend, and battling against his own son, Kell. He had seen the king struck down, as the sagas told, defeated and slain by Kell.

These were scenes from history that he knew so well he felt as though he had watched them happen before. The Sjonacaidh spun the tales and wove their words across the lands, and even in his long exile Cerle had never forgotten them.

Then, the dreams had changed, and the visions of those ancient battles of history faded and blurred. Through the eyes of his wife's dreams, Cerle found himself watching more fighting, and this time he knew he was seeing the future, instead of the distant past.

Green fields were stained with red. Warriors of the Claihed in their thousands marched to war. Set against them were beasts of shadow and darkness. And over the whole scene was a greater dread. Something feral, and furious, something that had slept long and was now awake. Something that threatened to destroy Banahgar.

These were the visions that plagued Indaella, and they had filled Cerle with horror too, once she had found a way of sharing them. It was not just the disturbing and violent scenes that were so affecting, but the feelings that came with them: terror, hopelessness, defeat.

And yet, there was a slender thread of hope, and this was what Indaella had pleaded with Cerle to consider: the Riversword. It was well known that the Riversword had vanished with Kell, but Indaella saw it in her dreams and when she did the emotions she described were of victory and of peace. Of hope.

Now, though, their grandson Eain had also appeared in her dreams. How was he involved? The timing of this revelation was…odd.

The door banged open and a lean figure in a long, dusty coat entered the room. He doffed his broad brimmed hat and hung it on a hook beside the door. Cerle stood.

'Master Tann,' he said, showing respect to the owner of the house.

'Sit, sit,' urged Carilton Tann, moving over to the bench. 'And you can drop the "Master" business, too. "Carilton" is just fine. Any news?'

'No?' said Cerle, a slight question in his voice as he looked to Indaella.

'No,' she said.

Carilton Tann sat down.

'So,' he began. 'Do you know what you're going to do? And can we help?'

Cerle and Indaella had arrived at Tann's isolated farmstead on the back of a trader's wagon as the surrounding plains were drenched by the indigo wash of night. Lamplight flickered behind shutters, slender shafts of yellow lancing through the gloom.

Footsteps had sounded, approaching rapidly from the darkness, and then the figure of a man had loomed into the glowing circle cast by the wagon's own lantern. His face was revealed as he looked up towards them.

He was a man of middle years, skin lined and darkened from a life spent outside, and his hair, the same colour as the dry soil of the surrounding plain, was thinning from his forehead. His eyes, though, were sharp and pale as he peered up into the glare of the lamplight.

'Who goes there?' he asked. 'Who comes at this hour?'

'My name is Mayapree,' said the travelling merchant, the unfamiliar accents of Tayo on her tongue. 'My moons are known to the master of this place. I am filled with relief now that I have arrived and am safe from the dangers of the plains. I come with goods, and with travellers seeking shelter for the night.'

That was the moment that Cerle had vaulted down from the wagon bed. It was proper to introduce himself, but he wanted to do it quickly. Indaella needed to rest. Before he could say a word, though, the farm owner turned towards him. Then he said one word that filled Cerle with confusion.

'Eain?' asked Carilton Tann.

The name had shocked through the still evening air, and Indaella had come to Cerle's side while the stranger before them who somehow knew their grandson's name was still gathering himself.

'No, no,' he said, looking more closely at Cerle's face. 'No, you are not he. But when you came into the light I thought…you'd best come up to the house.'

'Aye,' said Cerle. 'I think we better had.'

The house was a broad, single-story timber hall. Their feet beat on the wooden boards of the raised veranda, a hollow drumming as they filed towards the door. Within, the room was dark and warm, the glow of a dying hearth casting the corners into deep shadow.

The man, who Cerle assumed to be the owner of the smallholding, busied himself rummaging out a small oil lantern and lighting a spill from the embers. As he silently used the burning reeds to light it, the brief yellow flames washed his face with dancing light.

His brows were deeply furrowed as if in thought and his features cast with shade. It was not an unkind face, but it showed concern, and worry. He set the spluttering lantern down on the table in the centre of the room and straightened. Cerle moved and wrapped an arm around Indaella's shoulders.

'My name's Carilton Tann,' said the man. 'And this is my place—'

'You called me Eain,' interrupted Cerle. 'Why?'

How can you know that name? he thought.

Tann took a deep breath. 'Some weeks ago, a young man passed through here. In the dark, you looked a little like him. Now, I see you're not he. His name was Eain.'

'Eain was here?' blurted out Indaella.

'*An* Eain,' replied Tann, glancing from face to face. 'Assume you know someone with that name?'

'Eain is my grandson,' said Cerle, and was unable to keep a tremble from his voice. 'You met a boy who looked like me, bearing that name. Did he have the surname "Connow"?'

Tann stared. He shook his head slowly, then sat down on one of the benches.

'How?' he said, eventually.

Cerle grimaced. 'I don't know.'

Tann gestured to the opposite bench. 'Come, sit. I think there's a tale to be told here, and I know I won't sleep 'til I've heard it.'

'I want to hear your tale first,' replied Cerle, leading Indaella to the bench and sitting as she did. 'I need to know how, by the Brothers, my grandson came here, and where he is now.'

'First off,' said Tann, meeting Cerle's glare with his own level stare, 'I don't rightly know how he came here. Don't know where he came from. If someone don't tell me then I don't go asking. But, I do know that he'd come from fear. From battle, and death. It was there, in his eyes.'

'The war,' said Indaella, and Cerle nodded. Tann went on.

'He didn't even speak the Common Speech when he arrived, but he learned fast and settled in just fine. But, whatever had happened out there—' he gestured beyond the house, away eastward, 'was still with him. He knew no peace.'

'Poor Eain,' gasped Indaella. 'He's still so young. Too young to be sent out to fight.'

Cerle hardened his jaw. When the call came, you answered. That was what it meant to be a Banahgarian, and a member of the Claihed.

'This proves it though.' He said. 'You Saw war, and this shows it's true. Banahgar is under attack. Eain must have been fleeing it, for some reason.'

'Saw?' asked Tann.

Cerle fixed his eyes on Tann again. The man was sharp, and had not missed that word or the emphasis that Cerle had placed on it. The ability his wife possessed. The curse she carried, to dream of the past and the future. They had always been so careful to hide it, but now this man, this stranger, had asked the question.

Cerle made a snap decision.

'My wife,' he began. 'Dreams. And what she sees in those dreams is…real.'

'No, Cerle,' protested Indaella. 'Don't—'

'It needs told,' said Cerle, firmly and calmly. 'I think we can trust Master Tann.' He glared at Tann, hoping this stranger would prove him right. Tann said nothing, but nodded.

'She has seen danger,' continued Cerle. 'Dark clouds gathering, war brewing. Our own country is threatened and maybe yours too. Maybe every country. It's not clear.'

'Your country?' asked Tann.

'Aye,' said Cerle. 'Banahgar. Over the mountains to the east of here.'

'Across the Wolfteeths?' There was wonder in Tann's eyes.

'So you name them, aye. Few ever cross those mountains.'

'No, they do not,' said Tann, thoughtfully. 'There are always rumours about what lies beyond. The stories have wild giants there, wielding thunderbolts.'

Cerle spread his arms. 'We are but normal men and women. And we wield simple steel, when there is the need.' He nodded over his shoulder to where the hilt of his greatsword still loomed, strapped across his back.

'Banahgar,' said Tann, the word unfamiliar and awkward on his tongue. 'And you are at war? With who?'

'Kotev,' answered Indaella. She turned to Cerle. 'It must be Kotev.'

'Aye, the Kotevari will be the ones who have attacked,' Cerle confirmed. 'They have always envied our lands. Their ships sail up Osturfjord from time to time.'

'Yes, that makes sense,' said Tann. 'Rumours have reached here of Kotev building a fleet and strengthening their borders. It was feared they would strike at Anish again.'

Cerle shook his head. 'Nay, nothing but a feint. They posture on the border but they would not break the peace of Re'Emsser. Banahgar is apart from that, though, and they think they can conquer us and become rich enough to do without it.'

'You know of Re'Emsser?' Tann was surprised.

'Aye,' said Cerle. 'I'm an exile. I've spent the last twenty years on the eastern border of Anish.'

'Eastern border?' mused Tann. 'But those forts are manned by the Royal Sentinels.'

Cerle returned Tann's open, wide-eyed look with a level stare. Moments passed.

'You served with the Royal Sentinels?'

'Twenty years,' replied Cerle. Tann blew out his cheeks in surprise.

'So,' he said, shaking his head. 'There's a war in Banahgar, and you mean to join it?'

'Aye, but the winter snows will block the high passes soon. So we can't tarry.'

'But what about Eain?' asked Indaella.

'What of him?' asked Cerle.

Tann looked at Indaella. 'You think he might be involved?'

'It's possible. It seems too much of a coincidence that he was here.'

'He can't be involved,' said Cerle quickly, but he was not convinced. 'Is he safe?' he added, looking at Tann.

'He was healthy when he left here,' said Tann. 'I can tell you that much. But it's dangerous out there these days. And—' he hesitated. 'The boy was in a lot of pain. Whatever had happened, whatever he'd been through, it had left deep scars.'

'We cannot just abandon him,' urged Indaella. 'Our own grandson! Our son's son. We must know he's safe. We should find him, and take him home.'

Cerle clenched his fists, pressing his fingernails into his palms. They could hurry eastward across the mountains into Banahgar before winter arrived, and the weather turned, or head back westward to pursue Eain across the plains. They could not do both.

'We can go in neither direction this night,' said Cerle. 'We have travelled hard to get here, and we must rest. If you have beds for us then we can put our heads down, and consider the problem anew when the sun is in the sky.'

That conversation had been three days ago.

Every night since, Indaella's sleep had been wracked with more troubling dreams. Rest eluded her and her days had been filled with exhausted uncertainty.

She had been in no state to travel, or to even help decide about which way to go. Cerle had chafed at the delay, but had passed the time walking in the sandy hills above the farm and speaking with Tann. He wondered if they might end up spending the whole winter there. Achieving nothing.

So, it had stirred his hope to see Indaella up and smiling that morning. Maybe, today they could travel.

'How can we help?' repeated Tann, and Cerle knew that the man was being genuine. He had sensed that he felt guilty about letting Eain go. He was not to blame, but Cerle understood.

Eain had arrived at the farm full of guilt, grief and regret. Cerle could only guess at what had happened, but Tann had done everything he could. Eain had needed to move on.

Should Cerle go after him, though? Or leave him to his fate? That was the question.

'You have already done plenty,' said Cerle to Tann, before turning to Indaella. 'Our quest this side of the mountains is done. Over. We thought we could find the Swords, but we failed. I think our path must be back to Banahgar.'

To my redemption, he thought.

'The Swords?' asked Tann, surprised. Cerle glanced at Indaella as he cursed his tongue. This had not come up so far, and he had intended to keep it that way. The truth would sound like insanity.

'The Twin Swords,' said Indaella, and Cerle pressed his teeth together. 'Or one of them, at least. We thought that the Riversword might be what was needed to fight against the darkness that is coming. We hoped that we might find it. My dreams…' She tailed off.

'But they are just a story,' said Tann. Cerle and Indaella looked at one another. 'Just a story…'

'Banahgarian sagas have much to say about the Swords,' said Cerle. 'How they saved the country, and doomed the king. How they set father against son. How they were lost. But I believe they were real and may exist still, and if they do then they are powerful and dangerous. They must be found.'

'But you couldn't find them?'

Cerle shook his head ruefully. 'Kell, a Banahgarian hero, brought the Riversword with him when he went into exile. We followed his trail to Anish, but no further. Wherever he went afterwards, no tale tells.' He shrugged. 'We failed.'

'Sounds like you were chasing a myth,' said Tann, but his voice contained no criticism.

'Maybe,' replied Cerle.

'So, what now? We can give you supplies and furs if you mean to attempt to cross the mountains. If you have abandoned your search for good.'

'Or, we go after Eain,' said Indaella. She looked pained, and agitated.

'Aye,' agreed Cerle. 'Either way, we give up on our search for the Swords.'

Indaella stretched out her hands, fingers twisting together on the age-darkened boards of the table.

'Or...' she said, then closed her lips. Cerle reached out and placed one of his hands over hers.

'Tell me, my love.'

'I had a new dream, last night.'

What now? thought Cerle, his inner voice laced with irritation. He dismissed it. He trusted his wife.

'Tell me about it,' he said, gently, and noticed Tann also leaning forwards, listening with interest.

'More battles,' began Indaella, screwing up her eyes as if to remember better, as if to see it once more. 'The Riversword shining. Kell standing against the darkness, but...' she paused. Her eyes opened. 'There was a new name on the wind.'

'Eain.'

Cerle and Indaella both turned to look at Tann, who had uttered their grandson's name in a low voice. 'I knew I shouldn't have let that kid go. I'm sorry.'

'I don't know why,' Indaella went on. 'But I think Eain is going to be involved in whatever happens. He's important, or he's in danger. Or both.'

Cerle pressed his fingernails into his palms once more. This was a test. Did he dare hope that he could yet find the Riversword? That he could be the one to save Banahgar? Was his grandson truly at risk?

On the other hand, he had the opportunity to return to Banahgar, to the country he loved, and to draw his own sword to defend it. He could prove at last that he was no deserter, no coward.

He knew that this decision rested on him.

East, or west?

PART THREE

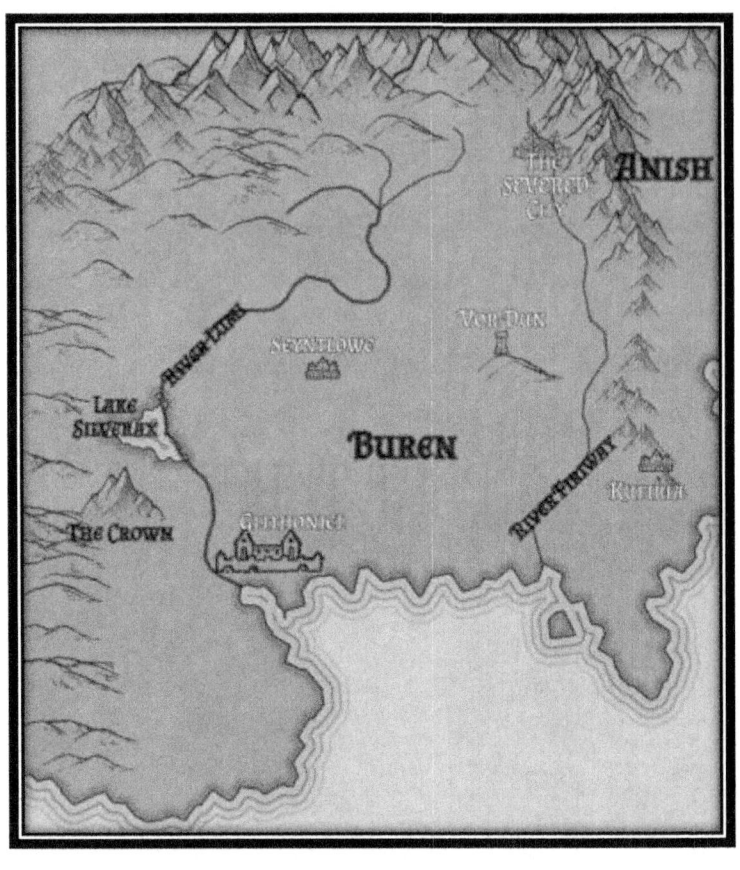

BUREN

FIFTEEN

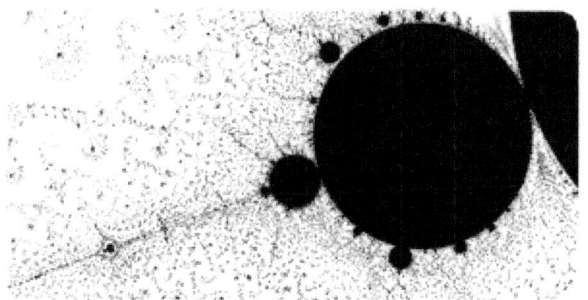

The rusty nail was rough in Nastja's hand. Dawn light chinked through the walls of the barn, the interior gradually brightening from pitch black to cold grey.

She lifted her hand once more, pressing the sharp point into the aged wood of one of the thick columns that supported the roof. One, two, three lines that intersected at the centre. A six-pointed star.

It was significant, she knew. She just did not yet know why.

She blinked in the growing light, eyes gritty. Had she slept this night? She was not sure. She had been so deep in thought that awake and asleep, thinking and dreaming, had intertwined and become impossible to distinguish.

The *pentang*, cut at the base to turn the five-pointed star into six points. The body of the innkeeper sprawled on the path, his lifeblood staining the ground. Ellyah's shocked face, eyes wide at the scene of violence. Her brother, backing away through the doorway of their house, face creasing into tears at what he had just witnessed…

She shook that thought away. It was not relevant, not anymore. A closed, locked box. It was not part of her present.

A rustle of movement disturbed the stillness; a cow climbing awkwardly to its feet. Beside her, Ellyah muttered and stirred. A moment later, her eyes opened.

'I've been waiting for you to wake up,' said Nastja. She felt impatient. 'I'm sure this is important. Look.'

Ellyah blinked slowly as she looked at Nastja, before turning to look where she was pointing. As she took in what was on the wall, her eyes widened.

Scrawled six-pointed stars studded the dark timber. There might have been a hundred or more, scratched deeply into the wood and rust-stained by the point of the nail.

'What in the Five…' breathed Ellyah.

'Making six cuts wasn't an accident, Ell,' Nastja went on. This was important. Ellyah had to understand. 'Whoever did it spread the man out into the shape of a star and cut him at six points.'

'Maybe they were just having a bit of sport,' said Ellyah, her voice thick and toneless with sleep. Nastja shook her head.

'No, or they wouldn't have bothered to be so precise. Six deliberate cuts at the six points of a star. A *pentang* with an extra point, coming down towards the ground.'

She turned and scratched another identical symbol to emphasise the point.

'*Pentangs* need that one,' said Ellyah. 'Or they'd fall over.'

'It's more than that!'

Why couldn't she see the significance? It was obvious!

'And, there's something else that I think is important.'

'Oh. Really?'

'Yes. The order of the cuts,' said Nastja, a note of triumph in her voice. This, she knew, was the proof.

Ellyah sighed. 'Once the poor man had his throat cut, I don't expect he was worried about what else got cut.'

'That's just it,' continued Nastja. 'That's the crucial thing.' She paused, making sure Ellyah was listening properly. This is what would make her take notice. 'They cut his throat last. He was still alive when they made the other cuts.'

'How can you know that?' Ellyah snapped back.

'The cut across his throat was really clean, like it was done slowly and carefully. The cuts on his wrists and the backs of his legs were messier, like he had been writhing. Like they had been holding him down.'

Ellyah's brow furrowed. 'And his…fiddle?'

'I think they cut that part off first.'

'Charming,' said Ellyah, wrinkling her nose.

'That's the main pole of the *pentang*, isn't it?' Ellyah smirked. 'They did that on purpose. The first cut of the six. It's significant.'

'So, what does it mean?' asked Ellyah, sitting up and reaching for her smock.

Nastja frowned this time. 'I don't know,' she admitted. 'Yet. But it's definitely important. It might tell us something about who's chasing us. What they can do, and what they want.'

'It might,' agreed Ellyah. 'It shows that they are ruthless, and that we can't be sure what their motivations are. So, let's make sure we stay ahead of them.'

'Yes,' agreed Nastja, although she was suddenly confused. Was Ellyah taking her seriously, or was she being dismissive? It was often hard to tell.

'Morning is here, hen,' said Ellyah, rising. 'We should be getting back on the road.'

They packed up quickly, breakfasting on a crust of bread with some dried fruit. Moments later they were riding towards the road, leaving an isolated farmstead at their backs.

From the village where the murder had occurred they had ridden as far, and as fast, as they had been able. Ellyah had only been concerned with putting distance between them and any pursuit, and had not worried about the direction they were heading. Nastja had chosen not to argue.

Mounted, they could move quickly and by the time dusk had fallen that first night, they were deep into the Bureno countryside. Golden tones surrounded them on all sides; yellow and amber of leaves on the turn, soft brown of bare fields and rich gold where ripe crops awaited the reaper's hook.

'We've got to find somewhere to spend the night,' Ellyah had said, peering uncertainly into the darkening woodland near the road.

'There,' said Nastja. 'Over there.'

A track led into the woods, the trees trimmed, and the lower foliage hacked back. They followed deep ruts left by the wheels of laden wagons until faint light was seen shining weakly through the trunks ahead.

'If we sneak around the back we can hide in the barn,' said Ellyah, dismounting and squinting into the gloom.

'No,' said Nastja. 'Follow me.'

She dropped down from her horse and headed towards the front door of the farmhouse. It was a dark square in the gloom, framed by square, heavy timbers. Bureno houses always seemed to be built on a square plan, blocky cubes of wood or stone.

The door itself was an ill-fitting rectangle of rough-cut planks, and Nastja approached it confidently. They had nothing to fear. She raised her fist to knock on the door.

'What are you doing?' hissed Ellyah from a few paces back. She was on the balls of her feet, ready to run back for the shelter of the trees. Nastja knocked on the door.

A moment passed. Nastja waited. Ellyah twitched.

'Who is there?' came a voice from within. A woman's voice with the slight crack of age.

'We are just travellers,' replied Nastja, slipping once more into her feigned Bureno accent. 'And we ask your help.'

The door opened a crack. The last glimmer of light in the evening sky fell upon a sharp eye in a brown-skinned face. The woman looked from Nastja to Ellyah, suspicion clear in her expression, but then the door opened slightly wider.

Nastja knew that Ellyah's first thought would be to lie, but sometimes it was necessary to tell the truth. Or at least, part of the truth.

'We are hunted, mistress,' she said. 'We were wrongly blamed for a murder in a village north of here. It was not us, we are simple travellers, heading for Glithoniel, but the elders of the village needed someone to blame and we were strangers to them.'

Nastja could almost feel Ellyah twitching with unease, sense the heat of her disapproving stare on the back of her head. She would understand why Nastja had done this, later.

'Tis the way of things these days,' replied the homeowner. 'So much suspicion. Not like the old days. Was it those Kingseye Guards who pointed the finger at you?'

'Yes,' said Ellyah, before Nastja could do any more than open her mouth.

'No better than savages, the lot of them,' snapped the woman, acid in her tone. 'Who do they think they are? Poking into everyone's business, asking so many questions? They care nothing for truth or justice, just so long as they can string someone up!'

'Can we sleep in your barn?' asked Nastja. 'We'll be gone in the morning. And we can pay.'

Exactly who or what the Kingseye Guards were, was a question that would have to wait.

The woman nodded, but her eyes narrowed. 'One thing first. Do you abide by the Five? Do you live in fear and hope for merciful judgement by the Veil?'

Once more, Ellyah was quickest to respond. She stepped forwards.

'Kaled, Tureank, Conferan, Ome and Mordea,' she intoned, pressing the splayed fingers of her right hand to her breast. 'The Five await, limitless and wise.'

'Quite so,' replied the old woman. 'You can use our barn for the night. Some of those northerners still hold to the old pagan gods, like those Tayan savages across the border. Can't be too careful.'

That had been what had got Nastja thinking about the *pentang*, and those questions were still turning over and over in her mind as they rode away the following morning. Five gods, but six points to the star. What did it mean?

'Do you know the way?' asked Ellyah, disrupting Nastja's train of thought.

She thought for a moment. 'Where are we going?'

'Glithoniel, eventually,' replied Ellyah. 'So, south. We will have to hope we have lost any pursuit from the village. How are our supplies?'

Nastja opened her bag and rummaged inside. There was half a hard-baked loaf, some strips of dried goat meat wrapped in leaves, and a small sack of dried fruit.

'A couple of days' worth, no more.'

'Let's head towards the nearest town,' said Ellyah confidently. 'We'll need more food to get as far as Glithoniel, and I think we'll stand out more if we stay out here in the countryside. We can blend into a crowd more easily. And there might be news of that thief.'

Of course, Ellyah had not forgotten the tall fighter from Ben Gedrin. He must be at least a day ahead, and could probably move quickly. Nastja was keeping her worries about the chase to herself, though. Ellyah would not want to hear about her doubts.

Even if they could find one man, however distinctive he was, in Buren, the biggest country in the civilised world, what then? Overpower him and rob him of the jewel, assuming he still had it? It would not be easy.

Ellyah would come up with a plan, though. She always did. And, if they could reclaim the jewel and sell it for what it was truly worth then they would be wealthy enough to escape all of this for good. They could run away to the deep country, together.

The thought filled Nastja with a warm glow that was tinged with worry. Would Ellyah want her to be there? Was she just a companion with a useful set of skills, or was she…more?

If she could help Ellyah recover the jewel, would she look at Nastja in a different way than just as a helpful friend?

She shivered, and steered her mount onto the southward road.

They travelled in near silence for the rest of the morning. The few other travellers they saw paid them little attention, although Ellyah stiffened whenever she heard hoofbeats on the road behind.

The landscape was soft, the chalky road weaving between slopes of green grass dotted with the occasional small tree. Their leaves rippled and waved in the breeze although the day was bright, and the sun slipped past wispy white clouds as it travelled from their left to hang directly ahead.

Heading south was straightforward, and they rode easily. The Bureno clothes they wore felt unfamiliar but were not uncomfortable for riding.

It was past noon when they crested a slight rise and followed the road down into a shallow sided valley. When Nastja saw what awaited them below, her stomach clenched with worry.

At the base of the valley a small but fast-flowing stream gurgled and splashed along a deep-cut, stony channel. A simple bridge of stripped logs spanned the small gorge, and a junction of two roads lay on the opposite bank.

The far end of the bridge was guarded; men and women in baked leather stood by a lowered bar.

This squared-off pole of pale wood blocked passage, and was matched by three more across each of the roads beyond. All were guarded.

'Shit.'

Ellyah's voice was not raised much above a hoarse whisper, but Nastja felt the same. They had walked into a trap. To turn around and return from where they had come would look too suspicious, now.

They had no choice but to join the queue which had formed across the bridge and back up the slope.

'Stay in line!' barked one of the guards, a short spear held at his side. 'Names,' he demanded of the group of travellers at the front of the queue. They shuffled forwards and the guard lowered his head to speak with them, too quietly to hear at this distance.

Nastja bit her lip. She wanted to know what Ellyah had planned, but did not dare ask. Their whispers would be overheard, and she did not want to draw any more attention to them than necessary.

The bar was raised and the group, a family, moved through and turned to head south. The line shifted as the bar slammed down once more.

Why was this here? What were they worried about? Could this be here for them? Nastja's foot jiggled in the stirrups as she waited. She could not suppress the worry that this could be the end of their journey. There would be no escape if they were apprehended.

'Name,' called the guard once more, boredom tinging his voice. The next in line, a scruffy man travelling alone, mumbled a reply that she could not hear. A moment later, the guard went as though to lift the bar.

'Wait. Stop.' A new voice rang out. Nastja peered forwards.

A figure had advanced from the centre of the crossroads. Mail of a thousand tiny metal scales flashed and rippled in the afternoon sunshine and a pale tabard over their chest displayed the symbol of the pawprint of a hunting cat.

This was a Bureno knight.

Her hand hovered close to the hilt of her longsword as she approached the bar. Even from this distance, Nastja could see the sharpness of her eyes as they were framed by the ornate cheek-guards of her helmet.

She was a tall woman and at a glance could be mistaken for a man, with broad shoulders and a firm jaw. A slight sway to her gait revealed her gender.

'Say your name,' she said in a firm voice 'Your true name.'

Nastja could not catch the response of the scruffy man, but the knight immediately reached forwards and grabbed him by the front of his smock. It was a rapid, aggressive action.

'You're a liar,' she seethed, face suddenly twisted into a grimace of distaste. 'I know you. You are Dintar of Mahric's farm. You are known as one who speaks falsely, spreading tales about your own lord and even against the High King himself.'

'I never!' protested Dintar, as the guards stepped forwards to seize him. 'I never!'

'You lie even now. You have turned your back on the Five.'

'I hold to the Five!' Dintar's voice was desperate and quavering as the guards dragged him across the road, one of them readying a rope with which to bind him.

'Your words are heresy,' cried the knight, loud enough for all to hear. 'The High King has commanded that all heretics and dissidents are to be rooted out. You shall face justice for your crimes now, and again when you are judged beyond the Veil.'

Nastja turned and met Ellyah's eyes. The worry she saw there was clear. All they could do now, though, was stay calm.

The bar raised and lowered, and the line shuffled once more. Nastja and Ellyah dismounted and led their horses across the narrow bridge. The thick planks, bound together with rough rope, creaked and groaned as a counterpoint to the soft, bubbling voice of the stream below.

'Names.'

The same burly guard stood before them, grim and impassive. His face was jowly and pock-marked, with a single pale scar that ran from the corner of his left eye down to his chin. A fighting man. Nastja opened her mouth to speak.

'Jeka and Kajej,' said Ellyah, quicker to speak. 'Of Marenah's farm.'

Nastja shut her mouth again. She had been about to say their own names but had to admit that the Bureno names that Ellyah had used were less conspicuous. Marenah's farm was where they had stayed the previous night.

Nastja had not noticed Ellyah paying any attention to the introductions at the farm. She could be surprising at times.

The guard responded with a grunt, disinterested. 'What's your business?'

'Marenah has sent us out to buy provisions,' replied Ellyah.

'And where're you headed?' shot back the guard, a sharp question. Ellyah hesitated. She could not say they were headed for Glithoniel. It was too far away, and would reveal their lies.

'Seyntlowe,' said Nastja, as the name of the town suddenly jumped into her mind. The farm owner, Marenah, had mentioned it in passing as the nearest town, but neither Nastja nor Ellyah had paid much attention as it was not on their route.

Now, it would have to be.

'Go with the Five,' said the guard, lifting the bar. He gestured towards the eastward road that spurred off on the far side of the crossroads.

They remounted and heeled their mounts into motion, leaving the bar behind. The gritty road led steeply uphill, towards the top of a green, tussocky rise. Nastja was grateful to ride away.

'I'll be much happier when we do get to Glithoniel,' said Ellyah, riding close and leaning over. 'We can get under cover in the city and hide from these lunatics.'

Seyntlowe felt busy after their journey through the countryside. The town walls, a mixture of mortared rubble and timber palisades, loomed above them as they approached, the pale stone and dark wood streaked with moss and dirt.

Nastja noticed the long, solid lengths of several hanging poles resting across their tall trestles as they approached the town gate. Dark stains of blood on the ropes showed that they had been used, and recently. She turned away.

A once-white statue of a nobleman, carved in pale stone and flecked with dirt stood by the gate, and once through they were surrounded by tall, blocky buildings that loomed over streets packed with people. The crowds jostled closer. Nastja felt suddenly anxious, even though she was above them while mounted.

Ellyah reached across and took her hand.

'Let's find a quiet spot, hen,' she said, raising her voice over the hum of the crowd. Nastja could only nod.

Ellyah took the lead, steering her horse into an empty alleyway between two tall buildings. One was a townhouse, and the other had iron bars hammered into the masonry around the windows to form a tight grille. A prison.

They dismounted and stood close to the mouth of the alley. Just beyond, the main street from the town gate opened out into a wide square. Stalls and barrows filled every available space as people thronged through the market. Too many people.

'We're fine, hen,' said Ellyah. 'Safe now. We just need to find some stables and somewhere to get away from the crowds, then we can plan our next move.'

Nastja nodded, but stiffened as she gazed out into the ever-shifting crowd.

'What is it? What's wrong?' Ellyah huddled closer, face creasing in an expression of concern.

Nastja had just seen a face. A face she recognised. It was like their escape with the jewel over again, and the pursuit that would never cease.

She had just seen the same woman that had been waiting for them in the village on the hill. The one who had left the inn just after their arrival and had somehow framed them for the murder of the innkeeper.

Once more, they were the quarry, and the hunters were closing in.

SIXTEEN

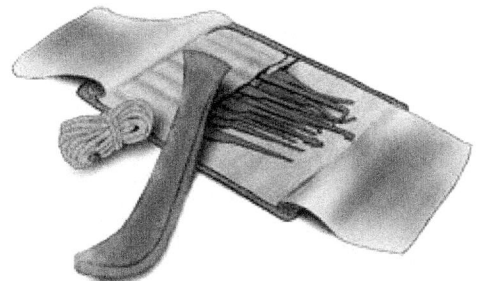

As Nastja shrank back against the rough stone of the building, Ellyah peered out of the alleyway, eyes searching for the danger.

The reassuring warmth of her horse, which she had decided to call Ghurta, was a solid presence against her shoulder.

'What, Nastja?' she asked, urgently. 'What is it?'

'It's her,' replied Nastja. 'The woman who was waiting at the inn. She's followed us again. They are here.'

'Which one?' asked Ellyah, not concerned with whoever Nastja thought "they" were.

'Short. Cropped hair. Simple smock with a dark cape over the top.'

Ellyah spotted her straight away, although by now the view was of her back. Her dark hair was cut very short, even shorter than Nastja's, in a style that was becoming more common for men and women alike. Most commoners still wore their hair down to their jaw, though, so she was easy to pick out of the crowd.

As the woman moved further away into the marketplace, Ellyah knew what she needed to do.

'Wait here,' she said.

Nastja began to protest, but Ellyah had already slipped from the alley and out into the street. Nastja's words were lost in the noise of the crowd.

Ellyah had recognised the woman, and after everything that happened over the last few days - the abduction and murder of the innkeeper and their apparent pursuit - she now shared

Nastja's concern. But, she was also curious. The pursuers did not seem to be the Mackems. So, who were they?

This could be her chance to find out. In this disguise she was just another Bureno face in the crowd. She could follow this woman, and hopefully learn who she was working with, and what they really wanted. The knowledge might help them escape.

Nastja might fret for an hour or so, but it would be worth it.

As soon as she began moving through the swirling crowds, she started enjoying herself. People moved in all directions, often paying little or no attention to those around them, but she could see and feel the rhythm and flow of the throng, and moved in time with it.

She stepped calmly this way and that, not hurrying but neither dawdling. She had business this day, but it was not urgent. Just one more body in the crowd. She felt completely at home, but made sure to keep a careful eye on the progress of the short-haired woman.

Weaving through the crowd, she moved along the main street with deliberate purpose, and into the open square where the market was in full swing. This was a very different affair to the raucous and chaotic covered markets of Carhinn or Kereva, and a far cry from the shady backstreets of Ben Gedrin.

Though the square was busy, the market operated with orderly calm. People waited in neat lines before the most popular stalls, and Ellyah did not hear any raised voices or arguments. She moved closer to watch transactions taking place, fresh produce or small sacks of rice being exchanged for snips of copper money rings. There was no haggling. No banter. It was so familiar, but at the same time alien.

But it was not an idyllic scene. Each entrance to the square was guarded by solid-looking guards in thick leather, hard eyes scanning the crowd. More were standing at each corner, spears in hand and with an attitude of impassive readiness.

The people bustled past them as if they were not there, gazes averted, but the authoritative presence loomed oppressively over the square. Eyes were tight with fear, no one wanting to stand out from the crowd.

Blending in was what Ellyah was good at, though, and she quickly adjusted to move with the same attitude of those around her: eyes down, shoulders slumped, defeated and deferential.

Her eyes were nevertheless alert. Her quarry was still a score of paces ahead, weaving through the crowd and seemingly unconcerned about standing out. She was easy to follow.

Her path took her all the way across the square, and towards the grand building that sprawled at the southern extent. It was a columned temple, like those of southern Anish. Ellyah remembered slinking between the stone columns of the Westgate temple in Carhinn after stealing the jewel from the Mackems, all those months ago.

The temple of Seyntlowe was built on a different scale, however.

The front façade seemed to span the entire south side of the square, an imposing wall of pale stone pierced with five-sided windows and a grand double doorway. Above the door a long, straight pole had been pinned to the masonry, the wood so clean and white it seemed to shine. It rose several feet above the ridge of the roof, pointing straight up at the clouds, and two more poles crossed it at diagonals to form a huge and looming *pentang*.

It rose above Ellyah's head, soaring towards the heavens as she climbed the steps and passed through the doorway, still trailing her mark.

Entering the building was possibly foolish, as there might not be an escape if she was spotted and recognised, but her curiosity outweighed her caution. What could this woman want in a temple?

The space inside seemed dark in contrast to the flat daylight. Ellyah blinked rapidly to let her eyes adjust as she stepped into the main hall. She held her head high.

Walk normally, do not skulk. Move like someone with a right to be there and that is how others will see you.

Even with this mantra repeating in her head, her palms were clammy and her heart hammered in her chest. Where was the mysterious woman?

Then she saw her.

Candle lanterns set in alcoves in the thick stone columns cast pools of light across the room, but plunged the spaces behind into deeper shadow. Small windows, high up near the slanting ceiling, cast little light to reach the floor below. The atmosphere within was still, and unwelcoming.

The glimmering orange light from the lanterns revealed that there were twelve columns in this room, to match the twelve thick pillars that supported the floor beneath. Each was built from chiselled blocks of pale stone, rising from the wooden floor to the beams of the ceiling above.

With her dark clothes in the dark space, the woman was difficult to pick out, but Ellyah saw a flash of movement as she passed between two of the trunk like columns on the other side of the room.

She was heading towards the far end.

Ellyah stepped forwards to follow and her eyes fell on the space between the columns. A congregation was there, sitting on the bare floorboards, and many pairs of eyes turned to regard her.

They were just glances, not stares. Her presence was not surprising or unwelcome, but it had been noted. She must continue to act exactly as expected if she wanted to blend in, if she wanted them to forget she was there.

Dressed in robes and wearing embroidered caps, they knelt in rows, facing towards the far end of the columned hall. Ellyah was glad that Nastja had remembered to carry a couple in her bag. She noticed though, that while hers was a simple peasants cap, the hats and clothes of those gathered was fine. Hopefully, in the gloom, her poorer garb would not draw attention.

Without hurrying, she moved forwards and knelt at the rear of the group, one of the thick columns looming at her right shoulder.

At that moment, a voice rose from the other end of the room, and Ellyah looked up.

'Today we will read of the mercies of Mordea, the Mother,' they said, and Ellyah realised that this must be a Charterist congregation. The new worship that seemed to be spreading across Anish was here in Buren too.

The priest was dressed in long, blue robes of silk, embroidered in gold thread. One hand rested on their narrow chest, five fingers spread in prayer, while the other turned the pages of a large, bound book that sat on a wooden lectern before them. The congregation quickly shuffled their own books to find the correct page. Some shared, but most seemed to have their own. Ellyah edged closer to her neighbour, looking down at the book she held as if they were sharing. She hoped that this woman, well-dressed and clearly well off, would be too polite to say anything.

As the priest read aloud and the congregation repeated sections in a gloomy monotone, Ellyah joined in, but her mind worked furiously. Where had that short-haired woman gone? Why had she come here at all?

She tried to keep her face down, following the lines of runes scratched in thick black ink on the yellow parchment, but her eyes darted around, trying to pierce the gloom behind the looming columns. Then, a brief shaft of light shone out from the back of the room, several paces behind the priest, and was gone again the next instant.

A door at the rear of the room, opening and shutting, with a dark figure passing furtively through. Now Ellyah knew where her quarry had gone, but had learned nothing about what she was doing here, or why she had been hunting Nastja and herself in the first place.

She needed answers, and for that she needed patience. Lowering her eyes, she found her place in the text and concentrated on joining in with the congregation.

Sometime later, the priest led the people before him to the conclusion of the story, and closed his book. He now looked directly towards the congregation and spoke into the sudden stillness.

'All here abide with the Five through these words as written. They hear our prayers and know our faith is strong. Limitless and wise, they wait beyond the Shining Veil. May their blessings be upon us all.'

'May their blessings be upon us all,' repeated the gathered congregation. The service was familiar to Ellyah, but also different. She had heard the same stories of the gods, memories from when they walked the earth. They had made the same prayers. But there was no singing or even simple chant. Apart from the repetition of phrases from the text, their voices were never raised together. It felt wrong.

Those around her began to climb to their feet. This was her chance.

Without hesitation, she jumped up and thrust herself backwards between two of the imposing columns and into the shadows that lay beyond.

Move quickly and surely, and people would often disbelieve their own perception.

If her neighbour in the congregation noticed her sudden disappearance, she would convince herself that she had left through the door, or even that she had never actually been there. People fooled themselves very easily.

Still moving, she walked back and to the side, keeping the columns between herself and the others. Her hands groped out behind her until they touched rough, hard stone. The wall. She shrank against it, staying as still as possible to become just another shadow.

Blinded by the lights on the columns, the few that glanced in her direction would have seen only darkness. She watched as the stream of people passed out through the doorway and the room emptied.

She huddled against the wall, motionless, and barely daring to breathe. The slap of footsteps against the wooden floor became the repeated thud of those same feet descending the stone steps, before dying away.

In the stillness, the muted sound of a single pair of feet moving at the rear of the room was loud. The priest.

Ellyah heard the door latch and then saw the glare of light from the room beyond, growing and then receding as the priest moved through the door and shut it behind him. The sound of it slamming reverberated through Ellyah's being. Answers were behind that door.

She had to know.

On soft feet, she edged around the walls to reach the doorway. Her eyes scanned the room after every few steps. She thought she was alone in the room now, but she had to be certain.

The stone was cold against her shoulder as she paused by the doorframe. The indistinct murmur of voices came from behind the dark planks. She could learn nothing from that. Cautiously, carefully, she pressed her ear to the rough wood of the door, straining to catch the words.

'…it is still a risk for you to walk in here, in broad daylight,' a man's voice was saying. The voice of the Charterist priest.

'Less of a risk than sneaking in at night,' retorted the woman. Her tone was flippant and dismissive. 'The guards only notice people who are sneaking around or running away. I bet they didn't even see me today.'

Ellyah noted this with interest, seeing the sense of her words. Her quarry was clearly a woman after her own heart, and therefore a potentially dangerous adversary.

'Hmph,' grunted the priest, unconvinced. 'You came here to report on your mission, I presume? So, report. Did you find them?'

'I found them,' said the woman. Ellyah listened even more intently. Were her and Nastja "them"? 'But, the brothers screwed up. Or the girls heard them coming. Either way, when they broke in to grab them, they'd gone. So, they grabbed the landlord instead after he woke up and saw them.'

'What? Why?'

'He'd seen their faces. And he'd spoken with one of the girls that night. The taller one.' Ellyah's breath caught. She was now certain that she was their subject. Her stomach clenched as she realised that what the woman was suggesting was that the landlord had died because of that brief conversation.

'If he had seen your faces, then you had no choice,' said the priest. There was no surprise and not a hint of remorse in his voice. 'You performed the rite?'

'Yes.'

'And?'

'It was weak, as would be expected. It showed us that they were close, but no more than that. We already knew as much. Once the villagers found the innkeeper missing we had to get away fast, so we could not risk a proper search.'

The priest clicked his tongue in frustration. 'We must find them, quickly, and place them under restraint. The orders were very clear, and my master's patience is running out.'

'Why are they so important, anyway? Do they carry something valuable, or have some profitable knowledge?'

'It should be enough that the order was given,' said the priest, with forced patience. 'But I believe they have knowledge, which can be used. This is why they must be captured, and alive.'

'They cannot have gone far,' said the woman. 'They were travelling south, yes? So, they are probably bound for Glithoniel.'

'Perhaps. If so, it is important that we overtake them before they arrive there. It'll be too easy for them to hide in the city, or find passage on a ship. If that happens, we shall all suffer punishment. We must make another attempt to locate them. The rite must be performed once more.'

There was a moment of silence. Ellyah listened in rapt incomprehension. There were undercurrents here that she did not understand. Her body was tense, and primed to move at the first sound of footsteps returning to the door.

'You have found a suitable subject?' asked the priest.

'Yes,' said the woman, and for the first time there was a slight hint of reluctance in her voice.

'This *must* be done,' urged the priest. 'It is the only way we will find them. Go to it, and return with the brothers, the subject, and the others at midnight.'

'It shall be done as you say,' said the woman.

Footsteps.

Ellyah did not stop to think. She did not need to pause to look for a hiding place. Her plan was ready.

Without taking the time to turn, she backed away into the corner of the room. Hands pressing against the walls, she stepped quickly right and left, and her soft-soled shoes found minute edges in the stone for footholds.

By the time the door opened, spilling a shaft of light out into the room, Ellyah had climbed up into the roof space. Arms and legs spread to brace herself amongst the beams, she looked down.

The dark-clad, short-haired woman strolled across the room, heading for the main door out to the marketplace. The priest's head appeared in the doorway.

'Do not fail in this,' he called after her. She did not turn.

He muttered under his breath, exasperated, before turning and locking the door with a long key of dark iron. He was still grumbling as he left the hall in the same direction, and Ellyah noticed that he carried a large, wood-bound book under one arm.

She waited until she heard his even tread descending the steps and then counted fifty slow breaths. Getting caught out by someone suddenly returning for a forgotten item was foolish and amateur.

Eyes fixed on the doorway, she swarmed back down the wall and stole across to the locked door. Her hands went to the soft leather tool roll that she always kept strapped around her waist, even as she bent to examine the lock.

Leaving the temple and returning to Nastja without breaking into this office and searching it did not cross her mind.

Without needing to look away from the lock, she drew two specific metal rods from the toolbelt, slim probes with hooked ends. Her fingers manipulated them in the lock with easy familiarity, and moments later there was a muffled click. She returned the tools to her belt as the door swung open.

She glanced back down the hall at the bright square of light created by the doorway to the outside. This was dangerous. If anyone were to come back, and who knew who else apart from the priest had a key, she would be trapped.

But, she could not leave without finding out what was going on here. This could be her only opportunity. She knew for certain they were hunted, now, and who by. If she found out why, it could help them escape. And she was equally curious about the rite. What was it?

She slipped through the door and pulled it closed behind her.

It was a simple office, but what surprised her most of all after the gloom of the main hall was that it was lit with natural light. A small window was set in the wall opposite the door. It was barely shoulder width and secured with a grill of iron bars, hammered into the joints between the stones of the frame.

There could be no escape that way.

It did not matter. She was alone in the temple and there was no reason for her to be interrupted. She forced herself to relax and began to examine the room.

Ellyah was good at looking for things. Better than Nastja. Nastja would want to check every scroll and tablet, reading every word, but Ellyah concentrated her search on places where things could be hidden. It was pointless examining anything left in plain view; these things would not be important.

And plenty of things were in plain view.

A narrow desk stood beneath the window, little more than a smooth-topped table. Writing implements were arranged neatly in clay pots: quills for ink on parchment and hardwood styluses for inscribing runes onto clay tablets.

Rolled scrolls were in an orderly stack to one side, but when Ellyah examined one it was covered with lists of numbers. Her eyebrows rose when she saw the total at the bottom of the page.

If she failed to recover the jewel, she should get into the business of selling books. It seemed like an easy way to line your pockets with silver.

She shook her head, clearing the thought and trying to focus. There was no version of the future she could entertain where she did not find, and then sell, that jewel. It was everything. But first, she had to see if there was anything here that could indicate the identity of their pursuers, anything that would aid their escape.

Rolling the scroll up carefully, she returned it precisely to where she had picked it up. Leave no trace.

The room's stone walls were clad in dark wooden panelling, rubbed smooth and oiled to a shine. Otherwise, the room was undecorated, and the only other furniture was a sturdy chest in one corner. It was secured with an iron lock with a thick shackle. Moments passed as she felt around the inside of the mechanism with her hooked tools once more.

One by one, the pins dropped and eventually she was able to lift the lid.

'For Fate's sake...' she muttered in frustration. The chest was full of books. Just books.

She opened one and flicked through it. Stories of the Five and the glory of the Veil filled the pages, in neatly scribed runes. She had seen the silver money rings changing hands for these heavy, ornate books, but knew she would never pass for one of the Charterist preachers, even if she had the mind to go into that business. She did not have the beard for it.

Could she take one? She paused with it in her hands, the bulky weight a reminder of the value of this object of parchment, leather and wood. No. It was too bulky, too heavy, too easy to trace.

Reluctantly, she placed it back into the chest and closed the lid. That some people had so much wealth, and she did not, had always seemed unfair.

She locked the chest once more and straightened. Something made her head snap round, and her body stiffened. Had she heard something? With catlike caution she crossed to the door and listened. Holding her breath, she strained her ears for any sound beyond.

There. The subtle patter of feet on stone. Someone was climbing the stairs to the temple. She crouched to peer through the keyhole, and fought to restrain a gasp.

Several figures were silhouetted starkly in the doorway, and were walking directly towards the office. She was trapped.

SEVENTEEN

'Perfect,' grunted Skane, glowering down at the barred bridge in annoyance. Jhari responded with an indistinct noise that Skane took for agreement.

This delay was not what they needed. He had hoped to be well along the southward road towards Glithoniel by nightfall.

Lines of people, afoot and mounted, stretched up the side of the valley towards them, and away in all three directions beyond the narrow bridge. The ground to either side of the dusty road was a rough mess of tussocky grass, impossible terrain for a wagon. In any case, they needed to cross this stream to make progress towards Glithoniel.

Skane bet it was the only bridge for miles, and so it made sense as a site for a checkpoint. To check for what, though?

'Could just break through,' rumbled Jhari, leaning in close to make sure Skane heard. 'There's only ten of 'em down there, and the knight.'

Skane knew. He had already counted the Bureno soldiers wrapped in thick leather and shimmering scales, in the knight's case. They were all well-armed, too. Their own cudgels and small knives were no match for spears and swords.

Jhari would not care about that, though. One word, and he would charge in like a raging bull, snapping those spear shafts like twigs. A wry smile creased his face. That would be fun.

He sucked his teeth, expression creasing to a frown. They could not risk it, not the risk to their lives, or their freedom, or the success of their mission. Orders were orders. He knew his reputation was as one who did what he was asked, however hard it was, however unpleasant it seemed. He hoped to keep it.

'I think you did enough breaking at the last village,' he replied, and Jhari chuckled.

They had trundled slowly up the slope to the hilltop village to find the gates pulled shut and a couple of burly men standing before it, gripping notched wood axes with white knuckles.

From their garb of short smocks and dirty hose, they were farmers or labourers, not warriors, and their eyes were nervous as the wagon approached. Both were broad and muscular though; the best the village could find as guards.

'Open up, friends,' called Skane, reining in the wagon several paces away. 'We have places to be!'

One of the guards muttered something in reply, too quiet to hear and spoken in too much of a rush.

'Speak up!' called Skane, cupping his hand to an ear to make the point. The man scowled, clearly thinking that Skane spoke in mockery.

'I said, you must state your names and your business. Our village is no longer open to any outsiders.'

'But you're on the main road,' argued Skane. 'It's the High King's road, not yours. You can't just shut it.'

'We've got to check everyone,' said the other man in a sullen tone. 'Can't have any more trouble.' His partner shot him a glare, before turning back to Skane.

'State your name and your business, or turn your wagon around and head back to Tayo.'

Skane was immediately aware of Jhari beside him, muscles tensing and fists clenching. The huge half-elf was getting irritated, and that usually resulted in things being broken and people getting hurt.

Lifting a hand from the reins, Skane held it, palm outstretched towards the half-elf, as he addressed the gate guards.

'Not from Tayo,' he said. 'We're traders from the Riverlands. We're carrying yarn, beans and dried herbs, and I can do you some good prices if you let us through.' The men at the gates glanced at one another, unsure. 'Come and have a look if you want to check.'

Skane kept his hands on his lap as one of the guards approached. His dark hair was cut in a straight line around the back of his head, level with his ears, and the olive skin of his chin was covered with a patchy beard.

Not a wealthy man.

His arms were thick, though, and his hands looked powerful as they gripped the axe protectively across his chest. A worker.

The rear of the wagon was piled with boxes and sacks; produce and goods that the Mackems had bought before leaving Ben Gedrin to help them pass as a trading caravan. The local man pointed at a long crate which was nailed shut.

'What's in there?'

'*Strommin*,' replied Skane. 'You know, that rotted fish they eat up in Timmers? The dwarves and elves down here love it. Don't open the crate! It stinks to the Veil!'

The man backed away, raising a hand to his nose.

'Open the gate!' he called to his friend. 'These traders can pass through.'

'Thanks, friend,' said Skane, swishing his reins to stir the horses into motion once more.

In truth, there was only a thin layer of the smelly, slimy fish packed into the top of the crate. Beneath, wrapped in oiled cloth, was a bundle of short swords and war axes. They needed to be armed but would attract too much attention to travel with such weapons openly. Hopefully, the threat of the vile stink of the aged fish would put off any others who tried to open the crate.

The gate creaked open, and the wagon trundled through.

Skane could tell immediately that something was wrong. There were people out in the street, going about their business, but as he and the other Mackems passed through the gateway heads snapped anxiously round to stare at them. Worried, haunted eyes watched them carefully.

'What's wrong with 'em?' asked Jhari, without bothering to lower his voice.

Skane shrugged. 'Dunno. Nothing that's our business. Let's keep moving, though.'

'Traders!' roared a voice from behind them. One of the gate guards had called out, and the hesitance of the crowd melted away, and they surged forwards.

Within moments, the rear of the wagon was surrounded by Bureno peasants examining the goods they carried and clamouring for attention. Jhari stood, striding back to stand atop the wagon bed. Skane cursed under his breath. This was supposed to be a cover story to provide easy passage across Buren. He had not intended to run a market stall.

Then it had happened.

A couple had clustered beside the wagon, behind Jhari's back. They were close to Skane's right shoulder and talking to each other urgently. Skane could not make out the words as they hissed to one another.

Out of the corner of his eye, Skane saw the man reach forwards, grabbing for something in the wagon. He realised, with a sudden jolt of fear, that the man's hands were on the long crate of weapons.

Jhari saw the crate move near his feet, and realised quickly what was happening.

'Oi!' he roared. 'Get your filthy hands off that!'

His fist swung. Skane had felt the force of Jhari's fists, more than once, while sparring or scrapping on the streets of Carhinn. He could only liken it to being struck by a blacksmith's hammer.

The man of the pair flew backwards, clutching at his face. His woman slapped angrily at Jhari's arm, so he punched her too. He must have pulled the blow though, because she stayed upright, staggering backwards with blood oozing from the corner of her mouth.

The crowd roared in rage, and fists flew at the Mackems who were gathered on foot around the wagon. They brandished their clubs in return, striking back. As Skane turned his head, he saw the burly gate guards advancing.

This was a disaster. The idea had been to pass through Buren unnoticed and to find the trail of the girls from Ben Gedrin. Now, they would learn nothing about whether they had even been here, and they would be lucky to escape this village. They had to get out of here.

'Jhari!' he bellowed. 'Clear a path!'

The huge half-elf brawler immediately knew what was needed, vaulting down off the side of the wagon and barrelling around to the front. His shoulders rolled as his fists lashed out. The village folk fell back in fear and dismay.

'Come on!' yelled Skane to the other Mackems, as he swished the reins. The wagon surged into motion, the other gang members running to keep up. A frantic running battle had ensued, but they had broken free.

Skane hoped there would be no repeat of that violence as they approached the bar across the river. They could not afford any more delay, and the presence of armed and armoured soldiers suggested that they would not be able to escape so easily if another fight broke out.

'We're traders,' announced Jhari as soon as the commoners before them had passed beneath the raised bar, and it was their turn. The soldiers at the bar rolled their eyes, disinterest clear in their attitude.

'State your name and your business,' stated one in a bored monotone. Fortunately, his voice was loud and clear enough for Skane to hear him first time.

'Name's Taureb,' he replied. 'I'm a trader out of the Riverlands.'

He always gave the name "Taureb" as an alias. It meant "friend" in the Old Tongue, and it amused him to tell all those he met that he was a friend, when his intentions were often quite unfriendly.

'Trading what?' asked the guard.

'Nothing but simple produce from the family farm,' waving an arm towards the wagon's bed. The guard's eyes followed the gesture, taking in the haphazard stack of boxes and sacks.

'What's in the long crate?' he asked abruptly, and Skane cursed inwardly. The crate of weapons. Why did it get so much attention? He kept his face calm, but wrinkled his nose.

'Just some of that *strommin* stuff,' he replied, dismissively. 'That rancid fishy stuff. It's disgusting, but elves and dwarves both pay well for it. And there are plenty of those folks in Buren, I've heard.'

The guard curled his lip. 'Very well.' He moved to lift the bar.

'Wait,' came a different voice. A female voice.

She moved forwards to stand before the bar, a fine coat of scaled mail glittering. Her left hand rested easily on the hilt of the longsword at her hip, and there was a density about her shoulders that suggested physical strength.

'You have *strommin*?' she asked.

'Yes,' replied Skane. Her eyes bored into him, sharp in the shadow cast by her decorated helmet. 'Sir,' he added.

'I will take it,' she said, turning and gesturing to another guard nearby. 'Unload that long crate from this wagon.'

Skane's heart sank. He needed those weapons. 'But,' he protested, raising his voice, 'it's really stinky stuff. Only elves and dwarves would ever want to eat it. Sir.'

The guard hefted the heavy crate and passed it down to another who was standing beside the wagon.

'I am aware,' replied the knight, in an icy tone. 'And as such it will be a fine gift for my lord Earl Yuvakudu and his mother, the Duchess Telivaina. Who are elves.'

Skane ground his teeth. Losing the weapons would be a major setback. He figured that their path would take them to Glithoniel, and did not like the thought of arriving in an unfamiliar city unarmed. Buying more could bring unwanted attention.

Also, once the crate was opened, which could be any time from now, their cover as honest traders would be blown. Would these lords send soldiers to hunt them down? Skane would rather not find out.

'That's my profit from this trip gone,' he complained. 'I can't afford for you to take that.'

The guards ignored him, carrying the awkward crate past the bar and away. The knight fixed him with a glare.

'Do you hold to the Five?' she asked, sharply. 'Do you live a life of humble obedience, so that you may be judged kindly when you pass the Shining Veil?'

'Of course,' muttered Skane. What else could he say?

'In that case, you can consider this proof of your conviction,' she said. 'Generosity and respect for your noble leaders are worthy qualities.'

She turned away, waving a hand dismissively to indicate that they be let through. Skane clenched his fists around the reins. He could do nothing more.

'Get on!' he shouted towards the horses and the wagon trundled into motion. He turned onto the southward road, leaving the bar and the soldiers, and their precious weapons behind.

His shoulder blades twitched as he felt the soldiers' stares follow him and the rest of the Mackems as they rolled away.

Skane ground his teeth against the pain. He made no sound, but his eyes widened in surprise.

This had not happened before.

It was night. They had continued south along the well-made road through central Buren until the evening began to draw in.

'Shut up the moaning!' Jhari had said suddenly, earlier that afternoon, turning towards the gang members who trailed along behind the wagon. He leaned back to Skane.

'They won't stop complaining,' he explained. Skane had heard muttering but had not been able to make out the words.

'Again?' said Skane. He kept his voice calm but felt his blood heating. His fist clenched on the reins of the wagon until the leather creaked.

Jhari nodded.

'Who?' Skane asked.

'Maris. And Axvyer.'

Skane raised his voice. 'Stopping here for the night!' He yanked on the reins and the wagon trundled off the road. It jounced and rocked as the wheels jolted over the tussocky grass.

Tall cypress trees, like long green feathers, screened a small grassy clearing from the road. The Mackems began unloading their camping gear as soon as the wagon halted, not waiting for an order.

Skane would remind them why they needed to do that.

'Axvyer! Come here!' he barked, swinging himself down off the wagon's high seat. 'Maris, you too. Now!'

They ambled over, Axvyer a tall, shambling man with long fair hair he wore loose, and Maris a short, stocky woman with her dark hair in tight braids. He would put his copper on Maris in a brawl or fistfight, but Axvyer had apparently served a couple of seasons as a soldier on the Kotev border.

'I hear you've been complaining,' said Skane in a mild tone. Axvyer shrugged and Maris opened her mouth as if to protest, but said nothing.

With a flash of sudden movement, Skane bunched a fist and swung it into Maris's midriff. In the same motion, he lashed out with his left hand, chopping at Axvyer's throat. He pulled both blows, but Maris doubled over, winded, and Axvyer clutched at his throat, gasping for breath.

'You both need to remember,' Skane snarled, loudly enough to carry to all in the camp, 'why you're still here. You all got out of Ben Gedrin alive because of me. You get food in your bellies every day and copper in your palm because of me.

'We're invaders in a foreign land, in case you've forgotten. Our enemies are everywhere. If you want to survive, you need to follow me and do as I say.'

He drew a few calming breaths, and when he spoke again his voice was quieter.

'Our master is hard on us, but they are working towards a mighty goal. We are part of that and if we follow orders and work hard, the payday at the end will set us up for life. If you don't fancy that—' he pointed away in a direction he thought must be approximately east, 'Anish is that way. Off you go.'

No one moved.

'Right. Let's get set up then.'

They had strung a wide length of canvas over the top of the wagon to form a makeshift tent, and Skane had gone inside to wait. He knew his master would want a report.

As the sun set and the autumn sky faded from a crisp indigo to charcoal grey, the air inside the wagon-tent had shimmered and a purple portal had appeared. This otherworldly, uncanny phenomenon now felt commonplace, and Skane had stopped even thinking about the whys and the hows of it.

He had admitted that he had lost the crate of weapons, and the punishment from the masked figure in the middle of the portal had been immediate.

Needles pierced his body, head to heel, as if driven by a strong arm and heated by a raging furnace. Yet, nothing could be seen, neither in the air around him or on his flesh.

Even through the teeth-clenching pain, Skane was deeply unnerved. This was not natural, not right. He recalled the horrific deaths suffered by the former leader of the Mackems of Carhinn, Bryn Gallit and his merchant accomplice, at the hands of the same masked sorcerer. He felt lucky that pain was all he was made to suffer.

It would not hurt when it was gone.

'This cannot be undone,' said the voice from behind the mask, when the torment subsided. 'And the risk that you will now be pursued as criminals in Buren is one that must be borne.

Continue on to Glithoniel as planned. I have work there for you. You may yet find the trail of those girls on the way, too.'

Those girls. Skane cursed inwardly. He had hoped that events might have made them no longer relevant. He was tired of trailing them.

'They are still to be sought?' he asked.

'Yes!' came the voice, shrill and laced with impatience and irritation. 'You have had your orders, that they be captured, and I expect you to continue to follow them.'

Skane had no idea where they were. Not anymore. They had lost their trail and the near riot at the last village had forestalled any attempt they might have made to gather news. Maybe there would be more chance of overtaking them on the way to Glithoniel, or locating them once they had arrived at the Bureno capital.

Skane sighed. 'I'll do what I can.'

'You will.'

'Are we done?'

It was impolite but Skane's patience was wearing thin. He felt like a hound chasing a stick, or one of those puppets on the end of a rod, dancing and bobbing in a shadow-play. Control of his own fate was slipping from his grasp.

'One more thing,' came the voice. 'I have a new target for you, as well as the girls. Another one to find and capture. Others may be looking for him too, but if we can be the ones to take him then there will be rewards for us both.'

'Who?'

'His name is Styoyan Jukeev,' answered the floating mask within the eerie ring of purple light. 'The youngest son of the ruling house of Kereva and Fordon.'

'Heard of him.'

'Would you recognise his face?'

'I know a noble when I see one. The rings, for a start.'

'Quite. He has likely crossed from Anish to Buren, and recently. If you hear any news of such a one, ask questions. Find out where he is, track him down and take him. Alive, like the girls.'

'Why's he come here?' Skane was curious about more than that but knew he wouldn't get away with asking too many questions.

The reply was terse. 'That is not your concern.'

Typical. Every boss he had worked for had been the same. They acted like everyone else was stupid, and did not deserve to know all the facts. Skane had just about enough of it.

'Right,' he said.

'Make it so,' said the masked figure, before the swirling portal collapsed in on itself, and the mask withdrew and disappeared.

Skane made a fist.

He was tired of being a puppet.

It was time to break free of the rods that would make him dance, even if just to show he could.

It would begin tomorrow.

EIGHTEEN

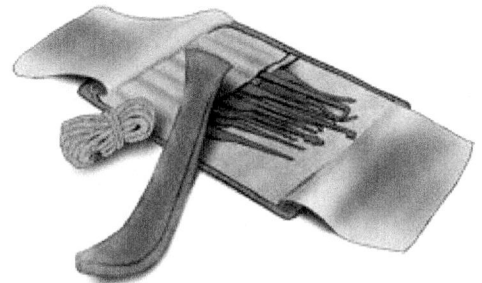

Footsteps. Coming closer. More than one person was moving through the temple and towards the door of this room. And Ellyah had let herself get trapped in it.

Fool! She thought, cursing herself. *Only an idiot goes in somewhere new with only one way out.*

What was she going to do now?

Bars on the window, forming a grille about wide enough to permit an arm, prevented any escape that way. They were forged of iron, thumb-thick and impossible to pull out or bend.

The volume of the padding steps increased. They were almost at the door.

Think!

That was when she saw it.

The room's wood panelling was finished with a dark stain, bringing out the grain in distinct stripes, top to bottom. She did not know why she noticed it in that moment, perhaps desperation, but she saw that some of the rich brown lines in the corner behind the door were not wood grain; they were tiny gaps.

Two strides took her to the wall, her hands groping across the joints, barely visible even this close.

The footsteps grew louder still, then stopped.

Her fingers found a small square of otherwise blank wood, with discreet joints on all four sides. She pressed it.

The sound of a key in the lock of the door to the room was loud in the stillness.

A narrow panel, barely the width of Ellyah's shoulders, swung open into the room. There was a dark void behind it.

The door to the office creaked open as Ellyah darted into the small, secret space and pulled the panel closed behind her. The click of the hidden door shutting was mercifully quiet. Barely daring to breathe, she huddled in the inky darkness of the hidden void, and listened as the people entered the room.

She had been foolish. That had been far too close. But, she hated not knowing who was hunting them and why. She wanted to know what they were up against.

'My apologies again, Earl Yuvakudu,' said a voice she recognised. The priest. 'As I said, had I known you were coming I would have arranged a better welcome.'

'That is not necessary,' said another voice, rich, bassy and melodious. 'This needs only be a quick visit. I became curious how matters were progressing?'

Ellyah thought that the newcomer might be an elf, especially considering his name. His voice was accented and had that resonant authority that elven nobles seem to possess naturally.

He spoke again, but his words were muted as though he had stepped out of the room.

'None are to enter.'

So, there were guards outside the door. Worth knowing. She could be safe here, but an escape route might still be useful.

'Be seated, please,' said the deep voice, louder again and there was the scrape of wood on wood as chairs were pulled back. He went on. 'You have not forgotten the task I gave you?'

'No, no, my duke,' blustered the priest. 'Of course not! All of my energy is directed towards finding them.'

Ellyah's lips parted as she listened even more intently. *Them.*

'And yet? Where are they?'

'Close, close. They must be close.' The priest's voice sounded near to panic. 'The rite was performed near the village of Dombtuun, and the signs indicated that they were near at that time.'

'I heard about that. Your agents were clumsy. It left quite a mess. Quite a…drama.' The deep voice of the earl remained smooth and calm, but there was a subtle edge of irritation.

'The murder was blamed on the two outlander women,' said the priest, confirming Ellyah's fears. This was about her and

Nastja. They were "them". 'My agents escaped without suspicion falling on them, and now the Kingseye Guards are seeking the girls too.'

'In this, you have been fortunate, not adept,' said the earl. 'Doubly so, for I also have agents in the Kingseye, so if they do chance to be taken then they will still be brought before me as is needed.'

'Fate wills it,' said the priest.

'*I* will it!' snapped the earl. 'And at this moment, *I* am your fate. If results are not forthcoming, *I* will be your end. Where are those women, and what are you doing to bring them to me?'

'I am thankful for my earl's continued patronage and patience,' said the priest in a small, contrite voice. 'And they will be rewarded. My best agent assures me that they are near. They may even be here, in Seyntlowe The rite will be performed again tonight, and we will find them.

'This I swear, on the name of our master.'

'Do not speak it!' warned the earl. Who was this master? Who would this earl refer to with such fear and apparent reverence? 'Who will perform the rite?'

'The same agent will do it. She must. The ties of blood will be invoked.'

There was a pause. Then the earl spoke once more, and his voice was calmer.

'If this is so, then it will greatly increase the power of the rite. They will surely be located, wherever they hide.'

'It is so. They will be found, and brought to you.'

'Do not fail again.'

'Yes, my earl.'

'We have other business,' the earl continued, brisk and purposeful. 'Are you getting good numbers attending your Charterist sermons?'

'Yes, my duke,' replied the priest, clearly grateful for the change of subject. 'Nearly as many as when I was leading a purely Chanterist congregation. And they are a better class of people altogether. Silver flows from their fingertips.'

'This is good news. You have the ledgers?'

There was silence then, but for the furtive rustle of paper, and Ellyah was quickly bored. She had already seen the calculations and the sums of money taken against money spent.

These people, these Charterists, who hunted her and Nastja for reasons yet unknown, were rich as dwarf lords.

Envy and greed warred with curiosity about why they were so keen to find her, as well as a stab of fear about this mysterious rite that would be conducted this evening. The earl seemed reassured that it would locate them. It must be late afternoon already: she did not have long.

She moved her head from the panelling for the first time and glanced around the dark, claustrophobic space. Her eyes must have adjusted to the low light, and she was amazed what she could now see.

Where she stood was a small, square alcove which was bound by stone walls on three sides. The fourth was the rear of the office's wood panelling and was the same height as the room next door. What made Ellyah start was what she saw in the floor.

Sturdy stone flags were beneath her feet, but in the far corner was a void. It was a small square hole in the floor, and beneath the level of the flagstones a steep and twisting staircase led downward.

She had been quite lucky not to fall down it in her haste to escape the office. But, luck was often mistaken for experience and judgement, so perhaps she should take the credit.

What could be down there?

The murmur of voices continued through the panelling, and Ellyah pressed her ear to the planks again.

'I continue to obey, and to serve,' the priest was saying.

The earl ignored the courtesy. 'Do what you have been ordered to do. That is all.'

'Yes, of course. Thank you, my earl.'

Footsteps sounded, then the door opened and closed. Shortly after, the chair in the office creaked once more.

So, the mysterious elven earl had left, but it seemed as though the priest remained in the room. What should she do now? Break free?

Against one man, and with the element of surprise, she might be able to overpower him and make her escape. But, it was risky and would reveal her presence and her location.

No, she thought. *If I open this door and he sees me, he must die.*

Could she do it? Morally, yes and with no regrets. Physically? It remained too much of a risk.

She could stay put and wait for the priest to leave. But what if he did not? What if he had reason to open this hidden door? He must know of it, and if he did then she would be cornered and at his mercy.

So, trying to leave the way she had come and staying where she was were both fraught with risk. That only left one option.

The dark staircase below her feet.

She thought for a moment before moving. The temple was raised on columns, as was customary, so the only way a staircase could descend through the floor was inside one of them. Recalling her approach to the temple, she had noticed that the columns were unusually thick, and could probably accommodate a narrow, spiralling staircase like the one below.

Her curiosity was piqued, as was her hope.

It must either lead down to ground level or descend below. Either way, it could provide an escape route. It was her only sensible choice.

Moving silently came without conscious thought as she eased her foot down the first tall step, shrugging into the low gap. Blocky stairs led down, their edges just visible in the low light but gradually fading away into absolute darkness.

Ellyah took a breath and gathered her courage. Slow, careful steps would take her safely down. She began to descend.

The light was quickly left behind, and her only sensations were the rasp of stone against her fingertips and through the soles of her shoes.

Down, and down.

She quickly fell into a rhythm. Feel for the edge of the step, toes curling over the stone, her heel sliding down the riser to find the next tread. As she repeated this motion her hands reached out to either side, feeling her way and bracing herself.

There was only her, the cold stone, and the darkness.

The twisting staircase descended further than she expected. It was hard to be certain, but she felt like she must be below ground level already. Where was this leading? Her fear was only outweighed by her curiosity.

Then a vague glimmer of light showed beyond her feet. It was not bright, not the glare of a candle lantern or even the oily glimmer of a rushlight, but it began to define the stair edges with an inky silhouette. It was enough to suggest that there was something else below.

A few more steps, and an arch opened over her head. As she ducked beneath, her eyes widened at what she saw.

This was not a simple basement or cellar, or anything that had been built or made. This was a cave; a broad, arch-roofed cavern that disappeared into shadowy darkness at the edges of Ellyah's vision.

That was the strange thing. She was clearly underground but could see, a little. There was just enough light shining in from somewhere. Where?

That answer would have to wait. The important thing was that it was not shining on her. If there was anyone else in this unexpected underworld space, then they would not see her. She would be just another shadow.

With her usual caution, she stepped forwards out of the archway. She found herself on a raised platform, seemingly formed from a natural outcrop of smooth, cracked rock. Before her was a stone-built lectern, a murky finger in the gloom.

She edged around it and stepped down silently from the boulder. Still wary of unseen eyes, she stayed close to the wall behind her as she looked around the space.

The main dome of the cavern was perhaps thirty paces in each direction, with a ceiling of rough rock that sloped down towards the edges, so she had to stoop slightly as she stalked the perimeter. The light filtered down from somewhere to her right; the distinctive pale glow of daylight, but that was not what caught her eye. Her attention was drawn instead to the floor of the cavern.

A symbol was carved into the rock of the floor, the lines of it at least twenty feet long. It was a symbol she recognised. She had last seen it scratched countless times into the wall of a barn, by Nastja.

It was a *pentang*, but with the lower vertical cut short to form a star with six points. The deep incisions left no room for doubt, this was deliberate and meant something significant to someone.

Those that hunted them?

She needed to find out, but she also wanted to escape this place. Daylight meant a route back to the surface, and so she set off to find it.

It was a natural cave. The space she had found herself in was just one large cavern, and smaller alcoves and blind passages led away in many directions. They were pitch black and Ellyah was not prepared to risk entering any of them. Not when something else was lighting up the cavern.

Edging around the twisting walls and sometimes moving between eerie pillars of smooth, lumpy rock that glistened wetly, she made her way gradually towards the light. Halfway around the perimeter from the entrance and the pulpit rock, narrow tunnel opened off to the right. After the gloom of the deeper cave, the light was bright.

Ellyah hurried up the slope, pressing close to the wall in case there was anyone else down here. This passageway must return to the surface, somehow. She turned a corner, hand trailing against rock which bore the scars and angles of miner's picks, and stopped.

The glow was brighter ahead, natural light filtering down from somewhere above, but the tunnel was blocked. Heavy, wrought iron gates stretched from wall to wall, anchored into the rock itself.

Ellyah hurried forwards and was unsurprised to find the gates barred and locked. She was already reaching for her toolbelt as she looked for the lock itself, but stopped when she saw it.

'Shit,' she muttered into the darkness.

The lock itself was protected by a finer grille, the squares too small to admit a hand or even fingers, and in too wide a circle around the lock to reach past. Ellyah half-heartedly tried to twist her wrist around the cold metal, but knew it was useless.

Was this place a prison?

The hinges were also solid, the gates too heavy and too close fitted for her to shift in any direction.

Once more, she was trapped.

She wandered slowly back down to the main cavern, giving her eyes time to adjust again. What was she going to do now?

She was satisfied that she was alone down here, but also that there was no easy route of escape. Now was the time to stop, and think.

Examine your surroundings, she told herself. *What is important? What can you use? Where is the danger?*

She would hear anyone unlocking the gates, and she was sure that the priest would make enough noise descending the stairs to warn of his approach. Ellyah briefly considered climbing back up the spiral stairs to check if he was still in his office, but the thought of meeting him on his way down filled her with dread. She would be completely at his mercy.

Think!

She moved into the centre of the cavern. The ridges of the great carved symbol felt deep beneath the soles of her soft shoes. Then, she noticed dark stains across the pale rock. It was not damp, not fresh. Could it be...blood?

Glancing around, she noticed that the nearest flowstone pillars had carved niches, which held the contorted stubs of old candles. So, this place was used, and lit, and blood was shed here.

The rite.

Six points. Six cuts. The dark, pervasive stain of blood. The rite that was going to be used to locate herself and Nastja.

Curiosity and a surge of red rage burned through her fear and worry. Who did these people think they were, and what ungodly games were they playing?

She had to know.

Acting quickly and decisively when she had a plan was one of her strengths, but she also knew when patience was required. Glancing around, she picked an alcove with a good view of the cavern but screened by a pillar of lumpy, shining rock that rose to touch the ceiling. Gathering her cloak around her and huddling against the wall, she thought about Nastja for a moment.

She would be worrying. Worrying deeply. But, she was an adult and could take care of herself for the rest of the afternoon. And afterwards, Ellyah would return knowing exactly what they were up against.

She made herself comfortable, as much as she could pressed up against cold stone, and did her best to become just another shadow.

NINETEEN

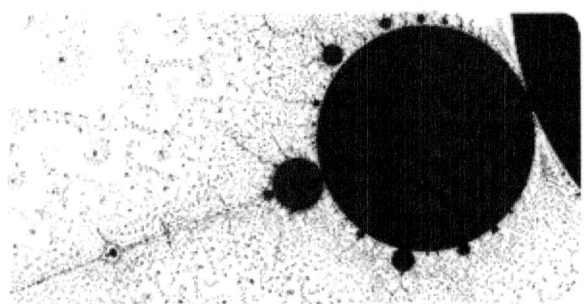

Nastja stepped forwards, beyond the mouth of the alley. She stepped back again. Chewing her lip, she stepped forwards again.

No, she thought, as she moved back behind the horses once more. Ellyah had told her to wait, so she would wait. Ellyah probably knew best.

The thought gave Nastja some comfort, for a moment. She had been told what to do, and could just do it. She did not have to make a decision. Ellyah would know where to find her when she returned, and for the moment she was safe enough. It would show Ellyah how she could be trusted.

Her fingers twitched on the reins of the two horses, who were standing placidly.

But, what if Ellyah had got herself into trouble? The woman they had seen was hunting them, although they did not yet know why, or for certain that it was related to the jewel. It was possible, though, that these people believed that Ellyah and Nastja still possessed it.

Ellyah might have walked straight into a trap. She would have been back by now, otherwise. Nastja stepped forwards again. She could not decide what to do.

What would Ellyah do?

Nastja pursed her lips in thought. Ellyah would make a plan. She would decide what she needed to do, then do it. So, what did Nastja need to do?

She needed to find Ellyah, and try to help her. Where to start? Ellyah had slipped through the crowded marketplace towards the looming temple on the far side of the square. Nastja should do the same. But, leading a couple of horses through the crowds would be awkward and would attract attention. So, first, to find some stables.

They would be by the walls, close to the gates. She turned her back on the square and the temple, and led the horses back in the direction they had come.

As she walked, her mind worked like an abacus, and she tried to stave off panic. What if Ellyah had been captured? What if they treated her like the innkeeper? What if she was already dead?

She screwed her eyes tight shut for a moment. Ellyah dead. It could not be the case. She must have time. Nastja could not bear the thought of being alone. Not again.

Hurrying towards the sprawling stable buildings, a ramshackle series of lean-tos against the pale walls, she slipped a silver money ring from her wrist.

'I need them,' she pointed back at the horses, 'in there.'

A woman with her dark hair cut into a severe bob came turned. 'Eh, what?' she said, brow crinkling. 'Yer in a tizz. What do you want?'

'I need these, in there,' Nastja repeated. It was clear. She wanted to put the horses into the stables. The ostler still looked puzzled.

Of course, she was worried about Ellyah and had forgotten that most people needed more explanation than that. They needed more words to make them feel comfortable about their part in the transaction.

She paused. She spoke.

'I need my horses looked after, for a time,' she said, remembering to affect a Bureno accent this time. 'Can you fit them in? Please?'

The ostler raised an eyebrow. 'I got room. It'll be a silver section for the day.'

Nastja held out the money ring again, but remembered she had a few sections in a pouch at her waist. She should use those up first. Slipping the ring back over her wrist, she rummaged in the pouch while the woman crossed her arms.

'You want to be careful flashing so much silver around here, miss,' she said. 'There are all sorts of criminals around. They wouldn't think twice about taking advantage of a tiny thing like you.' She took the snipped silver pieces from Nastja's hand and put them into her own money pouch.

'My mistress Marenah has sent me out to buy linen and thread,' said Nastja, repeating the cover story Ellyah had devised. The ostler's eyebrows rose once more.

'Right you are. May the Five protect.'

'Yes,' said Nastja, turning away.

She felt very pleased with herself. The horses were no longer an encumbrance, and she had successfully passed herself off as a Bureno commoner on an errand from her mistress.

It was the middle of the afternoon, and the grey clouds above were shifting and swirling in the slight breeze to reveal fleeting patches of clear, pale blue. There was a golden tint to the feathery edges of the clouds which promised a swift, autumnal dusk.

Nastja headed back along the main streets, past tall, blocky buildings and through thinning crowds. She was forced to step back as a pair of burly men manhandled a woman across the street in front of her.

'This is a mistake!' she yelled as her shoulders writhed against the strength of the men holding her. 'I hold to the Five! I have done nothing wrong.'

She wore her hair in an intricate braid and her smock was long and embroidered. It was the garb of a merchant or craftsperson. She looked prosperous, her appearance well-tended.

'Lies won't help you now,' grunted one of the guards as they forced her into the building on Nastja's right. It was the one made from heavy, pale blocks and with iron bars over the windows. The prison.

Either Buren was beset by heretics and troublemakers, or the nobles and rulers of this land were afraid of something. Nastja wondered if that something included people who murdered innocents in bizarre blood rituals.

If not, it should.

She entered the square, where the traders and hawkers were folding up their awnings and beginning to roll their barrows and wagons away. Without the crowds, the temple loomed even larger over the scene.

There was a solid and eternal look about the building, and Nastja could not help wondering about the months of labour needed to move the heavy stones into place, and the skill of the masons to ensure they would not fall. Even resting on tree-trunk thick columns, it appeared as though it was floating.

As she moved through the square, her eye was drawn to a pale structure in the very centre. It was another memorial house, like the one on the outskirts of the hilltop village, but on a much grander scale.

Were it hollow, which Nastja knew it was not, it would be large enough to be used as a real house for a small family. As it was, the solid white marble dominated the square, its blocky shape an echo of the larger buildings lining the perimeter.

It reminded Nastja of the dead man, lying on the path before the village's memorial house. Dead, and deliberately cut before he died. A specific sequence of cuts.

Ritual, or functional? To send a message, or to fulfil a purpose? There was one thing it was not, and that was an accident. And neither was the presence of the same woman here a coincidence.

Nastja looked up at the façade of the temple, noting the huge *pentang* that hung there. The five-sided symbol stared down at her. What exactly was going on?

That was the moment that Nastja saw her again.

With her short dark hair and matching clothing, the woman was immediately noticeable as she trotted down the steps of the temple and headed back across the square without a glance in Nastja's direction. She was the key to it all, Nastja was sure. If she could follow, she might find out where Ellyah had gone.

A few moments later, before Nastja had moved, a well-dressed older man with long hair and a beard that was neatly groomed appeared in the same doorway. His cloth was fine, and cut long, and he carried a thick book beneath his arm.

Did that mean that the temple might now be empty? Was Ellyah still inside?

Nastja wrestled with the decision for a while. If Ellyah were in trouble she might be able to help, but if Ellyah was in the middle of something Nastja bursting in might be an unwelcome disruption. Ellyah might not even be there at all.

In any case, Nastja wanted to know more about that woman. To follow, she needed to be unobtrusive.

Think.

What about her stood out?

Her garb was nondescript, that of a simple Bureno peasant, but she carried two dusty travel bags, hers and Ellyah's, over each shoulder. That might seem unusual.

Glancing around, she spotted a castaway sack in a pile of marketplace debris, and grabbed it. No one looked at a peasant carrying a sack.

As she held the mouth of the sack open to stuff the bags inside, she paused. The cobbles were littered with other discarded items. Cabbages rolled in a gutter while bruised pears lay here and there alongside other unidentifiable fragments of green and brown.

It was wasteful. There were full meals there, just dropped or thrown away. She stared at the mess. For a moment, she considered gathering some of the food up, but as she saw the street grime and footprints that fouled them she recoiled. She could not make herself touch them.

Loud hoofbeats caught her attention and reminded her of what she was supposed to be doing. She thrust the other leather travel bag inside the rough sack and flung it over her shoulder before shuffling across the square in the same direction as the woman.

As she scurried away, back bowed and head down in a posture of deference, a group of riders reined in before the temple. Out of the corner of her eye she saw the bearded priest returning, hurrying to the head of the group and bowing.

Words were exchanged but Nastja was too far away to hear, and could not risk being noticed, so carried on walking. However, as she got to the edge of the square and turned into a narrower street, she caught a glimpse of the lead rider as he dismounted.

She could not help herself staring for a moment.

Nastja had never seen a person quite so tall. He overtopped the priest by a head and more, maybe even by a foot. She had time to notice his coal-dark skin and long, colourful robes before her steps took her further into the alley and he was lost from view.

The priest had lowered his head, bowing in deference and the tall man had been followed by a retinue who were more simply dressed. Just the way he had dismounted and stood had radiated confidence and authority. Nobility. So, who was he and how was he involved in all this?

Perhaps he was just a follower of this new Charterist creed and was just buying books. Perhaps.

'Oi! Daydreamer!' came a shout from near Natja's face. 'You'll get run over by a cart if you stay standing there!' A smooth-cheeked young man in a short smock was waving a hand before her face.

Nastja realised she had been standing still in the middle of the street, staring up at the sky in thought.

She forced herself into movement once more, veering towards the edge of the street. She had to stay inconspicuous. And, she had to find that woman.

Square-fronted buildings lined the street on each side. The pale, heavy stones of each rose high above Nastja's head and gave the route the feel of a canyon, quarried through solid rock. The darkening sky was a slim strip of patchy blue-black, high above.

Ahead, a solid line showed where this street ended before the city wall. The only turnings were into narrow alleyways between the buildings, probably leading to rear yards.

Nastja knew she could not check them all, so she kept walking, heading for the end of the street.

In the fading light of evening there were fewer people around, and so about halfway down the long, straight avenue she got a glimpse of a small, dark-clad figure darting around the corner at the end, then turning right.

Was that her?

Nastja increased her pace, switching the heavy sacks to her other shoulder and remembering to keep her face down. A downtrodden peasant.

She wanted to edge around the corner and sneak a glimpse at what was there, wanted to be forewarned. But, why would a peasant out on an errand do that? So, she continued around the corner with a gait that was idle and unconcerned.

And, there she was.

Her back was to Nastja and she was strolling towards two guards in baked leather who were stood to either side of a small postern gate in the wall. The men, both burly and running to fat and with dark hair that stuck out from beneath their simple helms, had been deep in conversation. They looked up as the woman approached. There was an arrogant sway to her hips, and she had her thumbs tucked into her belt with her elbows jutting.

Her shoulders and neck were tense, though. Beneath the bravado, there was anxiety.

'Hail, cousin,' she called, stopping before the two men.

Cousin?

Nastja continued a few paces more, keeping out of the woman's eyeline, before dropping her sacks and bending her back, miming a stretch after the discomfort of the heavy load. It was not hard to feign; her shoulders were sore. The bags were heavy.

'I'm working, Majleyn,' said one of the men. 'I don't have time for your shit right now.'

'Looks like all you're working on is your knowledge of local gossip,' she sneered. 'And it's not *my* shit that should worry you. Captain Trekjy sent me to get you.'

The face of Majleyn's cousin was suddenly serious. Nastja slung her sacks onto her shoulders again, reckoning that to linger any longer would attract too much attention.

'Why would Trekjy talk to you?' he asked, as Nastja began to walk away.

'Because I'm a big deal in this town,' she replied. 'And, because he trusted me to get a message quickly to my waste-of-space cousin.'

Why was she taunting him so?

Nastja walked as slowly as she could to remain in earshot.

'What you are,' replied the guardsman, 'is a common criminal. Everyone knows it and you'll be lucky not to end your days with your neck being stretched outside the walls.'

'You're the one who will end up on the end of a rope if you disobey orders again.'

Again. There was some background here.

'I just find it hard to believe anything you say.'

'Can you afford to risk it?'

The guard sighed. 'Where is he?'

'Yard of the Clothbolt Tavern,' replied Majleyn. 'He told me to take you there.'

Nastja walked on, and around the next corner.

She had seen the Clothbolt on her way through the town. It was a narrow-fronted building near where cloth traders and seamstresses had their shops. A ragged, stained bolt of yellow cloth had been pinned beside the wine barrel that hung above the door.

She could find it without following them. That might be safer.

Nastja turned right down the next street, which was little more than a lane behind yards that were fenced in with wattle or scrap lumber. The ground was rutted and muddy, and as Nastja hurried on the sounds of animals in pens and people talking washed over her.

'Get them chickens in the coops, the foxes are about…'

'You been drinking? You know you ain't supposed to drink no more…'

'…is this all there is for supper? Crime would feed the children better than your trade!'

So many conversations, so many stories. They assaulted Nastja's ears and as usual she was unable to screen any of them out. The noise threatened to become overwhelming, and her breathing quickened, even as the temptation grew to stop and listen, and learn.

Ellyah's face swam into her mind, and she forced herself onwards. Still gripping the sack, she pressed both hands over her ears to shut out the insistent cacophony.

The lane opened out near the main square, and Nastja turned right and right again. She was back on the same street. Crossing to the far side, she hurried along, heading in the direction of the walls once more.

Dusk was closing in and what light there was spilled from upper floors of the shops that lined the street. Businesses had shut for the night and the owners had gone upstairs to eat, then sleep.

Nastja was little more than a shadow in the gathering gloom.

Halfway up the street, orange cracks of light from shuttered windows cast triangular shadows across the cobbles. The Clothbolt Tavern.

Nastja was surprised to see more guards stood beside the doorway, and another couple before the alleyway at the side. Taverns were not normally guarded, as far as she knew. Maybe Buren was different.

Their aggressive stance and the way they eyed any who passed seemed to suggest that the inn was closed. Yet, the lights were on.

Before Nastja had time to ponder this new mystery, movement at the mouth of the alley caught her eye. The guards glanced around, then turned.

'Hey!' exclaimed one. 'What's going on here?'

Here she comes, thought Nastja.

Right on cue, the woman, Majleyn, sauntered from the alley mouth and turned to address one of the guards.

'My dearest cousin is drunk on duty, again,' she announced. 'We're taking him to Captain Trekjy. This can't go on.'

As the guard muttered an uncomfortable assent, two burly men sidled out of the alley with an unconscious figure slung between them. Majleyn's cousin.

His head lolled and his feet dragged in the mud as they hauled him out into the street. A third broad figure, dressed all in black like Majleyn and the other two men, shouldered his way out between the two guards.

Majleyn's cousin had been sober and on guard just a few moments ago…so what had happened?

One of the tavern guards stepped forwards. 'One of us should come along, as he was on duty…'

The two big men dragging Majleyn's cousin did not pause, but the third turned to face the speaker, blank faced. His black shirt and jerkin were tight and the outline of his body beneath was powerful, with thick, bunched muscles. The other two men had the same shape, and the same complexion.

Brothers?

'No,' said Majleyn, simply, and walked away.

Nastja had a moment of doubt.

There was something strange going on here. Something underhand, and probably illegal. The woman Majleyn had lied to her own cousin and then had lied to the guarding militia, and was now abducting the man with the help of these three brutal looking brothers.

She had been looking for them at the village back on the hill, that was certain, but was this business anything to do with them? There was no way to be sure.

Helping Ellyah was the important thing. Nastja felt panic rising at the thought of her friend trapped or hurt or…worse. She suppressed it but could not escape the gnawing feeling of worry.

Could finding out what Majleyn was doing help Ellyah? There was no clear reason why it should, but Nastja's instinct told her it might. In any case, she had nowhere else to start and was now filled with simple curiosity.

Why had she singled out her own cousin? Where were they taking him? Was the militia captain, Trejky, involved too?

Hefting the sacks once more, Nastja began following along the street in the same direction as the group ahead.

The gloom of dusk cast the streets into deep, forbidding shadows. More lights shone from windows; the flickering, pulsing glow of cheery fires and smoky rushlights stabbing out across the cobbles. Fewer people crossed Nastja's path as the streets quietened.

The day was nearly done, for most people.

Nastja bit her lip. If any of the group glanced back, they would see her. This would not be a problem when the streets were thronged with people, but now she would stand out. They might even recognise her from earlier.

'If you're worried about being spotted, don't follow,' came Ellyah's voice from Nastja's memory. She had a habit of dispensing sage advice after a successful pickpocket or minor heist. *'Work out where they are going, and be there waiting.'*

Nastja increased her pace and crossed the street, stepping out confidently from the shadow of the buildings, but keeping her shoulders slumped and her face down. She overtook the group and headed off to the left.

She remembered reading that towns in northern Buren often had street plans that resembled the spokes of a wheel. The central square, the hub, had been a meeting place of many roads and an obvious marketplace site. Houses had been built along the roads and filled in the spaces in between, and the town grew.

She skirted the very edge of the square and headed off down a side street. It would put her out of sight of Majleyn and the brothers, and hopefully out of their minds. Nastja had guessed where they were going, and if she was right then she could get there without needing to follow, then find a place to watch what they were doing.

Turning right, she hurried down a grimy alley. She switched the sacks to her left shoulder to keep her right hand free, in case she needed to use her belt knife. Shadowy figures moved in darkened doorways, but she kept her head down and kept moving.

Leaving the alley for another gloomy street, she turned right again. As she had expected, the square was now before her once more. Guards stood beside glowing braziers around the perimeter, and the dancing flames cast shifting shadows across the cobbles.

The memorial house in the centre glowed with an eerie light, the white stone ghostly in the night. Voices came from Nastja's right and she shrank into an unlit corner, doing her best to merge with the shadows.

'Your cousin's heavy,' came a gruff voice from nearby, sharp with irritation. 'Must be someone else's turn by now!'

The woman, Majleyn, strode into view, before pausing and turning. The speaker was one of the heavy-set brothers, still half-carrying, half-dragging the unconscious soldier in their leader's wake. Nastja's hunch had been right; they were heading in the direction of the temple.

'I'm the lookout,' said a different voice, as the last member of the group came into view. He loomed in his dark clothing, a solid black shape against the glow of the braziers.

'Maybe our leader should take a turn,' he said. 'She's always telling us how she's as strong and powerful as any man.'

Majleyn sniffed. 'Power is a lot more than having big arms.' The men groaned, as though it was something they had heard many times before. 'Anyway, I need to save my energy.' She took a deep breath. 'After all, he's my cousin so I've got to be the one to perform the rite.'

'And it'll work?' asked one of the brothers.

'It has to,' she replied. 'The blood tie will make it stronger than last time. We'll find them, and when we do, we'll all share the rewards.'

She turned and walked away, the brothers following awkwardly beneath the weight of their limp burden.

Nastja remained frozen in the shadows. Her mind worked furiously. Like misshapen stones being slotted together to build a drystone wall: what she knew, and what she could guess began to stack up to form a clear picture.

She would struggle to put it into words, but suddenly she understood what had been going on, and what was about to happen.

And she had to stop it.

TWENTY

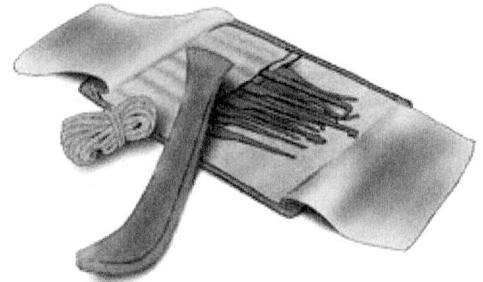

Waiting. Watching. Listening and remaining ready while her body was still, and at rest. Patience.

Ellyah was good at it and had had a good teacher. Savfa. She thought of him and smiled into the silent darkness.

She could recall every angle of his face, as though he was stood before her at that moment. The pinched hollows of his cheeks, the strong line of his jaw and the expressive thickness of his brows. They could be raised in surprise or amusement, or lowered in concentration or anger. They would always show her what he was thinking.

As a young girl, he had been everything to her.

'The best opportunists know when and how to wait and watch,' he had told her, more than once. He had never used the word "thief" but they both knew what he meant. 'And they know when to move, when to act. When to strike.'

As a foundling in the dark slums of Kereva, he had been a father figure to her at first, but more like an older brother later. He had become a lot more than that to her in the end

He had taken her under his wing as an apprentice, and as an assistant. As her teacher he had shown her the way, but had also acted as her guardian, and as her master. In truth, he had been her idol, and she had always aspired to match the masterful way he moved easily through the shadowy, dangerous underworld of the city.

Every line of his lean, strong body radiated confidence, agility and control.

Her lover? Never, although she had dreamed of it; a secret hope she could never share.

And then he had left her.

Left her for the job that he had decided was too dangerous for her. She had wept when she heard the news of the failed robbery. Hot, bitter tears had fallen in the knowledge he would never return.

Much later, she had learned that the raid had been a success, after all, and that the robbers had all escaped as rich men. But he had never returned for her. She had been drawn in and then abandoned.

She remembered every lesson he had ever taught, but the last had been the most powerful; work only for yourself. Trust no one but yourself. Everyone else will desert you when a better offer comes along. Everyone.

Her smile faded as she stared into the cold darkness of the cavern. His lessons about patience were the important ones, now. Silence surrounded her and all she could do was watch and wait.

She guessed that the hours were sliding past, the afternoon wearing away, up in the town. Up in the lands of the living. It was hard to be certain down here, though, in the unchanging, unmoving darkness of this lonely place.

The clash and rattle of a key in a lock was abrupt, but Ellyah did not startle or stir. A sudden movement like that, even a sharp intake of breath, could give her away and make her patience pointless. But, she opened her eyes wider, curious about what was about to happen.

The subtle groan of greased hinges in motion was followed by a steady slap of feet on stone. People were approaching down the tunnel. A group of them.

Ellyah peered out from her rocky alcove as the walls around the cavern were suddenly washed with throbbing yellow light. Harsh shadows were cast. The newcomers had brought lanterns.

Her skin pebbled with anticipation as a group of figures came into view between the flowstone columns. Each was dressed in black from head to heel, hooded and cloaked. As they neared, one of the shrouded figures glanced in her direction, and Ellyah's breath caught in her throat.

They were wearing a mask.

Dark eyes stared out, bare holes through a full-faced mask that was mostly black but striped with silver-grey. It gave the wearer a menacing, inhuman appearance. Another masked figure, shorter than the others, strode ahead and into the centre of the cave. Her gait betrayed her gender. A woman.

The woman? Thought Ellyah. She stared.

'Bring him forward,' she commanded, her voice muffled and distorted by the mask, the sound deadened in the underground air.

The bigger, taller people who were following behind stepped forwards into the light. They carried something between them, a limp bundle that they dropped unceremoniously at the woman's feet. It was a man's body; already dead or just unconscious.

Before, when Ellyah had seen people who were that limp but still living, they were either blind drunk or had been drugged. She watched on, fascinated.

'Make him ready,' snapped the woman. 'Guard him in case he wakes.'

The other figures detached themselves from the shadows and Ellyah could see that there were three of them. They kicked the prone shape over onto its back, and positioned directly on top of the six-pointed star carved into the cavern floor.

Her blood chilled as a feeling of bleak foreboding stole over her.

'Legs,' grunted one of the three men, and they spread out to stand by each foot, with the speaker remaining at the head. The prone man on the floor did not move or stir.

The woman herself took a few steps further, towards the stone pulpit, then stopped. She paused before the stark rocky finger, hands crossed before her. Waiting.

'Dusk falls,' she said in a low tone. 'The rest will be arriving soon. And *he* will come, too. Then, it will be time.'

Ellyah felt as though she was speaking as much to herself as to the three masked men. She seemed tense. Nervous?

On cue, the hinges creaked once more, and the sound of footsteps broke the oppressive silence. Ellyah counted them as they arrived. Not including the unfortunate lying on his back, the original four were joined by an additional seven figures, all hooded and masked.

They filed in silently and took up places around the edge of the icon carved into the floor. A couple broke away to light the candles in the carved niches, and the blank faces of their masks were burnished by the flickering flames.

If the presence of the prone man caused any surprise, they did not voice it, and any reaction was hidden behind the masks. For several long heartbeats, all was still.

Silence spread uncomfortably, like a wave that radiated from a placid pond to swamp the banks. Ellyah barely dared to breathe, and even then it felt like her heartbeat must ring like a warning bell from her hiding place.

One of the masked faces could turn in her direction at any moment.

Instead, they turned to face the pulpit. Footsteps echoed from behind where it stood, the footsteps of someone descending those steep spiral stairs.

Ellyah could just see the dark rectangle of the doorway between the edge of the alcove and a bulging, dripping column, and when the priest appeared there it was as an inky black shape that was a deeper shadow than the void behind. As he stepped forwards, the dancing candlelight lit the silver stripes of his mask with fire, and shone from a six-sided star on his breast, hanging from a chain around his neck.

That made twelve.

The eleven gathered below looked up as the priest stepped forwards to stand at the pulpit rock.

'Desya is present,' he said, in a quavering voice that echoed but died swiftly.

'Desya will be praised,' said those below in a monotonous chant. 'Desya will be served.'

The priest's next words were spoken in a more familiar tone. 'I see you have brought a subject. The ties of blood...?'

'This man is my cousin by blood,' said the woman.

'This is well. You know what must be done?'

'I must perform the rite,' she answered. Her voice was falsely flat. 'I am ready.'

'Then let it be done,' stated the masked priest, raising his arms. 'This time it shall be done properly, with the full cabal present and in the presence of Desya himself. The women will be found and brought before him for judgement, and we will receive our eternal rewards.'

No one spoke, but several of the masked figures shifted from foot to foot, nodding.

The priest's voice rang out once more. 'Prepare for the rite. Secure the subject.'

The two men at each foot stooped and clamped their hands over the unfortunate man's ankles, pulling his legs out wide and straight. Another two stepped forwards to grasp his wrists. The still-limp figure was now stretched out in a star shape, which Ellyah was sure matched the carved sigil on the floor.

She thought back to the pale, deflated shape of the mutilated innkeeper, and knew what she was about to witness. The question she had to answer was: why?

A sudden gleam reflected the candlelight. The woman, stood just inside the circle, had drawn a wicked, serrated knife. The pulsing and swaying of the candle flames made the whole cavern throb like a heartbeat. The atmosphere changed with the appearance of the blade, as though the temperature had dropped.

'Desya is here,' said the priest again, in a low, sonorous tone. 'Desya is all. Desya will be served.'

Dull, short-lived echoes came from the shadowy corners as the chant was repeated, over and over. They gave the impression that a much larger congregation was gathered, just out of sight. The effect was eerie. Ellyah felt the hairs on the back of her neck rise as the woman stepped closer.

Her hand tightened on the blade, knuckles whitening around the handle. Ellyah knew what was about to happen, but could not intervene. The unfortunate man pinned to the ground was already doomed, and Ellyah knew that to be discovered was to die with him.

She had to stay silent, stay hidden, and try to understand.

The woman knelt between her victim's legs, and Ellyah could see her chest and shoulders heaving with deep, raking breaths. Her distress was clear.

'Desya is here. Desya is all. Desya will be served.'

The woman's lips moved as she muttered the chant. The tension was a physical force, pressing down on Ellyah's chest. The man on the floor remained motionless and silent.

'Desya is here. Desya is all. Desya will be served.'

The woman reached out an unsteady hand and gripped the waistband of the man's hose. In one sudden, hasty movement, she wrenched them down and lunged forwards. The knife worked.

This forced him to wake. Now, he screamed: a piercing, keening wail of pain and shock. A cry of agony.

'First for Desya,' intoned the woman over her companions' continued chant. 'Our god and guardian, who will be restored.'

'Fate's eyes!' roared the man on the floor as his body writhed against the restraining hands. 'What are you doing? Stop! Let me free!'

She ignored him, taking a deep breath and moving to his right leg. The blade sliced mercilessly across the back of his leg, behind the knee. His scream of pain was sharp, and cut off his pleading.

'Second for Kaled,' she said, raising her voice over the sound. 'Who is fated to fall.' Another slashing cut to his other leg. 'Third for Conferan. Her courage will fail.'

Ellyah strained to keep still. Every instinct was urging her to move; either to flee this place or to intervene. But, there was nowhere to go, and nothing she could do without being revealed. She forced herself to watch as the rite went on, grimly curious to know what it was they were doing.

Majleyn moved around and stopped beside the arm of the man, who was sobbing and wailing. The knife flashed once more, cutting deeply across his wrist.

'Fourth for Tureank,' chanted Majleyn. 'The hunter will become the hunted. Fifth for Ome,' another cut, slashing the other wrist, 'who shall finally face his own death.'

'Desya is here. Desya is all. Desya will be served.'

The woman was bloody handed in the gloom, moving forwards to kneel beside the face of her own cousin. The jagged blade was raised one final time. Ellyah's fists clenched, in the knowledge that this poor man's suffering was about to end.

'Sixth for Mordea, brood mother and oppressor.'

The knife cut. Bright, arterial blood spurted and flowed. The man writhed as bubbling, gurgling sounds came from his ruined throat and gasping mouth.

'A life dedicated to Desya, the blood ties invoked. A prayer to Desya, that he might share his power.'

Majleyn moved back to stand before the pulpit, still clutching the bloody knife. She bowed her head, hands in front of her body and Ellyah could once more see her lips moving as she repeated the chant.

Ellyah did not know what to think. What was going on? Why had they done this?

For several long moments, nothing happened.

Then, *something* happened.

A greenish-yellow mist rose from the body. It shone in the gloom like tiny fireflies, or motes of dust caught in a shaft of sunlight. It gathered and swirled in the centre of the cave, then flowed like pouring water towards the motionless figure of Majleyn.

All Ellyah could do was gape.

The colourful cloud coalesced above the scene. The chanting continued. Eyes closed tightly, the candlelight casting her features with bright ridges and dark shadows, the woman was engulfed by floating sparks.

She extended her arms out before her, lips still moving, and raised her palms. She spoke, and the words were startlingly loud.

'Desya most wise, help me find them. Show me those who have defied you.'

Her outstretched arms stiffened, trembling with concentration and effort. The green-tinted specks of light danced and flowed around her like a cloud of spray raised by a cascading waterfall.

Then, the movement stopped.

Ellyah had seen flocks of starlings swarming around their roosts in the golden light just before dusk. Countless numbers of the birds like a dark, feathery cloud and as they twisted and turned, shapes would abruptly appear and vanish.

The way the sparkling cloud moved around the woman was like that. One moment it was a slow-moving haze, the next it had flashed into indistinct shapes that orbited her head.

Ellyah stared.

The grainy images merged and became more distinct, and the first that she could make out was the outline of a man. He moved as though striding along, although his luminous green feet moved on empty air. The shape was gauzy and translucent, as though at a great distance.

Another shape appeared and hung in the centre of the cave. This one was also moving, a darting, anxious scurry that spoke of haste, and fear. The glowing dust was packed more densely, giving this shape's appearance more solidity.

Ellyah could make out the shoulders and head, and something about the way they moved suggested that it was a woman. Then, their head swung and Ellyah was able to see their profile, and her breath caught in her throat.

It looked like Nastja.

The shape was no more than an outline formed of green light, but the proportions of the figure made Ellyah sure that somehow, she was looking at an image of her friend.

'This is one of the women!' gasped the woman through clenched teeth. Her arms were still outstretched and now her whole body was trembling with exertion. 'She is here, in Seyntlowe!'

Was the rite casting a spell to locate them? Was the image of Nastja a view of her now? How could this be? A sinking feeling stole over Ellyah, like a heavy weight pressing down on her shoulders.

A third figure had formed, closer to Ellyah still. The glittering dust poured in to form the shape, filling it like wine in a glass until it was solid and opaque. It was in a hunched pose though, which made it difficult to distinguish details.

Ellyah stared at it, studying it carefully as it formed from the air. Gradually, she was able to make out that the shape was that of a hunched, seated person. Their knees were drawn up to their chest and their head was bowed, as though they were attempting to make themselves as small as possible. Or as if they were trying to hide.

Ellyah raised her head slightly, looking out past her knees.
No.

'The other is here too!' gasped the woman. 'She is very close.'

'Concentrate on the spell!' urged the priest. 'It is almost complete. In a few moments it will show us exactly where both women are.'

In a few moments.

In a few moments these swirling lights would show these people, whoever they were, that Ellyah was not only in the same town but in the same room. Should she get up and run? The tunnel that led back up the surface was over on the other side of the circle.

Flight would be hopeless.

She would have to try it before much longer, though. She could not let herself be captured.

The woman continued to chant: 'Desya most wise, help me find them. Show me where they hide,' while her whole body, knees upwards, quaked and juddered with the effort.

The bright outline that Ellyah knew represented herself grew, and floated towards her. There was just no way she could hide from it. She could already feel the eyes of the chanting congregation following it as it drifted closer and closer to her hiding place.

Was this going to be the end?

Voices. Raised voices. A confusion of noise filtering from somewhere above and resonating around the space. Heads turned. Masked figures shifted uneasily. The woman continued chanting doggedly and the growing outline of Ellyah's hunched figure loomed ever closer.

Words were suddenly clear in the commotion above: 'Fire! Fire!'

The chanting faltered, then ceased.

'Fire?' was the murmur around the room.

'Do not be distracted!' ordered the priest, stretching his hands towards the figures below his pulpit.

But it was too late. The words of the spell died on Majleyn's lips, and the sparkling images faded away. Moments later the glittering green dust had also gone, vanishing as though it had never been.

Who would believe this? How could she explain what had happened, and how close she had been to a disastrous discovery?

With a swishing of dark cloaks, the circle broke up. A couple of the bulkier figures dashed across and grabbed the woman as she sagged. Hoods were swiftly raised and as a group they darted towards the tunnel.

Ellyah had escaped from enough tricky situations to see a fleeting opportunity when it arrived. She rose and wrapped her cloak around her shoulders. It was dark grey, but in this low light it would appear as black as the others. Ducking down into her hood, she strode confidently across the carved icon on the floor, avoiding the pools of drying blood, to join the rear of the group.

She strode past the two men who had their arms beneath Majleyn's armpits and headed for the shallow slope of the corridor, becoming one more hooded figure in the crowd.

'They are here! In Seyntlowe,' Majleyn was saying. 'We have to try again. We were so close!'

'Something's on fire,' came the grunted response from one of the men.

Ellyah kept her face down as she followed the rest of the cloaked figures. They filed through the gateway, now wide open, and onwards up the tunnel.

She noticed that the others were removing their masks and hiding them away beneath the thick folds of their cloaks, while pulling their hoods deeper over their faces. That was good. She would not stand out, not with her face likewise hidden by her deep cowl.

Smoke filled the top of the tunnel, and the hooded figures had to stoop to breathe clear air. Coughing came from up ahead, and with every step the heat increased; and with it the ominous crackle of burning timber.

'Hurry! Hurry!' urged voices from ahead in the smoky gloom. 'The back shed's afire. Come quickly!'

The group suddenly halted. Before them, and to either side were sheer, angular walls of mined rock. A small square of light above head height showed the way out. One by one, the cabal from the cave climbed towards it, making use of steps carved into the rock walls.

The smoke above was thicker.

Ellyah kept her head down like the others, until it was her turn to climb. Feeling her throat burn from the fumes, she swarmed quickly up and through the hole above.

A soot-smeared pair in the armour and garb of town guards helped her up, and she found herself in a small, timber-built lean-to. Hungry flames swarmed all over the walls, and the ceiling was lost in a pall of swirling smoke.

'Go! Get out!' urged one of the guards. The other reached out to help and Ellyah was suddenly filled with fear that he would knock her hood aside. That he would recognise her as a stranger. Darting towards the way out, she gave him a quick and hearty shove to the chest, and before he could say or do anything else he stumbled backwards.

Another doorway opened through a stone wall, and she hurried through it. Beyond was a house. The way led through a kitchen, now deserted, and along a passageway past well-furnished rooms. This was the home of a person with wealth.

Ellyah itched to pause and explore, but felt the threat of pursuit at her back. And the fire still raged behind her. She kept moving.

Straight ahead, she could see the street through an open door but the cloaked figure she was following turned away, heading towards a side door. Once outside, in a narrow, gloomy alleyway, they scurried away into the shadows without a backwards glance.

A secret society would have rehearsed how to scatter and hide in an emergency like this. Preserving their anonymity was crucial. At this moment, that helped Ellyah. She turned right, away from the brighter lights of the main street, and then left down a narrower alley.

Get away and stay out of sight.

A dark figure rose up from the gloom, and she jumped back, hand going to her belt, searching for the hilt of her knife.

'It's you,' said a voice. A familiar voice.

'Nastja?'

Nastja stepped closer, her face shadowed by the overhanging buildings, but a vague smile on her lips.

'It worked,' she said.

'What...?' Ellyah began, then stopped to think. 'You started the fire?'

'Like you did to save me in Ben Gedrin.

Ellyah almost laughed. 'I didn't...it doesn't matter. It worked. Thank you.'

'What was happening in there?' There was concern in Nastja's voice. Ellyah shuddered at the memory of the events, still recent and vivid. She could not explain it, and did not want to even describe it. Not yet.

'We need to go,' she said, instead. 'Someone might realise that one extra person left through the house.'

'Go where?'

'Glithoniel, like we planned. We can put these freaks behind us and get back on the trail of the jewel.'

Nastja's nod was an almost imperceptible motion in the darkness. Ellyah smiled down at her.

'We're still alive, hen,' she said, softly. 'Let's go.'

She reached out and took Nastja's small hand in her own, and moments later they were gone, two shifting shadows in the night.

TWENTY ONE

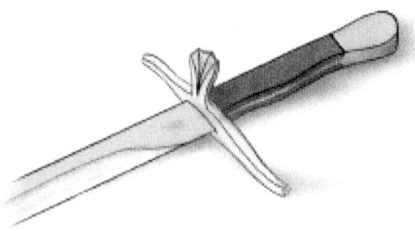

The high stone walls of the fortress town of Vor-Dun rose from the crags below as if the earth had thrown them upwards with the same shuddering force. Rounded, bulging cliffs of pockmarked rock towered over the sparse forests and green farmland at their feet. Bright yellow and vivid orange merged with plainer browns and greys, as though the rocks were smeared with honey.

The afternoon sun warmed the pale stone of the fortifications and their craggy foundations, but Styoyan's eyes were drawn to the spear points and burnished helmets that gleamed on the ramparts. This place, this Bureno settlement, was defended with a purpose despite being many leagues from the border with Anish.

It called to Styoyan. He had a sudden urge to be within the walls, to walk the narrow streets and to try to understand the politics at work.

He heeled Mahdesht into an easy walk, heading for the gritty road that wound up the steep slope to the north of the town.

He had followed no plan or map to get here, to the warm hills and downs of eastern Buren. All he had wanted was to leave the dirty streets and the humiliation of that border town behind. He needed to get far away from the scene of that ambush, that he might forget his foolishness, and his shame.

He had ridden heedless of direction, at first, just following his need to keep moving. To pause was to feel the pain of what he had lost, to remember anew the force of his father's contempt, and to risk surrendering to the urge to return.

But he could not yet right those wrongs.

His poor mother…

'*The truth will free you, however much it may hurt,*' had been one of Morehai's frequent sayings. The stern, greying elf usually reserved it for when he was about to deliver a scathing critique of Styoyan's fencing.

The honesty *had* forced Styoyan to learn, though. To understand himself and to confront his weaknesses.

Railing at the elf, arguing against his hard words, never achieved anything. Styoyan had grown and improved through reflection and self-awareness, never by anger or denial. Lessons learned, but learned hard.

His mother…

Styoyan longed to return and to force her to confront the truth. He often regretted holding his tongue at their last meeting but he knew that brutal honesty would not have solved his mother's problems. It was too late. Her mind was fragile, like a fine porcelain vase that held withered flowers, a brittle reflection of what had been.

To try to make her realise this would be like trying to open such a vase with a hammer. It would shatter into a thousand pieces. She would be broken beyond repair.

To protect her, he had to leave her behind.

And as for his father…

His father would never be swayed by mere words. To impress Earl Gevrin Jukeev, actions were needed.

Styoyan knew what he had to do. He would be like his noble ancestor, Steyfan. The story of Steyfan and Helein was ingrained in his very being. He saw himself in it, and a path to redemption.

Steyfan too had been driven into exile, and had returned from it a hero. He had become a great general, though none of his army had known his true identity, and had ridden back to Fordon in triumph.

Styoyan could picture it.

He would ride to the gates in armoured glory, leading his victorious retinue. His father would watch him come. Gevrin would not need to say anything, but would nod from the gateway to the keep, and give a slight smile.

That is when he would truly be home.

He shook his head to clear the fancy. There was a long way to go.

The fortress town lay directly ahead. A pale ribbon of road led along the crest of the ridge towards the first gatehouse. To his left and right, folded land stretched away, green and fertile. More frowning crags faced the looming walls across a deep valley where a river frothed and foamed.

As Styoyan looked out south, beyond the town's highest watchtower, the land flattened out into plains and fields bounded by hedges, the rich farmland that comprised the breadbasket of Buren. The horizon was a misty line between green and blue, hazy in the far distance.

Taller hills rose to Styoyan's right. Another deep valley lay beyond the nearest ridge, the path of the Firiway River cutting a swathe along the border between Anish and Buren, all the way to the sea.

The road was busy. Heaped wagons trundled up the hill and along the ridge carrying supplies to fill the granaries and larders of the garrison and the surrounding town. Empty carts passed Styoyan travelling in the opposite direction.

He turned at the sound of deep voices. A small party of dwarves were hurrying along the road, and soon overtook him. They were all wearing knee-length skirts of pleated wool and had short capes around their shoulders, their only apparent concession to autumn's deepening chill.

Styoyan had heard many tales of the dwarves of the region, and knew they could be both allies and adversaries. Partners in trade or bitter rivals. Peaceful neighbours or an aggressive presence in the land. He guided Mahdesht aside and gave the group plenty of room to pass.

Beyond the gorge of the Firiway River, jagged hills rose to peaks which marked the border, but further north these steepened into the huge, sheer cliffs of the Schism. It was still too distant to see from here, but the menacing, vertiginous crag hung over northeastern Buren. Unclimbable, impassable and eternal, it split the northern extents of Anish and Buren.

Between them, beside and within the rock of the Schism lay the Severed City. That great dwarf settlement that spanned the river near its headwaters, and also burrowed deep into the Schism's ancient cliffs.

It lurked at the edge of both Anish and Buren, in uncomfortable peace, but stubbornly refused to be part of either. Fortunately, conflict between the Severed City and the human lands that bounded it was rare, and if the stories were true then the dwarves were more likely to fight amongst themselves within the walls of their own city.

Other travellers stepped aside as the heavyset group approached, keeping their distance. Styoyan followed, trailing the dwarves as they approached the fortress town.

Doubt nagged at him as the first gateway loomed closer.

What was he doing here? How would he even begin to make a name for himself in this strange place?

He had to go somewhere, though. He needed a meal and bed for the night and at the very least he could find those here. Opportunities might come along though, so he had to remain alert.

He rode on.

The first gate was set in a sturdy wall of ochre stone that blocked further passage along the ridge. Pentagonal towers at each end sprang from the bulging cliffs, making approach from either end impossible. Soldiers in sturdy leather armour and bearing long spears defended the gateway. They wore pointed caps of iron with thick nasals that obscured much of their faces and gave them an inhuman appearance.

Those wanting entry were forced to wait as the guards questioned each party. As Styoyan reined Mahdesht in, the dwarves ahead were milling around before the gateway.

'Of course we follow the Five,' the leader was saying, irritation adding force to his words, his brows lowered. He held up one of his big, meaty hands and pressed it to his chest, fingers spread. 'Yer offend me by lumpin' us in with that heathen ilk.'

'No offence is meant, and none should be taken,' said the guard, voice flat. 'These are troubled times and the duke is careful.'

'We bring nobbut peace and honest trade,' grumbled the dwarf. 'And yer always treat us as foes.'

'Be calm, be at peace,' said the guard. He handed over a slim wooden plaque, branded with a complex rune. 'Take this token to the main gate and you'll be let through. May the Five bless your labours. Next!'

Still grumbling, the group of dwarves filed through and were lost to sight beyond the gate. Soon, it was Styoyan's turn. The guard glanced down at Styoyan's hands.

'Anise, eh?'

Styoyan nodded.

'What business brings you here?'

Styoyan swallowed. 'Seeking work. Just looking for a way to make a little silver. Is there any work here?' He realised he was gabbling. The leader of the guards looked down to where Styoyan's sword hilt protruded from his cloak, near his hip.

'Garrison's full but you might find a bit of guarding work at one of the taverns. Not today though, obviously.'

'Guarding taverns,' repeated Styoyan, nodding. 'Not today though, of course. Why not today?'

'It's a holy day, isn't it?' said the guard, as if speaking to a child. 'Conferan's day. I guess maybe it's a bit new for you Anish folk.'

The guards laughed and Styoyan felt his ears burn.

If only they knew who I truly am, he thought. But, he must keep that truth hidden. For now.

'Of course,' he said, trying to regain his composure. 'I had lost track of the days.'

The guard passed him a token and waved him through.

A clear space had been left between the first wall and the next, which was higher and enclosed the buildings of the town. A deep ditch had been dug, the soil at the base still bare; pale brown and spotted with pale, chalky flecks.

A narrow causeway carried the road to the next gate. It was barely wide enough for two carts to pass one another, and would leave any attacker who had breached the first wall horribly exposed as they attempted to assault the second.

Angular bastions protruded from the rear of the first wall, looming over Styoyan as he rode across the causeway. The ramparts on top were empty, now, but could be packed with archers who would be safe and able to shoot, even if an enemy had passed the first gate.

Styoyan was left feeling that any aggressive force in this area would be better off going around this town and attacking somewhere else. His next thought was that, of course, this was the point of such a fortification. The people of the town and surrounding areas must feel safe and secure knowing that this mighty refuge was there. It reminded him of Fordon.

'Who is the lord here?' asked Styoyan as he was waved through the next gate, after handing over his branded token.

'This is the home of Duke Vorban,' replied the guard.

'Vorban?' Styoyan had not heard that name before.

'Finest general in Buren,' explained the soldier. 'They say that a town defended by Vorban is saved. A town attacked by Vorban will be lost.'

This sounded like the sort of man Styoyan needed to meet.

'Does he take petitions?'

The guard snorted. 'He might. From nobles. But he's not here.'

'Not here?'

'No, he's been summoned to Glithoniel as an advisor to the High King. Spends half his life there.'

Styoyan thanked the man, and passed through the gate and into the town.

Within the walls, everything was built from stone. The streets were cobbled and all the buildings were of solid masonry, straight and square.

Little to catch or spread a fire, thought Styoyan

Bright colours filled his eyes, though. Streamers of yellow and pale blue cloth danced in the breeze where they hung from shuttered windows and in many of the doorways. Back at home, the festival of Conferan was subtle. It was a time when sources of clean water were revered, and before the day's feast there would be a ceremony where hands and faces would be washed.

It was a time to wash away regrets and look forwards to the new year, and to think about ways to ensure you passed the Veil with a light heart and pious soul.

Here, the celebrations filled the streets. People stood outside buildings in yellow smocks and robes, with great ewers of water in their hands of pewter or clay. Styoyan slipped from Mahdesht's saddle to walk on the same level as the revellers.

'Would you be washed clean, child?' called a voice from his right. A white-haired woman with creased skin and clear, dark eyes held up her jug and water slopped from the spout. Wordlessly, Styoyan moved closer and held out his hands.

'The past is the past,' she said with a smile, tipping her jug to send a stream of water over his outstretched hands. 'Let it wash away. Rain falls, tears drop, rivers pour endlessly to the sea. None can return from whence they came. All that matters is what is downstream.'

'Thank you,' muttered Styoyan, shaking the drips from his fingers. There was much in his past he would like to forget. And yet, could he?

'And your head?' asked the woman. Along the street, Styoyan could see others bowing low as the ewer-bearers wetted their hair. He copied. Chill water gushed through his long hair, and he shuddered as rivulets trickled down the back of his neck, beneath his robe.

'Be clean, be fresh,' intoned the woman as water dripped from Styoyan's nose and cheeks. 'Be renewed. Go with the blessings of the Five this day.'

He stammered his thanks again and wandered on through the streets. The water chilled his skin, and the experience of the washing had been surprising. He felt dazed and disorientated. What was he looking for here? Where was he heading?

Music lilted on the gentle breeze, and Styoyan let his steps be guided towards the sound. The keening melody of plucked strings mingled with the swell of voices raised together in song. He was unable to keep a smile from twitching his lips.

The style was different from the traditional, slow chanting songs of Anish, but music and song never failed to lift Styoyan's spirits.

A tavern stood on the corner, at a junction of cobbled streets. Wide doors on each side were thrown open, and a crowd of brightly clad people were gathered around the doorway, peering inside. They were singing a song that Styoyan had never heard before, along to a cheerful tune that soared out over the background noise. The words were of rebirth, renewal and forgiveness. It was sung with pure joy.

A moment later, though, the music faltered, and then ceased, and the harmony was shattered.

'What d'yer mean there's no ale?' roared a voice from within, and the crowd was flung aside as a huge shape surged out into the street.

Styoyan gaped.

It was a huge figure; broad and so tall they had to stoop to pass beneath the doorway. Their skin was dark as mahogany and as they lumbered into the street Styoyan noticed a slight upsweep to their ears, and that they wore slim rings on several fingers.

A half-elf, from Anish.

'I just want ale!' he bellowed.

A local woman was following him out, hands raised in a placating gesture.

'I'm sorry, but it is a holy day,' she said, in a worried voice. 'We cannot drink ale or wine on holy days, by order of the High King himself.'

'Stupid holy day!' roared the huge half-elf. 'Stupid king!'

There were gasps of shock and disapproval from the crowd. A leather-clad guard stepped forwards from where he had been standing against the wall.

'Mind your tongue, outlander,' he said. His fingers gripped the haft of his spear tightly.

The half-elf lunged out, his movement swift and powerful. An open hand the size of a plate struck the man in the chest, and he was flung backwards to land sprawling on the cobbles. The crowd shrank away, and several more guards rushed forwards, spears levelled at the huge troublemaker.

Styoyan took a step closer too, dropping his hand to the hilt of his sabre.

The looming half-elf eyed the spear points and the watching crowd, his head swinging from side to side like a hound on a scent. The very air crackled with the tension of the moment.

His eyes met Styoyan's, and his stare hardened.

'What?' he bellowed, head jutting forwards aggressively as he shouted the words into Styoyan's face. Despite himself, Styoyan took a step back. 'I'll get ale somewhere else,' grumbled the giant, before slapping the closest spear tip aside and striding away down a side street.

Styoyan blew out his cheeks. His heart was racing. What would he have done if the towering half-elf had turned on him? His hand felt tense, the skin clammy, as he released the grip of his sword and forced himself to relax.

He left the shocked crowd outside the tavern, now silent but for the hushed tones of anxious chatter, and walked on, leading

Mahdesht deeper into the town. His feet led him away from the busier streets with their sprays of colour and noise, and towards a quieter district near the southern walls.

Music still rang in the air, but it was distant and behind him. A louder rhythm pervaded the air, hammer and anvil, saw through timber. The sounds of industry. The heartbeat of a living, growing town.

Passing a narrow alley, a flicker of movement caught his eye. A dirty wagon, covered by a dirty sheet, stood at the far end, and as Styoyan halted his steps and looked more closely, a dirty youth wriggled out from under the cover. He darted away, up the alley towards where Styoyan stood.

As the boy got closer, Styoyan could see that his face was streaked with filth, his clothes were ragged, and his feet were bare. He clutched a bulging sack in his arms. It must have been taken from the wagon.

A thief.

The youth, a year or so either side of fifteen, looked up, noticing Styoyan for the first time. Their eyes met.

Styoyan had a second to decide what to do. By the time the dirty thief had turned to run, he was already moving in pursuit. His reactions had been honed by training with Morehai, his muscles built by swinging a sword. Where the lad was gaunt, Styoyan was well fed and rested.

A bare handful of heartbeats passed before Styoyan was close enough to grab the boy's wrist. He squirmed wildly as Styoyan clamped down with a firm grip.

'Get yer hands of us!' he moaned, in the clipped accents of eastern Buren. 'I'll clock yer one if yer don't let me go.'

Styoyan twisted his wrist hard, ignoring the boy's cry of pain. A moment later, a deft lift and shove had the boy's arm jammed behind his back and the sack fell to the floor.

'Thieving is no life,' he hissed in the boy's ear. 'You'll soon learn that, once you face justice.'

'I've got a big brother,' said the lad. 'He'll show you. Let me go…'

Styoyan ignored his protests and stooped, picking up the sack in his free hand. It was heavy and rattled as though it held dried beans, or peas. Not valuable, but still theft. Shoving the boy, he moved towards the wagon.

On his right, a gaping doorway opened off the alley, the boom and roar of the furnace and the rattle and clatter of metal on metal signalling that this must be a blacksmith's shop.

A group of people, men and women attired for travelling, were sitting on boxes and barrels near the door, around two men standing and in conversation. They both ceased and turned when Styoyan shoved the thief through the doorway. One of the men was bulky in the way that smiths often were. Cords of muscle rippled in his bare forearms and he wore a soot-smeared apron of thick leather across his broad chest.

The other was also broad, but with the heavy shoulders and thick legs that spoke of training rather than labour. He was shaped like a brawler, with fists like chiselled rocks and a flat face. A high forehead shone faintly above prominent, jug-handle ears. Pale eyes regarded Styoyan intently as he entered.

'I caught a thief,' said Styoyan, thrusting the youth forwards. 'Stealing from your wagon.'

'You bastard!' said the thief.

'What did he say?' asked the brawler, turning towards the group.

'Caught a thief,' said one of them. The big-eared man beamed.

'You saw him stealing?' he asked, in a loud and nasal voice. Styoyan had heard speech like that before. 'What did he steal?'

Styoyan raised the hand holding the sack, and gave the boy one more shove. The brawler's hand shot out, fast as a hawk's stoop, and he pulled the thief close.

'You got lucky,' he said to the boy, voice loud even though they were standing close together. 'You ran into an honest man.' He fixed Styoyan with a stare. 'Not many honest men around.'

He drew a knife from his belt and handed it to the smith.

'Heat that up,' he instructed. He looked towards Styoyan again. 'This man could have offered to share the spoils, or just taken them off you and not said a word. But he's an honest man.'

Styoyan remembered. One of his father's best fighting knights, Sir Kalek, had spoken the same way. The man had taken a heavy axe blow to the helm, and from that day on had struggled to hear anything, including his own voice.

'And you're especially lucky that this honest man brought you to me, and not my mate Jhari. Jhari isn't as kind as me, or as forgiving. If he'd caught you, he might have broken your arms or just busted your head open, if he was in a bad mood or thirsting for ale.'

The smith returned with the knife. It glowed red, and the thief tried to shrink away from it. The deaf man's grip must have been strong as iron, and he did not budge.

'I'm kind,' he said again. 'I'm going to let you walk away, with all your limbs still attached. And I'm going to let you go with a friendly lesson, so you won't forget.'

At that moment he pressed the point of the red-hot knife against the back of the youth's right hand. There was the hiss of searing flesh, and the boy gave a howl of pain that Styoyan found chilling.

'Don't go thieving,' finished the brawler, before releasing the boy. He dashed from the blacksmith's shop, sobbing and clutching his hand.

'We've all been there,' laughed the burly man, before raising his own hand. A pale, arrowhead shaped scar stood out from the darker skin on the back. The others laughed.

Something rose from the depths of Styoyan's memory, then. Another of Morehai's lessons.

'There is a manner of speech without words,' he had said. *'We will learn it together.'*

Like with all things, Morehai had taught it in a way that left no chance of forgetting.

Styoyan found his hands moving, remembering the shapes that he had practiced with his elf sword-master, during long hours where Morehai would refuse to speak with words.

You are deaf, he signed, pointing at the brawler and cupping his hand over one ear. The man's bluff, craggy face split into a wide grin.

Yes, yes, he signed, before striding over and throwing a thick, meaty arm around Styoyan's shoulders.

'An honest man,' he exclaimed, 'who knows hand-speech. Could do with someone like you around. You looking for work?'

Before Styoyan could respond, a wordless roar came from the street outside. The doorway was filled by a tall, broad shadow and then a dark-skinned, pointy-eared head was thrust into the room.

'No ale in this whole stinking town!' complained Jhari.

TWENTY TWO

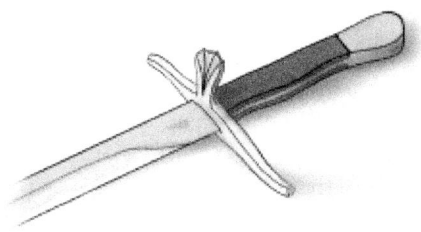

This place is a dump,' growled the towering half-elf, stalking across the room with a couple of long-legged strides before casting himself down to sit on a crate. It groaned beneath his weight. 'When are we leaving?'

'Soon,' replied the broad-shouldered deaf man, who Styoyan took to be the leader of this bunch.

'Who's this?' asked Jhari, nodding to Styoyan.

'New man,' replied the leader. 'He's an honest man, and I'm guessing he knows how to use that sabre.' Styoyan glanced down self-consciously. The hit of his sword had been hidden beneath his coat, but this man had spotted it. His eyes were sharp. 'I'm thinking that an extra guard to help us get to Glithoniel won't hurt.'

Jhari shrugged. Styoyan straightened, interested. Glithoniel, the famous capital of Buren. The oldest and largest city in the world, where Duke Vorban was meeting with the High King.

A city of opportunity.

The leader's fingers moved.

You want to come with us?

Styoyan signed back quickly. *Yes.*

'What's your name, friend?' asked the leader, aloud. Styoyan thought. He could not use his real name, not yet. He must be anonymous, just like Steyfan had been.

'You may call me Kalek,' he said, using the name of his father's deaf knight. 'And you?'

'I'm Skane,' said Skane. 'And these are my…colleagues You'll get to know them soon enough. Now, though, there's work to be done.'

He turned to the smith, who had been loitering in the background.

'Are we ready to load?'

'Let me check that my apprentices have put everything in the box.' He turned, and lifted a curtain before calling into the back of the shop. 'Arek! Rentav! You filled that box yet?'

Moments later, the shuffling of feet was heard, and two shabby youths in matching leather aprons appeared through the curtain, manhandling a large, square crate between them. They set it down in the centre of the floor and backed away.

'All there, master,' said one, ducking his head in subservience. 'All counted, sharpened and oiled.'

The smith shooed them away. 'Off you go.'

Styoyan looked into the crate. Low light reflected off the flat planes and sharp edges of an array of weapons. Short swords, battle axes and long, jagged knives. It almost looked enough to arm a small militia.

'Hands off!' ordered Skane as a stocky woman in dark clothes stood and reached towards the crate. 'These are for Glithoniel, and only then if we really need them. We've seen how twitchy the soldiers and knights are around here. If we get caught with a crate of weapons they'll lock us up if we can't fight our way out.

'We don't want that. Not yet.' He clapped his hands together. 'Get it on the wagon and let's make ready to leave.'

'So soon?' asked Styoyan.

'Yea,' replied Skane. 'They ask too many questions around here. And, I'm guessing Jhari has already made his presence felt.'

He glanced towards the huge half-elf, who just shrugged.

A couple of the group climbed to their feet and hefted the crate. As they carried it into the street, Skane turned and passed a clinking bag into the smith's sooty hands. The two men shared a swift handshake before Skane turned and herded the others towards the door.

'Let's go,' he said, in that distinctive nasal voice. His fingers worked as he signed towards Styoyan.

A journey.

As they gathered around the wagon, Styoyan felt a heavy hand on his shoulder. He turned to find himself looking closely into Skane's sharp, pale eyes. He leaned in close to speak into Styoyan's ear, pitching his words more quietly this time.

'What did you say your name was again, friend?'

Styoyan hesitated, but just for a moment, before replying. 'Kalek.'

'Kalek! That's right.' Skane's face broke into a wide grin. 'I'm good with faces, terrible with names. Welcome to the team, Kalek. It's going to be a fast trot to Glithoniel. Hope you're fit.'

'I have my own horse,' said Styoyan, gesturing to where Mahdesht waited patiently further up the alley.

Skane's grin did not falter. 'Very good, very good.' He peered past Styoyan towards where Mahdesht stood. His brow creased. Turning back, he signed:

A very fine horse.

Laughing, he clapped Styoyan on the back.

'The others will be jealous of us riding when they have to walk. Like we're the lords and they are the commoners, right?'

Styoyan laughed weakly. Skane hit too close to the mark. With a display of surprising agility for one so heavily built, he vaulted up onto the carts high seat and seized the reins.

'Let's roll!' he shouted, and his own horses tugged at the traces. Styoyan swung up onto Mahdesht's saddle and heeled the stallion into motion as the wagon wheels began to turn.

'Been to Glithoniel before?' asked Skane, passing Styoyan a clay flask. Styoyan took a sip then winced as the fiery spirit breathed a furnace trail down his throat. It gave him a chance to think up a convincing response.

'No,' he replied after a few moments, suppressing a dry cough. 'I have come straight from Anish. Like you.'

Skane shook his head. 'I wish. Been a long time since I was in Anish. We've been chasing six-legged horses across the world. Still are.'

A few days had passed. Styoyan had ridden easily behind the laden wagon, while the others, who called themselves the Mackems, walked alongside. Skane had led them on a route that followed twisting, ancient lanes bordered by grasping thorns and overhung by leafy boughs.

The coppiced woodland to either side were bursting with the flame of autumn; foliage of flaming red and orange danced in the breeze, but the going was slow.

Styoyan wondered at the unnecessary delay caused by the wandering route, when well-stoned turnpike roads ran between the towns and villages, until a narrow track opened out before a small town ringed by an earthen bank.

Skane reined in and the group came to a halt around the wagon.

'Look,' he had said, pointing with one thick finger.

Styoyan gazed out towards the dark brown banks that rose abruptly from green pastures. It took him a moment to realise what Skane was pointing at, but then slight movement caught his eye.

Thick poles had been driven into the bank, at an angle, and dark shapes swung at the ends.

Bodies.

Half a score or more lifeless shapes were dangling, ropes around their necks. A display. A warning. Crows and kites swooped in and flapped away again, feasting.

'I told you,' said Skane. 'They are twitchy around here, and getting twitchier. High King is nervous about something. Best to avoid the knights and their roadblocks.'

He turned to Styoyan, fingers moving in a simple sign:
Safer.

They skirted the town and followed another narrow, muddy trail through sparse woodland and between thick hedgerows, before the fading light forced them to halt for the day. Maris got to work lighting a small fire and a long-haired man named Axvyer made a stew of beans and shredded kale leaves before Skane passed the jug around.

'All over the world,' repeated Styoyan, once he had got his breath back. 'Why?'

'None your business,' snapped Jhari, almost invisible in the gloom beyond the ring of firelight.

'Jhari, it's fine,' said Skane. 'Kalek here is a friend. We were on a trading journey, obviously.'

Laughter rang out from the group at that, and Styoyan found himself laughing too. There was clearly more to this group than honest trade. They were not merchants. But, what were they?

'Truth is,' Skane went on, as the chuckles subsided, 'someone stole something from us. Someones. Pinched something very valuable from right under our noses and made off with it. We had no choice but to go after them.'

'Who stole from you?' asked Styoyan.

'Thieves,' rumbled Jhari. There were more sniggers.

'Three girls,' replied Skane ignoring Jhari or perhaps just not hearing him. There were groans.

'Give over, Skane,' said Maris. 'Don't…'

'What? I got no shame admitting we were done over by a group of girls. They were brave and smart, and led us a merry dance. If it had been one of you, I'd have told the tale with pride. They did well.'

There was an uncomfortable silence.

'Master wouldn't like to hear that talk,' muttered Jhari, after a few moments.

'What? Speak up.' Skane cupped a hand to his ear.

'You shouldn't talk like that,' said Jhari, more loudly. 'Master wouldn't like it.'

'They ain't here,' snapped Skane. 'And I'd like to think I'm safe to speak my mind around you lot without one of you reporting back.'

There was another silence, and the group stared at the ground or examined their fingers. A branch snapped in the fire with a crack and a sprinkle of rising orange embers.

'So, you'd sell me out?' Skane demanded, jaw tense. No one spoke in reply. Styoyan felt the urge to fill the gaping, edgy silence.

'Did you catch them?' he asked.

'Still on their trail,' said Skane, ruefully. 'We followed them into Buren from the north, and we've been a couple of days behind since.'

'They'll be further ahead since you led us in the wrong direction,' said Jhari, displeasure evident in his tone. There was an edge to his annoyance that carried through the group as though he had drawn a blade. Skane did not turn his head.

'We needed arms,' he said, calmly and patiently. 'And you know that's the truth. We'll catch up with them in Glithoniel. They can't be going anywhere else.'

'Yea,' agreed Maris, and the others nodded. Jhari was silent.

'When they try to shift the jewel, which they will, like they did in Ben Gedrin, it'll make a stir. We just need to be ready to jump when that happens. We can pass it straight onto the Master, get our silver and be gone.'

'She wants those girls, too,' added Jhari.

'Find the jewel and we've found the girls. Then it won't be our problem anymore.'

'What about that other mark you said we was to look out for. The lordling.'

'Yea,' said Skane slowly, deliberately. 'The noble Baron Styoyan Jukeev of Kereva.'

Styoyan's blood seemed to freeze. He stared fixedly into the fire, not daring to look up, terrified of meeting any of the others' eyes in case his guilt was obvious. He felt it must be shining from his face.

Jhari leaned forwards, the hard planes and angles of his face highlighted a soft russet in the low firelight.

'You said he was important. As important as the girls. How're we going to find him?'

'He's a rich noble from Anish,' replied Skane, with a dismissive wave. 'From the description I've got he's barely old enough to be shaving, and a bit of a wet blanket. He'll stand out like a struck thumb.'

Styoyan managed to feel slightly offended though his worry, but his overriding emotion was of fear. This group of men and women were tough and uncompromising, and were hunting him. What chance did he have if they discovered his identity? He did not even know why they might have been given his description.

Could his father have sent them?

He remembered his father's warning that refusal to do his duty would be considered treason. Could hunters have found him so quickly?

No, he assured himself. They did not know who he was, or this conversation would not be happening. He had time. But how long?

Could he buy them off?

He had plenty of money; a silver ring on each wrist and gold in his money pouch, but his father had far more. His best chance was to continue to play the part, and to keep his true identity hidden while he looked for a way to escape.

'Kalek?'

The name intruded through his whirling thoughts. That was him. He was Kalek.

'Yes?' He turned to Skane, before anyone had to repeat the question.

'I was asking if you had seen or heard any tell of this Baron Styoyan when you came through Anish?'

'No,' replied Styoyan, as Kalek. He had to think of that name as his own. 'Talk was all of Kotev and whether they meant to start a new war. You reckon this baron is in Buren now?'

'It's the way he was heading. And if he crossed the border, there's only one place he'll end up.'

'Star City,' said Jhari, sitting back again.

'Yea, Glithoniel,' said Skane. 'That's where he'll go, and that's where we'll find him.'

'I'll come that far with you,' added Styoyan, wanting to make sure they thought he had no reservations. 'I have always wanted to see Glithoniel.'

'We've a good trot to go,' said Skane. 'I'm going to get some sleep. We'll make an early start.'

The Mackems stood and began unrolling blankets onto the forest floor, and the noise of dead leaves crackling beneath their weight filled the air. Styoyan copied, but as he stood he had the unsettling feeling of eyes upon him.

Skane had frozen, half-turned on the felled log which was his seat. His eyes were on Styoyan, on his body. Styoyan looked down and realised that the rough cloak he wore had fallen open and the ornate hilt of his sabre was exposed.

Skane's eyes were fixed upon it.

Styoyan pulled his cloak back around himself, covering the sword and turning away, trying to convince himself that Skane could not have seen anything.

Styoyan was shocked into waking. His eyes snapped open. The stars were shrouded by a bulky shape, darker than the night sky.

It loomed closer, stooping down and reaching for him.

He heard a terrified gasp escape his own lips, and he reached for his sword which was lying at his side, wrapped in a fold of his blanket. His attacker was quicker.

They dropped and Styoyan felt thick fingered hands clamping powerfully over his own as a knee pressed down onto his legs. He was pinned to the ground, helpless.

Styoyan struggled, straining against the pressure on his hands. It was useless. His attacker was bearing down with a solid weight and an irresistible strength. All Styoyan could do was to wait for the blade.

His heart thudded.

Pressure lifted from one his hands, but he remained unable to move, his sword arm still clamped to the ground. As they shifted, the attacker turned slightly, and their profile was outlined by the faint glow from the dying campfire.

It was Skane.

The Mackems leader glanced around, then looked back down towards Styoyan. He raised a finger and laid it across his lips; a clear sign that Styoyan should remain quiet.

Styoyan nodded, but fear still thrilled through him like an icy stream. He had no idea what the man intended, and no idea what he was capable of. He could not help but fear the worst, however.

Skane lifted his other hand, although the pressure on Styoyan's body was still firm, and his fingers moved in hand-speech.

Do not move.

All Styoyan could do was nod. His eyes were wide, wanting to take everything in. Skane reached down and twitched back the edge of Styoyan's blanket.

The hilt of Styoyan's sabre gleamed with a dull light. Skane pointed at it, then when he knew Styoyan's eyes were on his finger, he moved it closer and pressed it to the hilt. Styoyan almost groaned. He knew now what Skane had noticed, what his thick fingertip was now pressing against.

His father commissioned several smiths who worked within Fordon to produce weapons, armour and other metalwork for the household. They were obliged to finish their work with a maker's mark, which was a version of their sponsor's crest.

His father's crest. The Jukeev house crest.

It was only a subtle form, five splayed lines, but it was well known across Anish. The motif was repeated on the sabre's short ricasso, and marked the wielder clearly as a member of the Jukeev family, or as a thief.

Skane had clearly come to the correct conclusion. He signed again.

I know who you are.

Styoyan considered denying it but quickly decided it would be futile. He did not know the signs, anyway, and did not dare to make a sound.

Skane gestured around the camp, towards where the Mackems slept.

They do not know.

Styoyan sighed. That was something. But as soon as Skane told them…

Skane lifted his knee from Styoyan's body and sat back. He could suddenly breathe again. The solidity and strength of the man had been sobering. Skane's hands moved again.

You must go. Fast.

Styoyan felt his breath coming in gasps. He needed to be calm. Skane was giving him a chance, which he had to take. He lifted his own fingers to sign back.

Why?

Skane shrugged.

You know hand-speech. You are an honest man.

He stood and extended a hand. Styoyan took it and let himself be helped up. Avoiding the deepest piles of dead leaves, the path vaguely lit by the campfire's embers, he screwed up his blanket and gathered his things.

Skane beckoned, urging Styoyan to hurry. Moments later, Styoyan was mounting Mahdesht as Skane held the reins. He passed them up and signed again.

Go quickly. I will lie.

Styoyan nodded, then signed back haltingly, thinking hard to remember the signs.

Thank you.

Skane's fingers moved.

One chance. If we find you again, I can't help.

Styoyan understood. Skane could cover for his disappearance now, but Styoyan's identity would be revealed. If the Mackems found him again, they would not have forgotten his face.

Why do you hunt me? signed Styoyan.

Skane shrugged, then with deliberate slowness made a gesture that was not hand-speech, but was nevertheless completely unambiguous. He drew one finger across his throat.

Styoyan gulped and turned silently, touching his heels to Mahdesht's broad flanks, and left the dark camp behind him.

They said that Duchess Telivaina was a seer. She was rarely surprised and her ability to foresee the way events might play out often seemed mystical.

She raised herself from a well-padded chair as she heard hoofbeats approaching along the drive. They came to halt before the house, and she rose. Her son was home.

As she moved through the house, servants hurried to get ahead of her, to prepare for the arrival of the earl. They kept their heads bowed and moved with the stiff energy of those nervous and anxious to please.

All knew the rumours and Telivaina did nothing to dispel them. Fear, respect and obedience were what she required from those who served her. Those who failed to show those things learned what she was capable of very swiftly.

Many years had passed since she had taken this house, this comfortable well-built manor, from its former occupant. He had thought he could play this game of power and be victorious, but had not reckoned on an opponent of Telivaina's guile.

Until she had defeated him, he had barely known of her existence.

The household and the local people still spoke of her triumphant arrival in hushed tones. Their previous master had not been liked, but to see him replaced so quickly and so decisively by this mysterious, dark-skinned elf had been a shock.

Whispers of sorcery and otherworldly knowledge still lingered, and she let them.

She entered the hall, daylight streaming in through the open front doors. A moment later, the doorway was filled with the huge shape of her son, Earl Yuvakudu. She smiled in welcome.

Duchess Telivaina was not a mystic, or a seer, or an oracle. She merely watched, listened, waited and considered all ends before acting. And when she acted, it was always swift, decisive and final.

Right now, her son had returned from his business in Seyntlowe later than anticipated, which meant that something unexpected had occurred. One look at his expression told her that something was awry.

She spoke, loudly enough for the gathered household to all hear. 'Be welcomed, my son. I fear you bring ill news from Seyntlowe, however.'

One of Yuvakudu's black eyebrows rose, and several of the servants raised their hands in alarm. She saw eyes widen. Maintaining her reputation did no harm at all.

Yuvakudu ducked beneath the doorframe, his towering height obliging him to do so to enter the house, before he inclined his head once more, this time in deference to her age and status.

'My heart is full to be with you once more, my mother and duchess,' he said in his rich, baritone voice. 'And, as always you see true. There was a disturbance in the town while I was there. The captain of the guard's house was attacked with fire, and the arsonists escaped.'

'The town survives?'

'Yes. The blaze was small. It is the unpunished crime that fills me with regret and anger.'

Telivaina nodded. 'I will have to inform the council of the High King. He already fears insurrection.'

'He may tighten his grip still further.'

'Indeed.'

'The people already complain of injustice. Of tyranny.'

'Do they indeed?' Telivaina raised an eyebrow, the barest smile twitching her lips. 'Put out further notices reminding them that these things are done in the name of the High King, who only wishes for innocent citizens to live in peace and safety.'

Yuvakudu bowed. 'It will be done.'

'Let all my knights know of this. They may need to muster their forces quickly should the situation…escalate.'

Yuvakudu said nothing, but his eyes were knowing.

'I bring a gift,' he said. He turned and gestured to one of his bondsmen who were waiting on the drive. They hurried forwards bearing a small but weighty box. 'One of my knights confiscated a crate of *strommin* during a wagon inspection at Fletford Bar. They thought of you.'

'How kind,' said Telivaina. 'You have their name?'

'Of course. Are you hungry?'

'Somewhat. Open the crate.'

A prybar was found and the lid of the crate was levered off. A powerful, fishy smell filled the hall but something about the packing caught her eye.

'Lift that layer of cloth,' she ordered.

Duchess Telivaina was rarely surprised, but when Yuvakudu's bondsman stepped forwards and lifted the cloth that wrapped the fish, her eyes widened.

The crate was filled with weapons.

The wicked blades of axes, short swords and jagged knives gleamed, packed tightly in the bottom of the box.

'I did not know—' began Yuvakudu, bewildered.

His mother cut him off with a long, loud peal of laughter that echoed from the ancient stones of the hall.

A true surprise could be a rare joy.

PART FOUR

TWENTY THREE

Snow swirled incessantly from a sky that was a perpetual, leaden grey. The ground was white, features rendered indistinct by the freezing blanket cast across this land.

The landscape had been painted with colour when Halok had marched proudly across the countrey with the great army of Kotev. Fertile green fields had led to hills purpling with tough, springy heather and speckled with yellow sprays of prickly gorse.

No longer. Autumn had turned swiftly to winter as the Kotevari advance was slowed by the constant ambushes of the red-clad giants with their fearsome swords, then halted as the first snows swept down from the menacing northern mountains.

'The land itself fights against us,' Halok had complained.

Now, he stood shivering as he guarded the perimeter of one of the advance camps, as high and as deep into the hills as they dared to venture. A forged brazier stood between him and his companion, Guston, but the paltry embers did not warm him at all.

He stamped his feet in leaky boots that were roughly wrapped in furs.

'We should have been home by now,' said Guston, echoing Halok's thoughts. 'They promised. Duco Buzurg promised. They'd never see us coming and we'd sweep them away. All the *tecati* said so.'

'They can say what they like, can't they?' replied Halok, bitterly. 'They could have said anything. It's not like we had any choice then, nor any choice now.'

Guston sniffed. 'Did you get a scarf? I didn't. Got pushed out of the way when they brought the last load up from the south. I'm freezing.'

'Have mine for a bit,' said Halok, with a sigh. 'I'm not feeling too cold.'

He handed over the strip of dark fur and Guston passed him his short-hafted spear as he draped it around his neck. It was not much, but it might help get him through the grey hours until full light was in the sky.

When the forces of Kotev had first swept through the outlying Banahgarian villages, the houses had been ransacked in an excited search for gold and jewels. They had found little. Now, what raids could still take place through the grip of winter were for supplies of food and warm clothes.

Halok had never valued scraps of fur so highly before.

'What was that?' said Guston, gripping his spear more tightly and peering out into the bleak whiteness. Halok scanned the area too, squinting as tiny icy flakes settled on his eyelashes and chilled his cheeks.

The camp was in a dell, which provided slight shelter from the driving wind and bitter cold. Lumpy slopes rose beyond their position, their features obscured by the white blanket, and tall evergreen trees rose in clumps.

Snow clung to their needles like bulbous, rounded limbs, reaching out hopelessly. Halok could not help seeing them as frozen gargoyles, and shivered as he tried to put the campfire stories of the wild beasts of this savage land from his mind.

Wolves, bears and worse could lurk just out of sight, teeth and claws ready to tear.

All was silent.

'It was nothing,' he said. 'Just the snow settling.' Nothing would be moving in this weather, surely.

The snow continued to sift down, pale specks against a leaden grey sky. Back in Tayo, Halok laboured in a granary. The fine white flakes reminded him of the pale, powdery flour that coated his hands and sleeves at the end of a day.

'One big push,' he said, turning to Guston. 'One hard march in spring, once all of this has thawed, and the country will be ours.'

'You believe that?'

'The *tecati* are confident, and we'll be reinforced in the spring. Won't matter how good these swordsmen are, if they are outnumbered a score against one. They'll lose numbers, they'll lose ground, then they'll surrender.

'Then we can go home.'

He turned back and a creature of shadow and frost burst from the snowy bank before him. It loomed over them, covered head to toe by dark fur. Snow seemed to cling to the creature and swirl around it, obscuring its appearance.

Guston grunted in fear but lowered his spear and thrust it towards the apparition. He struck nothing but empty air as the attacker seemed to flow around the point, closing in.

A shining blade appeared in its fist and lashed out. Guston fell, blood gouting from his throat and splattering onto the snow, the pure white sullied by the shocking crimson spray.

Halok brought his own spear to bear with trembling hands, desperately moving to defend himself but it felt as though he was moving through deep water. The towering creature of snow and fur turned and palmed his thrust away with dismissive ease.

Snow swirled into his eyes as Halok tried to dodge back, to defend himself, but his attacker was as swift as a shadow. He saw a twitch in the figure's broad shoulders, but never saw the blade that struck him.

Pain lashed across his neck, and he felt the damp warmth of his own lifeblood pouring down his chest, and soaking into his clothes. His mouth opened but he could not draw air into his lungs. His knees sank into the snow as he collapsed, darkness spreading to fill his vision.

As he died, his last thought was that the camp was truly under attack by a demon of the wild woods. A creature of the cold waste.

Nothing human could move that fast.

Morgan Blane straightened after cleaning his seax on the jacket of one of the dead *hafioh* spearman. He noted that it had been made by Banahgarian hands, like the furs that wrapped around his own wrists and ankles.

These invaders had taken so much.

He sheathed his blade and took a moment to examine the scene. The bulk of the Kotevari camp lay away to his left. It was close enough to see the thin plumes of smoke from their paltry fires but not near enough for the fight to have been overheard.

Not that it had been much of a fight.

If either of the Kotevari had thought to shout a warning instead of pointlessly trying to attack him, he might have been forced to flee back into the snowy land. But, instincts of self-preservation could be relied upon to outweigh logic in most people, especially those without proper training. He had applied the lesson of the owl; the teachings of the owl-headed god of wisdom, Glemme. Strike hard, before your enemy knew you were there and be gone before you were in danger.

He had struck silently and fast, and it meant that he had a little time.

The pair of spears were javelined up the slope and out of sight, before he stooped to their dead owners. They were small, slight men and he was able to heft one of them up over a shoulder with ease.

Stooping, he wrapped a hand around the ankle of the other, and trudged away.

His boots were wrapped in heavy fur and fitted with a stiff wooden sole, wider than his foot. With the underside also furred he could walk easily on soft snow without sinking in. What tracks he left would be difficult to identify.

The snow fell in thicker flurries as he skirted the camp, the upper slopes of the dell to his right, the smoke still rising to his left. That was good. The fresh snow would cover the bloodstains.

Let them talk, spreading more tales of creatures who could drag men away into the snow without leaving a trace. Fear was a powerful weapon against the weak and credulous.

At the other side of the camp, he found what he was seeking.

It looked little more than a snowy mound at first, but Blane had been watching carefully and knew what it hid. He had not acted until he was certain. Dropping the body from his shoulder, he dragged the other onwards and laid it at the edge of the heap.

Another surge of snow blew across on the icy breeze, and the mound shifted slightly. A face stared up at Blane. Its eyes were glazed, and the skin was blue. It was the face of a frozen corpse.

This was a pile of Kotevari dead; lost to the cold when the ground was too hard to dig graves. They had been piled here, just outside the camp, instead. It was a pitiful sight and a sign of their weakness. He would report on this.

After adding the other body to the pile he stalked away, a silent fur-clad shape moving through the blizzard.

These men had been led here with false tales of plunder and conquest, and now their bodies lay with just a thin blanket of snow covering them. Unburied and unburned, their souls would find no escape from this earthly realm. They would remain in eternal dishonour.

There was a word in Banahgarian for those unhappy, unworthy dead who would never rise to the great halls of the ancestors, or be reborn into the land itself: *draugr*.

These unhappy spirits lingered in the liminal places of the land. They dwelled in dark, wild woodland, atop the highest peaks or beneath the dank, still waters of upland pools. They hated the living and their cruel, grasping hands were always ready to claim the unwary.

He brushed past the branches of an isolated fir tree, branches heavy and drooping with the weight of snow. *Draugr* could lurk within the twisted shapes of these trees, he knew, and sometimes their leering faces were visible in the white-blue shadows.

At this time of year they were frozen, though, safely encased in snow and unable to harm the living.

Huddling in the lee of one such tree, he looked down at the Kotevari camp where it spread across the bowl-shaped vale. Flimsy, conical tents clustered around guttering campfires where the damp timber smoked and spat.

The men stayed close to one another. Their morale was low, and their postures showed that they were dispirited. They were weak and getting weaker. A swift raid could break a camp such as this and drive their lines further back, if only he could convince the Grandmaster to spare the men.

Few could move as quickly through this landscape as Blane, though. He took no particular pride in this; it was just the plain truth.

Blane would listen to the Grandmaster's words. They were always founded in deep wisdom, and beyond reproach.

The Grandmaster's insight had shamed him, last time they had met. As much as a man could ever be shamed by the truth. The true shame would be grasping the lie like a shield to protect your pride.

'Eain Connow,' Helden Haradsson, the grandmaster of the Claihed, had said.

All twelve of the masters were gathered in a *claidah* off the great hall in the fortress of Osturbrost. Clad in simple singlets, they sat cross legged in a wide circle, facing inward. The room was warm, with a great fire roaring at each end and Blane felt his weary muscles throbbing and stretching in the heat.

He had returned to the capital that day, running the forty miles from the Dall and avoiding Kotevari patrols as he went. A short sparring session had followed, and now he was ready to give his report.

'There was no sign of the boy,' replied Blane. 'The villagers spoke of Claihedehlar arriving and driving off some of the Kotevari, led by Connow. And the trail led to a box quarry, where there had been a battle.'

'All dead?' asked Skyle Burns, the oldest Claihed master.

Blane shook his head. 'One escaped. I found another trail from the top of the quarried wall. Led westward, through the hills and towards the mountains.'

'Connow,' said Caedmon Skaarn, who was sitting next to Blane. He had been Blane's sparring partner this morning and even sat still his thick arms bulged with muscle. He was slow, but strong.

'There's no way of knowing that it was Connow,' replied Blane, shaking his head. 'Only that one Banahgarian seemed to escape.'

'I'd say if one of that group had the skill to fight his way clear,' said Burns patiently. 'It was Connow.'

'Perhaps,' said Blane.

'What else did you find?' asked the Grandmaster.

'The trail led to a high pass through the Beinuirm Skele. And then…' Blane hesitated. 'It led out of Banahgar. I did not follow it further.'

'You went far enough,' said the Grandmaster. 'So, what are your conclusions?'

Blane sighed. 'If it was Connow, and I agree it's possible, then like his grandfather before him he has deserted the Claihed. He disobeyed direct orders, led his command to battle and death and then ran.'

He bowed his head. 'It was my decision to select him. I take responsibility.'

'You hold Connow to blame for all this, then?' said the Grandmaster softly.

Blane paused. Like all the Grandmaster's questions, it was loaded with meaning. It was a challenge, an attempt to provoke thought. The correct answer would not always be evident.

'I hold him responsible for the deaths of those he led,' he answered, eventually. 'Had he followed the orders that I gave him, they would have been safe.'

'Our orders,' replied the Grandmaster, 'were what led him to be there in the first place. Only our direct instruction put him and those unfortunate young men on that road.'

They had sent Connow and a group of younger soldiers away from the front line. The fleet of Kotev had sailed up Osturfjord to attack the harbours of the River Ostur. The Claihedehmore were to be sent there to prevent them gaining a foothold on the shore, and so it made sense to send the younger, more inexperienced soldiers in the other direction. Out of harm's way.

'But,' began Blane. 'We did not know—'

'Ah,' interrupted the Grandmaster, but in a mild tone. 'We did not know. It is true. We did not know that there was another army marching through the Dall. We did not know that we were sending those young men directly into their path. We did not know that Eain Connow would face the most terrible choice, between defending innocent Banahgarians and following orders.

'We did not know, we who call ourselves "masters", and yet we judge young Connow so harshly?'

Blane felt as though the Grandmaster was peppering him with physical blows, but everything he said was true. These were just facts. He could feel Skaarn next to him, the shadow of a smile on his face at Blane's obvious discomfort.

'He ran,' said Blane. 'He ran and he did not return.'

'That is true,' said Haradsson. 'That is one of the facts. What other facts are available to us? What are the ends of this unfortunate event? What can we learn?'

'Connow's decision to disobey orders saved many,' said Burns. 'Those in the village and others nearby. It gave them a chance to escape, a chance to spread the alarm.'

The Grandmaster nodded.

'He told off the young ones when he went to help the village,' said Maichen Munrae. His voice boomed in the confines of the small room. 'A Claihedehlar named Haefrad arrived at Vekwicc with the Hniffare, messages from Sudvirke and a warning. We sent a force down the Dall road as soon as we could, and slowed the Kotevari advance.'

The Grandmaster nodded once more, and Blane once more saw the hard truth. His focus had been on Connow himself, and not the consequences of what he had done.

'And what of Connow himself?' asked the Grandmaster, as though reading Blane's thoughts. 'What can we learn of him? What can we guess?'

'He lacks courage,' replied Blane immediately. There was a frosty silence. It was as though a cold wind had blown through the room, and he knew that he had misspoken.

'We know this?' asked the Grandmaster, quietly.

'We do not know,' admitted Blane. 'But we know he ran.'

'He did. He ran away from the village. He ran away from the road. And what happened?'

'The Kotevari army followed him.'

'Quite.'

Blane was silent as he thought this over. He had not considered what the Grandmaster was suggesting: that Eain's flight was a deliberate attempt to lure the enemy away. Intended or not, it had saved lives and bought time.

'If that is true,' replied Blane, words edging out slowly. 'Then where is he? Why has he not returned? He's capable of sneaking past the Kotevari lines, just like I did.'

It was the Grandmaster's turn to remain silent. He closed his eyes, his back perfectly straight and his thick-fingered hands resting easily on the knees of his crossed legs. He was a picture of calm and serenity; at peace and yet ready.

Blane opened his mouth to speak again but paused. He knew there was something else coming, and after several heartbeats more, the Grandmaster spoke again.

'There is an opportunity for you to learn something from this tale, if you are open to it.'

Connow ran. He ran to lead the enemy away from the nearby villages, and to delay their advance. He sent another Claihedehlar away to carry the messages and sound the alarm. Blane understood all of that. What he could not understand was why the boy would not return when the danger had passed.

The path to the self was through learning. To learn required the humility to admit your ignorance, to admit that there were things you did not yet know or understand. In this instance, there must be something more than the facts on the surface. Something about Connow that Blane had yet to consider.

What would I have done? he thought, and that question itself suddenly gave him the insight he needed. He was second-guessing Eain's actions through his own experience. Experience had shown him that they were very different people. In what ways were they different?

'He felt more than fear,' said Blane. 'A stronger force than just being afraid. He felt shame at what had happened and...' Blane searched for the right word as he tried to imagine Eain's feelings, in that moment. 'Shock.'

The Grandmaster nodded. 'His first command in action. His first time seeing bloodshed. Likely as not, his first kill.' He looked around the room. 'What had we done to prepare this boy or any of our young soldiers for that? Who in this room remembers the first time you killed another?'

There were nods from some, while others shook their heads. Maichen Munrae looked down at his huge hands.

'I felt like a monster,' he said, his voice thick and gruff. 'I knew it was the right thing to do, for my country. But I heard them die. Heard the last breath leave their lungs. Saw the light in their eyes go out.'

'And we let young Connow go through that as the eldest, as the highest rank present,' said the Grandmaster. 'The blood of his friends on his hands and the blood of enemies on his blade. Is it any wonder he felt that he had failed? Is it any wonder he fled?

'We taught him to fight but gave him no instruction on how to kill.'

The Grandmaster's astute observation had troubled Blane from that moment to this, through the months that had passed from the first chill winds of autumn to the heavy snowfall of winter.

His mind had been closed about the fate of the boy, and what had troubled him most was how he had clung to his initial conclusion rather than the mistake itself. There was no shame in being wrong, only shame in refusing to admit a mistake.

He needed to meditate further upon this lesson.

But not now. He had counted the tents and noted their disposition, and it was time to return north to Vekwicc. The other Masters must be told what he had seen.

The war was not over, and even if many of the Kotevari froze to death as the cold fist of Banahgarian winter gripped the land and squeezed their encampments, they would be reinforced in spring and the Claihed would be hard pressed once more.

He squinted against the tiny specks of ice that were driven into his face by the gusting wind and moved past the pile of bodies once more. Snow had drifted across the two men he had just killed, and soon they would be little more than two indistinct frozen lumps on the heap.

His footprints were already half covered, shallow dishes filling with snow, and the splatters of blood were just pink shadows beneath the surface. The signs of what had really happened here would remain, to the eye of a skilled tracker, but nothing Blane had seen so far suggested that any among the Kotevari had that expertise.

Retracing his steps, he stepped over the broken snow that marked the entrance to last night's hiding place, a burrowed snow hole. For many the cold night cocooned in ice would have been an unbearable ordeal, but, Blane was not the same as most. It was already less conspicuous, tucked between two heavily laden fir trees, but he stamped the area flatter before moving on.

The blizzard would do the rest.

As he loped away, he should have been focused on what he had just seen, the strength and number of the enemy, but once more he was distracted.

Try as he might, his thoughts kept slipping back to the fate of Eain Connow.

TWENTY FOUR

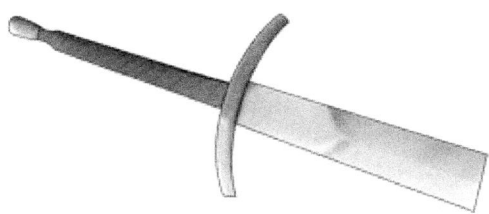

The sword felt unfamiliar in Eain's hands.

He had owned it for many weeks now, handled it often and had used in battle more times than he liked to remember. It had tasted much blood. But this morning it felt alien.

It was a bright day. The low hanging clouds had been blown away by a lively breeze from the south, and the sky was blue. Eain knew that the first snows could have arrived in Banahgar by now, but he stood here in his shirtsleeves and felt the sun warming his back. Ice touched his heart, however.

Morlen lay on his back, shoulders pressed down onto a flat boulder. Two heavyset warriors held him there, although Eain could see his eyes rolling wildly. A length of cloth tied between his lips served as a gag.

The others who had conspired to kill Daeron Teleri were similarly restrained and gagged, all lined up on the edge of this rocky plateau. They had all struggled and writhed as they had been dragged into place and forced down, but now they were all held still.

Their throats awaited the sword.

'I do not know if I can do it,' Eain had said to Klay, as they sat huddled together in the grey light just before dawn.

'Hold yer sword, swing,' replied Klay. He had woken just moments before and his pale eyes were screwed up against the morning light. 'Try ter 'it the neck.'

Eain sighed. He should have expected such a response. Perhaps he should have held his tongue, but his hands were already shaking with dreadful anticipation. He had needed to speak to someone.

'I mean, to execute them. To kill them. I don't know how to make myself do it.'

Klay shook his head. 'I don't see 'as yer've got a choice, youth.'

'Could someone else do it instead?' he said. His words sounded weak even as they left his lips. He could not hold them back, though. 'Do they really need to die?'

'This is Tayo,' said Klay, blinking and fixing Eain with a stare that was at once patronising and filled with pity. 'When yer've caught a hornet, yer don't keep it in yer cupped 'ands. Yer crush it afore it stings. To do owt else would make you a fool.'

Across the camp, people were beginning to stir as the early morning light brightened the ragged sky. The clouds that had hung over the camp that night had scudded away, revealing a sky that was shifting from a colourless grey to the palest cornflower blue.

Eyes were narrowed against the light, as the fog of sleep faded into the slow, uneasy wakefulness of a new day. A day that promised blood.

Klay stood and Eain was surprised to feel one of the dwarf's heavy hands on his shoulder. Clearly, he had learned by this time that it would not lead to either of them ending up with broken arms.

'Ah've known plenty of men like Teleri before,' he said. 'He won't truck with those as disobeys him. Not one inch. You've got two choices. Swing the blade, or put yer own neck on't block.'

Eain had been forced to accept the simple truth of this, no matter how little he liked the choice.

Daeron Teleri had been a remote, distant figure that morning. He had stood apart as the camp was struck, surrounded by the usual guard of Eagle Sisters. Their eyes were veiled and even in the camp they had arrows nocked to the strings of their bows. Teleri was taking no chances.

Klay stomped off and Eain watched him go.

Though he was a foot or more shorter than even the Tayan men of the camp, the top of his head barely reaching chest height on most, his shoulders were much broader. His retreating back was a solid square beneath his thick leather arming jacket.

Eain still did not know what to make of the dwarf. He was irritable and abrasive, and the way the other mercenaries deferred to him spoke of respect edged with fear. Many of the camp went to great lengths to keep out of his way.

But he knew of Holt Cookson and clearly cared for the man's fate. He had cursed the foolish nobility that led Elras to his death, and Eain felt that it was driven by genuine grief.

Klay and Elras had seemed close, as close to friends as mercenary fighters ever were.

'Not yer business,' had been Klay's reply when asked anything about his past before their meeting. Eain knew that the dwarf had been born in Tayo and had recently returned from Ben Gedrin. Klay refused to tell him anything else.

Could he be trusted? Could Eain really trust anyone? His choice remained the same; continue as he was or to find a way to change something. But, what?

'Up! Move!' barked Klay, his voice harsh, as he forced Morlen and his cronies to their feet. Their hands were bound and strung together, and they started forwards in a shuffling march as a long line.

Their faces were grey as though sleep had been elusive, their eyes rimmed with red.

'The Five curse you, dwarf!' snapped Morlen, and the words were followed by a hollow thump and a gasp, as Klay's fist hammered into his belly, driving the air from his chest.

'Get 'im up,' growled Klay to the soldier assigned as Morlen's guard. 'Keep 'em movin. Don't let em lag behind or you'll have me t'answer to.'

It had been an uneasy column that moved away from the grassy plateau a short while later. The mercenaries followed Daeron Teleri and the Eagle Sisters as they took a small track through the forest, hugging the steep hillside.

They kept the prisoners under a close eye, but it felt like they were all guarded in turn by the red clad archers who followed behind and ghosted through the trees to either side of the trail.

None rode, the path too rough, but the horses that had survived the ambush were in use as pack animals and were being led along at the rear.

Morning sunlight filtered through the surrounding forest, casting alternating shadows and golden shafts like spears of pure light. All was still and heavy with damp, droplets gleaming on leaves like so many scattered jewels.

Eain felt a heaviness on his shoulders and brow at the thought of jewels, and his mind turned to the ruby he had buried at the bottom of his pack. For reasons he could not have articulated, its presence filled him with dread.

He could no longer remember exactly why he had seized it, back in Ben Gedrin, but recalled a vague feeling that it was the right thing to do. The groups striving to possess it had shown themselves to be criminals; thieves and murderers with no honour. He had made a snap decision that they should not possess such a treasure.

And now? Carrying it brought him no joy. He told himself that it could be traded if he needed coin to escape from this, if such an opportunity ever arose. It must be very valuable.

He knew he would not find such an opportunity.

The path turned, following the curve of the hill, and the column followed in single file, like a gigantic snake winding in sinuous curves through the forest. The trees thinned and soon rocky slopes were visible through the trunks ahead.

The mercenaries followed Teleri out onto this broad space of ochre rock; a sombre, dun expanse amid the verdant surrounds of the forest.

Uphill, Eain noticed several strange structures built from rounded stones. These boulders, each too heavy for a man to move, had been piled into domed mounds. Moss grew in the cracks as though they were of great age.

As Eain watched, several of the priestesses broke off and moved over to one of the rocky mounds. Together, they rolled a wheel-shaped stone at the toe of the mound away, and revealed a dark space behind as though the dome was hollow.

'The graves of the ancient Tayans,' said Klay, in a low voice at Eain's elbow. 'Years and years old.'

'Is something going to come out?' asked Eain. He remembered the dead man walking on the outskirts of Ben Gedrin.

Klay answered with a bark of a laugh. 'No, but summat's going t'go in.' He looked meaningfully towards where Morlen and the other prisoners were being held down, faces up, over some square boulders. 'Get yer sword ready.'

A tremor of cold dread swept over Eain as Klay mentioned the sword. Suddenly, it felt heavy, a deathly weight across his shoulders.

'Soldiers of Tayo!' rang out the voice of Daeron Teleri. He was standing on a small boulder, addressing the gathering force. 'I know you are loyal. These,' he pointed towards the row of men who were pinned down, 'are not. They are traitorous and worse, as their treachery was clumsy and ill-conceived.

'It brings me true sadness that Tayans would be so foolish, and that justice must rest with me. A leader must always be on their guard, and they must always be just.'

Eain glanced down towards Klay. He had a feeling he knew where this speech was heading.

'Tayo,' muttered Klay, under his breath.

'I ask you,' continued Teleri, 'would you see justice done?'

There were cheers.

'Would you see traitors punished?' More cheers. 'It must be done. It shall be done. Captain!'

Teleri waved in their direction, and it took a moment for Eain to realise he meant Klay. The dwarf stepped forwards.

'Follow,' he hissed, and Eain hurried to keep up. Klay paused before the line of stones, and turned to address the crowd.

'The men before you are proven traitors,' he said in a flat voice. 'Penalty for treachery against a Tayan lord is death. It shall be done by sword.'

That was when he had beckoned to Eain, and he knew that his time had run out. He could not avoid or escape this fate. As if in a dream, Eain slid the long, heavy sword from the scabbard across his back and held it level, and ready.

'*Control! Control!*' barked a voice from the depths of his memory. The voice of Morgan Blane. '*Any woodsman can hack with a blade! A soldier of Claihed uses his weapon like he uses his body and his mind. With control. With purpose, and understanding of the consequences.*'

The *claidah* was around Eain in that moment, the scent of bodies damp with sweat mingling with the pervasive odour of steel and blade oil. He heard the gentle clatter of weapons being handled and touching, along with the occasional swish of a greatsword sweeping down in a cut.

To use a sharp sword required practice, and the cutting drills were supervised by Morgan Blane. There was little chatter or laughter during these sessions. The use of live steel with a keen edge was taken very seriously. Blane did not tolerate the slightest misbehaviour, or anything he considered a lack of application.

Laid between two benches was a long, rounded bundle; birch twigs wrapped and bound with damp reeds. As the young soldiers of the Claihedhlar watched, Blane raised his famous blade, The River In Flood. Long but slender, the quillons were forged into flowing shapes and the pommel was a quartz-flecked river pebble.

'Observe,' said the tall Master.

The great blade swung in a smooth arc. Eain barely saw the impact as it hit the bunched straws and wood, but a moment later it fell in two neat halves, cleaved through apart from a few strands of reed that kept the two pieces joined together.

'That,' said Blane, 'is control. Cutting the reeds is akin to cutting flesh. You must understand how that feels. Connow! Step forward!'

Now it would be Eain's turn, and a chance for Blane to humiliate him if his form was not perfect.

He had raised the sword, a simple Claihed stock blade, sharp and forged with expertise but identical to hundreds of others. He could feel Blane's eyes on him as he prepared himself to strike; judging, and anticipating failure. Eain tightened his grip. He was determined to avoid the man's scorn this day.

The blade came down, the tip whistling as it parted the air. He felt the resistance in his hands and wrists as the keen edge sliced through the reeds and then the core of birch twigs.

He paused, blade low, and looked towards the mat. The bundle split and the loose end toppled, to be held for a moment by a single uncut strand of reed. A heartbeat later it snapped under the weight.

Eain felt a smile twitching his lips.

Blane's voice seemed to come from a long distance. 'Good, Connow. But we go again. Control is the result of practice, and focus…'

The words faded away into the past, and Eain found that he was staring down at Morlen's face instead. A strip of stained cloth was tied tightly between his teeth, but his eyes rolled and bulged.

Klay stepped forwards and took a firm grip on the Tayan's long, dark hair in his thick fingers.

'It's time, youth,' he said. 'In the name of Duke Teleri, justice must now be done,' he added in a louder voice before whispering to Eain: 'Them or you, youth.'

Eain despaired at the truth of the dwarf's words. These men were traitors, criminals and betrayers. Morlen had tried to kill Eain himself on their first meeting, and Eain was sure he would have done it with no remorse.

There could be no forgiveness for what they had tried to do. Not this time.

He gripped his sword tightly, then brought it down. Control.

The blade was heavy, the edge sharp, and Eain felt little resistance through his hands and wrists. Red blood flowed beneath the blue sky.

Klay moved onto the next and Eain followed, dumbly. Horror and revulsion screamed from somewhere deep in his mind, but he shut the door on that frantic voice. Four more times his blade rose and fell. Four times a voice that Eain could not acknowledge wailed, from deep within his being.

Red blood. Blue sky.

'Justice is done!' boomed Daeron Teleri, when it was over.

> *The rocks still rise to the sky*
> *and the great river flows to the sea.*
> *Our lives are fleeting, but the land is eternal.'*

At his words, in the now-familiar poetic style of Tayo, the mercenaries turned as one to stare out southward. For the first time, Eain let himself take in the view.

The rocky plateau clung to the hillside and the land flattened out far below, rippled and green like a felted blanket. The river wound across the verdant plan like a huge serpent, glittering in the sunshine. Further south the whole land shone, great areas of wetland catching the sun and gleaming like polished blades.

Eain turned away.

Klay was standing beside him, and as Eain moved past the dwarf reached out, his lips parting to speak. With a sudden surge of anger, Eain slapped Klay's hand away and strode off.

He needed distance.

He felt sick. Sick of the dwarf, sick of this army and sick of Teleri. Most of all, he was sick of himself. Repulsed by the damage he caused, everywhere he went.

Stretching his legs, the desire to leave the plateau and the blood behind drove him on. The priestesses raised their eyes to watch him pass, pausing in their work of moving the bodies into the rocky dome that they had opened earlier. They would lie there alongside the dusty, ancient bones. Unburied, unremembered.

He stormed past and headed for the higher slopes.

The rounded summit was littered with boulders, like a population of twisted creatures all turned to stone during a chaotic battle. Curved, bulbous shapes loomed everywhere he looked. Eain swung around a block the size of a bull aurochs and sat down.

He realised only then that the bloodied sword was still dangling in his grip, clutched in his hand. It rang on the flaky rock as he let it fall.

To his left, more bare hills stretched away to vanish from view in the hazy distance. Dark mountains smudged the horizon, and everywhere else Eain looked was green, from the swaying forest canopy to the grassy plains of the lowlands.

He sat on a bald island in the middle of a rippling lake.

His thoughts seethed. Different voices shouted for attention, some angry, some hollow with guilt, and others wailing in self-pity. All in his own voice.

Ever since he had left Tann's farm, far to the east, he had been trying to regain control of his life. Trying to silence those voices. So, why did he feel more helpless than ever? Why were the voices growing louder?

His hopes of finding meaning and purpose had been betrayed. He was surrounded by people he could not trust, forced into actions he would never choose. All at the whim of his new master, Daeron Teleri.

Eain could not decide what to make of the man. His words had inspired, and for a time Eain had been filled with optimism and purpose at the thought of playing a part in Teleri's war. But the man was unpredictable and ruthless. He had killed, and had others killed, with no mercy and no apparent remorse. Eain's stomach churned as he thought of the executions he had just been forced to perform. Here, there was little value given to life and it seemed as though he had no choice but to become a part of it.

He shifted against the rock as he noticed something digging uncomfortably into his lower back. His laden pack was still on his back and the contents were being crushed between his back and the hardness of the boulder.

He knew immediately what he had felt.

It was the object that had caused the chaos in Ben Gedrin. The item that so many were prepared to kill to possess, and that Eain had felt compelled to take, telling himself that he must deny others from having it, from using it.

The jewel.

It was the reason he had fled south, and the reason he had ended up here, amid all this violence and blood. A powerful emotion gripped him as he thought of it. He begrudged its influence, and regretted having it with him. He should have just cast it away. Maybe he still could.

And yet…

Almost without intention, he unslung his pack and delved inside. The wooden box was simple and unimpressive, and felt slightly warm between his hands. His fingers trembled slightly as he undid the clasps, and opened the lid.

It was like nothing he had ever seen before, fist-sized and a deep, blood red. Sharp facets caught the sunlight and made the whole jewel glow, lighting the inside of the box and bathing Eain's face in crimson light. Stabs of red lanced out from the ruby's heart like blood-soaked daggers.

It was valuable, that was obvious. Probably worth a heap of gold. If Eain were to use it to barter or trade, he could end up with enough in his pockets and on his wrists to get away from here. He could be safe.

Or, said a more insidious voice, *you could become powerful.*

He could become Teleri's right hand man. He could become a general. Then he would be the one giving the orders and making the decisions.

He shook his head. That was not what he wanted, whatever value this jewel had.

Maybe it was more than that. Maybe a jewel like this had a power that could not be balanced against simple silver and gold. What if it could be wielded, like a weapon or a totem? Could it be used to enact change?

His hand edged closer to the surface of the jewel, the crimson glow washing over the skin of his fingertips.

A new voice, one that was not his own, whispered of a new beginning. Strength, power, and for the first time in too long, control of his destiny. He would be able to make his own choices.

It was there, within his grasp.

His fingers twitched, moving into the gaping mouth of the box. The glow seemed to strengthen and pulse, outlining the shape of his splayed hand. The surface was an inch away from his fingertips.

'Eain!'

A gruff voice barked his name from nearby, and was followed by the clatter of heavy boots on stone.

'Eain?'

Klay's bearded face appeared around the square side of the boulder. Eain's hand jerked back and he slammed the lid of the box shut. He looked up, guiltily.

Why did he feel guilty? He had done nothing wrong.

'Yer've got t'come, now,' said the dwarf, and there was an unusual edge of tension in his harsh tones. 'We're about t'move out.'

'Move out?' asked Eain? He realised that his heart was hammering in his chest.

'Aye,' said Klay. 'Hurry.'

Eain stood, gathering his bag and thrusting the jewel's box deep inside. He stooped to retrieve his sword, forcing aside his reluctance to touch it and sheathing it across his back once more.

'We're marching,' said Klay, bitterly, as Eain caught him up. 'Heading down't lowlands.'

'Marching?' asked Eain, but he knew what it must mean.

'Marching t'battle. Teleri has decided it's time to start his war. So, make yourself ready to start fighting.'

TWENTY FIVE

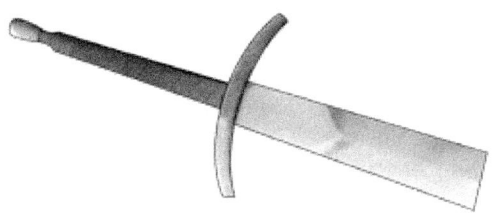

The light of dawn sliced across the dark horizon like a silvered blade. A fitful wind sighed in the branches overhead, a mournful voice that was full of woe.

Eain moved alongside the front rank, slipping through the band of trees like lost souls. Each muted metallic clatter of a weapon, or the snap of a twig underfoot was jarring and overloud in the tense quietness.

They were moments away from launching their attack.

'The first strike,' Teleri had said, climbing onto a tree stump to address his ragtag army, 'must land somewhere they do not expect and yet, somewhere that will hurt them. Somewhere with rich pickings that we do not need to occupy.

'We will strike somewhere that will lead to the word spreading. And that word is resistance. There is a way to fight against this tyranny, and together we will prove it to the rest of Tayo!'

They had marched for several days to get here. An atmosphere of tension hung over the camp each night.

'Who will he have killed next?' muttered some.

'He'll lead us into death,' said others.

Many more of the men and women of the army still watched Teleri with eyes full of awe whenever he passed. Despite what he had done they looked to him to lead, to show them the path to tread.

'He's told 'em what they want t'hear,' explained Klay, when Eain had asked. 'Most Tayans hate Buren, hate being part of Re'Emsser, hate that their ways of life have been trodden on.'

'Was it that bad?'

Klay shot him a hard look. 'Imagine your country is invaded, thousands dead, villages being razed all along't border. Then, when peace is finally made, you're forced into an agreement which doubles taxes for everyone apart from for those nobles what signed the treaty.'

Eain stared. He *could* imagine that. Part of it, anyway.

'For Buren and Anish,' Klay went on. 'And for Kotev too, Re'Emsser keeps 'em safe and rich. Because it keeps Tayo weak and poor. And that's wi'out talking about the other new laws. Language banned, worship of the old gods outlawed.

'Tayo's 'ad enough. They are ready to boil over. Just needs a man like him to stir the pot.'

Eain saw the truth in Klay's words, and they were shackled to Teleri now. His fate was their destiny. The horror of the executions had faded, and Eain was now able to see Teleri's actions in a different light. He was a leader doing what he must.

'I still wouldn't trust him, though. He's saying one thing and meaning t'other. He only wants his home back. He said as much. He's no crusader.'

Still, Eain could not help but have sympathy with the Tayans. Teleri's words had much to do with that. When he spoke, he painted a picture of a glorious future, a better time when the country was once again in control of its own destiny, when its people had the freedom and prosperity that Re'Emsser had denied them.

Believing Teleri was fighting a just war gave Eain a feeling of purpose he had been missing.

When Teleri spoke, Eain could imagine the future and could stop dwelling on the past.

'And Penaram?'

It was the name of the settlement they would be attacking.

'Trading post,' said Klay. 'A rich one. Silks and spices, weapons and gems. I reckon Teleri thinks he can give out a bloody nose by smashing it open, and fill his treasure chest at the same time.'

'So, just a raid?'

'Aye. It's reet noble, this trade.' The dwarf grinned, a humourless grimace. 'The gods give no one the right to love their trade, so the best we can hope for is survival.'

Survival.

The word bounced around Eain's head as they crept through the dawn-lit woodlands. Dead, brown leaves crunched beneath their bootheels, the only sound punctuating the stillness. The weather had changed as they marched south. Chill, gusty winds blew from the east bringing thick, angry clouds which roiled across the iron-grey sky.

'This weather,' muttered the Tayans, huddling more tightly into their capes and glaring accusingly upwards. 'Not natural.' It felt like autumn had fallen into winter overnight, the leaves curling and browning at the edges.

They advanced through the band of trees, bare branches stark silhouettes against the lightening sky. At the eaves, Klay lifted a fist into the air to signal a halt. When he spoke, it was in a hoarse whisper, hands cupped to his mouth to direct the sound.

'Hearken to Duke Teleri. He'll give orders and I'll be mekkin' sure they're obeyed.'

Amongst the clustered trunks and low branches, Eain saw many eyes as the ranks of soldiers turned towards the sound of steady footsteps. Teleri approached. Their leader, their general, had come to send them forth.

The dawn light washed the colours from his fine robes, but his height and the intensity of his hawkish gaze lent him the same commanding power. Eain's doubts seemed to burn away whenever he was in the presence of this man.

Teleri spoke quietly, but clearly: 'The hour has come at last. The hour when we will draw weapons together, brothers and sisters of Tayo. History will recall this as the day when it began. A new dawn for Tayo, and those who are not yet with us will wish they were!'

There were no cheers, not this close to the enemy, but feet shuffled and hands tightened on the leather wrappings of weapon handles.

'The war will not be won today, my friends,' he went on, 'but it will begin. The future holds more than simple raids, much more, but today we will deliver a jab that they will not, and cannot ignore.

'Go with speed, go with glory, go with the wings of the Skyfather himself spreading above you. Strike as fast as lightning and as hard as thunder, then return to me. Klay.' He motioned to the dwarf, and stepped back.

It had already been made clear that neither Teleri himself, or the Sisters of the Eagle, would be part of this attack. Neither could be risked in open battle, not yet, although the priestesses had their bows and would guard their retreat into the woods afterwards.

'Easy job,' said Klay as the soldiers huddled around him. Teleri had given him his orders and faded away into the woods. 'In and out. We'll march straight up yon causeway to the gates, and right through. Gates stay open, carts go in and out all day.'

'Sounds simple,' murmured Eain. The words burst from his lips, almost unbidden. Klay shot him a look.

'Aye, should be if we stick together and use our heads. No dashing off, no heroics. Stay behind me to the gates. Once we're inside we deal with any guards then drive away any loaded wagons we can. Burn what we can't. Got it?'

There were muffles of assent.

'Teleri will tell you that the righteousness of our noble goal will drive your fear away, but we all know he's wrong. What'll keep you alive is yer savage will to live. If you see someone swingin' at you, you swing 'arder, and faster, and stick that bastard first. And the next.

'They'll not know what 'it 'em. Now let's get to it.'

Warriors spread out into the trees, forming vague ranks. Eain jolted as a fist grabbed the front of his jacket and yanked his head down. He found himself nose to nose with Klay.

'You,' hissed the dwarf, 'will stick with me. Do what I do. Do what I say. Don't do anything bloody stupid. Got it?'

'Yes, yes,' said Eain, taken aback.

'Reet,' said Klay, calm once more, and lifted a heavy rimmed helmet onto his head. Eain copied, pressing a domed helm of sturdy iron over his hair. It felt awkward and unfamiliar, the stealthy sounds of movement as the advance began made tinny by the metal covering his ears, but it did make him feel safer. He also wore a padded jacket, as much armour as he could manage while still being able to move swiftly at need.

Most of the other mercenaries had their own armour, and he had none, but Klay had managed to find spares that would fit. His jacket had a ragged hole just below the chest, surrounded by a dark stain, but Eain had not wanted to ask the obvious question.

A bitter wind sloughed through their ranks as they left the cover of the trees, and Eain shivered despite the bulk of the armour. The sword across his back was a dead weight, and he knew he would have to use it soon.

Klay set the pace.

'Keep up with me,' he called over his shoulder. 'But don't run. Be ready.'

Boggy land that was dotted with puffs of pale cotton-grass that danced in the breeze, gave way to shallow slopes as they left the trees behind. Up and to their right a cart track ran along the crest of a ridge to the town itself, which crowned the summit.

Low banks of earth ringed the small settlement, but it was the high timber palisade which provided the stoutest defence. Logs of dark wood had been driven into the banks at a steep angle, so that the walls overhung the bank and ditch which encircled them.

The whole town resembled a crown set atop a bald head.

A sturdy gatehouse of stripped logs straddled the road where it passed through the bank. They joined the road at a fast walk and began closing the distance to the gates, which were thrown wide open.

Eain's stomach churned.

Guards at the gates had just noticed the advancing column and were peering out as if to identify the newcomers, hands shading eyes against the strengthening light of day.

'Now!' roared Klay, breaking into a run. Eain accelerated to stay at the dwarf's shoulder. Klay was surprisingly quick, and as he ran he managed to move the Capper into his hand without Eain noticing how. He reached for his sword, grasping awkwardly over his right shoulder as his feet pounded a war-drum rhythm on the track.

At that moment, the gate guards realised their peril. They shouted the alarm and began to close the gates. They were too slow.

Klay accelerated.

In a heartbeat he was in the gateway and the Capper was lashing out as though the Brothers guided his hands. It was a blur. The dull crunch of bones breaking and the breathless moans of those struck were a song to accompany his dance of death. Eain had not seen such skill since leaving Banahgar.

The other mercenaries dashed forwards to hold the gates open, and to form a line across the gateway, spears, maces and short swords rising to strike at the defenders. Eain joined the fight.

His sword was in his hands, angling across his body to deflect the thrust of a short-hafted spear, and then twisting in riposte. A jolt through his wrists. A cry of pain. A splash of blood.

Red.

His thinking mind receded as his instincts took over. Block, step back, strike forward. A curtain seemed to fall between his thoughts and his actions.

He could hear the grunts of effort, the clash and rattle of weapons striking and the moans and wails of those in mortal agony, but he was remote from it. It was as though he acted through another's hands.

A stride to the left, sword swinging horizontally to take the throat of a bare-headed man who was stabbing Klay, even as the dwarf pivoted right and struck at another with the Capper. The two attackers fell, and Eain looked down, meeting the dwarf's eyes. Klay nodded.

Eain breathed hard as he raised his sword into a high guard and took stock. A lull had fallen.

The mercenary force had won the initial collision, the element of surprise and the speed of their charge carrying them beyond the gateway and within the walls. They gathered, shoulder to shoulder, in a rough semi-circle enclosing the gate.

The ground behind them was strewn with the dead and groaning wounded. Eain tried to ignore the pitiful sounds that came from friend and foe alike.

Before them was a broad yard, an open area between the gates and the first buildings of the small town. Many of the structures were raised on piers of stone or timber, clearly granaries or storerooms rather than dwellings.

A couple of carts with horses still in the traces stood placidly beyond the battle lines, oblivious to the bloodshed. The drivers and handlers had wisely scattered at the first sounds of alarm. The town's defenders, a lightly armed bunch, backed away to huddle in the mouths of the nearest streets. They were outnumbered and outmatched.

Klay turned to address Teleri's mercenary raiders. 'You, and you, get on those wagons and get 'em out of here.' He pointed to a couple of fighters that were loitering near the back, before turning his gaze to a different pair. 'And you two, get torches lit and put fire to a couple of these sheds. Teleri ordered us to leave a mark.'

He turned back to face the town, before raising the Capper skyward.

'Forward! Let's give these soft bastards another taste of our steel!' He led the line's advance and Eain followed at his shoulder. The defenders fell back, turning to vanish between the buildings. Warriors on either side of Eain jeered and laughed.

'Lost their guts!' they cried. 'The day is ours! The Steel Hounds!'

The streets ahead of them were suddenly empty.

'Where's everyone?' muttered Klay. He wrinkled his hooked nose and sniffed suspiciously. 'Summat's not right.'

'They retreated,' said Eain, hoping that the day's fighting was done. A couple more souls had been added to his grim tally, and he could see the blood darkening on the grey steel of his sword.

'Aye, but a town like this should be defended more staunchly. Summat's amiss. Halt!'

He held up a hand and the advancing line halted, at least the ones Eain could see; the width of the streets had forced them to split, and half was moving down a parallel way. Their footsteps halted, the sound fading away to leave stillness and silence.

But only for a moment, because now Eain could hear marching feet, crunching on the ground in time. It was a heavy, slow drumbeat. And it was getting louder.

'Aw, shit,' muttered Klay, looking around anxiously. It was the first time Eain had seen the dwarf express anything close to fear, and it was immediately disconcerting.

Footsteps thudded more loudly, the sound emanating from the streets ahead.

Klay gestured over his shoulder. 'We need to back up. Now.'

'Retreat?' called another voice. 'But we have won the gate. They flee before us!'

'Now!' bellowed Klay.

But it was too late.

Around a corner, the source of the sound emerged. Eain stared, and moans of fear came from those around him.

'They've got a garrison of the Gluttons here,' said Klay, as he urged the front line to back away. Eain stepped backwards, trying to understand what he was seeing.

They were many, and they marched shoulder to shoulder. The front rank was three warriors wide, but so broad and thick-bodied that they filled the street. Their faces were hidden behind heavy, riveted helmets and curved plates of grey iron covered broad shoulders and deep chests.

They were huge, and their relentless march seemed to shake the ground.

'Back! Back!' roared Klay and the lines hurried towards the gates. Eain felt a new stab of fear in his belly at the cracks in Klay's normally stoic demeanour. Cries and the clash of weapons rang out from the next street. Eain hastened his retreat, and could feel the panic growing in those around him.

At that moment, one of the Gluttons, as Klay had named them, barked a sharp command and they surged forwards. Their armour rang like thunder, and their turn of speed was surprising.

The lines clashed and soldiers all around Eain were flung back. Each of the Gluttons bore a square shield with a heavy iron rim, and a brutal flanged mace. They lashed out with both, and helmets were marred by huge dents, ribcages smashed with sickening sounds, and most of the front line seemed to fall. Groans and screams filled the air, while the Steel Hounds' own weapons skittered off the heavy armour.

A few heartbeats later, the rout began.

A flicker in the corner of Eain's eye was the first sign, and he risked a glance around. Mercenaries were breaking from the rear ranks and sprinting away, their courage vanishing in the face of the assault of these iron-clad giants.

At the same time, the front rank was crumbling. Eain was keeping his attackers back with sweeps of his sword, but could do little more. They were moments away from being overwhelmed. He made a snap decision. Take control.

'On me! On me!' he cried, stepping back from the melee to take up a new position in the centre of the courtyard. Warriors were edging away through the gateway behind them, but he ignored them, and ignored the easy escape. Raising his sword in the air, he turned to face the oncoming Gluttons.

Fleeing mercenaries slowed, gathering behind him and a momentary pause in the Gluttons' advance let others break away. A ragged line formed across the gateway in the brief respite. Klay was beside him.

'We're done for now, youth,' he grunted, between deep breaths.

Eain stared at the scene. The bulky shapes of the Gluttons strode forwards as flames licked up the dark timbers of the nearest storehouse. The hard planes and edges of the Gluttons' maces were stained, slick with blood.

This had been an ambush. Somehow, they had been expected.

'Go,' said Eain. 'Go now. Lead them away.'

'If we turn, they'll fall on our backs,' said Klay.

'They won't,' replied Eain. 'I'll hold them back. Slow them down.'

Klay was silent.

'You won't need long,' Eain continued. 'I can give you that. Go.'

Klay reached up and patted Eain's elbow.

'Steel Hounds!' he shouted. 'On me!'

Eain heard feet hitting the track as the escapees passed through the gateway, armour and weapons clattering and fading. The front rank of the Gluttons stepped forwards. A deep, shuddering breath hissed from Eain's lips, and he raised his sword.

His legs were spread, a wide and stable base as he lifted his arms above his head. The point of the long, heavy blade angled back towards the gateway. A ready stance. A deadly stance. Kell's stance.

The Gluttons' advance slowed in the face of Eain's calm readiness. He knew, and they knew, that the first to attack would die. Heavy armour or no, that great blade would cleave down like a thunderbolt.

Heartbeats passed, enough time for the others to have put plenty of distance between them and the town. Just maybe, no one else would have to die here today.

Words floated across his mind from deep in his memory.

'The true victor is he that does not need to fight.'

The voice of Helden Haradsson, Grandmaster of the Claihed, as he had addressed Eain and the other new recruits. It felt like a lifetime ago.

He edged towards the Gluttons, the tip of his blade twitching as he aimed a strike. The front rank shrank back, raising their shields. They would overcome him in time, but none of them wanted to be first.

But Eain's advance was a feint. As soon as his opponents leaned back, Eain pivoted on his heel and ran.

He had bought the rest of Teleri's ragged army the time they needed to escape, and now he could follow. He had been ready to sacrifice himself, but only at the direst need. His other weapon could now be use: his speed. His boots pounded on the hard-packed trail as he sprinted away from the gateway.

The rattling, rumbling sound of heavy boots and clattering armour told him that he was pursued.

He had bargained on his speed keeping him safe, but his legs quickly felt watery and weak, the weight of armour holding him back as though a great hand pressed against his chest. His sword, carried awkwardly in one hand, was an unhelpful, unbalancing weight.

For a moment, he considered casting it aside but could not bring himself to do it. He was too used to it. He ran on instead, gasping for breath, but felt the pursuit gaining. The huge, bulky warriors of the Gluttons moved with a speed he had not expected.

Should he turn and face them, or keep running and risk being struck down from behind? He could not think straight through his fear and exhaustion. It felt as though they were breathing down his neck.

Before he could make any sort of decision, something rose from a ditch beside the road to vanish behind his back. There was a roar of alarm, a thud and a clatter, and a moan of pain.

Despite his fear, Eain slowed and turned.

Klay was standing in the centre of the track, the Capper spinning in his hands as he faced down the ranks of the Gluttons. Two were down already, sprawled across the ground. One had a huge dent in his thick breastplate, and heels that hammered as he gasped for breath, and the other's helmet was cracked. Blood trickled down the small part of their face that was exposed, and they lay absolutely still.

The others had paused, eyeing the dwarf carefully, as he spun the Capper in slow circles. Eain stepped forwards, sword raised once more as he moved in time, daring the Gluttons to face those two deadly weapons.

'Now what?' he hissed to Klay.

'Now,' said Klay, the bloodstained head of the Capper hovering and circling like an angry hornet, 'we run like hell. Go!'

He darted away, off the track and down the hillside, and Eain followed behind. An angry roar, like the baritone growl of a huge, furious animal, came from the ranks of the Gluttons as they gave chase.

Eain despaired once more, certain that they would be overtaken before reaching the beckoning sanctuary of the woods, when a dark cloud rushed over his head. Instinctively, he ducked. Shrill whistles turned to metallic thuds, then groans of pain. Eain half-turned to see the Gluttons' pursuit halted as the front ranks clutched at black-fletched arrows.

Only then did he notice the line of red-clad figures at the edge of the wood. As he watched, the priestesses shot another volley over their heads, and more Gluttons fell or were stopped in their tracks.

'Keep fookin' running, idiot!' yelled Klay, and Eain followed as he darted towards the eaves. As soon as the grasping fingers of the bare branches were above their heads, the priestesses melted away between the trunks.

Straining to put one foot in front of the other, Eain kept running until Klay slowed to a walk. He cocked his head on one side, listening intently to assure himself that the chase had relented, as Eain sheathed his sword and leaned against a tree.

That had been far too close. His lungs and legs burned, and there was a shivering, hollow exhaustion in his arms and shoulders that he knew would be a deep ache tomorrow. But, they had escaped. A smile was just cracking across his face, when Klay's fist hit him in the chest.

He staggered back.

'Bloody fool!' hissed the dwarf. 'Why risk getting yerself killed like that?'

Eain stared, lost for words. Had he not helped everyone else, Klay included escape? Had Klay not come back for him? But the dwarf had not finished.

'Heroes get dead. Right? End of story. And next time yer try some shit like that I'll not come back for you. I'll let the worms feast.'

And with that, he turned and stormed off, deeper into the woods.

All Eain could do was follow.

TWENTY SIX

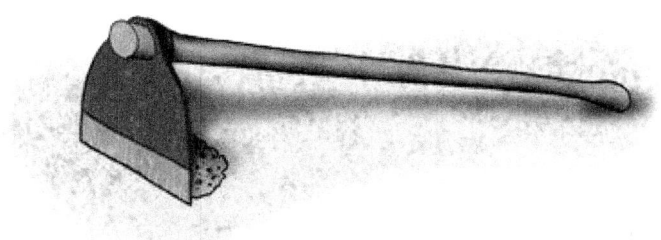

This had been a mistake. Carilton Tann saw that now. It was clear as day.

He had been so keen to travel with the two strangers. So keen to head east, to leave his farm, his home, far behind.

'You sure you know what you're getting yourself into?' his mother had asked as she stood on the veranda, the brisk, chill wind whipping strands of iron-grey hair across her face.

'We'll travel safe,' he had said. 'And fast. I'll be straight back. This is something I need to do.'

And he had convinced himself. Convinced himself of the rightness of the journey, the necessity.

The camp of the first night of their journey had convinced him yet further.

The fire crackled, casting their faces into sharp but shifting relief. Cerle reached into his bag and found an extra cape of russet beaver fur, and insisted Indaella wore it around her shoulders.

'I'm fine,' she said, with a slight laugh. 'I'm warm enough here before the fire.'

'Aye, but the chill will come in with the night.' She accepted the fur without further protest, and they both leaned back against the wheel of the wagon as the orange flames made the shadows dance around them.

Tann had a question, and had been holding it in ever since the conversation around the table in his hall. He was not a man who pried. By habit, he let people keep their secrets and tell him what they wanted him to know. But he felt like this one mattered, and understanding the answer would help him to help them.

'Indaella,' he began. Her pale eyes turned on him, wide and almost childlike. 'I have to ask. When you say you can "See" things…what do you mean? How do you see them?'

Cerle scowled instantly, but Indaella laid a soothing hand on his arm.

'Master Tann has placed his trust in us,' she said, 'and I believe we should show that we trust him. Because we do.'

Tann looked down self-consciously.

'They are dreams, mostly,' she said. 'Dreams which unfold into scenes that are vivid and real, and that I can place in the real world. It's the feelings that go with them, though…' She paused, staring into the fire. 'So real. So strong. Like memories, but of things that have not yet happened. I think I See possibilities.'

'And that's where you've seen Eain?'

She nodded. 'Seen, and felt. He's my grandson, my blood. There's a strong link there and so when I See him, in my dreams, I feel the emotions around him very powerfully. I can't explain how I know, and it probably sounds like I'm losing my mind. But I know.'

'I believe you, Indaella,' said Tann. He did believe her, and knew that it was important to both her and Cerle that he did.

'When the emotions are very strong,' she continued, 'there are times I can feel them with a touch. Or show them.' Cerle nodded at that. Indaella looked straight at Tann after saying that, her eyes knowing and bright. 'Let me show you,' she said, after a moment.

'There's no need,' Tann began. 'I believe you—' but Indaella had climbed to her feet and was moving around the fire. Cerle shifted uneasily

Indaella closed her eyes and gently pressed her fingertips to Tann's temples. She stood there for a moment, seemingly not breathing. Then she broke the contact and stepped backwards, and what she said next made Tann's jaw drop.

'Elsia,' she said. Tann said nothing, as he could think of nothing to say. He merely gaped up at the small woman, and she stared back with sympathy in her eyes. 'I am so sorry about what happened to your wife, Carilton. You must not blame yourself.'

His wife's name. His wife, who was murdered, all those years ago, and whose name he had not spoken aloud for a long time. She was ever in his mind, though. That wound would never heal.

'Your pain is still very strong,' said Indaella, by way of explanation, before she sat down again, leaving Tann choking back tears.

Tann had been convinced. He vowed to follow the Banahgarian couple and do whatever he could to aid them, but his conviction had just evaporated like a shallow pool beneath the summer sun. He realised his mistake the moment that Cerle Connow pointed north at a cloud of dust rising on the horizon.

'What's that?' asked the old, rangy warrior. His eyes, as always, were narrowed and hard. They were like chips of ice or splinters of quartz. Pale, sharp and cold.

'Dust,' said Indaella, and Cerle's eyes softened, for a moment. 'But what's making it? What say you, Master Tann?'

Tann looked out at the approaching cloud and back to Cerle, fear a fist clenching in his gut.

'Nothing good,' he replied. Cerle nodded, only a tightening of his jaw and whitening of his knuckles betraying his concern.

They had been on the road for a week or more, and all the while the arid, endless plains stretched away to the north while dusty, featureless hills rose to the south. To Tann's eyes, they were both familiar and alien; alike to the slopes that surrounded his farm, the backdrop to so many years of his life, and yet different. A world away.

He had been perfectly happy where he was, out in that remote corner of the Lands of the Great River. He was so far from civilisation that the only evidence he ever saw of the turmoil and strife of the wider world were the waifs and strays who found their way to his doorstep.

He had never seen any dilemma about welcoming them without judgment, and a small community had grown around his farmhouse, all working that hard land together and supporting one another. It was idyllic, although the living was never easy.

So, what had possessed him to leave that behind? He knew.

Eain Connow.

The arrival of that young man, haunted by horrors he could not express had been the first sliding pebble that had brought the landslide. At first Tann had thought that being at the farm could heal the boy, help him find peace. But as time went on it became clear that Eain's demons were still too near, too strong.

He had made his own decision to move on, and Tann had encouraged it. That had been his first mistake.

A few weeks later, the boy's grandparents had turned up, horrified by the story Tann had told and desperate to find him and return him to their mysterious northern country. What else could Tann have done but to offer his help? And now, this.

Cerle raised a long, muscular arm and pointed towards the side of the road.

'There. Put the wagon there.'

He was pointing to a space to the right. A slope of pale, sandy soil rose just beyond. Ochre rocks and boulders dotted the hillside as it climbed steadily to join the undulating ridge that bounded the southern edge of the road.

'You want me to stop?' asked Tann.

'Aye,' replied Cerle as the wagon rolled to a halt in the lee of the slope. 'Whoever or whatever it is, they are gaining on us. We won't outrun them.'

So…what? They were going to fight?

Cerle jumped down off the wagon's high front seat and raised a hand to his forehead, shielding his eyes. Then, he moved around to the rear and helped Indaella climb down.

'Head on up that slope,' he said to her, voice immediately softer. 'I'll send Master Tann up with you. Stay there until it's over.'

'What are you going to do, my love?' she asked.

'What I always do,' he said. 'Protect you. I'll see them off.'

She nodded as though the outcome was not in question, and began to climb, loose pebbles skittering down the slope where her feet disturbed the soil. Cerle reached down into the wagon and seized his sword belt, which held his mighty greatsword. He cast the belt over his shoulder and began fastening the buckle.

'Cerle,' Tann began, and was met with an icy glare. 'You know it's likely Wild Elves? And you know what they will do to us?'

'I know what they will try to do,' replied Cerle. 'I just need you to protect my wife while I stop them. Take your sword and shield and go.'

Tann nodded.

Cerle had quickly worked out that Tann had once been a soldier, and insisted that they both travelled armed. Tann had never mentioned it, but Cerle had just known. He had found a square Tayan shield in his store, and a single-edged Anise sabre.

He had been desperate not to need them. Not to use them.

How could you explain to a man like Cerle Connow, a man who radiated physicality and strength, that you could no longer fight? That you had been a warrior, once, but had been so sickened by the bloodlust and rage that lurked within yourself, you had vowed to never hold a weapon again?

'You'll put yourself before her,' said Cerle. A flat statement of what would be. 'You'll guard her like she was your own kin.'

Tann reached for the armaments, buckling on the sword belt and hefting the shield onto his left arm. He had not been there when the tides of war had taken his own wife, and had wished he had been every day since, even if all he could have done was to die at her side.

He could use the shield, at least.

'Cerle,' he said, and the tall warrior turned. 'Be careful. Please.' Cerle merely nodded, and Tann began to climb the slope towards where Indaella sat.

She watched him as he laboured up the loose, shifting slope, face expressionless, but just as he reached the top she surprised him with a slight smile. He stared, and she fixed him with her wide blue eyes.

'Do not be afraid,' she said, softly. 'All will be well. There is something about this place...some feeling. We are not alone.'

She looked perfectly content, but he was not. This felt like a very lonely place to make a stand. Not another living soul was within sight, apart from the dark shapes that could now be seen galloping before the rising cloud of dust.

He gripped the thick leather strap that formed the handle of his shield, and planted his feet on the loose, sandy soil.

'Besides,' came Indaella's voice from behind him. 'Whatever it is that approaches, they will never have encountered anything like my husband before.'

Tann blinked.

He recalled enough of his days as a soldier to remember what it was like to be in the presence of hard men, skilled fighters. It felt like a lifetime ago but those faces and the memories that went with them were still vivid.

He had met very few, though, with the uncomplicated aura of solidity, coupled with absolute confidence in his own ability, that surrounded Cerle Connow.

Despite his age, the man's muscles were like iron, his whole bearing stiff and unbreakable. It was though a coat of the toughest, thickest leather had been stretched over a frame of aged oak. And he handled that great sword, as long from pommel to tip as his wife was tall, as if it was another limb.

Still, he was just one man, and it looked as though the approaching force numbered a score or more. And Tann was now certain that they were a party of Wild Elves.

Cerle appeared unconcerned, slowly drawing his greatsword from where it hung on his back, before placing the tip on the ground. He leaned on it like a farmer on a hoe. For several moments, the tableau was still.

The drumming of hooves on the hard earth got steadily louder and soon Tann could see individual riders. The coats of the horses were as dark as the riders' skin, approaching the lone, grey-haired figure with menacing inevitability.

Tann had never encountered Wild Elves himself, and for that he thanked Fate. What he knew had been pieced together from the tales of travellers and merchants who moved across the Lands of the Great River regularly. Their attacks left few survivors.

Most of the stories said the same things, though: they attacked without warning, appearing suddenly from the dust of the plains and striking at any in their path. They left none alive and those that were not killed quickly died slowly, cut to ribbons as part of the elves' blood rituals.

There would be no mercy.

As the elven riders reined in, forming a loose semi-circle around the wagon, a fitful breeze tugged at the brim of Tann's hat. Apart from a loose strand of grey hair, dancing in the same gust, Cerle might have been a statue.

The elves paused, clearly unsure about what to do. They were probably used to those they assailed panicking and trying to flee, not standing calmly and waiting.

The scars that crossed their bodies, pale, livid weals on their dark skin, showed clearly as they dismounted. One stepped forward, a leader perhaps. She was shaven-headed and her chest was bare, like the men. Her dark, intense eyes were fixed on Cerle as she advanced, a short-hafted spear held loosely in one hand.

'Begone,' came a firm voice, carried on the wind. He had not moved, still leaning on that long sword but he spoke clearly. 'Begone if you would live. We have nothing worth taking. All I can give you is death.'

If the Wild Elves understood his words, in the Common Speech, they gave no sign. Two more elves, both male, stepped forwards to stand at the leader's shoulder. One bore two long knives, the other an axe with a curved, notched blade.

They were all on the balls of their feet, ready to strike. The leader drew her own arm back, just slightly, as if about to attack.

Cerle was quicker.

The old man launched into action so quickly that Tann was not sure what had happened. He barely seemed to move, but that great blade whirled up, out and around in a cutting arc. It took the blink of an eye and left the leader staggering back with dark blood gushing between her fingers.

There was a shocked moment, then the rest of the elves reacted. The two closest lunged forwards, daggers stabbing and axe swinging. They were elves and they were fast, but Cerle moved even faster.

They attacked, and he was abruptly somewhere else. One big stride to the left took him out of range of their short weapons, and his sword was still moving. A flash of red showed where it bit flesh, the point weaving a serpentine path through the air. The elves spread out to try to surround him but the mesmerising sweeps of his greatsword kept them at a distance.

Their numbers could not be brought to bear as he strode back and forth around the wagon, his sword swinging right and left, high and low.

Tann had never seen swordsmanship like it.

An elf with two short axes, like a pair of cleavers, surged forwards. The axes rose, and without breaking stride Cerle turned his sword into a low thrust, and the elf was impaled by the force of his own charge. Cerle tilted his sword down and moved back with firm strides as the body collapsed off the point and onto the dusty ground.

His sword whirled again, and the Wild Elves ducked back.

Tann took the opportunity of the brief lull to glance behind, expecting to see Indaella looking on anxiously. Instead of watching her husband fight for his life, though, her eyes were closed.

She seemed oblivious to the flash of weapons and the cries of pain, her face turned towards the sky. Her lips moved as though in prayer. Tann dared not interrupt her.

Shouts from below pulled Tann's attention back to the fight. Several elves already lay dead or dying, their blood darkening the sandy soil. Cerle remained badly outnumbered, though, and surrounded.

Should he go down to help? He could not leave Indaella alone. If Cerle fell, he needed to defend her. And if he did descend the slope, what could he do? Would he be able to draw his blade and cut flesh with it? He bit his lip.

Cerle still held them at bay with great sweeps of his sword, moving with fluid grace from one position to the next. But he was hard pressed, backing up towards the wagon.

A female elf darted away, and a heartbeat later she was standing atop the wagon. Throwing herself off, she lunged at Cerle's back with her broad-tipped spear. A warning rose to Tann's lips, but he did not have time to speak the words aloud.

They were unnecessary, in any case. Cerle's head snapped around and the point of his sword followed. The leaping elf was run through, the tip of the blade bursting from her back. The weight of the body dragged the sword down, and in the moment it took for Cerle to pull it clear another elf darted in and stabbed out with a jagged knife. Cerle dodged away but the blade lashed across his thigh.

The greatsword came down, fast as a thunderbolt, and the elf was struck down in a bloody spray. The elves still had numbers to spare and attacked with little fear, and now Cerle was injured.

How much longer could he hold out?

Tann wondered if he should take Indaella and flee. Without glancing around, he could hear her muttering under her breath.

Cerle whipped his sword to the right, then circled it over his head to point to the left. The elves had seen what he could do now, and were gathering themselves for a massed attack. He could not guard in all directions at once. He would be overwhelmed.

Tann's hand inched towards the hilt of the sword, and acid filled his guts.

Something whined overhead. An elf grunted and fell back. Then again. Elves sank to their knees, clutching at themselves in pain. Small red weals bloomed on their skin.

Tann turned, and his eyes widened. Indaella was sitting bolt upright, eyes open and a smile on her lips. To either side of her, a line of tall, grey-clad figures was advancing along the hillside. Casually, easily, they dropped small rocks into woven straps they carried. A swift whirl around their heads and a stone was cast down towards the road. One by one, the Wild Elves fell, peppered by small, sharp rocks.

If Cerle was surprised, he gave no sign. He moved back to stand close to the wagon, sword angled down in a patient, ready pose. A shrill whistle split the air, like the shriek of a hunting hawk, and the grey figures began to stream down the hill. Now, Tann finally understood what he was seeing.

The Walking Birds. The Meculvy Dutsch.

Tann had never seen these people before either, but everyone knew of them. They moved through the hills that fringed the southern extent of the Riverlands, grey hunters that were silent apart from the bird whistles that were their language.

'I told you we were not alone,' said Indaella as she moved past him. Tann followed, shaking his head.

On and around the road, the grey-robed Meculvy Dutsch were moving amongst the fallen Wild Elves with long knives, putting an end to those that still drew breath. One was standing beside Cerle, apparently in conversation. Tann noticed that the hooded figure was of a similar height to the warrior of Banahgar.

They handed Cerle something, then gave an ululating cry, a bird's alarm call. Their grey robes swished like spreading feathers, and the Walking Birds turned and hurried away up the slope once more. Moments later they were gone, as though they had never been there.

Tann felt completely unsettled. He had not expected any of the events of the last few moments, and was struggling to come to terms with what had happened. Cerle's brutal skill, Indaella's confident prediction and the mysterious arrival of the Meculvy Dutsch…it had been a long time since Tann had been so surprised, and now he felt a little overwhelmed.

He cast the sword and shield back into the wagon with relief. He was glad he had not been forced to find out whether or not he would be able to fight. Leaning back on the wagon as his breathing returned to normal, he was rewarded with the sight of Cerle unfastening his belt and letting his trousers drop to the ground.

'Need to bind this,' he said by way of an explanation, pointing to a ragged gash across his left thigh. It was bleeding freely. 'I'll stitch my trousers later, no need to get them soaked in blood.'

Tann saw now that what Cerle had been given by the apparent leader of the Meculvy Dutsch was a roll of pale linen; a bandage. A bulging sack had also been left on the ground nearby.

Indaella stepped forwards to help Cerle wrap the linen over the wound, around a thigh with pale skin but ridged and knotted with hard muscle. Apart from that single cut, Cerle bore no other mark from the battle. The man was extraordinary.

'The Wild Ones don't use poison,' said Cerle, pulling his trousers back up and buckling his belt.

'Pardon?' asked Tann, taken aback.

'I asked the chief of the Meculvy Dutsch,' explained Cerle. 'She said the wound wouldn't be poisoned. I had to check.'

'You spoke with them?'

'Aye.' Cerle's answer had a slight question in it, as if he found Tann's question strange.

Tann shrugged. 'I've never heard of anyone managing to speak with the Walking Birds before. Any outsider, anyway. I didn't know for sure they could speak, to tell the truth.'

'I wonder how many have ever bothered to listen,' replied Cerle. He chuckled slightly, and heaved himself back up onto the wagon. 'Explains why you all fear this landscape so much, if you won't even treat with those who have lived here longest.'

'You've spoken to them before?'

Cerle did not answer the question. 'Time to move on, Master Tann,' he said instead. 'We still have a long way to go. I don't fancy seeing if another tribe of Wild Elves might try their luck.'

'Not seen him this season.'

Carilton Tann sat silently for a moment. It did not make sense.

'Are you certain?' he asked, leaning forward across the small round table. 'You know who I'm asking about? Tressin Oke. He always comes here on his way west. Usually raises the roof when he's here.'

They had arrived in Annida. The Meculvy Dutsch had appeared from nowhere again, just before they had to steer the wagon away from the hills, and their gifts of provisions meant that the three travellers were able to pass the Dry Leagues easily.

Cerle had remained tight-lipped about his history with the Walking Birds, but then the man could be as communicative as a rock at times. Whole days of travel could pass without Cerle saying a word apart from when he spoke softly to Indaella.

Arriving in Annida, bustling with people and raucous with noise, had been very welcome for Tann. Cerle and Indaella had wanted quiet though, and went to find a room while Tann went to every inn and tavern in town. He asked the same questions everywhere he went.

'Of course I know Tressin Oke! Do you take me for an idiot?'

Tann raised his palms. He had spotted this man by his stained apron and brimmed hat. A yard manager, one who oversaw the loading and unloading of goods from the steady stream of wagons and boats that trundled along the many roads which converged on Annida, and from the docks on the Great River.

One who was bound to know Tressin Oke.

'And you've not seen him?'

'He ain't been here,' replied the burly man, cracking his knuckles before draining the last of his ale.

'But he set out from my farm a couple of months ago,' said Tann, half to himself.

'He didn't make it to Annida,' said the yardsman, standing. 'The plains can be dangerous.'

As he moved towards the door of the inn, Tann's heart sank. It was true, and he knew it. If Oke had not made it to Annida, where had he gone? It also meant that Eain's trail had gone dead.

Dead.

Tann dropped his elbows to the table and put his face in his hands, his tiredness adding a keen edge on his despair. He stayed like that for a long time, mind churning over the need to take this news to Eain's grandparents. Dark thoughts tumbled through his head as the time passed, until he became aware of someone calling his name.

'Carilton Tann? Is there a man by the name of Carilton Tann here?'

He looked up, slowly, scraping his hands away from his face. 'That's me,' he croaked.

A messenger was in the doorway, a girl in simple breeches and a vest; one of those who earned strips of copper running errands around the town. Her hair was the colour of dry straw, and her eyes were confident as she approached him.

'There's someone outside saying your name,' she said. 'But they won't come in.'

'Fine, fine,' muttered Tann, rising and heading for the door. She moved to block his path and held out a pale hand. He grunted, before delving into his pocket and passing her a copper section. She smiled sweetly and hurried away.

Stepping outside onto the street he was confronted by a large wagon, drawn by a pair of sturdy draft horses. He immediately recognised the cunningly hinged design as belonging to the Weica, the travelling people.

A family of three rode on the wagon, man, woman and boy-child. All were fair-haired and wore woven bands around their heads, as was their way. The woman, wearing a headband of twisted copper rods, looked down at him.

'You are Carilton Tann?' she asked. He nodded. 'You have been asking about a tall outlander? A travelling stranger?'

'Yes,' said Tann. 'I am searching for such a man.'

'I have seen him,' she said. 'I can tell you where he went.'

TWENTY SEVEN

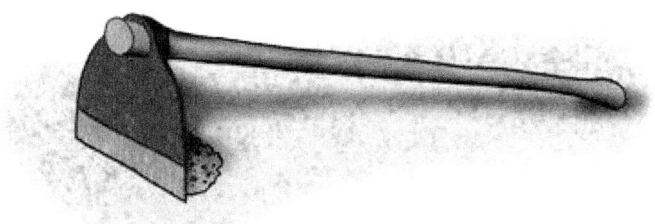

Holt Cookson could not believe what he was seeing.

The day had started as most did, with early light piercing the comfortable darkness of his house as the sunrise peeking through gaps in the shutters. His eyes opened slowly as his hands reached out, arms wrapping around the warm shape beside him, snug beneath the blankets and furs.

Luara.

After all those years sundered from her, she had returned, stealing into his house in the dead of night. His heart had almost stopped. Or perhaps, that was the moment it finally started to beat once more. He had spent so long telling himself that he did not need her, that he had been a fool for ever thinking of it, of thinking of them together.

All lies. He had lied to himself, day after day, so that he could continue to live his life without breaking down over what he had let slip through his fingers.

'Morning is here,' he said, whispering softly into her ear, stroking her head as her long chestnut hair tangled in his fingers. 'I should rise.'

'Stay,' she replied, voice husky with sleep. 'Just a few moments more.' Her hands reached for him.

More than a few moments later, he was dressed and about his errands in the village of Feorhryc. The people looked to him to make decisions, settle disputes, and to be the voice of authority. He had never wanted it, but he knew someone must do it, and for one reason or another the people trusted him.

It was mid-morning when he saw it.

The day was grey and the cool, heavy clouds hung oppressively over the wide landscape like a heavy woollen blanket, hiding the southern mountains from view. Holt had paused near the village inn when movement on the eastward road caught his eye. Travellers approached, atop a wagon.

That was not unusual in itself, as this was the main road and well-used, the only way for any trader or traveller to move between Annida and Ben Gedrin, or to visit any of the villages between.

What made him stare was the figure driving the wagon. Those broad shoulders, that familiar wide-brimmed hat. Could it be? Holt started forwards as the wagon's wheels rumbled on the bridge.

'Holt?' came a familiar voice from the wagon. A voice that remained familiar, even though an age seemed to have passed.

'Carilton Tann!' replied Holt as he dashed forward. 'By the Five, it really is you!'

Tann let the wagon roll to a halt as he leapt down and hurried forward. He thrust out his right hand and Holt grasped his wrist.

'Holt Cookson!' exclaimed Tann, his pale eyes creasing and a broad smile splitting his weathered face. 'I never thought I'd find you still here. You've grown.'

'I'm no taller,' replied Holt with a smile.

'I mean, you've grown up. You weren't much more than a kid when I last saw you.'

Holt's smile faltered. 'A lot of things changed after that.'

Holt had not forgotten how Carilton Tann had aided them when the village had been raided and occupied by Wolt Wose and his bandits, but also the blood and death that had been the result.

'You know I'm sorry—' Tann began.

'Don't,' said Holt, with a wave of his hand.

'I should have been honest with you. From the start.'

'Without you,' said Holt, 'Wose would have carried on doing whatever he wanted.'

'And without you,' replied Tann, moving closer and lowering his voice. 'I don't know what I'd have ended up doing.'

Holt was silent for a moment. At the climax of the battle it had emerged that Tann had only agreed to help Holt and Fionn so that he might take revenge on Wolt Wose, the bandit leader.

Holt had never spoken about it before, not with Tann, nor with anyone else. The aftermath of the battle had not felt like the right time, and then Tann was gone, travelling east to his farm and had not returned.

'He killed your wife,' said Holt. 'You had every right—'

'To torture him?' snapped Tann.

Tann had duelled Wose, one on one, but in his victory had not killed the bandit leader outright, but had instead set out to give him a slow death. Watching on, Holt had been horrified. Impulsively, he seized the sword of a slain bandit and had run Wose through, ending the battle.

'We were both tested,' said Holt, after a moment's thought. 'And together, we prevailed.'

Wordlessly, Tann reached out and grasped Holt's wrist once more, gripping it tightly. His eyes shone.

'That old sword still hanging in the inn?' asked Tann, in a lighter tone.

'Funny you should ask that,' replied Holt, reminded of the unusual encounter at the inn a few weeks before. But before he could tell Tann about it, and the sword's onward journey, a shadow loomed over them.

'Ah, I'm forgetting my manners,' said Tann, turning towards the newcomer. 'This is my travelling companion, Cerle. Cerle Connow. Cerle, this is an old friend of mine, Holt Cookson. You can share your moons later.'

Cerle reached out a hand to grip Holt's, wrist to wrist as Tann had. The strength of the man's grip was stunning. It was as though Holt's wrist had been clamped in a band of iron.

He stood several inches taller than both he and Tann, with a rangy physique that suggested a life of training. Looking to the deep creases of his face and the steel-grey in his long, bound hair, Holt thought it must have been a long life.

The man must be about seventy years old.

'Well met, Holt Cookson,' said Cerle. 'This is my wife, Indaella.' He turned and gestured towards a third figure who was approaching from the wagon.

Where Cerle was hard and craggy, his wife was soft, with a heart-shaped face and wide, pale eyes. She was at least a foot shorter than her husband and delicate, her open gaze knowing and bright.

Something tickled at the back of Holt's mind. Something about a name...

'We've come a long way, old friend,' said Tann as Holt stood silently, wracking his brains. 'A seat and something to drink would be welcome.'

Connow.

'Wait,' said Holt, the pieces sliding into place. 'Say your names again. Please.'

'Cerle and Indaella Connow,' said Cerle, eyes suddenly hard and suspicious. 'Why?'

Eain Connow.

'You'd better come inside the inn and sit down. There's something we need to talk about.'

'He was your grandson?' asked Holt, again. He could not hide his surprise.

'Is,' corrected Indaella. 'He *is* our grandson. He has not gone from the world.'

They were sitting at one of the long tables of the inn. At Holt's request, the innkeeper had lit an early fire in one of the big hearths that lay at either end of the great hall. A blackened iron kettle hung over the dancing yellow flames, steam just beginning to swirl from its spout.

Holt had sat them down and told them about the other Connow he had met recently, the haunted outlander warrior who named himself Eain Connow.

'You met my grandson?'

The question had snapped savagely from the lips of Cerle Connow. Holt had leaned back before continuing the tale.

Cerle looked like a man hewn from stone, and at the mention of Eain's name his knuckles had whitened as he pressed his fingernails into his palms. He looked like he was ready to punch a hole through the wall.

'Eain's the reason we're here, Holt,' said Tann. 'He was at my farm for a time, and he went off with Tressin Oke three months ago.'

'Oke!' said Holt brightly, recalling the jovial wagon master. Drink always flowed and songs rang out whenever Oke and his caravan passed through Feorhryc. 'There was a grand feast, last time he was here.'

'He was here?' asked Tann, eyes suddenly bright.

'Yea, six months ago I guess. He was heading your way.'

Tann's face fell. 'And you've not seen him since? He wasn't with Eain?'

'No, I've not seen Oke. Or heard any tell of him. Eain was alone.'

The three newcomers looked at one another, the atmosphere in the room suddenly cold and anxious.

'What happened when Eain was here?' asked Cerle, pale eyes fixed on Holt's face. 'And why is he not here still?'

Holt gathered his thoughts, recalling that strange day. 'It was quite something, to tell the truth. He arrived one morning, half-starved and dry as an old bone. I brought him in and he ate and drank his fill. Sat at that bench right there.' He pointed at the spot. 'Couple of hours later, some toughs came in. They were bandits or something, but said they were chasing some thieves across the Riverlands. I didn't believe a word, but they seemed set on causing trouble.

'Anyhow Eain saw them off. Woke up, grabbed the Wose blade off the wall—' once more Holt pointed, this time at the empty brackets protruding from the old stone, 'and made the bandits back off. They left in a hurry with him glaring at them, that sword in his hands like he was ready to use it.'

Cerle and Indaella shared a meaningful look.

'Then what?' asked Indaella. 'Where did he go?'

'He decided to tail them. We both knew they were up to no good, and he decided he wanted to stop them.'

'And the sword?' asked Cerle. His voice was smooth and old, a blade in itself.

'I gave it to him,' Holt admitted. 'It just seemed to…fit him.'

'So, you sent my grandson off,' said Cerle. 'On the trail of some dangerous bandits. You not only let him do this, but you armed him too?'

'I…' Holt floundered for words. 'I couldn't stop him. He was determined, cold as ice. If the folk he saw off were dangerous, he was more so. You've seen the size of him!'

'No,' said Cerle. 'I haven't. I'm starting to wonder if I ever will.'

Holt felt that icy stare on him, and Cerle's words were thrown as though they were physical blows. It did sound as though he had acted without care, but Holt remembered the steely look in the young man's eyes, and his conviction in continuing his onward journey.

'He certainly handled that sword like he knew what he was about,' said Holt.

'I should hope so,' said Cerle.

'Where was he going?' asked Indaella.

'He was following those bandits, so his road was wherever they led. I'd be surprised if they didn't end up in Ben Gedrin, though.'

'He won't be there now. Not if he's got any sense,' chimed in a new voice from the inn's doorway. Holt looked up to see Luara approaching the table.

She was dressed in rider's leathers, as she had not done for a long while, with snug trousers and a sleeveless vest over a pale shirt. Her long chestnut hair was tied back and her sharp blue eyes scanned the newcomers.

Tann had turned at the voice, and Holt saw his eyes widen.

'Fate curse me!' he exclaimed, as he rose. 'Luara Orsini! I hadn't thought to run into you again.'

'It's been a while,' she said, moving over to stand beside Holt and placing a hand on his shoulder. He wrapped an arm around her middle, resting a gentle hand on her waist. Tann's eyebrow's rose. 'So what are you doing back here? Stirring up more trouble?'

Tann gaped for a moment, eyes flicking between Luara and Holt. Holt got the impression he was desperate to ask, but knew it was against his nature to pry.

'I'm travelling with Cerle and Indaella,' he said, eventually. 'We're looking for their grandson, Eain Connow—'

'I've seen him,' cut in Luara. 'At least I think I did. In Ben Gedrin. A tall, outlander man carrying that big sword that used to hang on the wall, there?' She pointed.

'You saw him?' asked Indaella. 'Was he safe?'

Luara laughed. 'No one in that whole Fate-cursed city was safe that night. But he seemed to know what he was doing. I saw him on his way to the gates, so I think he got out.'

She eased herself back onto the bench, turning to press her back against Holt's shoulder, and drawing her knees up to her chest. She had spoken sparingly of what had happened that night in Ben Gedrin. The gangs had fought in the streets, and the Demonsnight festival had ended in chaos and fire.

Holt got the impression, though, that there was something she had not told him. Something that scared her.

She had remained cagey about her reasons for being in Ben Gedrin at all, although she had at least owned up to stealing three horses from the village. Or, borrowing, as she put it.

'If he went to Ben Gedrin,' Cerle was saying, 'and left the city, where would Eain have gone next?'

'South?' replied Tann, with a slight shrug. 'He's not come back this way, has he? And if he left the city, the only ways are back here or south.'

'I think he did,' said Luara. 'Everyone was dashing for the gates.'

'Right. So, we can rule out him hopping on a boat across the lake to Timmers.'

'So, south from Ben Gedrin,' said Cerle. 'What's south? Buren, and Tayo.'

'There's new rumours of trouble in Tayo,' added Holt. 'I've seen plenty of mercenaries heading that way. They can smell when there's money to be made in war, and something's brewing there.'

Indaella reached for Cerle's hand and clutched it.

'Wait, wait,' said Luara. 'Why are you all chasing this kid? Is he not old enough to look after himself? He looked as strong as an ox when I saw him.'

'It's not that,' said Tann. 'He's…important.'

'Important?'

Indaella's brow creased, pained. 'I have Seen…things. Futures. Eain is in them. I feel that he is in danger, and there's something he will need to do. To save our country from whatever is coming.'

'Futures?' asked Holt. This already sounded like nonsense.

Cerle rounded on him. 'My wife has the Sight.'

'The Sight?' Holt was incredulous. 'Are you serious?'

'Holt, don't,' said Luara softly, reaching to lay a hand on his upper arm. 'Let her speak.'

There was a tone in her voice he did not recognise. He could not understand it. There was no such thing as the Sight, just like there was no such thing as magic, or the Shining Ones. They were all stories for children.

'Something is moving in the world,' began Indaella. 'Changing. Something dark. I See it in my dreams. Armies marching, people dying and behind it all, a powerful darkness.

'I can't tell you any more than that because I don't know. It's not clear. I can only tell you what I feel and that is that Banahgar, and the other countries of the world, are in great danger.'

'Can't you feel it?' demanded Cerle. 'It has already begun. Armies march in Banahgar, Kotev and Tayo. Dwarves are on the move, Wild Elves too. Something is building. Something that comes from the shadows.'

Holt shook his head. He could not help himself. This was ridiculous.

'I know this sounds crazy,' said Tann, before Holt could speak. Cerle's eyes narrowed. 'I know it does. But you have to believe it. Indaella has shown me some things...' He tailed off. 'Whatever you think, you've got to admit that things are happening. War everywhere, conflicts escalating. And that boy could be stuck right in the middle.

'We should try to help him, as we were the ones who let him walk into it. We should try to get him home.'

'Thank you, Carilton Tann,' said Cerle. 'If I remember right, the next village is not more than half a day away. If we leave soon, we can make it before dusk.'

'You're leaving so soon?' asked Holt. He had not seen Tann in ten years, and he could not believe the man was going to pass through with barely a pause.

'My grandson is out in the world, somewhere,' said Indaella. 'We must help him, and we must hurry.'

Holt felt a stab of guilt. He was partly responsible: he had armed the boy and watched him walk away into the sunset. Half of him had wanted to go too, to escape the mundane confines of this village, but his common sense had won the day. His regret threatened to overwhelm him.

A surge of anger flared instead, and he stood.

'I wish the three of you well,' he said, keeping his voice level. 'May the Five guide your steps. I hope you find him.' He turned away.

'Are you leaving?' asked Tann.

'I've got work to do. Maybe I'll find time to wave you off.' He strode out through the open doorway of the inn and away up the street. He had nowhere to be, in truth, but could not trust his own tongue.

Footsteps sounded behind him, a rapid tapping on the hard earth. Before he could turn, Luara was beside him and lacing one of her arms through his.

'Calm down,' she said.

'I'm calm,' he replied, walking on.

'I could see you getting grumpy,' she said, with a swift smile.

'They were talking nonsense,' he said. 'The Sight, and mysterious danger, lurking in the shadows. Kid's tales.'

Luara shrugged. Her face was suddenly very blank.

'They believe it,' she said.

'Then they're all fools! The boy will have to look after himself. There was no mystery around him. Just another soul lost in the world.'

She said nothing, but those wide-set, blue eyes pierced him. With a simple look she could ask many questions without needing to say a word.

'What?' he spluttered. 'It's nothing to do with me! Was I supposed to physically restrain him?'

She laughed, but just for a moment, before her face was a blank, serious mask once more. 'Their grandson met Tann, then met you, and then I saw him. Five of us, including the Connows, all tangled up with the journey of the same lad. Don't you think that's at all strange?'

'Just coincidence.'

'Maybe.'

They had wandered along to Holt's own house, and Luara led the way to the door. Once inside, Holt slumped into his chair as Luara went through to the back of the house.

Holt closed his eyes. He was right. This was nonsense and none of his business. He would feel better once these people had moved on and were gone from his presence. They would quickly pass out of his mind.

So, why did he have a nagging sense of guilt?

Sensing movement, he opened his eyes and looked up. Luara was standing before him. His eyes widened.

'What are you doing?' he asked, stunned.

She had flung her cracked leather travelling coat around her shoulders, and a bulging knapsack dangled from one hand. Her twin shortswords were in place on a broad, well-worn belt that sat on her hips.

'I need to do this,' she said.

'What? No. Why?'

She kicked a chair aside and sat. Leaning forwards, her lips parted as she gathered the words.

'I never told you this,' she said, eventually. 'But I was lucky to escape Ben Gedrin. The city was torn apart, and the two girls I travelled with were caught in a double-cross.'

'The other horse thieves?'

'The same. The gangs would have killed them both to rob them of what they were trying to sell. And I'd have been next.'

She took a deep breath.

'That man, Eain Connow, he saved them. I don't know exactly how, or why, but he went into a meeting with the girls and one of the gangs, and only they came out.'

'He might have robbed them himself,' said Holt.

'He left them with a bag of gold,' replied Luara. She shrugged again. 'It was chaotic. I don't know anything for certain, but I know what I feel. And that's that I owe him something. If I can help, I should.'

Holt gaped. He did not know what to say. He knew how determined she could be, once she had made a decision. Life without her was unthinkable.

'But what about us...'

'I know, Holt. It's been perfect here. And it will be again when I return. I promise.' She touched cool fingertips to his cheek and her lips brushed his. 'I love you, Holt Cookson.'

'I love you too,' he said. 'Please, don't go.'

She smiled. 'I must.' Wrapping her arms around his shoulders, she kissed him softly once more, before heading for the door. It shut behind her with a solemn click, and his head dropped. Loss and guilt overwhelmed him.

He could stop her. Order her to stay. Maybe she would, maybe she would still go. It was pretty likely she would punch him in the face for trying to order her around. And she would be right either way: he had no right to tell her what to do, however painful it would be to live without her.

There was only one solution.

He began to pack a bag.

Tann watched, arms folded against the biting, insistent wind as Luara Orsini approached. He had thought she might.

'Joining the fun?' he asked as she stopped beside him.

'Shut up,' she said. 'That big outlander looked handy, but you might need some more swords to help you get to him. And more brains.'

He grinned. She had not changed in the years that had passed, still bright and breezy in the toughest of times.

'Listen' she went on. 'I have to do this. Don't ask me why, because I don't know. I just know it feels right. Feels like there's a debt I can pay off. And Holt is going to come too.'

'He doesn't have to—' he began.

'Of course he doesn't!' she snapped. 'But we both know he will. And it's not my place to tell him to stay here. Not again.'

Tann just nodded. He understood something of what she meant. When they had first met she was not ready to settle down, and had left Holt behind in Feorhryc. Tann could still remember vividly the pain he had seen in both of them at the time, all those years ago.

'You look after him, you hear me?' she hissed. 'We both know this could be dangerous. I want your word you'll keep him safe.'

'Sure, you have my word.'

'I mean it,' she said, and her smile was gone, the delicate features of her face suddenly as hard as a rock face. 'If he gets hurt, I'll kill you.'

TWENTY EIGHT

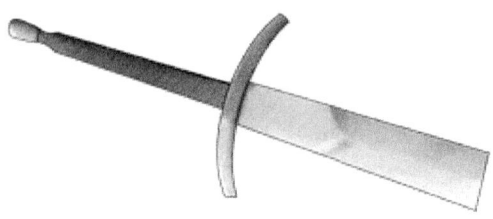

Eain could not bear it. He could not stand its call: a crimson tinted siren song.

Take me.

Take me, use me.

The voice echoed in his head, promising to grant him the strength he lacked, to solve all the problems he faced. Whispering. Another voice spoke as a counterpoint. A voice from his past.

'*There are no short-cuts, no ways to cheat.*'

It was the voice of Morgan Blane.

'*Hard work, dedication, courage. These are the paths to success. Any voice that offers you what you want without needing to train, and study, and practise is a voice that must be ignored.*'

The interior of the tent was lit a lurid red, as though the sloping canvas walls were drenched with fresh blood. The lid of the box was open, and Eain could see the glassy gleam of the jewel itself as it laid within.

He was sitting on one of the bunks, staring into the unearthly light, with his hand halfway towards the shining gem. He hesitated.

'At least we live, lad!' Klay had boomed as they surged through the trees, leaving the fort town and the Gluttons far behind.

Barely, Eain had thought, sucking air into his lungs. And many had not. The fort's courtyard had been strewn with bodies, friend and foe, as he had fled.

Such waste.

They had met the ragged survivors in a grassy dell, screened by tall tree ferns. The Eagle Sisters stood apart from the Steel Hounds, eyes still bound and bows slung across their shoulders.

'Victory!' cried Daeron Teleri, climbing up onto the bed of one of the stolen wagons. 'We have struck a great blow, one of plunder and fire! This is just the first bloody nose to the Taosach and her forces. She will hear of this, and her sleep will not be sound!'

There were a few cheers, but many of the assembled fighters remained silent. They had all lost comrades, friends, and many bore injuries.

The woman next to Eain groaned. 'Don't feel like a victory.' She was a Bureno soldier with dark hair cut in a severe line level with her jaw. One hand was clamped to an oozing wound in her side, and an arm around her neighbour's shoulder was all that held her upright.

'Eat, drink, rest,' continued Teleri, oblivious to the grumbles. 'We will move on soon. Captains, to me.' He beckoned, and Klay started forwards, muttering under his breath.

'You are hurt,' said Eain, as the woman slumped to a sitting position with her back against a tree.

'Caught a spear point under my ribs,' she replied, with a gap-toothed grin. 'Not too deep though, and the bastard felt the bite of my sword before he could stick me any worse.' She chuckled, slapping the hilt of the sword that hung at her waist.

She squinted up at Eain. 'You're that big outlander, aren't you? The one that held the gates for us to escape.'

'I am Eain Connow,' he replied. 'And I am from…far away.'

She chuckled again. 'I'm Caree Mione, and I'm from the wrong side of the river. It's getting sore,' she said, turning to her companion, a Bureno man. 'Pass the wine.'

She grasped the proffered wineskin and took a deep draft, before sloshing another measure over the still-bleeding wound. With a sigh, she sat back against the tree and closed her eyes.

A few moments later, Klay stomped over. A scowl even heavier than usual lowered his brows until his eyes were little more than slits. His fists were clenched.

'We're heading south!' he bellowed, loudly enough for the company to hear. 'Rest a while but be ready. When the horn sounds we move, waiting for none. Wounded can find a space on't wagons.'

He moved over to Eain and glanced down to where the injured Caree lay, eyes closed as if sleeping.

'Give us that,' he said, reaching for the wineskin. 'I need a bloody drink.' He upended it and the dark wine moistened his beard and moustache as he drank deeply.

'What's wrong?' asked Eain, sensing that there was something that had irritated the dwarf. It would be better if he got it off his chest.

Klay lowered the wineskin. "E' knew. Bastard knew.'

'Who? Knew what?'

'Teleri,' replied the dwarf, lowering his voice and shuffling closer. "E' knew that we might find that fort held by the Gluttons. He sent us in anyway, to spring the trap.'

'What?' Eain was shocked. 'Why would he do that?'

'Word had gone around that he was dead, reet? That they'd send a company of Gluttons this far east tells us that the Taosach knows it in't true. They were sent to guard against him, to crush any forces he might have been able to gather.'

'So why send us in there, if he thought that was the risk?'

"E' 'ad to be sure. Now 'e is. What Teleri did made sense. Callous sense. If I 'adn't given me word...' He eyed the treeline as though thinking about making a dash for it.

'Where would you go?'

'Ah, ah'll stay put. But I don't have to like it, youth.'

Eain did not know what to think. Teleri had deceived them, or at least withheld the truth. Could you follow a leader who you could not trust completely? Now, though, Teleri knew what he was up against and seemed to be leading them away from the danger. It made a cold, hard sense.

'But so many died,' said Eain, barely realising that he was speaking aloud.

'Eh?' grunted Klay, squinting up at him. 'Yer'll go mad if you start thinkin' about that too much. This is the game we're in. Those that fell knew what they were getting' into. Yer can't mourn 'em all.'

Eain shook his head. 'I'm not sure I can do it. I can't just forget—'

'You 'ave to!' hissed Klay, grabbing Eain's front and pulling him closer. This time, Eain's fingers did not even twitch towards a counterblow. 'If you want to survive, you 'ave to. Forget what's gone. There's two types of folk in this game, the tough and the dead.

'Yer good at this. Yer've got good instincts and know what you're about with that cleaver.' He nodded towards the sword, hanging heavily on Eain's back. 'Yer'll survive if yer smart, and if you make yerself hard to it. Think of it as a suit of armour.'

Eain nodded. Could he do it?

'You'll be grand,' said Klay, just before the company war horn blew. The wagons began to roll, and Eain saw Caree being helped onto the back of one, still clutching her side. He and Klay fell into step together, as the army marched south in a narrow, disordered column.

They followed an overgrown, serpentine path through woodland which was tinged with gold; the russet of fallen leaves that crunched underfoot, and the hazy amber of watery sunshine through breaking clouds.

'Who are the Gluttons, anyway?' asked Eain. Everyone else in the Steel Hounds had been horrified by their very presence.

'Taosach's personal guard,' replied Klay. 'Used to be the Kingsguard until the last border war, when Buren executed the King and banned that title. Gluttons remained, but under orders from the Taosach instead.'

'What are they?' Eain recalled the huge figures in their imposing armour. They seemed inhuman.

'Just men, nobbut men. Big bastards though, eh? Spend the whole time eating when they're not training or sparring.'

'They looked...' Eain searched for the right word. 'Fat.'

'Aye, they are that. But don't be fooled, youth, they're all strong as bulls, men and women alike. And they know what they are about in a scrap. Disciplined, organised. Teleri has the right of that. We'd be better to avoid 'em as long as we can, until our army is stronger.'

'And when's that likely to be?'

'If Teleri carries on being right, soon.'

They marched south for a few more days. The mood was uneasy and fractious. Fights broke out on several occasions, with Klay wading in to break them up, quickly, violently and efficiently. Eain saw more than a few warriors drifting off silently through the trees when no one else was watching.

Deserters.

Was Teleri's campaign falling apart so quickly?

Eain often found himself following behind where Caree, the injured Bureno, was riding.

'So, where *are* you from?' she asked on the second afternoon. Her wound was clearly still troubling her. She clutched the area with a clawed hand, and each bump and jolt of the cart produced a whimper of pain.

'North,' said Eain, giving the same answer as always.

'Riverlands, or something?'

'Or something.' Eain did not want to be drawn into saying more. He did not want to think about Banahgar. It was behind him, gone. 'And you?'

'I'm from northern Buren. A duchy called Telivaina.'

'It is like here?'

Caree let out a short bark of laughter, which turned to a whimper of pain.

'No,' she said eventually. 'No, nothing like this. Green hills, rich land, lords with honour.'

'So, why are you here?'

She shrugged. 'I got tired of being told what to do. Of being treated like I was worth less. This is my choice.'

They continued in silence.

Camping in a small stand of trees beside a still lake, Teleri posted sentries along their back trail, ready to warn if they were followed. Eain saw fewer trees in the distance as he looked south, but water gleamed. Chains of lakes merged with marshes and swamps, grey in the reflected light from the sullen sky.

The mercenaries strung oiled canvas between trees to shelter from the biting wind. Fires were built and kept well fed, and competition for the warmest places was fierce. Caree cast a forlorn figure, slumped in a darkening corner as night fell.

The next day was colder still. Dew shone brightly on drooping leaves and blades of grass. It felt as though frost could be near.

Caree lolled in the back of the wagon, eyes glazed. She did not speak, but moans occasionally emerged from her pale lips. She was mostly left in peace, the cart rolling along even, well-used tracks that were slightly raised above the damp land all around.

They left the trees behind and to Eain it seemed like they were dangerously exposed. He could see for miles in any direction, although little seemed to be moving.

Occasionally, he thought he saw the heavy blue shapes of buildings, far away to the west, but they were quickly left behind in the chilly haze. Little else changed throughout the day and Eain walked alone for the most part, lost in his thoughts.

They camped in the open, from pure necessity. There was no cover, no trees or even low shrubs. Just waving grass and marshland stretching away for miles. Flimsy shelters were thrown up along the verge of the track, just a few steps away from the filmy bog.

Eain was spreading out his own blankets when Klay bustled over.

'Bloody murder keeping this lot in line,' he grumbled. 'And Teleri wants us pushing harder still.'

'Where are we heading?' asked Eain.

'Bit further south yet. He reckons he'll find more support from the people down here. Farmers and peasants. I reckon he might be right. Again.'

'Caree isn't doing well,' said Eain, pointing to where the Bureno woman lay. Her head lolled and when they had pulled aside her robe, the flesh around the wound had been a livid purple and hot to touch. 'Is there anyone can help her?'

'Someone's probably got a bottle of rice wine,' said Klay. 'Get her to sup on that til she's blind drunk.'

'I meant medicine.'

'Ent no time to worry about that,' said Klay, before stomping away.

Caree was dead in the morning.

Eain had heard her moaning through the night, a mournful sound. But he had done nothing. Her stiff, grey corpse lay beside the marsh, dew in her hair.

He went to tell Klay.

'Tekk her weapons, boots any money rings she's got on and then roll't body in't swamp,' he said.

'That's it?' Eain was shocked. 'She was one of us.'

'And now she int. "Us" are the ones who are living, at least for't moment. We ain't got time to fret over't dead.'

'I just thought we should do something…'

'Listen, youth,' growled Klay, moving closer. 'Ah'm sayin' this for your own good, right? You need to put all them cares and worries in a box, and lock 'em away. They ent helpful.'

At the mention of a locked box, Eain thought of the one in the bottom of his knapsack. He still carried that mysterious jewel.

'Yer a good soldier,' Klay continued. 'But, yer need to worry about what you can fix, and forget what you can't control. That's if you want to stay alive.

'All that other stuff is just a distraction, and if yer can't get over it, someday soon it'll be your bulky corpse I'll be shovin' in't swamp. And, I'd rather not 'ave to.'

'I…understand,' was all that Eain managed to say in response.

'Right,' said Klay, as though the matter was settled.

'Listen up!' he bawled, moving to stand in the middle of the track. 'We'll be moving out soon! Be ready.'

They were back on the road as dawn broadened into the flat grey light of a wintery morning. Chill gusts chased fleeting ripples across the surrounding wetlands, and it was easy to imagine the spirits of the dishonourable dead stirring in the murky water, watching them as they passed.

The *draugr*.

He shuddered the dark thoughts away and marched on.

Noon brought a barely perceptible brightening of the leaden sky, and the pace quickened as a village appeared ahead. The houses were flimsy, little more than domed huts of woven twigs. A heavy thatch of trimmed reeds sat atop each one, and the walls were of dried, reddish mud.

The village was set about a small hilltop, barely more than an area of dry land raised above the surrounding wetlands. Folk garbed in bright colours moved through the marsh, wading through the still waters, although Eain had no idea what they were doing.

The sound of many voices came from ahead and Eain saw Teleri riding at the head of the column, approaching a large group of people gathered on the hilltop. As one, they raised their hands in welcome.

Clearly, they were expected.

A buzz of excited conversation greeted the mercenary army as they filed into an open area surrounded by similar ramshackle huts. Clustering to one side, they found themselves facing a crowd of Tayans in peasant garb. Children darted around their parents' legs, pointing at the warriors and talking excitedly.

Teleri jumped down from his horse and stepped forward, with the High *Offerad* beside him. Two women and a man were standing a pace ahead of the other villagers, their robes plain but woven with bright colours. Each had their head bound by a vivid scarf like Teleri's.

'Is this he?' asked one of the women, turning to her neighbour but speaking loudly enough for all to hear. Her face was creased with age, but her eyes were large and shone with intelligence.

'Yes,' replied the other woman, with equal volume. 'This must be he.' She was shorter, and slighter, with hands like bird's feet that clutched shakily at the sash that ran around her small waist.

'I expected more,' put in the man in a croaky voice. There were uneasy glances among the mercenaries, but Teleri had not moved, had not batted an eyelid.

'Much more,' said the first woman. 'From him, and from those he leads.'

The second woman gestured weakly with those twiglike hands. 'So few. He brings so few, yet I expect he will ask for our aid.'

'Who does he think he is?' said the man, white beard jutting as he raised his chin.

'I am Duke Daeron Teleri,' he said, speaking at last. 'And I will ask you for nothing. I come with an offer.'

'Offer!' spat the taller woman. 'Pah! What can you offer us?'

'Protection,' he said. 'My guardianship. My promise that I will fight against the oppression that grinds you into the dirt. When they come, I will put my body in the path of their march.'

'We will only need protection because of your presence!' wheezed the old man.

'If only that were true,' replied Teleri. 'But you must be old enough to remember the days before Re'Emsser? When all Tayans could live well on their labour? When we were one country. Do you remember?'

The old man's head dropped, his chin bobbing in a simple nod.

'I remember,' Teleri continued, raising his voice to address the crowd. 'I remember what was. What should have been. What has been stolen from you, by the Taosach and her forces.

'They line their pockets with the profits of your hard work, and would see you living your whole lives face down in the dirt. Even now, her forces are coming south not to follow me but because they fear you. They know the strength that resides in this land as well as I do, and even far away in their tall towers of stone they tremble.'

'You say she sends forces here?' said the smaller woman, in a shrewd tone. 'Why would they come here, if not for you?'

'She wishes to stamp down anywhere that resistance grows,' said Teleri. 'And do you not resist her? Do you not hate her? So she will come, sooner or later. But this is not a threat. This is an opportunity! She does not yet know your strength, but I do. I will add my support to your resistance and together we will show her the true Tayo.

'Together,' he raised his hands, 'we will fight!'

A roar of approval rose from the villagers and mercenaries alike. Once again, Teleri had turned a crowd to his will, leaving them feeling as though his ambition was their idea.

'I know there are many of those among you,' continued Teleri, 'who still know the old ways, the old skills. Send the word out. Let there be a muster. All those who are willing and able should come forth, for now is the time that their country needs them most.'

Just a few days later, Eain found himself packed tightly between other soldiers of the Steel Hounds. Klay was beside him. The morning breeze was chilling.

An ominous rumble came from the track ahead as heavy boots thudded on packed earth.

They were standing on a broad causeway which led through the wetlands just north of the village. The waters all around them were as still as if they were frozen, no birds or beasts moving in or out of the dense reed beds that lined the track. Teleri had predicted that this was where the first hammer blow of the Taosach's reprisal would fall.

In the distance, the iron fist that would wield that hammer appeared; a company of the Gluttons, moving ever closer at a brisk march.

'Hold your ground!' came Teleri's voice, from where he sat astride his horse behind the rear ranks. 'You have nothing to fear from the Taosach's terriers this day! They do not belong here. We do. Our fight is righteous and the old gods will watch over us.

'Hold your ground!'

'You heard't Duke,' added Klay. 'Yer all know what yer need to do. We cannot let them through. Not today.'

The dwarf was wearing a heavy-rimmed helm of dark iron and armour of overlapping bands covered his shoulders and chest. Eain had found a conical helmet with a thick nasal guard and was wearing several layers of baked leather. It felt uncomfortable and hot despite the cold air, but it at least afforded some measure of protection.

Neither bore shields as their weapons needed both hands, but warriors to their left and right did. Eain felt as though he was part of a stone-built wall. He knew what he had to do and was as ready as he could be. He just wished that his hands would stop shaking.

On came the Gluttons.

Eain could see them clearly now. Each warrior carried a square shield and heavy, flanged mace. Each was encased in curved plates of thick iron, adding even more bulk to their huge bodies. The very ground seemed to shake as they closed the distance.

Deep helms left little of their faces exposed. Their faceguards came down lower than their eyes and heavy mail hung down over their mouths and necks. They seemed more than mere men; the closer they got the more they were like titans cast from solid metal.

'Not a backward step!' bellowed Klay, just when Eain felt the courage of those around him begin to falter. 'Yer fighting for those villagers. Those that can't fight for themselves.'

It was enough. The line held. Shields were raised. Eain gripped the hilt of his sword as the Gluttons slowed. They came on more cautiously now, step by step.

They were in no hurry.

Eain could hear the plates of their imposing armour clanking together as they moved, hear the metallic swish of the mail skirts they wore, as each heavy step brought them closer.

In a few moments they would charge. The power of their surge forwards would be ferocious, and would sweep the lightly-armoured mercenaries away.

'Now!' yelled Teleri, his voice startling some drowsing waterfowl into urgent flight. As the flapping of their wings sounded over the marshes, the water beneath erupted.

From the long grass and red beds on both sides of the track, dripping figures emerged clad in oiled skins that shone in the morning light. They rose from the murky water and went on rising, taller than any man.

The Gluttons spun towards these unexpected, lanky bog creatures who swooped down on the banks on long, spindly legs. Before the Taosach's troops had a chance to do more than stare, missiles were cast at them from both directions.

Some of the newcomers threw nets, weighted at the edges with rocks, while others cast javelins into the milling ranks of the Gluttons. Eain could read the confusion even as the Gluttons tried to counter the attack, lunging to the sides at their new opponents. They splashed into the muddy water, sinking immediately to their chests.

They were quickly easy pickings for the marsh warriors, stooping down to strike at the floundering figures. Meanwhile, more appeared, racing through the swamp with their unusual long-legged gait. The Gluttons did not know which way to turn.

Even knowing they were nothing more outlandish than Tayan peasants on stilts, the marsh walkers still looked alien to Eain. They had done their work well, too; many of the Gluttons were still struggling to be free of the heavy nets, and some already lay still on the track, pierced by javelins.

'On me,' said Klay grimly, raising the Capper, and the ranks of the Steel Hounds swept forwards.

The Gluttons were now in total disarray and this time it was the mercenaries who caught *them* unawares. Eain's blade rose and fell, and this time he felt nothing. He was remote from the bloodshed as if watching it through another's eyes. The fury of battle quietened the voices in his mind.

It was over in moments, the Gluttons all struck down or driven off the track into the marsh. Some were pressed beneath the water by the combined weight of their thick armour and the nets that they could not shake off.

Teleri rode forward as the last few were dispatched. Cheers rose into the cold air and the waters nearby were stained with red.

More victories followed. The heavily armoured troops of the Taosach had been unable to match the craft and agility of the locals, and the ambush tactics they were able to use caught them off guard again and again.

Eain had learned that this was how they worked this damp land as farmers: striding across the waterlogged fields on those spindly stilts to tend their crops of rice, spinach or taro. It was also how they hunted, and how they fought. And as the word of the victories spread, more flocked to Teleri's banner.

His strength grew as his fame spread.

Eain should have been happy. For once, he was on the winning side. He threw himself into each skirmish eagerly, relishing those frantic moments where his mind was totally focused on the present and the pain of the past ceased to exist.

As he fought, he felt his body becoming stronger, the muscles of his arms and shoulders growing, and hardening. He was hardening himself on the inside, too.

Like a blade being heated in the forge, the guilt that had become part of him, and any horror he felt at the blood he spilled burned away what was left behind was little more than a weapon. Beaten steel with a lethal edge.

Why, then, did his guts churn and his hands shake when the fighting was over, and he was alone?

The ruby called to him anew.

Take me. Hold me. Use me.

It held such power, and it could all be his to command. The war could be over, and he could return to Banahgar at last. He could leave the blade behind.

His fingers twitched towards the box.

'*Be strong,*' came a different voice, and Eain started back. '*Have courage.*'

His vision seemed to swim, and he thought that there was someone else in the tent with him. He could feel their presence and a pair of large, liquid eyes stared into his.

Anndra? No.

Was it one of the Eagle Sisters? He felt dizzy and confused, but his hand withdrew from the box.

'Youth! Yer decent?'

Klay's voice disturbed his thoughts, and there was a swish of canvas as of someone leaving in the other direction.

With guilty haste, Eain lunged out and shut the box before shoving it beneath his makeshift bunk. The flap rippled and a stab of cold air touched the back of Eain's neck. The squat, solid figure of Klay was outlined in the doorway. His eyes scanned Eain's face for a moment before he spoke.

'Come on, no use sitting her stewin'. Be glad for what yer've got. We're winning and we've got a lord who seems to know what he's about. We live, for one more day at least.'

Eain sighed. 'Yes, you are right.'

'They've rolled out a barrel. Bureno wine. Come and have a drink. Mebbe's it'll help yer forget.'

Eain stood and followed Klay out, letting the door of the tent flap back into place.

Beneath the bunk, locked in its unassuming box, the jewel pulsed with crimson light as though it lived and had a heartbeat of its own.

TWENTY NINE

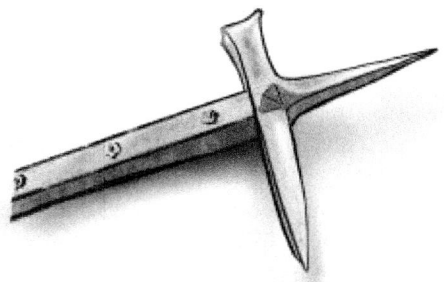

Dusk came swiftly, the sun plunging through the wispy grey clouds towards the distant horizon. The expanse of grey-green marshland was momentarily lit with shimmering fire as the sun set.

As Klay bustled through the camp, he noticed other soldiers huddling down for the night in layers of sackcloth and the odd scrap of foraged fur. It was not even that cold, yet.

So soft, he thought.

Eain followed silently behind.

Teleri had moved his army to another village built around the nearest thing to a hill these parts afforded. The slight elevation meant there was a small space on the outskirts where the soldiers could make a camp without risk of drowning in the night.

'Here he is!' rang out a jovial voice from beneath a shelter of stretched canvas. 'The dwarf captain himself.'

'Shut yer mouth,' replied Klay, but made his way into the shelter and sat on the floor. Eain followed, tucking his long legs beneath him.

A blazing fire warmed the air, but the thin twigs that twisted and crackled in the flames would burn through quickly. Kay wondered if there was any peat for burning in this damp corner of Tayo.

'Cold night coming,' said the first speaker, a short but burly Bureno named Gardas. He sloshed a measure of dark wine into a clay cup and passed it across.'

Klay sniffed. 'It'll get colder still, yet. Can smell it int' air.'

'Hope not,' replied Gardas. 'Never usually gets this cold this far south.' He filled another cup and passed it to Eain, who took it with a word of thanks. The shelter was full, with a handful of Tayans clustering in to try to absorb a little of the warmth.

'Load of fuss,' said the man sitting beside Gardas. He shook his head and long grey hair whisked across a face that was craggy with age. Ivhar was Anise, and thin rings of a variety of different metals shone on each of his fingers. 'It's just winter. Shouldn't surprise people.'

'Yer know yer talking dung,' said Klay, and Ivhar grinned. Both he and Gardas had spent years in Tayo and knew the country as well as any, but it was Ivhar's way to stir the pot.

They were hard men, seasoned fighters who had served with local militias and nobles' armies, before deciding that if they were going to risk their lives on a battlefield, they might as well earn as much as possible doing it. So, they ended up in Tayo.

'We should raise our cups to the blade captain, too,' said Ivhar, raising his own towards Eain.

'What?' Eain was clearly surprised.

'Shut yer hole,' snapped Klay, at Ivhar.

Some of the fools were muttering that Eain should be made a captain, or a bannerman. He was one to follow, they said. This "blade captain" nonsense was their name for him, and it was starting to spread.

It was daft. He was just a warrior, however effective, and to burden those shoulders with a responsibility, or even such a title, might be enough to break him. Klay was not blind. He had noticed the way Eain's hands shook after each battle, and he had heard him crying out in the night.

More wine flowed and the Tayans began to sing. These were warriors from the southern lands and the songs were cheerful, with frivolous melodies. Klay knew, though, that the words in Tayan spoke of injustice and oppression.

They were songs of hope, tinged with bitter memories.

Gargas and Ivhar followed by singing an old folk song together. It was well-known in both countries, telling the story of a princess who was turned into a bird as a test for her would-be lover. Klay had heard it before, and thought it was silly.

'Your turn, dwarf,' said Ivhar afterwards, voice thick with drink. 'Sing us one about wolves or mines or whatnot.' He cackled, and Gargas laughed with him.

'Yer a pair of mule's arses,' said Klay, but he was laughing too. They were drinking Bureno *folwine*, rich and strong. Even Eain had a warm smile across his face. 'I know a poem though. I'll tell that.'

He took a moment to recall the words, then recited these lines:

> *'Blood on stone, brazed in our stock*
> *Forged as one, forever toze*
> *Mem'ry and his'try*
> *Melded, hammered out*
> *Cracks in rock, can't be welded*
>
> *Sundered kin, swaled back to roots*
> *Green shoots nestled in grey rock*
> *Withies twisting strong*
> *Winding round t'ruin*
> *Time binds, together once more.'*

He sat once more.

'They are good words,' said Eain, breaking his silence.

'Well, I 'ad to translate it. It wasn't perfect.'

'It is very good,' said Eain. Klay could see the effects of the drink in his eyes. They were unfocused and heavy-lidded, as though ready for sleep. 'What is it about?'

'I'll tell you another time,' said Klay quickly. He did not want to talk about it.

'And you, swordsman,' said Ivhar, pointing an unsteady finger. 'Your turn. Sing a song.'

Eain said nothing, but put his cup down carefully on the ground and stood. He took a deep breath. Then, he started to sing.

At first, he sang in a low tone, in a droning language that recalled Dwarvish, although Klay could not understand any of the words. Nevertheless, the song conveyed a sense of deep loss and sadness. A bright light, long extinguished, never to be seen again.

Then his voice rose to a higher pitch, singing a simple melody but putting his whole heart into the song. His eyes were screwed up tightly and his voice trembled. Klay could see the gleam of tears on his cheeks.

There was silence when he sat down again, and he took a deep draught of wine while his cheeks reddened.

Later, Klay helped Eain to his feet and watched as he swayed off into the darkness, heading vaguely for their tent. Klay walked over to the edge of the marsh to empty his bladder before trying to sleep.

The boy was such a contradiction. On the battlefield he was fearless, and brutally efficient, but when the fighting stopped his hands shook, and Klay could see the pain and regret that filled him. It could not go on. Klay had fought alongside others like him before, and the truth was they were the dead walking. Sooner or later, usually sooner, their luck ran out and they found the oblivion they seemed to seek.

How much longer could Eain last?

He turned, and stopped. A dark shape stood nearby, motionless but watching him. The Capper was at his tent, but his hand dropped to his belt knife.

They stepped forward.

The red of their sleeveless robe was muddy in the low light, but Klay recognised one of the priestesses as the firelight glow played on her face. Her hair was dark and curling, tied to one side in the Tayan style. Dark eyes stared at him, wide and unblinking.

'You must not give up on him,' she said, her voice oddly toneless.

'What you mean?'

'You know who I mean,' she replied, taking another step closer. 'He.'

Eain. She must mean Eain.

'He's none of my business,' he said, making as if to walk away. 'Just another soldier. Some live, some die, I can't do nowt about that.'

'You know that's not true.' She took a step as though to follow him, or to get in his way.

He sucked his teeth.

The truth was that with Eain Connow beside him, he had never felt so safe on a battlefield.

Klay had been a soldier a long time, and resigned himself to the inevitable fact that one day, however strong he was and however much he practiced with his weapon, he would meet his end in battle. An unseen arrow, a well-aimed javelin or simply an opponent who outclassed him.

When fighting alongside Eain, that day seemed further away.

His ability to perceive threats from any direction, and to counter them, was like no one else Klay had ever met. It was like the boy could see out of the back of his head. Anything within the arc of his great sword was also guarded. That usually included Klay.

Despite himself, Klay had grown accustomed to it, used to the comforting feeling of the big warrior beside him and in turn he did everything he could to guard Eain's back. He owed him that much.

'So, what?' he snapped back at the priestess.

'He needs someone to be there,' she said. 'Someone to guide him along a path of life. He sees the door of death, but he must not go through it. Not yet.'

'Yer think I want to dig a pit for that great big corpse?' he snapped. The priestess merely stared back. 'I'll do what I can. I always do.'

'You must,' she replied, simply, and then was gone into the night with a swish of her robes.

The next day started bad and got worse.

Klay had lain in the darkness instead of rising before his second sleep, and the chill air bit his nose as he listened to Eain's breathing. When the light of dawn threw the tent interior into grey relief he rose and moved to the doorway. The laces of the flaps were crisp, and the heavy canvas crackled with the heavy frost. Overnight, the landscape around them had been transformed.

The paddy fields and marshes that stretched away in every direction had been stilled. Nothing moved, and not a ripple disturbed the surface, which was now covered with a flat, white sheen.

It was all frozen.

The grass was jewelled with crystalline frost, and the blankets and furs of the soldiers sleeping outside glittered in the new day's light.

Klay sucked his teeth. A chill like that could have killed people overnight, and that might not be the worst of it. He would have to check the piles of blankets and hope that none now contained frozen corpses. An uneasy feeling grew, as though the cold wind foreboded violence.

He strolled over to the shelter where he had been the previous night, thinking to rekindle the embers of the fire to warm up his breakfast. Frumenty porridge, like always.

Gargas was stirring as Klay approached.

'You were right about the weather, old friend,' he said, twisting up into sitting position.

'Don't have to sound so bloody surprised,' muttered Klay, feeding kindling onto a small area of fading embers and blowing softly. Soon, a small tongue of flame flickered into life.

Eain joined them as Klay was stirring his small pan of lumpy porridge, walking slowly over from his tent and scanning the frozen world he saw with a deep scowl.

'Ow're you feeling, youth?' asked Klay.

Eain's scowl deepened. 'My head hurts. I need water.'

'Come here and have a bite and a sup,' said Klay. 'Yer'll feel better soon.'

Eain took a step forward then paused, staring in the direction of the southern horizon.

'I see smoke,' he said. 'A lot of smoke.'

Klay scrambled to his feet to see for himself. A thick, billowing column of black-grey smoke was rising towards the clouds.

'Shit,' muttered Klay. It was too big to be the cookfires of a village, too big even for a bonfire. There was only one thing it could be.

All around the camp, others were rising and staring in the same direction. Hands drifted to the hilts of weapons.

'Captain,' came the rich, deep voice of Daeron Teleri. Klay turned and nodded. 'Gather those that can be made ready quickly so we can march to find out what burns. I must know the cause. Be quick!'

The sun's indistinct glow was barely a handspan higher when Klay led a cohort of fifty or sixty southwards along the road. Grass and reeds along the verge were still, frozen white. Eain marched at his side, and Gargas and Ivhar had been coaxed from their blankets. Teleri walked with them, silent and aloof.

The rest of the group were mostly Tayans, men and women in bright shirts partially covered by scraps of leather armour.

The mood was tense.

As the miles passed, the smoke cloud grew in their vision, a swirling column that reached up to darken the sky above. Klay feared what they would find, although he already had a suspicion.

They did not have to wait much longer to find out.

As they got closer to the source, the familiar scent of woodsmoke was pervasive. Ash fluttered past their faces as though the clouds had released the first snows of winter. Another smell mingled with it, though, a sharper, stranger smell that Kay wished he did not recognise.

Burning flesh.

They found the first bodies a handful of paces further up the track. An avenue of spindly trees screened the track, and several limp, bloody figures in the bright robes of Tayan peasants were sprawled between the bare, swaying branches. The bodies of old men, women and children among the slain. He thought he recognised some of their faces. None had been spared.

Beyond the trees a causeway led back to the first village, standing on a spur of higher ground. As they set eyes on the scene, the Tayans in the company moaned in grief and horror.

'They've done it now,' muttered Ivhar as they approached. 'They've gone too far.' Daeron Teleri was silent, and Klay did not dare to look at his face.

The village had been razed. The flimsy houses of dry willow and reeds must have gone up like torches, giving those inside no chance to escape. Bodies lay everywhere Klay looked, the blood that oozed from their mortal wounds pooling black on the frosty ground.

Why do this? Klay asked himself. *And why now?*

'The fields,' said Eain in an undertone, moving to stand close. 'They are frozen.'

Klay looked again. The boy was right. Footprints stood out on the icy surface in all directions. The Taosach's raiders had attacked the village by approaching across terrain that was normally an impassable bog.

The Tayans searched through the wreckage, but none had been left alive. Whole families had been roasted alive inside their houses, or struck down as they tried to flee. Klay saw the village elders huddled together in death, bodies broken and limp. It was brutal.

'This is my doing,' said Daeron Teleri abruptly, breaking what had been a tense silence. Heads turned. 'I have caused this, by my actions, and by my presence. The Taosach has punished those I have tried to help.'

He raised a fist, clenching it so tightly his whole arm shook.

'They would have us surrender, but we will not! They would strike us with fear, but we will not bow down. They would have the land turn against us so we must fight back harder to prove ourselves.'

He raised his head, and his voice. 'Gather my army. We march north to avenge this crime. Blood will be repaid in blood!'

To Klay it just seemed like a waste. A waste of life and a waste of effort. These people had done nothing; nothing to support Teleri and his resistance and nothing to harm the Taosach. Yet, she had decided that they must die.

It was a message. Klay understood that. It was an attempt to hurt Teleri, and to provoke him into doing something reckless. And it was meant to turn other villages in the area against him, to encourage them to withhold their support through fear.

Maybe it would work, but was there not another way?

Teleri would not reconsider.

'Can we not wait a few days?' asked Klay, speaking as bluntly as he dared. 'Gather more numbers. Grow our strength.'

'Have I not made my orders plain?' he snapped. His voice was cold.

'Aye, but—'

'Question me once more and become my enemy, dwarf.'

Klay held Teleri's frosty, blue-eyed stare for as long as he could. A few heartbeats later he looked away, defeated. He knew that arguing further was pointless. Teleri had made his mind up, and Klay feared that any proof that he was wrong would come too late.

They stood before the stark silhouette of a watchtower.

It was more than a mere tower, in truth. It had a high lookout point on a tall tower of sturdy logs, but a fortification had grown around its base. Timber walls - topped with spikes - rose from the frozen ground, and a single well-guarded gateway provided the only access. The interior was screened by the walls, but Klay knew there would be buildings inside for the lord's chambers as well as a decent-sized garrison.

All those that could stand and wield a weapon were behind them. The Steel Hounds that still lived had marched together, eyes lowered and the blacks and browns of their leather armour matching their mood. Marsh warriors of the Tayan lowlands came, wearing simple robes, but fervent in their enthusiasm. And, standing slightly apart, the Sisters of the Eagle were implacable behind their black eye bindings, bows slung across their shoulders.

It was all they had. It was a paltry force with which to lay a siege. Teleri mounted his horse once more, and Klay moved to stand beside Eain.

'Why do we do this?' asked Eain.

'Teleri's guilty conscience,' muttered Klay, but pitched his voice so that only Eain could hear.

Eain shook his head. 'So, we have to die?'

''E 'ad to do summat,' said Klay. 'Yer saw that village. What are we supposed to do? Wait for 'em to do it again?'

'He does fight for what is right, for the people,' said Eain, as though reassuring himself. 'We serve him, or...' he tailed off.

'Or we scarper,' added Klay. 'And there's no chance of doing that just now, youth.'

Dusk was painting the sky an ochre grey. Away from the marshes of the far south, and in the grip of the sudden winter's chill, all was quiet. Klay cast his eyes along the ranks, noting their fear and their suppressed nerves, before turning back to see Daeron Teleri riding forward to within a bowshot of the sturdy walls.

'I address the lord of Cas-Ghad,' he announced, his deep voice booming out across the open land. 'Come down! Open the gates and treat with me. A peace can be found.

'Until that time, you will be besieged. None may leave or enter this place.'

He rode back easily, passing through the lines close to Klay and Eain.

'Get a camp organised,' he said to Klay as he passed. 'Set sentries in all directions. Be alert.'

Klay nodded, keeping his face blank and trying to hide his growing unease.

Several days had passed. No sign of movement had been seen from the tower. The frost deepened across the surrounding lands. All was still.

'They have not tried to leave,' Eain was saying as they huddled around a paltry fire one grey afternoon. His face was pinched and pale, his eyes weary. 'Or to break the siege.'

Gargas and Ivhar laughed.

'They don't need to, lad,' croaked Ivhar. 'They're warmer in there than we are out here. Probably got more food and a nice big cistern of water. Don't need to go anywhere. They can just wait until we run out of strength.'

'We're the ones who are trapped,' said Gargas, smiling pleasantly.

Klay was not laughing.

Food was running low. Water was becoming increasingly hard to dredge from the frozen, dirty waterways nearby. Sick soldiers coughed and wheezed in the chill air, and there were never enough furs and blankets to keep everyone warm at night.

Gargas was right. All they were achieving here was starving themselves out.

'Teleri knows what he's about,' he said. 'Trust his judgement.'
And don't think about the other companies of Gluttons that are camped just out of sight.

He glared out into the sparse trees that ringed the clearing. He knew they were there. They must be. But there was no need to risk lives by attacking Teleri's ragtag army just yet.

Gargas and Ivhar knew this too, but were aware of what a fragile thing an army's morale could be. He was grateful that they kept their mouths shut. That thought guided Klay's eyes to Eain's face. The boy was close to despair. His dreams of a noble war of liberation had not looked like this.

Poor lad.

'If they are happy to wait, then we should attack,' said Eain. 'Soon!'

'Aye, youth,' replied Klay. 'Expect we'll get orders to move any time now. Keep that blade sharp.'

Afternoon dulled swiftly to evening, the temperature dropping as the clouds seemed to frown lower. The light was sucked from the sky, colours washing out to leave a grey-toned twilight. It was a scene for ghosts and spirits, not living men.

'Evening, captain,' called sentries from their positions near paltry, spluttering braziers. They reeked of burning dung. They covered their noses where they stood, lonely figures in the gathering dark.

He stopped at each position to share a few words, a joke, or a quick story. Someone had to. These folk did not deserve a fate that seemed unavoidable.

Words threatened to tumble from his lips, like: 'See yon treeline? Run for it and don't look back.'

Yet, he said nothing of the sort. He had been assigned his task and would stick at it. His oath was given.

'The hammer did not stop when the rock was hard', as the old Dwarvish saying went.

The sky was black by the time he returned to the tent he still shared with Eain. The boy was already in a fitful sleep, gasping and moaning, so Klay was careful to be silent as he wrapped himself in his own blankets.

Sleep took a long time to arrive.

His waking before second sleep was abrupt, as though something had disturbed him. Someone was talking, near at hand. Talking in a low, urgent voice.

'No, no no...I don't want to!'

Eain's voice.

Slowly, without moving his body, Klay opened his eyes. He managed not to gasp aloud at what he saw. The inside of the tent was illuminated, blood-red. The source of the crimson glow was a box, perched on Eain's knee where he sat on his blankets.

His face was cast in stark relief as he stared down, features twisted in desperation. Fingers twitched towards the opening of the box.

'I don't…' he sobbed. 'I don't want to.'

Klay could not bring himself to intrude. This struggle was Eain's, even though Klay could not understand what was causing the red light. The hopelessness of their situation was clearly weighing down on the boy.

They could either starve to death in this nameless field or be hacked apart when the lord of the tower deigned to sally forth. If they escaped those fates, then all that was left was to be bound as prisoners to await the headman's blade.

Was it a worthwhile way to spend their life blood?

They could go. Him and the boy. Foreswear those oaths and flee. The thought pained him, and even the thought was dishonourable, but it would let them live. In his long life, he had done worse and he remained breathing.

He was just about to break his silence, when Eain hissed a definite 'No!' and slammed the lid of the box shut. The red light vanished, plunging the tent into darkness.

There was the swish of stiff, heavy canvas and a stab of cold air as Eain left the tent. A moment later Klay was free of his blankets and on his feet. He would follow.

By the time he had tugged on his boots and ducked through the flap himself, Eain was little more than a shadow slipping away across the camp. Klay followed at a distance, making as little noise as he could. He was bulky and his boots were heavy, but he could move in near silence when he needed to. He needed answers.

The camp was disorganised. Soldiers sprawled in ragged clumps across the frosty ground. Some had tents, others had spread canvas sheets on cut poles as simple lean-tos, while many more slept rolled up in blankets and furs, huddled close to one another and as near as they dared to fires that burned low.

Eain passed these low, silent campers quickly, moving towards the centre. Klay already had an idea where he might be heading, but could not think of a reason.

Then, Teleri's own high-sided tent loomed ahead, lit by a pair of braziers, and Klay's suspicion was proved correct. He paused, ducking into the shadow of a low shelter made from animal skins pulled over simple sticks, and watched.

'I must speak to Teleri,' Eain was saying, speaking in a low hiss that nonetheless carried easily to Klay's ears. Two of the Eagle Sisters barred his path. He loomed over them, a head taller and as broad as both put together, and yet they did not flinch.

'He sleeps,' said one. 'Come back in the morning.'

'This cannot wait until then! I have something to give him. Something he must have, and now.'

Even this far away and in the low light, Klay could see their heads shaking, bodies moving to block his way.

'It could save us all!' Eain's voice had grown more desperate. Klay could not look away. The priestesses were unmoved.

Eain lunged forward. They caught him, one grappling with each of his arms. Klay was just about to move forward himself to intervene, when the tent rippled, and the flap was pushed aside.

The hawklike profile of Daeron Teleri was outlined by the pulsing light of the brazier. He said nothing, glaring out at the struggling figures. Eain pulled his arms free and faced up to the tall lord.

'I have something I want to give you. Need to give you.' He raised his hands, and Klay saw that he was holding that same small wooden box. As Teleri looked at it, Eain opened the lid.

Daeron Teleri's face was suddenly bathed in light, and his dark eyes shone. This light, though, was of the deepest, richest crimson as though the box contained a dying sun.

He smiled.

THIRTY

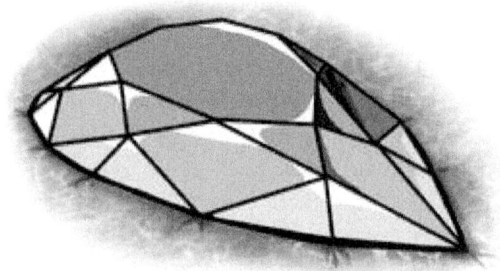

Mayreen struck the door with the back of her fist. Once. Twice. A third time.

'Yes, yes!' came the voice from within. 'Patience! Have some patience. I am coming.'

She fought the urge to hammer on the door again. Her ears strained to catch any sounds of movement inside the room. Whatever was happening was taking too long.

The door opened a crack, and the seneschal peered out.

'You?' His voice was indignant. 'Why are you here?'

'The servants have all been struck down by a plague,' she answered, watching his horrified expression with delight. 'Not really. Duke Sarnayu summons you. The besiegers call for negotiations.'

Seneschal Tomen sighed. 'I do not know why he deigns to treat with that rabble.' He reached down his headscarf and pulled the door closed behind him.

'Because he wants to,' replied Mayreen, walking along beside the small, twist-bodied seneschal. 'And I want to see what happens.'

'I see,' said Tomen, eyeing her with disdain. 'And this is why you are now the messenger of the tower?'

'I *am* a bard,' she replied with a grin.

'Maybe one day you will learn your place,' said Tomen, turning towards the great hall. 'You are not my keeper, nor the seneschal itself. I hold that position for a good reason.'

'Because out of all the boring old men, you're the oldest and most boring?'

Tomen hastened his steps, turning his face away and declining to respond.

Mayreen bounced on her toes as she strode along beside Tomen, with his awkward shuffling gait. Teleri and his ragged army had been camped pointlessly outside the walls for a week now, and Duke Sarnayu had insisted that they were to be ignored.

To acknowledge their presence would have been an admission that they were a threat, although one worthy of little more than contempt.

'Let them sit,' the duke had said. 'Let them starve. Let their water freeze. We'll wait until they come to us begging, and then we'll capture Teleri and destroy those who cling to his robes.'

Something must have changed, because the duke was now preparing to go out and meet his opponent. Now, Teleri would beg.

'You will talk yourself into trouble one of these days,' said Tomen. His hands were clasped beneath the voluminous sleeves of his formal robes, and his chin was raised. He thought himself superior, but Mayreen did not care.

Her mind was humming with the anticipation of being present when the events of the coming days unfolded. To be the first one to describe the battle, the slaughter, and the capture of the rebel leader. That was all any bard wanted: to see events of great moment with their own two eyes and then to recount them. Across the land, audiences would hang on her every word, and riches, honour and prestige would be hers to command.

Now was her time.

She would be there to see the lines sweeping together, hear the crunch of impact and the cries of pain, to see the blood flowing. And afterwards, she would walk amongst the slain and fix the scene in her mind.

The hall of the tower was not large, or grand; the fortification had been built to enforce the Taosach's laws, not to provide luxurious accommodation for its lord. Nevertheless, painted timbers curved overhead, three spans or more, to meet above like the entwined branches of a colourful forest.

The seneschal led the way, and as they entered through a narrow side door the duke's high seat lay to their left. The duke and his underlings were standing near the chair with several huge captains of the Gluttons, and servants clung to the walls in subservience.

'Ah, Seneschal Tomen,' said the duke. 'You arrive at the right time. We make ready to meet with the rebel Teleri.' The Duke Sarnayu was a compact, lean man with a creased face the colour of aged oak and a dark, drooping moustache.

Mayreen knew that he had a reputation as a rising star in the Tayan military, and his posting here was likely a stepping stone to a grander, more prestigious position further north and closer to Taosach Wenas herself. So far, he had treated Teleri with the contempt the rebel's insurrection deserved.

'Quite, sir,' replied the seneschal with the slightest of bows. 'Although, I do not see why you lower yourself to treat with him. I only see risk to your person, and little reward.'

'What risk?' scoffed Mayreen. 'They are a starving, freezing rabble. Our forces surround them on all sides. They are an upturned beetle, waiting for the boot to fall.'

'Know your place!' snapped Tomen.

'My place is here, where I can gainsay your cowardice.'

Tomen's brows lowered, mouth opening in sudden anger, but Sarnayu raised a hand.

'Peace. Peace! That's enough from both of you. Foolish words come from the wisest mouths when they open in anger.'

Lowering his hand, and his voice, he turned to address them both.

'You speak as though I have not given this due consideration. Not given thought to the risk that Teleri poses, and what I must do to ensure he is utterly defeated.'

The seneschal bowed his balding head, but Mayreen gazed evenly toward the duke. She had said nothing that was not true.

'Yes, he has put himself in a position of weakness,' continued Sarnayu, 'and yes, we can crush him and his army with ease. But, he is of more value if taken alive.'

The duke leaned back, clasping his fingers together across his lap. 'The Taosach would be well pleased were I to deliver Teleri to her, alive and able to face her justice. She could bring him low and show all Tayo how further revolts would end. We would all share in the rewards.

'I have been perplexed, unsure of how to put down their rebellion and end their puny siege while ensuring Teleri was taken and not slain. And Fate delivers. He begs for an audience. Says he has something to trade, something of great value with which he intends to bargain. No doubt he would try to exchange it for safe passage, but in doing so he provides a perfect opportunity to capture his offering and the man himself. Then we order in the Gluttons against his army.'

'It's brilliant,' said Mayreen, unable to hold her tongue. She would be able to look Daeron Teleri in his traitorous eyes as he realised that he was doomed, and that those he had led here were about to die. Her breathing quickened.

'Is everything prepared as I instructed?' asked the duke.

'Yes, sir,' replied one of the servants, an underling of the seneschal. 'The pavilion has been erected before the gates, and the Cask of Conquest has been brought out.'

They gestured towards the main doors where a square wooden chest, bound with black leather, had been laid. The skulls of Duke Sarnayu's defeated enemies lay within. Once, Mayreen had been allowed to open the lid and look inside. The memory was a shining jewel.

With slow control, as of a sword being drawn, the duke stood.

'Let us proceed,' he said.

The well-trodden path from the sturdy gates was still frozen at this early hour of the morning, the wagon ruts and footprints solid and uneven. The procession moved slowly, and in strict order. Servants bearing the Cask of Conquest led the way, followed by the seneschal. Duke Sarnayu walked behind, flanked by his squires and guard-captains. Mayreen walked to the rear, resisting the temptation to unsheathe her long-handled sword.

She had to watch, listen, and remember.

A pavilion had been erected in the flat space that the towers overlooked. Study poles had been driven into the frozen mud, and between them, large squares of dyed linen were strung as screens, as was customary.

He was there already.

As they approached, he remained standing. At least he gave Sarnayu due respect. Mayreen found she could not take her eyes off him, although she knew he was less than nothing. He was a weak enemy.

Sarnayu waited while a servant brought forward heated water in an iron jug, then Tomen poured it into a decorated pot. Steam rose and the delicate fragrance of jasmine tea filled the cool air. Tomen shared it between two matching clay cups before adding in a dash of rice wine from a small flask. His work was slow, as always.

'Duke Teleri,' said Sarnayu as he finally sat. 'I have heard much of you in recent weeks. Mostly that you are a rebel against the Taosach and a traitor. You have nonetheless earned quite a reputation. Sit.'

Teleri opened his mouth, then closed it again. He sat.

'Duke Sarnayu. I wish I could return what I presume to be a compliment.'

A silence followed. Mayreen noticed a smirk twisting the corners of Sarnayu's mouth. He had not missed the subtle insult. He let a few heartbeats pass before he spoke again.

'Your presence here is an assault on this tower,' he said in a tone of disinterest. 'And will be dealt with as such. It would be best if you surrendered. You may do so now.'

Teleri did not miss a beat. 'I have not come to surrender. I have come because I must. I represent all those who the Taosach would have as slaves. Slaves to Re'Emsser, slaves to her pride. I have come to fight, to fight in their name, and fight I will.'

'Fight?' There was a laugh in Sarnayu's voice, and others in his entourage laughed too. 'You come to fight? You do not have the numbers, or the strength. I see mercenaries who will flee as soon as you are short of money rings to throw at them, alongside peasants from the swamps. There will be no fight, my friend. There will only be slaughter.'

'Ask the captains of the Gluttons who led the assaults on the southlands about my numbers, or my strength. Ask them how they fared when faced with peasants from the swamps.'

Daeron leaned back. 'Ask them, but they will not answer. They all lie rotting beneath the swamp, along with those they led.'

Sarnayu's face hardened. Mayreen had heard the tales, although she did not know of any bards who had actually been present. Many companies of the Gluttons had marched along the causeways through the low, wet southlands and most had fallen to ambushes launched from the marshes. Hundreds had been slain. It had been an embarrassment.

'You requested this audience,' said Sarnayu, a snarl in his voice. 'Said you had an offer. Make it, so we can be done.'

Teleri's gaze was level. 'I have come to give you the opportunity to surrender.'

There was another moment of silence, and then Sarnayu erupted into incredulous laughter. The other nobles joined, and Mayreen found herself chuckling too, hand touching her open mouth. Surely, he spoke in jest. Only Seneschal Tomen remained unmoved.

'Surrender? To your rabble?' Sarnayu's voice was shrill with amusement.

'It is the sensible thing for you to do,' continued Teleri, oblivious to the reactions. 'It is the only way further bloodshed can be avoided. Enough Tayan lives have been wasted already.'

'That blood is on your hands, rebel!' spat Sarnayu, amusement snapping to annoyance. 'You have broken the Taosach's peace and now assail lands under my protection. I have no fear of you. I see no reason to agree to anything you say.'

'The Taosach will have your head!' shouted Cinco, one of the minor nobles standing behind Sarnayu's shoulder.

'Quite,' agreed Sarnayu. 'But not until you have witnessed your petty rebellion put down by the forces at my command. You are surrounded.'

'Not so,' said Teleri, unconcerned. 'What you see in my camp is a fraction of the numbers I command, a small part of my power. The others are scattered across the southlands, and have their orders.'

He leaned forward, staring at Sarnayu. 'Should we fall, they will command an uprising. Every village will revolt, every outpost and garrison in the southlands will be assaulted by vast numbers.

'Yes, you can capture me today and defeat *this* army, but if you do that it will plunge southern Tayo into a brutal, crippling war. That will be on your hands. Will the Taosach extend her thanks, and her favour, if that is what you provide as well as my head?'

There was a stony silence at that. Mayreen studied Teleri's face. His blue-eyed gaze was trained unflinchingly on Sarnayu's, and there was not the slightest flicker to betray his emotions. Sarnayu ran his tongue across his teeth.

'I don't believe you,' he said.

'Can you risk being wrong?'

Mayreen could not take her eyes off the two men. It was like observing a duel, or a game of *sadawch* between two masters. Each tile laid was a parry or counter. She tried to memorise their words, their attitudes and the thrill of the exchange, so that she would be able to recount it all perfectly.

'I'm not wrong, so I'll take the risk,' replied Sarnayu, after a pause. 'I think all you have is what I see—a pathetic band of yokels and sell-swords on the verge of starvation. That and your brass neck. I cannot and will not let you just walk away.'

'The country will be in flames—'

'I don't care if it is!' bellowed Sarnayu, losing his temper. 'It is you who have encouraged them to break the Taosach's peace, and the Taosach's laws, and they deserve to burn for that, along with you. You'll all face justice sooner or later, and I will not be held hostage by your empty threats. I will take you in, and reap the rewards *I* deserve.'

Teleri chuckled, a low and cynical sound. 'All for a taste of the Taosach's favour? All this to get just a little closer to that golden teat?'

'Why do we do anything?' replied Sarnayu, spreading his hands. Teleri put his own on the edge of the casket, leaning slightly forwards.

'For the good,' he said, 'of the country. That is why I do what I do. For Tayo, and for her people.

'I cannot leave them to their fate, not now. I cannot let them down. So, I cannot let you take me. I'm sorry, but it cannot be.' He leaned back again and raised his palms. 'Let me go, with my army, and no blood needs to be spilled this day.'

Mayreen found herself nodding along with his words. She believed every one. If only she could remember them exactly, her performance of this speech would make her famous. She had even forgotten about her desire to watch the battle, the glorious slaughter that had seemed inevitable.

Sarnayu laughed, breaking the spell as though it were a boulder heaved into a still lake.

'You still try to bargain? All the strength is with me. The fortress at our back is mine. The garrison ready to march forth answers to me alone. And the legions of Gluttons that surround your camp are waiting for my orders. It is over. You have nothing.'

Teleri's face remained impassive. 'I have more than you know. Remember, I suggested this audience with an offer. You will take what I offer, and in return I will ride away.'

'You have nothing I want.'

'You will want this.'

Sarnayu glared at his adversary, and Teleri met his gaze unflinchingly. Swords locked; parry and counterstrike forcing the combatants into a deadlock. It was as though sparks flew from clashing blades.

'You have nothing I want,' repeated Sarnayu.

'I can offer you something more valuable than my head,' said Teleri. Sarnayu threw his own head back, rolling his eyes. 'Something you will be desperate to possess, something that will place you even higher in the Taosach's estimations, were you to present it to her as a gift,'

Sarnayu's eyes flicked back to Teleri. 'You have this thing with you, now?' Mayreen also craved an answer to that question. Despite Teleri's fraught position he remained so calm, so measured, that he must truly hold something valuable.

'Yes.'

'Then you are a bigger fool than I thought,' said Sarnayu. 'I will take everything you possess, soon enough. I have no need to negotiate.'

'Let's just kill him now!' urged Cinco. 'This is a waste of time.'

'I never waste time,' said Teleri. 'But your time is up. My archers will have moved forwards by now, and are covering this position. One cry from me and they will shoot.'

Mayreen leaned around the edge of the pavilion. Red-clad figures were spread out across the clear ground surrounding the tower, a long bowshot from the walls. Once more, Teleri spoke true.

'You would be ordering your own death,' said Sarnayu, voice shrill with disbelief.

'No,' replied Teleri. 'I would be ordering yours. If I lose my life in exchange, so be it.'

'Madness,' muttered Cinco.

'Negotiation,' replied Teleri. 'I am offering a peaceful solution, and the item I would trade for my freedom is truly of great value. But, if you try to take it before I am clear of this field the sky will blacken with arrows.'

Sarnayu gaped. Mayreen saw how he had been outmanoeuvred. Everything Teleri said had seeded doubt and unsettled his opponent, though he was one against many, though his army faced greater strength.

Now, Sarnayu did not know where to turn. Had he any choice but to accept Teleri's offer?

'What is this…thing?' The words were forced from his lips, his tone a mixture of cold fury and desperation. 'What is it that you would stake all of our lives upon?'

Teleri said nothing, but reached into a cloth bag that had been sitting unnoticed on the floor between his feet. He lifted out a wooden box, a little more than a handspan to each side. He placed it carefully on the Cask of Conquest, then withdrew his hands.

'That's it?' Sarnayu was doubtful.

It did not look like much. Plain, unadorned wood formed its sides and lid, with simple hinges and a fastening. The thing had not the weight nor the size to conceal gold or silver in any significant quantity.

'Inside,' said Teleri. 'Take a look.'

Sarnayu paused for a moment, his gaze moving from Teleri's face to the box, as if considering where a trap might lay. He reached out slowly, and a simple twist of his fingers unfastened the latch.

His hand hovered near the lid as heartbeats passed. Then, with a flick, he pushed it open. Everything changed.

The pale canvas walls of the pavilion were immediately dyed with blood. Bright red light streamed from the box and cast the outlines of the onlookers as hard, looming shadows, fringed with crimson.

'I don't believe it…' began Sarnayu, before tailing off. He was staring down into the box and as Mayreen followed his gaze, she saw what had him transfixed.

Within the snug confines of the box lay a ruby. This was clearly no ordinary gem, though. It was large as a man's fist, or perhaps a heart, and it burned with scarlet light, bright as a morning star brought to earth.

It called to her. She wanted it. Her whole being strained to possess it, to hold it, and she even felt her fingers twitch in the direction of the box.

Sarnayu was quicker.

His eyes wide with avaricious intent, his right hand descended into the box and emerged clutching the jewel. His fingers could not close fully around it, and the radiance pulsed powerfully between them.

A pang of jealousy began in Mayreen's belly at seeing another holding it.

Then the screaming began.

A high-pitched wail, laced with agony, poured from Sarnayu's lips. Others backed away as he writhed, feet rooted to the spot and his hand still clenched around the jewel like a claw. His whole body convulsed.

Teleri's eyes widened, and he backed away. The sounds that Sarnayu was making were almost inhuman, a shriek as that of an animal in pain.

Louder and louder, his cries reached a crescendo, veins bulging in his throat as his head tipped back, and then he collapsed forwards to lie over the casket. His body was limp but the hand and arm holding the glowing jewel were still rigid, grotesquely tense.

Stepping forwards, Teleri grabbed the jewel, holding it lightly between finger and thumb. He pulled it free and a moment later dropped it back into the box.

There was silence.

Sarnayu's body lay where it had fallen. There was not the slightest flicker of life from the limp, twisted form. He was clearly dead.

'You killed him!' moaned Cinco, raising a hand to his mouth.

'Yes,' replied Teleri, voice unfeasibly calm and face impassive once more. There had been a moment of surprise and confusion as Sarnayu had been engulfed, but just a moment. Now, he looked absolutely in control.

'Yes, I killed him. I warned him that he should let me go, and he wouldn't listen. He forced me to use the power I possess.'

He raised the jewel's box and held it out at the onlookers. Some flinched back as the red light washed over their faces.

'Never forget this,' he went on. 'Never forget what I can do. Do not think that I will hesitate to use this power again, if I am defied.'

There were mutters of assent, and many stared at their feet.

'By my victory here, I claim control of all that Sarnayu commands—this tower and his forces. Send out the word. You, bard—' he pointed at Mayreen. 'Go forth and tell this tale. Tell of my name, and of my power.'

'Yes, my lord,' she replied. The tale would spread quickly, she knew. It would sound fantastical, but she had been there. She had seen it and would make all who heard it believe her words.

With her own two eyes she had seen the sorcerous power of Daeron Teleri.

Or, as she would call him when she told the tale: The Demon Teleri.

PART FIVE

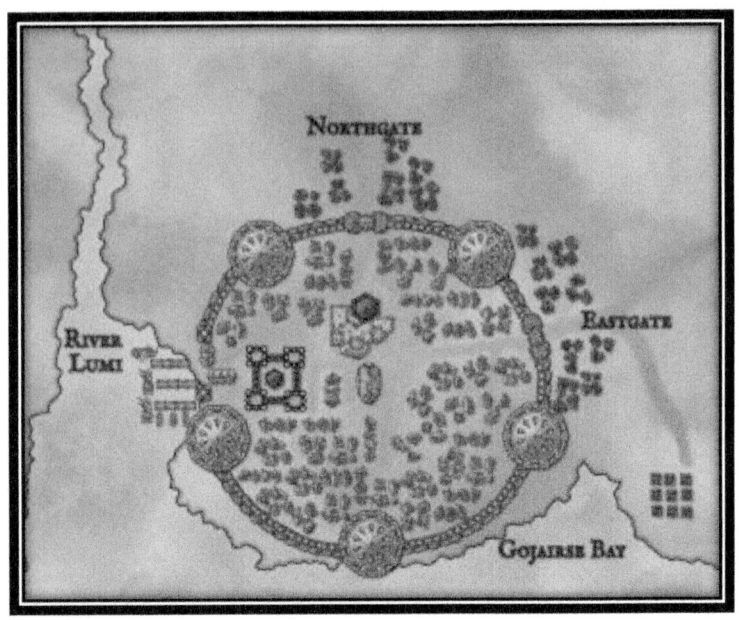

GLITHONIEL

THIRTY ONE

She had seen it all, even though she had been sitting in meditation. It was not like a dream, gauzy and insubstantial, but as though the images had been forced into her mind. They were impossible to ignore.

Evane Claes opened her eyes.

For a moment she sat unmoving, eyes staring blankly at the wall of her bare cell before her mind managed to encompass what she had seen. Then, she blinked and the reality of it hit her. She clapped a hand to her mouth to stifle a gasp.

It was happening.

The stones of the floor were like blocks of ice beneath the soles of her feet as she rose. Hurried breaths misted in the air, pale wisps of cloud in the low light. She ignored everything outside of her body and concentrated on her thoughts.

She could do this easily now. Practice had eased the path, and her strength had grown. All that mattered was her faith in Desya, and as she focused on that she felt the power rise and blossom inside her.

Recitation of the catechisms was unnecessary. The concentration came naturally. For something this momentous, a summons was not needed. She knew where to find him, and he would want to hear this.

As she drew on the power and released it in the familiar spell, her sense of self in space shifted. Somewhere in her consciousness she could still feel the cold flags beneath her feet, but her other senses told her she had dropped into the earth.

Not falling but…descending.

Even through her resolute focus she burned with eagerness to share the news. His time must surely be close at hand. A time when she would rise above the others around her.

Then, the sense of movement ceased and a vast space was around her. This cavern was deep beneath the earth, a subterranean cave that could have been real, or could have been…something else.

As she knew too well, what happened here *felt* very real, but left no mark that could be seen in the world above. It was the centre of her world.

She took a step forward.

You come.

His gritty, bass voice seemed to shake the walls. Or was it just her that shook?

'I had to,' she replied, lowering herself to kneel before his vast bulk. '*It* has been found.'

The sentence did not make sense; the jewel had been uncovered many months ago, but she knew what she meant. It had been found and claimed by one who would wield it, as the demon had predicted.

Tell me.

'The jewel woke,' she began. Explaining how she knew this, or what it felt like would have been difficult, but this was nevertheless what she knew to be true. 'It took another soul.'

There was a pause.

Yes. I feel the strength.

'But then, something else happened. Something different.'

She hesitated, thinking how to put what she had felt into words.

'I felt another through the jewel. A presence. A soul was not taken but a link was formed. It was not like the others.'

One has claimed the Tear for their own.

'Yes!' she exclaimed, in sudden realisation. For an instant she had felt the intent of the one who was now linked with the Demon's Tear, who must now possess it.

We have waited for this moment.

Claes was filled with sudden excitement. Whoever this person was, they could command the jewel. They could be the one to lead the army that Desya would need. Perhaps they would also be the one to find and bear the Twin Swords, in time.

Then, she paused to recall the brief sensation of that other that she had felt through their brief contact with the jewel. The memory made her slump to her haunches with a gasp.

'The power...' she muttered, trying to understand what she had felt. 'They are just so *strong*!' What she had felt made her own ability with the power in the earth seem like a candle next to a bonfire. 'They could burn all the world.'

They will burn it in my name.

'Yes. Yes, my lord Desya,' she said but fear had grown like a dark, menacing pit in her belly. She had not ever imagined such a one could exist. 'I have prepared for this moment. I am ready,' she said, although the size of her task now felt like a white-tipped mount to climb.

Find them. Guide them. Do this in my name.

'Yes, great Desya.'

She released the power and returned to her cell as though in a drunken haze.

Being back in her own body filled her with a sudden chill. She had spoken the truth, as she knew she must; preparations had been made. Now that the moment was here, though, she was filled with nerves.

She must not fail in this.

There was no time to waste, no time to stop and think. Checking her door was secured with a small wooden wedge, she reached into the secret space beneath her narrow pallet bed and pulled out her striped mask.

Donning it, she found the required focus with the ease of habit and drew the power into herself once more. It was stronger now, more vibrant, and she trembled with the intensity of the sensation as she forced it to do her will.

A portal, purple-tinted and swirling with discontinuous patterns, rose in the air before her and it took a mere twitch of thought for it to open like a window.

This time it was a window to a location nearby, a fact she had to keep hidden from those she was about to meet. An attic room in a barn-like building was before her, and a lone figure dozed in a ladderback chair.

A whip of red power woke the boy with a shriek, and he whimpered as he stood. This close to her physical location she could direct the power easily, and with great strength.

'I'm sorry—' he began, about to bore her with a lame excuse.

'Be silent,' she snapped. 'Fetch your leader to me. Do it now. And say that you are to be punished for your laziness.'

The gangly youth nodded awkwardly as a poor imitation of a bow, then threw himself down a nearby ladder and out of sight. Voices mumbled below, high and low, and a few moments later she could hear someone climbing the ladder.

A head appeared, dark hair cropped severely at each side, followed by the rest of a dwarf. Even by dwarf standards this one was broad, with bulky shoulders that stretched his rough shirt tight. Fists like boulders swung at his sides.

'Yer've got news?' asked Hack, his voice low and grating like rusty metal dragged over rock.

'You will address me properly,' hissed Claes. She bore all the responsibility for their work, and answered directly to Desya himself. Respect was the least she deserved, especially from a brawler of his ilk.

Hack merely shrugged.

With a flash of irritation, Claes struck him with the power. It was the same lash that had made the boy howl, a whip of air heated with fire, but Hack did not make a sound. One slow blink was the only acknowledgement he gave of the strike.

She stifled a growl, annoyed at forgetting that this one was not easily cowed. Not by pain alone, in any case.

Another head appeared at the top of the ladder, this one sparsely thatched with pale hair and with ears that sprouted from the sides of his head like jug handles. Skane swung easily from the top rungs to stand beside Hack. He overtopped the dwarf by two heads, and yet Hack's bulk made even the blocky Mackem appear slight.

'Master,' he said, in that voice like thick treacle. This one, at least, had learned something about respect.

'Events are moving on,' she began. 'The time has come for us to enact what has been planned. Have you made the preparations as I requested?'

'Won't be easy,' grumbled Hack. 'But we've found what you asked. The royal metalsmith uses blue-black for rings, got a delivery coming soon.'

By blue-black, Hack meant the precious metal *pluitone*. Dwarves alone knew where to find the elusive ore and how to smelt it, and had been trading small quantities with the Anise royal family since the days of the Many Kings and the country's subsequent unification.

Only royalty was allowed to wear *pluitone* finger-rings in Anish, the nobility having to be content with simple gold or silver. In recent times, the royal family of Buren had not wanted to be left behind by their simple Anise cousins, and had taken to wearing heavy rings of *pluitone*, as well.

'I must have it,' said Claes. 'It is absolutely essential that you obtain this metal, and soon, as is finding a smith who is capable of working it into the design I have provided.'

'Yea, I found someone. They're as baffled as I am. No idea what yer about. Looked like the setting for a jewel but big enough to clamp me fist.'

That was exactly what the pluitone was for.

'None of that is your concern. Obeying is your concern, if you want the gold.'

'Aye, aye,' said Hack. 'It shall be done, and soon.'

That was Hack's weakness: greed. His full, round belly revealed that much.

'Skane,' she said, turning to the Mackems leader. 'As you are here, am I to assume that those you lead are here too?' Skane nodded. 'You are prepared? You are armed?' Another nod. 'You will work for Hack from now on. Follow his orders as if they were from my mouth. Retrieve the *pluitone* and do as I have commanded, or you will both suffer the consequences.'

Skane's face was impassive, and Hack shrugged again. She held her temper with an effort. Soon, she would have the power to make brutes like this tremble.

'The other task you were given,' she continued, carefully studying Skane's bluff face. 'Am I to take it that you have still not found those you were supposed to capture?'

'We lost the trail of the girls,' said Skane. 'But we know they were heading south. If they are still trying to trade the jewel, they'll have to come here to do it.'

Claes nodded, brow wrinkling behind her mask. Skane did not need to know that the girls did not have the jewel, or that it had been found by another. That information was valuable, and hers alone, for now.

'And the Jukeev brat?'

'Folk in east Buren spoke of him, or of seeing someone matching his description. He was looking for work, looking for a garrison to join. Posh boy. I reckon he'll head here, too. We'll find him.'

'You must. Share their descriptions with Hack and those he commands. Once you have them, they are to be held but not harmed. When it is time to move, you will bring them too.

'I will send further word when I need more of you. Go, do my bidding.'

Without another word, she let the portal close and her view of the two thugs winked out. The moment they vanished, fatigue hit her. Her knees buckled as though the muscles in her thin legs had turned to water. She managed to direct her fall onto her bed rather than the stony floor, although it was not a great deal softer.

Slumped on the coarse blankets, she breathed in great rasping breaths, narrow chest heaving.

This was it. She had managed events and soon her time of triumph would be at hand. Lords and kings would bow before her, and those who had doubted her or shown her disrespect…well, they would die.

Skane followed Hack down the ladder, waiting halfway as the dwarf dropped his heavy frame onto the floor. The building seemed to tremble as he landed.

Above their heads, long timbers formed a high, pyramidal roof which was covered with wooden shingles from the peak to the ground. The attic hung as a mezzanine, halfway up to the roof, and the building provided ample storage.

It lay mostly empty now, though, and the few crates and barrels left behind were in use as seats by the Mackems and the larger number of Hack's followers. The dwarf himself made a beeline for the youth who had been on watch duty in the attic. He pointed a thick finger.

'Kippin on't job again,' he said, and Skane noted how the lad's face fell. 'Up.'

The boy stood, all gangly limbs and slumping shoulders. Even before he had straightened fully, Hack struck. His meaty fist swung from low, a brutal uppercut to the lad's midriff. The sudden expulsion of breath was harsh.

A second blow to the chin spun him to fall back into some of the onlookers. They pushed him away, faces blank. The youth staggered in Hack's direction and the dwarf hit him again, low and hard. The blow must have been enough to break ribs, and the boy emitted a plaintive sound that was half grunt, half moan.

Hack was not finished.

Still silent, he grabbed the front of the lad's smock and struck him a sharp jab, right between the eyes. A dull crunch and a howl of pain spoke of a broken nose. Blood streamed down, over the boy's mouth and lips, dripping onto his chin like dark wine.

No one had moved or spoken since the start of the attack. No one had reacted in any way that suggested that this was an unusual occurrence.

Hack stepped close, driving a fist into the boy's belly again. This time it was hard enough to drop him to the floor. He lay still, body curled agonisingly around his middle.

'I'm only leavin' yer fingers whole because I still need yer to work,' said Hack, folding his arms. 'But next time yer slip up, ah'll break 'em all.'

'I think he's learned his lesson,' said Skane, unable to hold his tongue. Hack's head snapped around.

'You tellin' me 'ow t'run me own business?' he snapped, reaching up to shove Skane firmly in the chest. Skane took a step backwards, but just a step. 'I'm in charge round here, remember that. What's yer name, anyway?'

'I'm Skane.'

'Skane? Some buttfuck Anise, eh? And what's wrong with yer voice? Simple or summat?'

'I'm deaf.'

'Huh. Well, you'd better listen hard, because if you cross me again you'll be dead as well as deaf.'

Skane did not react. He had dealt with bullies like Hack before, and knew he was itching for Skane to argue because it would give him an excuse to throw his fists around some more. Jhari, though, stood up. His heavy brows were lowered, his huge fists curling.

'You can sit back down too, lanky,' sneered Hack. 'We've got work to do.'

Skane caught Jhari's eye and shook his head slightly. Jhari subsided, folding his long frame back onto a crate. His scowl remained in place.

'We've already talked enough about what we need to do,' said Hack, tucking his thumbs into his belt loops and facing the group. 'Time has come to get on wi' job. Are we all set?'

'Yea,' said two of those present, speaking at the same time. One was a man of nondescript build, with dark hair trimmed in a severe bob level with his jawline, and the other was a teenage girl. Her face was grubby, and she wore a simple peasant's smock and snug hose.

'I've been runnin' as many errands for Master Harios as he'll give me,' she said, her face sullen but her eyes sharp. 'An' listening while I'm waiting. He's still expecting some blue-black to arrive from the north in a couple of days.'

'We've got to be ready and waiting for that wagon,' said Hack. 'Sylav, Gerran, watch the north road in shifts. I don't want one of you without eyes on that road from now on. We need to know as soon as it's close to the city.'

Two youths of similar ages stood. Skane thought they must be brothers.

'Why not hit the wagon on the road?' asked Skane. Hack swung round.

'What did I just tell you about questioning me?'

'It's a good question,' came Jhari's bassy growl. There was menace in his tone. 'Answer it.'

'We were going to,' said Hack, subsiding slightly. 'But then the Kingseye patrols got heavier. We could lift the blue-black, easily, but we'd have nowhere to hide in the country, no way to get it back to the city. If we hit them here, though...'

He turned back to the man who had spoken at the same time as the girl. 'Lacka, are you ready?'

The man, Lacka, nodded. 'Master Harios has asked for extra guards for the next few days. I'll be able to get myself where I need to be.'

'You have to,' said Hack. 'It all depends on you. If you fail, we fail. And if we fail, I'll break your legs.' Lacka nodded, face expressionless.

Hack turned to Skane once more. 'I need you and yours to be extra muscle. When we hit the wagon we'll need all the bodies we can muster. You've got weapons and I'm going to have to trust that you know what to do with them.'

'You don't have to worry.'

'No, but you do. Because if you don't pull your weight I'll cut your throat.'

Skane kept his face blank, but in his mind's eye he drew back his fist and smashed the dwarf's yellow teeth in. His fingers twitched.

He could do it, and perhaps he should. Hack kept this group in line through fear alone. If Skane were to beat him senseless, would they follow him instead?

In the end, the only thing holding back his hand was the fact that he did not know the city. He could not hope to pull off this raid by himself, and all in all Skane would rather be on the winning side.

'After we've helped you move the metal,' he said, instead, 'we've got some people to find.'

'Ah, right,' said Hack. 'Those three lost souls that are in such demand. I've had my orders about them.'

'And? Got a plan?'

Hack bristled. 'Of course I've got a fookin' plan! Yer think I'm an idiot?'

'We can't let them get away again.'

'No, and we won't. The young Jukeev lordling is on his way, right?'

Skane folded his arms, and nodded. 'From what rumour says, I reckon so.'

He avoided meeting Jhari's eye. They had not discussed this, and if the huge half-elf had any idea that they had travelled with this man they sought and Skane had let him go, he had not said. And he would not have been shy about expressing his concern, probably with a swift fist.

'He'll stick out like a scalded hand,' said Hack. 'We'll have people watching the gates, and we'll grab him as soon as he arrives.'

'And the others? The two girls?'

'They are together, right? And one of them is the infamous Ellyah Jerim?'

'Yeh, that's her.'

'Thought so. Don't worry about them, we'll winkle her out. We've got a special surprise waiting for Ellyah Jerim.'

THIRTY TWO

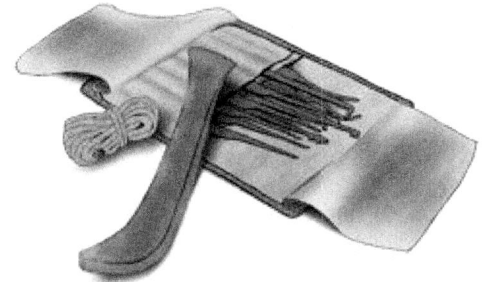

Ellyah had too many questions, and no answers.

Would that tall warrior be in Glithoniel?

Did he still have the jewel?

How could they find him and get it back?

These had circled her mind for weeks now, ever since they had fled the chaos of Ben Gedrin and travelled south. New questions had joined these since the troubling encounter in Seyntlowe.

Who were these people hunting them?

Who, or what, was Desya?

And, most pressingly, how long would Nastja be in this state?

They had been in Glithoniel several weeks, and so far Ellyah had experienced it alone. Nastja had barely moved from the bed in the tiny garret they had been able to rent, and she did not seem able or willing to speak.

The flight from Seyntlowe, with more buildings burning at their backs, had been frantic. Ellyah was certain they would be pursued, so did not dare risk returning to their horses. Hand in hand, they had fled southwards through the narrow streets, and then climbed over the city wall at a low point.

'We could go back,' panted Nastja as they hurried away into the darkness of the surrounding countryside, 'to that farm from a few days ago. We were safe there.'

'No, Nas,' replied Ellyah. Her eyes were scanning the gloom for any hint of an onward path, her ears pricked for the calls and footfalls of pursuers. 'We have to keep going. South. Onto

Glithoniel.' *Onto wherever that thief has taken the jewel, and away from that bloodthirsty cult.*

Nastja said nothing, but gave a soft moan. Ellyah encouraged her to keep moving, a firm pressure on her hand. A thought occurred.

'Nastja,' she asked, as they took a narrow path through a leafless olive grove. 'Have you ever heard the name Desya?'

'Desya?' repeated Nastja. 'A person? A place?'

'A person, I think.'

'No. Why?'

'Oh, nothing. Just something I overheard. Come on, let's move a bit faster.'

They had, through that night and the days that followed. Ellyah did not dare let them pause, not out in the countryside where they were so obvious. They could hide, and rest, in the city.

Glithoniel.

Ellyah had heard the tales of its size and wealth, its grand, ancient towers and soaring walls. But the stories had not prepared her for the reality.

Tinged with exhaustion, in the grey light of a dusky evening, she had seen it for the first time. Despite her worry, her fatigue, and the brooding silence of her travelling companion, her breath caught in her throat.

The track they followed sloped down to join a broader road. This ran into a wide vale, dotted with farmsteads and patched with fields. Away to their right the iron-grey gleam of a broad river sliced through the green, and to their left the sheen of the ocean butted against the underside of the heavy grey clouds.

In between was the biggest city in the world.

Five towers rose like the points of a star around the city. Each was circular at the base and rose to a domed summit, three hundred feet or more above the surrounding land. Alternating courses of coal black and honey yellow stone striped the looming structures.

They seemed to grow taller as Ellyah neared, and she found it hard to conceive of the will and discipline to build such huge structures. How could people think of bringing such things into existence, and how many hands, for how many hours and days and months had laboured over their construction?

As the light dimmed in the encroaching evening, a dark silhouette against the skyline caught her eye. Another wonder. A bridge, narrow but impossibly high, ran from the city and away towards the hills. Raised up to cross the city walls, the structure was carried on slender columns of carved stone.

This was not a bridge, but was the great aqueduct of Glithoniel. Streams that gushed and bubbled from the green hills that loomed over the vale had been diverted into this channel, from where it crossed over the fields and poured into the city; fresh, clear and holy.

It was hard not to stare in astonishment.

The great walls rose above them as the pale road straightened towards the city's north gate. The walls were of dull grey stone, almost colourless in contrast to the creamy yellow of the towers, but rose sheer with hardly a chink or a crack. Unclimbable, and virtually unassailable by force.

'We need to find somewhere to stay,' she said, turning to Nastja. 'Do they have guest houses here like we used near the river? Or cheap inns, like back home?'

Nastja's only response was a weak shrug. She was slumped low in her saddle, shoulders hunched. Her eyes were down and her whole manner was withdrawn as though she was trying to shut out the world.

She had remained like that while Ellyah had steered them through the ramshackle streets of the foregate town. As in Carhinn, the city spilled out beyond the walls, although the presence of solid stone buildings amongst the timber houses and huts suggested more permanence and more prosperity.

Many of the buildings were circular, small replicas of the towers that rose high above, and one of these turned out to be an inn. A white structure, with smooth curving walls and a domed roof, it stood near the huge iron-bound gates which opened into the city itself.

'I hope they've got some rooms, hen,' said Ellyah as they approached the front door. 'I'm ready to drop.'

Once again, Nastja gave no reply beyond a weary nod.

They soon left a common room which was almost deserted, after handing over what felt like an extortionate amount of copper for a single night, and threw themselves down to sleep without another word to each other.

They had kept a low profile since then, Ellyah venturing out in her Bureno clothing to find them a cheaper place to stay. In end she had managed to rent this poky room, above a hatmakers shop and close to the walls. Nastja had barely moved since.

And Ellyah was bored.

Leaving Nastja huddled on the bed she descended steep, creaking steps and hurried across the shop floor to the door. The hatmaker was a chatty woman and Ellyah was not in the mood to stop for a conversation.

Fortunately, she was busy measuring a customer's head with a strip of leather, and did not look up as Ellyah left through the door.

The air outside was chilly and a glance to her right provided a view of the surrounding hills, shadowed by a glowering mass of iron-grey clouds. Rain or worse could be on the way if the clouds poured down off the hills and over the city.

Huddling into a thin cape, she turned away and towards the gates. She had already noted that they were well guarded during the day and shut at night. If you were trapped on the wrong side of the gate at dusk, there would be no escape.

As it was daytime, she passed the guards without challenge or comment and headed for the inner city. A tunnel breached the wall behind the gate; a stony passage that revealed the thickness of the walls. It must have taken twenty paces to pass from one side to the other.

Then she was through, and the cold gloom was behind her, and inner Glithoniel was before her.

Round buildings in neat rows formed broad streets, the main avenue leading away from the gates, and smaller ways crossing at angles. Most were covered in smooth daub and whitewashed, so the city appeared clean and new. To Ellyah, it was startling.

She strolled down the main avenue, an even road paved with flat cobbles. A row of young bay trees grew down the centre, their leaves waxy and green even against the oncoming winter.

People flowed in every direction, commoners in smocks and nobles in longer robes. She heard no raised voices, no arguments, and there were no beggars on the streets; no obvious evidence of poverty. True, the low areas were those outside the walls, but Ellyah had still never imagined a big city could be this calm, this ordered.

At the end of the street the road split to pass a huge building, and Ellyah stared up in wonder.

The same honey-coloured stone, set in broad columns, held up a rounded roof, like half of a barrel. She had no idea what this huge building could be until she passed further around and heard many voices raised in song.

A colonnaded space before the front of the building held a crowd, all facing a dais at the foot of a broad flight of stone steps. A figure, hair shorn almost to the skull and clad in simple grey vest and breeches, was leading the crowd in chant.

Ellyah knew that this was a priest of the Veil, so this must be a temple.

She stopped, unable to resist listening as the song rose, swelled and ebbed. It was a lament, full of sadness that the gods had departed or drifted into slumber, and could no longer touch the world.

The melody was tinged with hope, though, that they still lived, that they watched and guided those with faith, even though their touch might be weakened and subtle.

She lingered next to one of the columns. Her lips moved silently as she recalled the words. She must have heard it in Anish, and she remembered how she had hung around the temple in low Kereva as a scrappy orphan as somewhere to keep warm. The songs had washed over her.

They had made her feel that even though her parents were gone and the man who had adopted her was little more than a common thief, she was not alone. There was a light in the world that shone on everyone, no matter how small. Somewhere, even if it be beyond the Shining Veil, there was care.

'Profanity!' came a voice from just outside the colonnade. 'Heresy! This noise is disrespectful to the gods. Thou shalt be judged.' The words were not shouted, but pitched loudly enough that many turned to look.

'The gods must be honoured by the written word,' they went on. 'This chanting is low worship. Base! It should not be tolerated.'

Ellyah was unsurprised when she looked towards the speaker. His robe was long, in smooth blue cloth, and his well-kempt hair and beard were the grey of ash. In his hand he clutched a heavy, wood-bound book and a linen sack beside him bulged with angular shapes which must be more.

'Profanity. Heresy,' he repeated.

None challenged him. None spoke back. They were many and he was but one, and he was old. They could easily drive him off. Ellyah did not understand.

Then she noticed several flinty-eyed men, each stood far enough away to be unobtrusive but close enough to quickly intervene. This Charterist had hired guards. It would explain the tolerance of his presence, and his barbed words.

Ellyah tried to ignore the burly, hard-jawed men but she could feel their eyes boring into her back as she turned away. It was unpleasant reminder that she was still hunted, and could not relax.

She was also still a hunter. Could that fair-haired thief be here?

The city was unfamiliar, unknown. She needed to explore first, to listen and watch, and get a feel for the place. That knowledge might guide her steps in his direction.

She headed south, towards the centre. She was a normal Bureno commoner going about her business, and need not attract a second glance.

It was only when she was well clear of the temple that she raised her gaze from the cobbles, and beheld one more wonder of the city. Her eyes travelled up, and up and despite herself she gaped.

Rising as high as the encircling conical towers, this was a simple column of smooth black stone, barely wider than the houses at its base. And it gleamed. Even in the dull light of this wintry afternoon, the pillar's sheer sides rippled and shimmered as though it were alive. But the gentle sounds coming from that direction revealed what cloaked the sides of the monolith.

Water. The column ran with a cascade of water. The Glithoniel aqueduct led to the summit, high above the city, and the water gushed over the edge, falling into pools below in a spectacular, eternal display.

The palace of the High King sprawled below, but the grand buildings of yellow and black stone looked insignificant in comparison. Ellyah drank in the view for a few more moments, then moved on.

She wandered the city for the next few hours, and although the shops had closed for the Waesful-day afternoon there was still plenty to see and hear.

More Charterists passed in fine robes and carrying sacks of heavy books, turning their gazes from Priests of the Veil who looked cold in short vests and breeches. Knights rode briskly along the streets, the scales of their mail shirts glistening like freshly caught fish, and with their retainers following on behind.

Most of the people she saw were human, but a couple of knots of dwarf craftsmen hurried past in skirts, loose shirts and jackets of thick grey wool, while a pair of elves stood at a junction in intense, quiet conversation.

As she left the centre behind, the buildings became less grand and shops and houses were replaced by dirty workshops and storerooms. There were more half-elves here, dressed in the work-worn smocks and aprons of labourers or dockers. They hurried past with their wide-spaced eyes down.

There was one thing that she could not help noticing, and that was even though it was the half day rest of Waesful, she saw no one drinking or revelling. In fact, she could not remember seeing an inn or a tavern inside the city at all. In Kereva, crowds would be hanging out of them by now, deep in their cups and raising unsteady voices in raucous song. The quiet calm here was unsettling.

Now that she was looking for it, though, she saw the odd building - often at a junction or overlooking a square - that was shut up and empty. And there—yes, she saw ragged holes in the wall as though something had recently been torn down. A tavern sign, maybe?

Curious, and worth investigating later.

Her steps took her further south, where the streets were quieter still and gangs of children in rags sang and played, before turning towards a mass of taller buildings in the south-west corner. These were more robustly constructed of bare stone and with crenelations on the higher towers. They were unmistakeably military buildings.

As she got closer, the mass of them stretched out, left and right, and she could see open areas where soldiers exercised and sparred with one another, even while the city rested for Waesful. She kept walking. Soldiers and armies were not of interest.

The garrison stood on the brink of a slope, and as Ellyah stopped beside a sturdy stone tower and looked down the hill, she beheld the docks of Glithoniel. A broad gap in the huge walls gave a view down to where the broad River Lumi poured out into Gojairse Bay, and the Southern Ocean. Even from this distance she could see that the docks were bustling with activity, and in the water beyond ships and boats of every size and shape bobbed, crawling with even more people.

Tiny fishing craft, barely large enough for two people were tied next to vast, ocean-going ships with masts like forests and banks of oars down each side, like the legs of insects. Ellyah knew little of boats but was impressed, and intrigued. Docks were interesting. Lots of money and lots of goods changed hands where the land met the water. A fortune could be made.

If she had time, she would return. But the light was dimming as the evening drew in.

As she paused, a man mounted on an impressive horse approached from behind. She had heard the sound of hooves on cobbles a few streets back, and was now worried he was following her. Without turning to look directly at him, she turned a corner and hurried away. Her heart was beating faster but no sounds of pursuit could be heard. Warily, she continued through the streets and away.

Returning north, she noticed something that made her slow, then stop. Braziers were being lit on each street corner, orange flames dancing merrily behind patterned iron screens. She had stopped before a large building, square built and with a flat roof. The doors were tall and elaborately carved, and a bored-looking guard stood outside.

This could be the answer. This could bring Nastja back from wherever she had gone.

As she hurried away, full of new purpose, eyes watched her from the shadows. Eyes that knew her very well.

It was time to cast a net that would ensnare Ellyah Jerim.

'I've found something,' said Ellyah. 'Something you'll want to see. In the city.'

Another night had passed, and morning had come. Ellyah had woken early, excited, and had waited as long as she could before waking Nastja. She had to pick her moment.

'What is it?' asked Nastja listlessly. At least she had responded. A few groaned words were better than continued sullen silence.

'Ah, that's the thing. I can't and won't tell you. You've got to see it. See it for yourself.'

Nastja sighed. Ellyah had tried appealing to her better nature and found it missing. Her new plan was to appeal to her curiosity. Nastja hated not knowing.

'It's something only someone like you could appreciate,' she continued, pressing her advantage. 'It would be wasted on people who don't have your intelligence. You know—normal people.'

Nastja's head rose, and her eyes shone with the light of interest for the first time in days.

'Is it the Tower of the Veil?' she asked, meaning the central pillar which ran with water. 'I've read about that. Or the High Temple?'

Ellyah could have danced. It had worked.

'I saw both of them. They are amazing. But it's not that. It's even better.' She hid her glee behind a bland expression. 'Come on, get your things.'

'Yes,' said Nastja, rising from the bed and grabbing the Bureno cap that completed her disguise.

Moments later they were strolling towards the north gate together, the bulk of the city wall rising before them. Nastja maintained a patter of talk as they walked; a stream of information about everything they saw.

'…and the walls were completed about two hundred years ago, during the reign of King Karamar. Of course, that predates Re'Emsser so the title of "High King" was not yet in use. Karamar oversaw the completion but work was begun during the reign of his uncle, King Madarn. They say he foresaw the threat of Tayo and the wars to come, but maybe he was just paranoid. Anyway, he died in the coughing plague when only the foundations had been laid, which began the decade of the succession crisis.

'Karamar triumphed in the end and took the crown, although the tablets I've read are silent on how…'

She went on without seeming to draw breath, and Ellyah let it wash over her. Nastja had been silent for nearly a week and perhaps she needed to catch up.

'No one knows for certain how old the towers are,' Nastja was saying as they passed the High Temple. 'Which seems stupid. It must be possible to find out, by looking at the foundation stones or something. Anyway, I read the annals of the Kings of Glithoniel and the towers must be at least two thousand years old, because that's how far back the records go and they were already standing then.

'Did you know that the towers predate the city?' Ellyah managed a vague shrug before Nastja ploughed on. 'None of the buildings are anywhere near that old. Some scholars think the towers were built first, and the city sprang up in the space in between.

'Ah, and there's the Tower of the Veil. That could be older still. No one is even sure *how* that was built.'

Ellyah gritted her teeth and kept walking. It would be worth it, in the end. She needed Nastja engaged and alert, so that they would have the best chance of finding the thief and tracking down the jewel. It pained her to admit it, but she could not do this alone.

'We're here,' she said, loudly enough to cut across Nastja's diatribe. She gestured ahead.

Nastja looked. Her face was blank but her eyes flicked over the grand façade, the honey coloured stone pillars, and the huge ornate doors. She blinked.

'This is…'

'Yes, it is.'

'It's the Grand Library of Glithoniel. Do you know what they have here? Tablets predating Re'Emsser and all the history we know. They say there are records dating back to the age of legends…'

'Yes, I know,' said Ellyah patiently.

'I need to have a look inside,' said Nastja, eyes so wide they bulged. 'Can I have a look inside. Please?'

'Of course you can, hen,' said Ellyah. 'But I don't think they'll let you in like that. Got a better disguise?'

'Yes. Yes, I do. I'll go and change, now.'

She scurried away, looking for an alley to don the outfit and Ellyah stepped back to lean against an adjacent wall. She was sure Nastja would be able to talk her way inside, and exploring the library would keep her busy for a while.

But after that…

She started as a shadow loomed over her. Arms rising, she was already backing away, ready to run, when the approaching figure said her name.

'Ellyah? It's really you, Ellyah,' they said. 'I don't believe it, after all these years.'

Ellyah stared in amazement, her hands falling to dangle uselessly at her sides.

'It cannot be…' she managed.

That face, that familiar face that she had known her whole life, and had thought she would never see again. Her teacher. Her mentor. The one who had raised her from nothing and taught her everything she knew.

The man who had been the centre of her life.

'Yes, Ellyah,' said Savfa. It's really me.'

THIRTY THREE

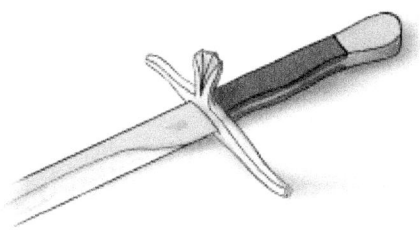

Styoyan was lost.

As the road had broadened and the traffic upon it thickened, he knew he was getting close to the famous Star City. In his imagination it was something like Kereva; a haphazard sprawl of buildings enclosed in a defensive wall. Or perhaps something like Fordon but on a bigger scale.

Glithoniel was nothing like either of those Anise cities.

It sat at the base of a broad vale like a round shield on a crumpled green cloak. It gleamed, pale and vast. Either of the two settlements huddled before the gates, north and east, was bigger than Fordon. The sheer size of the place gave him hope that he would find what he was looking for.

The walls reared above him as he approached, Mahdesht at the steady walk he could maintain all day. The towers bounding the north wall were higher still. Styoyan noticed they sloped inwards from the base, rather than rising vertically. They would not have been built that way if they were purely defensive.

He rode on and through the gate.

The last few days of his journey had been tense, and he felt another pang of anxiety as he left the gloomy tunnel behind and rode forward into the city. There were so many people. So much danger.

He had travelled with care, avoiding the main road as much as possible and keeping a careful watch on the way ahead, as well as his backtrail. He felt the hunters on his heels. His escape from Skane and his band had been fortunate; without Skane's intervention he would have been captured, or worse.

As Styoyan had ridden through the rolling green and brown patchwork of central Buren, it had been this puzzle that occupied his thoughts. Who were these hunters? He could only think that they had been sent to find him by either his father or by councillor Coril.

That Skane had indicated his life was in danger assured him that Coril must be behind it. However harsh his father's words had been at their last meeting, Styoyan could not, and would not believe that his own father would order his death.

So, Coril.

It made perfect sense that Coril would send out hunters. She would benefit more than most if he never returned, if he was never found. By now she would have assumed stewardship of the barony.

The thought made his hands tighten on the reins, but he knew he could do nothing for now except to evade capture. The title was his birthright, and when he returned in glory and honour none would deny his authority. Even his father. Coril would face his wrath on that day, just as Seneschal Tsvethan had cowered from Steyfan Jukeev all those years ago.

The thought added steel to Styoyan's resolve, and reminded him why he was in Glithoniel. He must find the garrison and arrange an audience with Duke Vorban. A military command would be the first step on his road to a triumphant return to Fordon.

It was past noon and the streets were busy. The Waesful markets were in full swing, as they would have been in Fordon or Kereva, and barrows and stalls lined the streets. A few passing commoners glanced up at Styoyan as he approached, but they did not give way before the heavy bulk of Mahdesht. Mahdesht, for his part, slowed his steps patiently.

It would be a very different story if he was being heeled into battle.

Styoyan let the stallion walk slowly as they left the walls and mighty towers behind. Buildings as large as the keep of Fordon loomed everywhere he looked. He passed a long building that must be a temple before the expanse of the High King's palace spread before him.

Circular towers of smooth, pale stone surrounded a dark, cylindrical pillar that reached up towards the very clouds. He knew this was the famous Tower of the Veil, which ran with holy water. Styoyan could imagine the gods gathering at the summit, just beyond the clouds, and looking down at those below.

Watching. Waiting. Preparing their judgement.

I serve you, thought Styoyan, and his mind went to Queen Conferan, patron of heroes. *I will not be judged wanting.*

The presence of the palace could serve Styoyan another purpose, too.

Guards in heavy leather hauberks sewn with iron plates, were standing nearby. Some were stationed at the gates while others held sentry positions around the perimeter. Styoyan saw still more watching over the queue of people in commoner's smocks who were waiting at one corner of the palace clutching large ewers and waterskins.

As he watched, a grey-haired woman scurried away, arms wrapped tightly around a tall pitcher that was full of water. The holy water of the Veil, available to all.

He nudged Mahdesht into a walk once more and approached the gates. The guards regarded him with disinterest, but Styoyan noticed their grips tightening on the spears they bore.

'You there, sentry,' he called down. 'I seek General Vorban and the garrison of Glithoniel. Will you aid me?'

The guard eyed him, lip curling. 'And I'd quite like a chat with the High Priest of the Veil. Don't mean it's likely to happen.'

His companion sniggered, and Styoyan felt his cheeks heating. He tried to hold down his temper.

'I am of noble blood, and a battle-trained knight,' he said. 'And I wish to offer my services to Vorban. I have heard he is here—'

He was interrupted by both guards chuckling.

'Noble blood, eh?' said the first with a laugh. He gestured at Styoyan's hands. 'If you're from Anish, don't that just mean you've got the biggest farmyard in your village?' They both laughed harder.

'I am the Baron of Kereva!' stormed Styoyan, forgetting in his surprise that he was trying to keep a low profile. He lowered his voice, forcing himself to calmness. 'I am only asking for your advice, as soldiers of this city. Please.'

Laughter subsiding, the first guard waved a placating hand. 'All right, all right. Only having a little joke with sir. The garrison is above the docks, just in from the west wall. Head for the southeast tower.' He gestured away, over Styoyan's left shoulder. Styoyan tugged on Mahdesht's reins, and the stallion began to turn.

'You have been most helpful,' he called back towards the guards, trying to keep any edge of sarcasm from his voice.

'Yes, yes,' replied the guard. 'Pass on my regards to Duke Vorban.'

Styoyan rode away, teeth clenched against the hot shame in his breast. He barely saw the rest of the city as he let Mahdesht walk roughly south. The disrespect that the guards had showed him rankled. He should have dismounted and shown them that disrespectful behaviour had consequences.

His hand drifted to the hilt of his sword, firm and reassuring. He would have his time, and soon.

Stewing over what he could have said and done differently occupied his thoughts, and when he looked up he had no idea where he was. The streets around him were quiet and mostly deserted, with no sign of the vibrant markets he had passed on the way into the city. Round town houses with shuttered windows, or workshops which were lifeless and deserted for Waesful lined the streets.

He had not found the garrison, and had no idea whether he should keep heading south , or turn off to go further west. Styoyan was not even sure that west was to his right. He had been letting Mahdesht wander and barely paying attention.

Just ahead, a woman in a simple smock and wearing a peasant's cap darted from a side street and crossed his path. She looked purposeful, and for no other reason than that, he followed.

Leaving a respectful distance, he walked Mahdesht slowly along behind her. The street was broad and all sorts of buildings stood to either side. Shops, smithies, houses and halls. But no inns.

It was not long before taller, squarer structures rose ahead, and Styoyan realised that by pure luck he had found the city garrison.

The woman turned away at the end of that street and headed off in what must be a northerly direction. Styoyan paused at the junction.

He stood on a slight ridge, with the ground ahead sloping down towards the city wall. Fortified buildings of bare stone lined this street, connected by a defensive wall. A tall gateway passed through the wall nearby, and Styoyan could hear the familiar clatter and thud of weapons practice from within.

This was where he needed to be.

He turned towards the gateway, noticing as he did so that the woman had stopped at a corner, just a little further down the street, and was gazing down the hill. A moment later she turned away. He gave her no further thought.

The gateway loomed over him as he approached, and more guards in heavy leather stepped forwards from the shadows beside the gate. Braziers burned with a merry orange glow, bright in the gathering dusk.

'What's your business?' asked the guard in a flat tone with, fortunately, none of the frivolity of his previous encounter.

'I am a noble of Anish,' he replied, sitting with a straight back and hoping these guards would not stoop to teasing. 'I have military training and experience and would offer my service.'

'From Anish?' asked the guard. 'Which part?'

'I hail from Kereva. Is Duke Vorban here? I would offer him compliments. His reputation is great throughout this land and I would be honoured to serve in his army.'

'I can't speak for him, or for any duke,' said the guard, 'but Captain Skeer will want to see you. I'll take your horse to the stables.'

Styoyan dismounted, dropping easily to the cobbles beneath the arch of the great gate. The guard took the reins.

'Vakher will show you the way,' finished the guard as he passed the reins to a small, grubby girl who had seemed to appear from nowhere. 'She'll take care of your beast,' said the guard in response to Styoyan's raised eyebrow.

'Follow,' said the other guard, Vakher, and walked away through the gate. Styoyan followed, watching Mahdesht being led away with a vague sense of misgiving. The guard continued directly ahead while the stable girl turned and headed right.

The stables were away in one corner of this fortified compound, and open areas to either side of the path held soldiers engaged in weapon drills. Knights in colourful tabards watched over the practices, occasionally barking commands.

Styoyan noticed that every one of the knights bore the same weapon; a longsword. He had heard that the longsword, longer than his own sabre and with a hilt sized for two hands, was popular in Buren and here was the proof.

Perhaps, if he stayed here, he would get a chance to train with one. He could take this Bureno style back to Anish, later.

The hurrying guard led him past ranks of spearmen, thrusting forwards in synchrony, towards another fortified building. Like a keep, this stood at the centre of the garrison and rose high above the practice fields below. The height of its narrow windows suggested several stories beneath a conical roof of timber shingles.

The guard led him to a doorway at the base, and then inside.

A roaring fire burned at the opposite end of the first room, which was a hall that spanned the ground floor of the tower. Tapestries depicting military scenes hung over the stonework and a long table of smooth, polished wood stood in the centre. Several knights sat around the table but barely looked up as they walked in.

Styoyan was immediately impressed. The furniture was simple but well-crafted and gave the room a sense of understated finery.

'Up this way,' said Vakher, turning towards a staircase at one side. At the top a narrow corridor ran between two partition walls, a single door in each. Another staircase at the far end climbed up and out of sight.

Vakher knocked on one of the doors, and waited.

The single word 'come!' rang out from inside, and the guard reached for the handle.

'Wait,' he said, as he went inside. Whatever he said was inaudible, but moments later the guard came out again, and held the door open. 'You can go in now.'

Styoyan felt that the guard gave him an odd look as he went past and back down the corridor, but put it from his mind as he walked into the room. It did not matter.

He found himself in an office. The walls were bare stone and once again decorated with tapestries, but a large map of Buren also hung on one wall.

'Come. Sit.'

Styoyan started forwards, eyes drawn to the man who sat behind a heavy timber desk, strewn with scrolls. He resembled the desk in some ways; aged, worn and heavily built. His nose was bent and hooked, his eyes with the flat, hard stare of one who had seen war. Styoyan realised the man reminded him of his father.

'Hail and well met,' said the knight, his voice rough and accented of a region that Styoyan did not know, but guessed might be southern Buren. 'I am Silav Skeer, one of the knight-captains of this garrison. Vakher says you've been asking for Duke Vorban. May I ask why?'

Styoyan looked at the captain's hard, lined face and then to the longsword that was leant in the corner. It had a solid, disc-shaped pommel and the black leather hilt wrappings showed the cracks and marks of heavy wear. He decided to be as honest as possible, not wanting this man to catch him in a lie.

'I am a knight of Anish,' he began, 'and a disagreement with my father encouraged me to go out in the world and seek my own fortune. I can fight, and I can lead. I will earn renown and prove my honour, if I am only given the chance.'

'I see,' said Skeer. 'And that's why you're here?'

'Vorban's reputation as a leader and a general reached my ears, so I thought to seek him out as one worthy to offer my services.'

Skeer raised an eyebrow. 'The duke will be thrilled to hear it.'

'Is he here?' asked Styoyan, eagerly.

'He is a very busy man,' said Skeer. 'But I can see if I can get a message to him. What is your name?'

Styoyan hesitated. *The truth, this time.*

'I am Styoyan Jukeev, Baron of Kereva in exile. Once more, I offer my service.'

He inclined his head and as he looked up it was to see Skeer leaning forwards eagerly.

'Do you speak true?' he asked. 'Styoyan Jukeev, Earl Gevrin Jukeev's youngest son?'

'Yes, that is me. You have heard of my father?'

'Of course. We are allies, are we not? The strongest leaders of Anish are part of the might of Re'Emsser.' Skeer paused, narrowing his eyes. 'I think Duke Vorban is going to want to see you, after all.'

He stood. Styoyan made to rise as well, but the captain waved him back to his seat.

'No, you stay there. You have travelled far to be here. Rest your legs. I will go and inform Duke Vorban about your presence, and I expect he will come down to greet you himself. His quarters are in this very building.'

'Oh!' Styoyan was surprised, and delighted. The reputation of his family had truly travelled far. 'I look forwards to meeting him. Thank you.'

Skeer crossed to the door and opened it. Before stepping out into the corridor he paused, and half-turned.

'Stay right there,' he said. 'Don't move.' He flashed a brief, toothy smile and was gone. The door closed once more with a solid click and Styoyan was left alone.

He leaned back in the chair, pleased with himself. It had been a difficult journey and he had been forced to leave much behind, but now he seemed to have found what he was looking for. Somewhere he could belong. An opportunity to prove himself.

His mind drifted to his mother, and a mix of emotions filled him as he recalled their last meeting. Her optimistic, blind delusion but also her unwavering faith in him. He would do everything in his power to return to her, and make her proud.

The room was comfortable, and clearly well-used, but a stillness and silence had settled over it since the departure of Captain Skeer that made Styoyan feel uneasy. He thought back over the conversation with the knight, hoping he had not said anything untoward.

In his excitement, he might have seemed too eager, too desperate, and he began to worry. Maybe Skeer was laughing about him, even now, just as the guards at the palace had.

No, he thought. *That could not be the case.*

Skeer had been pleased to see him, and even more so when he had found out his name. It was surprising that the fame of his father and his family had carried all the way from a minor earldom in northern Anish to here, in the capital of Buren.

Was that *too* surprising?

The walls of the room seemed to shrink in around him, and he felt suddenly vulnerable. Another reason for the captain to have heard his name, and to have been excited to see him had just occurred.

His name was known to some here, he knew. Some who were hunting him, on behalf of Coril. He recalled the deaf trader, Skane, drawing a slow finger across his throat in a sign that left no doubt as to his potential fate. Could that danger have followed him here?

His whole body tensed with the agony of indecision. Meeting with Vorban could be everything he wanted, a first step on the road to glory. Or, he could be sitting in a trap. Doubt seethed like a nest of sharp-toothed rodents in his belly.

Still fretting, he rose and crossed to the door. He tried the handle, and the worry became the stinging cut of a jagged blade. It was locked.

He could think of several reasons why Skeer might have locked him in, and none of them were good. If Styoyan was still here when he returned, with Vorban or not, his chances of escape would be gone.

Defiance rose. He would not wait just to be taken. He could be in danger where he sat, but trying to escape could be worse. The warring emotions threatened to freeze him into inaction.

He took a deep breath. What would Steyfan Jukeev do? He would disregard the risks and come up with a plan to retain his freedom. He would not restrain his blade. That is what Styoyan needed to do.

The lock. How would it work? He had no idea but bent over to peer at it, and to examine the tiny chink of light between the door and the frame. It seemed to be a simple wooden bolt, just enough to hold the door shut. It might be possible to smash it open but that would be noisy. A lever to pry it open might work just as well and without alerting the whole building. His eyes darted around the room until he saw what he needed. He smiled grimly.

Moments later, he was before the door once more, the hilt of Skeer's longsword in his hands.

This had better work, thought Styoyan. If not, Skeer would have another reason to want Styoyan in chains.

He pushed the keen point into the gap between door and frame, then forced the hilt away from himself. The gap widened slightly. Gritting his teeth and flexing the muscles in his arms, he pushed harder. The frame bent away a little more and the point of the sword forced the door inward. Pressure built against the wooden mechanism of the lock.

Please don't bend. Please don't bend, pleaded Styoyan inwardly, hoping the sword was as well forged as it looked.

There could be footsteps in the corridor outside at any moment, and then he would be caught.

With a dull crack, the latch gave way and the door burst open, swinging into the room. Dropping the longsword to the floor with a clatter, Styoyan darted out of the room and towards the stairs. He barely dared to glance back, but when he did the corridor was still empty.

Forcing himself to breathe deeply, he descended the stairs. They creaked beneath his tread and the air seemed to groan in and out of his lungs, as though his tension made the simple act of breathing an effort. He kept his face blank as he entered the hall.

The knights at the tables glanced around as he headed for the door. He tried not to look at them, keeping his eyes fixed straight ahead and attempting to walk with a confident gait. He could feel their gazes on his back, an uncomfortable prickle between his shoulder blades.

Styoyan had just reached the door, and was extending his hand towards the handle when he heard the sounds he had been dreading. Feet on the floor above, a door opening and then banging shut, followed by the thunder of steps hurrying down the staircase.

'Stop! Stop him!' Skeer's voice rang through the room as the man's feet came into view.

Styoyan did not pause to see the rest of him again, wrenching the door open and throwing himself through it.

At first, he headed for the gate at a brisk walk, but then the sound of the door being wrenched open came from behind, followed by Captain Skeer's roar.

'Stop that man! Seize him!'

Styoyan ran.

His feet pounded on the hard packed dirt as he surged towards the gateway. He was aware of heads turning in surprise as he passed the practice grounds. The confusion gave him a slight advantage, and he had to use it.

The gateway loomed ahead, freedom beckoning. He looked towards the far corner, realising with a stab of regret that he needed to abandon Mahdesht here if he wanted to escape. There was no way he could retrieve the stallion with the whole garrison raised against him.

I'll return for you, old friend, he promised.

One of the gate guards stepped out into his path, spear held mercifully upright, but his offhand extended.

'Halt—' he began but Styoyan did not slow, using both hands on the man's arm, wrist and shoulder, forcing him aside. Another guard thrust out his spear horizontally, like a bar, but Styoyan's momentum pushed it aside as he ran through.

He burst out on the street and kept running. His saddlebags containing everything he owned aside from what he wore were with Mahdesht. He could not pause to worry about that now.

The soles of his boots skidded on the cobbles as he turned left and kept running.

He needed to find somewhere he could quickly lose himself, somewhere the soldiers of the garrison would struggle to give chase. As he rounded the corner of the next building and looked down the hill the broad expanse of Glithoniel harbour filled his vision, and provided him an answer.

The docks.

THIRTY FOUR

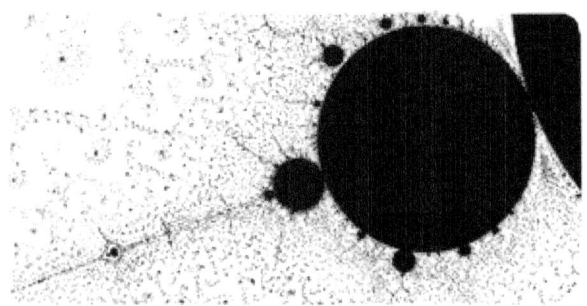

Nastja dressed hurriedly, delving deep into her pack to pull out the things she needed. It paid to be prepared. She had never understood why other people were not able to think and plan ahead as she did.

The long robe she had worn to escape Carhinn went on first, pulled over the peasant smock. It made her outline bulkier, which might help. A belt with thin plaques of polished bronze was wrapped around her waist. It was actually cheaply made, but people rarely looked past the gleam of shining metal. As always, she felt a pang of unease switching her finger rings, but it needed to be done.

She was already on her way back out of the alley as she pulled a soft Anise scholar's cap onto her head. She was very glad she had thought to obtain this, and to keep it with her.

One of her many jobs in the time between leaving home and meeting Ellyah in Kereva had been as a scribe; a scholar's assistant tasked with writing down their thoughts and copying the wooden tablets. It had taught her to read and write, had provided a very broad education and when she decided to leave, she had stolen her master's cap.

It had been worth more to Nastja, and she knew the scholar could afford to replace it.

As she crossed the street towards the library's grand entrance, she looked like a prosperous Anise scholar. She clasped her hands at her waist and raised her chin in an attitude of educated superiority. It came easily.

She thrilled with bubbling excitement as she approached the grand doors but hid it beneath her scholarly demeanour, walking past the guard as if he was not there. She did not even spare him a glance as she knocked firmly on the dark, aged wood.

For several heartbeats there was silence, then she heard a bar being lifted. She prepared herself to act her new part, with a voice to match. This was using dishonesty as a tool.

The tall, heavy door opened a crack, just wide enough to allow a face to peer out.

'Yes?' they said, the tone clipped and impatient. Nastja knew she had to be strident, to make this person doubt themselves so they did not doubt her.

'Are you going to open the door for me, or not?' she demanded. 'Or must I remain like a beggar in the street all day?' She tried to radiate a self-important impatience, irritation that her will had not already been done.

'The library is not open for casual visitors—'

'Do I look casual? Do you think I come here by pure chance?'

'Well—'

Nastja interrupted once more. 'I have travelled here from Savin Tides to carry out research on behalf of the great Anise scholar Philien Aramar.' Nastja knew that this was a real person and had read enough of his tablets and scrolls to answer any questions the librarian might ask. She hoped they did ask. Aramar had made some fascinating philosophical claims, and his reasoning for them was exquisite.

'Will you make me ride all the way back to Anish to tell my master that his ambition to educate and inspire the world was thwarted by a simple…librarian?'

Nastja flinched inwardly at her own words, knowing that most people liked to believe they had importance. But, it seemed to work. The door opened a handspan wider.

'And you are?' they asked.

The librarian was a woman of middle years, with an owlish face. Her robes were long but of plain cloth. This was someone with status but not wealth. Nastja took an immediate liking to her.

She could not show it, though. Not yet. Her show of arrogance had opened the door, so she had to carry on until she was inside.

'I am under-scholar Caralys Masojn of the college of Aramar in Savin Tides.' Nastja took a step towards the door, and the librarian stepped back. It was not quite a welcome, but she was almost inside.

'There are strict rules about what you can touch—'

Nastja spoke over her again. 'I'm quite aware. Do you think I would risk damage or degradation to these ancient writings, just from carelessness?'

The librarian bobbed her head, now apologetic and subservient. 'Of course. I am sorry. Come on in, and quickly. The door has been open long enough.'

Nastja ducked inside, the door closing behind her with a hollow boom. She looked at the room beyond and despite herself, despite the aura she was trying to project, her eyes widened in wonder.

'It's quite something to see for the first time, isn't it?' asked the librarian.

Nastja could only nod.

The interior of the library resembled that of a temple, in style and in grandeur. Two rows of columns marched away from the door down a long hall, rising to support an elegant, vaulted ceiling. Light filtered through from high above, tinted green by small panes of glass set in frames of oiled wood. The glass alone was worth a small fortune.

To either side of the long walkway formed by the avenue of columns, alcoves were divided by tall banks of shelves. And every shelf was filled with writings. Nastja could see stacks of linen scrolls rolled tightly, next to other parchment in simple folds.

Further on, wooden tablets stood neatly on the shelves, some wrapped in oiled clothes to preserve the ancient text beneath. And deeper still, towards the back of the room were the blocky grey shapes of clay tablets, covered with tiny, incised runes.

The knowledge that lay beneath this roof. The stories, the histories, and the cold, hard facts that most people would be unable to comprehend. It was all before her, just waiting to be read.

'Newer scrolls and papers are at this end,' said the librarian. 'Then wooden tablets further down, and the oldest clay tablets are at the back of the hall. What are you researching, if I may ask?'

Nastja noted how her manner had changed since they had first met. To all intents and purposes she was now a different person, all because of some perceived hierarchy between them. Was this how normal people lived, in lies and unfounded guesses? Everything they did was based on how they viewed their own place in the world. It made little sense.

The librarian had asked a question, Nastja remembered. She thought quickly.

The six-pointed star came back into her mind. That was the question she needed to answer, and the knowledge she needed must be here. But, where to start?

'Pagan beliefs in the old gods,' she said. 'My master wants to know how those beliefs came about, where the stories began.'

'A fascinating subject. You'll want to look at the earlier tablets, down at the far end.' The librarian gestured down the aisle, and Nastja started walking in that direction. Further down, a rank of plain tables was set in a strict line between the pillars, and a handful of scribes were sitting at them, carefully copying scrolls.

'Still scrolls?' asked Nastja. 'Not books?'

The librarian pressed her lips together. 'You have seen these Charterists, then?'

'Yes.'

'Their books are no more than propaganda. They have used their wealth to create these things, filled with false faith and rhetoric, then have the gall to take silver from people who have been fooled into wanting to read them. You will not find one fact in those pages, scholar Masojn. No substance at all.'

'I see,' said Nastja. She had seen the Charterist preachers several times now, but had disregarded them as fanatics exploiting other fanatics. 'They would replace the Chanterist congregations?'

'I think they would like to,' replied the librarian. 'With each person having emptied their pockets of silver for one of their books. It is little more than a scam, but the numbers of their congregations grow. I worry. People are looking for answers in these trying times, and the Charterists offer them, for a price. It matters not that they peddle falsehoods.'

Nastja nodded. There was a void, which grew in the absence of the gods. For every person who believed that the gods waited silently beyond the Veil, there was another voice who asserted that they were dead and gone.

Spending a little money for words that spoke of the glory of the gods and their triumphant return might seem a fair deal, for one who was desperate.

'Wait,' said Nastja, and turned off to her left. She had seen something that stirred her excitement too strongly for her to hide.

'I don't think those are the records you need,' said the librarian. 'That alcove is for—'

'Prathin Pra Mithrin,' said Nastja, reading the runic label on a prominent shelf. The first legend. The story that began all stories.

She approached the shelf, and her tongue moistened her lips in thrilled anticipation as she saw an age-darkened clay tablet with tiny runic inscriptions.

'Is this what I think it is?' she called over her shoulder, eyes fixed on the scratched letters.

'Yes, indeed,' said the librarian. 'One of our most prized texts. We believe it may be the original. The first version in writing, of course. It was first written down several hundred years after the event…'

Nastja read, translating the angular runes of the Old Tongue in her head:

> *Sing, muses of life and death, of war and peace.*
> *Of betrayal and hope, of two brothers and of the forging of the swords.*
>
> *In the shrouded dark before the great dying of the world, when man and beast strove as equals and the birthing of miracles was as a summer downpour on the coasts of Geth.*
> *In the time of the giving of names.*
> *In the wild of the land.*
> *In the gathering of doom when the great spirits and demons vanished or hid from mortal eyes. In the great diminishing.*

> *Then was strife brought to bear on the three peoples, to make war, to join with one another, to survive or fall.*

'That tablet itself could therefore be around two thousand years old,' finished the librarian, her voice interrupting Nastja's reading. 'The world would have been a very different place when those words were written down.'

The Twin Swords, those mythical artefacts of terrible power. In the Age of Legends, the swords were passed from hand to hand, each time causing war and destruction, and driving the great events of the time.

Then, the magic faded in the Diminishing, and the Swords vanished. Plenty dismissed the tales as myth but Nastja believed them. The gods had walked the world in those days, but had vanished at the same time as the Swords.

'The older texts are this way,' said the librarian.

'Of course,' said Nastja, and followed.

> *The land, lay beneath the sun*
> *Newly formed, the long night passing*
> *Creatures grew, in water, on grass*
> *Thriving and learning, with no threat or fear*
> *A great Council, the foremost of each kind,*
> *Was made. The masters of earth, air and sky;*
> *Wise salmon, cunning snake,*
> *Mighty bear, fearless boar…*

Sunrises and sunsets had passed unnoticed, Nastja's concentration on the angular writing and all else forgotten. She was vaguely aware of eating and drinking things that the library staff must have laid on her desk, but she recalled no hunger or sensation of taste; her body merely did enough to maintain its functions. Occasionally she napped, still seated at the desk or curled up on the floor, before waking and continuing with the task.

She rubbed a weary hand across her face, leaving dark smears of ink across each cheek. This was exhausting work.

She had found the tablet high on one of the furthest, highest shelves and the librarian had helped her reach it down and carry it carefully to one of the tables.

'The only copies of this are in wood,' she said, apologetically. 'And few remain. It is very old.'

'No scrolls?'

The librarian shook her head. 'Maybe there were, but they've all been lost to the years. No one has shown any interest in these writings for a long time.'

So, Nastja began the laborious task of translating the ancient, faded markings, writing notes on a scrap of linen parchment as she went. The writing was hard to read; small runes incised in the clay that had faded over time, and written in an archaic form of the Old Tongue where one rune could mean a whole word, or several words, depending on the context.

She skipped over a few lines of text, which seemed to be a list of the main types of animal, trying to find the important parts of the tale.

> *Lastly the King, with feathers crowned*
> *Lord of the skies, ancient Skyfather*
> *Laws were made, lives were lived*
> *Peace for all, before the Others arrived*

This was interesting. Nastja leaned back, thinking hard. The Others. She thought that was the correct translation, but the rune was smudged and unclear.

The Others were myths, folk stories. Creatures of superstition. If something went missing, or someone had a streak of bad luck, the Others were blamed. And here they were, mentioned in one of the world's oldest histories. Curious.

She read on.

> *Mysterious folk, many they were*
> *The creatures feared, of what was to come*
> *To defend their lands, the lords gathered*
> *Speaking and listening, desiring safety for all*
> *Soldiers were needed, steadfast warriors*
> *A band of guards, stationed at borders*
> *Simple creatures, called and raised high*

Strength was given, relentless and savage
They chased and harried, those that would do harm

Nastja wrinkled her brow. She had wrung the meaning of each line from the faint impressions in the clay, and had to read her own writing several times afterwards to make sure she understood the full meaning.

The animal gods, or their high council, had brought into being creatures that were to be their guardians. Their army?

It was impossible to know how much was myth, and how much was allegory. She also had to consider that it could be true, or at least believed true by those that had told the tale, and those who had first written it down.

As she continued reading, she felt as though she was travelling into a strange new world, where anything was possible and the distinction between fact and fiction was musty and indistinct.

The brocken fought, battling without cease
Against all. Uncontrolled aggression
Claw and tooth, no creature was safe.
And they grew, gaining size and strength
As they killed, consuming one another
Fewer and fewer, the fighting never ceased
Until a day, when the sky darkened
Only one remained, the ruler of the guards
Dominating all. And his name was Desya.

THIRTY FIVE

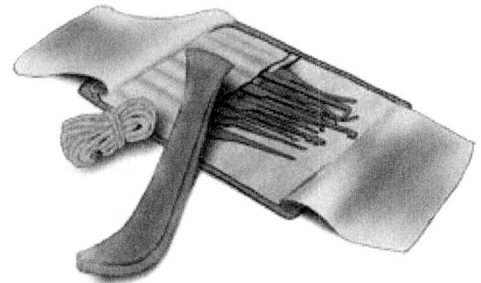

The rickety bed rocked, the frame thumping rhythmically against the wall. Ellyah did not hear it, lost in the sensations, and the long-forgotten feelings of being safe and protected.

Lost in the arms of Savfa.

They moved together with increasing urgency, her arms and legs wrapped tightly around his lean body. His face was twisted in concentration and pleasure combined, beads of sweat on his brow.

And then it was over, the pair of them crying out in unison and then falling together onto the bed, blankets knotted messily around their heaving bodies. He sighed, a happy expulsion of air beside her ear.

Catching her breath, she leaned over and feathered a light kiss to his brow, the salty tang of fresh sweat mingling with the clean taste of his skin.

'I've been hoping for this since you left,' she said. 'I always thought you'd come back one day.'

He wrapped his lithe arms around her. 'I always meant to. Once the heat had died down. Once it was safe.' He sighed. 'I've been imagining this, though, through all those years of running and hiding.'

She leaned into his embrace, slipping her own hand around his side and feeling the strength in his slender body. His touch, his tender caresses and his presence made her realise how alone she had felt.

'You're here now,' she said.

As the words left her lips, she realised how trite they were. A meaningless platitude. But Savfa reminded her of the way she used to be, all those years ago when she had felt safe and secure beneath his watchful eye. Back when her abilities had value beyond the copper and silver they could earn.

No one else had ever made her feel that way. No one else had ever said 'Well done' or given her a hug when she had shown her skill and smarts. No one but Savfa.

'Yes, Ellyah,' Savfa had said. It's really me.'

She had been unable to do anything but stare. The surprise had triggered her deepest instincts and she was fill with the urge to run, to escape from the situation. But it was him, the one person she never expected to see again, the one person who haunted her dreams.

He was exactly as Ellyah remembered him; a couple of fingers taller than her with a slim but powerful build, dark hair and olive skin. His hands were long fingered and clever, and he still wore his thin Anise age-rings on several of them.

The moment stretched.

Sudden emotion filled her, and Ellyah launched herself at him, fists beating against his chest in anger and frustration. He made no move to defend himself.

'You left me thinking you were dead!' Ellyah cried, heedless of who might overhear. 'And you knew I'd find out you weren't. And that was worse!'

He raised his arms, palms outwards in a gesture of surrender.

'Don't you think I'd have come back if I could? Don't you think that I was desperate to return and use what I'd made from that robbery to take us both away, buy us a new life?'

Ellyah was silent for a moment, still simmering with rage.

'I thought you'd made it yourself, and just didn't care enough about me.'

His eyes softened in sadness and he reached for her. She jerked away.

'I thought about you every day. But I was hunted. We all were. The leader of the trade caravan was a villain too and was able to call in favours from some very serious people. They caught us, one by one, and took back what we'd stolen, one way or another. The ones that died quickly were the lucky ones, from what I've heard.'

She imagined him then, cowering in barns or caves in the wilderness, the heavy pouch of coins nothing more than dead weight; an anchor that would drag him down to oblivion, sooner or later.

'You should have come back to Kereva,' she said. 'We had strength there. We'd have kept you safe.'

He shook his head, that familiar smirk playing on his lips.

'He had watchers everywhere. I'd have been snagged as soon as I walked through the city gates, but more likely they'd have waited until I thought I was safe then grabbed me and anyone who was with me.'

His stare pierced her, and she knew what he meant.

I was protecting you.

She also knew that Savfa could make almost any lie sound this convincing, however much she wanted to believe him. She folded her arms.

'So what brings you here now? Are they still after you?'

'I'm safe,' he replied. 'For now. It cost me everything I owned and now I'm in debt. But those I paid have the strength to protect me. I've got to work for them but it's better than being dead. I just need to keep my head down, like you are.' He glanced around the streets in an exaggerated fashion, before turning back to her, eyes flicking over her disguise. There was a question in his eyes.

'I'm keeping a low profile too,' she said. 'Had a bit of trouble in the north which is still on my tail.'

'Trouble? From who?'

She frowned. 'Oh no. No, no. You're not going to stroll up to me and have me tell you everything. I'm not stupid.'

'Don't you trust me?' he said.

'Don't. Just don't.'

He smirked, like he always did when he had been caught out.

'I need to go,' she said.

'Go where?'

'Away.'

'Great.' He made as if to follow, although she made no move. 'Please Ellyah, you can't just walk away from me after all this time.'

'I can, and I will,' she said. 'If I was to let you follow me so easily it would mean I'd forgotten everything you'd taught me.' He said nothing, but smirked in that familiar way. She was still furious with him, but his presence near her was still strangely comforting. He pulled to her in a way she was struggling to ignore. 'Come here at the same time tomorrow. If you're on your own and haven't been followed, you might see me again.'

She felt his eyes on her back as she walked away, and suppressed a smile as she turned a corner and lost herself in the crowd.

He came back the next day. She knew he would.

Nastja remained shut up in the library and Ellyah approached the front doors with her usual caution. She had changed her disguise for the mid length robe of a trader, with her hair still hidden beneath a different cap. The urge to run into Savfa's arms was strong but she knew she could not trust him. Not yet.

They strolled the streets, talking idly, trying to avoid questions about where they had both been since Savfa had disappeared. Ellyah could not forget his abandonment, even if he said had been doing it to protect her. She knew not to trust him. Not fully, not yet.

Despite that, she relished the hours she spent in his company. Years had passed but little had changed. He was still light-hearted and made her laugh. She had almost forgotten what that was like. Her cares melted away and she found herself wanting to share some of her experiences, the way she had applied his teachings.

Still unable to find a tavern, they held small wooden cups of thin stew in their hands as they hunched in a corner of a street where no one would notice them. She could not hold it in any longer.

The thought of sharing her story of the theft of the jewel and their subsequent pursuit seemed dangerous and thrilling. It had been her secret for so long, her own treasure trove to find and keep, but she suddenly wanted to tell Savfa about it. He would be just as motivated by the riches on offer as she was.

'I'm on the trail of something special, Savfa,' she said. 'Something so valuable that the Mackems chased it from Carhinn to Ben Gedrin.'

'Oh?' he replied, his interest understated. She knew he was listening, though. So, she told him about her heist in Carhinn and the frantic escape through Anish and over the Rujrweh Pass to the Lands of the Great River. Told him of the gang fights and fire in Ben Gedrin, and about that tall, fair-haired thief who had played them all at the game and won.

His lips twitched occasionally as she spoke.

She chose to leave out how she had witnessed the jewel killing a man from a single touch.

'So,' he said, after a while. 'This tall warrior still has the jewel?'

'Yes,' she replied. 'He must have it. He killed the gang leaders and ran off with it.'

'And you think he's here? In Glithoniel?'

'Where else? He can only want to fence it on, or use it to bargain? And either way, where better than here? He was definitely heading this way after he left Kiraband.'

Savfa was silent for a moment.

'You'd recognise him if you saw him,' said Ellyah. Tall, broad, carries a two-handed sword. Pale and fair-haired, looks a bit like a Riverlander.'

Savfa shook his head. 'I'm not sure about this Ell. I've only just got myself out of trouble.'

She felt an immediate stab of frustration. 'You owe me this.' Savfa laughed, a short, mirthless bark. 'This is a big one, Savfa. I know you've been running, but so have I. I'm tired of it. But if we can pull this off, it'll be the last one. The only one we'll need. I know we can do it if we work together, me and you against the world. And then we can disappear.'

Savfa gazed upwards towards the taller towers that surrounded them, expressive lips twisting into a thoughtful pout. 'I'll think about it, Ell,' he said, eventually. 'That's the best I can do. I've got to be careful.'

'I understand. But I'm not going to stop looking, and if I find it without you I'll need to leave quickly.'

'Same time tomorrow?'

'Yes.'

He sloped away into the crowd and Ellyah watched him go, mind racing.

'I've found him!'

Savfa's eyes were bright as he dashed across the street to where Ellyah lounged against the wall. He spoke excitedly and with no preamble. 'I've seen that big warrior you described to me.'

'Really? Where?'

'Spotted him in the docks. Didn't approach – if what you've said is true he's a dangerous bastard.'

'Yeh, he's a fighter. And we need to be careful not to spook him now we know where he is.'

'What do we next, Ell?'

She glowed as he asked her opinion, deferring to her as though he was in charge.

'It'd be too risky for us to try to take him. The man is a killer. I've seen him fighting. We need more bodies if we're going to take him down and take the jewel.'

Savfa was silent for a moment, chewing his lip in thought.

'Wait!' he said abruptly. 'I've just thought of something. Those people I mentioned – the ones I'm hiding out with? They asked me to help with a job. I turned them down because I didn't want the risk, didn't want any more heat. But if I helped them they would owe me a favour. And they have plenty of muscle available.'

'Would you do that for me?'

'For us. And, of course. But it might win them over if you help too. Someone with your smarts and skills would be really valuable.'

There it was again, that glow that came from Savfa's praise.

Grow up, Ellyah, she said to herself, but did not hide her smile.

'We're going to do this, together,' he said and his arms were wrapping around her and as she looked up at him their lips met. It was like a spark to a lonely candle, a flash of colour in a grey room. They paused, both looking at each other in mute, curious surprise. Then their mouths pressed together once more and some moments later they were hurrying back to Ellyah's attic room and she was lost, lost to Savfa's touch.

They lay together, later, consumed in a contented glow.

'This is going to work,' she said. 'I just know it. We'll get that jewel back, fence it on and be gone together.'

There was a rattle at the door.

Savfa turned as Ellyah pulled the blanket protectively up past her chest. The door rattled again, then the sound of a fist pounding boomed through the room.

'Ellyah. Ellyah! It's me, Nastja. You can open the door.'

Ellyah sighed, and Savfa chuckled.

'Nastja? Still?' he said.

'She's useful. She's saved my life more than once recently.' She grabbed a loose sheet and wrapped it around her body. 'I'd better let her in.'

She moved to the door and raised the latch. The door exploded open, and Nastja bustled in.

'I know what's going on,' she said, stopping in front of Ellyah. If she noticed that Ellyah was clad in just a sheet, she gave no sign. 'I know who is after us, and it's not the Mackems.'

Ellyah said nothing, raising an eyebrow and returning a hard stare that she hoped Nastja would read as a hint that this was not the time.

She did not.

'Desya. You said that name yourself and I didn't know what it meant, but it's mentioned in some of the oldest texts in the library. Which means that they are the oldest texts in the world. It's amazing, the writings they have there. So interesting.

'Anyway, I know who and what Desya is now. In the early days of the world, before elves or dwarves or men, there were the animal gods. The old gods. The ones the pagans still worship, who were first in the world.'

Ellyah sat on the end of the bed. Nastja clearly needed to get this off her chest and it would be pointless to try to interrupt.

'Something happened that scared them. The texts say it was the arrival of the Others, but the stories have always described the Others as peaceful, so I don't really understand that part. In any case, the gods decided they needed guards, soldiers. So they created them.

'Either they made a new race, or changed one that already lived, but in the end they had an army of creatures ready to fight with tooth and claw. They were ferocious.

'But they went too far. The creatures were too aggressive, too savage, and impossible to control. They fought ceaselessly, at first as the council of the gods directed but then against each other. And with each victory they grew, getting bigger and stronger until only one remained. They called it Desya.'

She paused, staring at Ellyah with wide eyes and slightly spread hands, as though expecting her to jump off the bed, screaming an alarm.

'Right,' said Ellyah, feeling that some response was required or else Nastja might remain frozen in that position until the day of doom. 'And that tells us...?'

'They created Desya. They created a new god, a demon of rage and violence, and unleashed it on the world. Desya is who this cult still worships. The rites they perform are done in his name. That's the reason for the six cuts. I was right.'

'Wait,' said Ellyah. 'If they worship this terrible beast, where is it? I don't see it rampaging around. And I don't understand why the six cuts is anything to do with this.' Ellyah wanted to dismiss this out of hand, blocking out what she had seen and heard in the temple basement, but Nastja was too intent on the detail to be ignored.

'Desya is chained beneath the earth, so the writings say. As his power grew, the elves were summoned from across the Southern Ocean and at the same time the dwarves awoke beneath the mountains in the north. They all saw the threat that the demon posed, so an alliance was formed.

'The Others, the young elves and the newly-woken dwarves banded together, and found that the power of the demon was balanced by a new power within them. Magic.

'The old gods fled in fear but the other races joined together to work magic. The leaders of the Others were raised up, strengthened. Made into something...new. Can you guess their names? There were five of them.'

Ellyah frowned. 'Five.'

'Mordea, Tureank, Conferan, Kaled and Ome. They began as mortals but became the Five. Maybe their names were rendered differently then, but that's how we know them. The language was different back then, nothing like the Common Speech—'

'Nastja,' said Ellyah. 'The point?'

'Yes, right. The Five confronted the demon and together they overcame it. The battle was ferocious, though, and shook the earth. The ground split. They threw all the power they had at the demon but could not destroy it, so they drove it deep underground and shackled it with huge chains of pure iron to restrain its magic.'

'And that was the end of the story?' Ellyah hoped so. Savfa's hand was creeping gently up and down her spine, and the urge to slip back beneath the blankets with him was strong.

Nastja shook her head. 'Not quite. Even chained, the demon was still powerful and filled with rage. His struggles against the chains split the earth further, and caused fire to spit from the top of the mountains. Forests burned and smoke filled the air.

'The Five summoned the elves and together they worked one last spell together. They cast a great magic to seal the earth, to put out the fires and blow away the smoke. It took all the power they had, and when the smoke had cleared the Five were gone, ascending to the heavens, and the Others faded away. But they'd made the land safe, and left the demon bound and asleep.'

Ellyah's patience was running out. 'What does any of this have to do with us, Nas?'

'The demon was not forgotten, in the same way that the Five were not. And while we worship the Five there have always been those who pray to Desya. That same cult has existed through the long ages since, secretly worshipping the demon. That cult is who hunts us.'

'But...why?'

Nastja looked awkward. 'I'm not actually certain. But it must be something to do with the jewel.'

'What?'

'You know why it's called the Demon's Tear?' asked Nastja, and Ellyah braced herself for another lecture. 'It was formed in the last shifting of the earth that imprisoned Desya. They say it contains the last remnant of his rage and power, before he fell into his long sleep. We carried that thing for a long time. There's a connection.'

'There'd be a better connection if we got it back—' said Ellyah, hoping to steer the conversation away from fairy tales, but Nastja interrupted.

'Maybe they think we do. It would make sense. Or maybe they just think we know where it is. Either way, we're in danger from them, and we don't even know who they are.

'You remember what happened to the innkeeper? That will be us, if they catch us.'

And the unfortunate man in the temple's basement in Seyntlowe, thought Ellyah, but kept the thought to herself. She had still not told Nastja the full horror of what she had seen. The magical force, conjured by a bloody rite, reaching out to find her.

She tried to dismiss the thought, telling herself that it did not matter now, and once the jewel was sold and she had escaped with Savfa, it would never matter again.

'We just won't get caught,' she said.

'You can't be sure of that!' said Nastja, her voice rising. 'They could be anywhere. They could be on the street outside, waiting for us!'

At that, Savfa let out a small chuckle at the thought of mysterious enemies crouching in dark corners. Nastja's eyes went to him and widened, as if noticing his presence for the first time.

'Who's this?' she snapped.

Ellyah moved a little closer to him, stretching out a hand to pat his thigh beneath the blanket. It was slender, and firm.

'This is Savfa,' she said. 'You must remember him.'

Nastja's face was blank as she stared at Savfa, before returning her gaze to Ellyah.

'He's the one who walked out on you,' she said.

Ellyah stiffened. Nastja just could not keep her acid tongue behind her teeth.

'He didn't walk out on me,' she said. 'It was complicated.'

Drop it, she thought. *Do not do this in front of him. Do not shame me.*

'It wasn't complicated,' said Nastja. 'You told me all about it, many times. You hated him for it, said you'd have preferred it if he had been killed like you first thought.'

There was a heartbeat's worth of silence.

'Get out.' Ellyah could hear the wobble of cold fury in her own voice, although she tried to stay calm.

'What?' replied Nastja, brow creasing in confusion.

'Go. Just leave me alone.'

Nastja blinked owlishly, mouth working as she thought of what to say. Eventually, she managed: 'Where should I go?'

Ellyah lost her temper and shouted: 'Somewhere you won't annoy me for a long, long time!' She forced herself to calm, quietening her voice. 'You have money. Half of the share. You can find somewhere else to stay, away from me. Leave. Now.'

Another horrible, awkward moment passed with Nastja staring at Ellyah, barely blinking. Then she turned, leaving without another word and shutting the door behind her.

Ellyah stared at the rough boards of the door as Nastja's clattering footsteps faded away down the rickety staircase. She had brought this on herself, and if she could not see why then it was not up to Ellyah to explain.

'She's not changed, then,' said Savfa, a laugh in his voice.

Elyah shut her eyes. 'She just can't see that other people don't find this stuff as interesting as she does. She thinks that just because you know something, you have to say it.'

'Like how you wished I was dead?'

Ellyah squirmed, then shuffled back on the bed. Reaching out, she ran a placating hand across Savfa's brow, stroking a loose curl of his dark hair.

'I never meant it,' she said. 'Not like that. I just thought you were dead for so long…I'd made peace with it. Understanding you had abandoned me was harder.'

'I can imagine how you felt,' he said. 'But I couldn't risk showing my face.'

She had found out all that she could about this, gently questioning him about their time apart. He painted a picture of a life spent looking over his shoulder, the riches he had earned weighing down his pockets but with no freedom to enjoy it.

'It's just us, again,' she said. 'Us against the world.'

He laughed, face splitting with happiness. 'That's right!' Lowering his voice he looked deep into her eyes, expression full of meaning. 'It gave me quite a thrill when you were so firm with Nastja, too.'

He pulled her close, holding her tight enough for her to feel the evidence between their bodies. In moments Nastja, and the rest of the world beyond the confines of the bed, were forgotten.

THIRTY SIX

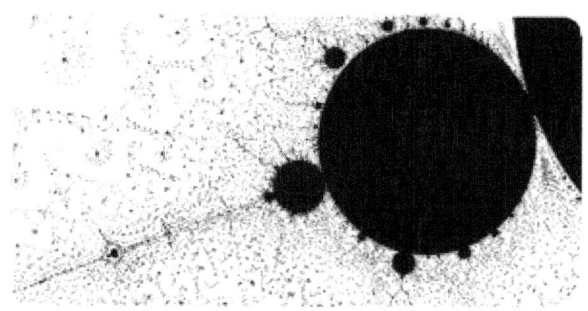

'Go. Just leave me alone.'

Ellyah's words rang in Nastja's mind as she strode toward the Northgate. *'Go somewhere you won't annoy me for a long, long time!'*

Her boots were spattered with dirt. The black mud sullied the brown leather, and the urge came over her to scrub at the dirty marks with a sleeve. But then her sleeve would be muddy.

No, no, no.

She had been given an instruction and would follow it. She understood Ellyah well enough to know that she had spoken in anger, but it had nevertheless been direct and unambiguous. The words had been said and that was enough. Nastja would go.

'Just walk away, like you did before', came a different voice from the depth of Nastja's memory. She ignored it.

She paid little attention to where she was going, her feet choosing their own route, dwelling instead on what exactly Ellyah had said and why. She knew the signs of anger, but swam in incomprehension as to the cause. Why had she upset Ellyah so much?

She walked through the settlement that hugged the outer wall of the city, the buildings becoming more ramshackle the further from the main road she walked. Small huts, like conical tents but roofed with rough thatch, not reeds, dotted the outskirts, and she spared them barely a glance.

Everything she had said was the naked truth. Bare facts, which explained what had happened since leaving Ben Gedrin. The cult of Desya still existed. They had not forgotten their dark, chained god any more than the rest of the world had forgotten the Five.

Something that was true should never be forgotten.

A vague path led between scrubby fields and away from the city, heading vaguely south. Nastja followed it towards a green bulge of higher ground. The day was wearing to a chill, wintry evening, watery sun flowing beneath the clouds and picking out the yellow in the stone of the towers. Nastja turned her back on them, walking away.

Something had changed in the time between Nastja going into the library and returning to Ellyah. Ellyah had changed. She had not wanted to listen, not tried to understand, even though she must have known that everything Nastja was saying was the truth. Ellyah was not being honest with herself.

Why?

Savfa.

Nastja had been surprised to see the man lying in the bed, but had guessed who he must be before his name had been spoken. She had hoped it was someone else, anyone else, because Savfa was not to be trusted.

Savfa was a liar.

'And you would know one.'

Even back in Kereva, his ability to put marks at ease had been well known amongst the underworld. He could bend the truth as though it was soft as silk in his hands. Ellyah knew that, and she must realise that his presence here, now, was far too convenient to be a coincidence. Nastja mistrusted everything about the man.

She had arrived at the top of the grassy rise. It was a broad headland that stretched out around the south of the city like a grasping hand. Iron grey ocean gleamed below her, the few vessels riding the choppy swell scurrying back towards the city like tiny toys on strings.

Beside her was a low wall of pale stone, and beyond that was a graveyard.

Tall, stone-armed *pentangs* stood in neat rows like trees in an orchard. Beneath, generations of Glithoniel's wealthy dead lay buried, their souls flown to the Veil. Would their wealth in life ease their passing through the Veil? Would it weight the judgement they received?

The priests said so, but called it service. Wealth was the reward in life, and the gods' love was the reward in death.

'*And for your lies,*' went on that voice, '*you deserve neither.*'

She knew the voice all too well. It was the voice of her brother. They were words he had never said, but she had earned.

Leaning back against the graveyard's low boundary wall, she pressed her palms to her face. For others, this would be a pose of despair, but for Nastja this was not the case. It was to let her concentrate; to block out everything external and to find clarity.

What was important?

The answer came to her quickly: Ellyah.

Despite her incomprehension, the knowledge that her words had upset her friend filled her with sadness. She had done it before; speaking what she knew was the truth and watching as people reacted with shock and anger. Ellyah was usually more understanding.

Nastja did not want to leave; she wanted to stay with Ellyah, but she could not ignore what her friend had said. What she wanted was not important; what mattered was respecting what Ellyah wanted. She had spoken, Nastja had to listen.

She had to go.

She rose to leave, but as she stood that same voice filled her mind again.

'*Walking away from the mess you made, again?*'

The voice of her brother. Challenging. Accusing..

'That's not the way it was…' she said to herself but as she spoke the ghosts of the past came to haunt her. She remembered the moment that had changed everything.

Her father, drunk. His fist, swinging and thudding into her mother's jaw. Nastja watching helplessly as she tumbled down, down, down. It was all over by the time she hit the ground. The life that Nastja had known was gone, forever.

And not just hers.

In her memory she allowed herself a glance to the side, recalling the wide eyes staring through from the next room. The eyes of her brother, Arjden.

'*You tried to deny my existence,*' he said, bitterly inside her mind. '*By lying to yourself about what really happened that day.*'

'No, I never lied,' she replied to the memory, knowing that she was only talking to herself. 'I just didn't want to remember what happened.'

She saw it now, though, the events playing out vividly in her mind. She forced herself to watch; she had to be honest with herself if she were to understand why others lied.

Her father had looked down at the limp figure of her mother, his fists still bunched as though fearing she would rise again. He swayed unsteadily, mind muddled by drink, unable to grasp the finality of his blow.

Nastja had stared at the back of his head and her thoughts had come with pure, cold logic. She was not sad for her mother, not yet. Her suffering was over, but a crime had been committed.

A life for a life.

The knife had been in her hand in an instant, and the keen point slipped into the flesh at the base of father's neck with ease. She remembered the disgust she had felt as his lifeblood gouted down the handle, dirtying her fingers.

She was already looking for a cloth to wipe them clean as her father's body went limp and toppled to the kitchen floor. He lay unmoving next to the body of her mother. Nastja had wiped her hands clean.

'*Do you remember what happened next?*' asked Arjden's voice.

She gulped, the guilt fresh and clean. There was blood on the floor, and on the knife, and pooling around the bodies of both of her parents. Arjden had stepped forward, his young eyes wide with horror. There was a long, terrible, silent moment. Then Arjden had spoken:

'Get out. Get away from me. Get out!'

She had looked down at herself, the bloody knife in her hand and her father's lifeblood staining her hands and her clothes. She knew she must be a vision of terror to her young brother. He could not mean those words, though. He could not truly want to be left alone.

But they cut her like the knife had cleaved her father's flesh. In the shock of the aftermath, she had taken him literally, obeyed his instruction, and had fled without another word.

That was the truth.

She expected to hear Arjden's voice once more, berating her further, asking her questions, but he had fallen silent.

Arjden had not wanted her to go, but it seemed as if Ellyah had. Their words were so similar. The difference was Savfa.

Nastja could have returned to Arjden and she could admit to herself, now, that she probably should have. If she returned to Ellyah while Savfa was there it would only cause more upset. Ellyah had replaced her with Savfa, and Nastja was right to do what she had told her to do.

She needed to go.

The graveyard felt cold, so Nastja left it behind and followed a well-used path that led down towards the city's Eastgate.

'*Leave me alone,*' Ellyah had said, and Nastja had to believe she meant it. She knew sometimes people spoke words they didn't mean, but if Ellyah had not meant it, she should not have said it. She knew Nastja would take them literally.

Why had Ellyah been so upset, though?

Nastja had questioned Savfa's presence and his motives, and it had been that which made Ellyah lash out. She had reacted emotionally to being reminded of the way he had abandoned her. Being reminded of her own grief, her own anger.

What did that really mean?

The Eastgate loomed over her, and she tried to think as Ellyah would. Ellyah was stubborn, and needed to feel like she was in control. She hated being wrong, hated changing her mind and hated admitting to either.

Was that it?

The return of Savfa had forced her to change her mind, and she found that difficult to acknowledge. She did not want to be reminded of it.

The grand buildings inside Glithoniel's city wall loomed over her, her feet choosing a path as her mind worked on the problem. She still had to decide what to do.

Had Nastja been wrong, or untruthful? No. Was there any way that Ellyah would admit to the truth? No, she was too invested in the lie she had told herself. All Nastja would achieve by trying again would be to hurt Ellyah, and to make her angry again.

The truth was the problem and the persistence of a lie was the solution. It made no sense. Nastja was the bearer of that truth, and so indirectly she was the problem. She had hurt Ellyah simply by stating facts, and she knew that she would do it again. Her heart hurt to think of it.

What, then?

Leave. Now.

Ellyah's last instruction was something that Nastja could follow to the letter. She could leave. The problem would be removed.

She had just begun to walk west with a more determined stride when something ahead made her duck aside and shrink into the nearest alley. Three figures were coming towards her down the street, and she recognised two of them far too well.

One was well-built, with fists like hams and jug-handle ears, while his companion was freakishly tall and with skin like scorched mahogany. Skane, the leader of the Carhinn Mackems and his right-hand man, the half-elf Jhari. There was a shorter, squatter figure alongside them in a leather vest; a dwarf that Nastja did not recognise.

She watched them pass, heading east and walking with casual arrogance. The few people out on the street as evening closed in avoided them, dodging to the side to get out of their path.

The Mackems were here. Hunting for Ellyah and herself? There was no way of knowing, but it was unlikely to be a coincidence. Another puzzle. It changed nothing, though, so she put them from her mind and carried on westwards, towards the docks.

The streets were quiet now, and she padded through the lengthening shadows. She clung to the sides of the streets, moving in a way that was unobtrusive with the ease of habit.

Yellow light shone behind shuttered windows as night fell. A cold breeze nipped at Nastja's nose and fingers, and she pulled a pair of woollen mittens from her pack as she walked on.

Part of her wanted to stop and listen at each window, each bolted door. It must be fascinating to listen to the tales people told each other, fooling themselves that their lies were the truth. She had to leave, though, so she kept walking.

The city garrison loomed ahead, the solid, blocky buildings little more than black squares against the night sky. Narrow windows were lit from within, like a hundred cat's eyes, slitted and yellow.

Here was something interesting, though. Braziers lit the main gateway and showed it to be thronged with guards. She had expected to see a handful but there were enough for a full rank to be formed across the width of the gateway. From within came the noise of activity: horses nickered and their hooves thudded, metal rang and clattered as though an army mustered beyond the walls. To Nastja it sounded like the garrison was roused and making ready to march to war.

One more puzzle this night

She could not wait around to find out more. *Leave*, she had been told, and leave is what she must do. Turning the corner around the northeast tower, she followed a broad lane downhill.

The docks spread below her, and they did not sleep.

Lanterns and braziers gleamed around the buildings, along the wharves and on the boats like fireflies in the branches of the spreading tree. If she hurried, she might find a ship that sailed with the dawn tide.

Warehouses guarded the entrance to the docks, huge timber sheds with conical roofs, and as Nastja passed them noise washed over her. Voices warred for attention; shouts and yells as goods were unloaded, dockers singing as they coiled ropes and scrubbed decks mingling with the hum of people chattering.

Nastja looked, and understood.

A row of mighty ships was tied to sturdy posts, with high prows and many masts. Their beams and rails were decorated in bright colours. These were the ships of the Teliyade.

Gangplanks led from each, down to the blackened wood of the wharf, and a steady stream of people passed up and down them past bare-chested sailors with lilac-tinted skin, and upswept ears.

'Come one, come all,' shouted the nearest, perched on the gangplank. 'Fine wines and rum from across Re'Emsser on board. Nowhere better to drink and sing than the Batasari!' His voice had an unusual, lilting accent.

Floating taverns. The High King had ordered the closure of the city's taverns, but on the water of the harbour these boats were not in the city. The sound of raucous singing came from within.

Nastja approached the half-elf sailor.

'*Namaskaram*,' she said, hoping she was using the correct Elvish dialect. 'I'm looking for a ship taking passengers.'

'*Manci prasangam!*' he replied, with a laugh. 'Fine speech, lady. Passengers? I don't know about that. Can ye haul? Can ye scrub? If ye can then the Goppagali is looking for hands. Next one along. They are sailing with the dawn.'

'*Dhan'yavadalu*,' she said, thanking him, and moved along.

A stream of people flowed along the wharf, mirroring the river that flowed past the bay. Nastja joined them, a small figure in the crowd. The Goppagali was a taller, longer vessel than the Batasari, and workers in rough smocks joined merchants in robes on the broad gangplank.

'Music! Tales! Merriment!' called the sailor at the foot of the ramp, balancing easily on the slanting top of a barrel. 'Come ye aboard the Goppagali and drink your troubles away! Or drink yourself into trouble, makes no odds to us!'

Nastja stood next to the barrel, and tapped the half-elf lightly on the side of his bare foot. He looked down.

'A child of the land!' he exclaimed. 'Why do you be touching my foot, child of the land?'

'Passage,' she said, before remembering more was needed. 'I'm looking for passage on board. As a passenger.'

He crouched down, bringing his face closer to hers. 'Aah, you'd sail aboard the Goppagali?'

'*Miru nannu kaligi unte*,' she said. 'If you would have me. The crier of the Batasari said you sail at dawn.'

The sailor's eyes widened, and his face split into a delighted grin. 'And you have the Elvish on your tongue! I'm sure we can find a berth for one who speaks so sweetly.' He laughed, like the splashing of clear water.

Nastja made as if to come up the gangplank. He stood up and thrust out a warning hand.

'Not now,' he said. 'No, no. Not the right time. It is busy now, loud time.' He gestured over his shoulder to where the deck was thronged with people. Music was playing but almost drowned out by the raucous sounds of voices in loud conversation. 'You must go, then come back. Just before dawn. We will expect you.'

'Yes,' said Nastja. She had learned something. 'I will come back. *Vidkolu*.' She added a farewell in Elvish, and turned away.

'Sarasamaina gali mim'malni surakṣitanga castundi!' he called, towards her retreating back. It was a traditional saying of the Teliyade: 'May a fair wind see you safe.'

Dawn was a breath away when Nastja returned to the wharf. *Leave*, Ellyah had said, and she still intended to. *Go and come back*, the sailor had said, and that is what she had done.

The night had been chilly and uncomfortable, but the docks were a warren of alleys and yards. There were plenty of nooks and crannies to hide away, if you were careful. She had wrapped herself in a blanket from her pack and wriggled beneath an old sail behind some empty crates.

Her belt knife had felt hard in her hand, protection in case anyone found her and thought to take advantage, but she had not been disturbed and had even slept a little.

Her eyes felt gritty, and she blinked in the growing light, but she could sleep aboard ship. The important thing was getting away. It was better if she was on her own, now, and could not cause upset with the things she said.

The wharf was quiet, compared to the night before, and she had barely taken three steps on the rough planks before a figure detached from the shadows behind a pile of crates and followed her. The movement was clear in the corner of her eye. Nastja took two more long strides, then stopped and turned around.

The figure stopped suddenly, standing before her on the wharf with an air of guilty indecision.

'Yes?' asked Nastja.

The young man hesitated, mouth opening and closing like a dying fish. His eyes darted, as if thinking of running but confused about whether he should be intimidated by a girl he overtopped by a hand or more.

'I was just walking along the dock,' he muttered eventually. Interestingly, the accent of Anish was clear on his tongue.

'You were hiding behind those crates,' said Nastja, calling out his pointless lie. 'And as I walked this way you followed me. You couldn't have made it any more obvious. You either wanted my attention or you're really bad at being stealthy.

'Either way, I'm curious now as to what you're up to. I don't want to have you following me around.'

He opened his mouth again, an angry scowl creasing his face. Then, he blew out a breath and his expression softened.

'I overheard you asking about the ships,' he admitted. 'I was hoping to do the same. I need to get away from this place. But I didn't know how.' His face twisted in shame at this last admission, before he fixed his eyes on her again. 'So, I followed you so I could learn what to do.'

He was definitely from Anish, and well-spoken. She took the time while he was speaking to study him and his garb.

Smooth-cheeked, he was certainly young. Nastja guessed that he had twenty years or fewer; slightly younger than Ellyah. His hair was raven-dark and tied back, but long enough to suggest that he was more than a simple labourer. If his drab, cheap clothes were a disguise then he should have also cut his hair short.

At least it was not still held in place by silver pins, but to Nastja it made his class obvious.

He was wearing a grubby smock and hose, but Nastja noticed the collar of another robe beneath. It was a deep blue and in a rich, smooth cloth. So, he had donned the smock over the top of his own clothes, being unwilling to throw them away.

This boy was a fool.

'Why are you staring at me?' he asked. Nastja did not reply, still preoccupied with his appearance, his true identity and his amateurish attempts to conceal it. He wore fine riding boots in expensive leather, which did not surprise Nastja one bit. The sword hanging from his belt, which did, the hilt tucked beneath the smock.

Nastja had a sudden suspicion, and reached out to grab the hem of his smock. Lifting it, she took a quick look at the hilt of the sabre beneath, before letting it drop. The boy just stared in silent outrage.

Like a blacksmith's puzzle, all the pieces fit together to reveal the intricate final shape.

'Good morning, sir,' she said. 'I name you Styoyan Jukeev, son of Earl Gevrin. Should I bow?'

'What? No!' spluttered the boy. His discomfort was obvious, but Nastja could not understand why. 'I'm not...I mean...How did you know?'

'Why would you think I wouldn't?' replied Nastja, but stepped closer so they would not be overheard. 'Your rings and your voice show you're Anise. I mean, you've swapped your rings at least, but still...You did not get rid of your coat or your boots or cut your hair which all show you are from wealth. You're too young...nineteen?' Styoyan nodded.

'Too young to have made money,' Nastja went on. 'So, you're noble born. The Jukeev crest on your sabre names your family, unless you overcame the owner and stole it, and...no, not likely.'

'But—' began Styoyan, but Nastja was still talking.

'You're not Gevrin, and if my memory serves me right then Sylen, Nadez, Dostoy and Umeylo are all closer to thirty which makes you the youngest brother, and names you as Styoyan. Pleased to meet you.'

She extended a hand. Styoyan's eyes darted from side to side as though he expected a horde of people who had recognised him to rush forth and seize him. Then he sighed, and took Nastja's hand.

'Is it that obvious?' he sighed.

'No. Not to most people.'

'But you aren't most people?'

Nastja just shrugged. 'I pay attention to what I see. A lot of people don't.'

'Clearly. I'm Styoyan.' He gave her a level look.

'Yes,' she replied. 'I just said that.' They had been over this.

'And you are?' he asked, after several moments' silence.

She understood. It had been one of *those* stares. A facial expression that was actually a question, the words unspoken.

'My name is Nastja Mjette,' she replied.

There was another pause, the young man staring at her while the morning's business of the dockyard gathered pace around them. None paid them any heed. Was there another facial expression for her to identify?

'Shall we see about getting that ship, then?' asked Styoyan.

'Oh. Yes. That's what I was doing, yes.' She turned and continued towards the Goppagali. Styoyan fell into step at her shoulder.

'Do you have somewhere you need to go?' he asked in a casual tone. 'Or something you're trying to get away from?'

She looked at him again, surprised. It was a perceptive comment. Maybe she had underestimated him. Maybe he could be, at least, interesting.

'I was told to leave,' she replied.

'Oh. By who?'

'My friend. Well, we used to be friends. I don't know what we are now. I didn't stop to ask.'

'If he threw you out without telling you why, he doesn't sound like much of a friend.'

'She.'

'She. Sorry.'

'Oh, I know why she wanted me to leave. That's one thing I have an answer to. The problem is all the other answers I still don't have.'

They walked on, approaching the gangplank of the Goppagali. Another bare-chested elf stood beside it, this time overseeing the loading of cargo rather than crying the quality of liquor on board.

Styoyan cleared his throat. 'If you didn't get the answers you need, have you wondered if maybe you were asking the wrong questions?'

Nastja stopped mid-stride. His words rang around her head, a pointless line of small talk. It was meaningless in and of itself, but...

'... *asking the wrong questions?*'

And she was.

The day played out again in her mind: the library and the histories, Ellyah and Savfa, and then the appearance of the Mackems, against the backdrop of their relentless pursuit. Once again, it was as though she was twisting the pieces of a blacksmith's puzzle into place, slotting them together to form an intricate and surprising shape.

It was all there, and now she could not leave the city. She needed to put this right. She hoped she was not too late.

'I've changed my mind,' she said, turning on her heel. 'I need to go back.'

'What? Why?' Styoyan made as though to follow her.

'I'll be back soon. Hopefully this evening,' she replied. 'Take a ship now, or wait for me. I will return.'

Styoyan called something after her as she dashed away down the wharf, but she was not listening.

She had something important to do.

THIRTY SEVEN

Skane stared longingly at the back of Hack's head. As the dwarf spoke, he imagined slamming his fist into the base of that thick, rounded skull, then trampling him into the dirt.

'Today's the day, youths,' Hack was saying. 'This is the one we've been waiting for. One big raid, one big payday. One more time to show who really controls this city!'

His eyes were bulging, spittle flying from his lips in his rabid enthusiasm. Even Skane could hear every grating, bellowed word. And he was sick of it.

'The wagon carrying the blue-black will have left Seyntamros-o-the-Hill at dawn, so will arrive just after noon. We need to be ready. We all need to be ready.'

'We're ready,' said Skane, and Hack swung round. His brows drooped, and yet his pupils were wide enough to make his entire eye look black. Skane had seen him swigging heartily from a flask of rum or *folwine*, even this early, and had a suspicion that the dwarf might also have been chewing on mushrooms.

'You're not ready!' snapped Hack. 'You're not ready. You need to go and tell the smith to be ready. Ready. The work needs to be done and with our master by nightfall.

'So, you need to go and remind them. Put the fear of the demon on them so they don't think about shirking or running. Right?'

'Why's that my job?' asked Skane. He could not have said why he felt the need to question Hack's orders, apart from that he was sick of the dwarf, and because he could. This whole thing stunk.

'Why?' roared Hack? 'Why! Because I bloody said so is why!' Skane saw his shoulders hunch, his fists clenching.

Come on, short arse, he thought. *Throw a punch. I bloody dare you.*

Jhari had seen it too.

'Hack's the boss here,' he said. 'We got to do what he says.'

I see how it is, thought Skane. Jhari's allegiance had always been to the most savage dog.

'Don't get into any fights while I'm gone,' said Skane, as he headed for the door.

It was just past dawn, the low cloud an oppressive grey, the colour and apparent weight of beaten lead. The cold was biting. Skane had been forced to buy a winter coat while here, thick wool with a rabbit fur collar, and he huddled down into it as he strode towards the Eastgate.

He knew full well why keeping the smith cowed and ready to work was important, but he had had just about enough of being bossed about, especially by the likes of Hack. If he wanted to lead, let him lead. Let him work for it.

The streets were quiet, quieter than they had been when he had strolled in the opposite direction the previous night. The work of the day was just beginning for many, and smoke spiralled lazily from chimney pots as hearth fires in houses, shops and factories were kindled into life.

This particular metalsmith had a small workshop attached to the back of her house, which was beyond the Northgate in the shadow of the towering, curving city wall. It was well away from the main district of smiths, crafters and artificers, which made it ideal.

The place was discreet, unlikely to be searched once the *pluitone* was stolen, and the smith was very skilled at the delicate work required. Skane just had to persuade her that sticking around in the city and doing the work was a better option than making a run for it.

It was not true, but what did truth matter these days?

He went to cross the north street near the central temple, but something gave him pause. There was a vague sound in the air, but with it a rumbling vibration that he felt through the soles of his feet. It was getting louder, closer. He leaned back against a nearby wall, curious.

Others had stopped too, gazing south as a flock of children appeared up the street. They dashed north, then stopped to look behind before running on again. Behind them came the source of the noise. Skane stared.

First came a company of mounted knights, proudly wearing coloured tabards emblazoned with animal insignia over rippling scale mail. Hard eyes stared straight ahead beneath gilded helms with cheek guards, all brightly polished and gleaming. Behind them marched the standard bearers, one bearing a tall *pentang* and the others carrying embroidered banners displaying the emblems of the barons and earls who must command this force.

Those nobles rode close behind: three men whose skin was creased with age but whose eyes burned with authority. In the middle was a tall man on a dappled grey stallion of imposing size. Gilding shone on his helmet, the trappings of his scabbarded longsword and on the collar of his mail coat.

His expression was almost predatory, like the implacable stare of a hawk.

'What's all this?' asked Skane, turning to a skinny woman in a plain smock who had come to stand beside him.

'That's Vorban, innit,' she drawled, her accent unfamiliar and difficult to understand. Skane leaned in close, watching her lips carefully. 'He's leading the garrison.'

Behind the lords of Buren came the rank and file. Foot soldiers, marching in tight, neat ranks with spears pointing at the sky. The pounding of their feet made a percussive, heartbeat rhythm. Grey clad Veil priests walked alongside, sprinkling water from polished ewers beneath the marching army, escorting them towards the gate.

'But, where?' asked Skane, raising his voice over the insistent thud of the army's footfalls.

She shrugged. 'Dunno.'

A man who was walking along beside the column paused, overhearing Skane's question.

'Marching to the west border,' he said. 'Trouble in Tayo. You not heard?'

Skane and the woman shook their heads, and others nearby leaned in to listen.

'There's been fighting,' he began. 'Near the border, so they say.'

'It's Tayo,' cried the woman. 'When is there not fighting?'

'This is different. There's a rebellion against the Taosach. And they're winning. They say their general is a genius, and led a bunch of farmers and sellswords to victories against those

Gluttons, all across the southeast. He's captured forts and towns, and his army is still growing. The Bureno nobles who own land in the Swarthland are sweating, I can tell you. Feels like civil war brewing and whoever wins will have the scent of blood.'

'Gah,' said another. 'Same thing all over again. There'll be a few battles then they'll make a peace.'

'This time it's different,' insisted the first man. 'This time it's making the lords and knights nervous. Their general is a giant of a man, and the commoners love him. They call him the Demon, and they say he's a sorcerer.'

There was laughter. 'Get on!' cried the first woman.

'Vorban wasn't laughing, was he? This general, this Demon, called out one of his opponents, a favourite lord of the Taosach, and froze the skin off his bones. Killed him dead, like that!' He snapped his fingers.

'Can't be true, can it?' asked the first woman, laughter dying on her lips.

'High King's taking it damn seriously. He's emptied the garrison and got them all marching to defend the border. Not taking any chances.'

Skane listened quietly. A few months ago he would have been laughing too, but since then he had seen people killed by dark magic and watched the dead walking. Only last week he had been tortured himself by someone who was many miles away.

There were strange forces at work, and it stank. But, he had a job to do.

He turned his back on the column still snaking up the street, continuing on his way.

As he got further from the High King's palace, the central temple and the Northgate, the buildings around him dwindled in size and grandeur. Most were still circular, and the daub on the walls a crisp white, but as the northwest tower loomed above him most were a single storey. These were the dwellings of simple folk.

The metalsmith's workshop was at the back of one of these small houses, with rounded walls and a conical roof of timber shingles. The workshop itself was a lean-to extending into the back lane; barely more than a wooden shack.

Skane opened the door without knocking, and stepped inside.

The workshop was empty, with a dull orange glow showing the residual heat of the small furnace. Small pieces of metal hung on hooks and stood on small shelves around the room. These were the decorative yet functional pieces that were the smith's speciality.

Belt clasps, necklace settings for precious stones, ceremonial torcs, that sort of thing. Skilled, honest work. However, he needed to find the smith herself.

A simple wooden door led from the workshop into the main house. He opened it. The room beyond was circular, the interior walls white as those outside but hung with embroidered cloths. A small hearth burned merrily on the far wall, and the room felt homely.

Three people were sitting at the table in the centre of the room, and all three turned to stare at him. Two children stared blankly, still chewing, while the woman who must be their mother fixed him with an expression that was keen with fear.

Crusts of bread on wooden plates told of a breakfast being finished, and a tall clay cup stood between the three. A jug of oil stood to one side, and one of water to the other as though they had been mixed in the cup. Five candles were arranged neatly around the cup, flames flickering in the draft.

He had interrupted them in prayer. That could not be helped.

'You can't just come in here!' blustered the woman, rising. 'This is my home—'

'It's about the job,' said Skane, interrupting. 'You know which one. We need to talk. Now.' He held open the door and motioned through it.

She hesitated, shoulders tense, lips thin. Then, she sagged.

'Go and get your day clothes on,' she said to the children. 'I need to talk to this man about work. I won't be long.'

The children got up from the table, heading for a chest near the beds. The woman gestured towards the open door and Skane went through, back into the workshop. She followed him, then pressed the door shut with her back and leaned on it heavily.

'Hack sent me—' began Skane.

'I know what I need to do,' cut in the woman. 'He doesn't need to keep checking up on me. You needn't be here. I'm not going anywhere.'

'He does need to check,' said Skane. 'He needs to know you're ready. The blue-black is arriving today.'

'Today?'

'Yea. The work needs to be finished by nightfall.'

'That's...a hard ask.'

'There's no choice. It needs to happen.'

'Yes,' she said, ruefully. 'I have no choice.'

Skane did not have time for pity.

'You got the design? Know what you need to do?'

'Yes, yes, it's all prepared.' The woman put a hand to her brow.

'Show me,' said Skane.

She sighed, then went over to a cabinet set against the wall of the house. Opening it, she drew out a long shape, wrapped in sacking, as well as a tight roll of linen parchment.

'Here's the piece so far,' she said, unwrapping the sack cloth. 'It's just waiting for the *pluitone*. I have to say, I still don't understand what it's for.'

'You don't need to understand,' said Skane, gruffly, but he shared her confusion.

A steel rod, the length of his arm, lay on the workbench. The top broadened into a polished head with spaces for three fittings. Skane glanced at the drawing, noting that the *pluitone* would be forged into three arms that attached to the head and curved inwards to grasp at empty space.

He looked again, then back at the unfinished rod. The space at the top was about the right size to fit a fist-sized object, with the *pluitone* arms as clasps. Perhaps a fist-sized jewel.

This business kept getting darker and stinking worse, although he still could not see what his master was trying to achieve. He just hoped he would be able to walk away with clean hands at the end.

He rolled up the parchment and handed it back to the metalsmith. She wrapped the rod up again, and returned them both to the cabinet.

'The blue-black will come here this afternoon,' he said. 'Could be with me, could be with someone less polite. Be ready.'

She said nothing, but nodded miserably. Skane pitied her, then.

'I'm sorry I interrupted your prayers,' he said.

'It's fine. We were done.'

'You pray to Kaled?' he asked.

'Today we do. And maybe for many days to come. My husband marches to Tayo this day.' Skane nodded. The call to war was harder to bear when it came in a time of apparent peace.

'I hope Fate protects him,' he said.

'As do I,' she said. 'But I am afraid. There is something in the air, these days. Something…dark.'

'I know what you mean.' Said Skane, and he did. Too well. 'You will be free of us soon, in any case. Just do what you need to do and it'll all be over by this night.'

'Perhaps,' she replied, her tone flat.

'Be ready,' he said once more, then left the workshop.

Shre Evane Claes had been one of the delegation of priests sent to escort Vorban's great army to Glithoniel's Northgate that morning. Even as she had chanted the catechisms of the Five and washed the road beneath the soldiers' feet with sanctified water her keen eye had spotted a familiar face in the crowd.

Skane.

She knew that flat, jug-eared face so well, and yet this was the first time she had seen him in the flesh. He looked like little more than a thug.

Forced to stand outside the temple once the army was on the road to the Tayan border, her skin pebbled with the cold as she dispensed the blessing of the Five to all who queued up. She ignored the cold. As a priest of the Veil she was meant to rise above such earthly discomfort.

As the first disciple of Desya, soon she would not need to.

Power would be her reward, and while with power came wealth what she craved was respect, and comfort. She had been confined in this life of faceless, ascetic servitude for long enough.

Tonight, things would change.

She was still performing her duty outside the temple when Skane strode past again, in the opposite direction. It was mid-morning by then, but no warmer. A wry smile spread across her lips, despite her discomfort, because she knew where he must have been. Which meant that her plans were all falling into place.

In a few hours, Hack and his band of criminals would have stolen the *pluitone* she needed, and passed it to the metalsmith. Shortly after that, the finished sceptre would be in her hands and she would be riding a swift horse after Vorban's army.

She needed to get to the Tayan border, and then into Tayo itself. Somehow, she had to contrive a meeting with the Tayan general, the one they called The Demon.

As soon as he had claimed the jewel, owning it and its deadly power, she had known him. Her connection to the Demon's Tear, through Desya, was so strong that she was aware of him through even her waking hours.

She closed her eyes as fear and excitement thrilled through her once more. He was so strong, much stronger than her, but as yet he knew nothing of what he could do.

He must be found, then controlled; his power harnessed. And the sceptre was the key. With it, he could bear the jewel as a weapon and as a totem, and through it she could guide his hands. Guide his power.

With him at the head of an army, they would be truly unstoppable. Soon, the demon would rise.

THIRTY EIGHT

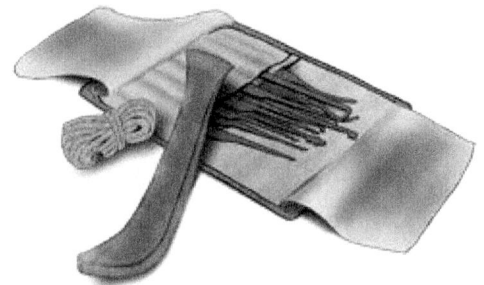

Ellyah clutched Savfa's hand as they moved through the crowds. People pressed in on all sides, but Savfa guided her confidently through the streets. She thrilled with the excitement of the familiar and the unknown. All her senses were heightened, ready for what was to come.

The garrison marching out through the streets just after dawn had caused a huge amount of interest and excitement. And speculation.

'Tayo is rising,' said some. 'They'll be swarming into the Swarthland next.'

'It's just politics,' said others. 'The High King needs a victory to strengthen his rule. That's all there is to it.'

But the most pervasive rumours were about the Tayan general who led the rebels, about who he was and the mysterious powers he held.

'They call him The Demon,' said a woman in a fine robe, silver hair unbound. 'He can work dark magic, raze towers and scatter armies with a wave of his hand.

'My brave son marches to fight him, though, so we can feel safer.'

Her reassuring words were betrayed by the pinched anxiety of her face. Her hands twisted together, and she looked towards the west.

'What do you think of these stories?' asked Ellyah as he dragged her away and onto a quieter street. He did not turn.

'It's good for us. Less soldiers in the city, and their leaders' attention will be elsewhere. It'll probably help.'

Ellyah wanted to pursue the conversation. At the mention of dark magic her thoughts had turned to the dark rite she had witnessed in the basement in Seyntlowe. But something made her keep that to herself.

Savfa would just laugh it off, anyway.

The High King's jeweller was a few streets away from the palace itself. Savfa pointed out the route the wagon would have to take on its way there from the north gate.

'Along here, and past the front gates of the palace,' he said. 'Don't look! Don't give the guards any reason to suspect anything.'

'I didn't look,' she said.

'Don't answer back,' he snapped. 'Who's in charge here? Me.'

'Where are we going?' asked Ellyah, biting back an angry retort.

Savfa tutted with impatience. 'Do I have to tell you everything?'

'I just want to be ready.' Ellyah tried not to let it show, but she was hurt. Savfa's manner had changed completely since they had left her rooms this morning.

'Fine. I need to check the ambush site, make sure it's not watched. And I need to make sure you end up in the right place.'

He stopped abruptly, and pulled Ellyah into a recessed doorway. His arms wrapped around her and his lips feathered kisses along her cheek and towards her ear. Instantly, her heart beat faster.

'What—?' she began.

'Hush,' he said, as a small group of labourers in dirty smocks walked past behind them.

Ellyah realised that this embrace was a cover; no one looked too closely at a couple entwined, but that did not mean that she should not enjoy it. She breathed in his fresh scent, felt the wiry strength in his arms…

'Tell me how it's going to go,' she whispered, lips close to his ear. 'Tell me how we're going to win today.'

He sighed. 'Look left and right,' he hissed. 'The wagon needs to turn a sharp bend there, with narrow streets in every other direction. That's where we hit them.

'We'll be hiding around these alleys, and when we hear the wagon we come running. There's enough of us to block the streets, and when we've got the blue-black we can scatter into these lanes and they won't know which way to chase.'

She had missed this. The anticipation of action, the fluttering of fear in her belly, the strong hand of Savfa guiding her...

'Now, we split up,' he said, interrupting her thoughts. 'You go north, I'll go west. Go. Now.'

He broke away from the embrace and began to walk away.

'Be safe,' she hissed as she went in the other direction. He did not reply, or even turn his head.

Ellyah made sure not to look back as she walked away herself. A glance over a shoulder, however quick it was, was one of those gestures that drew unwelcome eyes. Like Savfa had said, they could not give anyone a reason to be suspicious.

One by one, they would gather and find a hidden spot, then when the time was right they would strike....

Ellyah's instincts gave her a fraction of a moment's warning before a tall shape detached itself from the nearby doorway and grabbed at her. She dodged back but another pair of strong arms seized her shoulders, gripping tight.

She tried to twist away, but the strength in those unseen hands was like steel. As she wriggled they slipped down her arms to her wrists, pinching them painfully together behind her back.

The tall figure before her lunged forwards at her, a loop of coarse rope in his hands. He went as though to slip it over her head, but she leaned back against the other attacker and kicked out, hard. Her heels bounced off the huge body as though striking seasoned oak. He came in again, ignoring her kicking, and the rope went over her head. It was dragged down to her mouth and drawn tight between her teeth.

It was filthy, and tasted rank. She gagged against it, but it would not shift, and she could not make a sound beyond a furious groan. Desperate panic fluttered in her breast. These men were so strong, and she was utterly helpless and at their mercy.

If only Savfa was closer...

The rough, squeezing sensation of another loop of rope being tied tightly around her wrists made her gasp, and the giant figure before her stooped to bind her ankles. As he straightened again, the light fell on his features and her ragged breath caught in her throat. She knew him.

'Got you at last, missy,' said Jhari, the huge half-elf brawler.

'Stop struggling,' came the thick, nasal voice of Skane from behind her. 'You're coming with us, one way or another. No need to make it harder.

'Lift her legs, Jhari.'

Together, the two men manhandled her across the street and into the doorway where Jhari had been waiting. As they forced her up a rickety staircase and into a grimy attic, their brutal strength was impossible to resist.

They could do anything they wanted with her.

'Get her on the chair,' said Skane, and they twisted her body into a sitting position before dropping her onto a wooden chair A few tight turns of rope around her middle and thighs rendered her immobile.

She had ceased struggling. It would just be a waste of energy. Even if she somehow slipped the bonds, she would not get far. She could not overpower either of these two, let alone both at once.

Fear still bored a hole through her guts, but she tried to master it. If they had wanted her dead, they could have easily killed her already and left her body in the alley.

They wanted her alive. That was something she could cling to.

There are worse fates than death.

Skane drew up another chair and sat while Jhari stood guard at the top of the stairs.

'Now,' said Skane in his loud, distinctive voice. 'Me and you are going to stay here until the others have knocked that wagon over and lifted the blue-black. Then, we're going on a little journey together. Ever seen Tayo? I've heard it's lovely.'

Ellyah glared at him, powerless and furious.

'Look at her,' said Jhari. 'Still thinks she's better'n us.' Two long strides took him towards her and one of his great fists swung. Blinding pain shot through her body and she gasped against the gagging rope.

He drew back his fist for another swing, but Skane stood.

'Enough,' he said. 'If you kill her by accident it all goes to shit.' Jhari glared at Ellyah, a snarl on his face. Then his head swung round in the direction of the street. Ellyah heard raised voices outside, too.

'Hear something?' asked Skane.

'Yea,' replied Jhari.

'Go. She ain't going anywhere.'

Jhari turned and hurried down the stairs without another word. Ellyah was relieved to see him go although she had no reason to think Skane would be any kinder. Her ribs ached already, and she could only breath in short, painful gasps.

The door clicked shut. If she was going to try to escape it had to be now. It was her only chance, and she had no idea what fate awaited her. If she could get to the street, maybe Savfa would find her.

She threw her weight forwards, rocking the chair onto its front legs. As her feet touched the floor she kicked down as hard as she could. She left the ground, still attached to the chair and came crashing down a moment later.

As she had hoped, her weight smashed the flimsy chair to pieces. Pain stabbed through her like a knife to her injured ribs, and she screamed noiselessly against her rope gag. The bonds around her thighs and middle slackened as the chair broke apart, and she ignored the pain as she wriggled free and stood.

Mirthless laughter, like stone sliding over rock, filled the ensuing silence.

'You're a bloody idiot,' said Skane, who had moved to block her path to the staircase. 'What are you going to do now?'

Still bound at the ankles, and with her hands tied behind her back, she knew she would have more hope of escaping by running through the wall. If she had the use of her mouth, she might have admitted that she had no idea. At least she was no longer tied to a chair.

Skane chuckled again, but the mirth died on his lips as soft footsteps sounded on the stairs below. He turned and backed away, and as he moved to the side Ellyah saw who was coming. It was not Savfa.

Nastja.

She advanced on Skane, her outstretched hand holding her small belt knife. The Mackems thug's brows rose in an expression of curious surprise. He was not afraid.

'Afternoon,' he said, voice loud. Ellyah knew he had lost his hearing after taking too many blows to the head as a prize-fighter. He got by, watching lips to work out what was being said but it had left him with a voice that was nasal and often overloud.

'Yes,' said Nastja. 'It is afternoon.'

'Come to help your little friend?'

'Yes, I think so.'

'How'd you find us?'

'It wasn't hard,' replied Nastja. Her belt knife was still aimed at the thug, but he had put his hands in his pockets. Ellyah knew that even together they would not be able to get past him. If they tried, he would be forced to fight back and would not pull his blows. It would be very dangerous.

'There are people hiding in every dark corner and doorway out there,' said Nastja. 'And I saw a drunk dwarf who was hissing "Hide! Hide!" to anyone who passed.' She frowned. 'Maybe he was worse than drunk. His eyes were all wrong.'

'That'd be Hack,' said Skane. 'He's one of theirs, not one of us. He's a bloody liability.'

'Don't worry,' said Nastja, in a reassuring tone. 'You'll still get away with the *pluitone*.'

Skane stared. 'How—?'

'You've timed it perfectly. The garrison is empty and everyone is looking in the wrong direction. It's far too convenient for coincidence.'

'I meant, how did you know about the *pluitone*?'

Ellyah could hardly believe what she was seeing. She was still bound and gagged, standing awkwardly in the centre of the room, unable to do more than hop. And here was Nastja, in conversation with her captor as though they were old friends.

Had they forgotten she was even there?

She took a deep breath and forced it out as loudly as she could through the gag, in the form of a furious groan.

They turned.

'Sorry, Ellyah,' said Nastja with a total lack of surprise or alarm. 'The reason I came here was to talk to you.'

It was Ellyah's turn to stare. Nastja was unbelievable.

Skane laughed. 'So you thought you'd just break in here while we were in the middle of a robbery, and have a quick chat with your friend?'

'Yes, exactly,' said Nastja, oblivious to Skane's sarcasm. 'Thank you. It won't take long.' She turned back towards Ellyah.

'I realised—' she began, then stopped to correct herself. 'Someone made me realise that I lacked answers because I was not asking the right questions.

'I thought I'd made you hate me. I knew that I'd hurt you with what I said, but I didn't know why. And I wanted to know. Needed to. I needed to know what it is about me that's so…wrong, that when I try to help, try to tell the truth, I just cause pain.'

Ellyah grunted against the gag.

Stop it, Nas! She wanted to yell. *For Fate's sake, you drive me crazy at times but I'd never hate you!*

Nastja continued. 'But those were the wrong questions. They were distracting me from what was really going on. I was looking at a symptom, but ignoring the cause of the disease. And the disease is…everywhere.

'He's part of it,' she said, pointing at Skane. 'Part of it and he doesn't even realise how big it is. Doesn't realise what he's working for.'

'You're an expert, are you?' scoffed Skane.

Nastja nodded. 'Yes. I think I am.'

Ellyah laughed, a muted snort into the gag, and the sound finally caught Nastja's attention. She strode across and a moment's work with her knife released the filthy gag. Skane did not react, but when she also cut the cords that bound Ellyah's wrists and ankles, he hefted his cudgel and stepped forwards.

'Hey, hey!' he said. 'Think you're going somewhere?'

'Yes,' replied Nastja. 'We're leaving. I think you're going to let us.'

Ellyah stretched her wrists and legs, the relief immediate, before throwing her arms around Nastja's neck.

'I love you, hen,' she muttered into her ear. 'But unless you have a very good plan you're going to get us both killed.'

Nastja was stiff, staring at Skane as though Ellyah was not there.

'You're stealing *pluitone*,' she said, 'but you don't know why. You chased us from Carhinn to Ben Gedrin, then all the way here to recover that jewel, but you don't really know what it is. Your master is desperate to bring all these pieces together, but you have no idea what they are trying to make. No idea. Correct?'

Skane looked down at his feet for a moment. 'Got some idea.'

'Some idea. But really, no idea. You don't even know what you're part of.'

'I'm in the Mackems,' he muttered.

Ellyah was transfixed. Nastja had walked in here and now had this brutal man, twice her bulk, hanging on her every word and mumbling like a boy caught scrumping.

'Very much not the Mackems,' replied Nastja. 'They were swallowed up some time ago by something much bigger, much darker, and much older. They just didn't tell you, because they wanted to use you. They're not interested in petty thieving or protection rackets. They want to change the world.'

'Nastja, what is this?' asked Ellyah. The line between loving Nastja and being driven crazy by her rambling was so very close.

'Let her say on,' said Skane.

'In ancient times,' she began. 'There was a demon. It was born with a single purpose, to destroy the Others and return the earth to the domain of the animals. That was all it knew.

'Eventually, the Others, the elves and the dwarves worked together to defeat it, control it, and bind it beneath the earth. It sleeps there still and its name is Desya.'

'Not this nonsense again, Nastja,' said Ellyah.

'Is it nonsense?' asked Skane.

'If it is, or if it isn't, there were many who believed it to be true. Through the long years that have passed since those days they have remembered Desya, revered the demon and its rage, and vowed to bring it back.'

'And?' asked Skane, brow furrowed.

'And that is who you are working for,' said Nastja. 'Those are the people who have driven you all this way, through all this risk. The jewel is called the Demon's Tear, and they say it can take a person's soul and bind it to Desya. Others in the cult practice death magic, in the hope that they might draw power from the demon.

'I've seen the evidence myself. And Ellyah has seen it happen.' She looked at Ellyah.

Ellyah did not know how Nastja knew, but could not deny it. She nodded.

'And the *pluitone* must be something to do with the jewel, too. Maybe as a setting, or as a handle. Because the jewel can't be touched directly. And it must be something to do with this new leader in Tayo, too. He's involved. He must be.'

'This all sounds...crazy,' said Ellyah.

'You were part of it, too,' replied Nastja. 'That's why they sent Savfa to find you, to win you over. They used him to bring you to them.'

'Savfa has nothing to do with any of this—' she began to retort.

'Of course he does!' said Skane and Nastja in unison. They eyed one another then looked at Ellyah again.

'They knew about your smarts, your skills,' said Nastja, more gently. 'They knew how good you are at vanishing. So, they found your weakness. The one thing that would make you let your guard down.'

Ice gripped Ellyah's whole body. Not Savfa. Not this. Ellyah felt her face crumple, unable to stop it.

'This can't be true. I know him. He wasn't one of them.'

'He was,' said Skane. 'I never trusted him, but he was in real deep. Turned up saying he knew you, knew how to bring you in.'

'It's true, Ellyah,' said Nastja. 'You know it is.'

Ellyah's body slumped, and a little light that had been burning inside her guttered and died. The hard thing was not that Savfa had fooled her, again; used her and abandoned her, but that she had probably known all along. Deep down, she had known that he was a trickster, a confidence man, and even though she suspected that she was just part of another scheme, she did not care.

She had just wanted him; wanted his attention, and had blinded herself to anything else.

That was why Nastja's words cut her so deeply. She knew that they were true. With her head spinning, she was suddenly desperate to be away from this place, but, once again, she was trapped.

'Well...now what?' asked Skane.

'This is when you let us go,' said Nastja, with forthright confidence.

Skane just grunted.

'Say we had help. Say they overpowered you,' she said. 'Just give us a hundred heartbeats to escape. That's all we need.'

There was a long, uncomfortable pause. Urgent sounds filtered in from outside; yells, screams and the pattering of running feet. Skane's brow furrowed deeper as the moment slipped away.

THIRTY NINE

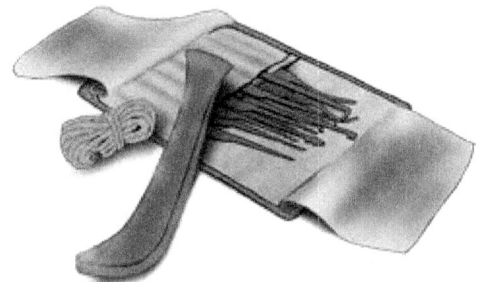

'If you walk out, I'll have to disappear,' said Skane. 'They'll never believe you got away without me letting you.'

'Maybe that's what you want to do,' said Ellyah.

'I swore oaths.'

'To people who have only deceived you. Your masters are driving you along without telling you anything. You're stumbling blind. Darkness is coming and you're in the middle of it. You need to choose a side.'

'Hah!' Skane barked a laugh. 'Even you can't believe there are sides in this.'

'Maybe, maybe not,' said Ellyah. 'But if there are, you're on the same side as demon worshippers.'

That did it. Skane's shoulders sagged, and he took a step to one side.

'Clear off, then,' said Skane. 'Don't want to see either of you again. Go.'

Nastja opened her mouth to speak, but Ellyah grabbed her hand before she could get started.

'Time to leave,' she said, giving her a tug towards the stairs.

Ellyah winced as her ribs stabbed pain through her body. Every step down was a challenge. She drew a deep breath.

'Well,' she said. 'Where now, hen?'

'The docks,' replied Nastja, with no hesitation.

They paused at the door to the street, listening before they stepped out. Yells and other sounds still came from their right. Without speaking, Ellyah caught Nastja's eye, nodding in the opposite direction before rolling her eyes.

Head north then double back.

They left the doorway and strode away, neither looking back.

Ellyah gripped Nastja's hand tightly. Happy as she was to be free of the Mackems and to have her friend back, she could not forget Savfa's deceit, and the fool she had been to fall for it.

She had known what he was like. Why had she let herself believe a word he said?

Nastja was probably just waiting for the right moment to say: "I told you so", and when she said it, Ellyah would scream. It would be driven by anger but born from shame.

It was not her fault.

She brooded as they strode through the streets, hand in hand. Waiting for Nastja to speak, waiting to meet her words with fury. But Nastja remained silent.

The evidence of the *pluitone* robbery was everywhere. Small knots of guards marched past, eyes darting towards dark corners. Every now and again a solitary figure would dash across their path, skulking from alley to alley. Their postures were hunched and furtive, their attitudes of prey in flight.

As Bureno commoners, the two women were ignored, and gradually left the noise and the chaos behind as they headed steadily south and west. The dreary grey chill of the afternoon darkened as they walked.

Lost in thought, Ellyah was startled when Nastja tugged hard on her hand and pulled her into the mouth of an alleyway. Another stab of pain from her ribs made her grunt.

'Give me some warning, Nas—' she began but Nastja clamped a hand over her mouth and pointed.

It took her several heartbeats to see what Nastja was pointing at, and several more to understand it. When she did, a moan escaped her lips into Nastja's hand, a sharp pain touching her heart to match the agony from her ribs.

Savfa was there. He was stalking along the street, coming from the north, while his eyes scanned left and right. Searching. Looking for her. And *she* was at his side. The woman from the village, and from Seyntlowe, was here. She wore the same dark clothing and had the same severe haircut. She was unmistakeable.

Her presence was proof of Savfa's lies, and Ellyah hated it. She looked in the other direction, face colouring with embarrassment that she hoped Nastja did not see. If she did, she said nothing, and led them onwards down the alley, and out into a broader street on the other side.

'You actually have a plan?' asked Ellyah, as they hurried across the gloomy street and into another alley.

'Yes,' replied Nastja. She paused, looking left and right, then headed for a gap between two round, single-storey houses. Ahead, the city wall loomed hard and dark in the oncoming dusk.

'And do you feel like sharing it with me?' Ellyah could not hide the irritation she felt.

'Get to the docks, then get away from here,' Nastja's response was bland, not noticing Ellyah's tone.

Sounded simple. Ellyah felt like it might not turn out that way. They were still being hunted.

A rough track ran beside the wall, curving so gradually as the wall continued its huge arc that it seemed straight. The southwest tower was just behind them, and they got the occasional glimpse of the south tower through gaps between the houses.

Beyond that, Ellyah knew, was the wide ocean and freedom. Then, a thought struck her and she halted.

'Nas, the jewel! What about that thief and the jewel? Savfa said he saw that thief here, in Glithoniel.'

Nastja looked at her scornfully. 'Weren't you listening?'

'Yes. Well, mostly...'

'I don't think the jewel even came this far. It's somewhere else. It'll be wherever they take that *pluitone*.'

Savfa was lying about that too, thought Ellyah.

'Couldn't we follow them—' she said out loud, denying the realisation.

'To touch the jewel is to die,' stated Nastja. 'You know that, you've seen it. With these people chasing it, you'd never escape with it anyway and even if you did there's no way you could sell it. If that thief still had it when they caught him...' Nastja shook her head. 'He's worse than dead. You need to let it go.'

Ellyah pulled away from Nastja's hand and slumped against the nearby wall. It was cold and dusty, but she could not make herself care. She had worked so hard to get her hands on that jewel, and stay one step ahead of her pursuers.

For nothing.

It had all been for nothing. She was empty handed and she knew who to blame: that fair-haired thief. If he had not interfered in the jewel trade, this would all have gone differently.

Yes, you'd be dead, said a calm voice in her head that sounded suspiciously like Nastja's.

'We're not done yet, hen,' said Nastja, moving to pat Ellyah gently on the arm. As an attempt to be reassuring it felt awkward. 'We can still get out of this, if we stick together.'

Ellyah nodded wearily, and they continued.

The wall ran downhill, and the docks sprawled ahead of them. Darkening streets ran towards black water, while the lights of lanterns and braziers studded the view like jewels on a fine gown. People were moving in every direction. They swarmed over the boats, loading or unloading, and thronged the streets. Any one of them could be the hunters.

'I hope you know what you're doing,' hissed Ellyah. Nastja said nothing.

They crept through the gloom between hulking warehouses, edging closer to the waterline and the hubbub of the docks. At the corner of one building, Nastja paused.

Beyond was the open land before the wharves. Many lanterns cast long, shifting shadows as people moved back and forth. Too many people, too many eyes.

'We need to get to the Batasari,' said Nastja, pointing at one of the large boats at the end of the jetty. 'It's sailing with the next dawn. Maybe we can bribe the crew to let us hide there until it leaves. It'll take us back to Anish.'

'Right' said Ellyah. She did not have the will or the energy to say more.

'I think we should separate. They are searching for a pair. If we're alone they might miss us. It might at least buy us a little time.'

'Right.'

'You go first. If I see any danger you'll hear a seahawk cry.'

This time, Ellyah just nodded, then walked out across the dockyard. No one spared her a second glance, and she just…walked. No sneaking, no studied posture or gait. She was just herself, a woman who meant nothing, walking away from defeat and into obscurity.

The ships towered over the wharves, almost like tall buildings of aged timber and trailing rope. Their round bellies rested in the black water, and even the thought of those hulls filled with treasures from around the world failed to excite Ellyah in her current mood.

She walked past the bare-chested half-elf sailor perched at the foot of the gangplank, and then up the ramp.

'Come one, come all aboard the Batasari,' he called out across the crowded wharf. 'The finest wines, ales and liquors from all across Re'Emsser, and a warm welcome. Hurry on in, young lady. There be plenty of room inside.'

The ship's deck was furnished with tables and chairs of simple scrap lumber, and a longer table towards the stern served as a bar. Beneath a broad, pale canopy made from a stretched sail, people were sitting, drinking and talking just like in any tavern.

A couple of pot-bellied stoves sat near the rails, flickering with jolly flames and belching warmth across the deck. Ellyah took a seat at a small round table, choosing a spot where she could see anyone arriving up the gangplank but would not be in their immediate line of sight.

Unintrusive music came from a corner near the bar. A couple in dark robes played, one blowing pipes and the other tapping an accompaniment on a set of small, tuned drums. Half-elf crew members lounged along the rails, their postures relaxed but their eyes sharp.

Had circumstances been different, she might have been enjoying herself. But her frustration with the day's events was a heavy stone she could not put down.

The tapping of footfalls on the gangplank caught her attention, and she looked in that direction from the corner of her eye. Nastja appeared through the gap in the rail, but she was not alone.

A boy trailed behind her, slightly younger than Ellyah and with long dark hair and wide, frightened eyes. Rings on several fingers revealed he was from Anish, and while he was dressed in the rough clothes of a docker or labourer his hands and face told a different story.

'Who in Fate's name is this?' she demanded, as Nastja and the newcomer sat.

'Someone else who has got caught up in this and needs to escape,' replied Nastja.

'I will fight to aid you,' said the boy, formally, his hand dropping to the hilt of the Anise sabre at his hip.

'Doubtful,' said Ellyah, scornfully.

The boy looked hurt but before he could respond, Nastja butted in. They were in this together, now, and all needed to understand what they were up against. So, she explained everything she had learned about the cult of Desya and the Demon's Tear as the boy's eyes widened and Ellyah frowned even more deeply.

She was just finishing her tale when the sound of heavy treads on the gangplank rang out. The owners of the boots appeared a moment later, and Ellyah's heart sank.

That hulking half-elf, Jhari, swaggered onto the deck followed by a heavy-bearded dwarf who swayed slightly, bleary eyes squinting. A small group of men and women followed them, all with the bunched fists and lowered brows of hired thugs.

Jhari led the group to the bar and ordered a round of drinks. The half-elf barman poured them generous cups of wine, and Ellyah saw Jhari throw the half-elf a whole copper money ring. They spread out to lean on the bar and the ship's rail, every eye fixed on their table.

Jhari looked directly at her, and his flat, brutal face split into a grin. He nudged the dwarf and pointed, before raising his cup in her direction, a toast of mockery. So, they thought it was too public, too busy, to assault her here and now, but their message was clear:

We have all night. You're going nowhere.

'They've found us, then,' said Nastja.

Ellyah forced down the angry retort. 'Looks that way, hen. What's the plan?'

'Plan?'

Ellyah closed her eyes for a moment. 'Please don't tell me you've walked in here and trapped yourself, but with no way of getting out.'

'Well, the ship leaves on the dawn tide,' said Nastja. We just need to stay here until then.'

'They won't wait for dawn!' hissed Ellyah. 'They'll wait for it to quieten down, then grab us. We've got no chance against that many. And more might arrive, too, if we wait.'

Nastja paused for a moment. 'You're probably right. What are we going to do?'

Ellyah felt like screaming.

'Why don't we take a running jump over the side and into the bay,' she said, bitterly. 'Then swim to Tayo.'

'We'd never manage to swim that far against the current,' said Nastja. Ellyah drained her ale to stop herself shouting out loud. Jumping over the side and sinking to the bottom, and blissful oblivion, was beginning to seem more appealing when two more people arrived; the short haired woman, Majleyn and by her side: Savfa. Hot anger and shame gripped her as she stared at him.

'You should have done what you were told, Ellyah,' he called. 'I was just trying to help you.'

Even now, after everything he had put her through, she wanted to believe him. Wanted to dash across the deck to him and take his arm, to be by his side in whatever scheme he had planned. He would keep her safe.

She hated him for her own thoughts, that she could not seem to control; she hated herself. He made her so weak.

As though he had been waiting for their arrival, Jhari chose that moment to advance. His huge fists bunched and the dwarf swayed in his shadow, teeth bared. The boy at their own table stood, drawing his sword. It gleamed in the red light, a tongue of fire. Of danger.

'You will let us go,' he said, his voice melodic with a slight wobble that betrayed his fear. 'Now. No one needs to be hurt.'

'Wrong,' rumbled Jhari. 'You do.'

'Put the sword away, boy,' said the dwarf. 'You'll just end up with it stuck in you.'

The point wavered but the boy stood his ground.

The crew were on their feet now, sturdy hardwood staves in their hands. The dwarf spun towards them, producing a wicked knife, almost the length of his forearm, from somewhere beneath his coat.

'You all stay back!' he bellowed. 'This is private business. You get involved, you get cut up!'

One of the sailors who was not bare-chested, but wearing a waistcoat of fine silk, spoke up.

'You cannot fight here!' he said in a commanding tone.

Nastja turned towards the sailor and cried out a string of unintelligible syllables. It sounded like Elvish. The sailor stared at her for a moment before calling back in the same tongue. Nastja nodded and he raised his head and let out a long, high-pitched whistle.

The music had died away and all the other drinkers in the floating tavern sat as if frozen, staring at the dramatic tableau before them. No one dared move.

The boy edged closer to them, looking at Nastja.

'I'll fight a way free,' he said. 'I'll go for the drunk dwarf. If I can knock him down we can make a run for it.'

'That easy, eh?' snapped Ellyah.

'It won't come to that,' replied Nastja. 'We are going to escape. Together, like we talked about before.'

'I can't run,' she said, pressing a hand to her ribs.

'You won't need to,' said Nastja. 'Just follow my lead. '

She began to edge backwards, in the direction of the ship's bow. Ellyah moved with her, as did the boy, and Jhari closed in, seizing Ellyah by the arm. The others behind him surged forwards.

That was the moment the hollow thud of boots on the deck caused every head to turn. It was Skane. He stood at the top of the gangplank and his head swung, his flat face inscrutable.

'Where've you been?' grated the dwarf.

'Come on, let's get 'em!' shouted Jhari.

Skane crossed the deck and a hush fell. Jhari waited for his leader to arrive, and even Majleyn and Savfa watched him as though waiting for his approval to continue. Skane paused beside Jhari, his eyes flicking from Nastja, to Ellyah, and then onto the boy.

'The honest man and the thieves,' he said, finally, flinty eyes fixed on the boy's face. 'All those things she told me—' He nodded toward Nastja. 'Are they true?'

The boy swallowed before speaking. 'Every word,' he replied.

Skane took a deep breath. 'Then, I'm sorry about this, friend,' he said, before spinning and throwing a brutal punch that whistled over the top of Ellyah's head. There was the hard slap of flesh on flesh, and Jhari grunted. He fell back and his vice-like grip was broken.

'Go!' said Skane.

'Come on!' urged Nastja, but a sudden fury gripped Ellyah. Seeing her opportunity, she lunged forward, swinging a fist. It struck the woman, Majleyn, hard across the cheek and her head snapped around.

'Bitch!' growled Ellyah.

Nastja grabbed her hand and dragged her up the short flight of steps behind them. Looking down from the bows, she understood. A small riverboat was pressed up against the hull, bobbing on the gentle swell. The boy joined them at the rail and paused.

'Wait!' he said, urgently, before turning. 'Skane!'

The Mackems leader was standing at the foot of the steps, facing his colleagues, fists raised defiantly. Jhari was slowly climbing to his feet, an expression of fury across his face. Skane turned his head at the boy's cry.

Sheathing his sword, he moved his hands and fingers in a series of complex motions that Ellyah recognised as hand-speech. She had learned a few signs, but the boy's were too fast for her to read. She was surprised to see Skane return the gestures with a few of his own.

'Jump!' said Nastja. The boy jumped, landing with a roll on the deck of the boat waiting below.

Ellyah reached out and grasped her friend's hand, and they leapt from the edge together.

The sounds of fighting on the deck of the ship receded into the distance as the little boat moved away, sailors on each side pulling on long oars. Ellyah watched the wavering light of the docks of Glithoniel fade into specks as they sailed on, upriver and into the night.

PART SIX

FORTY

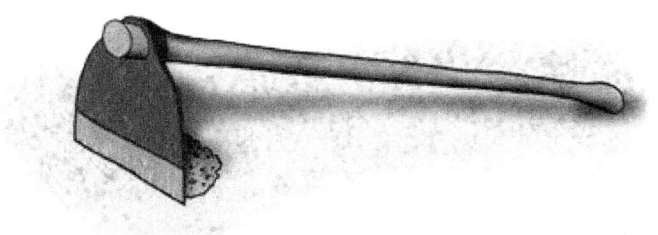

Carilton Tann's feeling of unease grew with every mile they went south. All five of them were worried, especially after what had happened to Indaella.

He pulled on the reins and moved his horse closer to the wagon, where Cerle Connow sat alone.

'How is she?' he asked.

'Same as she was,' snapped Cerle.

'I was just wondering if she'd said anything else—'

'If she had, I'd tell you.'

Silence returned. The big Banahgarian was tense, his mood brittle. It was only natural, but Tann worried about what it might drive him to do.

It was a bright, cold morning and they were heading south into Buren. The trees that lined the gorge and peppered the slopes above were bare, winter's chill and the southerly wind stripping the leaves away from all apart from a few hardy firs on the higher slopes. These made a green smear across the hillside against the iron grey of the rock, and the pure white of the snowy peaks that loomed above.

Holt and Luara rode slightly ahead, leaning in towards one another and speaking in low voices. Tann wondered if they were talking about turning back. He would not have blamed them, not now.

Luara had been thoughtful and withdrawn since leaving Ben Gedrin the previous morning. It was noticeable because her normal demeanour was so effervescent. Holt had shown his own concern by how attentive he had been.

'We know Eain's trail leads to Ben Gedrin,' Tann himself had said as they left Dunnbalc, a town to the west of Feorhryc. 'But we don't yet know if it stops there, or leads on someplace else.'

'We need to know,' said Cerle. 'We need to be certain.' He turned to address the whole group. 'How do we find out? Who will go in?'

'It has to be me, doesn't it?' replied Luara, immediately. 'I know the city better than any of you, and I was there that night. I know the questions to ask.'

By "that night" she meant Demonsnight, when the gangs had turned the streets red, the city had burned, and Luara had seen Eain in the thick of it all.

'Me and Holt will go,' she continued. 'I'll need to hide my face, but he isn't known.'

The decision was made. The couple had vanished into the city for a day while Cerle, Indaella and himself had made a camp in a small stand of trees just out of sight of the walls. When they returned, Luara seemed troubled but was convinced that Eain had left the city, heading south. Two women she knew, who she named as Ellyah and Nastja, had been seen following him.

So, they continued south.

The next decision they were forced to make was at the bridge to Tayo. Tann had seen it before, although the last time was long ago. He had even crossed it once or twice, but the sight never ceased to amaze.

That arching single span, leaping across the deep, rocky canyon that held the foaming river, always seemed impossible.

'How in the Fates did they build that?' he said, voicing his thoughts, as they approached.

'Perhaps it was not built,' said Indaella from her high seat next to Cerle.

'What matters,' added Cerle, before Tann had a chance to say anything else, 'is whether Eain crossed it or not. Which way would he go?'

'Tayo's a rough place,' said Luara. 'They never seem far from civil war.'

'That's what I've heard,' said Cerle. 'I wonder…'

He turned aside and paced to the verge of the road, which almost overhung the ravine. Tann had ridden straight past without noticing, but as Cerle approached it he saw there was a small shelter there, right on the brink, the roof barely rising above the height of the gorse that lined the road.

'Hey, friend!' he called, seemingly to the rough thatch of fern and moss itself. After a moment there was a rustle, and a face appeared in the small gap between the verge and the roof. Sharp eyes peered out, then the roof lifted and a tall, dark-skinned figure climbed out. Tann caught a glimpse of a space hollowed out of the cliff edge, covered by the rough roof.

'Loyanivah has no friends,' said the newcomer as he rose to his full height, several inches taller than Cerle. "Just people who pass him by.'

His upswept ears marked him clearly as an elf. His clothing was strange; a skirt of many knee-length strands, dyed a ruddy orange, and a sash of the same colour fabric tied diagonally around his body, shoulder to hip.

'I can be your friend, for a moment,' said Cerle. He reached into a pouch at his belt and pulled out a silver money ring, already part broken. With a quick twist of his thick, strong fingers he snapped a section off the ring and handed it over to the elf. 'You live in the cliff?' Loyanivah nodded. 'Good fishing down there?' Another nod. 'And you watch the road when the fish aren't biting?'

'My new friend sees much,' said the elf, gravely. 'He is wise as well as generous.'

'I need to know more, though,' replied Cerle. 'I'm trying to find someone. A family member. I think he passed through here within the last few weeks.'

'Many pass,' said Loyanivah. 'A great many.'

'You might have noticed this one, though. He was tall, like me. Hair the colour of a field of barley in the sunset. Would have been wearing a sword, a bit like this one.' Cerle gestured over his shoulder to the hilt of his greatsword.

Loyanivah gazed at Cerle silently, the moments stretching until Tann began to feel awkward. In his world, when folk stared each other down it was with the threat of violence. But he had forgotten where Cerle had been for the last decade. Who he had been with. He knew elves.

'Loyanivah has searched his memory,' said the elf, eventually. 'And he remembers a man like this. He came from the north and his strides were urgent, but full of doubt. He was escaping something.'

'That sounds like Eain!' cried Indaella, delighted.

'Where did he go, Loyanivah?' asked Cerle. The elf pressed his lips together, so they went pale over his gums. Then, he pointed to the far end of the bridge. Towards Tayo.

'He went there,' he said. 'He went there, and his steps were heavy with the promise of blood.'

'Are you sure?' began Tann, but Cerle waved him into silence.

'Thank you, my friend,' he said to the elf, bowing low. 'May peace bless your days.'

The elf returned the bow, and slipped back down into his home, recessed into the wall of the ravine. Cerle took a stride towards the bridge, and Tann was unsurprised to see the guards behind the bar stiffen to alert. Spear hafts were gripped more tightly and the knight in command of the small band lowered his hand to the hilt of his longsword.

Buren guarded this side, and a solid rank of Tayans stood at the other end. Tann could see their colourful clothes and the dull gleam of their weapons even from this distance.

'Passage across the bridge, if you please,' Cerle was saying to the knight.

He shook his head, eyes hard in the metallic surround of his helmet. 'Tayo is closed. They're at war. None goes in or out until there's peace.'

'I don't fear war, and I don't fear Tayo,' replied Cerle, and Tann saw the fingers of his right hand twitch. He hoped Cerle was not considering fighting his way through. 'I just need to pass.'

'You may not,' replied the knight, without heat. 'And even if you got past my bar, the Tayans would not let you pass either. Go back, and go with the Five. Friend.'

Tann saw Cerle's hands clench, fingernails digging into his palms, and could sense the big man's frustration. He stepped forward, but stopped short of grabbing Cerle's arm.

'Don't,' he said. Cerle's head whipped around, grey eyes sharp as swords. 'We don't need to go that way,' he continued. 'I know another way into Tayo. Another way to get to where Eain may be.'

Cerle's head swung, jaw clenched as he glared from Tann to the knight once more.

'Lead on, Carilton Tann.' He said, eventually. 'I trust you. You can tell me of this other way as we go.'

They moved off, continuing south. Tann's mind was busy. What had possessed Eain to go to Tayo? Surely the boy had seen enough of war. Perhaps he was escaping, running from someone and thought he could evade them there. Perhaps he was desperate to earn some money rings. They would have to find him to be sure.

That was the moment that it had happened.

'No!' gasped Indaella, in a loud, desperate tone. She stood up on the wagon bed, even as it rocked along the road. Her hands went to her face, mouth gaping open. Then she collapsed.

She had fallen unconscious, lying limp and unresponsive on the wagon bed. They gathered around the wagon as Cerle leapt back from his seat to check on her.

'He has it,' she murmured. 'He is coming. He is coming.'

'She's Seeing,' said Cerle. 'Having a vision. But I've not seen it take her like this before.' His craggy features were creased with worry, and Tann could see the pain in his eyes. He seized a blanket and wrapped it around her, leaning close to look at her face.

Her eyelids fluttered and her breath came in panicked gasps; she seemed unhurt but gripped by a fit or fever dream. Cerle watched her carefully for several heartbeats before straightening.

'We need to go on,' he said. 'This will pass.'

So they had gone on, Cerle driving the wagon while Indaella lay in the rear.

The harsh, rocky landscape of the river gorge slipped behind them, and soon they turned away from it and began to climb into the green hills that marked the border of Buren.

Dusk fell as a slope rose before them, and at the top they were confronted by a walled village with a solid gate that was shut and guarded.

'State your name, and your business!' called the guards, burly locals bearing wood axes. Tann hoped they did not provoke Cerle to action; his greatsword lay hidden beneath a blanket on the wagon bed.

Cerle recounted their names and explained that they were just simple travellers. The guards were reluctant to open the gates until Cerle beckoned them to look into the wagon.

'My wife is sick,' he said. 'I need a healer, and to find her somewhere warm to pass the night.'

The two villagers nodded to one another before finally standing aside. It was not quite a lie, but it was equally not the whole truth. It had worked, however.

There was a strange atmosphere in that hilltop village. People walked in a wide circle around them, staring with haunted, suspicious eyes. Trying to ignore the piercing stares, Tann dismounted and approached the inn. It was a bulky building with an arching extension that spanned the road like a bridge.

'What goes on here?' he asked a woman who had just emerged from the inn. Her eyes were wells of sorrow. 'We have just arrived, and are looking for rooms to pass the night.'

'Rooms and stables are available,' she replied in a flat voice. 'But the bar and the common room are shut.

'Order of the lord,' she added, in response to Tann's raised eyebrow.

They passed an uneventful night in the inn's simple but comfortable rooms, and Tann was delighted to see Indaella on her feet the following morning.

'Glad to see you up,' he called, as she headed towards the wagon. 'What—'

'Don't,' said Cerle, approaching from behind and cutting him off mid-question. 'Not yet.'

Tann waited as Indaella climbed up onto the wagon, then leaned in close to Cerle, lowering his voice.

'But what if she's seen a clue about Eain? What if she's seen exactly where he is?'

'If she had, she'd tell me,' said Cerle, folding his thick arms across his chest. 'And I'd tell you. She's only just woken. Have patience.'

Tann nodded, but there was acid in his belly.

This was his fault. That they were undertaking this great chase, travelling into danger and causing Indaella this distress, was his doing. He had let Eain go, encouraged him to leave the safety of his farm and head out into the wider world.

The danger Eain seemed likely to be in was a weight on his shoulders, and he was finding it harder to remain patient.

At the bottom of the hill, on the outskirts of the village, Tann found what he was looking for. The main road continued southward and westward through farmland; green where animals grazed and brown where crops had been harvested. A smaller track led right, hard to the south, cutting a vague green trail across the hillside and towards a distant ridge of hills.

'This is where we head for Tayo,' he said.

'Along that sheep track?' asked Luara, doubtfully.

'If we're sure Eain went to Tayo, this is the way we need to go,' said Tann.

'How can we know that?' asked Holt, reining in close to Luara. 'Even if he went there, and the bush-elf was right, how can we know he's still there?'

'Stop,' said Cerle, and everyone was abruptly still. 'We must all decide together. There's just too much that we're not sure of without making wild guesses about things we can't know.'

He turned to Indaella. 'What do you think, my love?'

She looked pained, brow wrinkling and eyes screwing up tight.

'It's confusing,' she said, after several silent moments. 'There's a new presence in the world and it's clouding my vision. Whenever I close my eyes, and try to See, all I See is red. That's what I Saw yesterday, too. Red. A pair of red eyes, and a red mist that covered everything. It's hard to be sure, but it feels like the presence is in that direction.'

She pointed south, directly along the line of the smaller track. Luara frowned.

'But,' she went on. 'I Saw something else, too. One vision. Two armies, separated by still water.'

'A battle?' asked Tann. The thought of Eain being near that red presence that Indaella had described, or being part of an army made him anxious. The boy had already seen enough danger, enough war.

'Not yet,' said Indaella. 'But maybe soon.'

'And Eain could be involved,' said Cerle. 'And if he is, we must help.'

'But,' said Luara, before taking a deep breath. 'The direction we need to go to find Eain is the same direction as this great danger. Is it a sensible way to go?'

'This is the choice we must make,' said Indaella.

Tann looked at her, staring hard as if he might read her thoughts, as though he could glean a clue of what she had Seen. He considered her words, and realised he knew a place where there was still water; a lake that lay near the border between Buren and Tayo.

'The place you mentioned,' he said. 'I think I know where it may be.' He raised an arm, pointing towards the ridge of hills ahead of them. 'That's the King's Arm. That ridge used to be the border between Buren and Tayo, before the Swarthland was taken.

'Follow it along, a day's ride or more, and there's a gap in the ridge. A stream runs down the gap and feeds a lake. It's right on the current border.'

'That must be it, then,' said Cerle. Tann knew he had great faith in his wife's visions, and he spoke now without doubt. 'If that's what you Saw, then it must be important. That's where we go, unless there are any objections?'

No one spoke.

Tann remained anxious. If armies marched, then they could only be from Tayo and Buren. That uneasy peace had held for years, but if open war broke out again it could tear the lands apart.

If Eain was there, they had to get him out before he was caught in the middle of it.

A blizzard roared outside, and even with shutters of tanned skins tied tightly over the windows flakes of snow swirled into the room. Inside, it was frostier still.

'Am I the only man here who sees sense?' Morgan Blane was coldly furious. 'Am I the only one with the will, and the courage, to take the fight to the enemy?'

'You doubt my courage?' roared Maichen Munrae, moving as if to rise from where he sat cross-legged.

'Peace,' murmured Graigor Farguson, reaching out to lay a calming hand on the huge man's shoulder.

'This has little to do with courage, or with will,' snapped Caedmon Skaarn. 'And nothing to do with sense. You've clearly lost whatever of that you had.'

'Brothers,' spoke up Skyle Burns. 'Stay calm. Let Blane say on.'

Blane swallowed down his impatience and thought anew about what to say, how to convince these men that what he suggested was the right thing to do. How to convince the Grandmaster, silent so far, to give his blessing.

'The weather worsens,' he said, and the wind howled its agreement against the shutters. 'And our enemy weakens. They huddle in their camps, low on food, low on furs, losing men to the cold. Their morale is low.'

'We know all this, Blane,' said Skaarn.

'They are on the edge of defeat!' continued Blane, more firmly, annoyed by the interruption. 'It would not take much to begin a rout. If they are forced to retreat from their forward camps the only place they will have to go is back to their boats.'

'What do you propose?' asked Burns.

'A strike. Several strikes. Hit their camps from the snow. Kill who we can, scatter their supplies, teach them to fear the Banahgarian winter. We know these conditions better than they do - we can be on them before they know we are there and gone before they can respond. We can win the war.'

Skaarn was shaking his head. 'It would be risky.'

'The risk is for them, not us. We are masters of this terrain.'

'No, Blane,' said Burns. 'You are a master of this terrain. For anyone else the danger of going out in this is great. Would you lead men of the Claihed to their deaths in the snow, or capture by the Kotevari?'

'Burns speaks true,' said the Grandmaster, Helden Haradsson, finally breaking his silence. 'And I would ask you to recall Stygg. Recall the lesson of the bear.'

Blane nodded; he knew all of the lessons of the gods. When the Sjonacaidh sang, he listened.

'If you would poke the bear,' continued Haradsson. 'Be ready for his claws. Be prepared to fight until one of you is dead.'

Blane understood. Kotev was the bear that they must be wary of. But right now the bear was half-starved, half asleep. They could at least wound the bear. If they wanted to win the war, they had to.

'Then let me go alone,' he said. 'I already know the way to the camps. I can move silently and kill many of them before they know I am there. And if they catch me, you have only lost one man.'

'Foolishness,' said Skaarn, shaking his head.

'You know I can hurt the enemy in this way,' Blane continued. He looked across the circle of seated men, locking eyes with the Grandmaster, those unreadable icy pools. 'Would you forbid this? Would you restrain my blade?'

There was a moment of silence. The Grandmaster returned Blane's stare as though he was a figure carved from stone. Then he blinked.

'I would not,' he said. 'But I would counsel you to recall Eftirfor. Remember the lesson of the wolf-god.'

Blane nodded to himself. He was determined to make this strike, and not to let the invaders think they were safe in their camps. He would be the wolf. He would be the hunter.

'I will make myself ready,' he said, rising. He rose, bare feet chilled by the cold stone beneath his feet as he moved towards the door. No one else spoke as he left the room, and the storm howled outside.

Soon, he would be the storm.

FORTY ONE

Eain Connow looked out over the field and sought to quell the discordant voices within.

So much fighting, so much blood, so much death. And more to come this day.

A broad, sluggish river lay at the bottom of the hill to his left. Klay had named it as the Swarthwash. Marshes glistened at the banks, still, cloudy water bristling with swaying reeds and bustling flocks of egrets and ducks.

Now and again, something would startle the birds, and they would all take flight, wheeling above the battlefield before returning to the riverbank. They were heedless of the violence that was about to happen.

The drier land uphill of the river meads rose in gentle grassy slopes and to Eain's right was the lumpy crest of a low ridge. On the undulating field ahead, the enemy waited.

'I 'ope Teleri knows what e's about,' said Klay in a low voice. 'There's nowhere to go but in't river if this goes wrong.'

'The Demon Teleri does not lose,' said Eain, bitterly.

Daeron's new nickname had stuck, his followers using it as a badge of honour and his enemies crying it as a curse, and since Sarnayu's tower had fallen he had led them onwards, carving a bloody path.

Eain felt sick to think of it.

The surrender of the tower and its garrison had been sudden and surprising. It had all happened behind the canvas screens of the pavilion, but it quickly became clear that the commander of the tower, Duke Sarnayu, had died by Teleri's hand.

The details were hazy, but after his death the minor nobles present had immediately bent the knee to Teleri as a conqueror. Whispers went around the camp of dark magic and sorcery, but never louder than a whisper.

Teleri's army had moved into the tower where the combination of a roof over their heads and full bellies after raiding the granaries had engendered a mood of celebration among the survivors. None wanted to question a lord who led them to such victory, and such spoils.

The troops of the garrison, previously loyal to the Taosach, had been given a simple choice: join Teleri's army or die. A few had slipped away into the surrounding countryside but most had sworn a new oath.

Better to have The Demon as your general than as your enemy.

Teleri had not let them rest for long. Pockets of the Taosach's forces remained, but now they were weak and Teleri's army had gained new strength. Isolated and outnumbered, the Gluttons and the peasant levies they commanded were hunted down and routed.

Victories came, one after another, and for the first time in months the soldiers around Eain felt safe.

'Fate smiles on The Demon!' they cried after driving their enemies into another rout, raising bloody weapons to the sky as the survivors fled. 'The Skyfather watches over him.'

Klay leaned on the Capper. There was blood on the dwarf's hands, painting his gloves, and smeared across one cheek. Eain was not worried; the blood was very unlikely to be Klay's own.

'Change 'o fortune,' he had said, beady eyes narrow. 'The gods be praised for granting our glorious leader such wisdom and such luck.' His tone was flat, and his face remained blank, without the faintest trace of a smile.

Eain looked away, flexing his hands and forearms. It stung. Tiny slashes across the thick leather of his gloves and bracers showed where he had been nicked in the melee. None felt deep.

'He killed the lord,' he replied, turning back to the dwarf. 'He killed Sarnayu, and the rest bowed down. That's how Tayo works, isn't it?'

'Sometimes,' said Klay, looking thoughtful. 'Depends on the way it 'appens.' He paused. 'So,' he went on, with a meaningful look. 'How d'yer think it 'appened?'

Eain looked away once more. 'I do not know.'

'Hm. Mebbes Teleri strangled him to death in front of all his captains and generals, while they did nowt. Or, mebbes he can do dark magic, like they say.'

Another pause.

'Mebbes it was summat else,' he finished. Eain knew exactly what he was getting at, although the dwarf could not have known the whole truth.

'Yes,' he said. 'Maybe it was something else.'

'Aye, that,' said Klay, turning away. 'I reckon you'd tell me if there was something I needed to know, right?'

Those words had stayed with Eain, over the days that followed.

He owed Klay, he knew that. The dwarf had saved his life more than once, and as much as he could trust anyone here, he trusted Klay. And yet, he struggled to put what had happened into words.

Teleri's change of fortune had been thanks to Eain giving him a magic jewel. It sounded ridiculous but Teleri had somehow turned that jewel into a weapon. It was unbelievable.

Eain could not have made himself say the words aloud. He tried not to think about it.

So they fought on, as Teleri directed, and their force gained in strength and numbers. As they marched through soggy villages, grey with frost, folk came out to cheer them, banging wooden drums and waving streamers of colourful cloth.

A great celebration for the liberating army.

Eain wanted to rejoice with them, but something nagged at him. Something sour in his gut.

Teleri.

He had changed. Or was now more confident to be his true self in a way he had not before. There was a fervent light in his eyes, and Eain thought he had seen the occasional glint of red there. Perhaps that had just been his imagination, though.

In any case, Teleri graciously acknowledged the cheers and adulation, swearing that he would right the injustices wreaked by

Re'Emsser and take the fight to the Taosach. In private, it was a different story.

'Turgon Fallas,' he hissed, addressing Klay and the other captains in his command tent. Eain had been present as bodyguard. 'Turgon Fallas is all that matters. We must win through before the full force of the Taosach's army falls upon us.'

'But we have beaten their troops back at every turn—' began one of the captains of the Gluttons, his loyalty newly sworn and his heavy armour gleaming like a winter lake.

'Idiot!' Teleri interrupted, face twisted into a snarl. His eyes flashed red fire that was not a reflection of the braziers. 'You know as well as I do that all we have faced so far are the outstretched fingers of one of her hands. Her fist will follow swiftly, mailed and sharp. Her next blow will crush us.

'We we need solid stone around us and beneath our feet. We must regain Turgon Fallas, and soon.'

Klay glanced around, meeting Eain's eye for a moment before looking away. He remembered what the dwarf had said, some months before.

'He only wants his home back. He said as much. He's no crusader.'

Turgon Fallas was a strong fortress, Eain knew. It would take all the strength they had to force their way through the doors, and the cost in blood would be high. And after that, what would happen to those pledged to him, assuming they even survived?

Nevertheless, Teleri had manoeuvred to a field of his choosing after fording the river, and the Taosach's army had marched from the north to meet them. Teleri needed to go that way, and the enemy had barred that road by making a camp that was fortified from the river to the ridge.

Battle was inevitable.

Klay and Teleri's other captains had supervised the ordering of the troops across the hillside, barking orders in the chill grey light that had followed dawn. Eain marched forwards to stand in the centre of the lines. Around him were the remains of the Steel Hounds.

Many had died. The faces of the fallen had gone from Eain's mind. He could not even remember most of their names.

He had chosen this life.

Two great blocks of Gluttons were positioned on the flanks, like the two fists of a prize fighter. Their disposition dictated the enemy's battle plan. They would try to avoid these strong wings and throw their strongest troops, probably their own Gluttons, at the centre. If they could rout the centre of the line, the flanks would be isolated.

The risk was also obvious, however. If the centre held, then the two wings would fall on the flanks of the enemy, crushing them. Hammer and anvil. Unless, this was in itself a feint and there was a strong reserve ready to emerge and attack Teleri's Gluttons while they were engaged.

Bluff and double bluff. Strategy and counter. Wheels within wheels.

It would need a brilliant enemy general to get the better of Teleri in this game. Eain leaned on his sword and waited.

'We'll be advancing soon,' barked Klay, addressing the massing ranks. 'Be ready.' He turned to Eain and lowered his voice. 'Teleri has only let on part of 'is plan. Don't seem to trust no one these days.'

'Many of his captains are new,' replied Eain. 'They were fighting for the Taosach not long ago.' Why was he jumping to Teleri's defence? Why did he feel responsible?

'Mebbes,' was Klay's only response before the horns blew from the rear and the advance began.

'Forward on me!' shouted the dwarf. Despite the softness of the turf, so many feet moving in unison could be felt as vibrations through the very earth. The sensation was ominous.

The Taosach's army was advancing too, and as the battle lines closed Eain could begin to pick out the disposition of the troops. From this distance, it appeared as though the entire front rank was made up of peasant levies, unarmoured apart from the odd iron cap or leather hauberk.

These people could not afford armour. They could barely afford food, and yet here they were in the vanguard of an army.

And the Gluttons were nowhere to be seen.

The ground undulated along the hillside, and as the front rank gained a slight ridge the horns rang out again. Klay raised the Capper aloft.

'Stand!' he called. 'Stand 'ere. Let 'em come.'

The peasant forces opposite kept coming, marching wearily over the spongy, damp grass. Eain peered out at the oncoming lines, trying to anticipate what was going to happen. His stomach clenched as he thought about the first clash of arms. Behind the advancing ranks of spearmen, though, something was moving. Figures in armour.

'Klay—' he began.

'To the right!' cried the dwarf. 'Look sharp't right!'

The spearmen were abruptly pushed aside, and a host of bulky figures muscled their way through, emerging at the front of the line and advancing rapidly. They massed to Eain's right, on the uphill edge of the battlefield.

The peasant spearmen bunched together once more, continuing their march directly towards Eain and the mercenaries while more and more Gluttons emerged from their rear, surging up the hill to sweep around the flank.

There must have been thousands.

'They were hiding their numbers!' Eain called to Klay.

'Think that's obvious,' replied the dwarf. 'But we've got our own problems.'

Eain looked ahead. As they closed, the spearmen bunched together. They came on with good discipline, marching in step and presenting a flat, solid front rank. Their levelled spears were like a hedge as they came ever closer, steady but relentless.

A clash of weapons came from the right, followed swiftly by shouts and cries. Eain glanced across. The Taosach's Gluttons had swept around to fall on Teleri's, surging out from behind the peasants to gain an uphill position. Now, they came down from the higher ground and Teleri's troops were immediately hard pressed.

'Eyes forward!' cried Klay. Eain looked to see a fence of spear points, now mere feet away. The spearmen took a couple more rapid steps, and then Eain's training took over.

Cutting from low to high, he lifted an incoming spear point and stabbed at the wielder. There was a cry, but he blocked out the sound and stepped forwards into the gap he had created.

His sword whirled, close to his body, to cut at the spears. He did not strike flesh but felt the harsh impact as his blade hit wood, pushing the spears aside. Into this fleeting gap stepped Klay. The Capper lashed out, left and right, and because of his height the enemy did not even see the blows coming. Ribcages smashed and legs were broken by the heavy, forged head as he and Eain danced around one another, dealing death.

Across the lines, other mercenaries were not so lucky nor so skilled. The number of spear points they faced was overwhelming, and the extra reach allowed the enemy to drive their opponents back, and find openings in their defences.

Eain could hear cries of pain as the bitter points thrust forwards, drawing blood and piercing flesh. Their line creaked, bowing inwards. It must not shatter.

'Back!' yelled Klay, as though reading Eain's thoughts. 'Fall back, on me!'

The Capper swept around and as the dwarf scuttled a brisk retreat, Eain followed. They were not defeated, not yet, and not in full retreat, but needed to make space between their own ranks and the oncoming spearmen.

They scrambled back and out of range.

Both sides paused for a moment, grateful for the respite in the bloodshed. Eain's breath came in great heaves as he glanced around.

To his left, a block of Gluttons was holding their position against the ragged line of peasants sent against them by the Taosach's generals, but to his right they were retreating. The greater numbers of the Taosach's Gluttons and their sudden attack from the higher ground was telling, and Teleri's flank was being forced back, step by step.

It seemed as though Teleri had been outmanoeuvred for once, and surprised by the enemy's subterfuge. Eain knew that the centre had to hold. If they gave any more ground, then their whole battle line could be driven down the hill and into the river.

That would mean death.

'Stand now, lads!' cried Klay. 'This is our ground, now. Right here. They come no further.'

The dwarf was forged in battle. He could see in an instant how the tide was flowing, and knew what needed to be said, and what needed to be done. Eain hoped the soldiers around him could find some of that steel.

The spearmen came on again and once more the clatter of metal and wood rang in the morning air, along with grunts of exertion and moans of pain. Now, though, Teleri's forces did not give ground. They could not, and Klay's words had hardened their will

Spears were trapped on the ground and smashed to splinters by blows from maces or axes as their wielders were dragged down. The battle lines pressed together as both sides wrestled for an advantage.

A dark-haired Tayan fighter surged forward beside Eain, raising a simple mace. He aimed a wild swing at the nearest enemy but a spear point from an unseen opponent thrust out and took him in the throat.

He died a horrible, gurgling death in the churned mud at Eain's feet. Eain looked away.

His sword was coated in a red sheen, darkening where it had dried, but even though the enemy shied away from him and Klay their line was weakening. The Taosach's Gluttons were pressing down the slope to the right and Teleri's ranks were bowing, breaking, and beginning to fall back down the hill.

Their position was becoming desperate.

'Hold! Hold yer ground or die!' bellowed Klay.

It was no use.

The lines had swivelled against the force of the enemy attack. Teleri's leftmost Gluttons had held, but had been forced to turn to face up the slope as the pressure told on the centre. The right flank had given way completely, retreating until the soft, wet river meads were at their back.

The fighters with Eain and Klay remained but their organised line was lost. Beset on all sides, they fought desperately but were falling one by one. Eain already bore bloody nicks and cuts to his face, wrists and forearms when a spear thrust slipped past his defence. It pierced the mail he wore and even as he twisted away he felt the keen tip scrape through his flesh and along his ribs. It was a line of fire.

He pulled away, gritting his teeth against the groan that tried to burst forth, and the greatsword technique of Kell's Rule Five, ingrained in his subconscious, slayed the spearman as a deadly riposte. Even so, Teleri's forces were falling all around him. Their choice was the blades of the enemy or the sucking depths of the marshes behind. The end was near.

'Back! Back!' roared Klay, but they could not go much further. They were on the very brink of the wetlands. The ground squelched and sucked at Eain's feet. A few more steps and he would sink into the bog, easy pickings for the oncoming enemy.

Then a new sound rose above the din of battle. It was partly a noise and partly a sensation; a throbbing, drumming feeling trembled through his feet and ankles, growing louder.

Something was coming.

Heads began to turn, fighters from both sides looking in the direction of the sound. Eain looked up himself, and was astonished.

Sweeping down the hillside towards the rear of the Taosach's army was a loose formation of warriors, advancing rapidly. All were mounted on horses, manes and tails streaming.

Before the enemy could turn or organise themselves, these horsemen swept in close and cast a volley of short-hafted javelins at their rear ranks. Still a distance from reprisals, they veered away before galloping around to attack again from a different direction. Each rider bore a long quiver on their horses' harness which held many such weapons, and they moved too fast to be attacked in return.

Now it was the turn of the Taosach's army to panic.

They faced attack from their front and their rear, and now that the pressure on them had eased the rightmost company of Teleri's Gluttons began to reform, advancing to attack from a new direction down the slope. The Gluttons on the left flank copied.

At a stroke, Teleri's forces had turned the tables on the Taosach's, and now they were the ones being pressed down towards the river. The ranks of spearmen huddled closer to the Gluttons, shying away from the rain of javelins and letting Teleri's forces attack their flank.

Pressed on the right and the left, and harried from the rear, the only way they could go was forwards. This led them towards the river and through Eain, Klay and the ragged remains of the Steel Hounds.

'Scatter! Fookin' scatter!' yelled Klay, and at that moment Eain realised that they had been used as bait. Their advance, and subsequent retreat, had put the enemy exactly where Teleri wanted them.

They had been a sacrifice.

Fury rose in Eain. Teleri kept showing what sort of man he was, even though Eain had kept trying to tell himself otherwise. He was a man who would cast lives away with barely a though if it would further his ambitions. One who saw others as tools and weapons, and not as people. One who did not care.

The centre of the field was now in chaos. The Taosach's forces swirled and surged, trying to push away from the river but being steadily driven towards it. The mercenaries were left as a shapeless, orderless mass and in danger of being crushed or driven into the bog.

The crowd near Eain parted with violent suddenness, and Eain looked down to see Klay shouldering a path. He followed through the gap, skirting the riverbank. Ankle deep in water and mud they forced their way south, fighting along the edge of the marsh and turning at bay to keep spears from their backs.

The dull thunder of hooves on soft turf came again, and this time the cavalry charged. Horns sounded and Teleri's Gluttons also thrust forwards. This was Teleri's death strike to the enemy, and it seemed that everyone else knew where and when it would fall; everyone except the mercenaries of the Steel Hounds.

The Taosach's army still had strength in numbers, but they were confused and dismayed at the way the battle had turned. The cavalry charge proved to be the last straw, and they turned to flee. Their only escape was into the boggy marshes of the river meads. They splashed into the murky water, many throwing their weapons away. The battle was over.

Only now did Teleri come forwards from his position on the crest of the ridge. He rode, his horse tall and black, and the Sisters of the Eagle surrounded him.

The army cheered at his approach, cheered the victory, even as the priestesses swarmed forwards, arrows aimed at the warriors floundering in the water. No muster and attack could be made from the sucking swamp without being cut down by a hail of arrows.

Weapons were thrown to the bank, surrenders accepted.

Teleri rode toward where the Taosach's generals were gathered. Teleri's new weapon, the cavalry, rode with him and a strong force of Gluttons marched behind.

The field, and the day, belonged to Daeron Teleri. The Demon Teleri.

Eain felt his knees buckle with exhaustion, and he sank onto the damp grass. Blood coated his hands, and some of it was his own. Cuts and nicks burned like lines of fire all over his upper body and the wound to his side was like an ember. He was exhausted.

Klay moved to stand nearby, and he could feel the dwarf's eyes on him. He kept his own down. He was in no mood for Klay's tough love or worse, his pity.

He was growing tired of being used like a pawn in a game, or a javelin to be cast and forgotten. But, he could not see a way out. He had sworn his oath, and chosen his side.

He was trapped.

FORTY TWO

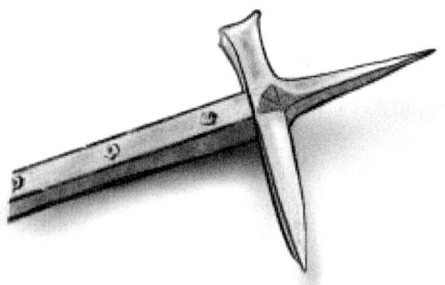

Klay Garrant marched across the hasty camp. He was still wearing his helmet and thick gauntlets, with the Capper held loosely in one hand.

The activity of raising tents and shelters, lighting fires and setting sentries buzzed around him, but he kept his eyes fixed to the ground, sucking his teeth ruefully.

Klay was uneasy, and he did not like it.

He preferred it when life was simple, and until the last few months he had managed to keep it so. Go where he was told to go, fight who he was told to fight, return, repeat. This life, which he had chosen freely, left no room for doubt or time for introspection.

That had changed, and there were two reasons. He could name them: Eain Connow and Daeron Teleri.

The boy had been troubled since they first met, and there was not much unusual about that. Klay was seventy years old and had been a soldier for the last twenty-five. He had seen countless other lost souls attempt to drown themselves in the sea of war in that time, to silence whatever horror was in their past with the thunder of battle. They usually found oblivion quickly.

But Eain had not drowned. He swam in the tides of battle with as much skill and wisdom as any veteran. The boy thrived in the maelstrom, however much he hated it. And Klay had allowed himself to be drawn into Eain's struggles. Despite himself, he found that he cared. He shuddered.

The fact was, the boy was following a path that would lead to his doom. And he had changed. When he had first joined the Steel Hounds there had been a darkness around him, and although that had lessened he now seemed…desperate. Bereft of hope and unconcerned for his own safety. It was dangerous.

Klay had no obligation to the boy. He needed to do nothing to help.

The camp had been sited on the hard, dry ground uphill from the battlefield. A hilly ridge ran from north to south, crowned with broken rock and clothed in brown heather and gorse. The army had marched to a low point in the ridge, a broad grassy saddle that gave a view across the Swarthwash and out toward the wide valley of the Great River to the west, and through the hills to Buren itself to the east.

Klay headed for a tent that was larger than the rest, square-sided and of bright yellow cloth. He was reminded of his summons, and the other reason his days were now filled with uncertainty and unease.

Daeron Teleri was a great leader, and the canniest general Klay had ever served. Klay would not have called him a good man, though, and struggled to trust him. Did either of these things, matter, though?

Teleri was ruthless, driven, ambitious and enigmatic. He led his forces as though he was a freedom fighter, a nationalist and a liberator, and yet whispers still went around the camp that all he wanted was to regain his home.

Turgon Fallas was said to be impregnable; would he throw their lives away storming its gates?

Klay shook his head. It was a problem for another day. He had given his oath. For now, his path was wherever Teleri led. It did not mean he had to like it, though.

Gluttons stood on guard outside the tent, the bulbous curves of their heavy armour making them appear as statues cast in the shape of warriors from ancient times. Their eyes were shadowed by their heavy helms.

Klay ignored them, and they him, as he passed inside.

Some generals considered themselves as lords or kings, and their dwellings were decorated as richly as any palace, including their tents while campaigning. Thick rugs might lie on the floor, intricate tapestries on the walls and furniture of heavy, polished wood.

Teleri was not like this. His bed was just a blanket laid on a mat of reeds, he had a single stool as furniture and the only decoration was a large square of linen parchment upon which the lines and curves of Tayo's rivers and hills were scrawled as a rudimentary map.

He was sitting on the stool and gazing at the map as Klay entered.

'Many paths, ever shifting,' he said, without getting up or looking around. 'Like a great game of *sadawch*, dwarf. And I am still searching for the right piece from the tangle, to take me home.'

Now he turned, and his eyes burned with intensity. 'Your report.'

'Report?' Klay was taken aback by Teleri's words, forgetting why he had been summoned.

'I wish to know how your company fared in the battle,' said Teleri, slowly and deliberately.

'Aye, aye. Yes, my lord.' Klay gathered himself. 'We lost many. With the Gluttons on the right flank in retreat we bore the brunt. We 'ad few spears of our own, and nowhere to go to escape theirs.'

He paused, hesitating. Then, he went on, unable to hold back the bitter words. 'And we did not know what yer'd planned. We did not know you'd strung us up as a straw dummy.'

Teleri rose. He was a tall man, almost Eain's height, and Klay had to look up a long way to meet his pale eyes.

'Do you bring a complaint, captain?' he asked. 'Do you question your general's wisdom? Do you question your lord, even though he has led you to another victory?'

Klay was not to be intimidated. 'Yer could 'ave told us what you 'ad planned. We could 'ave been warned.' These were words that needed to be said.

'I told you what you and your company needed to know, dwarf,' replied Teleri. 'I needed them to fight with tenacity. I needed them to be desperate. The battle was won because they gave everything to hold that position. Would they have done that if they had known what they were going to face? If they'd known I was planning to spring that surprise on the enemy?'

'Yer could've at least told me,' muttered Klay.

'A company follows its leader,' snapped Teleri, with sudden heat. 'You are their leader and you did what you had to do. I am *your* leader and I told you what I needed you to know to ensure victory. I should not need to explain this!'

He seized the low, three-legged stool and hurled it across the tent, his rage hot and sudden. It slapped into the canvas wall of the tent and dropped to lie on the floor.

'I doubt you not,' said Klay. 'I don't doubt that yer doing what you believe must be done. I don't doubt that you can win where others would lose. And I don't doubt you'd use any forces under your command like hurling a javelin. The warrior cares not for the fate of the javelin, so long as it strikes his enemy down.'

Teleri gave Klay a long level look, eyes sharp. 'True. But I do not see you as a weapon to be thrown. You are as a mace—' he nodded to where his own battle mace, of heavily ribbed grey iron, leaned against the wall. 'A simple, powerful weapon, and one you keep close to hand so that you can strike at your enemies again and again. Brutal, reliable, battle-worn.'

He paused, giving Klay a knowing look. Those pale eyes were alive, and for a moment Klay thought he saw red sparks swimming in their depths.

'The mace does not question the hand that swings it,' said Daeron Teleri.

Klay nodded. 'The mace does not question the hand,' he repeated.

'I'd tell you that your loyalty will be rewarded with riches, or with power, but I know that those things do not interest you. So, instead, I offer you something simpler. For you, Klay, I promise you worthy adversaries and the opportunity to exert your will over them. I offer you victory. And if my luck runs out, we will both get the one thing that may silence the screams that haunt our souls—oblivion.'

Klay was silent. Part of him raged at the presumptions this man had made. His fists clenched. How could Teleri know what he wanted? And yet, he did. Teleri was right.

'What of Eain?' asked Klay.

'What of Eain?' snapped Teleri, impatient at the question. His eyes were sharp.

'He was hurt in't battle.'

'He's a good soldier doing his duty. These things happen. Will he live?'

'Aye, he'll be reet. But, he's angry about what you did. Fuming.'

Teleri paused again, blinking. 'If a soldier is angry about plying his trade, then perhaps he needs to find a new trade. And if he questions his commander, his lord, then that is an issue of discipline that should be dealt with by his captain.'

Klay resisted baring his teeth in frustration. The man tied him in knots.

'And if one of my captains cannot keep his troops in line,' Teleri went on, 'then they will also face discipline. From me. Are we clear?'

'Clear as a mountain beck,' replied Klay. 'My lord.'

At that moment there was a rustle near the tent door.

'Envoys!' came the cry from without.

'Come,' called Teleri, and the head priestess of the Sisters of the Eagle strode in.

'I have been passed two messages that need your attention,' she began, then noticed Klay and paused.

'Continue,' said Teleri. 'My captains are entitled to know what I know.'

Klay suppressed a mirthless laugh. Men like Teleri seemed to twist reality to suit whatever version of the truth they wanted to present.

'The first message is from your watchers in the north,' she said. Klay was vaguely aware that Teleri had left a network of spies across Tayo as they marched south. 'The Taosach has marched out with her first legion. They are heading east, along the road to Turgon Fallas.'

Teleri closed his eyes, and Klay saw his fist clench. The dark skin across his knuckles whitened. A full legion outnumbered the Teleri's forces three to one, and they would march with companies of Gluttons, well-trained spear regiments and archers too.

They would be as a wall across Teleri's road to Turgon Fallas.

'All I want is to take back what is rightfully mine!' growled Teleri, baring his teeth. 'All I want is justice. The gods know my cause is righteous. Will they not grant me the strength I need?'

Klay was glad that the stool had already been thrown, and that Teleri's mace was out of his reach. Teleri ran a hand over his face.

'What else?'

'The other message was perhaps better news,' she said. 'A large force of the Bureno High King's army is camped on the other side of the Swarthland, on the eastern bank of Lake Takin.'

'How in the name of the Skyfather can that be good news?' roared Teleri, taking a furious step towards the High Priestess. She did not flinch.

'Because the message is from an emissary of High King Suten. They would meet with you to establish your intentions towards the Swarthland. They would sign a truce with you.'

Teleri looked up at that, interest sharp in his eyes. 'With me?'

Klay saw the implication as quickly as Teleri had. Buren wanted to treat with Teleri, as though he were a ruling lord. As though he spoke for Tayo. Such a treaty would legitimise his rebellion, and drive a wedge between Re'Emsser and the Taosach.

'She'll be livid,' said Teleri, with a sudden smile. Klay said nothing, but his mind worked. Such a treaty made little sense for Buren. Teleri led a small rebellion that would be put down any day. Why would Buren pay him any attention, or feel they needed to negotiate? They could just sit back and wait, and crush any attempt he made to move deeper into the Swarthland.

Untangling this was fortunately not Klay's problem.

'Very interesting,' said Teleri. 'I will meet with this emissary. The Envoys of War can often surprise, can they not?' He looked towards Klay. 'What are their terms?'

'The message says not,' replied the priestess. 'Only that the emissary will cross the lake soon. They have promised hostages as a gesture of their good faith.'

'Make the arrangements,' said Teleri. 'Klay, I want you to ensure an escort is ready for these hostages when they arrive. We have somewhere secure to keep them?'

'We're holding some captured soldiers at the edge of't camp. Ones 'as 'asn't bent the knee to you yet. Can put 'em there, keep 'em well guarded.'

'Very well. Make it so.'

Klay ducked his head before heading for the door of the tent. He thought he had seen a fiery gleam in Teleri's eyes again, as the man considered the opportunities that an agreement with Buren presented.

Suppressing a shudder, Klay left the tent and went out into the chill of the evening.

FORTY THREE

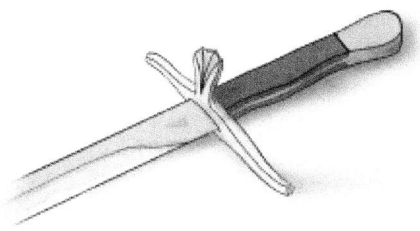

It had been a terrible mistake. He realised that now, and even as he lay wrapped in a thin blanket on a bed of wooden boards that swayed and rolled, he was filled with regret.

What a fool he had been.

Styoyan opened his eyes with reluctance, and stared upward, wondering what new disaster this day would bring.

The sky was a pewter plate, dull grey and charmless in the chill of dawn. The boat's sail was furled, useless against the steady breeze from the northeast, and six of the small crew were pushing the boat along with slow sweeps of the oars.

A hypnotic slap-slap-slap was the only sound as the wooden blades entered the dark water of the river. He watched their backs bending and straightening as he sat up and wrapped his rough cloak more tightly around himself.

One more regret. He wished he had thought to stash his own hose in the small bag he carried. The docker's trousers he had bought in haste by the waterside were cheap and rough. They itched.

The banks slipped past, brown hills in the distance to the south and east, and uninhabited lands of scrubby forests in between. Brown wastes of dead ferns bracketed meadows of long grass, painted grey by the morning's frost.

He yawned, stretched and turned to look north. Then he stopped, and stared.

The story was known all across Re'Emsser, of course. It was a wonder of the world. But to see it for real was still a shock.

The Crown.

An isolated range of mountains standing proudly and abruptly up from lowlands on the border between Tayo and Buren, the Crown was five conical peaks arranged in geometric precision like the points of a star. Or, like Glithoniel itself.

Some said that the conical towers of the Star City had been built as a replica of The Crown, or as a tribute. Or, perhaps for some ancient, mystic purpose that had been lost to time. Now the five identical peaks were almost eerie in their sudden size and symmetry, a landmark that was impossible to ignore.

'Raised by the Five,' said a bright, female voice. Styoyan turned. 'Their last earthly act before they ascended to the heavens.'

It was the small woman who Styoyan had tried to follow onto the Teliyade ship. The one who had found him passage on this small riverboat, saving him from his pursuers. The one who had seen through his disguise in moments and seemed to be able to speak fluent Elvish.

Nastja Mjette.

'Good morning,' he replied. 'Hope you slept better than I did.'

'Oh yes,' she said. She was sitting neatly on one of the benches, blankets already folded and stowed in her pack. 'I always sleep well on boats. I like boats.'

He had yet to learn the name of her companion, who was still a mere bundle of blankets in the base of the hull. Mousy brown hair showed above the folds, but little else.

'Is she well?' he asked. 'I noticed she was hurt yesterday.'

'The Mackems got hold of her,' said Nastja.

'The Mackems?'

'Yes. The ones who chased us off the boat. Skane, Jhari, and the rest.'

Styoyan stared. Those were the Mackems?

He had heard of them by their reputation in Anish. Criminals. Thugs. Brawlers. He was aware that there was a dark underworld in Kereva, and probably in Fordon too, but he had always done his utmost to keep his distance from that world. Of course, stories had filtered through even the thick walls of the keep of Kereva. To recall them made him shudder.

Those were the folk who had welcomed him as one of them, before they had discovered his identity. It was the Mackems who had been hunting him.

He had been lucky to escape. They had all been lucky. Without Skane's intervention, saving him for the second time, they would all have been taken. Despite the knowledge that he was a criminal, Styoyan hoped Skane had managed to get away. He hoped he had managed to find Mahdesht.

Leaving his horse behind had been a bitter blow.

There was a muted shuffling sound, followed by a groan and then an eruption of swearing. Nastja's companion was awake.

She pulled herself up into a sitting position, movements awkward and face twisting in pain, before peering out at her surroundings.

'Oh, shit,' she said. 'We're on a boat. I'd hoped the whole thing with the boat might have been a bad dream.'

Nastja and her companion were very different. Where Nastja was short, the other was tall; not many inches shorter than Styoyan himself. Her hair was an unremarkable brown, and her skin was a rich olive shade that would not look out of place anywhere across Anish or northern Buren.

All in all she was nondescript, especially with her hair bound up tightly and the signs of sleep still grey upon her face. There was something about her eyes, though…something bright and restless. Something that shone—

'This idiot is still here, then?' she said, glaring in Styoyan's direction. 'Hoped he might have fallen over the side in the night.'

'This is—' began Nastja, and Styoyan glared at her. She noticed his sharp look and went on: 'Styoyan. We both needed to escape Glithoniel and agreed to travel together. He can fight. He'll be useful, Ellyah.'

At least Nastja had not revealed his house and title, although Styoyan had feared she was about to. And now he knew both of their names.

'Well met, Ellyah,' he said, greeting her formally. 'I appreciate you helping me escape. I swear that I will repay the favour.' He inclined his head in her direction.

'That's lovely,' she said, her tone dripping with sarcasm. 'But thanks to you we might have the High King's army after us, as well as the Mackems.'

'If they are chasing us now, they always were,' said Nastja. 'We just didn't know it.'

Styoyan had told them about the odd events at the Glithoniel garrison and his subsequent escape in the breathless, exhilarated moments as the boat had pulled out into the river's current the previous night. Ellyah had been horrified, and angry that Nastja had brought him along.

Nastja herself had been calm. 'Whatever is going on, we're all in it together,' she had said, and repeated it now. 'These people want to capture us, and I think it's to use in one of their rituals. We can't let them.'

'That's one thing I can agree with,' said Ellyah.

'So what are we going to do next?' asked Styoyan. 'Where's this boat taking us?'

'There's a trading post with a wharf into the river at Lake Takin,' began Nastja. 'The Teliyade have agreed to take us that far. They don't like to get any further from the coast.'

'Then we can get off this bloody boat and go our separate ways,' said Ellyah.

'Buren isn't safe, Tayo isn't safe,' continued Nastja as if Ellyah had not spoken. 'So, I think we should take the road north. We could probably lie low in Ben Gedrin, or out in the Lands of the Great River.'

To Styoyan names sounded like places in a child's tale, one of faeries and magic. He was aware of their existence, but they seemed so remote as to be unreal.

'I will aid you in any way I can,' he said, hand slipping to the hilt of his sabre, hidden beneath his coarse smock. 'I can fight, if I need to. I can protect you.'

'Right now,' said Ellyah, tone bland and dismissive, 'you'll help me if you shut up.'

The day passed beneath a pall of awkward quiet after that. The low, grey sky pressed down on Styoyan's mood. He felt anxious and afraid, unable to put the fact that they were still being hunted from his mind, but also wary of his new companions.

Nastja was sitting with Ellyah, talking quietly but failing to elicit much of a reaction, as far as Styoyan could tell. He was left to sit in the bows, watching the banks drift by, the murky river water slipping beneath the boat.

Dusk was near when someone spoke, close to his ear.

'Dacadaniki samayam!'

Styoyan turned in uncomprehending confusion. The half-elf sailor laughed, then spoke again in accented Common Speech.

'I am sorry, young master. You must hide, now.' He gestured back towards the centre of the boat, pointing down into the hull. Styoyan stood and moved down toward Ellyah and Nastja, who were finding a spot deep within the barrels and crates that were arranged there.

'What's going on?' he asked. Ellyah rolled her eyes and snorted.

'We're coming up on Pike Wharf,' said Nastja. 'The Teliyade sometimes do a little trade there, and think there's a good chance of soldiers wanting to check the boat. So we need to hide.'

Styoyan felt a sudden grip of fear, and peered upriver as though he might be able to see the danger that loomed ahead.

'Get down, and get under cover,' snapped Ellyah. 'Over there.' She gestured to a pile of boxes closer to the stern, and Styoyan picked his way over, careful not to get in the way of the rowers.

A narrow gap between the rough, splintery planks of two crates would have to serve as a refuge. He grabbed a frayed scrap of canvas, stiff with salt, and wrapped himself in it as he squeezed beneath the crates.

One was a solid-sided chest, with a pungent, leafy smell that Styoyan recognised as tea. He was not certain, but thought that tea was grown in the south of Tayo. The other crate rattled as he moved against it, and had a strong, fishy odour. It seemed to be full of seashells.

Styoyan pulled the cloth down tightly, blocking out the fading light, and did his utmost to stay still.

The boat swayed and rocked to the rhythm of the oars as they swept through the water. Styoyan tried to guess what was happening from the motion, but it was impossible.

Then there was a thud, and a muted splash. The whole boat rocked before gradually coming to a stop. He heard the wooded clatter of the oars being stowed, and then the boat rocked again as the rowers stood. Stretching their aching backs, probably.

Low voices could be heard, speaking softly in Elvish.

'Hihi!' rang out a new voice, calling loudly in the Common Speech. 'Captain! Captain, come here.' Footsteps sounded, accompanied by the boat trembling as the captain, of whom Styoyan had not learned a name, moved over towards the wharf.

More talking, in voices too low to hear clearly. Styoyan guessed it was in Common, but for how much he could make out it could have been Elvish or Dwarvish.

'Are you certain?' asked the captain, his voice accented and distinctive and raised in surprise for a moment. Just for a moment, though, and then the volume reduced once more to an unintelligible murmur.

Styoyan's heart beat faster as he strained to hear what was being said, while willing his body to remain motionless. He needed to be ready in case the cloth was pulled suddenly aside.

After what seemed like many minutes, there was the soft but unmistakeable sound of money rings clinking. It must be the captain paying some sort of toll, or tax.

Shortly afterwards, the boat began to move once more.

The dawn was ragged, the sky a skein of grey wool torn across smooth blue silk. The swish and rattle of the oars sliding through the dark water was muted, and the rest of the world was silent.

The clouds swirled over either bank, hiding the hilly ridges to their left one moment and revealing them in the next; a spine of green and brown outlined against a fleeting blue sky.

Styoyan stared straight ahead, watching the river in front of the bow as they began the final stage of their journey.

By the time they were clear of Pike Wharf and the Teliyade sailors had called for the three stowaways to emerge, night had fallen. The banks on either side were barely visible, and the water was black. Another uncomfortable night followed, the boat tied to stunted trees at the water's edge. The current rocked the boat, gentle waves lapping all through the night, but Styoyan was not soothed.

He had walked blindly into danger, with every step since he had left Fordon, and even if the Teliyade set them down in safety, what then? All three of them remained hunted, and his fellow fugitives had no interest in an alliance. Perhaps he needed to prove himself to them, too.

The song of the rowers was an insistent lullaby, a contrast to the dull, grey sky. The Teliyade sailors sang whenever they worked: rowing, coiling ropes, or lifting and stowing crates and barrels. Their songs were nothing like the noble, soaring melodies that had filled Styoyan's ears and mind during his early years in the court of Fordon. These were simple and repetitive chants to fit the rhythm of their labour.

In the quiet cold of this morning, he found the sound unsettling.

'How much longer on here, Nas?' asked Ellyah, sitting up and stretching uncomfortably before clutching at her side.

'A few hours, yet,' replied Nastja. 'Three or four at the most. They will take us to the docks at the head of Lake Takin. The Teliyade call it Lake Silveraxe, the *Vendigod-al*, and the docks are a little further north where the waters meet. The river isn't navigable much beyond that.'

'So, today?' Ellyah's tone was flat and unfriendly.

'Yes. Today.'

'Right.'

One of the sailors walked back from the bow, where he had been staring down into the dark water. Bare chested and bare footed despite the cold, he walked with that familiar balanced sway of one who had spent their whole life on the water.

'Yes, you will see the Silveraxe soon. Very soon!' he said.

'Quiet!' called the captain from his position near the tiller. 'Back to work. Do not talk.'

The sailor ducked his head and returned to his position.

Nevertheless, his words soon proved true.

The banks on both sides melted away, although a low mist all about them hindered any view of what lay beyond. Styoyan got the impression, though, of space and of water. The subtle background sounds of wind hissing across moor and grassland, or stirring the bare branches of isolated trees, were gone. Small waves lapped, rising oars let drips fall, but all else was still and silent.

A breeze lifted and the clouds swirled, lifting slightly and providing a glimpse of the expanse of water that surrounded them. Grey as a blade and textured by small ripples, the shore spread away in a long curve to their right and vanished to a distant point to their left.

Hemmed by a shallow valley like the pages of an open book, the western end of the lake resembled a spear point, thrusting towards Tayo.

Even as he gazed out, drinking in the view of that mysterious, distant shore, he felt the boat turn. The steersman leaned on the tiller and they turned to the left, the bow heading towards the very point of the spear's tip.

'This is the wrong way,' said Nastja immediately. 'We're going the wrong way.' She stood. The Teliyade captain was stony-faced.

'We need to go north. This is west. Are you listening?' Nastja was frantic. 'Why are we heading west? We made a bargain.'

'What's going on?' demanded Ellyah, standing beside her friend. Styoyan jumped to his feet, too, hand moving to the solidity of his sword hilt, still hidden beneath his rough smock.

'Sit down, my dears,' said the captain. 'Calm yourselves. It's too late to change anything, now.'

'What do you mean?' asked Ellyah. 'What does he mean, Nas?'

'We did make a bargain, yes,' continued the captain. 'But at Pike Wharf I made a new bargain. Someone paid me more than you can afford to take you somewhere different. I'm sorry.'

'It's them, isn't it? You're working for them.' Ellyah was furious, fists clenched.

She meant the Mackems. Or the High King's army. Or were they both the same, now? Either way, if she was right, the Teliyade were taking them to be captured.

Styoyan darted a hand beneath his smock, and it emerged holding his sabre. The sharp steel shone, and he pointed it at the captain.

'Take us where you promised,' he said. 'Honour the bargain.'

The captain just laughed. 'Put down the spike, boy. No one needs be hurt.'

As he spoke, several of the crew stepped forwards. Styoyan had not noticed that they were armed, but now each had a punch dagger in their fists. A single spike, the length of their palm, protruded between their clenched fingers. They were brutal weapons designed for one purpose: stabbing someone again and again.

The lethal points gleamed as the half-elves stepped closer to the two girls. Styoyan was left with no choice. He could not fight them all, or risk one of the women being hurt or killed if he did. He slammed the sabre back into its scabbard.

'Disarm him,' ordered the captain. 'And check the girls for blades, too, before binding their wrists. We have a way to shore yet and cannot afford any accidents.'

They were not treated roughly, but the sailors kept their daggers bared as they took Styoyan's sabre as well as a number of knives that Ellyah had hidden about her person. Styoyan found his wrists wrapped with rough twine and tied at his back.

'Look what you've got us into now,' said Ellyah as they were forced down to sit in the bottom of the hull. Her glares towards Nastja and Styoyan were poisonous.

The rowers bent their backs, and the hills seemed to grow on either side as the head of the valley neared. The subtle sounds of small waves on the rocky shoreline could still be heard over the rhythmic slap and hiss of the oars when a shadow fell across them.

A much larger vessel, under full sail, was overtaking them. Looking up, Styoyan noticed the mast flew the colourful flag of the Bureno army. Now there really could be no escape.

Both boats veered towards the southern bank, and over the rail Styoyan could see a cluster of small buildings above a wharf of dark wood. The Teliyade captain brought them deftly into shore, bumping lightly into the fenders of thick, braided rope as sailors hurled mooring lines around the wharf's posts.

'This is where you leave us,' said the captain. '*Mi atma svecchaga undanivvandi.* Farewell and good luck.'

'*Vidkolu,*' replied Nastja. '*Sarasamaina gali.* Farewell and a fair wind.' Her tone was despondent.

The Teliyade sailors helped them to their feet, then lifted them onto the wharf. Styoyan noticed that the half-elves remained in the boat even though they forced himself and the two women forwards.

'Got any more bright ideas?' asked Ellyah bitterly. Nastja was silent, face blank.

The larger ship had been tied up nearer to the village, and a broad plank lowered as a walkway. Armed and armoured soldiers began trooping down onto the wharf, rank and file warriors in baked leather and armed with spears. They turned at a command, marching towards the Teliyade ship.

A firm grip from the sailor at his back bade Styoyan turn to face the oncoming procession. He, Nastja and Ellyah were held firmly as the captain stepped up onto the rail. He paused there, as though waiting for something.

Moments passed. Styoyan glanced around, briefly considering options for an escape. It was hopeless. Even if he could slip away from his guards, the only ways to go were onto the spears of those soldiers or into the chill waters of the lake.

The sound of shuffling feet, as the soldiers from the ship straightened, drew his attention back to the wharf. A figure was walking down the gangplank wrapped in a dark robe, and so deeply hooded that their face was entirely shadowed. They stepped down onto the dark planks and turned to walk towards them. They carried a long, narrow case beneath one of their arms.

They stopped a few feet away.

'You have done what was needed,' she said. It was a woman. 'Payment will be as agreed.' She produced a handful of silver money rings from one of her flowing sleeves, and passed them to the nearest soldier. A gesture was enough to instruct the soldier, and he passed the rings to the captain as several others moved forwards to seize the three captives.

Without another word, the cowled figure turned away and they were thrust along by the soldiers.

Styoyan could do nothing to resist as he was marched along the wharf, the planks throbbing like drums beneath their feet. The grey cloud hung low above their heads and the bare slopes of the valley sides faded away in the haze. It only added to the mood of despair and hopelessness.

The hooded figure walked in the midst of the soldiers, and the captives followed as they left the wharf and passed through the small, ramshackle waterside village. Clearly, this was not a prosperous settlement and if it had once thrived with trade, those days were gone.

A couple of families seemed to be all that dwelled there now, and a handful of ragtag children stopped to watch the procession as their parents sat beside the street. Some mended fishing nets, but most simply stared.

Styoyan knew that it must appear as though they were criminals, and the shame of it made his ears burn.

The road led onwards through the outskirts of the village, half-rotted houses and enclosures choked with weeds marking the boundary. The procession was forced to halt, however, by the presence of another force barring the road. Styoyan could not see them clearly through the forest of bodies and spear hafts, but the dull light gleamed on armour and weapons.

'Bring them forwards,' instructed the cowled woman. Firm hands on shoulders pushed them through the ranks, until they stood beside her.

Now she addressed the other group, raising her voice to be heard. 'I come as an emissary of Buren, representative of Duke Vorban in whom the authority of High King Suten resides. I would broker a meeting between my lords and your general, the honourable Duke Daeron Teleri.'

'The Demon,' hissed Nastja.

'These hostages are a gesture of our good faith, and will be a gift for your lord.' She gestured with one robed arm and the three of them were thrust forwards to stand in the middle of the road. Wishing that the ground would open up and swallow him, Styoyan waited.

Several figures came forwards from the opposing ranks, all attired for battle. Styoyan noticed that one was a dwarf while his companion was a towering, fair-haired young man with the hilt of a large sword rising above his right shoulder.

As they approached, Styoyan heard Ellyah gasp. He turned, and her face was twisted in a conflict of emotions: half shocked, half furious. She was staring at the young man.

'You!' she said.

FORTY FOUR

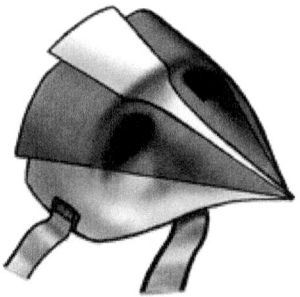

The nightmares were over.

The respite might turn out to be short lived, but those night terrors where she was dragged down beneath the earth and tortured mercilessly had relented, for now.

She had worked hard to keep her dark master satisfied, and now that she had a little freedom from pain and exhaustion she could work harder to make his long-held plans come to fruition.

Evane Claes stood in the bow of the boat and watched the hazy shore approach. The chants, cries and yells of the sailors were as the buzzing of insects in her ears. Insignificant. Like the rest of the world they were oblivious to her subtle labour, and her grand purpose.

The ranks of Bureno soldiers in the hull were the same. They could serve her purposes, but could not comprehend the part they were playing. The world teemed with them, little people in little houses, and they would probably welcome the firm yoke of Desya when the demon's time came.

And it would come soon.

Stepping down from the gangplank felt like crossing some invisible threshold. So much work had led to this point and now she could not turn back. Her road ahead led directly to *him*.

The one. A man with the strength of will to use the Demon's Tear, and claim it as his own. The only one to touch it and live. It seemed to Claes that with that brief contact he had passed something of himself into the jewel, and the ruby had not exacted its usual price: death.

She had known him in that moment, felt his presence through their shared connection to the demon and the jewel that contained part of Desya's essence. It had taken several days after that, though, for his name to reach her ears.

'A new power seems to be rising in Tayo,' Brother Hilass had said, his voice ringing out into the great hall of the temple of Glithoniel. 'Word says he uses sorcery and dark magic to overcome his enemies. He now leads a powerful army and I fear a new civil war in Tayo.

'His name is Daeron Teleri. We should all be afraid of what he may do.'

Claes' own sources had said more. Teleri had apparently drained the life from another Tayan lord with a mere touch. The story went that he laughed as he did it, and that the enemy army had immediately surrendered to him.

She paid little attention to the wilder tales, but knew the signs of the jewel. The demon agreed.

He has it. And dares to wield it.

Desya's voice had torn through her skull, as though the words were driven on the tips of needles.

'He is the one we seek,' she replied.

He will lead my army. It has already begun. You must guide him.

'I will go to him,' she said. She had already given much thought to her next action. 'I can guide him along the path we have discussed. It shall all be as you have instructed.'

The jewel.

It was a statement. This had been her problem to solve. The general they needed must bear the jewel, must be able to use it as a weapon. How could they hold an object that would kill them with a single touch?

'*Pluitone*,' she said, making sure that she spoke with a confident tone. 'Ancient scrolls tell of the royal metal being able to withstand and control magic. *Pluitone* can hold the jewel and let this man wield it. It shall be in the form of a sceptre of his new office.'

She thought it would work. She hoped it did.

Her hired thugs from Glithoniel, aided by the Mackems, had done their job and stolen the *pluitone* that was needed. The long case tucked beneath her arm held it, worked into a device. Now, she just had to reach Teleri and persuade him to take it.

What man could not be tempted by power, though?

The captains of her armed guard had their orders, and retrieved the hostages from the half-breed pirates who had remained stubbornly in their boats. Pushing the new prisoners before them, the small force marched away from the docks.

Delight warred with apprehension as she saw the ranks of Tayan troops arrayed across the westward road. Her message had been heeded, but she had a momentary flash of worry that these soldiers had been sent to bar their passage.

She must know.

'Bring them forwards,' she ordered, and the three hostages were dragged from the ranks.

Her face remained impassive, but she was delighted to see the two women restrained at last. Much of the pain and suffering she had been forced to endure could be laid at their feet. Their thieving and subsequent obstinacy at resisting capture had come close to seeing her dead at the hands of the demon.

She would watch them meet their end beneath the crimson glow of the jewel with great pleasure.

'I come as an emissary of Buren, representative of Duke Vorban in whom the authority of High King Suten resides. I would broker a meeting between my lords and your general, the honourable Duke Daeron Teleri.'

Of course, the meeting between Teleri and Vorban would be naught but a formality, a public display. The most important meeting would hopefully occur in the next hour, when she came face to face with the one they called The Demon.

'These hostages are a gesture of our good faith, and will be a gift for your lord.'

To her relief, the Tayan soldiers came forwards to receive the hostages. That boded well. She noted the taller of the two women, Ellyah Jerim, directing a string of curses towards her new captor.

Claes paid it little heed. It fitted what she knew of the woman's character: a petty thief with a stubborn streak and a foul mouth. Soon enough, her cursing would be silenced forever.

One of the Tayans, a scowling dwarf with a short, reddish beard, looked up at her and the Bureno ranks.

'Ah'm t'tek yer t' Duke Teleri,' he said, a thick accent making his speech almost incomprehensible. 'If yer follow, we'll lead you t'is camp.'

Dwarves.

'Lead,' she said in response, suppressing a shudder.

A vague path, little more than a grassy strip worn through the gorse and heather, led up the valley. Hillsides frowned over them on both sides, and a loud-voiced stream tumbled down beside the path to their right.

More tiny streams and rills carved twisting trails through the brown furze on the opposite slope, rushing down to the gully where the combined weight of the frothing water gurgled away to feed the broad grey lake behind them.

Ahead, a wide gap in the looming ridge was like a bite from the landscape. The angle of the slopes slackened to either side, and a grassy plateau lay between.

Claes could already see the conical shapes of tents, dark against the skyline, as well as the orange flares of braziers and the sentries huddled beside them.

This military encampment, this village of tents, was where the fate of the world would be decided. Her jaw clenched. Her approach to Teleri must be perfect; she could not be rejected. He was too important.

Against anyone else she would consider using the power that Desya granted to overcome them, to make them compliant to her will. But, she dared not try that against him. Whether he knew it yet or not, he was too strong in that same power. He could destroy her.

The ranks of Tayan troops passed the outer ring of sentries without challenge, dragging the prisoners away. But as Claes led the soldiers of Buren towards the same gap, they found their way barred.

The sentries hardly moved apart from to slightly lower their spears, but other figures melted out from the camp to block the path. They were clad in red and held bows, arrows nocked.

Despite herself, Claes shrank back.

She knew these red-robed priestesses for what they were: heretics. They denied the Five and would have the backward pagan worship of the animal gods preserved.

Beneath her cowl, she frowned deeply. This suggested something troubling about the man Teleri. Even if he did not follow this blasphemous, childish faith himself, he had sympathy for them. It could not be tolerated.

Their leader spoke. 'Your soldiers must remain outside the bounds of the camp. Attempting to force entry would be deemed an act of war.'

She addressed the words directly to Claes. Her bow was held loosely in one hand, and the arms that were visible beyond her sleeveless robe were lithe and muscular.

'What guarantees do you give that I will not be harmed, or taken prisoner?' asked Claes, attempting to project her voice with authority.

The head priestess gave a soft laugh. 'The same guarantee you give that you are genuine. You say you come with an offer for Duke Teleri. Make that offer and speak true, and you are safe. He knows it will be forfeit if he harms you.

'If you are false, though…' She let the suggestion hang in the chill air. The threat.

'My offer comes from Duke Vorban,' replied Claes. The haughty confidence of the other woman had needled her. She felt the urge to strike out with her power, make her beg for the agony to stop. 'And from the High King. I act in good faith. Any assault on my person will be as an assault on Buren itself.' The lies came easily.

'We understand one another,' said the High Priestess. 'Proceed. Duke Teleri awaits.'

Claes strode on through the camp, head high beneath her deep hood. She was aware of the muted treads of the priestesses following behind, but ignored them. To turn to look would reveal her unease, and she would not give them that satisfaction.

Teleri's tent was modest. A simple tent for a war leader in the midst of a campaign. Apt. And, though he knew it not, the war was about to turn in his favour.

She waited for the guards to announce her: 'The emissary of Buren arrives,' then ducked in through the tent door. The interior was sparsely furnished, almost bare, and its ascetic simplicity impressed her.

And then she saw him for the first time. And knew.

He rose as she entered, moving to stand a few feet away. A tall man by any standards, he would tower over most Tayans, and made Claes feel small. His head almost brushed the canvas of the tent's roof. He was physically imposing but no warrior: his shoulders sloped and there was a softness to his body, around his jaw and in the curve of his belly.

Then she met his eyes, and it took all her resolve not to take a step back. They smouldered with intensity, a bright intelligence and a restless rage. His whole face was twisted with mistrust, and she noticed that those blue eyes were lined with the grey of fatigue and worry.

'Is it common for emissaries of peace to stand before a lord hooded?' he demanded. She had forgotten herself with the shock of being in his presence.

As if unconcerned, she cast it back.

'I am much more than an emissary,' she said, attempting to match his glowering power with her own authority. It was difficult, more difficult than she had imagined, and she realised with a jolt it was because she was afraid. He raised an eyebrow.

'I represent Vorban,' she went on, 'but he is not my master. We do offer a treaty, as it serves our purposes to aid you in your war. Your cause is just and is but the first step on a long road. For you, power beyond comprehension lies at the end.'

Teleri was frowning. 'What do you mean?'

She saw his genuine confusion, mingled with curiosity, and was delighted.

'What do you want?' she asked.

He paused. 'From you? Surety that I will not have an army on my eastern flank as well as to the north and west. But, why do you ask? It was Vorban who offered this truce.'

'No. I was the one who offered the truce, and suggested a treaty. It shall be honoured, as I said, but it was in part a device so that I could meet you, to present you with an offer of much greater significance.

'I ask again—what do you want? Why do you fight?'

'For Tayo,' replied Teleri, without a pause. 'We have been oppressed for too long. By you. We are forced to serve those who would grind our way of life, our very essence, to dust beneath their boots. You.'

'What else? I do not ask as an emissary of Buren, and I understand your hatred of that regime. I ask as a friend who would offer aid.'

Teleri paused once more. His heavy-lidded eyes flicked over her, weighing her up, measuring the meaning behind her words. His instinct was to mistrust, she knew, but his purpose burned so fiercely within him that he would consider any offer she made.

'I want to return home,' he said, quietly. 'Amid all the injustices that is the first I would put right. The Taosach knows that the theft of Turgon Fallas is a needle beneath my skin, a thorn in my flesh. She would use it to lure me north.'

He sighed. 'And so she throws all her forces north to stand between my home and my army. If I persist, she will crush me. If I turn back, I will lose everything. My position is impossible and she knows this. So unless you are about to offer ten thousand Bureno soldiers and the knights to lead them, your treaty will just delay my defeat.'

His shoulders slumped. She thrilled inside. This was the moment.

'I can give you Turgon Fallas,' she said, her voice low and urgent. 'I can give you power worth many thousand knights. I will stand at your right hand and show you how to use it. None will stand before us.'

'What is this power?' He looked sceptical.

'The jewel,' she said, and his eyes widened guiltily. 'Do not deny it. I know you have it. I know you have used it. Stories have already spread of your power. Stories of fear.'

'I did not mean to—'

'No! You could not have known of its true power. You still don't. But it helped your cause, did it not? A battle went unfought because of what you did. Many lives were saved, and your campaign was rescued. Do I speak true?'

'You do,' he admitted. 'But I still don't understand what happened.'

'I do. The jewel has come to you for a purpose, and in the right hands it is a weapon more powerful than you can imagine. Your hands are the right hands.'

He stared at her. She had him, she knew. The jewel's power was obvious, but he had not truly thought he could wield it. The moment to capture him was now.

She pulled the long case from beneath her arm and held it out to him. He took it, but his eyes were hard, brow furrowed as they shifted between her and the long, plain case.

He feared a trap.

'This is no trick,' she said. 'It is a gift. Open it.'

Curiosity outweighed his caution, and he obeyed. His long, clever fingers worked at the catches before he slowly opened the lid. His eyes widened.

The length of his arm, the sceptre filled the case from end to end. The shaft was of simple steel, blackened with a dark patina. The head was a conical collar of silver, brightly polished and engraved with geometric designs. Atop this, three curving horns sprang from the end of the shaft, gleaming, blue-black *pluitone*. A metal that could bear the power of the jewel, and allow the sceptre to be carried as a totem and used as a weapon.

'What—' he began.

'You know,' cut in Claes. She had to ensure he acted as required. It would be a mistake to give him too much time to think. 'You know what this will do. Where is the box?'

He gestured to a small chest in the corner, but did not speak. All his attention was on the forged length of the sceptre, and he grasped it as he let the case drop to the ground, forgotten.

Claes opened the lid of the chest and could barely contain her excitement at what she saw. The box. And she knew, that after all this time, she finally had the Demon's Tear within her grasp.

As she lifted the nondescript wooden box she could already feel the throb of unearthly power within. It was slightly warm. She longed to reach in and grasp it, to claim the power for her own.

It would destroy her if she tried.

Taking a breath, she opened the lid.

The inside of the tent was instantly washed with scarlet. Teleri turned to look at the source of the light, and his face was cast with the same glow. Even his eyes seemed to shine with an inner red fire as they reflected the jewel.

As if it understood the important of the moment the Demon's Tear responded. It shone like a new star, casting vivid shafts onto the canvas that became as a shifting, blood-drenched galaxy.

Daeron Teleri knew the importance of the moment, too.

'What must I do?' he asked, in a hoarse whisper.

'Seize the jewel,' she replied, unable to raise her own voice above a breathy murmur. His glare was sharp, a question in his eyes. 'With the sceptre,' she added.

He nodded.

She set the box down, and he approached. Gripping the shaft of the sceptre firmly, he lowered the head towards the open mouth of the box. The *pluitone* fittings seemed to reach towards the source of the crimson glow like eager, grasping fingers.

They touched the jewel. There was a soft, metallic sound and then a click. Teleri raised the sceptre.

The Demon's Tear was now held between those blue-black claws as though it had formed there, or the sceptre had been forged around it. It blazed with light, with power.

Wisps of what resembled red steam or vapour rose from the jewel and flowed down the shaft of the sceptre. Teleri stared at it, open-mouthed.

The vapour swirled around the dark metal, edging lower until a hazy wisp of red touched Teleri's white-knuckled fist.

If it had shone fiercely before, now it was as though a furnace burned in its heart. It was no longer red, though. Now, it shone with a deep purple light that was almost too bright to endure.

And, as the tent was bathed in purple, Teleri's eyes snapped wide open. They too were painted a bright violet.

He screamed.

FORTY FIVE

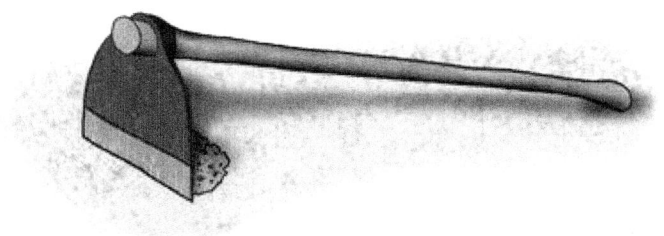

Indaella Connow screamed.

Tann could only stare as she clamped a hand to either side of her face and let out a long, keening wail. It came from nowhere, and the sound was harsh and grating. It was a sound borne of unseen horror.

Cerle turned and wrapped his arms around her, quickly enough that although her body went limp, knees buckling, she did not fall.

'What? What is it, my love? Are you hurt?' His eyes were wide as he stared at his wife's face. It was as close to panic as Tann had ever seen in the big man.

'Archer?' said Luara. She had drawn both swords and dropped into a low crouch, eyes scanning the landscape. Tann hefted his shield, moving to stand the other side of Cerle and Indaella. His hand went to the hilt of the sword he now wore, although he did not draw it.

Holt ducked behind him, close to Indaella.

'There's no shaft,' he said. 'No blood. She has suffered no hurt that I can see.'

'What is it then?' demanded Cerle, although Tann was not sure if he was asking them, Indaella, or the world in general. She was still slumped in his arms, eyes open and mouth slack, as though in a trance.

'What does she See?' said Tann, with an emphasis on the last word. Cerle looked up sharply.

'Aye, aye,' he said. 'Perhaps she Sees. Something that has happened, or is about to. What do you See, my love?' Indaella did not answer.

Tann gazed out south, sharp eyes alert for movement among the brown and rocky slopes. Away to his left, westward, a thick pall of smoke hung in the air. The sheen of dull daylight on water showed where a long, tapering lake lay. Another column of smoke rose over the brow of the nearest hill, where rocky escarpments crowned bare, brown slopes. The grey haze hung in the air, merging with the leaden clouds above their heads. A Tayan encampment lay beneath the smoke.

They had seen several travellers before leaving the wagon behind and continuing into the hilly countryside on foot, and all had confirmed that several companies of the Bureno army were camped on the western shore of the lake.

The news had worried Tann. He had fought on this ground himself, so many years ago that it seemed to be a different life. He knew the signs of war brewing when he saw them, though.

'Whoever the Tayan general is, he's trying to provoke something,' he had said, as the group began to slog over the slopes of knotted grass in the direction of the plume of smoke, earlier the same day.

'How so?' asked Holt. The lad had fought, but never led. It showed.

'No Tayan army should be here,' he replied. 'This is the Swarthland. Used to be part of Tayo but Buren took it as weregild for the last big border war.'

'Took it?' asked Cerle. 'Just stole it?'

'Occupied it,' answered Tann. 'A buffer against future aggression, they said. They built a wall and some forts along the hillside in the south, and a couple of Tayan villages gained Bureno lords.

'But hardly anyone lives up here, it's poor land. So, it's owned by Buren in principle. The Tayans know that and so leading an army here is provocative.'

'To provoke Buren?' asked Cerle.

'Maybe so. Or maybe it's a civil war brewing. Either way, Buren has answered. They aren't going to let that incursion go unchallenged.'

'What does that mean for Eain?' asked Indaella.

'Well,' said Tann. 'If that elf spoke true that he went into Tayo, and we're right in our guess that he's taken up as a mercenary, he could be about to be caught up in a battle.' Indaella's frown showed her worry.

'Let's find out for sure, before we do anything silly,' said Luara.

'Aye,' agreed Cerle. 'We can get closer, maybe we'll spot him. Or find someone to ask.' He clenched a fist. Tann could imagine Cerle being a very persuasive questioner, at need.

That had been the plan; the five of them would sneak up to the Tayan camp and see what they could see. If there was a chance to retrieve Eain, they would take it.

Indaella's sudden fit had changed that though. She was unable to speak, or even, seemingly, to move. Cerle still held her tightly, so she did not fall.

'She can go no further,' he said. 'Not like this.'

'I will stay with her,' offered Holt. Tann kept quiet, but the same words had been about to spring to his lips. The thought of having to spill blood if they needed to fight their way free already filled him with queasy dread.

Cerle stared at Holt, eyes hard. 'Do you think I'll walk away with my wife laid down on the cold grass? In a state like this?' His eyes blazed with fury, which showed just how worried the big man was. Holt looked away.

'I'll go,' said Luara. 'You stay here and look after Indaella, Cerle. I know what Eain looks like and I'll be able to get close.'

'I'm not letting you go alone,' said Holt. 'I'm coming too.'

Luara rolled her eyes. 'Fine. But you'd better tread more softly than you usually do, farmer.' Her eyes were smiling.

Tann looked at the pair of them and remembered what Luara had said before they set out from Feorhryc. He had sworn to take care of Holt, and he did feel responsible for the younger man. Once again, he had dragged the kid into danger.

'Let's call it three,' he said. 'The heroes of Feorhryc again. Just like old times.'

'So be it,' said Cerle. 'Do your best and we will meet back at the wagon.' As though she weighed nothing, Cerle hoisted his wife up in his arms and turned to retrace their steps. 'Take care of each other,' he said, as he walked away.

Take care of each other.

Tann had sworn to do just that. He would not let either of those two come to any harm.

Luara led as they skirted around a flat-topped hill to the north. The going was slow. There was no real path through the deep banks of dry, dead bracken and they were forced to climb over large boulders, or take a longer route around them.

Despite the chill of the afternoon, Tann found himself sweating beneath his long coat. His breath came in short gasps.

'Not as fit as you were,' he muttered to himself.

'And you were never that fit anyway,' said Luara, turning to give him a broad smile. She was breathing easily.

'Cheek,' he said. 'Your tongue is less sharp than your swords, though. I used to be strong as an ox. Could run all day, and fight at the end of it if I had to.'

'You just might, this day,' said Luara.

'Let's pray to Fate it don't come to that,' he said.

'Hopefully, we can talk our way in and then out again,' added Holt. Tann stayed quiet. That did not seem likely.

A steep outcrop of rough, grey rock leaned out from the hillside, and Luara paused beside it. Tann joined her and felt Holt arriving behind him as he stared over her shoulder.

The camp was below them, lying at the base of the hill and filling a flat saddle in the ridge. The sight of the cluster of tents and the indistinct shapes of people moving between them brought back vivid memories for Tann. The constant noise of voices calling and weapons clattering, the grass churned to mud underfoot, and the ever-present smells of woodsmoke and unwashed bodies.

The nostalgia was overpowering.

'Can we get close enough to see what's happening?' he asked. 'Does it look like there's anywhere we'd be able to sneak in?'

Luara pointed. 'There. Down there. We'll need to be quick and quiet.'

A cluster of boulders lay where the slope slackened. Rising from the brown furze, the rounded grey shapes were dressed in a mottled coat of moss and lichen. Tann nodded. They would get a better look at the camp from there, and were unlikely to be noticed, especially as the light faded.

'Quick, and quiet. Luara, you lead.'

She swooped down the slope. Her legs moved quickly as she raced over the rough ground, and Tann was reminded once more how easily Luara could be underestimated. Her bright smile hid the steel that lay beneath.

He hurried to keep up, and could hear Holt's rapid footsteps behind. Tann kept looking up towards the camp, praying that the alarm would not be raised. Hopefully, the sentries had got lazy.

In any case, they were only three. Clad in dark colours against the dun hillside they would barely show up. The sentries were watching for an encroaching enemy force or, as Tann knew from bitter experience, anyone inside the camp trying to escape. Deserters could not be tolerated.

They reached the boulders, each one taller than Tann, and he slumped against the nearest. Hands on knees, mouth gaping wide, he sucked cool air into his burning lungs.

'Take a while, Grandpa,' said Luara, and vanished around the corner of the boulder before Tann had time, or wind, to respond.

Holt chuckled. 'She only pokes fun at the ones she loves,' he said, then his face became serious. 'She's my world, you know?' Tann nodded. 'I couldn't live if anything happened to her. Not again.'

'Nothing's going to happen to her, Holt.'

'Hey!' Luara's head appeared around the boulder, and she called to them in a low hiss. 'Come and look at this.'

They edged around the boulder together, and Luara bade them to peer through a gap in the rough grey rocks. It gave a view down to the camp.

A sentry was before them, about thirty paces away; a simply armed Tayan warrior with a spear and wearing a leather hauberk. Left and right, Tann could see other guards. They were standing about fifty paces apart along the camp's perimeter, and each looked bored and inattentive.

'Not expecting any trouble, are they?' he said softly.

'Look further right,' said Luara.

Tann looked. Beyond the next sentry was what looked like a corral. High canvas walls screened this from the rest of the camp, and more sentries were standing on each corner, guarding what was between the fences.

People. Sitting on the ground and covering the grassy space were scores of people.

'Hostages, or prisoners,' said Tann. Tayo could be brutal but those who surrendered were still unlikely to be slaughtered out of hand. Warriors were too valuable to waste.

'What if Eain is in there?' suggested Luara.

'What if he is?' said Tann, eyes fixed on the makeshift prison. 'We need to get a closer look.'

'We won't get closer in daylight.'

Tann was quiet, thinking and watching.

'We're not thinking of going in there, are we?' asked Holt, anxiously.

'We don't have any choice, if we want to be certain about Eain,' said Luara. 'And Cerle won't be happy if we don't at least try.'

Tann was still staring at the corral. At the furthest corner he could see what looked like a cage of sturdy staves, lashed together. What it confined was hazy with distance, but could have been three figures. Three prisoners held apart from the others.

That was curious.

'We wait here until nightfall,' he said, eyes still fixed on the camp. 'Then, sneak in and see if Eain is being held there. If he isn't, we return here and think again.'

'It'll be fine, Holt,' said Luara. 'They'll never even know we're there. Trust me.'

As Luara moved away to hunker down behind the boulder with Holt, movement at the gateway to this segregated enclosure caught Tann's eye. A bar was lifted and several figures passed through, heading towards the corral. Tann swore.

Among the newcomers were a few large, rotund figures clad in armour of iron plates. He recognised them as the old Tayan Kingsguard and knew of their fearsome reputation. Their presence made stealth more important. Trying to fight them would be worse than foolish.

Alongside them were two others. One was small, slight and dressed in a long, dark cloak. The hood was thrown back to reveal short, cropped hair. A woman. The other was the tallest of the group, although he moved with slouched shoulders. His headscarf and hair revealed him to be Tayan nobility, and even from this distance the rich cloth of his robes stood out.

He was a grand figure, and the Kingsguard soldiers moved around him with wary deference. Was this the war leader who had provoked Buren into mobilising their army?

As he watched, the guards opened the pen, seized one of the prisoners and hauled them out. Tann guessed they were trying to persuade the captured soldiers to swear new oaths to the rebel general.

They dragged the unfortunate out into an open space beside the corral, close to the perimeter of the camp. A pair of the Kingsguard forced them to kneel, while the robed woman and the leader stood close. They seemed to be deep in conversation.

Only then did Tann notice that what he had taken for a war mace in the Tayan leader's hand was something different. Bright metal gleamed in the late afternoon light as he raised it, and the bulging head glowed.

Tann stared. For a moment, he thought it was a trick of the light, or that the Tayan held a burning torch, but the object he carried glowed a vivid purple. There was something unearthly about the way it crackled and pulsed. Something…unnatural.

The Tayan lifted the glowing mace, then lowered it to the prisoner's chest.

They screamed.

The sound carried to where Tann was hiding, but only faintly and he hoped Luara and Holt had not heard. He could see the prisoner writhing and thrashing against the strong hands that restrained them, but it was hopeless.

Purple light coursed along the length of the shaft to engulf the victim, and after a few heartbeats their screams died away.

The Tayan lifted the mace, still flickering, and the body fell to the ground, limp. Tann had no doubt that they were dead.

'What was that scream?' asked Luara. She had not seen anything. Tann thought quickly about what to say, and settled on a half-truth.

'Looks like they were forcing new oaths out of their prisoners,' he said. 'Killing the ones that refused. That's Tayo.' He could not bring himself to describe the way they had died. How could he begin to explain it? 'More reason to get in and find Eain as soon as we can. Tonight.'

'Tonight,' agreed Luara.

Tann took a deep breath and prayed to the Five for protection. He suddenly felt like they might need it.

They made themselves comfortable in the dead bracken between the boulders and waited while the light faded. Dusk came swiftly, and the grey roof broke for long enough for the western sky to burn briefly with the sunset, as though a furnace door had swung open.

There was precious little warmth in the air, though, and Tann and Luara soon opened their packs to dig out the extra furs and blankets they had thought to bring. They shared them with Holt, who had not.

Luara wrapped herself up snugly and quickly fell asleep, head on Holt's shoulder.

'How does she do that?' chuckled Tann. 'She could always sleep anywhere.'

'Inner peace,' replied Holt.

'Eh?'

'I wondered, too. How she was always so bright, so happy, despite the life she's had. I asked her one day, and she was surprised at the question. I asked how she blocks out all the questions, all the worries, all the regrets.'

'And what did she say?'

'She doesn't have any,' said Holt, and Tann scoffed. 'Really. It's true. She explained how she'd made peace with her past. Everything she had done was for a good reason, and was the best she could have done with what she knew at the time. She only ever looks forwards, and because of that she knows exactly who she is. She has inner peace.

'Don't you wish it was that easy?'

Tann nodded, thinking of all the things he regretted, all the mistakes, everything he would go back and change if he could. What he would do for the power to silence the worries that woke him in the long, lonely nights.

'Said she'd only ever had one regret,' said Holt. 'And that was walking away from Feorhryc, when she did. And she made sure to put that one right.' Holt was smiling, and his eyes shone.

'She's a fine, strong woman,' said Tann. 'You're a lucky man, my friend.'

'And don't I know it.'

Luara awoke when it was fully dark. Tann saw the gleam of her eyes as they opened. She blinked several times, and her nostrils flared as she seemed to sniff the air. Moving a little, she noticed Holt, asleep and slumped against her.

'Come on, lazy bones,' she said, prodding him awake. 'It's dark. Time to move.'

They ghosted down the shallow slope beyond the boulders, heading for the nearest sentry who was standing, shivering, beside a low-burning brazier. Tann was confident they would not be seen. Beyond the small circle of pale light, the darkness was a thick blanket.

Luara naturally took the lead as they closed the distance.

'No killing,' Tann hissed. 'Not unless there's no choice.'

'You know me,' she whispered back. That was the problem. He did.

She broke off to the right, moving silently across the heathland. In a moment she was invisible. Tann led Holt to the left, keeping well out of the light.

'Here we go,' he said to Holt, in a low undertone, then tapped the pommel of his sword against the rim of his shield. The sentry's head swung towards the subtle, metallic sound, their spear lowering.

A heartbeat later a dark figure stole into the light, and the sentry was dragged silently to the ground.

'Come on,' said Tann. By the time they got to the brazier Luara was back on her feet, leaving the sentry sprawled across the tufty grass.

'He'll be fine,' she said, in response to Tann's unanswered question. 'Just needed a little nap.' Tann knew better than to ask anything else.

'We don't know how often they change the guard,' he whispered. 'But we might not have long until they find him. Let's see how close we can get to the prisoners, in case Eain is there.'

Creeping closer was easy. Apart from the ring of sentries, the camp was not guarded with diligence. An attack out here was unlikely.

Enough light came from the nearest braziers to show that the corral, or the jail, was full of folk sprawled out on the floor, asleep. As Tann crept closer he could see that their hands and feet were bound, even in slumber.

Luara repeated her trick with the guard on the nearest corner and dragged his limp form out into the darkness. The three of them began to move along the fence line, peering in while keeping low and out of sight of the other sentries. The whole corral was surrounded by another fence line; those high canvas walls they had seen. Tann thanked Fate. Without them they would be exposed to the rest of the camp.

He moved further around the corral, in growing consternation. He would know Eain if he caught a glimpse; the boy's size, shape and complexion were distinctive. He strained his eyes against the darkness. The guilt was hot and heavy this night.

Luara edged off right as Tann went further left. The nearest sentries were close, but he had to take the risk. He needed to be thorough. He could not go back to Cerle empty-handed without knowing he had done everything he could. And he remembered the purple flash, and the dead prisoner.

Holt was ten paces behind as Tann neared the corner of the pen. Two sentries stood there, but their backs were to him and their heads leaned close in idle conversation. His eyes scanned the pen, but he only saw Tayans.

Beyond those asleep on the bare ground, he could now see into the cages. Another prisoner slumped in each; two women and one man. Why were they being kept apart? Another mystery. Tann thought they might be Anise.

Gripped by curiosity, he wanted to get closer. If he could distract the nearest guards, it might be possible to get a better look.

And free them, said a voice in his mind. Freeing all those bound Tayans had not occurred to him once. Was he still so twisted against that country because of what had happened all those years ago.

Yes, said the voice.

Shocked at himself, his prejudice, he took a clumsy step forward. The guards did not turn, but sudden light shone down on him, like the beam of a lantern from above his head. Except it was purple.

He stared up at it.

A spectral, violet image floated above his head, and he realised, as he took a step back, that the image was of him. It moved when he moved, shining out across the camp. A beacon.

At the same moment, horns rang out from the centre of the camp. Three short blasts, repeated. It had been a long time but for reasons he wished to forget he recalled the alarm call of the Tayan military.

They were discovered.

The guards were alert now, bellowing a challenge and levelling their spears at him. He had the barest moment to think as they approached.

Surrender would make sense. The alarm was raised, and soon more soldiers would arrive. He could run, but had no idea how far that damned light above his head would follow. Above all, he remembered the fate of that prisoner earlier. He could not let Luara and Holt be taken.

'Elsia,' he said, whispering the name to the night, and his sword was in his hand almost without thought.

He took a long stride left, using his shield to guide the first spear thrust away. Following up, he stepped around and closed, the sabre lashing down in a backhanded cut. It cleaved through the layers of leather the guard wore, and the man cried out and fell back.

The point of his companion's spear came at Tann but his sabre was already turning, point downwards, catching the shaft and guiding it away. He punched out with the shield, striking his opponent a solid blow with the boss. Even as the Tayan staggered Tann launched an overhead cut that hit the man where his neck met his shoulder.

The bitter edge cleaved flesh, and the men fell without a sound.

Tann stood for a moment, chest heaving and the point of the sabre dancing as his hands started to shake.

'I never wanted to fight,' he muttered to himself. 'I'm not a killer.' The bloody evidence at his feet said otherwise, and it had been so easy. So natural.

He was abruptly aware of Holt arriving beside him as the horns continued to blare their summons. It was their doom. Holt's eyes were wide and wild.

'Let's go!' he urged. 'Let's run!'

Tann shook his head, pointing up. 'You take Luara and go. If I come with you we'll all be caught. And we can't risk leading them to Cerle and Indaella.'

'I'm not leaving you here.'

Tann knew what he must do. He had to lie.

'Go now, Holt. Please. I need you to tell Indaella about this.' He pointed up once more. 'It might mean something to her. I'll distract them for a time so you and Luara can get away, then I'll surrender. I'll be safe with the other prisoners. We'll meet again when this is over.'

Holt hesitated. The sound of running feet in heavy boots was getting closer.

'Go!' bellowed Tann. 'Go now, or I'll kill you myself.' He took a step toward the younger man, and Holt bolted towards Luara. Good. This was the way it had to be.

Turning, he saw what approached and fear gripped his guts like an armoured fist. A rank of bulky Kingsguard in full armour had come through a gateway and were running at him. With a wry chuckle at the absurdity of it all, he raised his shield and charged.

FORTY SIX

The urgent sound of horns blasting out an alarm yanked Eain from an uneasy sleep. His eyes snapped open as voices shouting and the sound of running feet joined the cacophony.

'Get tha boots on, youth,' said Klay. The dwarf was fully dressed and armoured, already stamping into his own heavy, iron-clad boots.

Eain copied, tugging his leather hauberk over his woollens, wincing as it pulled the cut in his side, before slinging his coat over the top to keep out the chill of the night. If Klay thought they might need to fight, Eain would be ready. The dwarf's instincts were nearly always right.

Eain seized his sword and followed Klay from the tent. Soldiers dashed past; lightly armed mercenaries as well as lumbering Gluttons in full armour.

'There's a raid!' yelled some of the soldiers as they passed. 'Prisoners have tried to escape,' called others. The Gluttons said nothing, impassive beneath their heavy helms.

'Steel Hounds!' cried Klay, as the company began to gather. 'No rushin' off. I don't hear fighting, so mebbes it's all over. Mebbes it's not even started. We stand here, for now, and wait for orders.'

'The prisoners,' said Eain. 'The new prisoners…'

'Aye, youth,' said Klay. 'I thought about them too. Bit of a coincidence.'

Eain had been even more troubled than usual since the previous afternoon. The mysterious emissary from Buren had brought three hostages, who Eain thought would be political prisoners, or the children of nobles.

So when he had seen who was being passed across for him to guard, his mouth had dropped open.

'You!' she had said, eyes blazing with shock and hatred. Months had passed since they had last looked into each other's eyes, necessity forcing them to go in brief trust, and yet Eain had not forgotten her face.

Her long dark hair was tied up and mostly hidden beneath a fabric cap, and she was dressed differently, but those dark eyes that burned with fierce purpose were the same as those he had stared into in Ben Gedrin.

'I knew we should never have trusted you,' she spat, as Eain seized her arm and began walking her up the track towards the camp.

'You were about to be killed,' said Eain, but quietly. He did not want to reveal their shared history. Her animosity was surprising, though.

'So you robbed us instead,' she said. 'How kind you are. You must have lined your wrists with silver after you sold my jewel.'

'Keep those prisoners quiet,' ordered Klay, and Eain was left to silently wonder what the woman could mean. He spoke true, she would have been murdered by the gangs of Ben Gedrin if she had persisted in trying to sell that jewel. He had done the right thing. But now she thought he had robbed them?

He noticed that the woman's companion from that warehouse in Ben Gedrin was also one of the hostages. She was shorter, and with a darker complexion but fairer hair. She allowed herself to be guided along without a word.

Eain did not recognise the third, a slender young man with dark hair. He walked along with his head bowed, defeated.

Enemy soldiers had been forced to surrender after each battle. Most were willing to immediately swear a new oath to Teleri and became part of his army, but some refused. These few were held as prisoners in the hope they would change their mind.

'We'll hold 'em here, starve 'em out a bit,' Klay had said, in explanation. 'They'll all swear in the end.'

'What would that oath be worth?' Eain had asked, thinking back on everything he had learned of Tayo, that betrayal was part of everyday life. Klay just shrugged.

Now, the dwarf directed Eain and a handful of other soldiers as they guided the three new hostages towards this enclosure. It lay at the northern extent of the camp, screened off by high canvas walls and guarded.

Eain was surprised to see that in addition to the main fenced enclosure, three cages had been built from straight wooden staves. They forced the prisoners inside, one to each cage, and secured the doors by tying the staves together and knotting them so that the captives would not be able to reach the knots, bound as they were.

They stayed silent, but the taller woman stared balefully at Eain throughout.

That had been last night, and the surprise of her arrival and intensity of her apparent hatred had troubled Eain since.

Now there was a disturbance in that direction, and all he could do was wait and wonder. As Klay had said, there were no sounds of fighting. There was, though, a strange purple glow over the area, but Eain could not make out the source.

The coincidence was unsettling.

Aside from that glow, the night was deep. The stars were shrouded and only a vague, watery light through the clouds hinted at the direction of the moons, both waxing towards the full. Beyond the braziers the darkness was inky.

'Can we go back to sleep yet?' moaned Ivhar.

Klay ignored him, and Eain continued to wait impatiently.

Voices came from the left, up the slight hill leading to the prisoners' enclosure. Eain stared into the gloom. Then a fist of Gluttons appeared, firelight dancing in reflection on their armour. They were marching purposefully towards the centre of the camp, and Eain could see that they were dragging something.

'Problem appears solved,' said Klay as they passed. Two of the Gluttons bore an unarmoured man between them, arms clamped to his sides as they forced him along. His feet dragged limply but the strength of the warriors on each side held him up.

There was blood on his face and his head dangled. For a moment, Eain thought he might be dead, or just beaten into insensibility, but as the group went past he lifted his head, enough to give a brief glimpse of his face.

A terrible, freezing sensation gripped Eain's very bones, and spread out to immerse his whole body in a horrified chill.

The man they carried was Carilton Tann.

Eain could do no more than stare as Tann was dragged away. Questions about why he was here, what he was doing, and where he was being taken darted through his mind. Questions with no answers.

'I know that man,' he murmured, then looked down toward Klay. The dwarf's face was equally confused.

'Aye,' he whispered. 'So do I.'

There was no time to discuss this revelation, as another horn brayed from the centre of the camp. This time it blew Teleri's call. It was a summons. The camp was soon alive with movement as the soldiers already risen moved towards Teleri's tent, and those still in their own tents began to emerge.

Voices whispered and eyes were wide with curiosity and surprise.

Eain followed the shifting crowds, bewildered but trying to keep close to the short, solid figure of Klay. He was still shocked at the appearance of Carilton Tann, the man who had taken him in after his flight from Banahgar and set him on this path. A man he would call a friend.

Teleri's tent rose above the others around it, tall and pale. The canvas seemed to glow in the light of several braziers and a bonfire which crackled in the open space before the doors. By the time Eain and Klay arrived, Teleri had emerged. The cloaked Bureno emissary was beside him, and now that her hood was thrown back Eain could see she was a woman. Her hair was short and cropped, and although her features were delicate there was a hardness to her face.

The High Offerad stood Teleri's other side, and her face looked open and friendly in contrast.

A ring of Gluttons, standing shoulder to shoulder, had formed to hold the rest of the soldiers at a distance. The onlookers were forced to peer over shoulders and around the curving armour plates for a view.

Close by, two looming Gluttons held the sorry figure of Carilton Tann. One of his legs was twisted up uncomfortably as though it could not bear weight, and his face was bloodied and bruised. His eyes, though, were sharp. They were full of fear.

'Men. Women. Brothers and sisters,' said Teleri in a loud, grandiose voice. 'Our camp was assailed this night. The Taosach fears us, fears our strength, and sent this man as a spy!'

As he pointed towards Tann with his mace, Eain realised that it was not a mace. Teleri was holding something Eain had never seen before.

It was the same shape as a war-club, with a dull metal shaft the length of a man's arm. But it was ornate and highly decorated, and where the solid head of a mace would be was an object that glowed an unearthly purple.

He looked closer. The object was fist-sized, glassy, and cut with many shining facets. A jewel. Recognition came with a lurch. It was the jewel he had given to Teleri.

How it had changed colour and why Teleri had mounted it so were more questions that he could not answer. The presence of it caused a hollow dread to grow, though.

'This fool has chosen the wrong camp, and the wrong day,' continued Teleri. The light emanating from the jewel seemed to pulse in time with his words. 'Our enemies do not know our strength. Cannot understand how our power grows. But they will.'

He raised the short staff and the jewel blazed. A violet starburst, shining out into the night sky.

'This is the Demon's Sceptre! From this time it will be the totem of our campaign. It will be a symbol, a shield and a weapon. While I lead you on with the Sceptre in my hand, none will be able to oppose us. And, tonight, the world will find out what they are up against.'

'What's he going to do?' Eain hissed down to Klay. 'That's my friend. What's going to happen to him?'

'Dunno youth,' replied Klay. 'Nowt good. Nowt we can do to stop it, either.'

The Gluttons to either side of Tann took a step apart, gripping his arms tightly. He hung between them, helplessly spreadeagled. As Teleri moved forwards there was something unmistakably threatening about the way he brandished the sceptre, as though he was preparing to strike.

Eain could not bear it. The growing feeling of desperate worry felt like a cold pit opening in his guts. He had to do something, had to help.

Struggling to move forwards through the crowd, he managed a few steps before he came up against the solid wall of the Gluttons. He shoved with all his strength but they did not move an inch. They did not even react.

'Stop, youth!' urged Klay, still just a step behind.

'The world will remember this night!' cried Daeron Teleri.

'Please, no—' came the weak protest of Carilton Tann.

Teleri struck.

As though thrusting with a short spear, he lunged forward. As the violet head of the sceptre struck Tann in the chest it shone brightly, purple light lancing out over the stunned crowd and shooting up to touch the base of the clouds.

Tann screamed. It was a sound of someone in unspeakable, helpless agony. A glow began at the centre of his chest, where the jewel touched, before coruscating over his whole body.

The Gluttons holding him jumped back in surprise, releasing their grip. Tann stood still for a moment, arms outstretched and body stiff, before Teleri drew back the sceptre.

A flicker moved down the shaft, and vanished.

Eain looked at Tann in desperation, scanning his face for life, his body for movement. But, the light faded as Teleri stepped away, and Tann's eyes went black. A moment later he toppled forwards to thump onto the cold ground.

Eain sobbed as he tried to understand make sense of what he had just seen; a fact he was desperate to deny.

Carilton Tann was dead.

FORTY SEVEN

Eain's mind lurched away from his body. A dark pit opened around him and he plunged down, and down.

Every step he had taken, every decision he had made had brought him to this point, and every single one had been a mistake. Carilton Tann was dead at the hands of Daeron Teleri, and it was all his fault.

He had known that the jewel was dangerous. It radiated power, seductive power, but Morgan Blane was right. He should never have listened to its voice.

The crowd was still watching in stunned silence while Teleri talked, but Eain could not make himself listen to the words. They were the buzzing of a wasp full of the glory of its sting.

He pushed away, turning his face from the limp, slumped form of Carilton Tann. Guilt and horror drove him, filled him with new purpose. He knew what he had to do. As he moved away, Klay clutched at his wrist.

'Stay, youth,' he hissed, in an urgent undertone. 'Don't draw attention to thaself.'

Eain shook off the dwarf's grip and strode away without a word.

The camp was almost deserted, most having answered Teleri's summons even though it was the middle of the night. They would be heading back to their blankets soon, but for now Eain had a little time.

At his tent, he collected his pack and rolled his blanket up neatly. The churning waves of grief and disgust he felt did not reach his hands.

Lastly he slung his sword belt around his body before drawing the blade. He knew he would need it.

The night was still deep and the mumble of voices continued from behind him as he began to march up the hill. It was not as cold as it had been but the air remained chill, Eain's breath steaming as he walked.

Amid the horror, he felt a sudden clarity. He had been in such doubt about his actions and his purpose for months, but now he knew exactly what to do.

A pair of guards stood at the gateway of the enclosure, facing out towards the camp with the screens at their backs. They would not stop him.

'Been told to fetch a prisoner,' he said as an explanation, and they nodded him through. They ignored the naked sword in his hands.

The six guards around the prisoner's pen barely turned their heads as Eain entered, concentrating on watching those in the prisoner's pen. The captives were awake and Eain could hear the buzz of conversation. He steeled himself for what he needed to do next, reminding himself that the guards had all sworn allegiance to a cold-blooded murderer.

Like you, hissed a voice in his mind.

He gripped his sword.

'Put down your weapons,' he said, trying to keep the fear from his voice. 'Put down all your weapons and go over there,' he gestured to a corner with the point of his sword, 'and no one needs to be hurt.'

The closest guard stepped forward. 'Our orders are to guard the prisoners. How can we do that if we're unarmed?'

'I'm giving new orders,' said Eain. 'These people are to be prisoners no longer. Now, put your weapons down. Or I will make you.'

That got their attention. The closest man stared for a moment, then began to advance, spear levelled.

'You are the one who should be throwing down your weapon,' he said. The spear's tip aimed unwaveringly at Eain's chest. 'You shouldn't even be here. Teleri will hear of this.'

'No,' said Eain. 'He won't. I'm sorry.'

He rushed forward, sweeping the spear away with his blade, and a swift strike with the conical pommel caught the spearman by surprise. It rang off their helmet and they staggered and fell. It had left a visible dent. Eain doubted they would rise again in a hurry.

Now, though, the other guards were aware of him, and began to rush around towards the fray. Five against one were not good odds, but for the moment they were still spread out around the enclosure.

Eain dashed to meet the first attacker. The point of their spear danced as they rushed in, and he evaded it with a step to the side. The sword swung, but Eain turned his wrists to hit the man with the flat of the blade rather than the lethal edge. It thudded into his middle, doubling him over with an explosive outrush of air.

Another pommel strike to the back of his neck dropped him to lie face down on the ground.

A spear thrust at him immediately and even as he parried it away, sword held vertically, he noticed another guard approaching from the opposite direction. Time was running out.

Keeping the spear haft bound against his blade, he stepped forwards and ducked, guiding the point of the weapon over his head. Suddenly wrong-handed and off balance, the spearman was defenceless as the point of Eain's sword licked out to cut a gash across his chest.

Blood welled in the wound, and he fell back with a cry. Eain hoped it would not be fatal.

Without looking, he let the sweep of the blade continue behind his head and felt the sturdy contact between weapons as he turned an attempted thrust toward his back away. He swivelled, arms tense as he forced the weapon upwards.

Catching a fleeting glimpse of the man's desperate face as he stepped inside his guard, Eain let his sword flow naturally into a brutal pommel strike to his jaw. Bones broke beneath the solid mass of metal. The spearman fell, hands rising to clutch his face.

Two guards remained standing, one approaching from each direction. They advanced warily, having just seen four of their comrades fall in quick succession.

'Put down your spears,' said Eain again. 'I don't want to hurt you.'

'We can't do that,' said one of the guards. They would rush him, he knew. They had seen what he could do, but he could not defend against two spears at once.

He rose onto the balls of his feet, and a heartbeat later had broken into a full run towards one of the spearmen. He saw his hands tightening on the spear's haft. Over tightening. Panic stiffened his body.

The resulting clumsy thrust missed Eain as he charged in, and instead of swinging the sword Eain dropped his shoulder and body-charged the man. The Tayan gave away at least six inches in height and was much less bulky. The impact knocked him off his feet to sprawl onto the mud.

Stay down, thought Eain. He turned to the last guard. The others lay scattered around, some groaning, some silent. A tense moment passed, and then the guard threw down his spear and ran.

Eain closed his eyes. Part of him was grateful he had not needed to hurt the last man, but soon he would have a new problem. He needed to work fast, before the alarm was raised.

Hurrying over to the spearman he had body-checked, he placed a foot on the man's heaving chest.

'Stay down and live,' he said, and meant it. Now he had stopped moving, the pain in his side was a burning brand. He would need to avoid any more fighting.

Bending down, Eain took the man's stubby belt knife and turned away, opening the gate into the prisoner's enclosure. He bent behind the back of the first prisoner, a huge man with a shaven head and a bloated, jowly face. The soft flesh of the Glutton's thick wrists bulged around the thin cords of his bonds, his huge body folded awkwardly on the floor.

Eain cut the cords deftly and passed the knife to the big man, who looked around in surprise.

'Free everyone and run,' said Eain. 'You'll be dead if you're caught.'

The Glutton nodded his compliance and went to work. Eain drew his seax, his long fighting knife, and moved over to the cages.

'Get the hell away from me,' said the taller, dark-haired woman, standing at his approach. Her words were fierce, but her eyes were frightened.

Eain ignored her as he cut the cage open then reached inside. He twisted her around and slashed the cords binding her wrists with his keen edge.

'Ouch,' she said as she followed him out, rubbing her wrists.

Moments later all three were free from their confines and their bindings. They stared at him with puzzled expressions, but he had no time to explain.

'You need to get away from here, now,' he said. 'If you get caught again they will kill you. Don't ask me why because I don't know.'

He went to move away.

'Wait,' came the man's voice. As Eain turned back he realised just how young he was; a few years younger than himself with smooth cheeks and wide eyes. 'Where can we go? We don't know where we are, and have nothing with us.'

'That's not my problem,' replied Eain, in a harsh tone. 'Just go. I told myself I'd set you free and I've done that. I can't do anything else for you.'

'Are we supposed to run off into the dark?' snapped the taller woman, in a sarcastic tone that was becoming familiar. 'Fall off a cliff or just get captured again? Is that what you want?'

'I don't care!' stormed Eain. He was impatient and his anxiety was growing. The alarm would be raised again any moment, and the chase would begin.

The shorter of the two women moved closer. Eain could not help noticing that she seemed to be looking at a point several inches beyond his right ear.

'But,' she said. 'I think you do care. You've put yourself at risk to free us. You didn't need to. You must have had a reason for that. Why go to that trouble, if you're just going to leave us to be caught again?'

The moment stretched. The truth in her words were like a slap in the face. Eain was silent as he considered what to do next.

Ellyah rubbed her wrists to try to bring some life back into her prickling hands. All her senses were screaming at her, alarm bells ringing in her mind that urged her to run. To hide. She was in danger.

Those inner warnings had been noisy recently. When was she *not* in danger? If she was going to flee, just to be caught again, she might as well save herself the effort and just sit down on the ground right here and wait. But, however much she despaired and her instincts wailed, she was not ready to give up yet.

The pain from her middle might make a dash away impossible though, or at least slow and awkward.

She was furious to be in this situation. All her hopes and dreams were gone as though burned to ash. The jewel, her fortune, her escape from this life and even the affection of Savfa, past and present, had all been torn away from her and her hands were empty.

And it was all this young man's fault. He had robbed them in Ben Gedrin, and led them into this peril, and…

And what? Said a calm, rational voice in her mind. It sounded like Nastja's voice. Annoyingly, it always did. *He doesn't seem to have gained anything. He's not rich. He's not living in comfort.*

Ellyah pressed her lips together, willing that coldly sensible voice to stop. It went on.

And now he's put himself in more danger to rescue us, when he could have easily fled and left us to our fate. What if he was never to blame? What if he rescued us the first time, and he's doing it again, and he's as much a victim as we are?

If that were true, that left only one person to blame for this mess.

Herself.

She had led Nastja across the lands in pursuit of impossible riches; she had trusted Savfa when he was no better than a rat. It had all been her. She prided herself on always having a plan, always knowing the escape route. Savfa and her own greed had combined to dull her senses, and she had walked into trouble with no way out.

But maybe, however much it hurt her to admit the fault, even to herself, there was a way to make amends. A different way out.

'Please,' she said, and the words stung her throat as though they were formed of thorns. 'I've made some mistakes and got some things…wrong.' She swallowed. 'We won't be able to escape on our own. We need help. Will you help us?'

She forced herself to meet his eyes, those steel-grey pools that revealed nothing.

'Please.'

He blinked under her stare, and his lips parted to speak. Before he could say anything, though, the blare of horns rang out across the camp.

Three blasts, loud and urgent, repeated again, and again.

'That's the alarm,' said the tall swordsman. 'They are coming. We must go.'

He dashed towards the entrance of the enclosure, and she followed. Ellyah assumed Nastja and the dark-haired Anise boy would do the same.

The other prisoners were still busy cutting one another loose, and they began to stream away as well, dashing in every direction to vanish into the darkness beyond the camp. Ellyah's ribs stabbed her with pain every time she took a step, every time she breathed, but she had no intention of revealing her weakness. She did not need pity, even if she had been forced to ask for help.

As they reached the corner of the enclosure, Ellyah almost collided with the broad back of the tall warrior. He had raised his blade and was staring at the gateway, the entryway between those tall canvas walls.

Ellyah had guessed that the screens were to prevent the prisoners observing the goings on of the camp. Keep them isolated and they might be more inclined to surrender and bend the knee. A single gateway led out to the camp, and that was where their rescuer was staring.

Marching through the gateway was a rank of armoured warriors. Iron plates shone in the pulsing light of the braziers as they advanced. Each looked twice Ellyah's size; tall, broad and armed with brutal maces and heavy shields.

They were moving quickly, cutting off any chance of escape.

Once more, they were trapped.

FORTY EIGHT

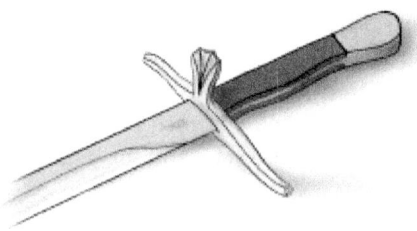

Styoyan stared at the oncoming warriors with a mix of terror and awe. Who were these huge soldiers? They looked more like statues brought to life than mere men.

The sandy-haired warrior, the one who had cut them free from the cages, raised his sword and took a step forward.

'Run, now,' he said. 'I can hold them back while you escape.'

Styoyan peered out into the darkness beyond the camp. He had no idea about the land that lay beyond apart from what he had seen as he was marched through the camp. Bare, rolling slopes of scrubby heather and bristling gorse had surrounded low grey crags. Nowhere to hide for miles.

If they just ran, with no supplies, no weapons and no guide, they would be found before dawn. Ellyah was right.

Yet, this man was prepared to at least give them a chance. Styoyan was struck by the heroism. This was noble glory worthy of Steyfan Jukeev himself. Styoyan clutched at his hip, wishing his sabre was there. If he had the blade he would stand at this man's side.

The oncoming wave of advancing warriors spread out. The swordsman raised his blade into a high stance, the point moving in controlled arcs as he pivoted on the balls of his feet. Always in balance, he was ready to strike at the first attacker.

The sword itself was unusual, oversized for a longsword with a blade three fingers wide at the ricasso and a hilt that he held with two hands but was long enough for three or four. A strike from such a long, heavy blade would cleave armour and flesh with ease.

'Go,' he repeated. 'Now!'

He had an unusual accent and Styoyan wondered if he was a northerner, maybe from the Riverlands.

'We should go,' said Nastja, backing away.

'We need him!' argued Ellyah.

Styoyan could tell from the change in posture of the advancing warriors, the way they gripped and hefted those murderous maces, that they were about to strike. He had to do something, had to be brave. He took a step forwards.

Then their heads were turning in confusion, looking back in the direction from which they had come. The high canvas walls that bounded the enclosure were tilting, leaning inwards. Then, they fell. The heavy boots of the massed soldiers moved desperately, but they were too slow.

The walls on both sides of the gateway toppled onto them, collapsing inwards to cover the whole group with the thick, heavy canvas. It trapped them as though they were netted. As they struggled, a short, broad figure came barrelling over the top.

'Klay!' cried the swordsman.

'Aye,' replied the dwarf, slowing to a stop. "Ad a feeling yer might be off't do summat daft.' His accent was thick, his speech difficult to understand. 'Ah guess this butter knife is yours,' he added, casting a long, slender object in Styoyan's direction.

He caught it, realising with delight that it was indeed his own sabre. With it in his hand he felt immediately safer, and empowered to play his part.

A hand in a heavy gauntlet inched from the edge of the fallen canvas, near their feet, followed by a head in a gleaming iron helmet. These huge, strong warriors would not be held down for long.

Without looking, the dwarf trod on the hand, the bones crunching beneath his boot. At the same time, he whirled the evil-looking polearm he carried and swung it down. The haft was as long as the dwarf was tall, and the head moved in a blur to strike the helmet, leaving a sizeable dent. The struggling figure lay still.

'Now,' he said. 'Let's put this mess at our backs.' He turned and started out in the direction of the darkness.

Ellyah had not moved. 'Where? Where are we going to go that will be safe?'

The dwarf paused. 'Ah were born in Tayo, miss. Ah know mah way round. Follow, or stay. Makes no nevermind to me. But I'm getting out of here.' He turned away.

The tall swordsman followed, hurrying to catch up with the dwarf, and Nastja trailed. Styoyan started after them, looking back at Ellyah.

'We don't have much choice but to trust them,' he said, meaning the dwarf and the swordsman. Ellyah rolled her eyes and made a disgusted noise in her throat before she also moved to follow.

The five strode out from the camp, which was alive with noise. The horns continued to blare, while furious voices roared in every direction. Klay's eyes were hard as they stared out into the enveloping darkness while the warrior glanced back often.

'I think we need to run,' he said, after a few moments. Styoyan looked back to see those huge, armoured soldiers breaking free from their canvas trap, and beginning to give chase across the rough heathland.

'Aye,' replied the dwarf. 'Let's 'ave us a little jog.' He broke into a run and Styoyan followed as closely as he could. Nastja ran beside him, with the tall swordsman just behind.

A grunt of discomfort made him turn. Ellyah was lagging, following them in a shuffling half-run. One hand was clamped to her side. The tall warrior had also paused, staring at her as she laboured awkwardly to catch them.

'I am sorry,' he said as she drew level with him, before bending and picking her up.

'Let go of me!' she cried, shock and annoyance filling her tone.

He ignored her and broke into a run, carrying her as he went. It was an impressive display of strength. His teeth were bared with the effort as he passed.

'Put me down right now!' Ellyah urged.

'Let me know if you need me to take a turn,' said Styoyan. The only response was a flat stare.

'Just run,' panted the warrior.

They ran.

'You're a bloody fool. You're a bloody fool.'

Klay cursed himself over and over as he ran. He had no reason to get involved in this idiocy. None. His oath was to Daeron Teleri and the sensible thing would have been to do nothing and watch Eain and these three idiots get captured again, even after witnessing the death of Carilton Tann.

Yet here he was.

A bloody fool, up to his bloody neck in foolish business.

It was the boy. That was the problem. The plight of that sad, lost soul trapped in the body of a killer had stirred something in him. Pity, empathy, care…all emotions the mercenary life gave no time for.

Klay could not help but recall his own younger days, remembering too well the steps that had led to him grasping the Capper and marching out to find a meaningful death. He knew what it was like to lose everything, including hope of forgiveness or redemption.

Even these thoughts were foolish; he could not save himself by saving the boy.

On he ran.

His vision was still good in darkness and he had no trouble finding a route through the patchy, ankle-deep heather and waist-deep ferns, so it took him a few moments to realise that the ground ahead was brighter. A vivid purple light was shining over the hillside, strong enough that he could see his own shadow.

He looked up.

'What the bloody hell is that?'

Nastja ran along happily, following the dwarf. Her legs were tired and her breath burned in her throat, but her mind was strangely calm.

Her time tied up in the cage had been a shivering nightmare of anxiety. They would be hurt. They might be killed. Ellyah might suffer, and she would be angry with Nastja for reasons that she would be unable to anticipate.

Events had moved away from her control, and she could see no way out.

That had changed the moment that tall warrior had cut them free. Every detail of him and his actions had been so vivid. His eyes were wide, darting and uncertain even while he was helping them to escape. His hands trembled.

The man was terrified, but the way he had moved to defend them with that great sword made her think it was not the immediate danger that scared him. It was something else. Something deeper.

He had seen something that he did not understand, something that his mind was struggling to accept. This young man was an interesting new puzzle.

She watched as he picked Ellyah up and carried her when he realised she was struggling to run. She shouted angrily at him, but he acted like he could not hear her. He must be desperate to escape this place.

The hair on the back of her neck suddenly rose. The sensation of *something* rising and brushing past her was enough to stop her in her tracks. It felt like a gust of wind, heavy with the promise of pending rain.

As it passed, the scrubby ground around her was lit with a ghostly purple glow. She looked up.

The impossible hung in the sky above them.

Four shapes were defined by twinkling clouds of sparks, the insides shifting like motes of dust caught in a sunbeam, but the outlines remaining solid.

Nastja knew immediately what they were. One was broad and squat. One was slender, and the other was a bulky shape that she knew to be two people, one carrying the other. The last was the exact size and shape of her body.

A reflection of her, that moved when she moved, cast into the sky above her head like a beacon fire.

Nastja had an open mind and was not reluctant to believe magic when she saw it. Any other explanation was so unlikely to be impossible.

'Keep movin!' bellowed the dwarf, breaking into a run once more. Nastja paused before following, gazing up at those shimmering violet figures.

Three were moving, galloping across the sky in time with the running figures below. Following, casting an unavoidable signal for their pursuers that they would not be able to outrun or evade.

A wave of panic washed over her. After all this, they were once again helpless against the relentless march of fate. She despaired, and opened her mouth to call to the others, to tell them to stop running.

What was the point?

However much she wished she could reach up and dispel those floating images, waft them away like a cloud of flies, they were untouchable. She was so focused on this idea, that of being able to wave those purple figures away, that she actually stretched out her hand as though to try.

The nearest figure to her, the one that resembled the soldier carrying Ellyah, flickered. Nastja blinked. A fan waved vigorously at a gout of steam might have had the same effect.

She stared at it, considering, understanding. Then she concentrated.

Picturing her hand as a fan, willing it to extend beyond her fingers into the cloudy sky, she raised her arm. *Something* filled her as though it were a cold chill rising from the ground beneath her feet. Her whole being buzzed with the sensation.

Forcing her will through her extended arm, she waved her hand through the air. Joy filled her, incomprehensible joy, as that lumpy purple cloud broke up and dispersed. All that remained was an indistinct cloud, like fleeing fireflies.

Before she had a chance to wonder about how, or why, before any doubt had a chance to grow, she turned to the other two images and repeated the trick. The same sensation filled her, of power rising, of a chill passing through her and projecting out as directed by her intention, and they blew apart. Dust in the breeze.

Lastly she turned her eyes directly upward, and directed her will towards the violet-tinted image of herself. Heartbeats later, it too had gone. The landscape was plunged into darkness once more.

'They've gone!' came Ellyah's excited voice. 'Whatever they were, they've gone!'

'Yes,' replied Nastja, as she hurried to catch up. 'They've gone.' Her insides thrilled with the thought of impressing Ellyah, but now was not the time to talk about it.

'They are still chasing us though,' cried Styoyan, looking back over his shoulder and pointing in the direction of the now distant camp.

The pursuit was flooding out across the dark moorland. More of those massive warriors were coming straight towards them, although the appearance and sudden disappearance of the purple illuminations had made them pause for a moment.

They had a head start now, but it would not last long.

'Do we make a stand?' The tall warrior was looking to the dwarf for a decision.

'Give 'em a choice as to kill us now, or kill us later, yer mean?' he snapped back.

'I mean, give these three a chance to get away.'

'Wait,' said Nastja. 'Look.'

They looked.

The pursuit had been closing in, spreading out in a line across the hillside as they strode across the heath. Then, abruptly, they were not there.

From one moment to the next, Nastja felt the sensation of a curtain being drawn across her vision, across her entire consciousness. All the pursuers, as well as the frantic sounds emanating from the camp, had gone as if they had never existed.

'What…' managed Styoyan. 'How?'

'I don't know,' said Nastja, but she wondered. Had she done it, somehow, the same way she had dispelled the hovering images?

She did not think so. Although she had felt something, the sensation had not come from her body. Even as this thought occurred, a heaviness began in her limbs and a wave of fatigue washed over her. She staggered.

'Let's not hang around until they come back,' said the dwarf, and turned away once more.

She took a few steps sideways, on the verge of collapse, but Styoyan was suddenly there and hoisted her up, carrying her like the other warrior carried Ellyah. She glanced back once as she drifted off, baffled and intrigued by the empty scene. There were no answers in the darkness, and her head lolled as Styoyan followed the others away.

A few moments later, they were lost into the night.

She lay on the ground, spent. The last of her fading strength had been used to cast that spell, and it was possible that her life force would now fail.

The short twigs of heather that hugged the ground prickled the skin of the form she had been using, and while the physical presence, only ever an illusion, began to fade away, the life that flowed in even these meagre plants provided a little sustenance.

The concept of self that formed her true name, the complex mix of emotions and experiences that combined to make her, wished to live on. But if she perished here then her fleeting consciousness would become part of the eternal earth.

It was a small comfort, but she would rather endure. Her work was not complete. And she wished to see her mother again.

She might regain her strength, in time, and return to the wild woods to report on what she had done, what she had learned, and what hope she had helped to survive.

Turning her gaze towards the five figures vanishing from sight over the brow of the nearest hillside, she felt a surge of satisfaction. Her task had only been to guide and protect one of them, but she could see that the five had power together; it was a strange symmetry.

Five was portentous. Five was powerful. Perhaps, this was the work of Fate.

Her vision faded and her consciousness was lost with that last thought.

Five were together. It was up to them, now.

EPILOGUE

Holt Cookson knew he could not go much further this night. Luara's quivering frame was a solid weight on his arm, and she leaned heavily on him as he pushed on, keeping them moving northwards.

'No!' she had shouted at him as they stood on the hillside overlooking the camp. 'We have to see what happens.'

'It's too dangerous,' he had urged. 'Tann did what he did so we could escape.'

'I'm not moving another pace,' she stated. 'If you want to go, then go. I don't care.'

She did not mean it, but he had stayed with her. He wrapped an arm around her shoulders as they watched their friend Carilton Tann being overpowered by the onrushing Gluttons, and dragged away.

Leaning in close, she had pressed a hand to her mouth as they saw him being held up before the massed ranks of the Tayan rebel army. He had drawn her into the firmest embrace, dragging her back to prevent her from running down the hill, as the Tayan general struck with that glowing mace.

They had both known immediately that Tann was dead.

His body had fallen, limp and lifeless, in a way that left no doubt. Carilton Tann had given his life to save theirs.

Luara's anguished weeping had cut into Holt's soul as though it were a serrated blade against his flesh. There was nothing he could do to ease her pain, nothing he could do to make it better.

The only thing he could do was to keep her safe.

So, he had dragged her away. Yard by yard, step by step, he had forced her to retrace their steps.

'Why?' she sobbed, over and over. 'Why, Holt?'

He had no answer.

They were safer as they travelled further from the camp, but the knowledge that they were leaving the body of their friend behind dragged at Holt with every step. It seemed unreal.

Cerle came to meet them, looming out of the darkness. One look at each other's faces was all it took for them to understand how bad things were; Tann was gone and Indaella was still incapacitated.

Their quest had ended in death and disaster.

'The camp was crawling like an anthill,' said Holt. 'They knew something was up. Hunters were going everywhere. We're not safe here.'

'Eain?' asked Cerle.

'I never saw him,' replied Holt. 'We can't stay though, or risk going back. We'd be caught and…' he tailed off.

Cerle nodded, his eyes darting to where his wife lay. He would never risk her safety.

'I think we should head back to the Riverlands,' he said. 'Indaella can recover while we keep our ears open for rumours. Maybe we'll get another chance to find Eain.'

Holt nodded. He just wanted to take Luara far away from this place.

They had reached the road once more, Cerle driving the wagon while Luara sat in the back with Luara, when they heard hoofbeats approaching from the south.

'What now?' said Cerle, reaching for his greatsword.

Holt's hand went to his own sword as a shape overtook them. It melted from the darkness as a rider, mounted on a very fine black stallion.

'Peace, friends. Peace,' said the rider, lowering their hood and raising their hands.

It was a man with a heavy-browed face and distinctive ears, like the handles of a jug.

'If you've got any sense, you'll keep heading away from all that.' He gestured back over his shoulder towards where Holt and Luara had come from. 'I'm getting as far away as possible.'

His voice was strange, his words slurred and nasal although he spoke in the accent of Anish.

'I know these lands well,' he went on, 'and I'd be happy to guide you and guard you, if you'll let me travel with you.'

Cerle and Holt looked at one another.

'You want to get far away from here, trust me,' he finished. 'I've seen what's going on down south, and I can tell you that it stinks,' said Skane.

Morgan Blane stood beneath the spiny branches of an ancient yew, barely daring to move and trying not to breathe.

The shouts and cries of the hunters were getting closer. Kotevari soldiers strode through the night in small groups, spears at the ready. Hunting for him.

He had made a mistake.

Creeping into the camp had been easy. The velvet darkness of the winter's night and the fresh snow on the ground had let him pass silently through the scrubby thickets near the campfires.

He was little more than a shadow.

Strike hard, strike fast, then ghost away faster than they could follow. Make them fear the night, the snow, the very land in which they stood as usurpers and invaders.

That had been his plan.

He should have been more alert, more suspicious. The dark gap where they had placed the sentries too far apart was deliberate. The inattentiveness of the watchmen in the outer ring was designed to lure him in.

It was a trap.

He had flowed into the camp, seax in his hand like a wolf's tooth ready to bite. His target was the command tent, and no eyes should have marked him as he slipped between the tents. Morgan Blane was not afraid, or even excited. His heart beat a slow, steady cadence and his body was tranquil. It was impossible to move silently and act decisively otherwise.

Then the alarm bell began to ring. Soldiers, already armed and armoured, began to pour from the nearby tents. They had been waiting for him.

He felt his pulse quicken, his eyes widening in surprise. Knowing he could not afford to either panic or hesitate, he turned on his heel and broke into a sprint, returning in the direction from which he had come.

Escape had become the only option.

The Kotevari peasants were forming a line as he dashed toward them. They tried to bring their spears to bear, but he was too fast, palming a couple of points away and barging between them. His speed and greater bulk knocked them back and he ran on before they could recover.

He had thought to escape into the night, but he could hear voices calling in all directions beyond the camp. A net had been spread to catch him. He had been foolish.

Diving into the sparse shelter of the trees, he caught his breath and decided what to do next.

If he ran headlong he risked stumbling into a group of Kotevari hunters. He could overpower three or four of them at once but they would be in groups greater than that, and the sounds of fighting would draw more. Even if he avoided them, his tracks would be clear for even such as these to follow.

He should do what they would not expect, and return to the camp. The surprise might give him the time he needed to reach the command tent and kill their leader.

Of course, he would never escape again. He would keep fighting until they killed him to avoid being taken as a captive. For Banahgar.

He was just about to emerge from his hiding place, ready to sell his life dearly, when sounds reached his keen ears from the snowy darkness away from the camp. Sounds of fighting.

Sheathing his seax and reaching over his shoulder for his greatsword, he moved out of the tree's shelter and towards the sounds. The white snow glimmered in the darkness, providing a chilly half-light. It was enough to see bloodstains on the whiteness, and where the huddled forms of fallen Kotevari soldiers lay.

Standing over them was a knot of figures, swathed in furs and with bared and bloody greatswords in their hands.

He knew them. The way each gripped their sword identified them as though they had written their names in the snow.

Caedmon Skaarn, Maichen Munrae, Skyle Burns and more. The Masters of the Claihed were here. A stocky figure detached himself from the group and stepped forward. He drew back his hood.

'Have you recalled the lesson of the wolf?' asked Helden Haradsson, Grandmaster of the Claihed.

Morgan Blane stared. 'The lesson of the wolf?'

The Grandmaster raised his blade. 'The wolf hunts in a pack.'

He stepped forward, and Morgan Blane followed.

The light of dawn fell on a chill, silent world. Beneath the bare branches new, pale sunlight touched the wintery desolation of the forest floor with delicate golden fingers. It came with precious little warmth, though.

Mateck the Healer huddled deeper into his cape of coarse wool, feeling the scraggy whiskers on his unshaved chin snag in the fabric. It did not help his mood.

'Help me with my rash, Mateck,' he muttered to himself as he scanned the dead leaves beneath the trees for what he sought. 'My guts gripe, Mateck. My precious child is afflicted with pimples, Mateck. Will you help?'

He snorted.

People.

He helped them, of course. Provided powders and salves for their aches, blemishes and general ills. And did they thank him?

Some did, he supposed. They said the words and passed him a few copper scraps, but they looked at him with contempt. They would miss him if he were gone.

A flash of green amid the dry, dead brown caught his eye and he swooped down onto it. A spray of *feverfew*, growing in the lee of a small holly bush. He gathered the leaves and stuffed them into one of the leather pouches hanging from his belt.

He could crush the leaves into a salve or brew them into tea, and sell it to those who suffered headaches or pains in their joints. It was not valuable enough to keep him in good quality wine, though.

The prize he really sought was always harder to find. Sometimes, impossible. He called it *barrenwort* but the local commoners called it horny goat weed.

He loved seeing the faces of the good and noble of Fordon when he asked if that was what they wanted. Maybe they could pretend it was because the shape of the bright pink flowers resembled a goat's curving horns.

But it was not.

He chuckled to himself. It was very useful in treating an affliction between couples that most preferred not to speak of, and that meant that it was worth its weight in silver. The thought of those rich men and women's embarrassment filled him with a warm glow.

That was when he saw it.

A sprouting plant with dagger-shaped leaves, and vivid flowers of bright violet. That single plant should earn him enough for him to eat well for a few nights.

He harvested it.

Looking around, he cried aloud with joy as he saw another *barrenwort* plant growing behind him. Now, he could treat himself to a flask of wine, too.

As he cut the stem and stuffed it into the pouch with the other, he paused. The second plant had been growing in a patch of earth that still held the clear imprint of the sole of his sandal. He had stood there mere moments ago, and there could not have been a flowering *barrenwort* there then. His brow furrowed.

Maybe dreams did come true.

He closed his eyes and imagined a burgeoning barrenwort, those purple flowers emerging happily from the forest floor just in front of him. He knew it was ridiculous, but he did it anyway.

He opened his eyes.

A *barrenwort* plant was growing between the dead leaves at his feet. He touched it. It was real.

Mateck staggered and sat back against the smooth bark of a young beech. Flowering plants could not grow from bare earth in a few heartbeats. It was just not possible.

Extending his arm, he pressed a palm to the coarse, dry leaf mould. Once more, he imagined a plant growing. A moment later, something tickled his palm. Spreading his hand, he watched incredulously as yet another *barrenwort* sprouted between his fingers, the new leaves brushing his skin lightly.

He giggled, and a sudden fatigue hit him. Still staring at the impossible plant, tiredness overcame him, and he drifted away into a swift sleep.

Mateck did not believe in magic, but his last thought before he lost consciousness was that he had just done it.

Another forest floor, far away. Winter's grip was strong, and where it was not blanketed with snow, the ground was grey with hard frost.

A frozen scene, a dead scene.

And yet.

Something was changing. Quickening. A pulse of life was present that had not been there before. And it was centred around an object that was entirely out of place.

The hilt of a sword.

Bound in leather and with gilding on the pommel and crossguard, it stood upright in a clearing, the blade thrust deep into the hard, icy ground. The snow had melted in a perfect circle around the point where it touched the earth and one who looked closely would notice that the blade was marked with sinuous, serpentine lines.

But no one was there, and any that might have been would very quickly find themselves in the gravest danger.

Footsteps. Something large and heavy approached through the trees, with slow, ponderous strides. Moments passed like glacial ages, then a hand that was twisted with unfathomable age reached out, and grasped the hilt.

THE END

OF

BOOK TWO

OF THE

JANTAKAI SAGA

GLOSSARY

ANISH – Country in the confederacy of Re'Emsser

BANAGHAR – Country in the north-east, isolated and encircled by mountains

BEN GEDRIN – Capital and only city of Kiraband

BUREN – Most powerful country in Re'Emsser

CARHINN – Capital city of Anish

CARILTON TANN – Farmer and smallholder in the Lands of the Great River

CERLE CONNOW – Banahgarian, disgraced former member of the Claihedehmore and Eain's grandfather.

CLAIDAH – Claihed training area (lit. 'place of the Claihed')

CLAIHED, The – The professional standing army of the country of Banahgar

CLAIHEDEHLAR – the rank of the Claihed below the Claihedehmore

CLAIHEDEHMORE – the upper rank of the Claihed

CONFERAN - One of the Five gods of the world, the god of heroes

CORIL FADUILE – Head of the High Council of Kereva

DAERON TELERI – Duke of Turgon Fallas, in Tayo

DEMON'S TEAR, The – A mythical fist-sized teardrop-shaped ruby

DEMONSNIGHT - Autumn fire festival, celebrated in the Lands of the Great River, Alrean Empire and Tayo

DERUFIN MOUNTAINS - The biggest mountain range in the world, running east to west and dividing The Lands of the Great River from Buren, Anish and Kotev

DESYA – Mythical creature and demon

EAIN CONNOW – Banahgarian, member of the Claihedehlar

ELLYAH JERIM – Anise thief and entrepreneur

EVANE CLAES – High priest of the Veil, title "Shre"

FORDON – Ancient fortified town in Northern Anish

GLITHONIEL – Capital city of Buren; biggest and oldest city in the world. Also know as the 'Star City' and the 'First City'.

GRAIGOR FARGUSON – Banahgarian, Master of the Claihed. Blind. Sword-Name – Eyes of the Sword

HAFIOH –The peasant levies in the army of Kotev

HELDEN HARADSSON – Banahgarian, Grandmaster of the Claihed. Sword-Name – Death's Face

HNIFFARE – the lowest rank of the Claihed

HOLT COOKSON – Village elder of Feorhryc in the Lands of the Great River

INDAELLA CONNOW – Banahgarian, wife of Cerle Connow and grandmother of Eain

JHARI – Member of the Mackems criminal gang in Anish. Half-elf

KALED - One of the Five gods of the world, the god of fate

KELL LEOWRACSON – Youngest of the Twelve Brothers of Banahgarian myth and founder of the Claihed

KEREVA – City in central Anish

KINGSGUARD, The – The personal guard of the Tayan Taosach, also know as The Gluttons

KIRABAND – Frontier region between the Lands of the Great River and northern Tayo and Buren

KLAY GARRANT – Dwarf mercenary soldier

KOTEV – Country in the east of the continent. Member of the confederacy of Re'Emsser

LANDS OF THE GREAT RIVER, The - A great land to the north and south of the Great River, in the north of the world. Also known as the Riverlands

LEOWRAC - Last king of Banahgar

LUARA ORSINI – Mercenary fighter from the Lands of the Great River

MACKEMS, The – Criminal gang in Anish, based in Carhinn

MAICHEN MUNRAE – Banahgarian, Master of the Claihed. Sword-Name – The Bear's Claws

MAJLEYN – Cult leader and agent, based in Seyntlowe in Buren

MANEG – Eagle-headed god of wisdom. Foremost of the gods of Banahgar

MECULVY DUTSCH - A mysterious tribe of the Lands of the Great River. Also known as the Walking Birds

MORDEA - One of the Five gods of the world, the "Mother"

MORGAN BLANE – Banahgarian, Master of the Claihed. Sword-Name – The River in Flood

MZINDA BISANI – A mythical dwarven city lost in the Lands of the Great River. Known as "The Hidden City"

NASTJA MJETTE – Anise polymath and entrepreneur

OME - One of the Five gods of the world, the god of death

OSTURBROST – Capital city of Banahgar

PENTANG – Five-pointed symbol of the Five gods

PRATHIN PRA MITHRIN- An ancient legend about the forging of the Twin Swords

ROYAL SENTINELS, The – A military organisation based in the southwest of Anish

SAVFA – Former mentor and guardian of Ellyah Jerim

SEVERED CITY, The - The dwarf city between Buren and Anish

SJONACAIDHAN, The – Banahgarian organisation of bards, historians and musicians.

SKANE - Member of the Mackems criminal gang in Anish. Deaf, former prize-fighter

SKYLE BURNS – Banahgarian, Master of the Claihed. Sword-Name – The Centre

STEYFAN JUKEEV – Anise historic figure. Former Duke of Fordon

STICASTS – A criminal gang based in Ben Gedrin

STYOYAN JUKEEV – Youngest son of Gevrin, current Earl of Fordon

SVERLAEGGARE– the rank of the Claihed above Hniffare

TAOSACH – the leader of Tayo, a post currently held by Taosach Wenas

TAYO – Country in the southwest of the world

TORRO – Bull's blood, drunk for luck as part of the Demonsnight celebrations

TUREANK - One of the Five gods of the world, the god of unity

TURGON FALLAS – Fortress town in northern Tayo, ancestral home of the Teleri family

TRESSIN OKE – Wagon train leader in the Lands of the Great River

VEKWICC – The northern fortress and garrison of the Claihed in Banahgar

WÖLFIN – Dwarf wolf-god

AUTHOR'S STATEMENT

I am an independent author. I am not represented by an agent or a publishing house. This means that I am free of any pressure to hit sales targets or to write to market. I am free to tell my stories in the way I choose.

Being independent also means that I have very little support for my writing. I carry out nearly every stage of the creative process myself, and the task of turning the story into a book also rests entirely on me.

I have no budget to hire professional help for development, editing, formatting or proofreading so I have had to do most of it myself, and rely on the generosity of friends from time to time.

I should also declare again at this point that I do not, and will not, use generative AI in any way during the writing and publishing process.

By reading this far you have already done a huge amount to encourage me to keep writing. I hope you enjoyed this book, and if you did, please tell people about it.

As an independent author my marketing budget is close to zero, but you can help me by leaving a review somewhere, or blogging about the book, or telling a reading group. These small things are huge for indie authors, and do more to spread the word about our stories than we can do ourselves.

Choose indie, and tell the world about it.

THANK YOU

The difficult second album. Of course this is not my second book, but the second book in the Jantakai Saga. I knew I had to keep the story going but also raise the stakes.

I could not have done this alone. My beta readers have offered invaluable support, encouragement and feedback: Rich P, Claire S, Carina Inkdrinker, Andrés da Silveira Stein and the relentless red pen of my proofreader, Sam G. Thank you so much.

The Secret Scribes have done more than they know to keep me motivated and writing; you're a lot more than a writer's group to me, you're friends, colleagues and sometimes, therapists. I've listed our growing catalogue of works on the next page. Why not just read them all?

Outside of the Scribes, I'd like to list some other great indie authors who have been there to support, cajole and sympathise: Eryn McConnell, Carolina Cardona, Tea Spangsberg.

Paul B – art, HEMA advice and my creative conscience. You know what you've done.

Lastly, I must thank my wife Claire, who has to put up with me living in an alternative world a lot of the time, and my son Jim who has endless curiosity for stories.

Thank you all.

R.E. Sanders – Summer 2025

SECRET SCRIBES

The Secret Scribes are an affiliation of independent fantasy authors. If you have enjoyed this book, why not check out some of the great authors and titles below?

Dave Lawson

The Envoys of War
The Pawns of Havoc

Bella Dunn

The Dreams Thief
Blood and Dreams
The Sorrow of the Wise Man
Darkness Unleashed

R.A. Sandpiper

A Pocket of Lies
A Promise of Blood
A Claiming of Souls
Heir of Water
To Touch a Silent Fury

Bill Adams

The Tenacious Tale of Tanna the Tendersword
The Godsblood Tragedy
Lady Drakeslayer
Unlucky Evens, Cursed Odds

G.J. Terral

Bloodwoven
Bloodbound
Bloodless

Sean O'Boyle

The Ballad of Sprikit The Bard (And Company)
Checks, Balances and Proper Procedure in Monster Hunting

L.M. Douglas

Gharantia's Guardian
Gharantia's Fury
Gharantia's Fate (2025)
Davga – An Endless War Novella (2025)

Damien Francis

The Tome of Haren

Alex Scheuermann

The Odyllic Stone

Althea Lyons

The Hiding
Reawakening
The Somnia

Lamia N. Bayen

The Wingspan of Treason

Tom Bookbeard

The Corsair

Also by the author…

R.E.Sanders

A Path of Blades
Tann's Last Stand
Demon's Tear

Printed in Dunstable, United Kingdom